THE SELECTED LETTERS OF WILLIAM WALTON

The Selected Letters of
WILLIAM WALTON

Edited by
MALCOLM HAYES

Oxford
9.iii.02

ff
faber and faber

First published in 2002
by Faber and Faber Limited
3 Queen Square London WC1N 3AU

Photoset by Agnesi Text, Hadleigh
Printed in England by Clays Ltd, St Ives plc

This work is published with subsidy from The William Walton Trust

A CIP record for this book
is available from the British Library

ISBN 0-571-20105-9

2 4 6 8 10 9 7 5 3 1

for Sally
who likes Italy too

CONTENTS

List of Illustrations
page ix

Introduction
page xi

1902–1929
page 1

1930–1935
page 51

1936–1948
page 103

1949–1954
page 173

1955–1963
page 259

1964–1976
page 341

1977–1983
page 433

Appendices
page 465

Chronology
page 481

List of Works
page 488

CONTENTS

Select Bibliography
page 503

Acknowledgements
page 505

Index
page 508

[viii]

LIST OF ILLUSTRATIONS

1 Louisa Walton, William Walton's mother.
William Walton Archive, Ischia

2 Dr Thomas Strong, Dean of Christ Church, and one of Walton's first mentors.
William Walton Archive, Ischia

3 WW and crew of the second boat, Christ Church College, Oxford, 1919.
By kind permission of the Governing Body of Christ Church, Oxford

4 Sacheverell, Osbert and Edith Sitwell, 1920s.
Photograph Cecil Beaton courtesy of Sotheby's London

5 Margot Fonteyn and Frederick Ashton dancing the *Tango Pasodoble*.
Photograph Gordon Anthony (V & A Picture Library)

6 Edith and Osbert Sitwell take some light refreshment in the 1920s.
Courtesy PA News Ltd

7 Imma von Doernberg.
William Walton Archive, Ischia

8 Siegfried Sassoon and Stephen Tennant, early 1930s.
Photograph Cecil Beaton courtesy of Sotheby's London

9 Edwin Evans, Leslie Heward, WW, Dora and Hubert Foss.
William Walton Archive, Ischia

10 Osbert Sitwell and Christabel Aberconway, 1930.
Courtesy The Graphic

11 Alice, Viscountess Wimborne.
Photograph Cecil Beaton courtesy of Sotheby's London

12 Benjamin Britten and Peter Pears.
Photograph Foto: Fayer, Wien

13 WW and Laurence Olivier.
Courtesy Mrs Muir Mathieson

14 Susana Gil Passo, 1944.
William Walton Archive, Ischia

15 Newly-weds Mr and Mrs Walton leave Buenos Aires for England,
January 1949.
William Walton Archive, Ischia

16 Christopher Hassall, WW and Sir Malcolm Sargent at the Royal
Opera House, 1954.
Courtesy Radio Times

17 Magda László as Cressida, first Covent Garden staging of *Troilus
and Cressida*, 1954.
Photograph Houston Rogers (V & A Picture Library)

18 Walter Legge, EMI's classical music supremo, and WW during the
recording of *Belshazzar's Feast*, Kingsway Hall, London, 1959.
Photograph Erich Auerbach/Hulton Getty

19 La Mortella, shortly after the house was completed, 1962.
William Walton Archive, Ischia

20 Recording the Violin Concerto with Yehudi Menuhin and the
London Symphony Orchestra.
Photograph David Farrell

21 WW with Edward Heath, the Prime Minister, early 1970s.
William Walton Archive, Ischia

22 Walton aged eighty, 1982.
Photograph Jane Bown

INTRODUCTION

Letters written by artists tend to fall into two categories. There are those composed with at least half an eye on how they will appear when they are published. And there are those which were addressed straightforwardly to those concerned, with little or no strategic interest in adding, at the same time, some useful building blocks to the monument of the artist's output.

Much of the appeal of William Walton's letters relates to their unpretentiousness. Together they assemble a self-portrait in words that is the more entertaining, and in its own way more informative, precisely because his letters were so seldom the vehicle for his deepest musings. He kept these for his music. In this book there is just one reference as to how a vintage Waltonian witticism – a naughty one, of course – might come across to the reader, if and when it were ever to appear in print. Walton's sense of humour was one of his most reliable qualities, and there is no reason to suppose that this momentary flirtation with the allure of publication betrays a deeper concern to immortalize himself in this way. His approach to the business of living and working was too practical for that. And his way of conveying it was spontaneous to the point of irrepressible roguishness. These are letters with the pollen still fresh on them.

This attractive scenario does not in itself make the task of compiling a selected edition of Walton's correspondence any easier. He liked to make out that letter-writing was something that he never really bothered about. This is true only in the sense that he almost never made copies of his letters, since most of them were handwritten. In every other respect the impression of the ultra-reluctant correspondent was another Waltonian joke. In the course of gathering material this book, I pre-selected a 'short list' of about one-fifth of what was available to me. Of that amount, not more than a quarter has ended up in the pages that follow. And this is without allowing for additional material that may or may not exist elsewhere.

Walton was indeed a tireless and voluminous correspondent. It was to some extent a necessary fluency, relating to the logistics of his life on the island of Ischia from 1949 onwards. He had moved there partly to extract himself from the time-consuming administrative commitments into which his position as one of England's leading composers was drawing him. He also wanted to start work on what was to be by far the largest and most complex single project of his life: his opera *Troilus and Cressida*. At that time telephones were an almost non-existent rarity on Ischia. Walton therefore had little choice but to keep in touch by letter with friends and colleagues, above all with the opera's librettist, Christopher Hassall. It therefore turned out that every detail of the creation of *Troilus and Cressida* was documented with astonishing completeness. Walton's and Hassall's letters alone take up eight volumes among those assembled in the Walton Archive at La Mortella, the home that the composer and Susana Walton built together on their adopted Italian island. And this mass of material concerns just one major work among an output that spanned more than six decades.

So how does an editor decide what to select? My priority at every point has been to choose those letters that show something of Walton's personality: at work or at play, cheerful or angry, charming or manipulative (or both), honourable or evasive, importunate or generous, shrewdly calculating or rampantly indiscreet, gracious or sarcastic, exhilarated or depressed, often very funny indeed, and sometimes deliberately and gratuitously unpleasant. A waspish side to Walton's nature is never far away, especially in relation to other living composers. With exceptions, he could not help regarding his contemporaries as competitors first and foremost.

Yet this flickering resentment of others' abilities could co-exist with a genuine respect for his fellow practitioners, and especially for their technical fluency (although how the creator of the Second Symphony and *The Bear* can truly have felt inferior to any composer in matters of technique is a mystery). I have been careful, however, to try to present Walton's nature within a perspective that the balance of the evidence indicates to be fair. His was a complex temperament, both musically and personally, whose sunny side was often subverted by a cold and ruthless streak of self-sufficiency – the artist's necessary containment, perhaps, but a quality that could be far from likeable for those who had to deal with it.

But I have also been much struck by the enormous and genuine amount of goodwill that surrounds Walton's memory, and indeed anything to do with a body of music that has brought so much to the lives of so many. A composer does not generate this level of retrospective warmth simply by having fuelled his talent at the surrounding world's expense. As Susana

Walton put it to me, happily remembering her husband's capacity for bringing off one successful ploy after another, 'William was always able to get everyone to do exactly what he wanted. I never understood how he did it.' When I asked Maureen Murray, my researcher for this book, whether or not the composer and his posthumous editor would have got on, her answer was instant: 'You would have liked his humour.'

Besides portrayal of character, there have been other factors to consider. This book is intentionally a self-portrait in Walton's own words, rather than an exercise in documentation. But I have not hesitated to include letters where the detailed information that they offer about Walton's music is both illuminating and interesting. There are more of these from the years after the Second World War than from before. Living in Ischia meant that Walton had to rely on letter-writing to oversee the technical preparation of his published scores, and the intricacy of much of this correspondence concerns only the specialist. But for interested readers with or without scores or recordings to hand, I hope that there is enough material here to shed fresh light on what lay behind the creation of some of Walton's best and most characteristic music.

I have concentrated in particular on *Troilus and Cressida*, the Cello Concerto, the Second Symphony and the *Variations on a Theme by Hindemith*. This is partly because Walton wrote much about them in his letters, and also because the works themselves, even now, are so much less familiar than they deserve to be. Besides, Walton's own perspective on them is more than vivid enough to appeal to readers who may be coming to them for the first time, quite apart from the obvious interest to those who already know and love this vintage period of Walton's music. He himself repeatedly said, in his correspondence and elsewhere, that he considered these four works to be among his very best. To date, received opinion has generally decided otherwise. But there was no shrewder judge of Walton's music than the composer himself.

Since the theme of the book is 'Walton by himself', I have tried to assemble his letters in a sequence that reads as self-sufficiently as possible, with no more recourse to editorial insertions and footnotes than is necessary. Sometimes these do need to be fairly abundant if the material itself is to make sense, but on the whole Walton's correspondence is well able to tell its own story. The one period when there appears to be little or no surviving material is, exasperatingly, the one that so many readers will wish to know more about. These are the years when Walton was making his way as a young composer in London in the early 1920s – living in the

Sitwells' house in Carlyle Square, and beginning to make the necessary high-powered contacts in the musical world. Meanwhile he was creating *Façade* and its sequence of exploratory successors – the early String Quartet, the *Sinfonia concertante* and others – which were all part of their composer's journey towards the self-knowledge of the mature artist.

It may simply be that Walton wrote very few letters at this time. His career was in its early stages; performances of his music were relatively few, and when he travelled abroad he almost always did so in the company of the Sitwells themselves. The situation changed thanks to the decision of Hubert Foss, the head of Oxford University Press's newly expanded music department, to start publishing Walton's music. This initiated a regular correspondence between the two men. From the time that Walton completed the Viola Concerto in 1929, enough of his letters exist to tell the story of his life and work in a sequence that is at least reasonably continuous. Posterity is fortunate indeed that Walton's letters to Siegfried Sassoon in the early 1930s have survived. Without them, we would have a much more fragmentary picture of his years in Switzerland, his relationship with Baroness Imma von Doernberg, and the long and difficult creation of the First Symphony.

It is the nature of human relations that all of us, to a greater or lesser extent, naturally adjust our responses to mirror the personalities of others around us. In that respect there are many different Waltons in the pages that follow. He is scrupulously laddish with Malcolm Arnold; bluff and genial with David Webster; insistent and sometimes hectoring with Christopher Hassall but seldom unkind; at his most intelligent and incisive with Walter Legge; flirtatious and richly amusing with Griselda Kentner; at once businesslike and entertaining with Dallas Bower; and by turns friendly, tough, ebullient and thoughtful with Alan Frank, his publisher for many years at Oxford University Press. I am sorry to have to disappoint anyone who may have been expecting a comprehensive exposé of Walton's various affairs with women, outside the three major relationships of his life. This is because there seem to have been fewer of those affairs than legend would make out – and besides, any potentially incriminating letters will very likely have been destroyed by either or both parties, while the always streetwise Walton would have tended to avoid writing those letters to whomever he was involved with, at least at the time. (Afterwards could be different.)

Something else is missing too. Walton's knowledge of classical music of all periods was as extensive as his talent would lead one to expect, and the evidence of this is abundantly clear in the pages that follow. But those who knew him were often equally impressed by his knowledge and understanding of the other arts also. By all accounts he could be a riveting conversationalist when discussing, for instance, Italian art and architecture – an interest whose foundations had been laid during those early years with the Sitwells, who would take Walton with them on their omnivorous culture-hunting trips across Europe. Next to nothing of all this, however, is apparent in his letters. This is perhaps partly for the same reason that he did not use letter-writing as a vehicle for metaphysical musings about the human soul and its place in the surrounding cosmos. Walton's instinct to steer clear of ponderous philosophizing is, of course, what makes his letters such a straightforward pleasure to read. But to the extent that they make so little reference to his artistic interests outside music, that pleasure comes at a price.

Another delight is Walton's way with the English language. In conversation he liked to make much of his near-illiteracy in these matters, at least by Sitwellian standards – the son of Oldham who had 'coom oop from Lancasheer', and who would insist that he ended up being a composer only because he was too stupid to do anything else. Behind this entertaining and self-deprecating mask lay a deeper unease – that of the Oxford undergraduate who never got his degree, and who then set about surviving as the Sitwells' semi-permanent house guest at Carlyle Square with a characteristic blend of contained, but winning charm ('I realised that I needed to make myself interesting to others') and streetwise determination. But whether or not he ever realized as much, his way with words was instinctive, and I hope it will give as much pleasure to the reader as it has to me while compiling this book. Walton's gift with language was an essentially informal one. Anything requiring a more serious approach – a programme note, for instance – was treated with alarm and farmed out wherever possible to someone else, usually to Hubert Foss or Alan Frank. Walton's thought-provoking memorandum regarding the future of Covent Garden's Royal Opera House in the years after the Second World War (Appendix 3) would almost certainly not exist if he had not been prevented from working normally by an eye infection, and had therefore found himself dictating it to Alice Wimborne. But the ease, freedom and intelligence of his letter-writing style are qualities that many a professional writer can only envy.

His letters tended mostly to be short, and wherever possible I have presented them complete. When he needed to, however, he could write at considerable length. The correspondence about *Troilus and Cressida* is a case in point, but Walton also wrote quite long letters to Siegfried Sassoon and others during his years in Switzerland in the 1930s, often when he was worried about something and needed to confide in a friend. I have always preferred to present his longer letters, too, as completely as possible, but there are many occasions where some editing has seemed necessary.

The oddities of Walton's letter-writing style create a series of problems that confound any standard notion of editorial practice. His approach to spelling was, to say the least, idiosyncratic. His equally bizarre concepts of punctuation and abbreviation were matched by a readiness to omit both individual letters within words, and individual words themselves. One might think that he never bothered to read through any of his letters before sending them, except that there are enough last-minute insertions of words and phrases to show that he must have done so.

One solution is to edit Walton's words in a way that approaches translating them into standard English. This is Michael Kennedy's judicious and convincing procedure in his *Portrait of Walton*, in the specific context of illustrating this outstandingly lucid biography. But an edition of the letters themselves is a different proposition, and one that surely requires that the reader be taken as close as possible to the moment of their writing. This means that a balance somehow has to be found between what is both legitimate and characterful on the printed page, and what risks becoming a source of cumulative irritation for the reader. After much experiment I decided that a consistent resolution of all the anomalies was unrealistic, and that each individual situation had instead to be assessed on its merits.

Wherever the sense of Walton's text is immediately clear, I have on the whole left it as it is. Examples of this include some of the composer's *idées fixes* regarding spelling. For instance he almost always writes 'dissapoint', 'dissapear' or 'dissaprove' – except that, in the letter to Gregor Piatigorsky dated 6 October 1956, he for once spells 'disapproval' correctly, since it appears alongside 'approval'. From start to finish 'amiable' always appears as 'aimnable' or, less often, 'aimable'. 'Dos'ent' for 'doesn't' is another almost constant presence, along with its equivalent siblings, but again there are exceptions: sometimes the apostrophe turns up in the accepted place, so that 'have'nt' can become 'haven't'. I have added missing apostrophes only where their implied presence is not obvious (for instance 'Ive' for 'I've' seems acceptable). Walton almost invariably omits the cedilla from *Façade*, but where he includes it, I have shown this.

From about 1918 the ampersand ('&') arrives in the Waltonian lexicon and hardly ever leaves it. The very few letters that were originally typed can be identified by their consistent use of 'and' instead of the ampersand. Among these are some dictated or drafted by Walton at Lowndes Cottage in London and typed by his secretary there, Sheila Perry. Sometimes Walton writes out what he feels to be an important letter in a tidy, 'Sunday best' manner, having evidently drafted it first, and in these he sometimes reverts to using 'and' rather than the ampersand, as in the letter to Gertrude Hindemith written on 4 January 1964 (but not, however, in the one written to George Szell on 11 May 1962). Where accidentally repeated words occur (e.g. 'something that that I saw') I have omitted the redundant one.

Walton elevated the use of initials to something approaching an art form. Where new ones appear for the first time or reappear after an interval, I have usually amplified them, but on the whole I have left them alone, provided that their meaning is immediately clear from the context. 'P.P.', for instance, can mean either *Portsmouth Point* or Peter Pears, two very different musical phenomena which fortunately tend to feature at different ends of the correspondence, so that confusion between them is easily avoided. The fun really starts with 'B.B.' Depending on the context, this can stand for Benjamin Britten, *Billy Budd* (hence 'B.B.'s B.B.'), 'Bloody *Bear*', Brass Band, and for good measure one of Walton's choice renamings of *Belshazzar's Feast*, 'Belli's Binge'.

Walton also constantly mixed up commas and full points, and was always liable to begin new sentences without a capital letter. I have generally corrected these, although exceptions have been made in Walton's childhood letters from Christ Church College, where it seems fair to give an indication of how his adult style was gradually forming. All visible editorial amendments of any kind – whether to clarify a name, to supply a minimum of necessary information, to add missing punctuation, missing letters or words, or to expand an abbreviation – have been added within square brackets. Words within round brackets are always Walton's own. (He himself uses square brackets only once, in his letter to Hubert Foss dated 7 November 1939. I have indicated this.) I have retained all of Walton's own underlinings: italics are editorial only. Unconventional spacings between words have mostly been retained, but sometimes amended.

Addresses and dates at the heads of letters have been standardized, but within the text itself they have been left as Walton wrote them. Dating several of the letters written before the Second World War is difficult.

Walton usually wrote down the day and the month, but often omitted the year, and sometimes a letter is not dated at all. This was not carelessness on his part: at that time local letters were routinely delivered on the same day that they were sent, and the addressee could assume this. Sometimes an original envelope has survived, providing a helpfully legible postmark. But as often as not the month or year in question has to be deduced from the contents of the letter itself. Fortunately, from about 1940 onwards, Walton increasingly added the year, besides the day and the month. All dates not in square brackets are those given by Walton himself. A year or a month, or both, within square brackets means that the letter itself does not show these, but that they can be deduced with a measure of sureness ranging from strong probability (a clear reference within the text) to certainty (a postmark). There are a very few examples – for instance the letters to Zena Naylor – where a likely guess is all that is possible unless further correspondence or other dated information comes to light. In these cases the estimated date is shown entirely within square brackets.

With very rare exceptions, Walton's letters are almost always easily legible. The facsimile reproductions in this book will give an idea of how widely and unpredictably his handwriting could change down the years – sometimes small, cramped and convoluted, sometimes so large and sweeping that a page will contain only two or three sentences. The first, childhood letter is written in pencil. Fountain pen and, almost always, black ink then dominate until Walton's move to Ischia, with rare excursions into pencil. Blue ink makes an appearance in the letters from 1949 onwards, to be replaced largely by blue ballpoint from about 1960. Some of the last letters experiment, clumsily and briefly, with a felt-tip pen. But whether the letters in this book were written by a small, sometimes lonely choirboy in Oxford during the First World War, or by an ageing master composer reflecting on past years under the Italian sun, the vividness of the personality behind the words remains strong, constant, and unfailing.

Maureen Murray's contribution to this book as its research consultant is referred to in the Acknowledgements (p. 505). But I would also like to record here my particular thanks to her, for her skill and persistence in locating a substantial amount of Walton's correspondence from sources which, I am quite sure, I would not have discovered on my own. The result has been a selection more wide-ranging than would have materialized without her outstanding professional support. The responsibility for the book's contents, including any errors, is of course my own as editor.

[xviii]

1902–1929

OLDHAM'S most famous son was born on 29 March 1902 to Charles Walton, a music teacher, choirmaster and organist, and his wife Louisa. The couple's other children were Noel, Walton's elder brother, and Nora and Alexander (Alec), his younger siblings. Charles Walton's work in the small but busy Lancastrian mill town – a community where almost everyone would have known almost everyone else – meant that the thriving tradition of English choral music was a regular background to his son's upbringing. As a small boy, Walton started out by singing in his father's choir, and began to learn to play the piano and organ (quite successfully) and the violin (much less so).

It was soon clear that young Billy was showing signs of an exceptional musical talent. Charles Walton spotted a newspaper advertisement for scholarships to be awarded to choral probationers at Christ Church College in Oxford University. In a stroke of good fortune, the first of several that were to garland Walton's long life, he was accepted. His accompanist at the piano during the voice trial was the organist at Christ Church College Cathedral, Dr Henry Ley, who was to become one of Walton's early supporters in the years of growth and struggle ahead. Another was Dr Thomas Strong, the Dean of Christ Church College.

Walton's letters to his mother give a vivid picture of life as a young chorister at a boarding school in the early years of the twentieth century. Outwardly it all seems unremarkable at first, although his gifts of sharp observation and economy of expression are already apparent. The constant presence of his signing-off statement – 'There is no more news' – stirs memories of my own life at a choir school some fifty years later.

It was a life built around routine. Included within the unvarying weekly timetable were the two hours that we were allowed every Sunday morning to write letters home. The evidence is that Walton's life at Christ Church ran along the same lines. It would have been a life that was constantly busy, with singing, classroom work, music lessons and sport following each other in a non-stop whirl of gregarious activity. Much would have been going on. But because it did so within the set routine, it would have been somehow difficult to write about in a way that made it seem interesting enough to parents who were not there to witness it. (I remember this feeling exactly.) So when Walton wrote, 'There is no more news', or words to that effect at the end of a letter that, as often as not, was quite impressively full of news, he meant that there was no more of what amounted to news from this particular 'boys together' perspective. But it is amusing to note that the same phrase sometimes crops up in the letters he was to be writing in fifty years' time.

The received notion that talented artists-in-waiting are bound to be misfits at an English boarding school is contradicted by the picture of his life that Walton paints in his letters. He seems to have been naturally skilled in the all-important art of 'mucking in', and this must have made it easier for him to conceal the underlying loneliness that (so he maintained in later life) he felt for much of the time. Given that Walton's aversion to physical exercise from the age of about twenty onwards was extreme, it is entertaining to see that as a youngster he was obviously good at sport, or 'games' as they would have been known. 'Games' were, and still are, an essential passport to social acceptance in the culture of English boarding schools and university colleges. But besides that allure from Walton's point of view, he must have been a quite promising young cricketer to have made 45 runs even at this modest level, as he reported on 15 July 1917. His ability to put bat to ball with the necessary timing and co-ordination is just one of a number of natural skills that marked him out as a true son of Lancashire. Walton's lifelong competitive edge is already modestly evident too, in his pleasure at being a ten-year-old member of the Christ Church Choir football team that had just put three goals past Marlborough House.

If the early evidence of his extreme musical gifts was cause for comment among his school friends, there is no direct evidence that they disliked him for it or, in the time-honoured boarding-school fashion, felt that he needed 'taking down a peg'. Perhaps this is because he learned early not to boast. But it is also likely that his lifelong capacity to channel his personal resources carefully was an innate skill that his years at Christ Church taught him to rely on very early. Even in the very earliest letters, a young boy's typical enthusiasm at his own success – for instance when showing his six-part choral motet to Henry Ley, who said that 'it had wonderful ideas in it' (10 September 1916) – co-exists with a much less typical refusal to exaggerate his own impressions and responses. A week later, he clearly

[4]

felt no need to impress either his parents or himself unduly when mentioning that his compositions had been sent to one of the most prominent and influential English composers of the day, Sir Hubert Parry, or when describing Ley's performance of young Walton's Chorale Fantasia: 'People said it was very fine, but I don't give my opinion.'

There was a war on, of course, as Walton's observations of the world around him also show. Some aeroplanes are seen looping the loop; the newsreels report the Battle of the Somme; the college gardens are used for growing vegetables to help with the war effort; a night-time air raid is cause for excitement – including an unscheduled gathering round the fire in the headmaster's drawing room – rather than fear. But generally the tone of Walton's earliest letters show that here was a boy whose instinct was to leave the impressions of his childhood world behind as quickly as possible. On one level he takes trouble to do his best to tell his mother as much as he feels he can of his day-to-day life. On another, he already shows signs of the tight-fisted self-sufficiency that was to be so typical of the ambitious composer of years to come, determined to survive and succeed in a profession as difficult and uncertain as anyone can choose. His already unmistakably sharp awareness of money matters, for instance, never left him for a moment in his adult life.

When Walton's treble voice broke in mid-1916, the choir school's headmaster asked Strong if a way could be found to allow him to stay on. Strong undertook to pay the balance of the boy's school fees himself, removing the immediate risk of Walton having to return to Oldham and, most likely, to the beginnings of a life as a music teacher somewhere in the north of England. Two years later Strong also arranged for Walton to enter Christ Church College as an undergraduate on an exhibition scholarship, at the age of just sixteen.

It must have been an intimidating transition from being very much the senior pupil at the choir school to becoming an undergraduate surrounded by others who would have been at least two years older than Walton himself – and, at that age, even a single year's difference is something of a psychological chasm. But again, if Walton found the experience destabilizing or even traumatic, there is no evidence of this in his letters to his mother. Instead of merely getting along easily with his former schoolfriends, he is now having tea with the likes of Roy Campbell, Herbert Howells and others who would become as famous in their chosen fields as Walton himself. He reports encounters of this kind matter-of-factly, and signs off as usual, 'There is nothing else to say.'

[5]

At this time he was composing some of the music – including two startlingly accomplished early songs, 'The Winds' and 'Tritons' – that helped to attract the interest of those who were to help shape his future: Sacheverell ('Sachie') Sitwell, a fellow undergraduate, also Sacheverell's brother Osbert and sister Edith, and Siegfried Sassoon. The Sitwells' invitations to spend vacations with them in London and abroad opened up a further new world. All three siblings were talented writers, and were heavily and contentiously involved in London's busy world of literature and the arts, where their penchant for rating their own notoriety at least as highly as the quality of the work they were producing kept them under the spotlight of publicity – exactly as they intended. Walton took instantly to this lifestyle of high culture and hard work. He also seems to have found his awareness of his own background – much more modest than that of the affluent and aristocratic Sitwells – to be a competitive spur to his own ambitions of success. Before long the young and astonishingly promising composer was being introduced to some leading musicians of the day: Eugene Goossens, Igor Stravinsky.

Against this new and exciting background, Walton had to grapple with some of the more mundane matters of day-to-day existence. Here he was, submitting some of his earliest orchestral music for consideration by Sergei Diaghilev's Ballets Russes, the star-studded company that earlier in the decade had given the first performances of Ravel's *Daphnis et Chloé* and Stravinsky's *Petrushka* and *The Rite of Spring*. Yet, at the same time, he had managed effectively to escape to London for the summer vacation without some of his tuition fees at Oxford having being paid. These two concerns nonchalantly rub shoulders in his letters to Thomas Strong, whose unstinting and far-sighted support of his young protégé must have been at least momentarily taxed by the ease with which Walton seemed able to shrug off responsibilities of this kind.

Walton must have sensed almost at once that the alluring world of London's musical and artistic life was where the key to his own future lay. Even so, his failure to complete his studies at Christ Church College was not entirely due to lack of interest or motivation. He passed his second B.Mus. examination in 1920, but the year before he had failed for the third time in the more general subjects included in Responsions. From the Michaelmas term of 1920 his exhibition scholarship was not renewed. The Sitwells decided to take him under their wing as a kind of honorary brother, and to let him live in an upstairs room at the family's house at 2 Carlyle Square in Chelsea. His life as a freelance composer had begun.

To Mrs Walton   [c. 1910?]

My dear mother I hope that you are keeping well I suppose, Nora and baby[1] will miss me. Noel is rather glad I am away. I am having a nice time. Loree [Laurie?] is going to buy me a bagpipe I lost a ball in the winter gardens.

　　With love from
　　Billie

Dear mother I hope you are ceeping well and is Noel well and baby Noel will be very glad that I am away[2]

To Mrs Walton   [17 November 1912]

Cathedral Choir House, Oxford

Dear Mother,

　　we have had a very nice time the fortnight. We had a lovely prize giving the being dressed up. One Saturday we went to the Deans[3] to tea and he showed us the State [Room] in which Charles I slept in. We went up the watch tower as well. We won our first match by three goals to none yesterday against Marlborough House. I did go down in class a fortnight yesterday I was ninth. I was sixth last week and I am now fourth The Trades Exhibition is being held [in] the Town Hall all next week. Will you send me some cash as I have none left. I got taken out in the half-term by Russel, Lindquest and Proger! Russel took me to the Picture Palace, Lindquest to the Scating Rink and Proger took me out to tea. I can skate quite well now. I went again on Monday and I can do the inside edge I did not no what that postcard ment and I threw it away But tell Mary that I was very pleased. Will you send me some jam for 'tuck' night as I have to use school jam or someone gives me some. I am going to close my letter here.

　　With much love
　　Billy

1 Walton's youngest brother, Alexander (Alec), born in 1910. His elder brother Noel was aged eleven at the time, and his sister Nora was aged two.
2 This apparent postscript is evidently an incomplete first attempt to write the letter.
3 Dr Thomas Strong, Dean of Christ Church College.

[7]

To Mrs Walton   11 July 191[5]

Cathedral Choir House, Oxford

Dear Mother,

I have had a very nice week. I can go to Ballacheys from Aug 3rd to
8th [?] can't I. He is awfully desent [decent] and if I can go I can learn to
ride a horse. I think Mrs Ballachey is writing to you about it. Say "yes".
There is hardly any news this week. I had a solo in Stainer in E♭ on
Tuesday. We went to the Baths. I nearly did [a] breadth in swimming.
We had a [cricket] match with Cothill on Wednesday. We lost. 80–50. It
was a ripping drive there. We went to the Baths on Thursday. There was
no practise. We had a full practise on Friday. There was a game yesterday.
I had the solo in "God of my righteousness" Greene. I had a solo in
Garret in D this morning Dr Watson preached. We are having "Praise
thou the Lord" Wesley.[1] I have got three out off the four solos. The
"Gym" Competion is on next Wednesday. I enclose another photo and
the vouchers etc.

With much love
Billy.

To Mrs Walton   23 January [1916]

Christ Church, Oxford

Dear Mother

Thanks very much for your letter. My weight is 5 st. 12 lbs. my
height 5 ft ¼ ins. It rained all day Monday. The non-choir boys came
back. We had the first "Gym" on Tuesday. on Wednesday we had a
[football] game. We won 10–2. On Thursday we had a game. I had solo
in "When Jesus our Lord". Bach.

On Friday we had a full practise. It rained all day. We had a game
yesterday. I had a solo in Arnold[2] in F. The Dean preached this morning.
We are having "When Jesus was born" Mendolssohn [Mendelssohn]. I
thing this is all the news this week

With much love
Billy

1   Samuel Wesley, nineteenth-century English composer and organist.
2   Samuel Arnold, eighteenth-century English composer and editor.

[8]

P[S]. Can I be confirmed

To Mrs Walton [10 September 1916]

Christ Church, Oxford

Dear Mother,

Thanks very much for the parcel and 1/-. H.G Ley[1] came back on Thursday. I showed my six part Motet. He said it had wonderful ideas in it. I showed him the others. Those were quite excellent especially the Fantasia which I had'nt finished copying out. A new Choral[e] Prelude and two others did'nt sound well on the organ but were fairly respectable on the piano. He is teaching me harmony free and is going over the the motets, and I thing we may sing them [in the] Cath[edral]. Machlin and Winnifrith have not yet come back. We went to Wheatley on Wednesday. Some areoplanes have been over. One looped the loop. Dr Sandy preached this morning. By the way, he is taking us to [a newsreel film of] the Battle of the Somme. There is no more news.
With much love
Billy

To Mrs Walton 17 September 1916

Cathedral Choir House, Oxford

Dear Mother,

Thank you very much for your letter. We have had a very nice week. On Monday I played tennis with Miss Brookes. We saw two areoplanes. On Tuesday I sent my compositions to Sir Hubert [Parry].[2] On Wednesday we went to see the king, I was only about three yards from him. He was inspecting the Flying Corp. Windle and I took invitations to the Sports all round the town. In the afternoon we went to Negus' for tea. It was quite respectable. The Non-choir boys came back on Thursday. We began work on Friday. I am in the Senior Class and the work is considerably harder. We practised for the Sports yesterday. There was a practice in the morning at 10.0. We had Communion this

1 Henry Ley, Organist of Christ Church Cathedral.
2 English composer, also Director of the Royal College of Music and Professor of Music at Oxford University.

Christ Church
Oxford

Dear Mother,

Thanks very much for the parcel and V₃. By #4 I came back on Thursday. I showed my aria part "Motet". He said it had wonderful ideas in it. I showed him the others. There were quite excellent, especially the Fantasia which I hadn't finished copying out. A new Short Prelude and two others didn't sound well on the organ but were fairly respectable on the piano. He is teaching me harmony free and is going over the them the motets, and I thing we may sing them Batt. Machlin and Wumfreth have not yet

come back. We went to Wheatley on Wednesday. Some aeroplanes have been over! One looped the loop. Dr Sandy headed this morning. By the way, he is taking us to the Battle of the Somme. There is no more news.

With much love

Billy

morning. Mr Ley played my Choral[e] Fantasia after service. People said it was very fine, but I don't give my opinion. The Dean said he wished he'd been there as he when looking at MSS said it looked very jolly. We are having "Save us O Lord" Bairstow[1] this evening. Dr Sandy is taking us to see the Somme Film. The Sports are next Friday. There is no more news.

With much love
Billy.

To Mrs Walton   8 October 1916

Christ Church, Oxford

Dear Mother.

The weather has been awful this last week. We have had hardly any games. I haven't had a letter this week. Two old boys have been staying at the Deans Garret and Baldwin both fine chaps. The Dean has been saying somethink to me about the Royal College of Music. He says it is unpatriotic to England to let slip such a Musical brain. I haven't heard from Sir Hubert yet but expect to before half term. Half term is on November 2nd, prizegiving on the 3rd. I have got one prize and I might have too. I have t[w]o Counterpoint lessons in the week and I expect to be able to do Florid Counterpoint in four parts before half term. Our first match is on the 18th against Magdalen. It rained on Wednesday our free day and so we spent a very dry afternoon. On Thursday we had a game. I scored six goals. We are having "Abide with me" by Ivor Atkins[2] for the anthem to-night. There is no more news this week.

With much love
Billy

N.B. Axtell [?] a friend of mine who lives in Oxford is asking me there for half-term.

1 Edward Bairstow, English composer, organist and conductor.
2 English composer, and Organist at Worcester Cathedral.

To Mrs Walton   12 November 1916

Cathedral Choir House, Oxford

Dear Mother

Thanks very much for your letter. I have had rather a cold since Wednesday. My new composition is a very great improvement, so Mr Ley says, and he has sent it to Dr Allen.[1] It is then going to Sir Hubert Parry. I've just finished a new pianoforte piece. I shall send my new thing to Sir C. V. Stanford[2] [. . .] in about a fortnight's time. We went to Dr Allens for tea on Tuesday. It was fine. He has my compositions. On Wednesday there was a game. We had Cath[edral service]. We had practise at 2.0 on Thursday. I had a harmony lesson. We should have had a match yesterday, but no team turned up. Dr Sandy preached this morning. We are having "The Wilderness" Goss[3] for the anthem to-night. I have heard from Muriel. She sent two packets of choclate, toffees and biscuits. It is jolly fine of her[.]

  With much love
  Billy.

To Mrs Walton   26 November 1916

Cathedral Choir House, Oxford

Dear Mother,

Thank you very much indeed for the parcel etc. We have had a most successful week. There was no game on Monday. I had a harmony lesson. We went to "Gym" on Tuesday morning. It rained. On Wednesday we had a match with Magdalen. We won 3–0. I got a goal. On Thursday we had another match with Bradfield. We won 7–0. I got some goals. I finished my Composition "For all the Saints" It rained on Friday. We had a game yesterday. I had a harmony lessons.

  The Archdeacon preached this morning. I had a Harmony lesson after Cath. We are having "Remember now thy Creator" Steggall for the

---

1 Hugh Allen, Organist at New College, Oxford, and from 1918 Professor of Music.
2 Charles Villiers Stanford, Irish-born composer. Professor at Trinity College, London, and also a teacher at the Royal College of Music.
3 John Goss, nineteenth-century English composer, also Organist at St Paul's Cathedral.

anthem to night. Tell Noel I'm writing, and I havent a Composition that he [?] could play just now.
 With much love
 Billy

To Mrs Walton   17 June 1917

Cathedral Choir House, Oxford

Dear Mother.

 I am so pleased to have your letter and to hear you are getting on well. Also thank Noel for his, and the fine photo. I enjoyed myself very much indeed. On Thursday we went to "Within the law" at the theatre. It was awfully good. It was free-day on Friday and March took me out. We were on the river all day and had dinner in the evening. I went to Dr Allens on Saturday morning. There was the Dean's tea in the afternoon. On Sunday Winnifrith took me out all day. We went to an Organ Recital at New College. Mr Brooke took us on the river on Monday. It was beautiful. We had prep in the evening. It was hard luck on some of the boys because they had German measles all half term. We settled down to work again on Tuesday. I played tennis in the afternoon. We had a game on Wednesday. There was no Cath. I had a piano lesson on Thursday. There was a practice at 2.0. We had a game. I went to Dr Allens on Friday afternoon but he being out I met Mr Ley who was going to practise for a recital, so I went with him. I saw Dr Allen yesterday morning. Apparently I am not leaving this term but staying on as <u>NON</u>. Choir. I shall learn the Piano and Harmony from Dr Walker. The rest as usual. We had Choral Communion this morning. Dr Scott Holland preached. I went to Dr Allens to be introduced to Sir Hubert Parry; but his car had bust down so am going at 3.30. The anthem to night is "Jesu, joy of man's desiring" Bach. I am going to an organ recital at New College to-night. Mr Ley is playing. There is a new Parry motet being sung by the Bach Choir. The Exam is on July 13th. I hope to be able to pull through. It is doubtfull with everyone. No more news.
 With much love
 Billy

To Mrs Walton   24 June 1917

Cathedral Choir House, Oxford

Dear Mother.

I hope you are getting on well. The weather has been stormy and
a little colder than last week. I went to see Sir Hubert Parry on last
Sunday afternoon and had quite along talk with him. He is an awfully
jolly old person. We had a game on Monday. I had a lesson at 10.30. I
went to see Dr Allen on Tuesday afternoon. He asked Macklin and I to
go to a rehearsal of the Bach Choir Orchestra at 8.30. We went and
heard Rimsky-Korsakoff's Symphonic Suite [*Sheherazade*]. It was grand.
We had no Cath on Wednesday. About ten boys went down with
German measles. I had a lesson at 6.0 on Thursday. We had a game. It
was the first time we went to the Baths. Beautiful warm water. It rained
on Friday. I went round the Broads. We have only five a side in Cath
now. Yesterday we went to the baths. There was a game. Francis Ma
[major] one [of] the boys has had an appendicitis and has undergone the
operation successfully.

I went to early service this morning. Dr Cooke preached. We went to
the Deans after Cath. The anthem to-night is "Comfort ye" Handel. The
exam is three weeks to-morrow. Will you ask Daddy to sent some of the
orchestral MSS from Middletons like he did last time. I don't think there
is any more news

    With much love

    Billy.

To Mrs Walton   15 July [1917]

Cathedral Choir House, Oxford

Dear Mother.

I hope you are now up and getting stronger after your long sojourn in
bed. The weather has been beautiful this week. Plenty of sun but awfully
hot. On Monday I had a lesson at 10.30. There was a practise at 2.0. We
had a game. I made 45. We had our last "Gym" on Tuesday. We went to
the Baths. Mr Allchin[1] came in the evening. He was very pleased with my
compositions. We had no Cath on Wednesday. There was a game, but I

---

1 Basil Allchin was Assistant Organist at Christ Church Cathedral.

played tennis. We went to the Baths. [. . .] We went down to the field this afternoon. The anthem to-night is "Te decet hymnus" Schumann.

Tomorrow the exams begin. I shall try very hard to pass. <u>Don't forget to send me the money, by return of post,</u> if not already being sent. There is no more news.

With much love
Billy

To Mrs Walton   30 September 1917

Christ Church, Oxford

Dear Mother

Thanks very much for your letter. We have had beautiful weather this week except on Wednesday which was the day we needed it most. I had a lesson on Monday. We went to practise for the Sports. There was "Gym" on Tuesday. I went to the Bodleian [Library] in the afternoon. We had the sports on Wednesday. It was not a very nice day, but the rain held off till just at the end.

I won the Senior Cup. And also the 100 yds ¼ mile ½ mile. And in the Jumps both the High and the Long. For the 100 yds I got a cup for the ¼ a jam dish, & for the ½ mile a silver tray. For the High Jump I got salt & pepper shakers. In the Long jump prize I changed my watch for a 7/6 Ingersoll which could be made into a clock or you can carry it in your pocket It is fine. I went to Dr Allens on Thursday. We began football on Friday. I went to Dr Allens yesterday. He played me most of [Verdi's] Otello. I went to early service this morning. Dr Ottely preached. The anthem to-night is "Where thou reignest" Schubert. There is no more news.

With much love
Billy

To Mrs Walton   21 October [1]917

Christ Church, Oxford

Dear Mother,

Thanks very much for your letter. The weather has been quite **good** considering. We have had quite an exciting week. Miss Allchins **burial**

was on Wednesday. Also we had Mrs Peake's[1] birthday treat. Football
went on the same. Our first match is on next Sat. We had great fun on
Fri[.] We went to bed at 9.0 & about 9.30 suddenly the lights went out
downstairs and the hooter began going. Then Mr Peake came up to us,
and the other dormitory which is on the top landing, and told us to go
down stairs since there was a raid. Having arrived down in the drawing
room (there were 11 of us) we sat ourselves round the fire, and had
candles for lights. Then the "specials" came round and said all lights
out and we were left in the dark. We stayed down till 11.30 but heard
nothing. We afterwards heard that they had bombed Bedford station and
were coming on further but lost their way. I have enjoyed my lectures
and got on well. I take my Mus Bac next June. I went to early service
this morning. Dr Ottely preached. The Anthem to-night is "The Lord is
my shepherd" Stanford. There is no more news.
    With much love
    Billy

To Mrs Walton   4 November 1917

Christ Church, Oxford

Dear Mother.
    Thanks very much for your letter. The weather has been much decenter
this week. I have been attending my lectures (4 a week) and seem to be
getting on well. There is a Serbian also amongst us. On Wednesday we
had a match against Magdalen [College]. I got the first goal of the match
and just before half-time they equalised. Just after we began again they
got another, so they were winning 2–1. Then in the last five minutes we
got two running. and so defeated them 3–2. [. . .] Half-term begins on
Thursday. Prize-giving on Friday. I have two prizes; The Deans and
Choir. Send me some chink to go to the opera with.
    With much love
    Billy

1   Wife of Revd Edward Peake, Headmaster of Christ Church Choir School.

To Mrs Walton   [December 1917]

Christ Church, Oxford

Dear Mother.

I have not much news this week as I only wrote on Thursday. I finished my lectures on Friday. with Dr Walker on harmony. Dr Iliffe says I have done wonderfully at my counterpoint, and thinks I shall easily be able to get through my 1st Mus bac in May.

[. . .] I have a solo in the anthem to-night. It is "Dies irae["], Mozart. I do hope Noel will be able to come. I told Dr Allen of the possibility & he said he would be pleased to see the brother of such a promising young composer.

There's no more news
With love
Billy

To Mrs Walton   17 February 1918

Christ Church, Oxford

Dear Mother.

Thanks very much for your letter. I am sorry not to have written last Sunday, but I had no time since Noel came up. He arrived on Sat night. I went up to the Peakes' for all meals with him. I took him round the colleges. He was awfully pleased with H. G. Ley. He went up in the [organ] loft with him. I saw him off about 8.30 and so ended a very enjoyable day.

Have been attending lectures same as ever. Working jolly hard. I went to the Musical Club concert and heard a Brahms Trio in B. and Dvorak Trio in F minor. There is not much news really, only the same things happen here from week to week.

With much love
Billy.

To Mrs Walton   3 March 1918

Christ Church, Oxford

Dear Mother,

Thanks very much for your letters, parcel, money and "tuck". I am so sorry to hear about Uncle Tom. I can hardly realise it. When the letter in the parcel came I thought he was going to recover; but your P.C on Friday told me of the end. I am writing Auntie. Grandpa and everyone must be terribly upset.

For the news here, nothing has happened much. I heard from Noel. He might be able to come up next week. Dr Allen is doing the "Creation" next Sunday so he might hear it.

We are all working hard in the garden, sowing vegetables and things. By the way <u>you must get</u> my ration card for the holiday. Don't forget.

My exam is on 19th. I hope to just manage to scrape through, but it will be a near thing. There is no more news.

With much love
Billy.

To Mrs Walton   5 May 1918

Christ Church, Oxford

Dear Mother.

Thanks very much for your letter. I have quite settled down by now. I hope you got over to [Lytham] St Annes, and had a nice time with grandpa. There is not much news. I began my lectures as usual. I am not going in for the Senior as I don't think I can manage both. We have had two games of cricket on fine days, but the other days were cold or rainy. I am doing nothing else but music now. Next term I hope to be organist at Brasenose College if I can learn enough by October. It will be rather good if it is possible to do it. I shall begin learning after my exam. Send a sweater when possible and Noels address.

With much love
Billy

To Mrs Walton   11 July [1918]

Cathedral Choir House, Oxford

Dear Mother.

I am writing to tell you that my fate hangs in the balance. The Dean is writing Dad to see whether I shall go into Ch. Ch. & get my Mus bac & B.A. (or go into an office). Mind Dad replies immediately in the affirmative (immediately). He will probably [be] asked if I shall be able to get on after with piano & you'd better say it would not [be] improbable that I should be able to get a post as organist at a public school if it was possible.

With love
Billy

To Mrs Walton   23 October [1918]

Christ Church, Oxford

Dear Mother

Thanks for your letter and the £1. I have been and am and shall be very busy. The Dean has made all arrangements about sheets etc. And I can go to him for money when I am without.

I have a most lovely Bechstein upright in my rooms. I am taking both organ and piano lessons from Mr Ley now as Mr Allchin is too busy with the military.

The "flu" is getting quite the rage round here, I don't know what it is like at home. Mr Marshall one of the choirmen got it and died last night.

I went to the Musical Club last night.

It was a fine performance. The Catterall quartett is coming soon. We are having a memorial service to Parry. Everything goes very smoothly. We havent had any fun worth speaking of. Except our Musicall quartett make a "hell" of a din.

I have been out to tea with Roy [Campbell][1] and he has been round to me. I have also been out to Mr Peakes and Mr Leys to tea.

There is nothing else to say.

With much love
Billy

1 South African poet and writer, who later lived for many years in France, Spain and

To Mrs Walton   29 October [1918]

Christ Church, Oxford

Dear Mother.

I am getting on splendidly now. It has been quite an eventful week.

It is rather good in a way, because Mr som[e]body or other real organist of Brasenose is coming back from the army for next Sunday, so I shall get six [?] guineas for 3 services. Short but sweet.

I have got everything in now. Cups & knifes etc. And I have a kettle & make coffee etc.

Mr Marshalls funeral was on Sat morn. It was in the Cath.

On Sunday I sang bass just to help them out. I made a hell of a shindy. I go to Mr Ley now for my piano lessons. I like it much better.

We have started a literary society. Last night we read Sheridan "Rivals". I took a part.

I cant think of any more news. Nothing much happens.

With love

Billy

Will you please hurry and send my boots as my shoes won't last much longer.

B y

To Mrs Walton   6 November [1918]

Christ Church, Oxford

Dear Mother.

Thanks very much for the letter & boots which I have received alright but no cheque.

I am sorry to hear about Nora, and I hope she will soon be better. Also about Mrs Lloyd.

Everything is going on steadily and peacefully. By the way we have hired a barrel organ for Peace day.

I sang a verse in Cath last Sunday.

—

Portugal. Author of *The Flaming Terrapin* and *The Georgiad* (poetry), and *Light on a Dark Horse* (autobiography).

[20]

I went to the Musical Club last night. The[re] was a trio by Brahms & one by Beethoven[.]

I have started rowing. It is great sport. Next term I shall cox the 'House' eight. I don't know whether there will be any races. Well, I cant think of anything else to say.

With much love
Billy

To Mrs Walton   27 November [1918]

Christ Church, Oxford

Dear Mother,

Thanks very much for the letters & 10/- [note] (I expected another).

I am so sorry not to have written before. But what with Peace demonstrations & making up for lost time also toothache in both sides (for which I have lost two teeth) I have had no time whatsoever. I come home a week on Saturday so remember to send my fare & something extra. Nothing has really happened in the last fortnight. I went to hear three operas at the Carl Rosa [Company]. Madam Butterfly, Faust, & Mignon. They were done very well for a travelling company.

It is awfully sad about Leslie. I will write if I can find something to say.

I wonder if Noel will be home when I am.

I heard from Anne. Poor old thing. Rowing is going on well. We are going to have races, next week. There is no more news.

With much love
Bill

N.B. The Governing body have given me a[n] exhibition of £85 a year.

To Mrs Walton   [postmarked: 5 December 1918]

Christ Church, Oxford

Dear Mother,

Thanks very much for the letter & £11. We have had a most enjoyable week. I shan't be coming home on Sat as there are 'Collections' & other affairs but shall arrive on Monday[.]

Last Sunday we had a big concert in the Sheldonian [Theatre]. We had Bach's Magnificat & other things.

I met Mr [Herbert] Howells[1] the great composer. and have had him to tea with Dr Allen.

We have had races for the last two days. We beat Campion Hall in the heats, St Johns in the Semi final & Balliol in the final[.] So we are the victors. We are having a 15/- [celebration] in the Mitre tomorrow night. There is no more news.

With much love
Billy

To Mrs Walton   12 February [1919]

Christ Church, Oxford

Dear Mother,

Thanks very much for your letter. I am glad to hear that Noel is getting on better. I am have still to work hard therefore I have not had much time to write.

The boat races are coming off at the end of this term. I am 'cox' of one of the "eights".

I went to the Musical Club last night. We had a fine concert.

I met John Masefield[2] & Siegfried Sassoon[3] the poets. They are great men.

I have no more news except the D'oyly Carte are up. Am going to see the "Mikado" tommorrow & the "Yeoman of the guard" on Sat.

With much love
Billy

1 English composer, whose major choral works include *Hymnus Paradisi* (1938).
2 English poet and writer, best known for poems 'Sea Fever' and 'Cargoes'. Poet Laureate from 1930 (succeeding Robert Bridges) to his death in 1967.
3 English poet and novelist, and for many years one of Walton's closest friends and supporters. He was twice seriously wounded in the First World War, in which he was awarded the Military Cross. He was a pacifist and his poetry includes the collections *The Old Huntsman* and *Counterattack*. Among his autobiographical writings are *The Memoirs of George Sherston, Siegfried's Journey* and *Memoirs of a Fox-Hunting Man*.

To Mrs Walton   11 March [1919]

Christ Church, Oxford

Dear Mother,

Thanks very much for your letter. I shan't be coming home till about next Monday week. You need not trouble Auntie Rose about my staying there as I am going to stay with [Sacheverell] Sitwell[1] at Chelsea. I am meeting a great many distinguished people.

You can please send the railway fare (it ought to be a big'un)[.]

We have won both our races so far, but the 1st boat have lost theirs. We beat Queens yesterday by 2 yds but B.N.C [Brasenose College] by about a 100. My wonderful coxing undoubtedly[.]

I must now trot off to dinner.

With much love

Billy

To Mrs Walton   15 May [1919]

Christ Church, Oxford

Dear Mother

Thanks very much for your letter and the parcel which arrived quite intact. I have heard from Annie.

The weather has been really wonderful for the last few days and it has been lovely on the river. The races begin on the 20th. It will be quite like it was before the war.

I am glad Noel is getting on well. Tell him I will write soon.

[Sacheverell] Sitwell came back the other day from Spain. I went to dine with him last night. We are busily arranging about the [Bernard] Van Dieren[2] concert which we hope to come off about June the 10th.

I went to the Musical Club on Tuesday night[.] The Elgar Violin sonata was played. There are very good concerts at Balliol on Sunday

---

1 Younger of the Sitwell brothers: poet, writer and biographer (of Liszt among others). His writings included *Southern Baroque Art* (1924), the autobiographical *All Summer in a Day* (1926), and the text of Constant Lambert's *The Rio Grande* (1927). He succeeded his brother Osbert to the baronetcy in 1969.
2 Bernard van Dieren, British composer of Dutch birth, much admired by the Sitwells. Among his better-known works at this time was his *Chinese Symphony* (1914).

nights open for the members of the university. I don't [think] the[re] is anything else to say, if so I'll tell you next time I write.

With much love
Billy.

To Mrs Walton   1 June [1919]

Christ Church, Oxford

Dear Mother.

Thanks very much for your letter. I am just about beginning to breathe after the turmoil of "eights" week. By the way my boat was very unfortunate in getting "bumped" every day. The weather has been perfect for the last fortnight or so, but it looks like a thunderstorm just at the moment.

Sitwell & myself have arranged a terrific concert for the 13th of this month. We are doing a lot of Van Dieren, and new songs by Delius & myself. If it is a success We ought to make about £20. But that is a mere detail.

Everything is really going on and on just the same as usual.

There was a bit of a "scrap" with some Magdalen fellows the other night. We sank about ten of their punts.

I shan't be leaving here till about July 3rd then I shall go to London for a month to see the best of the operas & ballet. One is unable to get a passport for Italy or France.

With much love
Billy.

To Mrs Walton   29 June [1919]

Christ Church, Oxford

Dear Mother.

Thanks very much for your letter. It is ages since I wrote but I hav[e] been so busy that I have no idea where I am. I am going to London on Wednesday to stay w[i]th the Sitwells. I shall be staying probably to the end of the month. as there will be a great deal to be seen at Covent garden and the Ballet.

If I were you I should take Auntie Nora's house. There will be one less to look after so you will have more chance of a real holiday.

Our concert never came off. We had everything ready, bills out & everything and at the last moment Helen Rootham who was going to sing was taken ill so there was nothing else to do but to postpone it. Anyhow the picture Exhibition has been going tremendously. However as a consolation some of my songs are going to be sung at Lady Glenconnor's [Glenconner's]¹ concert for "Slava week" in London on Friday. Also I shall be conducting two pieces for orchestra at the Russian Ballet[.] We all went to Gloucester for the day last Saturday. It is the most wonderful cathedral I have ever see[n]. I also heard a service.

There was a huge row in the town last night over the Peace. Bonfires & fireworks etc.

All sorts of people come up for hon-degrees. [Generals] Haig[,] Joffre etc. Rather interesting but very boring.

With much love
Billy.

P.S. Just had £40 as a little pocket Money for the vacation.

To Thomas Strong   25 July [1919]

5 Swan Walk, s.w.3

My dear Mr Dean.

Thanks very much for your kind letter, which I have just received. I am still in London and I have been hearing a great deal [of] music, including a wonderful opera by Ravel "L'heure Espagnole", which I heard last night. Also I am going to Borodine's opera "Price Igor" on Saturday night. I return to Manchester on Monday.

I have been working hard for responsions ever since I heard that I had failed.

I think also that there has been a slight misunderstanding about the coach, for if Mr Owen will meditate for a little, he will undoubtably remember, that it was he himself who advised me to change my coach

1 Lord and Lady Glenconner were the parents of Stephen Tennant, the artist who was a prominent member of the Sitwells' circle. The Glenconners often hosted concerts at their London home: Walton's 'The Winds' may have been sung there on this occasion. In 1926 Walton composed *Siesta* while staying with the Glenconners at Haus Hirth near Munich. He dedicated the work to Stephen Tennant.

and go to Mr Young as I could not get on at all with Mr Brabant.

It has been so unfortunate that my pieces for the orchestra have not been played at the Russian Ballet.

But it has been impossible owing to the shortness of the time, and the amount of other work which had to be rehearsed. However it is most probable that they will be performed in Paris at their season next month, which is really much better. Also Mr [Eugene] Goossens[1] is doing them in Manchester in October.

Lastly I must express how grateful I am to you for enabling me to stay in London and to hear so much music. And you may be certain that I shall go on working my hardest for responsions which I am most anxious to pass.

Yours very sincerely,
W. T. Walton.

To Thomas Strong   7 August 1919

93 Werneth Hall Road, Oldham

Dear Mr Dean,

Thanks very much for your letter. I have now been home for quite ten days, and I am getting on rapidly with the work for responsions. As regards Mr Brabant, I understood the college paid him, for after the Christmas term he said he had received his fee from the college. Also he sent no bill, so I thought he had been paid as before.

I shall most certainly try to make sure of getting through in September. One thing is, that I know what I am weak in, and hope to make my weaknesses strong enough for a pass.

Yours very sincerely,
W. T. Walton

1 English composer and conductor, and a supporter of modern music: he gave the British première of Stravinsky's *The Rite of Spring* in 1921. His brother was the oboist Leon Goossens.

To Mrs Walton   17 November [1919]

Christ Church, Oxford

Dear Mother

It seems ages since I have written, or heard from you. I have had an attack of 'flu and have been in bed for about 10 days, but I have quite recovered now. I hope you are much better also father.

Nothing much in particular has been happening. I went to hear Cortot[1] give a recital last Monday. He is simply magnificent. His programme consisted of a Concerto by Vivaldi, the Chopin Preludes some Debussy & the Li[s]zt Rhapsody no. 2.

Lady Ottelline [Ottoline] Morrell[2] asked me over to her house last Sunday. It was very entertaining.

I went to London yesterday for the afternoon. and saw the ballet "Parade". It was very marvellous, especially the scenery. The music was by Erik Satie, a Frenchman[.]

I am to meet Stravinsky next month or perhaps before, so that will be too ex[c]iting for words.

I am sending Noel the music etc by the next post.

With much love

Billy

To Thomas Strong   10 February 1920

2 Carlyle Square, s.w.3

Dear Mr Dean,

I am so much touched by your kindness in writing to me again. I realize only too well how much I owe you in the past, and whatever I do in the future will be thanks to you.

In answer to your question, I must tell you that I have no prospects, and absolutely no means of my own. After thinking it all over very carefully, I believe that a sum, if possible, of £3 or £3.10 a week would be enough to cover my expenses as they are at present.

It makes me very ashamed to ask you after all your kindness in the past, and the disgraceful way in which I have dissapointed your expectations

1 Alfred Cortot, French pianist, conductor, teacher, and editor of Chopin's piano music.
2 Society hostess and patroness of the arts, who lived at Garsington Manor, near Oxford.

over the matter of examinations. But I am working very hard at my music and I think I am making a great deal of progress.

Thanking you so much again for your letter.

Yours very sincerely.

W. T. Walton

To Mrs Walton   24 September [1920]

2 Carlyle Square, s.w.3

Dearest Mother,

Thanks so much for your letters. We are all very well & hope you are also. I am very busy at the moment. [. . .] having lessons from Ansermet[1] & [Edward J.] Dent.[2] [Eugene] Goossens has [Dr] Syntax but has not returned from his holiday so the date of performance is stil[l] indefinite.

Tell Noel not to bother about any more parts [?] but to send what he has done as Ive finished.

Sorry about Granpa Its not my fault. Love to all & to little Nora.

Love

William

¹ wi ite [?] Noel tomorrow.

To Mrs Walton   18 December 1921

2 Carlyle Square, s.w.3

Dearest Mother,

Thanks so much for your letter. I ought to have written before.

I am perfectly well & hope all [of] you are. They want me to stay for Xmas, but [I] will come home if you really wish.

I am glad you took a copy of Tritons. How do you like it. Did you see that "The Winds" was sung last Wednesday.

---

1 Ernest Ansermet, Swiss conductor who worked often with the Ballets Russes company, founded and run by the Russian impresario Sergei Diaghilev. The company appeared regularly in London at this time. In 1919 Ansermet had conducted the Ballets Russes in the world première of Manuel de Falla's ballet *El sombrero de tres picos* (*The Three-Cornered Hat*) at London's Alhambra Theatre.

2 English musicologist and music critic. Professor of Music at Cambridge University from 1926; also the first President of the International Society for Contemporary Music.

[. . .]
Love to all
Yours
William

I write Noel tomorrow.

To Mrs Walton   13 June [1922]

2 Carlyle Square, s.w.3

Dearest Mother,

We arrived back here [possibly from Germany] last week after a most lovely time. It is rather dull now, but [I] have settled down to work. I hope you are all as well as I am. There is really no news to tell you at present

Love to you all
William

WALTON'S surviving correspondence from his first few years with the Sitwell family in London is either rare or non-existent. It is probably fair to assume that the circumstances of his life at this time are themselves the reason for this period of near silence. When not sharing the Sitwells' company at home, or out and about in London, in the country, or abroad, Walton lived in his upstairs room at 2 Carlyle Square. There he studied scores, read widely, and worked relentlessly hard at his composing. His apparent abandonment of letter-writing at this time was certainly not due to any emptiness of events or ideas in his life. On the contrary, in later years he would insist that this period had been an experience of much richness, and the making of him as an artist. In particular Walton's love of painting and architecture developed alongside his burgeoning musical expertise as he accompanied the Sitwells on their intensive European cultural journeys – particularly to Italy, which he first visited in their company in 1920.

In terms of likely correspondents, too, his life had changed. We have no reason to doubt his respect and love for his mother, but already his earlier letters to her had betrayed how his affection for anything to do with

Oldham and his upbringing there had been becoming steadily more forced. Walton wanted to escape from all this; he had found a way of doing so, and he was determined, somehow, to succeed enough in his new life to avoid ever having to go back. It is possible that a collection of letters to his mother from this period may yet be discovered. It is also more than likely that, like so many youngsters breaking free of school and family life for the first time, he simply lost interest in writing home unless it was unavoidably necessary. That this was probably so would explain Charles Walton's sudden visit to London in 1920. Calling at 2 Carlyle Square, he found that Willie and his new friends happened to be away, but an elderly relative of the family was able to convince the anxious father of his son's well-being. A more than very occasional letter home would surely have pre-empted the need for Charles Walton to make what in those days would have amounted to a quite major journey.

Within a few years, too, Walton would have built up many of the personal contacts to whom he was to spend the rest of his life writing letters. But at this stage he would have known far fewer people, and those that he did know he would mostly have been meeting regularly, so that writing letters to them would not have been necessary. And while in the early 1920s the telephone was still something of a luxury, the Sitwells and almost everyone in their circle would have had one. So posterity is likely to remain with very little evidence in Walton's own hand of what was indeed to be the most formative period of his life.

The creation of *Façade*, for instance, seems destined to remain shrouded in mystery in this respect at least. Without Walton's occasional verbal reminiscences in later life of the work's genesis, we would know even less about this than we do already. *Façade*'s early performances were a *succès de scandale* of a kind that masked the brilliance of Walton's effective launch as a composer. His score had more in common with the crisp incisiveness of Stravinsky's idiom, and with the witty irreverence of Poulenc, Milhaud and other members of 'Les Six' in France, than with almost anything in English music of the time. What might be called the 'pre-first' version of the work was given its legendary first, private performance in the drawing room at Carlyle Square on 24 January 1922. Edith Sitwell recited her poems with the aid of a Sengerphone (an early species of megaphone) through a hole in a drop curtain, while Walton conducted the accompaniments. The first public performance of an already substantially reworked version was at the Aeolian Hall on 12 June 1923, and further numbers were revised or substituted over the next few years. Wanting the music to have a wider circulation, Walton also arranged the first of his two *Façade* suites for orchestra in 1926.

Façade's combination of technical virtuosity, steely musical strength, and anti-innocent sophistication marks it out as one of the most astonishing early achievements of any composer in any age. Walton followed it with a String Quartet, which was played in London in July 1923 (a previous version had been performed two years earlier). The following month he travelled to Salzburg, where the International Society for Contemporary Music's newly inaugurated annual festival was being held. Alban Berg, no less, was sufficiently impressed to take Walton to meet Arnold Schoenberg, who was holidaying at Traunkirchen by the nearby Traunsee.

Like *Façade*, if in a different way, the String Quartet is a radical work. Its passages of strongly chromatic harmony may well have been influenced by Schoenberg's idiom: there is evidence that Walton knew *Pierrot lunaire* from the printed score before he started working on *Façade*. (Schoenberg's provocative masterwork was first performed in England in 1923.) Berg had clearly sensed that this English composer might be, from the stand-point of the Second Viennese School, 'one of us'. It is interesting to reflect on how Walton's music might have developed if he had proceeded further along this path. But the climate of English concert-going life was even more conservative than that of its Continental counterparts. Like any young composer, Walton needed performances. He was unlikely to get many with works as idiosyncratic as *Façade* (whose original version had to wait until 1951 to be published), or as suspiciously modernist as the String Quartet.

So Walton began to explore in other directions. His experiments during the next few years included a *Fantasia concertante* for two pianos, jazz band and orchestra, written at the time he was making arrangements for the Savoy Orpheans, the resident band at London's Savoy Hotel. The *Fantasia concertante* remained unperformed, and the score appears to be lost. But Walton had more success with his overture *Portsmouth Point*. He started work on it in London and completed it during a stay in Spain with the Sitwells in 1925. When it was accepted for performance at the ISCM festival at Zurich in June 1926, Walton copied out all the orchestral parts himself. He dedicated the work to Siegfried Sassoon, who contacted Hubert Foss at Oxford University Press on Walton's behalf.

Foss's decision to publish *Portsmouth Point*, and also to sign a contract to publish other works by Walton over the next five years, was a shrewd and far-sighted move. But Foss would probably not have made it on the strength of a work such as the String Quartet. *Portsmouth Point* is a brilliant and breezy *tour de force*. It also offers cheerful and straightforward entertainment value that gives undemanding pleasure to audiences. For a composer who wanted performances, Walton was learning fast.

He was doing so in other ways too. Many years later, Walton liked to make out that in matters of romance he was a 'late developer'. The process appears to have been decisively speeded up by Zena Naylor, a free-wheeling friend of the Sitwells and their circle. Following the Sitwellian example, Walton had dedicated himself to a life of hard work as a composer in his room in Carlyle Square, and he was in no mood to allow anything else in his life to interfere for too long. But morals in London of the Roaring Twenties do indeed seem to have been as cheerfully loose as legend has it, at least if you moved in the necessary upmarket circles. The young composer's heart was susceptible. Walton habitually misspelled people's names, and there is no realistic doubt that the 'Zina' by whom he was so smitten, as his letters to her show, was indeed Zena Naylor. Their relationship appears to have been short but, for Walton at least, painfully sweet.

A deeper friendship helped to give birth to the Viola Concerto, which Walton completed in 1929. It was performed at the Henry Wood Promenade Concerts in October that year, with Walton conducting, and with Paul Hindemith as the soloist. (In the years to come, Walton never forgot this gesture of support from one composer to another.) The Concerto is dedicated to Christabel McLaren, the wife of Henry McLaren, later Lord Aberconway. The attractive society hostess was a friend of the Sitwells, and Walton's letters to her hint at something rather more serious than racy flirtation. Walton and Christabel were never lovers, although it seems that they both considered it. Each also seems to have subsequently been rather relieved that a relationship did not after all develop. They always remained friends.

Several years later Sir Hamilton Harty wrote to Hubert Foss about Walton's First Symphony and its composer. 'Enormously gifted – something further has to happen to his soul. Did you ever notice that nothing great in art has lived that does not contain a certain goodness of soul and a large compassionate kindness?' It is a perceptive remark, up to a point, in relation to the fraught and furious world of the Symphony. But it appears to overlook the astonishing speed and depth of Walton's development as a composer in the few years between the creation of *Façade* and that of the Viola Concerto. The musical evidence of this mature masterwork is that 'something' had indeed happened to Walton's soul. It was surely Christabel Aberconway who had caused it to happen.

[32]

To Mrs Walton   4 May 1925

2 Carlyle Square, s.w.3

My dearest Mother.

At last we are back. And we are all very pleased, we have been away so long. Though we have enjoyed ourselves very much during our stay in Spain. I shall however, be unable to come home until the end of the month, as there is the performance of my Toccata on the 12ᵗʰ and I shall have to superintend the rehearsals of it. Also I have to see what can be done with my concerto [*Fantasia concertante*]. with these Savoy people [the Savoy Orpheans].[1] Though I am afraid that there is only a remote chance of anything satisfactory coming of it. One can only hope for the best.

With best love to all
Yrs ever
Willie

To Siegfried Sassoon   [1926?]

2 Carlyle Square, s.w.3

Dear Siegfried

Here is the typescript I brought to Queens Hall the other night hoping to see you.

It is most awfully kind of you to do the parts. I will let you know exactly when the bill comes in.

Ansermet who I saw last week, is very pleased with the work [probably *Sinfonia concertante*]. I have taken the liberty of dedicating the full score of "P.P." [*Portsmouth Point*] to you, as a small tribute.

ever yours
William

---

1 Formed in succession to the Savoy Havana Band, which had been founded in 1920 by the American bandleader Bert Ralton. The Savoy Orpheans' regular arranger and conductor was Debroy Somers, who had commissioned Walton to make arrangements of foxtrots and other jazz numbers. Walton's *Fantasia concertante* for two pianos, jazz band and orchestra was evidently written with a view to a performance by the Savoy Orpheans, and was possibly commissioned by Somers for them, but it remained unperformed.

To Zena Naylor   Monday night [1926?]

Hotel Continental, Paris

My darling,

I do miss you so much. We had a most awful crossing in more ways than one, but everything is as calm as it could be now, & O & S[1] are really very fond of you. I have been behaving beautifully and show my feelings – not at all. If you know how difficult it is to do, when I want to tell everyone how marvellous and beautiful and divine you are. My Zina! how I wish I wish I could kiss you now but I am sure you know that I am doing it in spirit. If not I send them by wireless from the top of the Eiffel Tower (x x x x x x x x x). I do love you so much, my darling, you have been perfectly heavenly all the week. I have never enjoyed a week so much before. It has been perfectly marvellous and I shall never (x x), never (x x), never (x x) forget you. Write to me, darling, at the Hotel Europa, Salzburg. This will probably be my last letter before Wednesday night unless I find occasion to be able to write in the train. Good-night, my only love x, darling x, angel x and everything else that is wonderful.

    ever your devoted
    William x x x x x x x x x

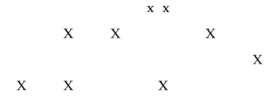

To Zena Naylor   27 September [1926?]

c/o Thos Cook & sons, Via Tornabuoni, Florence

Zina,

I am so distressed about your letter. You must know I wouldn't do the slightest thing to hurt you. I only meant to tease you. Can't you be teased, you silly baby? (if I may be forgiven for using that form of endear-

---

1 Osbert and Sacheverell Sitwell. Osbert, the older of the two brothers, was a poet, novelist, essayist and travel writer. He relished his role as the provocative intellectual leader of the Sitwell circle.

ment).. I know I must have phrased it very indelicately and clumsily, else you really couldn't be cross with me. Besides, fancy you crediting me with, believing anything the little bounder said; I was absolutely livid. He saw and shut up. One could hardly throw coffee over him in Florians, when his mother, Edith[1] etc, etc, were there. As it was I trod hard on his toe, as he went out, (better after all than doing nothing). Do tear up my letter, because I don't like to think that you may again [be] reminded of my stupidity, and forget all about it. I shall tear up yours because I cannot endure to have a letter from you which reminds me that I have hurt you, even inadvertently.

Do please forgive me and don't hate me too much. Will you write to me again?

I wouldn't have mentioned him, only I thought it might perhaps amuse you, and I was under the delusion, (I am rather dense in many ways) that you didn't dislike him quite completely. Don't let's mention it again.

Your reproachful letter has had a shattering effect on me: and what am I to do? I, who worship everything about you, who would run to the ends of the earth for you, in fact [do] anything for you, have only managed to hurt and offend you.

Anyhow what exactly do you mean by "bothering"? You know, that to fulfil your slightest whim, is my greatest pleasure. It is too cruel!!

Your abject.

Willie

To Siegfried Sassoon   5 October 1926

2 Carlyle Square, s.w.3

My dear Siegfried,

I am letting you know about the fruits of your labours. Hubert Foss[2] has taken not only those songs but also "P.P.["] [*Portsmouth Point*] also he has made a contract for 5 years to publish my works. Thank you so much for the trouble you've taken.

Yours ever

William (T. Walton)

---

1 Possibly Edith Sitwell, sister of Osbert and Sacheverell. Walton had set her poems for reciter and instrumental group in *Façade*. The work's first version had been premièred at 2 Carlyle Square in 1922, with Edith Sitwell herself as reciter.
2 Head of Oxford University Press Music Department.

To Mrs Walton   [early December 1926]

2 Carlyle Square, s.w.3

Dearest Mother.

It is indeed a long time since I have written to you, and I am very
sorry about it. But I have been so terribly busy this last month. I have
had to orchestrate four large numbers for Berner's ballet [*The Triumph
of Neptune* by Lord Berners[1]], and it has kept me hard at it.

Friday was a great night [–] the production of the new ballet, and you
will have read about it in the papers so I need not say more.

I conducted my "Facade" suite [No. 1, as an interlude between acts
of the ballet] with good success and again on Sat. Quite a surprise my
being asked to do it. I also conducted my piece "Siesta" at the Aeolian
Hall about a fortnight ago. Unfortunately I receive nothing for it, but it
is well worth doing for the experience.

We have arranged to go to <u>Rome</u> next Sunday. Owing to this unforeseen event of my conducting (I am doing every night this week) it seems
improbable that I shall be unable [*sic*] to come & see you as I had
intended to do, as the tickets are already booked and we are unable to
change them without a great deal of expense, which I can't bear being in
very low water, not having received very much for my orchestration.
And Sachie is in straits too, so I have to keep myself as much as possible.

However I enclose you £2 which I am sorry to say is all I can send
you. at the moment. I am also sending Alec another suit. I hope you
understand about my not being able to get over, but I shall be back late
in January I expect.

With very best love to all
ever your loving
William.

1 English composer, writer and painter. In 1920, along with the Sitwells, Thomas Strong
and Siegfried Sassoon, he had contributed to the £250 annual income which enabled
Walton to live and compose at 2 Carlyle Square.

To Zena Naylor   17 December [1926]

Grand Hotel Santa Lucia, Naples

My dear Zina,

Thank you so much for your thrilling letter. We have come here for a
few days for a respite, but return to Amalfi to-morrow. It has been quite
exciting, compared with the austere hermits life we have been leading for
the last two months. I am getting tired of celibacy. It really is one of the
things one can have too much of.

I was quite expecting by the time I got towards the end of your letter,
you would be telling me how Boonie, had either given you a black eye
or tryed to throw you overboard, probably both. It must have been
nearly too exciting. All the same you seem to have managed to throw
some oil on the troubled waters, though I am afraid it won't remain,
even on the surface, for long.

I trust that the "marvellous looking French boy, much taller etc etc"
was nothing more than a deck walker d – – – him. I wish I had been
there, you would [have] had no need for either Gus [?] or me. I should
have monopolised you completely, whether you liked it or not. (I am
feeling rather ferocious at the minute.) And what is more I shall do as
⸱⸱ᴏn as I come back which is probably sooner than we expected as
ᴊacne has to be back for the publication of his book on Jan 24th or there-
abouts. Now don't say that you'll have gone to Spain or somewhere. Of
course there is no truth in Mrs Howards gossip about Osbert.[1] She has
probably got mixed up with an announcement of O's cousins wedding.
O, by the way, is aimnably disposed but perhaps inclined to be a little
firm. I am so longing to see you again.

Much love
x x
Willie

1 Osbert Sitwell: aristocratic English novelist, poet and essayist, brother of Edith and
Sacheverell Sitwell, and provocative standard-bearer of literary, political and social ideas at
once right wing and anti-Establishment. His many books included *Discursions on Travel,
Art and Life* (1925), *England Reclaimed: A Book of Eclogues* (1927), and several volumes
of autobiography, including *Left Hand, Right Hand!* (1944) and *Laughter in the Next
Room* (1948). He selected the text of Walton's *Belshazzar's Feast* (1931) from the Old
Testament.

To Christabel McLaren[1]   4 August [1927]

Weston Manor [Hall], Nr Towcester, Northants

Dearest Christabel,

I really might have written to you before, but I have no news to tell you, nothing except what you already know, & what is supposed to be unwise to com[m]it to paper.

Life has been exceedingly calm and unruffled, in spite of the appearance of one or two awkward press-cuttings which have been airily and satisfactorily explained away, & except for one or two more or less ordinary domestic incidents life has been boringly calm; really rather nice if only the weather would behave. I have been undergoing the worst attack of sciatica that I've had, but thank goodness it is a little better today. Osbert says it is due to sexual overindulgence. I only wish it was.

I heard this morning that in spite of the old men the [Royal] Philharmonic [Society] are going to do my "Sinfonia [*concertante*]" in January.

I count the days till you come down here, it seems ages ago since I saw you.

Best love,
ever yours,
Willie

To Christabel McLaren   15 September [1927]

2 Carlyle Square, s.w.3

Dearest Christabel,

Thank you ever so much for your letter etc. It indeed brought me confidence and luck.

The performance [of *Portsmouth Point*] went off quite grandly and went down very well (I was recalled three times).

1 Society hostess and patroness of the arts. Married to Henry McLaren, later Lord Aberconway. Walton dedicated his Viola Concerto to her.
2 Walton's postscript in musical notation.

Though I say it myself I conducted quite magnificently, really ex[c]elling myself, the score, being enormous slipped off the tiny desk in the middle of the work, but quite unperturbed I conducted the rest by heart, – in fact a really well stage managed effect, though it might have been disastrous. My shares went up with the orchestra accordingly. My only wish is that you had been there.

The press has so far been extremely aimnable, – and it jolly well ought to be.

I am in London for good. Ring me as soon as you arrive. Am dying to see you.

Love
W.

To Zena Naylor   15 September [1927]

2 Carlyle Square, s.w.3

Dearest Zina,

It is indeed shameful that I haven't written you before, however this week has been a busy one what with one thing and another & Mother & Noel being on my hands, & the previous week I was seeing to the parts of P.P.

P.P. was a great event & I wish you could have heard it. It went extremely well & I conducted A1 in spite of the fact that my score being too big for the desk, fell off half way through so I had to trust to memory – a very impressive & well stage-managed incident. The applause was quite tremendous & I was recalled 3 times. Sir H.W. [Henry Wood][1] was very aimnable & liked it very much. My shares have gone up considerably with [the] orchestra over it all. The press has been aimnable without exception the "Times" only being a bit silly.

After P.P. we adjourned to the Eiffell, where I met Sir Thomas B. [Beecham][2] who was affability itself & wants the score of my Sinfonia to send to the Leeds Festival Committee. which is only a formality, so that performance is apparently settled.

1 English conductor, celebrated for his organization and leadership of the Promenade Concerts in London.
2 English conductor. Founder of the Beecham Opera Company in 1915, the London Philharmonic Orchestra in 1932, and the Royal Philharmonic Orchestra in 1946.

Also the Phil performance is definitely announced, & I heard from Ernest Newman[1] that Koussevitsky[2] was pressing [?] for my new work, so I sent it off also "Facade" suite & I am hoping he will do both in Boston as well as P.P. I shall probably [hear] from him in a day or two.

Otherwise no news. Sc[i]atica on the improve but not yet gone. I shall stay under Sharp [a doctor] for another month or so, if no definite improvement happens I will see Creasy. Hoping youve all been having a lovely time.

I am ever your
W

Best love to O. & S. etc.
P.S. Last week was an expensive week & I am rather poor.

To Stephen Tennant   [September 1927?]

2 Carlyle Square, s.w.3

Dearest Stephen,

According [to] Sieg's [Siegfried Sassoon's] instructions I have found a lovely piano with legs as near to Mrs B L's as possible. Also I have done it in style as it will cost 280 guineas (which is trade price). I may say it is a beautiful & seductive instrument to look at, like a sinuous panther black sleek & glossy, except for the legs, which are, as I've said, as near possible to Mrs B.Ls. I enclose specimen photographs, & I think you will agree with me that the legs are all that you could wish for.

Will you let me know as soon as possible what you decide, as they are keeping it for me for some days.

I saw the Dr again yesterday & my appendix is still on its best behaviour & very quiet.

My best love to you both
ever your
Willie

1 English music critic, and author of books on Wagner, Beethoven, Liszt, Elgar and Richard Strauss.
2 Sergei Koussevitsky, Russian-born conductor, composer and double-bassist. Conductor of the Boston Symphony Orchestra from 1924.

To Siegfried Sassoon [1927]

2 Carlyle Square, s.w.3

Dear Siegfried,

I hope that you will feel able to come and hear "Siesta" at the B.B.C,
Savoy Hill, on Sunday at 3–0 o'clock, I will leave a ticket for [you]
whether I hear from you or not.

The bill for copying has not yet come in but it is somewhere in the
nature of £18. Also I have a bill with Creasy amounting to £12–12–0
half of which is to you. This tiresome sciatica still hangs about, though
it is not so bad as it was. Hoping to see you on Sunday[.]

    Yours ever
    Willie

To Mrs Walton 12 November [1927]

Marlborough Club, Pall Mall, s.w.1

Dearest Mother.

It is indeed a long time since I wrote to you. I hope you are all well. I
am not yet rid of my sciatica though I have been having treatment from
a specialist. There is a rumour that I have a curvature of the spine. I was
X rayed yesterday & shall know definitely on Tuesday.

Otherwise my news is good. Sir Thomas [Beecham] conducts Facade
at the Albert Hall on the 27th. Also we are all very busy about the play
which is also on that date. Tell Alec I will send him a suit as soon as
possible probably in a day or two. Also I hope to be able to send you a
small cheque before long[.]

    with best love
    to all
    Willie

To Christabel McLaren   3 January 1928

2 Carlyle Square, s.w.3

My dear Christabel,

It is high time I wrote to you, especially as I have quite a lot to tell you.

Sachie and Georgia[1] gave the most lovely Xmas party consisting of Stephen [Tennant] and Cecil [Beaton],[2] Dick Wyndham, Siegfried [Sassoon], and alas! Elizabeth Ponsonby – . Baby, bless her had to go to Ireland. Stephen and Cecil were in fantastic form, especially the latter. We were dressed up the whole time, and did a lovely new film which we see on Thursday. I took the part of a boot boy, Sam Snigger, by name, and had a lovely scene seducing Stephen, one of the girls at the school. It was all the more fun as, when everyone should have left noone wanting to a bit, it was found to be impossible, owing to the snow, and we were unable to get away till Friday.

You have probably heard my best bit of news, – that Raymond Mortimer is engaged to Valerie Taylor. What Clive thinks, I haven't heard.

My concert [including *Sinfonia concertante*] is on Thursday. Do listen-in, if you possibly can, it is broadcast from all stations, so you can pick it up easily from Liverpool or somewhere. The first rehearsal is to-morrow. After the concert we are all being taken by Dick to the Chelsea Arts Ball, so I hope to finish the day well. Anyhow I will write and let you know how it goes.

Have you heard from Osbert? He seems rather depressed.

Do write to me if you have nothing else to do, or rather if you have a great deal to do, knowing that you are more likely to write the busier you are.

yours ever
Willie

1 Sacheverell Sitwell and his wife Georgia.
2 English photographer and designer.

To Christabel McLaren [9 January 1928]

2 Carlyle Square, s.w.3

Dearest Christabel,

Thank you so much for your letter. I am so distressed to hear that you have been ill, and do so hope you will be better soon.

I hope you didn't listen-in on Thursday, the performance was bloody, though the applause tumultuous. The work was terribly underehearsed, in fact the players just about knew the notes and that was all. There were only two rehearsals for such an enormous programme, and I doubt if more than an hour and a half was given to my work which needs very careful playing. However it went down very well, though the press has been not too good. All the big circulation papers were favourable and aimnable, but the "Times" etc stupid and unsympathetic, attacking especially the orchestration, which I'd prophesied would happen, owing to the lack of rehearsal. But all that hasn't bothered me, as so many intelligent people seemed to like it, particularly Oscar [Oskar] Fried, the conductor of the Berlin Philharmonic, who was so impressed that he is going to give it in Berlin probably with Schnabel[1] playing the piano part. I have about 7 other performances booked – at the Bournemouth Festival in April, the "Three Choirs" at Gloucester in August, Koussevitsky in Boston New York & Paris, & with Sir Thomas [Beecham] at Leeds (this is quite definite, I heard from the agents for the Festival) also at Oxford & Cambridge. So I haven't done so badly. The Supper after [the] concert was very "hair-raising". People made such complimentary speeches about me that I didn't know where to look and what was more awful, was that I had to get up and speak myself, which I did very badly, but was perhaps rather effective, from being so nervous and blushing, and my tongue cleaving to the roof of my mouth.[2]

After that I had a riotous time at the Albert Hall Ball and got home at 5–30 since when I've been feeling rather exhausted.

There are one or two further intriguing details about Raymond [Mortimer] and his 'bird' which I've unfortunately forgotten at the

---

1   Artur Schnabel, Austrian pianist, composer and teacher.
2   The reference is to the text of *Belshazzar's Feast*. Christabel Aberconway subsequently claimed that she researched this for Walton, although the final text of the oratorio was selected from the Old Testament by Osbert Sitwell. This private joke may indicate that Walton and Christabel had at least discussed the idea of the work earlier. Walton appears not to have started composing *Belshazzar's Feast* until 1929, when the BBC commissioned it.

moment, however she seems to [be] rather temperamental, having once been found with her head in a gas-oven.

The film is too lovely, not much approved of by Lady Grey,[1] and I think that Stephen & my big scene had better be cut. It is too genuine, – think of the great-grand-children.

Write to me again, & come back soon
love
Willie

P.S. I did say "alas Elizabeth", and what is more I say it again.

To Siegfried Sassoon [5 December 1928]

Hotel Cappuccini Convento, Amalfi

My dear Siegfried,

I am so sorry to have been so long in writing to you, but there has been no news of much interest to tell anyone, consequently I am much in arrears with my correspondence, and therefore in disgrace with not a few people.

I have been working hard at a Viola Concerto suggested by Beecham & designed for Lionel Tertis.[2] It may be finished by Xmas and is I think by far my best effort up to now. Hoping to be here till April, I imagine I may get the other works finished as well.

How long are you remaining in Paris? "Façade" entertainment is being done there sometime in January by the "Pro Musica" society, and the "Sinfonia" is being done on Feb 22nd by Ansermet with the new "Orchestre Symphonique de Paris".

"Portsmouth Point" has just be[en] given in Glasgow & Edinburgh so on the whole things are not going too badly.

I enjoyed your book immensely & look forward to the 2nd instalment.

How sad about Stephen's mother. He will need a great deal of looking after now.

I am sorry this is such a rotten letter
Yours ever
William

1 Stephen Tennant's mother, the former Lady Glenconner, since widowed and remarried.
2 English violist. He at first rejected Walton's Viola Concerto and then, after the German composer Paul Hindemith had played the solo part in the work's first performance in 1929, regularly played it himself.

To Siegfried Sassoon   2 February [1929]

Hotel Cappuccini Convento, Amalfi

My dear Siegfried,

I do so hate asking you, but do you think you could possibly do something about the enclosed letter. I shall quite understand if you don't, but will be more than grateful if you do.

Both Osbert and myself have been ill with a nasty attack of "flu" caught from the American tourists who descend on this place in their thousands – it is the only drawback of being here, but it is probably worse elsewhere. It has been a great nuisance as it has robbed us both of about three weeks valuable working time.

Nevertheless, I finished yesterday the second movement of my Viola Concerto. At the moment, I think it will be my best work, better than the "Sinfonia", if only the third and last movement works out well – at present I am in the painful position of starting it, which is always full of trials and dissapointments, however I hope to be well away with it in a day or two.

There is no news to speak of – "Facade" has been put off in Paris till April, which I am rather pleased about as I shall be able to be there, per-haps conduct it, on my way back from here. The "Sinfonia" is being done there on the 22nd of this month. I believe it is just out, and have written to the Oxford Press to send you a copy.

I have really got into this mess with the bank through the fault of the O.P. [Oxford University Press] as they hadn't informed [me] that they didn't pay out royalties till the work was in print, and I was expecting about £20 or £30 last October from the many performances here and [in] America, now I find I can't get [it] till next October, and I had over-drawn on that expectancy. So if you can wait till then, I shall be in a position, I hope, to pay you back.

I hope that you are working at your next book and that it is going well.

I am so sorry to trouble you, but there is this bill also for my piano – but I can hold it over till next quarter as they are aimnably inclined but I don't want it to accumulate into being an ungovernable amount.

It will be most kind of you if you can do anything about all this, and I shall be eternally grateful.

Yours
William

To Siegfried Sassoon   12 February 1929

Hotel Cappuccini Convento, Amalfi

My dear Siegfried,

Thank you so much for your letter, and a thousand thanks for the glad news – it is really most generous of you.

Almost by the same post as I received your letter, I had one from dear Stephen [Tennant], full of happiness at being at Haus Hirth,[1] and most kindly asking me to stay with him whenever I like. I am overjoyed at being able to see him & you & Haus Hirth and all its heavenly contents soon.

Quite what date I shall go is uncertain – it depends on the date of the performance of "Facade" in Paris which is sometime in April, I hope at the end, also on when Osbert and Sachie leave here. Sachie arrives here on the 24th so I shall be able to let Stephen know exactly about the date.

Osbert is very pleased about the "Max" and is writing to you.

Otherwise I have no news, except that I have started on the 3rd movement & hope to complete it soon.

Thanking you ever so much again.

ever yours
William.

To Siegfried Sassoon   3 July 1929

2 Carlyle Square, s.w.3

My dear Siegfried,

Your letter & cheque arrived at a most opportune moment, as I was just beginning to despair about my piano. Cash is not exactly plentiful anywhere at the moment.

I am so glad that Stephen is so much better and I look forward to seeing you both soon.

Scandal have I none, though lately I have been more abroad in the great world. I went to the new ballet "The prodigal son". Scenery by Rouault[2] music by Prokofieff. Lovely the former & mediocre the latter except for the end which is I think better than anything he has done.

---

1 The house near Munich formerly much frequented by Lord Glenconner, Stephen Tennant's father.
2 Georges Rouault, French painter, who also excelled in stained-glass work.

The dancing is very good very excentric & perhaps dull in patches. "Jaggers" [Diaghilev][1] has got a new friend, a composer aged 16 called Igor Markevitch.[2]

I saw Cecil [Beaton] there, and tactfully asked him if he was going to the "circus" party. He was furious, as he had originated the idea & was going to give [it], when some other young thing got in first.

There is very good news about my [Viola] concerto. Hindemith is playing it on Oct 3rd, myself with the "bâton". Also I wield it in the "Sinfonia" on Sept 15th. Both works are down for performance again in the autumn.

On the 12th I make gramophone records of "Facade" two double-sided ones for the new "Decca" company. Unfortunately I get precious little for it. However it will be a good advertisement.

I have more or less got to go to Germany to see Hindemith about the V.C. but how I am going to go, I can't think. He is going to be at the Baden-Baden Festival on the 25th & I hope to meet him there as it will be better than going to Berlin.

I gather that (via Eddie Marsh)[3] you won't be exactly popular for your sin by omission on the 12th.

Tchelicheff[4] is over here and Edith [Sitwell] is giving a party for him next week.

Otherwise no news. My best love to you both. I will write to Stephen soon.

Yrs

Willie

P.S. Imma [von Doernberg][5] has just rung in distress, saying that Alice [Moat][6] went to the "circus" party last night, came back at 6–oxclock [sic], picked up some clothes & left a note saying she had flown to Paris with a young man called George in his "Moth". I hope she comes back as she went.

1 Sergei Diaghilev, Russian impresario and founder of the Opéra Russe and Ballets Russes companies.
2 Russian-born composer and conductor. A prodigy in both capacities, he was already working regularly with the Ballets Russes.
3 Edward Marsh, diplomat, patron of the arts, and editor of the anthology *Georgian Poetry*. He was later to be the model for the role of Pandarus in *Troilus and Cressida*.
4 Pavel Tchelicheff, exiled Russian painter.
5 See pp. 53–5.
6 An American socialite, whom Walton had first met while staying with Stephen Tennant at Haus Hirth. She had also been staying with Edith Olivier at The Daye House, Quid-hampton, in June 1929, during the weekend when Walton and Imma von Doernberg had met for the first time (see p. 53).

To Ernest Newman   6 September [1929]

2 Carlyle Square, s.w.3

Dear Mr Newman,

I am rather diffident about writing to ask you a great favour.

The Decca Gramaphone Co. have just recorded "Facade", and I wonder if you could be so kind as to write a paragraph or so about it, for the pamphlet they propose to issue with the records. I am sure you realise what a help it would be in getting them over.

If you are willing to do this, I will send you the records, when they are ready, as there are several new settings which I think you hav'ent heard.

Can you also, by any chance, tell me Koussevitski's address? I am sorry to trouble you.

Yours sincerely
William Walton

To Ernest Newman   24 September [1929]

2 Carlyle Square, s.w.3

Dear Mr Newman,

I send under seperate cover the score of the first & last movements of my Viola Concerto. Unfortunately the second has not yet been returned from the copyist, but if it comes back in time I will forward it to you.

Will you return me the scores by, at the latest, Monday morning.

Yours sincerely
William Walton.

To Mrs Walton   [23 December 1929]

2 Carlyle Square, s.w.3

Dearest Mother,

Thank you ever so much for your lovely present. I am so sorry not to have written for such a long time, but the truth is, that there has been nothing of any interest to tell you, & you know that I am always well unless you hear to the contrary. I am off to-night to Amalfi to join Osbert[.] I am sorry not to be with you all over Xmas, but I must get away to begin work on this thing for the B.B.C. [*Belshazzar's Feast*] As anyhow, I don't much care for Xmas, I am spending it in the train, where one dos'ent notice it.

I am sending a small present for my nephew & niece, & I am afraid the rest of you, will at the moment, have to put up with nothing but love, of which I send a great deal.

Ever your William

All the usual and manifold Xmas greetings to you all.

To Sergei Koussevitsky   30 December [1929]

Hotel Cappuccini Convento, Amalfi

Dear Mr Koussevitsky.

I have sent to you under seperate cover, the score of my Viola Concerto, also a part for the player.

I am so sorry that I have been unable to send it before, but my publishers insisted on its going to press, and so I have only just had the score returned to me. The parts will arrive in Boston by the end of the month.

Thank you so much for giving the work its first American performance, and I only hope that it meets with your approval.

With best wishes for the New Year.

I am
Yours very sincerely
William Walton

1930–1935

WALTON met the Baroness Imma (Irma) von Doernberg in 1929. She was a young widow, the aristocratic daughter of Prince Alexander von Erbach-Schoenberg, and had formerly been married to the much older Baron Hans-Karl von Doernberg. Her spirited personality and graceful attractiveness had Walton falling in love with her almost at first sight. As their relationship developed, he naturally began to find life with the Sitwells at Carlyle Square too confining. Besides, loose morals indulged in behind closed doors were considered to be one thing in between-the-wars London, whereas openly living in sin was quite another.

This seems to have been a large part of the reason why Walton spent much of the next few years living abroad. Regarding his determined pursuit of success as a composer – a commitment that obviously required him to be a highly visible presence in London's musical scene – his decision to spend so much of his time away from England was risky indeed. But, as it turned out, his sure-footed instinct for successfully pursuing his professional life at this kind of long distance meant that his upward rise through the ranks of England's composers did not falter. The experience was to serve him in good stead, too, when he came to settle in Italy many years later.

Walton had met Imma von Doernberg in June 1929 at The Daye House at Quidhampton near Salisbury, the home of the benevolent society hostess Edith Olivier. His relationship with Imma now featured constantly in his letters to Siegfried Sassoon, in whom he confided with an openness and honesty that was not always to be his manner when writing to others in years to come. To judge from the postscripts that Imma added to Walton's correspondence, she was herself very fond of Sassoon, and was as genuinely grateful as Walton himself was for their friend's financial support whenever it was urgently needed.

By early 1931 Walton and Imma were living together in Ascona in Switzerland. Their situation was difficult. Without Carlyle Square as a regular base, Walton depended on whatever income he could earn from his music: royalties from performances, conducting fees, and his contract with Oxford University Press. If the life of a composer today is in many ways no easier than it ever was, far more potential sources of income, at least, are now available than Walton could then have imagined. Grants from the public sector; substantial commission fees; a realistic level of fees and royalties from copyright performances, gramophone recordings and radio broadcasts; the concept of business sponsorship by the private sector – all these lay far in the future. Hubert Foss's admirable determination to build up the strongest possible catalogue of composers at Oxford University Press required the laying of expensive financial foundations. Foss knew that it would be many years before the music of 'his' composers began to make money for the company, and while he correctly judged that Walton would be one of those composers, he was not yet in a position to pay him more than a quite small retaining fee.

Despite her aristocratic ancestry, Imma seems to have had next to no money of her own. But at least she and Walton could be together in Ascona, and Imma's parents were living near by. Walton needed to return to England at regular intervals to keep his career on course and, in the process, to earn whatever he could. Mostly he stayed either at Faringdon House, the Berkshire home of his fellow composer Lord Berners; with Edith Olivier at Quidhampton; or with Hubert and Dora Foss in Hertfordshire. Carlyle Square too remained open to Walton, and Sacheverell and Georgia Sitwell welcomed him to their home at Weston Hall in Northamptonshire. At this time Walton also wrote a film score, *Escape Me Never*. It was his first experience of a new medium which was eventually to provide him with a useful source of income. For now, though, it was back to Imma at Ascona and to more months of composition, against a background of constant worries about money.

Walton's letters to Sassoon on this subject should not be read as a form of unscrupulous scrounging. At this time there was a recognized tradition among those who were well off that supporting impecunious artists was an honourable and practical thing to do, and Sassoon and Walton would each have understood this from their respective viewpoints. (Later on in life, Walton was prepared not only to engineer similar support for others who needed it, but also to provide it himself. Once, when the young and impecunious Hans Werner Henze was living in Ischia in the early 1950s, he arrived at his house to find an envelope pinned to his front door. Besides some money, it contained a note from Walton that read, 'This is to keep the wolf from your door.') And, true to form, while Walton was asking Sassoon to help keep him and Imma afloat financially, he was also working extremely hard. *Belshazzar's Feast* had been commissioned by the

BBC in 1929, and Walton made early progress on it while staying with the Sitwells in Amalfi the following winter.

A hiatus then followed, probably caused in part by his realization that the oratorio had grown into a larger work than the BBC had expected. By early 1931, however, it had been completed. After the triumphant first performance at the Leeds Festival in October that year, Walton's thoughts began to turn to writing a symphony, an idea that had been suggested by Sir Hamilton Harty. The new work's extremely difficult genesis is vividly charted in Walton's letters. Its première was planned for December 1934, but by then Walton had run into such severe problems with the symphony's finale that he reluctantly agreed to allow Harty to conduct a performance of the first three movements only.

Apart from what can be gleaned from Walton's letters and a few reminiscences by his friends, we know extremely little about Imma von Doernberg. Did she exaggerate her health problems, which worried Walton so much, as a form of jealous attention-seeking? It is not really possible to know. Hers was evidently a difficult nature, but health problems can make any of us difficult. Was her capacity for warmth and understanding as reliable as her words to Sassoon seem to show? Any editor has to remain haunted by the thought that, stored in an attic somewhere in Italian-speaking Switzerland, there is a huge and undiscovered collection of Walton's letters to Imma and of hers to him. If those letters exist, they would help to shed much light on an evidently turbulent relationship which, however, neither party was easily able to bring to an end, even when it must have been clear to them both that this was inevitable. To judge from their letters to Sassoon and others, Walton and Imma seem to have understood quite early on in their relationship that they probably did not have a future together. But given the genuineness of the emotional bond between them, it must have been equally difficult for them to accept that their separation was a mutual trauma waiting to happen.

When Walton completed his First Symphony in 1935 after Imma had left him for another man, he dedicated the work to her. Its first three movements – in turn furious, spiteful and depressive – can be seen as charting an emotional relationship that was breaking up in extreme bitterness. The finale, on the contrary, radiates a triumphalism that appears to express Walton's state of mind – exhilarated, free-wheelingly optimistic, and not a little relieved – at the start of his new life with Alice, Viscountess Wimborne. But Walton's dedication, if at least partially ironic, was also honest. Without Imma, the First Symphony would not have come to life as we know it.

To Siegfried Sassoon   2 March [1930]

Hotel Cappuccini Convento, Amalfi

My dear Siegfried,

It must seem that whenever I write to you, that my letters consist of either of acknowledgements for favours granted, or for favours which I hope to be able to acknowledge – I need hardly add that this letter belongs to the latter category. The enclosed bill will show you what straits I am in, as regards my piano; but that is not my only trouble.

The question is, is how am I to exist between April 17th, when I leave here for Berlin, & April 24th when I get paid (Mks 500) for my concert, & incidentally how to get there even.

Osbert & David [Horner][1] are leaving here on March 19th, so I shall be alright here till I leave. You are enough in touch with the former's state of finance to know that to expect help from him is not easy or possible: so I am more or less forced to come to you again for help, as I feel it would be unwise to ask for my fee in advance, & unlikely that I should get it if I did.

Except for the Berlin concert I don't see that I shall be having anything coming in, until my royalties are due in October, unless, as I believe is possible, the B.B.C repeat my concert in London, – but anyhow that won't be till June. My hopes however for the autumn are comparatively high – I had a letter from C B. Cochran[2] hinting that he would like my help in his next revue!! both as a ballet & as a "jazz" merchant. I cordially accepted, & hope that something will come of it, but I suppose one shouldn't be too sanguine about it. My royalties also ought to be more this year, as I have been having many performances – that hardy-annual P.P. having been toured by the Chicago Symphony & played in New York by Koussevitsky, in Paris on "radio", in Birmingham by Boult![3] & even it has penetrated the forbidding portals of the Royal College. – the "Sinfonia Concertante" has done less well, but that is to be expected, only having been played in Paris, Geneva & London. It was a great pity that Beecham was ill for the latter performance. The Viola

1 Osbert Sitwell and the artist David Horner had recently begun to live together in a homosexual relationship.
2 Sir Charles B. Cochran, impresario and promoter of highly successful revue theatre shows. Nothing came of this first approach. In 1935 Walton was to compose his ballet *The First Shoot*, to a scenario by Osbert Sitwell, for Cochran's revue *Follow the Sun*.
3 Adrian Boult, English conductor, at this time much involved in English contemporary music.

Concerto is not yet out so can't really start its career till the autumn.

A de-luxe – signed-by-the-authour[sic]-&-composer edition of "Façade" is going to appear in the autumn 300 copies at £3–3–0 which I hope will do well, it ought to bring me in about £70. Incidentally the records are out this month, & it is being "broadcast" to-morrow by Edith & Constant [Lambert].[1]

Stephen [Tennant] may well blame me for my insipid letters, but here there is no equivalent of the exciting Siracusan life to describe so he can hardly expect anything else. It is good news to hear that he is so well – so pink & chubby & I hope that you are the same. I am writing to Tante Johanna[2] – I hope that it is nothing very serious. There is an epidemic of illnesses & operations going on amongst our friends, – Jean Fleming has been at the point of death for months, but I believe is getting better slowly – we have a wire to-day from Mrs Powell [the Sitwells' housekeeper] that [Sir] George [Sitwell][3] has to undergo an operation to-morrow.

Work [probably on *Belshazzar's Feast*] goes tolerably well, but I always am uncertain of its merit, anyhow at this comparatively early stage in its creation.

I hope that you have nearly finished your book & that it is going well. Otherwise there is no news. I will write to Stephen very soon.

I regret very much having to pester & bother, & I hate doing so, especially as I know what a help & relief you have been to O & S recently.

With best love to you both,

Yours ever

Willie

To Ernest Newman   5 March [1930]

Hotel Cappuccini Convento, Amalfi

Dear Mr Newman,

I am having sent to you the recently issued records of "Façade". There are several new numbers which I don't think that you have heard.

1 Gifted and erratic English composer, conductor, pianist, writer and critic. The first English composer to be commissioned by Diaghilev, with the ballet *Romeo and Juliet* in 1926, Lambert was the founder music director of the Vic–Wells Ballet in 1931, and a close friend and colleague of Walton. In 1934 he published his entertainingly contentious book *Music Ho! – A Study of Music in Decline.*

2 Resident at Haus Hirth near Munich, where Stephen Tennant regularly stayed.

3 The father of Edith, Osbert and Sacheverell.

Thank you so much for allowing me to quote from your article. Did you receive the record of "Portsmouth Point", incidentally none too good, which I sent you sometime ago? I only ask, because others, which I had sent at the same time, never reached their destination.

Yours very sincerely
William Walton.

To Siegfried Sassoon   [postmarked: Amalfi, 6 March 1930]
[postcard]

Thank you so much for your telegram. It is really too good of you.
Willie.

To Siegfried Sassoon   10 March [1930]

Hotel Cappuccini Convento, Amalfi

My dear Siegfried,

I can't thank you enough for your great generosity, & I hope that I shall live to be a credit to you. Also sweet Stephen, how angelic of him to give me such a present.

It is really good news to hear that he is feeling so well, I only hope that he will continue to feel so.

It is terrible about Tante Johanna. I do so hope that she will get alright. George we hear from Mrs Powell, has had a major operation and is in a very bad way & unlikely to recover. Which is all very worrying.

Osbert says that if possible you both ought to stay in Sicily, instead of going north, during at least some part of April, as you have no conception of how lovely it is during that month.

With thousands of thanks again
Love to you both
ever yours
Willie

To Mrs Walton [20 March 1930]

Hotel Cappuccini Convento, Amalfi

Dearest Mother,

I am so very sorry that it is such a long time since I wrote to you, but really I have had nothing much to tell you, as life is very quiet here.

I remain here till about April 15th when I go to Berlin for my concert which is on the 24th. I am in a bit of funk about it, but I think I shall manage alright, as I have four rehearsals.

I had a nice letter from Sir Ham. Har. [Hamilton Harty][1] about the "Façade" records, & I think I shall get more of a look-in at the Hallé [Orchestra] next season, in fact I believe he is contemplating playing the piano part of the "Sinfonia [*concertante*]" as he did in [Constant Lambert's] the "Rio Grande" which I see is having a huge & very well-deserved success, which makes me happy for Constant as he has not had much of a good life till now, & this ought to put him on his feet, both financially & otherwise.

C. B. Cochran is I believe contemplating asking me to write the music for his next revue. But there is nothing definite as yet.

[Sir] George [Sitwell] has had a severe operation, which he has got through alright, & Mrs Powell may have to have another. Really never a year passes without one of them being up to something. You might write if you have a minute to spare.

I hope that you are happy & comfortable in your new surroundings & that all goes well. I am sure it is a wise move, & that you will settle down soon enough. I hope the children & [are] better by now.

Thank Nora for her letters & give my best love to all & to yourself
ever your
Willie

1 Irish conductor and composer. From 1920 to 1933 he was conductor of the Hallé Orchestra in Manchester. In 1934 and 1935 he gave the first performances of Walton's First Symphony.

To Mrs Walton [May 1930?]

c/o Thos Cook & son, Zurich

Dearest Mother,

Thank you for your letter which was forwarded from Berlin. I trust Noel continues to improve.

You will be very sorry to hear that Mrs Powell died last Sunday. I am feeling rather upset about it.

Keep me informed about Noel. a P.C will do. After the 8th my address will be

> C/o Thos Cook & son
> Via Tornabuoni
> Florence.

With best love to all
Willie

To Dora Foss[1] [postmarked: Paddington, 18 June 1930]
[postcard]

Thank you so much – I shall be delighted to come on the 28th & I hope, to carry off the championship.[2]

yours
Willie Walton

To Siegfried Sassoon 8 March [1931]
[with postcript from Imma von Doernberg]

Casa Angolo, Ascona, Ticino, Switzerland

My dear Sieg,

I am writing this on the terrace in the sun. It is heavenly here & [I] am enjoying it very much, and am immensely happy. Also I am doing [a] vast amount of work, as you prophesied I would. I am now on the last chorus [of *Belshazzar's Feast*] – unfortunately at the moment it dos'ent

1 Hubert Foss's second wife, with her own career as a soprano singer.
2 At deck tennis, the preferred game of the Foss family on the lawn at their home at Nightingale Corner, Rickmansworth, Hertfordshire.

progress too well, but I hope to complete it, or practically do so before I leave, which I do a fortnight tomorrow.

It is a most frightful nuisance having to come back, just at the critical moment, as otherwise, if I could stay, I have no doubt that I could complete the whole work for my birthday (29th) as I promised Foss. Also at the rate I am living here, I could stay till practically the end of May & complete the orchestration.

As it is, I propose to return here as soon as possible, but the fare & expense of being in London, make a large hole in my fortune, consequently making my stay here much shorter.

I feel bound to return, otherwise Tertis will take such offence, and he has spent so much time and labour on the Viola Concerto that I feel it would be ungrateful of me [not] to be there, especially as I promised him I would and he would be dissapointed & offended. Incidentally I wish also to hear it myself, never having done so properly as yet. Also there will be some business with the Leeds [Festival] people, Sir Thomas [Beecham] & Foss to see to, but it is all a matter of a few days. So my plans are at present that I leave here so as to get to London for a rehearsal on the morning of the 25th, go with you that night to hear "On the plateau", to the "Phil" on the 26th, and leave London on the 29th & be back here on the 30th. I[t] seems a large expense for so short a time, but I feel it is absolutely necessary.

My other plan is that I shall bring you back here with me on that date.

To-day, Imma has heard from from Edith [Olivier][1] about Stephen's, I hope temporary, set-back and of the catastrophe with Nurse May. What a bitch. I am sure she's made him ill on purpose. I think Imma had better see her handwriting.[2]

It would be an entire change for you to come out here, if only for a fortnight or so, and I am sure [it] would do you good. It is a most lovely place, just what you would like, & you could settle down to some work.

I think also it would be worth your while to come to see if it wouldn't be a good place for Stephen to convalesce in, when he is able to move.

There is a very good new hotel owned by a German millionaire baron & it gets the sun all day. It is an unusual hotel in that it houses part of his picture collection of Picasso[,] Matisse, Braque, Chinese paintings etc. It is right in the country & very good mountain air, and as it is only

---

1 Novelist, patroness and supporter of artists, and society hostess. Her country home was The Daye House, Quidhampton. Distantly related to Laurence Olivier.
2 Imma von Doernberg was a graphologist.

2 miles from the Italian frontier it is not like being in Switzerland at all, though it has all the Swiss amenities of life.

I am sure it would take your mind off all this disagreableness & keep you quiet till it blows over, so do try and make up your mind to come back with me on the 29th. Let me know if you will, soon, so that I can book a room for you.

Before I left, I had supper with [Edward] Clark[1] of the B.B.C and there is little doubt that your dream about "Morning Heroes" materialised, as apparently when Boult came to rehearse it he just couldn't force it & land the onus on the choir, and Bliss[2] himself is conducting on the 25th. and I suggested that "Crikey" [the poet Robert Nichols] should recite the narrative part, but I have not heard whether that is definitely fixed. I hope it is, as the suggestion was treated and made in all seriousness.

Otherwise I have no news at all.

Let me know what you decide.

Best love

Willie

Dearest Siegfried,

I feel very sorry for you, that you have such a tiresome time with that beastly nurse, as Edith told me in the letter I got today. – What are you doing? I am afraid you feel very depressed about all this. – But I am sure, it will only be a temporary thing. – Willie and I would so much like to have you here for some time. – The hotel Willie described to you, is a five minutes walk away from our place, so we could keep a good neighbourhood. – Do try and come, it would be quite a nice change for you, also you should be able to settle down with some work. –

We are having a very nice and peaceful time together. Best love and I hope to see you <u>very</u> soon

Imma.

1 BBC radio producer, and a dedicated supporter of new music both in England and abroad. It appears to have been on Clark's initiative that the score of Walton's Viola Concerto had been sent to Paul Hindemith after Lionel Tertis had turned down the opportunity of playing the solo part in the first performance in 1929. That year Clark also arranged for the BBC to commission *Belshazzar's Feast* from Walton.
2 Arthur Bliss, English composer. His *Morning Heroes* for chorus and orchestra was composed in memory of those who had died in the First World War.

To Siegfried Sassoon   14 March [1931]

Casa Angolo, Ascona, Ticino, Switzerland

My dear Sieg,

Thanks for your letter. I am sorry that you have had such an irritating time and I am sure that you ought to come here for a bit. I have booked a room for the 30th. for you. It is the best I can get, as the hotel is already well booked for Easter.

I return on the 24th to Carlyle Sq, let me know where to meet you for the 25th.

I am sorry to say there is not a hope of my finishing this damn work before I leave, but I hope to have it under way, so that I can finish it quickly on my return here.

There is a really good specimen of a 33 inch bore, well worth coming for if for nothing else. The weather's been lovely, a little cold.

Imma is away for a couple of days, visiting her parents who are living at Lugano just over the mountains. Luckily [only] hours away.

With love
As ever
Willie

To Siegfried Sassoon   22 July [1931]

Casa Angolo, Ascona, Ticino, Switzerland

My dear Sieg,

This is going to be a somewhat alarming letter, but not, I consider entirely without some justification.

You will have received my postcard stating our safe arrival. Imma only just got out of Germany in time – you will have read the new decree about people leaving the country.

Her position is this: – this year, up to now she has been living on £15 a month, which has just been sufficient, and now she is reduced to £7–10 (a month), owing to her father being in that bank smash, and is consequently unable to allow her anything, anyhow for some time to come. She has £15 now, which has to last her for two months, after that she is uncertain what she gets. Consequently she can't afford to stay here, after I leave on Sept 6th. & proposes to take a small room & cook her own food till she leaves for Zurich on Oct 1st.

[63]

There she hopes to be able to find a job of some sort, & is starting lessons in stenography tomorrow to make herself more eligible, but it will take all the time she is here, to become efficient at it, I imagine. She will at the same time [have] to continue with her graphology when she gets to Zurich, with the Pulvers.[1]

I think it will be very difficult for her to find a job as there is the same amount of unemployment in Switzerland as elsewhere, but it will be easier [and] less dangerous here, than in Germany.

I haven't told her too much of your offer to help, perhaps you would write to her yourself.

In a moment of alarm & weakness, I sent a veiled & general S.O.S. to Steenies [Stephen Tennant's] for the first time!

That is her position, and now I want to outline the general horror of the coming winter & urge you to do something about it.

Even if the Conference in London does put Germany on her feet, the position, not only for Germany but for all countries is going to be worse.

I have heard that unemployment will in England reach 5 or 6 million & that there will be a general break-down about February 1932. Also that the value of the £ is bound to drop (inflation is anyhow proposed in the Macmillan report). I've been informed of this by several Swiss bankers, who say there is no confidence in England & that the only currencies to keep their value will be the American Swiss & Dutch.

Consequently I beg of you to consult with Lassade (who is sure to urge you that everything is all right) & move some money – a great deal, out here, while there is time, for a law is sure to be made preventing capital from leaving England. I should try to persuade Steenie to do the same, that is, if Glenconnor will allow, & if it is possible I should have him moved out here, for one has no idea how unpleasant it may become in England this winter.

In fact, it is so difficult to explain things, that I think you had better come out here for a bit again, if you are having a poor time of it.

It is heavenly here, not too hot, & empty[,] far less crowded than when we were last here, at any rate at the Monte [Monteverità].[2]

I am afraid, this will be the last time, for long ahead, that Imma & I are together, which is too sad for me to dwell on. There is, I feel, no doubt, that when I return to England I also should try & get a job of

1 Friends of Imma von Doernberg's family.
2 In this case not Castello di Montegufoni, the Sitwells' residence in Tuscany, but the nearby hotel to which Walton refers in his earlier letter to Sassoon: see pp. 61–2.

some sort, though what, heaven alone knows, as I think that it is more than possible, that however much my friends may want to help me, they will not be in a position to do so much sooner than any of them expect.

Of course, you will probably think that I am talking through my hat & without reason or authority. Only too true to some extent – but all I can say is, that I more or less foresaw this present crisis a long time ago, & I have been talking to several people here, who are in a position to know about these things, & lastly my instinct tells me as well. I only hope that it is all wrong.

Write to me soon & let me know what you think & how Steenie is (give him my best love) & yourself.

ever yours
Willie

P.S. Imma's visit to Leeds is presumably off, as she feels that in her present position that luxuries can't be gone in for, & that she could live for a long time on the money it would cost. I quite see her point, but that is too sad.

Imma sends her best love & has nearly finished the jumper for you.

To Siegfried Sassoon   31 August 1931
[with postscript by Imma von Doernberg]

Casa Angolo, Ascona, Ticino, Switzerland

Dear Sieg,

One of us ought to have written to you long ago, but we are both such busy creatures, Imma with her stenography (at which she is progressing very well) & I correcting hundreds of pages of parts [for *Belshazzar's Feast*] – the worst of that is over & I have been able for the last 10 days to do what I liked.

I have been lent a canoe & so spend most of the day paddling about on the lake & swimming consequently I am looking & feeling the picture of health.

Luckily the last ten days has coincided with lovely weather, it previously having been just like anywhere else.

I return on Sept 8th to conduct the V.C. [Viola Concerto] at the "Proms" on the 10th. Will you been in London then or still in the country? If the former we might meet after the performance. Let me know.

We were both so sorry that you couldn't come here.

Your letter makes depressing reading – I honestly don't what to make of Steenie, his behaviour is too complex & fickle to judge what will happen next – worse even than trying to see what may happen in the world crisis, which seems to be having a lull before an even greater storm.

The bankers, whom I have been more or less avoiding seem to think that it will be worse in England than in Germany. However we can but see.

Imma has recovered what money she had in the Danat bank & with care it seems that she will be alright to round about Xmas.

She is not going to Zurich till November & may not then, as she is not allowed, as an alien to get a job, but she can work with Frau Pulver at graphology. But that won't bring in much.

She heard yesterday from her brother-in-law that the [von] Doernberg estate can't pay anything for sometime to come & her father also will have to discontinue the small allowance he has been giving her.[1] Her Aunt dos'ent seem to be going to do anything about it.

All of which is very depressing for her & her nerves are consequently in rather a bad state, but she is much better than she was a month ago, generally speaking.

Edith O. [Olivier] [h]as asked her to stay as long as she can, if she comes over for Leeds, which is sweet of her.

I've not much news of the "Family". Osbert is at Toulon or somewhere near there with D. [David Horner] & Sachie & Georgia I imagine by this time will be somewhere in Sweden after having cruised & caroused through Portugal with the Duke. What a life!

With best love
Willie

My dearest Sieg,

I am thinking of you so often, since we got your sweet but so depressed letter. If we only could help you my dear! – I do hope you have a comparatively nice time in your country-house. – It was too sad for words, you could not come, as I was so much looking forward to see you again. – Willie looks very well indeed, since he stopped working. – We shall have another two weeks together before he has to go back. This time the parting will be rather sad, as one doesn't know, when and

1 Germany had imposed currency restrictions preventing its citizens, including Imma, from withdrawing money from the country.

if there will be another meeting again, for some long time. But I am very grateful for all those peaceful months we could spend together, which we entirely owe to you. God bless you for it! Do write to me soon again, how you are and how everything goes on for you.

All my love for you
from
Imma.

To Adrian Boult   1 December [1931]

2 Carlyle Square, s.w.3

Dear Dr Boult,

I must thank you very much for all the trouble you took over the performance of "Belshazzar", which on the whole except for (occasional) "nerves" on the part of the chorus, was admirable.

I am sure that the enclosed letter will charm you.

Yours very sincerely
William Walton.

To Siegfried Sassoon   12 December 1931
[from Imma von Doernberg]

Zürich 6. Offikerstr. 24, bei Dr. Pulver

My dearest Siegfried,

I must tell you again how much I enjoyed all the hours I spent with you last Monday. It was such a comfort to have that long talk with you my dear. – Since we have seen a great deal of each other at Ascona last spring, I very often think of you, and it is always very painful to think that you have to suffer to such an extent. – But I understand it so perfectly, but also I do hope you will find other things in life again, which are giving you an interest and pleasure. –

Willie and I had two more nice days at London, but the parting is always the most painful distress to us both, especially now, where the circumstances are more and more against us and it might be such a long time before we see each other again – I wish I could do more for Willie but I have the feeling that fate is at the end against the fact that our two lives settle down together. –

I hope you will understand these lines, it is still difficult for me to explain myself in English letters. There are so many things I would like to talk about with you. My very best wishes are with you always. I would so much like to have a nice photo of you. Can you send me one? – With much friendship and love I am yours

Imma.

To Dora Foss   21 December [1931]

Faringdon House,[1] Berkshire

Dear Dora,

Thank you so much for your letter. It is kind of you to ask me for a week-end.

Would it be possible for me to come instead of the dates you mention, for the week-end of the New Year? I that is too inconvenient I will come on Jan 15th.

It is sweet of you to ask the Baronin [Baroness] as well, but alas,! alas! she returned to Switzerland about ten days ago.

Here is one of the Songs ['Through Gilded Trellises']. Don't hesitate (because it is dedicated to you) to severely criticise it, if it dos'ent meet with your approval.

It is not so difficult as it first looks, especially the piano part which sounds difficult but is in reality as easy as Sidney Smith, & I may say not unlike.

However I hope you will like it. I will send the others as they are finished.

I've now to write a Xmas carol[2] by tomorrow morning for the "Daily Dispatch." It is bad to tempted by filthy lucre!

With all good wishes for Christmas & the New Year to you, Hubert & Christopher[3]

Yours

Willie Walton

1 The country home of Lord Berners.
2 *Make We Joy Now in This Fest.*
3 The young son of Hubert and Dora Foss.

To Siegfried Sassoon   [postmarked: Dorking, Surrey,
                                          29 December 1931]

Dear Sieg,

Here is "Crikey's" letter! It has been rather nice spending Xmas here.
We leave to-morrow & I shall go down to Faringdon again at the end of
the week. At the end of January I come & stay with Edith [Olivier]
indefinitely so I hope to see something of you.

Imma wrote and told me the good news you had written her. It really
is too kind of you – it is indeed something to look forward to and I feel
so unsettled at the moment both as to work & environment.

With all blessings for the New Year
Yours
Willie

To Dora Foss   12 January [1932]

Faringdon House, Berkshire

Dear Dora,

Thank you for your letter. I am glad my "effort" ['Old Sir Faulk'] has
not gone down badly. I had considerable misgivings about it.

Hubert will soon be joining the B.B.C dance band!

I don't mind a bit about the room, as long as Paddy [Patrick Hadley][1]
won't object to my seeing his wooden leg in the flesh, so to speak.

I will let you know what time I arrive.

I just had a wire from Harriet [Cohen][2] saying that as a token of ——[3]
she is playing the Sinfonia in Montreal & paying for it herself. Which,
all things considered, is extremely nice of her. Also I've had a very
aimnable letter from Harty.

yours
Willie

P.S The new song is not fit to be seen, & there's not much of it as yet.

---

1 English composer, mostly of works for chorus and orchestra. He later became Professor
of Music at Cambridge University.
2 English pianist. A dedicated performer of music by English composers, including
Arnold Bax and Ralph Vaughan Williams. She had been chosen by Elgar to play the piano
part in the first performance of his Piano Quintet.
3 The dash is as written by Walton, not an editorial emendation.

To Siegfried Sassoon   28 January 1932

Faringdon House, Berkshire

Dear Sieg,

Being on the verge of financial embarrarsment [*sic*], perhaps you will be so kind as to sign the enclosed form quaranteeing [*sic*] me an over-draft, as you said you would.

It is only as a safeguard as I am managing to keep my nose above water. As soon as the "Daily Dispatch" pays me for the Xmas carol I wrote for it I shall be alright, as I shall receive the magnificent sum of £10–10.

Also I deposited my 120 Decca shares with the bank & the manager seems quite pleased with them! Incidentally they are now mine, as dear Lil [Elizabeth Courtauld],[1] as I saw in her will, forgave all paltry sums that she had lent to various "down & outs". Also I've 200 Swiss francs in my bank at Ascona, but I don't want to withdraw them.

Last week, I was in Manchester & heard a marvellous (the first good orchestral part) performance of the Viola Concerto.

Harty has asked me to write a Symphony for him. So I shall start on that when I come to Edith [Olivier's]. A rather portentous undertaking, but the Hallé is such a good orchestra & Harty such a magnificent con-ductor besides being very encouraging, that I may be able to manage to knock Bax[2] of[f] the map. Anyhow it is a good thing to have something definite suggested & a date to work for.

I've been writing some songs for Mrs Foss during my stay here[.] They'll teach her!

I come to Edith [Olivier] about Feb 18th. We leave here on Sat. I shall stay in Carlyle Sq for the following ten days as I want to see Furtwangler [Furtwängler][3] & Klemperer.[4]

I hope all goes well with you, & I look forward to seeing you.
Yours
Willie

1 The late wife of the textile manufacturer Samuel Courtauld. Both were generous patrons of the arts.
2 Besides much other music, Arnold Bax composed seven symphonies between 1922 and 1939.
3 Wilhelm Furtwängler, German conductor and composer. He conducted regularly in London at this time, where his interpretations of Wagner's operas were of legendary quality.
4 Otto Klemperer, German conductor and composer. At this period of his career he was associated as much with contemporary works as with the classical repertory.

To Christabel McLaren
[4 February 1932]

2 Carlyle Square, s.w.3

Darling angel Christabel,

    I am completely overcome, and can only cry and pray.

    I do so hope that I shan't let everybody down. I must write a work really worthy of Lil & Sam's wonderful and unbelievable trust and generosity.[1] I hope I'm capable of it.

    Darling   I am so grateful.

ever yours

W

To Siegfried Sassoon
6 February [1932]

2 Carlyle Square, s.w.3

Dear Sieg,

    Thank you so much for your guarantee. I probably shan't need it, or anyhow it will only be necessary for the next month or two, for the miracle has happened. This [is] an absolutely dead and profound secret, known as yet only to myself, (Imma) & Sachie & Georgia & Gerhild who is to be my trustee & should be kept in the family circle.

    Dear angel Lil Cortauld [Elizabeth Courtauld] has left me in her will the magnificent sum of £500 per annum for life & with the disposal of the capital in case of my death. It seems quite unbelievable & I am feeling more than a little hysterical about it. It is too marvellous for words. I can hardly realise what it means to my life and really to every-one else to whom I have been a willing burden. I suppose it will take a little time before I begin to receive anything & if you can put up with me till then, I shall be more than grateful, as I am for all you have done for me in the past.

    I come to Edith [Olivier] on Thursday & shall look forward to seeing you.

love

ever yours

Willie

1 For details of this, see next letter below.

To Siegfried Sassoon [early February 1932]

2 Carlyle Square, s.w.3

Dear Sieg,

Having heard from Sam, I can't impress enough the necessity for absolute secrecy about the contents of my previous letter, not even to Edith, not that I really doubt her ability to keep it, but that if she knew, she might become a bit of a nuisance about marriage etc.

Yours
Willie (the will rather)

To Siegfried Sassoon [early 1932?]

2 Carlyle Square, s.w.3

My dear Sieg,

I am more happy than I can say to hear about the thrilling (& not to add unexpected) news of your engagement.[1]

All my love & congratulations for it, & I hope you will be as happy as you deserve.

I hear that she is the most ravishing beauty & I'm longing to meet her.

To-morrow I'm going to Abinger to see about the house I intend taking, I'm afraid it may fall through, in which case I shall be going to Weston next week.

I had a long telephone talk with Imma; she seemed rather better & I think it is now more than likely we shall make it up.

Let me know if you are in London this week as I long to see you.

Again many congratulations.

Yours ever
Willie

1 Sassoon married Hester Gatty in 1933. In 1936 they had a son, George; the marriage ended in 1945.

To Dora Foss   [*c.* February 1932]

The Daye House, Quidhampton, Salisbury

Dear Dora,

I am so very sorry to hear that you have not been well & I hope that by now, you are recovered.

Here is the last song ['Daphne']. I am sorry to have been such a time with it, but I could not get it satisfactory – this is the 3rd version – all I can say about it is that it is better than the other two.

I am here for some weeks, trying to start on a symphony. What I fool I am, treading where so many angels have come a "cropper". However I shall be able to be in a better position to judge, by April 1st.

I asked Edith [Sitwell] about the pronunciation [of the word 'Lucia' in 'Through Gilded Trellises'] she prefers "chi" to "cha", anglicised if incorrect. Are you going to have the Recital on March 20th?

yours.

Willie Walton

To Dora Foss   [*c.* February 1932]

The Daye House, Quidhampton, Salisbury

Dear Dora,

Thank you for your letter. I am so pleased to hear that you are better and that your voice is making a 'come-back'.

I feel that you both know best about giving a party for the songs, I personally feel that they are hardly worth taking so much trouble about. As regards the date April 9th would suit me best, if it is all the same to you.

About the concert, June 15th seems a good date, but whether I shall be back from Switzerland I can hardly say at the moment. It all depends on how expensive it is and how long my money lasts. It probably won't last anywhere near June 15th.

The Symphony is unspeakable, it has been christened the "Ichabod" or the "Unwritten", only time will decide which, if either are appropriate.

yours

Willie

To Dora Foss   [c. February 1932]

The Daye House, Quidhampton, Salisbury

Dear Dora,

I have been waiting to hear from Edith S. before I wrote you.

I heard from her last night, & I expect you will have also received a letter from her.

Her explanation seems adequate and genuine & I hope that you will accept it as such.[1]

I felt sure that there was some misunderstanding & that she was labouring under some misapprehension and non-realisation as to who the invitation was from. So I now trust that this unfortunate contretemps is amicably settled.

About the order of songs, I had conceived it as being –

① Daphne
② Through gilded trellises
③ Old Sir Faulk

but perhaps Hubert is right & 1 & 2 should be reversed.

Though I think my order better as I think "Old Sir Faulk" won't come as such a shock after ② as after ①.[2]

I don't think the matter of speed really enters into the question as ③ is quite sedate & altogether the styles of the songs are so different that contrast will be there in whatever order they appear.

---

1 Edith Sitwell appears to have over-reacted to the news that Walton had arranged these three songs from *Façade* for voice and piano. Probably she had not been informed in writing either by Walton or by Dora Foss about the arrangements. It is also possible that if she had heard informally (i.e. if Walton had simply spoken to her about the idea), she might have forgotten. Similar incidents regarding performances of *Façade* were to occur for many years. The reason was that no formal copyright arrangement had been drawn up between Walton and Edith Sitwell, either at the time of Walton's first settings of her poems in 1922, or subsequently during *Façade*'s several recastings and revisions. This meant that Edith Sitwell continued effectively to hold the copyright of her text in performances of the work's original version, and therefore that her personal permission had to be secured for every performance of this that took place. She herself had appeared as reciter in *Façade*'s first ever performance and several subsequent ones, and she was also extremely particular about how her poems should be recited in the context of Walton's music. So it may be that she was also a little suspicious (perhaps only subconsciously) of others doing this. Evidently she considered the situation regarding Walton's three song adaptations to be similar.

2 The final order remained as above.

I will arrive for lunch on the 9th & look forward to seeing you both.
yrs
Willie

To Hubert Foss[1]   17 May [1932]

Casa Angolo, Ascona, Ticino, Switzerland

My dear Hubert,

This is all very well. You know that my life is already an open book & I can't think of anything more which can with strict propriety be divulged to the public. However as you ask – here goes.

Perhaps it is wiser (& more profitable) to cast a doubt about the parentage,[2] only born March 29th 1902.

It is said that he could sing before he could talk (doubtless untrue).

Anyhow he remembers making a scene (tears etc) because not allowed to sing a solo in local church choir when about the age of 6.

Won probationership to Ch. Ch. Cath. Choir. at 10 (after being very sick on first long train journey).

First signs of composition "Variations for Violin & Pf." on a Choral[e] by J.S.B. [Johann Sebastian Bach] didn't progress (like his latest composition) more than a dozen bars. Not very interesting & wisely decided to stop.

However broke loose again about 13. & wrote two 4 part Songs "Tell me where is fancy bred" & "Where the bee sucks". After that fairly went in for it & produced about 30 very bad works of various species songs. motets, Magnificats etc.

First composition to show any kind of talent Pf Quartet (ultimately published not very much revised) by the Carnegie Trust – (very <u>black</u> mark in 1924.) though written in 1918.

At this date became undergraduate at Ch. Ch. & failed consistently in all "schools" & was ultimately ignominiously "sent down" (though he passed his Mus. Bac. exams like lamb, except the composition!!).

The most fruitful thing about that period was gaining the friendship

1 Foss had asked Walton for an outline summary of his life and works to date, for promotional purposes.
2 Constant Lambert had for some time been spreading the colourful rumour that Walton was the illegitimate offspring of Sir George Sitwell and the English composer Dame Ethel Smyth.

of the present Bish. of Ox. [Bishop of Oxford: Thomas Strong] & S. Sitwell & ultimately with the rest of that talented family.

Apparently idled away his time from the time he was sent down, (1920) though went to Italy for 1ˢᵗ time, till suddenly appeared as an unpopular "bolt from the blue" at the I.F.C.M. [ISCM[1] Festival] with a String Quartet at Salzburg 1923.

Though not too popular a work in England, nevertheless it excited the interest of the great Alban Berg, who took the shy & nervous young composer to see the even greater Arnold Schonberg [Schoenberg], who gave the little brute his blessing (luckily he has not to the composers knowledge heard any of his late compositions).

After this, the composer not knowing which way to turn produced some rather bad works in various styles (he is self-taught) now mercifully in the fire. And it was not till 1926. again at the I.F.C.M. this time at Zürich that he produced that exciting work P.P. [*Portsmouth Point*] on which so much of his fame wrongly rests.

This was all 'great fun' (as Dame Adrian [Boult] would say) for the composer as all the English musical world considered him dead & a "flash in the pan". After that with the production of "Façade" at the I.F.C.M at Siena in 1928 & again the Viola Concerto at Liège in 1930, the young composer seemed well on the lower rungs of the ladder of fame.

The rest you know & I hope really very much that sometime I shall produce a good work – till then with this pious wish.

auf wiedersehen
Willie

The Baroness sends her love to you both.

To Siegfried Sassoon   29 May [1932]

Casa Angolo, Ascona, Ticino, Switzerland[2]

Dearest Sieg.

You can see by the address where we are.

Imma has not been at all well since I came, in fact, as you know for months previously & last Tuesday she became so bad, that a hasty dash

1 International Society for Contemporary Music.
2 The letter is headed with this address by Walton, and written on the printed notepaper of the Hotel Garni, Zurich.

here was the only thing to do. It was lucky we decided to do so, as if she had left it longer she would have had to undergo an unpleasant if not actually serious operation. Owing to some stupid dentist her teeth had got an infection which was about to spread to the bones & all over her head. She was in [the] most fearful pain, but now after seeing specialists Xray's & the usual paraphe[r]nalia of illness & having some teeth extracted she is better & we shall be able to leave here in a day or two I hope.

By that brief paragraph, you will understand that life has been very worrying & such things as symphonies have fallen far into the background.

However as it is already decided that a performance of it is to be given here on next March 27th I suppose I shall be able to get away with it soon. Also a performance of "Belshazzar" has been arranged here for next November year. I am in negotiation about a Berlin performance but all choirs are so fearfully bankrupt in Germany that little hope of a performance seems to be forthcoming. However I think that the Berlin "Phil" are going to do the Viola Concerto & that a "broadcast" of "Belshazzar" relayed from Queens Hall will take place from some German stations when it is next performed in London. So I feel that so far so good.

To get on to even more material & worldly topics – which I feel is necessary for me to do to guard against the consequences of the coming world crisis – don't get alarmed (it probably won't occur) & listen quite calmly.

You must be sick of guaranteeing overdrafts – but I warn you, if you will be so kind, to guarantee mine for £300. The reasons being these – quite simple and won't involve you in any expense – I will pay the interest.

Life is just possible here at the present rate of exchange: if the £ goes down (& it is quite possible that it may be forced down much lower than it is) even a franc it becomes to be impossible. Therefore as I hope & expect to be here most of this year & of the next, I should feel very much safer about it if I had between £200 & £300 here always in a Swiss bank. If I have to be in England more than I expect it can easily be moved back, but all the same I should like some here as Imma's financial position is becoming more & more precarious & she will perhaps at times have to rely on me for support entirely, and I'm only too willing that she should, as you must realise how much she means to me. So if I could always have 6 months income here I should feel much happier & safer both as regards being able to get away to work & being able to see Imma.

[77]

As my income[1] comes in on Aug 1ˢᵗ & Feb 1ˢᵗ yearly, I can't overdraw it now, as I am sure it is wiser to do, without a guarantee, so though I hate asking you to & being such a bore & nuisance, I do hope that you can see your way to doing so.

When I hear from you I will write to the bank. I may say that even with the expense involved by coming here my financial position is absolutely sound so please don't think that I have any other motives than what I have stated.

Let me have news of you & how Stephen [Tennant] goes on & forgive me for bothering you about this. If you don't like the idea please don't hesitate to say so – & I can only hope that things will work out alright as they stand.

Best love from Imma & myself.

Yours ever

Willie

To Siegfried Sassoon   2 June 1932
[with postscript from Imma von Doernberg]

Casa Angolo, Ascona, Ticino, Switzerland

My dear Sieg,

You are an angel to do this for us. I can't tell you what a relief it will be to have a fairly substantial sum out here[,] not that I don't believe in the £ but that there seems little doubt that there may be a further crisis in England & though the £ may not lose value, it is likely that one won't be allowed to draw money out of the country.

I am delighted that you have taken to having a couple of days of "festive" gaiety each week, & I only hope it won't depress [you] too much.

It does seem that there is still some life yet left in Steenie. I imagine that Lord G. [Glenconner] is the one who might use most influence both with Snowden & Christopher.

We came back here two days ago & "her highness" is beginning to be her usual sweet self.

If we could only have some sun she would rapidly get alright but the weather has been beyond words awful[,] wet & cold – but it really can't go on much longer.

---

1 From Mrs Courtauld's bequest.

Imma is going to stay with Neil McEachran [McEacharn] at Pallanza[1] for a few days on Saturday, so she can lead a life of luxury. I'm not going, for one thing she is in a very nervous condition & it will be better if she's alone, which she more or less will be, as it is an enormous villa & she will have her own suite & need hardly appear even for meals unless she wants to.

And I must get down to this Symphony.

With many thanks again & love

Yrs

Willie

My dear Sieg,

How nice of you to send those photos. Silvermane looks to be in a very good form. How awfully sweet of you to guarantee W. the overdraft. I shall write next time more. We are missing you here very much indeed. Much love

Imma

To Edward Clark   [6 July 1932]

Casa Angolo, Ascona, Ticino, Switzerland

Dear Clark,

I've received a letter from Von Benda of the Berlin Rundfunk about "broadcasting" "Belshazzar" when it is next given in London & I told him to apply to you. I hope that is right & that you will be able to fix it successfully, otherwise I don't think there is a hope of it being done in Germany owing to the financial side of the question.

I saw Sir Henry W. [Wood] in Zürich who told me that there was a possibility of [Artur] Rubinstein[2] doing the "Sinfonia". I hope that is so – or is jolly old Hattie [Harriet Cohen] going to do it?

The Zürich performance of "Das Unaufhorliche" [*Das Unaufhörliche*][3] was magnificent – and what a terrific work.

---

1 At Villa Taranto, the home of Captain Neil McEacharn, whom Imma was eventually to marry.

2 Polish pianist. He had lived mostly in London during the First World War, and still played there regularly.

3 Oratorio composed in 1931 by Paul Hindemith, to a text by the German poet Gottfried Benn.

Let me know if there is any news.

yours

William Walton

To Siegfried Sassoon [10 August 1932]
[with postscript from Imma von Doernberg]

Casa Angolo, Ascona, Ticino, Switzerland

My dear Shakespeare,

We were delighted to hear from you.

I shall be back about Aug 28th to rehearse [the Viola Concerto] for the 3 Choirs [Three Choirs Festival],[1] & I go down to Worcester on Sept 4th with Foss, remaining there till the 9th – having I hope successfully dealt with P.P. & the V.C. on the 7th & 8th.

Do come over for those days, & you might drive me back perhaps putting me up for a day or two, or I might go to Edith [Olivier] again.

I then can try my luck with Stephen. It is marvellous that he's entirely rid of his T.B. & I am sure now that he will begin to get more normal once he can assure himself that no more haemorrhages will occur.

Imma is much much better, & leaves on the 18th for [Bad] Ischl for her final (at least I hope so) cure. We return here about Sept 15th & I think we shall take a flat & be here on & off till around March.

As regards that symphony, I must confess that I've been also doing a good deal more ruminating than actual work – nevertheless I've collected a number of symphonious bars which promise well.

I can't tell you how grateful we are for that guarantee – as you may have seen the £ has gone into a decline though not much at present.

I enclose a pretty little photo of the arrival of the Queen (for a fuller account see my letter to Edith).

All news when I see you.

Yours ever

Willie

1 Held every year since 1715, in and around the cathedral towns of Worcester, Hereford and Gloucester in turn. Choral music was (and remains) the Festival's central focus, but orchestral and chamber concerts also featured.

How are you my dear Sieg?

We enjoyed your letter so much – as I see you are still at the Ely house[.] How is Silvermane this summer? I am longing to see you again! Is there any chance? Willie will tell you soon all about us.

All my love
ever yours
Imma.

To Dora Foss   [postmarked: Salisbury, early September 1932]
[postcard]

I enjoyed so much being with you both, in fact I don't know what I should have done without your presence at that dismal [Three Choirs] festival which [i.e. whose other events] we so successfully avoided[.] We [Walton and Sassoon] arrived here [Quidhampton] somewhat late owing to a valve exploding, otherwise life is peaceful & pleasant.

Willie

To Dora Foss   [October 1932]

In the train.

My dear Dora,

You must forgive me, but I've had a rush of telegrams from the baroness asking me to join her at once. It is so difficult to know how bad she is, but I feel she must be otherwise I'm sure she wouldn't have wired for me.

I've had such a rushed two days getting ready for my unexpected return.

I am truly sorry that I shan't be present on the 10th[1] but I'm sure my absence will make no difference to the quality of the performance, & I'm sure all will go well. You have all my best wishes for a huge success.

I've done all I can in the way of 'propaganda' & I've written to Osbert to carry on the good work.

It seems very bad my rushing off like this, but I'm so distracted that I feel I've no option.

1 At the first performance of the *Three Songs*.

With kindest regards. I'm writing Hubert.
yrs
Willie

To Dora Foss [Ascona, 10 October 1932]
[telegram]

MISS DORA STEVENS WIGMORE HALL LONDON

ALL LOVE AND BEST WISHES FOR WONDERFUL SUCCESS MISERABLE AT
ABSENCE WILLIE

To Dora Foss [October 1932]

Casa Angolo, Ascona, Ticino, Switzerland

Dear Dora,

Thank you so much for your letters, and I'm delighted to hear that all
went well, though it is a distinct pity that it should have collided with
the Cortauld Concert. The cuttings Hubert sent me seem quite amusing,
but are chiefly pre-concert so I hope there will be some more.

I am really very sad at missing the recital, not only for my own songs,
and I am sure that it was a magnificent performance. But without doubt,
I hope, I shall be able to hear them again.

I must say that when I was sent the programme for the Music Club, I
nearly wired you to sing something more dreary. I can feel the shivers now.

What a good thing that the B.B.C has thought fit to allow Hubert to
broadcast on "B.F." I shall try & listen.

Will you tell him that I will try a[nd] produce a low masterpiece for
him, I don't know quite when, but miracles sometime[s] happen.

Imma sends her love. She is getting better slowly & I hope next week
that she will be able to go to stay a[t] Pallanza further down the lake in
Italy with some rich friends to recuperate.

Meanwhile the symphony shows definite signs of being on the move,
a little spasmodic perhaps, but I've managed to get down about 40 bars
which for me is really saying something. What hopes for it being completed for April I should hardly like to say.

I should like a pen-picture-post-card of Harriet [Cohen]'s goings-on if
you've time, now that you will be full of domestic worries.

[82]

[. . .]

It seems a pity that Christopher[1] should so truculently follow in his father's footsteps and refuse to take the floor. I secretly sympathise with him completely, embarrassing as it may be for you.

So with much gratitude to you both for all the trouble you have taken over those songs, I must now stop.

With love to you both,

Yours ever

Willie.

To Dora and Hubert Foss   [November 1932]

Casa Angolo, Ascona, Ticino, Switzerland

My dear Dora & Hubert,

Being in dire arrears with correspondence you will forgive me, I hope, addressing you both.

I adored your marvellous description of Harriet's concert & I have destroyed the letter but couldn't find heart to do the same with the drawing which I'm keeping.

I'm sorry the B.B.C. have this uncompromising attitude to your singing my songs. It's fantastic. Do you think it wise if I write a snappy little note to [Edward] Clark or do you think it too undignified.

I listened to "B.F" on the Radio from Berlin. It didn't come through too well – in fact I was horrified, but am considerably cheered up at receiving Hubert's letter.

From the point of view of "tempi" I didn't think it too good the slow parts being too slow & the fast etc too fast. But I'm glad it wasn't the "flop" I thought it was going to be. What have the notices been like, rude I suppose.

I heard from various people in Germany, it came through excellently & there is a good notice of it with Berlin "B-Z am Mittag".

Will you send two copies of the latest edition to bore Hans Reinhart as he still wants to have a go at the german version. Perhaps you might send the songs as well, he might try his hand a[t] translating them.

Alles gut

yours

Willie

---

1   Hubert's and Dora's infant son.

P.S. I heard Hubert well & how clear & resonant was his voice. Really what a broadcasting voice should be.

To Dora and Hubert Foss [late December 1932]

Casa Giachetti, Ascona, Ticino, Switzerland

My dear Hubert & Dora,

I know that it sounds unbelievable, but nevertheless it is quite true, that I had just taken up my pen to write to you when the telephone rang & Imma brought in your telegram announcing the glad tidings about Amsterdam.[1] Doubtless you are both as happy about it as we are – it indeed sets, what I believe is understood as, the "seal" upon it – "high-brow, lowbrow, rich & poor, one with another" that is undoubtedly the text, at least I hope so. We would get the Queen there, but she hates noise so we shall have to put up with Princess Juliana (a violin virtuoso) instead, that is if Imma can persuade her to come which I understand won't be very difficult. But really, high spirits & joking apart. I think it is good news & I hope that you will ultimately sell your 10th-thousand copy. When, by the way, is the Festival? All such questions as to who is singing, conducting etc will be settled later, I presume.

Now I ought to try and excuse myself for not having written you before & thanked you for your two news letters – if I had any adequate excuse I would glibly offer it, but the honest truth is that I haven't except to confess to sheer laziness & a certain shyness to owning up to the sad fact that this - - - - - - - symphony[2] is not getting on in the way, I feel it should do. You may remember in "Belshazzar" that I got landed on the world "gold" – I was there from May to December, (1930) perched, unable to move either to right or left or up & down, & I'm now in a similar distressing position, but it is not such a nice chord (in fact it is only an octave on A) – when I'm likely to move, is I regret to say, unknown.

I've written to Harty cancelling the April date & explaining every-thing, & how delighted I was with his taking so much interest etc. in B.F. & I must say he's behaved beautifully about it & seems to under-

---

1 *Belshazzar's Feast* was to be performed at the following summer's ISCM Festival in Amsterdam.
2 As written by Walton, not an editorial deletion.

stand perfectly, & we stand on extremely good terms. It is proposed, that the Viola Concerto shall be put in instead of the symphony – whether this will actually be I am, till now uncertain.

I'm delighted that the Manchester & Nottingham performances of "B." were so good – I'm sure that Harty is really the man for it.

We spent 10 lovely days in Rome (there is a 70% reduction on every-thing) & I had hopes that the change would perhaps freshen me up but alas as I've already said, nothing has happened until now. But in any case whether it might be finished in time for the April date, I consider it wiser to sit on it for some months longer & produce it next season.

I should like to hear your considered opinion on Bax's 4th [Symphony] & the new work. Instinct tells me that with the Bax, we have heard it all before at perhaps even greater length. Harriet told me it was so gay & just like Beethoven, but perhaps better than that master, but my instinct (or is it predjudice) tells me otherwise.

It seems that I've no other news. Life is very quiet, & under the circum-stances would be positively dull & nothing of any interest happens, except continual reminders from jolly old Hans [Reinhart], who is becoming a colossal bore to say the least.

[. . .]

Imma sends her love & so do I.

Yours ever

Willie

To Siegfried Sassoon   20 December 1932

Casa Giachetti, Ascona, Ticino, Switzerland

My dear Sieg,

How are you? It is a long time since I wrote to you but as you know life is not very eventful here.

The Casa Angolo being in the process of demolition for a new house to be built, we are now installed all by ourselves in a nice flat with Finni looking after us. I have my piano here as well, as it became unbearably cold in my room at the Monte which is quite empty. Though the sym-phony begins to progress a little I've no hopes of finishing it in time for the April performance so I've written to Harty cancelling the date. He has been awfully nice about it & I feel much relieved & now being fired not to be done in by old Elgar's No 3[1] I hope I shall produce something really good.

[. . .]

I hope you now see how right I was to change as much money as possible into francs – the exchange though improving is still very low, & we are both so grateful to you that you guaranteed my overdraft otherwise we should have been in a bit of a panic & probably a bit of a mess.

We spent a nice fortnight in Rome with Frau Oppenheim who paid for Imma. There was also a 70% reduction in fares.

We were about the only foreigners in the place[,] not even a ghost of an american voice & we managed to see a great deal in a short time & came back a little exhausted.

The weather is lovely and at the moment couldn't be better.

I hope that Steenie [Stephen Tennant] progresses. We have sent him a present c/o of [sic] you which I hope will arrive safely.

How does your work get on?

With all love & best wishes for Xmas & the New Year

Yours ever

William.

To Christabel McLaren   21 December 1932

Casa Giachetti, Ascona, Ticino, Switzerland

Dearest Christabel,

This brings you all my best wishes for a happy Christmas & New Year.

Though I've not heard from you I hope that my letter in reply to your last one reached you safely.

As the Casa Angolo is being pulled down & rebuilt we are now installed in what might be called a commodious flat & being looked after by the proprietress of the Casa A. It is nice to be alone for a change & we are leading a happy & comfortable existence.

[. . .]

I hear from O. [Osbert Sitwell] that he has gone to Corfu & let Carlyle Squ. till June, so I suppose that I shall be away till then also. For

---

1 The BBC had commissioned Elgar to compose a Third Symphony. Elgar was to leave only fragmentary sketches of the work at his death in 1934.

though the 1st performance of my symphony is announced for April 3rd the fact that there is not a hope of my finishing it by then, has made me write to Harty (who has been very nice about it, & may substitute your Viola Concerto[1] in its stead) cancelling the date & having the performance next season.

Meanwhile I have hopes that "Belshazzar" will keep my head above water in many respects. It's latest effort is to get itself accepted for the International Festival at Amsterdam next year, (my 5th work at these festivals!) & what with there being 15 performances of it in England & America & there being a prospect of it being put on the records, I hope that it will not only preserve my good name but replenish my depleted purse as well.

Imma, though she is much better than she was, is still not very strong. She has prospects of getting a rather good job in the spring & there are hopes that the estate from which she derives her money will start paying again sometime in the coming year, so we shall accordingly I hope be in a very much better position financially speaking if all that materialises.

What would be happening to us except for that providential happening,[2] heaven alone knows, & I'm full of gratitude & your slave for life (I was that before) for whatever part you may have had in it.

Dear Christabel, what should I do without you? I only hope that you are well & happy in fact have every blessing that should be yours.

Imma sends her love, as I do too, only more so

as ever

Willie

To David Horner   5 January [1933]

[Casa Giachetti, as from:]
Casa Angolo, Ticino, Switzerland

My dear David,

Thank you so much for your letter & pardon me so to speak for my negligence in not having written you before – but I got so bored with writing letters during Xmas & the New Year, that I could'nt have written you an intelligible one, not that this will be, but you must hope for the best.

1 Walton had dedicated his Viola Concerto to Christabel McLaren (later Aberconway).
2 Mrs Courtauld's bequest.

Corfu sounds a bit of A1 & I wish we were there as it is rather dreary & cold here, snow & black clouds, in fact it would be nice to go somewhere else. But "das Leben" [life] indicates our being here for sometime to come.

However life is "nicht so schwer" [not so difficult] as we are comfortably installed in a flat, the Casa Angolo being in a state of disintegration prior to re-building & the proprietress looks after us. Nevertheless you might look out if there is a tolerably good piano in Corfu which I could put in an out-house as it might be a good place for me to work sometime in the future.

Bertie's behaviour sounds to me "unglaublich" [unbelievable] & unseemly. You must be more firm.

I'm delighted that Carlyle Sq is let & that it will more than pay its way.

Anyhow I had no intention of returning before the middle of June as this "lovely!" symphony is nowhere near ready, in fact it seems to me it will in all probability be stillborn for though it is more than six months gone you would'nt believe it to look at it – not a sign of a swelling or even a protuberance.

Meanwhile jolly old "Belshazzar" will I hope, keep my head above water. Its latest achievement is to get itself taken for the International Festival in Amsterdam. The performance is on June 10th & I see by your plans there is not a bloody hope of either of you being there. I shall go there on my way back from here to London.

It is to be hoped that Georgia & Sachie may pop over, but I doubt it, – it will be a bit awkward about Imma coming without a chaperone in view of her royal relations who would be slightly surprised about her sudden interest in music. But we shall have to see how things work out.

Imma is much better, but still not strong & she is off to Zürich on Sunday to have a few wisdom teeth ejaculated. So I shall be alone for a couple of weeks.

By now we have a few friends here, Whitbrook etc[,] not too interest-ing, but pass the time.

You must come & see us in April & we will take you to see Elisariou & all the sights.

Meanwhile I'm in a stinking rage with Bertie about that there Fascist 'ymn. As Cimmie[1] wrote me I could hardly refuse but made the stipulation that I must have the words first (Onward Oswald, Onward) but if Bertie ever writes them I'll kick his bl—— ar——.[2] I hear that at a Fascist

---

1 Cynthia Mosley, the wife of Sir Oswald Mosley, leader of the British Union of Fascists.
2 The deletions are Walton's, not editorial. Osbert Sitwell had joined Oswald Mosley's

meeting in Grosvenor house Tom announced the fact of our writing this song. Anyhow it is the only possible thing that could "make" the party.

As an atonement for his errors, you can make him think about a subject for an opera & I hope by the time you've both hit on it I shall be ready for it.

This brings our best love & good wishes for 1933.

Yours ever

William

I gave O's address to a Frau Weissmann[,] wife of the late State Secretary in Berlin, who wishes perhaps to translate "Winters of Content",[2] I believe she's very good.

I should appreciate a letter from B. [Bertie] with an account of your goings on!

To Christabel McLaren   1 June [1933]

Casa Angolo, Ascona, Ticino, Switzerland

Dearest Christabel,

I'm delighted to get your letter & feel more than guilty that I've not written you for so long.

In fact so much has happened since I wrote you that I hardly know where to begin.

I can hardly believe it is true about dear Cimmie.[3] It is unthinkable that I shall never see her again. She really meant a very great deal to me, & I shall always regret that, owing to my stupid youth & "gaucheness", I never really appreciated her when I knew her best. But thank Heaven, we made it up & I tried to explain to her why I was so stupid & I think she understood, in fact I'm sure she did. But I must say I should rather anything had happened than this.

Between you & me, I've made a most idiotic mess of my life in the last year, but it is going better now.

---

fascist New Party in 1931, and in August that year had allowed one of its rallies to be held in the grounds of Renishaw Hall, the Sitwells' family home in Derbyshire. He subsequently began to lose interest in the party as its members became more notorious for street violence than for nationalist political idealism.

2 Osbert Sitwell's *Winters of Content. More Discursions on Travel, Art and Life* (1932).

3 Cynthia Mosley had died suddenly of appendicitis at the age of thirty-four.

Imma came back from Berlin (she'd been there since the middle of February) and we had a happy ten day[s] staying with Neil McEarchern [*sic*] at Pallanza. She's now in Zürich & start[s] her job today. Of course, it is wonderful that she should have got one these days & it will be a great financial help.

My symphony progresses & I hope will be finished when I next see you which I hope will be at Renishaw in August. Till then I remain here, except for an excursion next week to hear Constant conduct "Belshazzar" at Amsterdam & shall only be there about 4 days.

It is very sad about Malcolm S. [Sargent][1] Whose going to fill his place in the Cortauld [Courtauld] Concerts? I hope not Geoffrey Toye. Why not Sir Hamilton Harty? Perhaps a too dangerous rival. But you might see what you can do.

I've got so much to tell you that I can't write.

I'm delighted about the "Venus & Adonis["] idea. Ask Norman de Wills to write at once. It is only Harriet that I "tick off".

Bless you dear Christabel,

All love

your

Willie.

To Arthur Bliss [early 1934]

Weston Hall, Towcester, Northants

Dear Arthur,

Having just been going through your Concerto, urges me to what I've [been] meaning to do for ages, namely to congratulate you on your achievement, and to thank you for the handsome dedication of which I am exceedingly proud.[2] I trust that you will overlook my ungraciousness in not having written to you before about it.

---

1 English conductor, particularly noted for his expertise in choral works: he had conducted the brilliantly successful first performance of Walton's *Belshazzar's Feast* at the 1931 Leeds Festival.
2 Known evidence elsewhere indicates that Bliss's Piano Concerto was composed between 1936 and 1938. The score is dedicated to 'To the people of the USA'. Bliss's other works in concerto form do not date from the early 1930s, which is when Walton's letter must have been written, since it mentions his own unfinished Symphony. So either the 'Concerto' dedicated to him was a work that Bliss later withdrew, and which is now lost; or, as seems more likely, it was in fact an earlier version of the Piano Concerto of 1937. This had its first performance at the New York World's Fair in 1938, for which the première of

I prefer the first two movements, the second perhaps more than the first, – but altogether it is an admirable work, & I look forward to hearing [it] properly, as I've only heard it on the wireless & that is always unsatisfactory.

Also I should like to congratulate you on your protegé Benjamin Britten. I've been sent a copy of "A boy was born"[1] & though I've not been through it very carefully, it is obviously a rather remarkable work for anyone to have written let alone someone of his age & with luck he ought to go far as the saying is.

As for myself, I've just risen from an attack of "flu", & the gloom when I look at what there is of this wretched symphony & more so when I contemplate how much is lacking, is not to be gone into.

With many congratulations & thanks again
Yours ever
William Walton

To Adrian Boult   16 February [1934]

Weston Hall, Towcester, Northants

Dear Dr Boult,

There is, I am ashamed and dissapointed to tell you, quite definitely no hope of my finishing this symphony in time for its intended performance on March 19th. consequently as I've promised the first performance to Harty, it will be necessary to abandon the idea of performing it at the May Festival.

I am extremely sorry if this causes you much inconvenience, and I am sure you will realise that it is a rather painful situation for me to live down.

With kind regards
Yours very sincerely
William Walton

———

Walton's Violin Concerto was also at first planned (see pp. 113–15, 118). So it would seem that Walton's statement, in his letter to Bliss on 28 April 1938 (p. 113), that 'I don't think there is any complication about the dedication' must be in response to the re-dedication of the Piano Concerto, about which Bliss had written to him to explain.
1 One of Britten's early works for chorus, published by Oxford University Press (Hubert Foss would therefore have sent Walton a score). Shortly after its publication Britten left OUP and signed an agreement with the rival musical firm Boosey & Hawkes, which published his works composed between then and 1962.

To Christabel Aberconway [1]   [March 1934]

Weston Hall, Towcester, Northants

Dearest Christabel,

Seeing a glorious photograph of you in the papers this morning, reminds me how ashamed I am not to have written to you before to congratulate you on the safe arrival of your new son. How happy you must be & how lovely for you, & how delighted you must feel at it all being over.

I hope & trust in the goodness of your heart that [you] will overlook my remissness in not writing before.

Having been here just a month all alone I've decided to come to London on Friday staying till the Wednesday. I expect during this busy time you will have little opportunity for seeing me but I hope that you will be able to manage at least a minute or two sometime. Up to now my plans consist of the Kreisler [2] concert on Sunday, the Finnish orchestra on Monday & the opera on Tuesday. I shall be staying at the Cumberland Hotel so shall be just round the corner.

I enjoy very much being here alone & don't remember being so content for sometime, neither hilariously high spirited or low depression, just that nice midway balance.

The symphony progresses slowly & steadily & I've now completed the 3rd movement. You know how rarely I am pleased with anything I write, but with this particular movement I think (I hope I'm right) I've brought off something a bit A1. extra.

I've naturally not much to tell you, but if I think of anything I hope I shall be able to tell you in person very very soon.

Bless you
Best love
William

1 Formerly Christabel McLaren, now Lady Aberconway; her husband succeeded to the title of Lord Aberconway in 1934.
2 Fritz Kreisler, Austrian violinist and composer who later settled in America.

To Ernest Newman   22 June [1934]

Weston Hall, Towcester, Northants

Dear Mr Newman,

I am sending you three movements of my symphony under seperate cover. The third has yet to be copied but there is no particular hurry, so perhaps you would be so kind as to send it to Mr Foss at the O.U.P. in about a fortnights time – the other movements you can keep more or less any time till the end of July.

I am most grateful to you for taking an interest in the work, and I can assure you that any criticisms you make [sic] like to make, adverse or otherwise, especially the former, will be more than welcome.

With kindest regards and many thanks
Yours very sincerely
William Walton.

To Dora Foss   21 July [1934]

Weston Hall, Towcester, Northants

Dear Dora,

Thank you so much for your letter & the delicious cream.

In spite of my having progressed a little with this last movement I feel at the end of my tether & am longing to get off to Denmark for a few days. Actually the food situation will be better on my return as the cook will be back from London.

As a matter of fact I'm not at all sure that I shan't have to begin this movement all over again & only a chance remark of the gardeners wife as she brought in the famous ham saved me from destroying it already. "How pretty your music is getting – it sounds just like a great big band." Considering that it is more than likely she knows what she likes than I know what I like & perhaps it may be a piece for the mob at any rate I thought I'd keep it to see what Hubert thinks on Monday. But on the whole I feel pretty gloomy.

I hope you have enjoyed your holiday in spite of the adjacency of the Bliss's. I love your description of his studio & of course he is just like a moustachioed cod-fish so he will be in the right environment. I hope it won't make his music even more watery.[1]

Yours
Willie

To Ernest Newman   15 August [1934]

Weston Hall, Towcester, Northants

Dear Mr Newman,

Thank you so much for your letter and for the trouble you have taken in going through my symphony.

It is a great cause for satisfaction and encouragement that you should think so well of it.

There is, I'm afraid, no doubt that as you say, it will need most careful handling to secure an adequate performance, but I'm hoping for the best as Sir Hamilton Harty is insisting on a lot of rehearsal, not because the notes are in themselves so difficult, but so as to give the players a chance to get inside the work. Sir Hamilton himself seems to be very sympathetic & understanding about it (he has only seen the first two movements) & I'm inclined to think that he will do it well, especially as he is the only conductor who has ever given a good performance of my Viola Concerto, & that with extremely little rehearsal.

I will send you the fourth movement as soon as it is available[,] also I will try and let you see the rest again. Unfortunately there is only the one score, as Foss dos'ent want to go to the expense of making another since it is to be engraved.

I am so sorry to hear about the trouble with your eyes & I am afraid my manuscript must have been trying for them.

With ever so many thanks again for the interest you have taken in the work & with kindest regards to Mrs Newman and yourself.

Yours sincerely
William Walton.

1 Note by Dora Foss, in her unpublished memoir of her and Hubert Foss's friendship with Walton: 'I had merely described Arthur's studio as being made chiefly of glass and built on piles in the middle of a wood, and said that one felt like a fish in a tank. It was a lovely place and we had had a very happy day with them!'

To Patrick Hadley   9 November [1934]

Weston Hall, Towcester, Northants

My dear Paddy

Hearing your honeyed & seductive voice last night discoursing on my most detested composer (you almost brought me to feel I liked his music, a feeling, I'm perhaps a little ashamed to confess, which was quickly dispatched, on being switched back to Queen's Hall) reminded me that I owe you a letter, in answer to yours which was full of comfortable words.

You may or may not have seen in today's D.T. [*Daily Telegraph*] that Sir H. Harty is taking the unprecedented course of giving my symphony (if such it may now be called) minus a finale on Dec 3rd.

The great comfort to me is that the onus of this decision rests almost entirely on your shoulders, for there is little doubt I could have pumped out tolerably easily, a brilliant, out-of-the-place pointless & vacuous finale, in time for this performance, or I might have got Arthur Benjamin[1] to "ghost" for me! (Of course, please pass this tit-bit on!) But that is where you or rather your letter, stepped in. Instead of doing that, egged on by you, I persisted in finding something which I felt to be right & tolerably up to the standard of the previous movements. This involved me in endless trouble & I've burn't about 3 finales, when I saw that they were'nt really leading anywhere or saying anything. And it is only comparatively lately that I've managed to get going on what I hope is the last attempt. At the moment I need hardly add, that I'm held up, & my blood has turned to water & [I] see no hope etc, etc, & shall have to begin all over again. But it is more probable that I'm a bit "oopset" on the prospects of Dec 3rd.

Whether it is a wise decision to have arrived at, I hardly dare to think. Harty, who has behaved like a lamb, was more or less willing to wait till March, but the L.S.O. [London Symphony Orchestra] committee said that another postponement would be fatal, & that if I agreed, they would do it without the finale.

It being pointed out very forcibly, by my friends and advisers, that it was the lesser of two evils, I concurred. Anyhow I'm certain that it is better for it to appear like this, than with a bad or artificial finale. After

---

1 Australian–British composer and pianist, at this time known mostly for works written in a lighter style than Walton's tended to be.

all the worst that can happen is that it is a miserable "flop" & [one] that I'm prepared for, having seen it staring me in the face for sometime. As for a success, you know what I feel about that sort of thing by now. The only point of a success is the money it brings in, & in this work, no matter how much it had, it wouldn't bring much in, considering what kind of work it is. The only things that can be said about it are, either "Thank God, there's not a finale" or "What a pity there is'nt one" or the more subtle ones may say "I wonder what the finale will be like". And that is what I want to know.

For it is, for want of better words, what may be called the emotional and spiritual continuity that is worrying me & not so much the actual notes (but they are bad enough).

Luckily, however, in this work, it is not a case of it being "made" by the finale. The three existing movements, though I say it who shouldn't, are about as good as they could be & if I can bring "off" a finale as good as them, the whole symphony will be "a bit of orlright" [sic] which is, for me, saying a hell of a lot.

Anyhow I hope it won't come to the point where you will have to play V.W. [Vaughan Williams] to my [Herbert] Howells & come round & pat me on the back & say "I'm afraid, old chap, that that will not quite do." On the other hand, it would'nt surprise me, if that happened, especially when I think of ending up with that slowest & almost inaudible slow movement.

So, my dear Paddy, here I am calmly & dispassionately regarding the pit that I've dug for myself, but I look to you to be my staunch defender amongst the rats of the R.C.M.

I shall be in London soon & look forward to seeing you again & to a perusal of "La B.D. sans S.A."[1] after which I expect no obstacle to my completing my own god-forsaken work.

Forgive this long egotistical epistle, but I must do something, no longer being able to look at a piece of MSs paper without acute nausea, & you are (I hope,) one of my few understanding friends.

Yours,
William

1 Probably a private joke on Keats's poem 'La Belle Dame Sans Merci'.

To Christabel Aberconway [November 1934]

2 Carlyle Square, s.w.3

Dearest Christabel,

Having emerged from the flood of part-correcting I have a little time
to write & thank you for your suggestions & for the very handsome
volume of Donne.

They are difficult poems & I can't say I've made up my mind about
any of them, but at any rate it sets the mind working on some new track.

It was very sweet of you to send it & I thank you more than I can say.

You will, I hope, of course be coming to hear my "Unfinished"
[Symphony] on Dec 3rd. The fact that it is "unfinished" is not worrying
me as much as I thought it would, though the end as it is, is to say the
least, a trifle on the gloomy side. I'm now in London for at least 3 weeks
so perhaps you will do something with me.

Yours as ever,
William

To Christabel Aberconway 31 January [1935]

Weston Hall, Towcester, Northants

Dearest Christabel,

How very kind of you to go & see Sam [Courtauld].

Thank you so much & what an angel he seems to have been.

I telephoned my brother [Alec] last night & told him the news.

He was naturally delighted & said that as long as he got out of banking
he doesn't much mind if he stays in Canada, as long as it is not Eastern
Canada but of course he would prefer a job in England if that should be
possible.

It seems that it would be difficult to prolong his leave [f]or he doesn't
seem to like to feign illness & he should sail about Feb 20th. But I'm sure
that is a minor difficulty.

On the other hand if Sam has no job open for him just now, perhaps it
would be as well for him to go back to Canada & give in his 3 months
notice in the regular way (though it is not apparently obligatory to do
so). During which time Sam may have found something for him, either
here or in Canada. Of course if the job should happen to be here, there
would be the expense of an unnecessary journey.

I come up to-morrow & look forward to seeing you very soon.
With many thanks again
Love
Will

To Osbert Sitwell [April 1935]

Hotel Continental, Paris

Dearest Osbert,

What you can think about my not writing hardly bears consideration[.]
Here I am for one night & take the train for Bussaco tomorrow. I hope
there to find a piano & settle down & finish the finale of my symphony.

I expect to be away till the end of May.

I have had, as you may imagine a very rough time lately. The film people
kept me hanging about chiefly owing to their stupidity & inefficiency & in
the end I had to write all the music [for *Escape Me Never*] in four days.

Luckily while the house was being painted I was able to go & stay
with "Bumps"[1] who helped me out with the orchestration.

The film music anyhow can hardly be heard & is cut about very
badly. But however as they paid up it is their business.

It is very probable I shall do the music for "St Joan" & also Sir J
Barrie's new play [*The Boy David*] (on a theme suggested by Princess
Margaret Rose!!!). Money in every bar[.]

My symphony went extremely well, much better than the last time &
was really grand.

I don't see why I shouldn't do the music for your proposed ballet
[*The First Shoot*] & I think you might suggest it to [Leonid] Massine[2]
when you see him. I[n] fact I don't see who else to suggest.

Imma is beginning to do quite well with her new job & she work[s]
wonders with that "old-fashioned nose of mine", which incidentally was
worth £87.

I was unable to do anything for Alec, though I tried everything I
could think of. However it is more than likely that Sam will ultimately
get him a job in their branch in Canada.

1 Hyam Greenbaum: composer, conductor, former violinist in the Queen's Hall
Orchestra, and friend and colleague of Walton and other composers of his generation.
2 Russian-born choreographer, who had come to prominence with Diaghilev's Ballets
Russes company.

I went down to see the family who are getting on it seems rather better. I had to part with a lot, but otherwise everything more or less alright.

I hope you've had a lovely time in your wanderings. I got your book[1] for my birthday. It has had marvellous notices & is I see a best-seller.

How is little D.? [David Horner] Not too obstreperous I hope. Thank him for his letter & forgive me for not having answered same.

My best love to you both.

ever your

William

To Edward Dent   1 June [1935]

Casa Angolo, Ascona, Ticino, Switzerland

Dear Edward,

Your letters only reached me last night.

I will most certainly make out a list for [Hermann] Scherchen,[2] in fact I might go over and see him as it is not very far from here.

Constant [Lambert] is conducting "Belshazzar" at Amsterdam. It may seem a rash choice, but I'm confident he will make a good job of it.

I shall be in Amsterdam & look forward very much to seeing you again after such a long time.

Yours

William Walton.

To Hubert Foss   9 July 1935

Weston Hall, Towcester, Northants

Dear Hubert,

Thank you for your letters & the copy of E.M.N. [*Escape Me Never*] The cover is grand – if only the inside was as good!

The parts are in the possession of B&D. [British and Dominions][3] & I don't [know] whether they will part [with them].

I've been here some ten days or so & have produced this for the 3rd

1 Probably *Brighton* (1935).
2 German conductor, much involved with the International Society for Contemporary Music (ISCM), of which Dent was the founding president.
3 A film production company.

subject,[1] but am shivering on the brink about it I need hardly say.

I may be in London on the 18th for a day or two & then on to Renishaw for the week-end to discuss this ballet question with these Russian people who are coming also. I think it is almost as good as settled that I do it.

Love to Dora & yourself

yrs

Willie

What about going [with] the enclosed?

Has the score of the first two movements arrived safely? There are still one or two things in the 3rd I've not yet made up my mind about, but will let you have it soon for engraving.

To Siegfried Sassoon   21 October [1935]

56A South Eaton Place, S.W.1

My dear Siegfried.

How are you? It not only seems, but is ages since I've seen you. However I hope you will be in London for the complete performance of my Symphony at the B.B.C. concert on Nov 6th. Do come if you can. In some ways I think the last movement to be the best of the lot, at anyrate it will be the most popular, I think.

---

1 There are slight differences between Walton's sketch and the theme as it finally appeared in the published score.

There has been a slight chilliness between me & Carlyle Squ,[1] so I've settled down here & I must say I much appreciate being on my own. You must come & see me here.

I've several things chiefly commercial on foot. Firstly a ballet [*The First Shoot*] for Cochran with Osbert doing the libretto (in spite of the coldness) then music for the film of "As you like it" with [Elisabeth] Bergner.[2] & lastly music for Sir J. M Barrie's new play [*The Boy David*] with Bergner & Augustus John[3] doing the scenery. So I shall be able financially to keep my head, I hope, well above water for the time being.

Hoping to hear from you that you will be coming for Nov 6th.

With love to you both

Yours ever

William

To Bernard van Dieren   21 October [1935]

56A South Eaton Place, s.w.1

Dear Bernard,

I am hoping very much that you will come to hear the performance (complete) of my symphony on Weds Nov 6th. If you can manage it I will have tickets sent on to you.

At the moment I am engrossed in your book[4] which I find most interesting & inspiring.

With best regards to Mrs Van Dieren & yourself,

Yours very sincerely

William Walton

---

1 Walton's new relationship with Alice, Viscountess Wimborne, had created a rift between the couple and the Sitwells, although Alice and Osbert Sitwell had been friends until then.

2 Austrian actress, married to the director Paul Czinner; they moved to England in 1933. Bergner starred in the films *Escape Me Never* and *As You Like It* (both with scores by Walton), *Catherine The Great* and *Paris Calling*. Barrie wrote his last play, *The Boy David*, specially for her.

3 Welsh painter, draughtsman, sculptor and designer, as famous for his bohemian lifestyle as for his skill as a portraitist. His subjects included George Bernard Shaw, James Joyce, Dylan Thomas and Christabel Aberconway.

4 *Down Among the Dead Men* (1935), a collection of critical essays.

To Sir Hamilton Harty   7 November [1935]

56A South Eaton Place, London s.w.1

Dear Sir Hamilton,

I should just like to let you know how very grateful I am to you for the infinite trouble care & energy you put into the performance last night.

There is no way of describing it except by that well worn word "inspired" but it is certainly true in this case.

Hoping to see you soon & with many thanks again.

Yours ever sincerely

William Walton

1936–1948

WALTON'S position as England's leading composer of his generation had been confirmed by the success of the First Symphony. His financial situation, too, was improving, and continued to improve, thanks to his discovery that he could compose film scores with an ease and fluency that were a world apart from his difficulties with works written for the concert hall. He had bought a house at South Eaton Place in Belgravia, and now divided most of his time between there and Ashby St Ledgers near Rugby, the country house and estate of Alice, Viscountess Wimborne.

Alice was twenty-two years older than Walton. Her admirers were much impressed by the fact that she had the looks and allure of someone many years younger. She and her husband by now led separate lives, although they continued to entertain together in the sumptuous surroundings of Wimborne House in Arlington Street, where the private concerts they hosted were a regular fixture in London's musical calendar.

The start of Walton's relationship with Alice brought major changes to his life. Among these was the rift that now opened up between him and the Sitwell circle. The reasons appear to have been personal and trivial rather than at all rational. Alice and the Sitwell family had previously been on friendly terms, but Osbert Sitwell now seems to have reacted to the latest development in Walton's love life by nursing a mood of outraged possessiveness, on the grounds that Walton no longer even notionally depended on him for support. To her credit, Christabel Aberconway was one of the few who remained on friendly terms with both parties. But Walton now found that he was *persona non grata* at Carlyle Square and the Sitwell family's other homes. South Eaton Place was therefore a necessary London base as he set about developing his contacts in the film world. He and Alice did not live together until after the death of Viscount Wimborne in 1939, when Alice bought Lowndes Cottage in Lowndes Place as her new home in London.

Alice and Walton shared the same love of the Italian south. To help him convalesce after his double hernia operation in December 1937, she took him with her to stay at the Villa Cimbrone above Ravello. The view from there, down the steeply dropping coast to the sea below, remains enchanting today. To judge from contemporary postcards of sixty years ago, it was truly heart-stopping before the hillsides round the bay began to be covered with modern hotels. In these exquisite surroundings Walton found himself in a quandary, as he pondered whether to continue work on the Violin Concerto that Jascha Heifetz had commissioned from him, or to take up the latest tempting and lucrative offer of a film score that had come his way.

With hindsight it may seem easy to doubt Walton's integrity as an artist, if he really did find this decision as difficult as his letter to Hubert Foss of 11 May 1938 makes out. But that doubt would be misplaced. It is true that the world of classical music has been permanently enriched by the dreamlike loveliness of Walton's Violin Concerto from the moment of its first performance in 1939. It is also more than likely that his film score for *Pygmalion*, if it had been written, would now be of serious interest to film buffs only. But what should not be underestimated is the importance to Walton himself, as to any professional artist, of the practicalities of a working life. 'Going with the flow' is not automatically the soft creative option that it is too readily assumed to be by those admirers, however genuine they may be, who do not have to commit their own lives to doing the actual creating. Walton had a genuinely difficult decision to make. By now he would have been well aware of the formidable sums earned by some of the most talented composers of the time, from Gershwin to Korngold, in Hollywood's film studios. A few successes on that scale would have been enough to give Walton financial security for life. And he had already demonstrated that he had the fluency and technical skills to make film composing his main career if he wanted.

Posterity therefore owes Alice Wimborne a real debt, in that Walton's decision to persist with the Concerto had much to do with her persuading him that this was the right course to take. Walton later admitted that she was very good at 'standing over him and making him work'. The work is dedicated to Heifetz but, on a deeper and truer level, it is an unmistakable expression in musical terms of Walton's feelings for Alice. The survival of any of their correspondence to each other remains uncertain. Walton appears to have kept Alice's letters to him, and subsequently to have destroyed them. Nor is it clear that his letters to her are still extant. But there is a sense in which, thanks to the music of the Violin Concerto, posterity does not need them in order to understand at least something of the early years of their relationship.

As the Concerto took shape, its première was planned for December 1939 in Boston. In May that year Walton and Alice sailed to New York in order to meet Heifetz at his home in Connecticut. Details of the score, relating mainly to the solo part, were worked out between the composer and the great violinist, and Walton completed the Concerto in June. But his plans to return to America to conduct its first performances were subverted by the outbreak of the Second World War on 3 September.

To Hubert Foss   7 March [1936]

56A South Eaton Place, s.w.1

My dear Hubert,

As arranged, I talked to Loring about the Barrie play [*The Boy David*] & after much struggle got what I wanted (a pound a performance when & wherever it is performed) but in order to get [this] I had to repudiate you & take over the whole responsibility of the negotiations. I may add that I was told that I was a very hard headed & hard hearted business man!

Nevertheless I'm informed that I've not done as well as I should do over it – but more especially over the film contracts & have been recommended to an agency Messrs O'Brien, Dunfee & Linnet [O'Bryen, Linnit & Dunfee] who have great standing & command much respect from the film companies & in particular with London Film whom it is rumoured may want me for the music for René Clair's[1] new film.

I feel reluctantly that in the future I ought to do all my film business through them rather than through the O.U.P. as I am coming more & more to the view that it is absolutely necessary to have someone who really lives in, & understands the film world inside out. Only they can get the highest prices & know how to haggle & bully this gang of would-be tricksters. As I know you won't lose by this move I have no compunction in going to these people.

The negotiations about "As you like it"[2] begin tomorrow & it will be a tricky business, & I know from inside information that they were

1 French film director, whose pre-war masterpieces included *Paris qui dort* and *Sous les toits de Paris*. In 1935 he moved to England to make *The Ghost Goes West*, which made him world-famous. The film mentioned by Walton was probably *Break the News* (1937).
2 Walton had been approached to compose the music for a film version of Shakespeare's play, starring Elisabeth Bergner.

delighted to have got me for such a sum even for arranging only old music.

I realise we have both done as well as we possibly could, but the fact is I feel we are like two babes in the wood, as Sir J. Barrie would put it, wandering in a strange & predatory land.

I hope Dora is now really better & that you enjoyed your holiday. Hoping to see you soon

Yrs ever
Willie

P.S. The Barrie play as you probably know is off till the autumn.

To Mrs Walton [9 March 1936]

56A South Eaton Place, S.W.1

Dearest Mother,

Thank you for your letters. I am so very sorry not to have answered before but as you may have realised I have been most frightfully busy, though now owing to Miss [Elisabeth] Bergner's illness I [am] enjoying a respite.

How terrible about your ankle[.] I am so upset about it, do go & have any treatment the Dr recommends to get it right.

I've had no news from Alec & don't know quite what has been the matter with him. But [I] presume he must be better by now. Don't worry about him, he is sure to be alright.

No further news at present. Get well quickly & giv[e] my love to all.
Yrs
William

To Hubert Foss [February 1937]

Ashby St Ledgers, Rugby

My dear Hubert,

I suppose it was inevitable that a counter move should come from B & H.[1]

---

1 For Foss's reaction to Boosey and Hawkes's attempt to lure Walton away from Oxford University Press, see Appendix 1.

It says –

Clause 2. For the sum of £100, please read £150.

In clause 6. (clause 10 in O.U.P.) I had pointed out that I had my own agent for film, dramatic & stage works.

<u>Answer.</u>

"Your activities in the stage world can be: –

(1) Incidental & other music for stage plays

(2) Ballets & other works of a dramatic musical nature.

"In respect of the former, I do not think we should want any interest whatsoever, unless any of the material could be publishable in separate form, in which case it would come under Clause 3. (B & H)."

In regard to the latter royalties should be divided ⅓ to B & H. ⅔ to me.

I have been discussing with various people notably Sir H. [Hugh] Allen & Mr Courtauld the dilemma I'm in, & they were rather inclined to think that it would not be a bad thing for both the O.U.P & myself if I changed publishers for a while, reasoning that I should gain an entirely new shop window, so to speak & that that would help with my old works as well as any new & that there would be new channels of distribution etc, & that two firms would be working for the same object instead of one.

I write this for your private ear & I should appreciate very much what you think about it, & what you would do if you were in my place.

I shall be in London next Thursday for the day. So we must meet if it is possible for you.

Yours ever
William

P.S. [Louis] Kentner[1] would like a copy of the piano solo arrangement of the "Façade" Valse as he wants to play it at a concert soon.

To Mrs Walton   [19 February 1937]

Ashby St Ledgers, Rugby

Dearest Mother,

I hope you received my wire & have settled about taking your new house.

I am down here for some days trying to get going on my Coronation

---

1 Hungarian-born pianist and composer, who had settled in England in 1935.

March [*Crown Imperial*] for the Abbey so I'm pretty busy & have been for sometime what with one thing & another.

When you next write to Alec tell him that Lady Wimborne has very kindly written to the wife of the Canadian Governor General (she is her cousin) & if he's ever in Montreal & near the Governors special train, he is to write his name down & they will be delighted to see him.

Here is a cheque to be going on with. I expect you will be having a busy & expensive time.

Hoping that you are all well & have escaped 'flu.
With much love
as ever
William

To Benjamin Britten[1]   [October 1937]

56A South Eaton Place, s.w.1

Dear Britten

Having just listened to your "Variations" [*on a Theme of Frank Bridge*] I should like you to know how very excellent I thought them. It is really a fine work.

I do hope that the rehearsals for the Wimborne House performance will be enough, as it sounds rather difficult, & a doubtful performance would do a lot of damage to a work where every note tells.

Let me know what you think[.]
With many congratulations
Yrs
William Walton.

To Mrs Walton   [7 December 1937]

56A South Eaton Place, s.w.1

Dearest Mother,

Thank you so much for your letter & telegram.

I have been so very busy as you may imagine what with my concert & recording my viola concerto.

1 Britten's diary refers to a lunch together with Walton in July 1937. This seems to have been their first encounter, but there is no firm evidence that they had not met earlier.

Unfortunately tonight I have to undergo a slight operation for a tiny rupture[,] really nothing to worry about & I'm in the best hands. Will let you know how I progress.

With best love to all

William

To Dora Foss   16 December, 1937

The Clinic, 20 Devonshire Place, w.1

My dear Dora,

Thank you and Hubert ever so much for your telegram and the lovely flowers and present, which have cheered me up no end.

It was a bit grim for the first day or two, but I am much better now. I hope to be out by Christmas after all, as I am getting on much better than they expected, so perhaps you will give me a ring and let me know if you could come and see me some time, as I should be delighted to pass one of the weary hours in your pleasant company.

I do hope Hubert's voice is better – I know what a burden it makes life to lose one's voice.

Yours ever

William

To Benjamin Britten   23 December [1937]

The Clinic, 20 Devonshire Place, w.1

My dear Ben,

I am so very sorry not to have answered your letters before, not that I am [doing so] now, as I forgot to bring them here with me. But I'm sure you will understand.

It was a bit grim for the 1st week or so but I'm now getting on well, in fact I leave to-morrow for the country, but shall have to be in bed for another 10 days.

How are you? Better I hope, & I trust nothing more serious than overwork (which incidentally, I could'nt reprimand you too severely for).

I gather the Wimborne House performance was excellent & it went down very well. It was dissapointing that you could'nt be there, in fact that we both werent.

And I liked listening-in to "A Boy was born" & liked it much more than when I heard it last time.

I shall be away till about the end of Jan. Let me know how you are. Incidentally I saw Ansermet & the Variations are chosen for the next I.S.C.M. Festival along with Lennox [Berkeley][1] & [Alan] Rawsthorne[2] which is all to the good. Many congratulations.

All best wishes of Xmas & the New Year

Yrs

William

To Hubert Foss   [received 27 January 1938]

Ashby St Ledgers, Rugby

My dear Hubert,

[Walter] Legge[3] writes me that [Willem] Mengelberg[4] wants scores of the Symphony & Viola Concerto. He leaves on Friday, but you could send them round to Q.H [Queen's Hall] tomorrow (Thursday) where he's conducting the [London] Phil.

(Also Furtwangler [Furtwängler] wants the big score of the Symphony as there is an idea that he will do it at his concert of English music in June. C/o Prof. J. Plesch 40 Hereford House Park Lane will get him.)

"Morning sickness" is beginning, otherwise not much progress.

Love to Dora & yourself

William

1   English composer. A friend and contemporary of Britten: they had collaborated on the composition of their *Mont Juic* suite in 1936.
2   English composer, originally more prominent as a pianist. His output included two symphonies, two concertos each for piano and violin, and the cantata *A Canticle of Man*, to a text by the left-wing poet and writer Randall Swingler. He also composed twenty-two film scores.
3   Recording producer at EMI and subsequently the record company's Artistic Director. One of Walton's lifelong friends, he was to become and remain one of the most powerful forces in the recording industry.
4   Dutch conductor of the Concertgebouw Orchestra, Amsterdam.

To Arthur Bliss   28 April 1938

Villa Cimbrone, Ravello

Dear Bliss.

Your letter has just been forwarded to me, for which many thanks.[1]
The proposal suits me admirably, that is, if everything can be arranged.

You may or may not know that [Jascha] Heifetz[2] has commissioned
me to write a violin concerto for him & I have just got started on it. The
only question is if he will agree to the 1st perf. being under the auspices
of the British Council. I think he probably will do as it seems to me as
good a 1st perf platform as he will ever get.

My terms with him are that he pays me a certain sum for the right to
be the sole performer for a certain length of time.

I don't know if the British Council would insist on a British violinist
appearing in New York – if so I am afraid it would dish the whole thing,
or at any rate I should have to decide w[h]ether Heifetz or the British
Council took it. But it is obvious that the best arrangement would [be]
for the "world première" to be played by Heifetz under the auspices of
the British Council.

The financial arrangements you mention are entirely satisfactory to
me & I don't think there is any complication about the dedication.[3]

With many thanks again for writing to me.

With kindest regards
Yours ever
William Walton

To Osbert Sitwell   28 April 1938
[postcard]   [postmarked: Ravello, 30 April 1938]

I am so sorry to hear of your being so unwell. Do try "Naïodine" (a
French preparation) injections for the rheumatics – it acts like a charm
on me & keeps it off for months at a time. I am afraid I've done nothing
about the ballet & see no prospects of doing so for about a year, as I'm

1 Bliss had proposed to the British Council that it should commission Walton to compose
a violin concerto for the forthcoming New York World's Fair.
2 Russian-born American violinist. One of the great players of his era.
3 Probably of Bliss's Piano Concerto, which he dedicated 'To the people of the USA',
although an earlier version may have been dedicated to Walton: see p. 90 n. 2. Walton's
Violin Concerto is dedicated to Heifetz.

involved with a violin concerto for Heifetz to be played for the 1ˢᵗ time in New York at the World's Fair. Am being paid vast sums for it as well as being invited to N.Y. so feel I must put everything into it. Hoping to hear better news of you soon. [My] Mothers address: 26 Appleton Rd. Hale. Cheshire.

    Love to you both
    William

To Hubert Foss   11 May 1938

Villa Cimbrone, Ravello

My dear Hubert,

    This is a letter which I am writing for the sake of clearing my mind.

    In the last fortnight I've had weighty decisions to make & I do hope you will think that I have acted rightly.

    What has happened is as follows: About a fortnight ago, Bliss, authorized by the British Council, wrote me, for the moment in strict confidence, asking me to write a violin concerto for the concerts at the New York World's Fair adding that three others were being asked, himself for a Pianoforte Concerto. V.W. [Vaughan Williams] for a choral work & Bax for an orch. work. Terms being £250 for 1ˢᵗ perf only & no other rights being asked for except maybe the dedication. Also £100 extra for a trip to New York.

    I replied in the affirmative, stipulating that Heifeitz [Heifetz] should play 1st perf. The B.C.'s terms not clashing with Heifeitz, I felt I could try & kill two birds with one stone, for he can do whatever he likes about [it] after the 1st perf. (I've not heard that the B.C will accept H, or demand a British violinist.)

    This I felt settled the American question which has been worrying us previously & knocks out any "In honors" etc. Everything in the garden seemed lovely & I settled down to it, determined to undertake nothing else till it was finished. And knowing what I'm like it is not any too much time.

    Next occurs a telegram "Please undertake music Pygmalion" film terms 550 guineas. I answer "no". This started last Thursday & has been going on ever since, Pascal the producer not taking "no" for an answer.

    It takes too long to describe the temptations being [put] in front of me, the telephone calls (I might be Garbo) but I've persisted in saying no.

    The most difficult one to refuse is the offer of the next two pictures at the same if not a higher price. Which means refusing £1650. Within the next twelve months. But to accept would mean refusing the American offer, for I should have to return now, & there is about 30 mins music in this film & it is going to take a month to get through; & at least one other film would be ready by Xmas, & that would mean another month. – quite apart from the distraction & settling down again to the V.C.

But as I say I've turned it down. Whether it is a wise decision I am in some doubt. Consider the B.C.s american proposition again, financially with what I shall get from Heifeitz, I'm not much out of pocket if it concerned this one film only. But there are other doubts as well. Heifeitz may not like the work, he may have other dates & be unable to play. This I've not yet had time to find out, & at any rate H. is hardly likely to com[m]it himself until he has seen at least part of the work & at the moment there doesn't seem much to show him.

Of course I suppose in the case of H refusing, I can always find someone else, but it would be bad, I think for the work.

What, however, seems to me the greatest drawback is the nature of the work itself.

It seems to be developing in an extremely intimate way, not much show & bravura, & I begin to have doubts (fatal for the work of course) of this still small voice getting over at all in a vast hall holding 10,000 people. [I wonder] whether my original plan to have the 1ˢᵗ perf. with Cortaulds in the 1939–40 [season] at Q.H. [Queen's Hall] is not the best after all. At least there would be some in the audience who would know what I was talking about. In fact, under the american conditions, however good the work may turn out to be, I can't see it being a justifiable success at that particular perf. & that means the end of it, & of most of my works in America for some time to come.

Anyhow I think I can leave the idea of refusing the american perf. for a little while, at any rate till the end of July.

But as it is, it all boils down to this, whether I'm to become a film composer or a real composer.

I need hardly say that noone likes refusing the prospect of £1650, but on the other hand, with the O.U.P subsidy, my old royalties, & P.R.S. dues etc that what I've got of my own, I am fairly alright for the moment. In fact I think I can safely wipe out films, which have served their purpose in ennabling me to get my house etc.

Nevertheless I should like your approval & views especially on the american question. Even if I came to refuse that[,] I believe I'm right

about the film decision. Sorry to bother you with such a long letter.
    Love to you both.
    William.

To Hubert Foss [May/June 1938]

[Villa Cimbrone, Ravello]

My dear Hubert,

    I am so sorry to have been so long writing to you, but I have been undergoing the usual travail & have dropped at last the [Violin Concerto's] 1st movement. Not too bad.

    Having been bitten by a tarantula a rare & dangerous & unpleasant experience I have celebrated the occasion by the 2nd movement being a kind of tarantella "Presto cappricciosamente alla napolitana". Quite gaga I may say. & of doubtful propriety after the 1st movement, – however you will be able to judge.

    I return about July 5th having let my house till thereabouts.

    I am most distressed to hear about Dora & do so hope that she has made a good recovery. You must have been having a bit of a time of it what with that & the ISCM etc.

    I will let you know as soon as I'm back & we will meet.

    With best love to you both & looking forward to seeing you again
    Yours ever
    William

To Christian Darnton[1] [1938]

Dear Christian,

    Your score arrived just as I was about to write you. Having been in Amsterdam (for that miserable, music-forsaken festival) & Zurich I didn't get your wire till my return.

    I saw [Hermann] Scherchen in Amsterdam & with the aid of many others we arranged a programme for his [ISCM] festival including one of your works (the 2nd piano suite if I remember rightly).

    I'm sorry you've had to hurry over this work for nothing, but there

---

1 English composer. His style was more modernist than Walton's, and his Marxist political standpoint sharply opposed.

didn't anyhow seem much opening for a choral work, so I hope you won't be dissapointed.

I've taken the opportunity of having a good look at your score, & though personally I can't honestly say that this style of music appeals to me, yet nevertheless I can't help but admire its very many good qualities, particularly its clarity both of form & expression, also its good & lengthy line especially in the first part. It is to be hoped that the B.B.C. will give it a performance.

Many congratulations to your wife & yourself on the birth of your son. It must be a great happiness for you both.

I'm sorry that I've not been able to do better for you about this festival, but I'm sure you will understand what arranging these things is like.

Yrs

William Walton.

To Dora Foss   2 August [1938]

Ashby St Ledgers, Rugby

My dear Dora,

I am most touched by your kind thought of sending some flowers to my mother and for offering to go and see her. It really is too kind of you & I am most grateful as I am sure she is.

She seemed to be on the improve already when I left her and in good spirits.

With love to you both & ever so many thanks again.

Yours ever

William.

P.S. Would you ask Hubert to send [Leonid] Massine at Drury Lane min. scores of Symphony & Façade I.

To Hubert Foss   [February 1939]

Ashby St Ledgers, Rugby

My dear Hubert.

Here is something to go [on] with. Please get Nora to send details for guarantee. Are you getting the allowance alright from my accountant or not, as you should be doing.

[117]

Just heard that Heifetz has accepted my concerto.
Best love
W.

To Leslie Heward [1]   28 March 1939

Ashby St Ledgers, Rugby

Dear Leslie

I'm sorry not to have answered your letter before but what with having to give an unexpected performance of my Symphony & all this bother with the British Council, I've had rather a chaotic & distracted ten days.

As you may have seen I've withdrawn my Concerto from the World's Fair not as is stated because it's unfinished but because Heifetz can't play on the date fixed (the B.C. only let him know about ten days ago!). Heifetz wants the concerto for two years & I would rather stick to him. But actually I'm afraid there is little to be said for either the British Council or myself, so keep this "under your hat".

So I'm out of the World's Fair altogether. I understand that all the music programmes barring those of the B.C. have been cancelled & that nothing is happening at all.

Unfortunately I know very little about American conditions, but I am going over sometime soon to work with Heifetz on the concerto probably the same time as you, and I most certainly will scout around and unreservedly recommend you, which for once I can do with a clear conscience.

I could'nt sympathise with you more about Brum & opportunities here generally I must say are not too bright. But as I've said I will do everything possible when & if I ever get there.

Hoping to see you sometime soon.

Yours ever.

Willie Walton

1 Conductor of the City of Birmingham Orchestra (now the City of Birmingham Symphony Orchestra).

To Dora Foss   [postmarked: Le Havre à New York,
[postcard of SS *Normandie*]   15 May 1939]

Arrive tomorrow after a very good passage[1] in this miracle of a ship.
  Love to you both
  W.

To Dora Foss   [postmarked: Grand Central Annex, N.Y.,
                                    6 June 1939]
[postcard of aerial view of the Empire State Building, New York]

Shall be back possibly before you get this. All news when I see you both.
  W.

INSTEAD of travelling to America to conduct the first performances of his Violin Concerto, Walton had to be content with staying at home and reading the enthusiastic telegrams about the work's reception at Severance Hall in Cleveland, Ohio, on 7 December 1939. The start of the Second World War had turned his and Alice Wimborne's lives upside down, like those of millions of others. The 31 acres of Alice's estate at Ashby St Ledgers were now to be ploughed up to grow food for the war effort. And much of London's normal musical activity was suspended.

Two areas of this that began to become rather more active, however, were broadcasting and film-making. Both were seen by the war government as having substantial propaganda value. Through his contacts in the film world, notably the producer Dallas Bower, Walton quickly sensed which way the wind was blowing, and set about involving himself in various projects at the BBC and the Ministry of Information film unit. He also wrote his overture *Scapino*, to a commission from the Chicago Symphony Orchestra, and a number of smaller works. Meanwhile his longstanding friendship with the writer Cecil Gray drew him into considering a much larger project.

Walton's competitive streak was a part of his nature, and a significant factor in motivating him to compose. It is beyond doubt that his later

1 Walton and Alice Wimborne were *en route* to Heifetz's country farmhouse in Connecticut, US, to discuss details of the Violin Concerto with him.

determination to create *Troilus and Cressida* was fuelled at least in part by the international success of Britten's *Peter Grimes* after its first performance at London's Sadler's Wells Theatre in June 1945. But the facts also indicate that Walton had been thinking about writing an opera many years earlier. In a letter written to David Horner on 5 January 1933, Walton had humorously mentioned that Osbert Sitwell should start thinking about 'a subject for an opera' for him to work on. Perhaps this had not been entirely a joke.

For much of 1941, Gray and Walton put a considerable amount of time and thought into the idea of an opera about Carlo Gesualdo, Prince of Venosa (c. 1561–1613). This Italian composer's chief claim to fame, apart from the chromaticism of his music, was his arrangement of the murder of his adulterous first wife and her aristocratic lover. The project proceeded as far as an early draft of Gray's libretto. It therefore remains a cause for extreme regret that Walton abandoned the idea early in 1942, apparently without having written any of the music. The subject had the potential to suit him ideally, with its blend of interesting characters and high drama within a Neapolitan setting. And the possibility of integrating some of Gesualdo's own music (at that time almost entirely unknown) into an operatic score must surely have intrigued him. But for the moment there were more pressing demands on his time.

Early in 1942 there seems to have been a likelihood that he might be called up to some kind of military service, a prospect he wanted to avoid. Film production in wartime England was thriving, as the authorities seized on the value of this medium of popular entertainment as a means of raising patriotic morale at home and also of flying the national flag abroad. Walton now plunged into the world of film music. His house at South Eaton Place had been destroyed in the Blitz of May 1941, so during visits to London he stayed at Lowndes Cottage. But mostly he lived with Alice Wimborne at Ashby St Ledgers. There, working to a demanding schedule, he produced his incidental music for Louis MacNeice's radio play *Christopher Columbus*, and also several film scores. Among these was the *The First of the Few*, the story of the creation of the Spitfire fighter plane which had helped to repel the Luftwaffe's air attacks in the Battle of Britain.

The film's success put Walton in an ideal position to secure the commission of the music for *Henry V*, whose star and director was to be Laurence Olivier. Walton and Olivier became firm friends while working on what turned out to be one of the most spectacularly successful British films ever made. It is therefore unfortunate that they appear to have written no letters to each other during its creation. Muir Mathieson, who conducted most of Walton's film scores in the studio, remembered that he and Walton were so busy at the time that it was more practical for them to keep in touch by telephone. Probably Walton and Olivier did the same.

When the war eventually ended, Walton was at work on his String Quartet in A minor. He had been contemplating this for many years, partly as a disciplined antidote to the orchestral scores that had dominated his output so far. He evidently found the creative gear change between film scores and chamber music to be even more difficult than he had expected, but the Quartet was eventually completed in 1947. By then, opera was uppermost in his thoughts.

In 1944, as London began to make plans for its musical life in the postwar years, Walton was sounded out as to his views on the future of the opera house at Covent Garden. His memorandum on the subject (published here for the first time, see Appendix 3) would seem to have impressed those to whom it was sent for consideration, because in 1946 Walton joined the board of the newly created Covent Garden Opera House Trust. Its immediate tasks included the complex integration of the existing opera and ballet companies already connected to Covent Garden to some extent, but whose traditional bases were at theatres elsewhere in London. Walton found his time being increasingly devoured by these administrative demands. But they helped him acquire the useful contacts that he needed, and in 1947 the BBC commissioned him to write an opera of his own. The choice of Christopher Hassall as a potential librettist appears to have been suggested in the first place by the BBC. Alice Wimborne's acquaintance with the writer, however, was certainly a factor in persuading Walton that he and Hassall could work together.

Hassall submitted to Walton the outline scenarios of a number of possible subjects. Some were gloriously far-fetched, while others appeared to have potential. Among them were *The Duke of Melveric* (or *Death's Jest-Book*,) adapted from a never performed play written in the 1830s by Thomas Lovell Beddoes; *Hassan*, after James Elroy Flecker; *The Woman of Andros*, based on Thornton Wilder's novel; *Queen Jocasta* (or *The Scourge*), adapted from Jean Cocteau's play *La machine infernale*; *Volpone*, partially based on Ben Jonson; *Antony and Cleopatra*, after Shakespeare; and a project of Hassall's own, *Byron*. After much discussion throughout the summer, Walton and Hassall decided to revert to one of their earlier ideas. *Troilus and Cressida* was to be based on versions of the story from the Trojan War as retold by Chaucer and other writers, rather than on Shakespeare's play.

Walton and Alice then set off in September for a holiday together in Italy. They had travelled only as far as Lucerne when Alice became seriously ill. Cancer was suspected, but not at first diagnosed. Hampered by the foreign-exchange restrictions of the post-war years, Walton frantically tried to find a source of funds to pay for Alice's treatment in a Swiss clinic. Purely by chance he met Diana Gould, the future wife of his friend Yehudi Menuhin, on a train journey. On Menuhin's behalf she commissioned a Violin Sonata, to be played by Menuhin and Louis Kentner, who was married to Diana's sister, Griselda.

Walton took Alice home to Ashby St Ledgers, where her health deteriorated further as the winter wore on. By the start of 1948 it was finally clear that she had cancer of the bronchial tubes. She continued to take an interest in Hassall's work on the libretto of *Troilus and Cressida*, expressing some perhaps prescient doubts as to whether it was, after all, the ideal subject for Walton. Her harrowingly slow death on 19 April 1948 was one of the darkest turning points of the composer's life. Alice left Lowndes Cottage to him in her will. In May he went on holiday to Capri, and then worked further on *Troilus and Cressida*'s libretto with Hassall during the summer.

Some of Walton's letters during this unhappy period make for eyebrow-raising reading. In the preceding years he had been involved in more than one liaison. Alice must by now have understood that his behaviour in this respect was both compulsive and inevitable, but the evidence is that she had as much difficulty in coming to terms with it as one can imagine. It is perhaps best not to pass judgement on Walton's jocular anticipation of the pleasures of pinching Griselda Kentner's bottom, as he wrote to her on 3 March 1948 from Ashby St Ledgers while Alice lay dying. Everyone copes with personal grief in his or her own way. As Walton's correspondence shows, the ensuing summer brought yet another emotional complication. This continued as Walton travelled via Switzerland to Genoa, on his way to Argentina.

He had been asked to represent Britain at an international conference of the Performing Right Society in Buenos Aires. Argentina was not then a signatory to the Berne Convention on copyright, and the hope was that the presence of a powerful British delegation would prove influential in bringing this about. Walton's letter to Alan Frank, written on 31 October, radiates the new and sunny mood brought about by what he had expected to be no more than a tedious official visit. Susana Gil Passo, aged twenty-two, was working for the British Council in Buenos Aires, where she had been asked to organize a press conference for Walton and the other delegation members. Six weeks later, she and Walton were married.

To Hubert Foss   9 September 1939

Ashby St Ledgers, Rugby

My dear Hubert,

How are you & what is happening about you?

As for myself, I am now looking around for something to do & propose joining the local A.R.P [Air Raid Protection], also there is an idea I should help to supervise this estate now it is to be ploughed up; in fact [that] I become a war-time estate agent. I suppose, in addition to these proposed activities, there is no hope of the composers being used for propaganda purposes!

Meanwhile I've been trying, not too successfully to get going on this work for Chicago [*Scapino*]. But I've got quite a good scheme for the work. It is not to be a[n] overture, but a suite which I am titling "Varii Capricci".[1] There are to be five pieces, thus.

I.	Intrada	(full orch.)
II.	Siciliana	(Wood wind)
III.	Sarabanda	(Strings & harps)
IV.	Marcia	(Brass & Perc.)
V.	Giga	(full orch.)

It will probably work out a bit differently when & if I am able to get down to it, but that is the general outline.

Incidentally what is going to happen to the O.U.P.?

I suppose the copying of parts for the [Violin] Concerto is still in progress & I think the sooner the better, we get them off to America, as I presume things will go on there, more or less normally & Heifetz will still want to perform it sometime this season. So if there are any ready for correction will you send them here.

How is Dora? In the country I hope.

My love to you both

---

1 Not to be confused with *Varii capricci* of 1976, Walton's orchestral version of his Five Bagatelles for guitar (1971).

Yrs ever
William

The only good thing I can see in this situation is the suppression of musical criticism, though there is a bit of an "eyeful" in the "Times" this morning.

To Hubert Foss   7 November 1939

Ashby St Ledgers, Rugby

My dear Hubert,

I enclose the agreements[1] duly signed.

Did you get my letter in answer to yours of Oct 31ˢᵗ? About the week-end of Nov 26ᵗʰ, this morning I received an invitation to stay with Sir H.P.A. [Hugh Allen][2] for the same, and if you & Dora don't mind, I think it would be wiser to accept it, and I could come to you either the following week-end or any that suits you. He particularly wants me to meet some admiring undergruades [undergraduates] & give them a good talking to, & I think it might be as well to keep in with the young, not that there will any left shortly. It sounds from the way he puts it, that the symphony may be down as a score to be studied for one of the music examinations, so I think it might be as well if I accept his invitatation, if as I've said before[,] you & Dora don't mind.

I go to Manchester on Saturday to conduct Facade II & shall be back on Monday.

I've been wondering whether it might not be a good idea to get going on some performances of Facade in the original version. The programme might be as follows –

①	Canti Carnasc[h]ialeschi[3] (new)	10 mins	W.W.
②	Chinese songs[4]	10 mins	C.L. [Constant Lambert]
③	Pfte Concerto	30 mins.	C.L.
④	Façade	35 mins	W.W.
			(about 1 hours ½ in all with intervals)

1 With Heifetz, concerning the Violin Concerto.
2 Now Professor of Music at Oxford University. (See also p. 12, n. 1.)
3 Italian for carnival songs: specifically, a form of partsong for three or four voices, performed by masqueraders to accompany the procession of carnival floats in Florence in the fifteenth and sixteenth centuries.
4 *Eight Songs of Li-Po.*

(as regards 1ˢᵗ item see sheet with my plan of work for the "duration").

Constant has I believe orchestrated his songs for the same combination as the Concerto & Façade, & the Canti Carnasc[h]ialeschi would be for the same, a few short pieces to act as a curtain-raiser so to speak.

C. would conduct his own pieces & I mine. About Facade, I'm afraid C's voice is not quite what it used to be & I doubt if it would stand the racket now, so if say, someone like Parry Jones[1] was to sing the songs, he would in all probability be willing to do the reciting part in F. If guarantees were available we might arrange performances at the following universities, for that I think is where we should get most support. Oxford, Cambridge, Manchester, Liverpool, Birmingham, Cardiff, Bristol also perhaps one in London.

I think, however, it is not worth doing till summer-time comes in again & the time of the concerts should be 5–30 with the black-out at 7–30. so that would be in late April.

I've not yet approached Constant about it & maybe you also, will think it a bit too risky to carry through without loss.

This is my plan of work:[2]

Overture "Bartholomew Fair" for orchestra
(I'm not really decided about this title)

Alba, Pastorela et Serena for String orchestra
(These names are the Provençal [Italian] ones for aubade, Pastoral[e] & serenade)

Four medieval Latin lyrics for unaccompanied chorus.

Dämon et Thyrsis (after [the painting by] Giorgione) for Oboe solo,
       strings & harp   scene pastorale (in 4 movements)

(These [last] three I should like the B.B.C. to do as a single programme)

---

1   Welsh tenor. In 1954 Walton was to consider him as a possible cast member for the première of *Troilus and Cressida*.
2   This is the 'sheet' mentioned by Walton earlier. None of the works mentioned on it was to be composed, except for the String Quartet, which was eventually written between 1945 and 1947 (and which may or may not have been a later conception altogether). Unlike in the list earlier in the letter, the duration of *Canti Carnaschialeschi* and the other works is not given. Very unusually for Walton, the passage from 'This is my plan of work . . .' to 'What a hope!' is placed within square brackets. These have been omitted, to avoid confusion with the insertion of editorial square brackets elsewhere.

Varii capricci[1] (portraits from the Commedia dell'Arte)
for orchestra
(This is to be a rather more ambitious work than the original plan I had
for it)

Canti Carnasc[h]ialeschi (a curtain-raiser for "Facade")

String Quartet

Amoretti (which I've already mentioned to you)
This title, I shall use as a sort of musical waste-paper basket, into which
I shall throw the odds & ends, which occur in composing & which in
the past I've needlessly discarded. The only thing now is to carry it out,
which I am doing by the end of 1941. What a hope!

Looking forward to seeing you both
Yrs
William

To Hubert Foss   [early December 1939]

Ashby St Ledgers, Rugby

My dear Hubert,

Here are the cables: –

Concerto enormous success. orchestra played superbly you would
have been extremely pleased. Congratulations your most successful
concerto. Writing sending programme. Best greetings
Heifetz

Just heard terrific successful premiere so happy darling*(!!!since
when?)[2] writing details
Janet Goossens[3]

*I'm innocent of this endearment.

yrs ever
William

1 See p. 123, n. 1.
2 Walton's insertion.
3 Wife of Eugene Goossens, who at this time was conductor of the Cincinnati Symphony
Orchestra.

To John Ireland [1] 14 December 1939

Ashby St Ledgers, Rugby

My dear John,

It <u>appals</u> me when I see that the date of your letter is October 26th. I did not know time could fly so quickly in these days.

I appreciate very much all you say about coming to Guernsey, and doubtless I hope I shall find myself there, anyhow for a short time, in the not too distant future.

Actually life is not as bad here as you would think, and I feel, though probably I am wrong, that there is not much likelihood of there being bad air raids until the end of the War, and I do not think that is in sight for some years to come.

You will be interested to hear that I received the following cable: –

Concerto enormous success orchestra played superbly you would have been extremely pleased congratulations your most successful concerto Writing sending programme best greetings thanks

Jascha Heifetz

Isn't this fine?

Anyhow I could not come to Guernsey just yet as I have some film work coming on, which seems to be the only money I shall earn next year!

[. . .]

I wish you a very happy Christmas and many many more New Years.

~~Yours,~~

thine

William

To Hubert Foss 27 December [1939]

Ashby St Ledgers, Rugby

My dear Hubert,

The enclosed have turned up from O'Bryen [O'Bryen, Linnit & Dunfee]. Clause 8 in Samuel's [2] letter will be better discussed between

---

1 English composer, who had just retired from his teaching position at the Royal College of Music.

2 P. C. Samuel of Pascal Film Productions Ltd.

you so as you can find out exactly where you stand. He's just a bit slip-
pery. I send my contract so you can see what it is all about. Clause 8 in
the original contract I think is the P.R.S. one & cannot be changed.

With all good wishes to you both for New Year

Yrs

William

To Hubert Foss   [early 1940]
[letter on two postcards, showing Chartres Cathedral
& Schloss Monrepos, Ludwigsburg]

Chenhalls

Dear Hubert,

[. . .]

I've been asked by the M.O.I. [Ministry of Information] to arrange a
simple overture of popular music to run for about 8 mins. I don't know
as yet quite what they mean by "popular music" but presume it means
things like "Rule Brit" etc. You don't happen to know a volume of popular tunes (non-copyright) upon which I could draw. I suppose it ought
to be on the lines of Quilter's[1] Children's Nursery Tune overture or
V.W.s [Vaughan Williams's] Fantasia on Folk Songs.[2]

It might be a profitable thing to do. Anyhow I've got to do it.

Incidentally about V.W. you might see that he charges full rates £ ₅₀
for his next film (if not for gov. dept.) He's sure to get plenty of offers as
I hear 49th P. [49th Parallel] is pretty good & it is not a help for the rest
of the composers if someone of his calibre & reputation is asking half
what most of us get.

Yours ever

W.

1 Roger Quilter, English composer, best known for his songs for voice and piano. His *A
Children's Overture* was composed in 1919.
2 Probably *The Running Set* for orchestra (1933).

To Hubert Foss [early 1940]

Ashby St Ledgers, Rugby

My dear Hubert,

[. . .]

It appears that I'm definitely going to be offered the job of general music director of the Mo.I [Ministry of Information] film unit & although unpaid I think it wisest to accept it. I'm afraid it will involve more work than I first anticipated, but anyhow one can but see how it works out.

I'm still exercised in my mind about the title for the overture.[1] What do you think of "The triumph of Silenus", or "(T'was) Bacchus and his crew". I incline to the latter. See Oxford B of V. p.723 at verse starting "And as I sat," Keats.[2] If this and the following verse were quoted it might give enough of a clue without involving one in a "tone poem"?

I will talk to you more about your film idea when I see you which I hope will be soon.

Yrs
William

To Edward Clark 5 March 1940

Ashby St Ledgers, Rugby.

My dear Edward,

I think the draft [BBC radio] programmes to be absolutely splendid, & will need little if any attention in committee.

Offhand I've only these suggestions to make.

2nd Orch. Concert. You mention "Louise". What about Charpentier's "Mediterranean Sketches"? I'm not sure of the title, but it is a comparatively unknown work & rather good & right up Tommy's [Sir Thomas Beecham's] street.

3rd orch. concert. Won't the appearance of the Stravinsky add considerably to the cost without bringing much into the house?

1 This eventually became *Scapino*, on a quite different subject.
2 The references are to texts from Keats's *Endymion*.

3$^{\underline{rd}}$ N.G. Con. [National Gallery concert] What about trying to get J. Francaix [Jean Françaix]^{1} to write a work, or perhaps he has already written one for a vaguely similar combination (or his str. trio). Also perhaps there ought to be some songs by B. Britten included.

4th Nat.G. con. There you've got me! I don't know a good Eng. str. qt. Charles Wood?^{2} V.W.? or [Alan] Bush's^{3} Dialectic as originally written [for string quartet] instead of in last programme.

Mention of Gounod makes me long to include the Wind Symphony, but I don't quite see where, & it would be an added expense as I seem to remember it is for a fairly large number of players. Perhaps it would go in the 5th programme instead of the Satie & would be more popular.

When you send me the budget for these concerts will you also send one (no programme details) for the projected "Prom" season, so we can make the application to the Pilgrim Trust for both at the same time.

[. . .]

Another idea occurs to me as to whether it would be possible to devise some kind of "deffered payment" system for subscriptions for the whole series of concerts. If it were not too complicated, I think we could "cash in" on the National Gallery audience which by now must be pretty big if rather poor, & it might be inclined to jump at a "defered payment" idea.

You can drop a line to Milhaud^{4} c/o Mr Cavalcanti G.P.O Film Unit Bennett Park Blackheath, & it will get him when he comes over.

I may be coming up on Thursday[,] if so, I will give you a ring.

Further I think it would be a good idea to get in touch with the French Embassy also the Mo.I propaganda department as it seems to me that this is the best bit of Anglo-French propaganda that has been forthcoming since the outbreak of the "bore".

Yours

William Walton

---

1   French composer and pianist, best known for his chamber music among a large output.
2   Irish composer, resident mostly in England, and best known for his church music.
3   English composer. A member of the Communist Party, he had founded the Workers' Musical Association in 1936.
4   Darius Milhaud, French composer of prolific fluency.

To Hubert Foss   [16 May 1940]

Ashby St Ledgers, Rugby

My dear Hubert,

I saw Mr Feldman[1] on Tuesday and managed to calm him down somewhat.

In fact, barring a certain animosity against the O.U.P. generally he couldn't have been sweeter and we got on like a house on fire.

He was perfectly willing to discuss sharing the proceeds on the one piece only & in fact doesn't want to take any royalty on anything that doesn't strictly belong to him.

What had got his goat was that three months had elapsed without his yet having seen the figures we promised to send him, a legitimate grievance I consider, and we decided that the ratio of royalties can't properly be fixed until he has seen the figures. But there was no question at all of his not being more than willing to fix up the business absolutely fairly.

I think that not receiving the figures made him a bit suspicious we are

---

1 Bertram Feldman, of the publishing house B. Feldman & Co. Since August 1939 he and Oxford University Press had been involved in an extensive correspondence about the popular song 'I do like to be beside the seaside'. Walton had quoted the tune of this – without the words, and with his own accompanying harmony – in his setting of 'Tango-Pasodoble' in *Façade*, and in his orchestral arrangement in *Façade* Suite No. 1. Walton had used the melody without being aware that it was copyright material. In fact it had been composed by John Glover-Kind, and was published by B. Feldman & Co. in 1909. Having discovered this breach of copyright, Feldman, at first through his firm's general manager Felix Slevin, had been pursuing OUP for royalty payments. OUP, in the person of Sir Humphrey Milford – Publisher to the University of Oxford, and the supremo of the Press's London office which included the music department – had been refusing either to consider this, or to respond to Feldman's entirely polite requests for a meeting to discuss the matter (although privately Milford was prepared to consider paying a nominal one-off fee in lieu of all past and future royalties). It therefore fell to Hubert Foss to try to deal with the problem by stalling. The evidence of the correspondence is that Milford had instructed him to do this, in the hope that Feldman would eventually lose interest. Feldman, on the contrary, persisted, and on 11 December 1939 asked for 'a line of the profits to date' (although stating that he did not want the figure publicly disclosed). Foss reported this next day in a memorandum to Milford, who returned it to him with the added footnote: 'I am inclined to let this delightful Jew sue us.' In February 1940 an unofficial meeting took place between Walton, Foss, Feldman and Slevin, but the informal agreement they appear to have reached over royalty payments evidently foundered on Milford's resistance. In May 1940 Feldman, having had no formal response from OUP, threatened the company with an injunction restraining it from printing and publishing Walton's 'Tango-Pasodoble'. Walton's response was evidently to offer to visit Feldman personally and attempt to sort the matter out.

concealing something for he produced his own royalty sheet for what "I do like to be etc" produced in the last three months[:] a large sum of about £125 & I vaguely think that he thinks we arc getting the same. How I wish we were!

Anyhow I said we would both go & see him next week and finish the business once & for all. We have got to fix it by the end of the month, as he is keeping to his word about injuncting us if we don't do so by the date mentioned.

So I propose we meet him on Monday at 12 o'clock with the figures, if that is suitable for you.[1]

Personally I think it lunacy & immoral to have to go to law at a time like this when the money involved had much better be put into savings certificates!

Yours
William

To Hubert Foss

[December 1940?]

Ashby St Ledgers, Rugby

Dear Hubert,

I return to the Sieber[2] arrangement. I'm not quite happy about it & suggest you should see one made by Roy Douglas,[3] who showed it me

---

1 After this meeting between Walton, OUP and Feldman, the basis of a formal agreement was reached. OUP would pay a backdated, one-off sum of £50 in respect of past performances of *Façade* in its original and suite versions (£25 for infringement of copyright and £25 in lieu of royalty payments to 31 August 1939). The Press would also pay Feldman one-third of one-fifth of fees received for future performances ('Tango-Pasodoble' being one of *Façade* Suite No. 1's five movements). When Walton learned from Foss's telephone call that these payments would be offset against his own royalty income from OUP, his initial response was to cut off the conversation. A similar share of Walton's broadcasting and conducting fees through the Performing Right Society concerning performances of *Façade* were to be made over to Feldman. John Glover-Kind had died on 8 April 1918, which meant that 'I do like to be beside the seaside' remained in copyright until 8 April 1968. Feldman asked for a full royalty payment until 8 April 1948; on that date, prompted by OUP, he agreed to accept a payment of one-tenth of one-fifth of OUP's income from future *Façade* performances until 8 April 1968 (a reduction in line with the formula stipulated in Section 3 of the Copyright Act, 1911). The original version of *Façade* remained unpublished until 1951.
2 Probably Mátyás Seiber, Hungarian-born composer resident in England from 1935.
3 English composer. His all-round musical expertise was such that he was much in

when here last week helping me out over some extra orchestrations for Major B. [*Major Barbara*] It was still in a rough sketch but seemed to me much more like the original. So I've asked him to send it you.

[. . .]

About my nephew.[1] Here is his address.

Michael Walton
c/o Caryl Arnold
15 Governor's Rd
N. Rosedale
Toronto, Ont.

(As you know one can't do anything about sending money to support the children in Canada & Michael is being looked after by his maternal uncle who is not well off & has children of his own. My brother & so am I, is anxious that Michael's musical talents should not be neglected, but the uncle cannot afford to do more than keep him & I imagine send him to the board School or its Canadian equivalent.)

If you could pen a line to Sir. E Macmillan about him I should be very grateful. There may be some fund for evacuees education. At any rate I think without doubt someone could be found who would look after his musical education voluntarily.

Yours
William

To Roy Douglas [June/July 1941]
[postcard]

I expect I shall be needing you[r] help sorely about Sept. as I'm doing a film at Ealing [*Next of Kin*] & I believe a new Howard[2] film at Denham [*The First of the Few*] more or less simultaneously. Are you still a lot at

———

demand as an arranger, orchestrator, and copyist of the music of others, notably Vaughan Williams. Walton too was increasingly to rely on Douglas's meticulous technical thoroughness and intelligent advice, at first regarding his film scores and later during his work on *Troilus and Cressida*.

1 Son of Walton's younger brother Alec.
2 Leslie Howard, English actor and director. At this time world famous after his co-starring role as Ashley in the 1939 film of Margaret Mitchell's novel *Gone with the Wind*.

Oxford?[1] If you are you must come over before it is necessary for intensive work.

yrs
W Walton

To Edward Dent   6 October 1941

Ashby St Ledgers, Rugby

Dear Edward,

Thank you so much for your book which I shall study with interest and instruction.

I am, I hope, going to embark on an opera. Cecil Gray[2] is writing the libretto, based on the life of Gesualdo.[3] We have only got as far as sketching the scenes as yet, but I should very much like you to see them. I think I shall be coming to Cambridge to stay with Paddy [Patrick Hadley] fairly soon and I could show you what there is then.

We are all rather concerned about the future of opera and Sadler's Wells (when I say we, I mean people like Walter Legge, Cecil Gray & Sir H.[Hugh] Allen) and I feel we ought to get together to formulate some concrete plans to do in Christie[4] & his machinations, which won't be easy.

Yours ever.
William Walton

I send you a copy of my violin concerto which is at long last, out.

1 Douglas had been orchestrating film scores by Richard Addinsell (English composer of the *Warsaw Concerto* and much film and theatre music) in Oxford.
2 English poet and writer, often on musical subjects. His book *Sibelius* had done much to promote the Finnish composer's rising reputation in England.
3 Carlo Gesualdo, Prince of Venosa, Italian composer. A gifted and original amateur musician, he had his first wife and her lover murdered in 1590.
4 John Christie, who had founded Glyndebourne Festival Opera in 1934.

To Edward Dent

10 November 1941

Ashby St Ledgers, Rugby

Dear Edward,

Thank you so much for your letter. Indeed the acoustics of the Albert Hall are beyond words & when I tell [you] that practically all I could hear[1] were the cellos on my right & the solo violin on my left you may imagine what it sounded like to me.

However from a preliminary rehearsal at Bedford with the BBC. Orchestra I realised that it is an entirely different work from that heard at the Albert Hall.

Perhaps you may find time to listen-in on Weds at 8–0 when it is being broadcast along with a new overture.[2]

I am coming to Cambridge on Dec 17ᵗʰ to conduct half a concert so I hope we shall be able to meet & have a good talk about Sadler's Wells etc.

Yours ever
William Walton

To Dallas Bower[3]

21 January 1942

Ashby St Ledgers, Rugby

Dear Dallas

This is most irritating – there is nothing I should like better than to accept both propositions[4] (I can do the second, though no approximate date is mentioned). Unless you can get the Corp. [BBC] to postpone the date to mid-May instead of mid-March, I don't see how I can do it, as I'm at the moment doing a film [*The Foreman Went to France*] (a boring one & only just taken on as a "filler in") for [Alberto] Cavalcanti at Ealing. This should be finished by Feb 23ʳᵈ at the latest as I have also to

1 During the British première of the Violin Concerto, conducted by Walton on 1 November 1941.
2 *Scapino*: the British première in the BBC's Bedford studio, conducted by Walton.
3 English director and producer. He had been responsible for Walton's engagement to compose his first film score, *Escape Me Never*, in 1934; Bower had been the film's assistant director.
4 Incidental music for Louis MacNeice's *Christopher Columbus*, and also for W. B. Yeats's translation of Sophocles' *Oedipus Rex*.

do L.[Leslie] Howard's "First of the few" a first-rate one which I start on at once after the Ealing film. It won't I suppose be finished before the end of March.

If Christopher Columbus[1] could be shifted to even early May or late April I could manage it.

In fact I don't see how else you can do it, as there are precious few composers about nowadays. I don't suppose it would be possible to get Alan Rawsthorne out of the army again as he was given 8 weeks leave in Dec & Jan to do the "Golden Cockerel". He would be best, but as I've said I doubt the Corp. being able to get him so soon after, in fact they would'nt have got him at all if it wasn't for yours truly. But anyhow it would be worth trying & he is most frightfully good & would do it excellently.

Benjamin Britten is by way of returning [from the USA], – he may already be back, but I gather he joins the RAF music dept. on landing. Who else is there except the old gang of V.W. J. Ireland A. Bax if you want any of them.

As for the other I should like to do that as well. When would it be?

I enjoyed very much Al. Nev.[2] & meant to drop you a line, but I've been appallingly busy. A War Office film starting on Dec 3rd & finished by the 22nd 32 mins music followed by Macbeth[3] starting on Xmas day & finished on New Years day 20 mins[.] And not all of it bad either! In fact Macbeth is pretty good. Then the recording & rehearsing in Manchester. It is only the last day or two that I've had a moment to myself. Let me know what you think.

yours ever
William

& I'd like to cooperate with MacNiece [MacNeice] who I admire immensely[.]

---

1   At this time Bower was also working as a radio producer at the BBC. He had commissioned the English poet Louis MacNeice to write a radio drama to mark the 450th anniversary year of Columbus's discovery of the Americas, and had also approached Walton to compose the incidental music for this.
2   Sergei Eisenstein's film *Alexander Nevsky*, with Prokofiev's score.
3   Incidental music for a new production of Shakespeare's play in Manchester, by the English actor John Gielgud.

To Roy Douglas   25 January 1942

Ashby St Ledgers, Rugby

Dear Roy

Thank you for the "errata" [probably in the score of *Scapino*]. How stupid of me to have missed them, but the parts & scores are being made to tally.

I managed "Macbeth" by the skin of my teeth[,] 20 mins in 8 days & not too bad at that. Tomorrow I start on Cavalcanti's film at Ealing [*The Foreman went to France*], a rather boring one to fill in the time till the Howard film which I saw yesterday & is very good. That should'nt be ready for music till the middle of March[.] However you never know, so please let me know your movements. After that is over it will be about time I settled to something else. A String quartet? A Clarinet quintet? Perhaps neither.

Scapino has not yet gone to press, but I shall be most grateful if you will help me with the proofs.

Yours ever
William W.

To Cecil Gray   26 January 1942

Ashby St Ledgers, Rugby

Dear Cecil,

I am sorry about the 'flu and hope that you will be better by the time you receive this.

I think the sketch for the opening of Act I Sc I[1] to be just what needed and will give just enough to establish Laura Scala as a semi important character.

I hope that you will be left in peace. I sha'nt be rid of my film entanglements till the end of March & will then be ready for anything.

Yours ever
William

1 Of the projected opera about Carlo Gesualdo.

THE SELECTED LETTERS OF WILLIAM WALTON

To Dallas Bower   30 January 1942

Ashby St Ledgers, Rugby

Dear Dallas

Thank you for the sketch of C.C. [*Christopher Columbus*] I'm a bit terrified of accepting it, since you know what films are like & I'm worried that the Howard film won't be over in time to give this, the music it deserves. If it could be later than the end of April I would feel more confident about accepting it. For the music will have to be good & one can't rely on a quick film extemporisation technique for it, so it will need more time trouble & care. There will too, I imagine be at least a half hours music & not much of it repeatable.

So before I accept can you give me a rough idea of the extent of the music & what could be the latest possible date. I should have to have the music ready sometime before the date fixed, don't forget, because of rehearsing the choir copying etc.

Yours ever
William

P.S I should hate to have to deliver it to the tender mercies of V.W. though on the other hand he might do it rather well, but I must admit it is more up my street.

To Norman Peterkin [1]   [March 1942]

Ashby St Ledgers, Rugby

Dear Peterkin,

I've received today a letter from the Min. of Labour giving me deferment till Sept. It ends on a threatening note & more or less states it is my last 6 months.

I saw W. Legge for a second yesterday & he told me about the projected plans for [recording] "Belshazzar". To help I should like to offer a years retaining fee, especially as I have'nt produced anything for the last 14 months or so & now owing to this call-up business I shall have to try & throw a barrage of films round me & try & make myself as indispensable as possible to the film industry. So it is unlikely I shall be able to get down to any work of my own.

---

1 Hubert Foss's assistant at Oxford University Press Music Department.

So I feel that my offer should be accepted & if the O.U.P will put up the other amount for which I understand the Brit. Council asked[,] it might go through. The cost of the records would be roughly between £1100 & £1300 so if we put up £400 or £500 between us they will possibly do it. It is the only hope of it being done & I think eventually we might get our money back.

Please send the score of the Vl. Con. here.

Yrs ever

W.W.

To Dallas Bower [March 1942]

Ashby St Ledgers, Rugby

My dear Dallas,

Thank you for the rest of the script which I've not yet read.

I went to Denham [Film Studios, regarding *The First of the Few*] a week last Weds came back & started with 'flu the next day & have been in bed till yesterday. It has been the most foul not to say dastardly attack & has left me with double sciatica in[to] the bargain.

Nothing was definitely settled at Denham & I've as yet received no footages so "flu" has not stopped that. However I've not, naturally enough, been able to do anything about C.C. [*Christopher Columbus*] either. From a glance at the last page there is the last instalment [to come] I presume.

Now I don't suppose I shall be properly up & doing for another week and at the rate things are moving at Denham I don't think it possible to finish the music for Leslie's picture much before the ~~beginning~~ middle of May, so it is obvious that I can't get C.C. done by the end of May. It is going to take at least 6 weeks.

In any case the end of May is I should have thought a bad time for a play of this kind, in fact I don't see that it can be put on during the double summer time[1] at all, because noone is going [to] sit indoors listening for 2 hours to something they don't know whether i[t']s good or bad when they can be outside. I'm sure your B.B.C statistics will show you that noone listens in at all during double summer time.

---

1 During the Second World War, British Summer Time was set two hours ahead of Greenwich Mean Time, rather than the usual one hour, in order to allow as much daylight as possible for work on the land to continue in the evening.

However you probably wont believe me, so if you must do it at the end of May you must get someone else to do the music.

I can tell you exactly who should do it & would do it admirably & better than me in any case & that is (I know you'll think I'm dotty but I'm not) Victor Hely-Hutchinson.[1] He's come on no end of late at this kind of thing, also film music & is extremely good at it.

Actually from my point of view I can't treat C.C. in any way different from a rather superior film. That is, that the music is entirely occasional, & is of no use other than what it is meant for & one won't be able to get a suite out of it.

Which is just as it should be, otherwise it would probably not fulfil it's purpose. That is why I'm against my film music being played by Mr [Stanford] Robinson[2] or anyone else. Film music is not good film music if it can be used for any other purpose & you've only got to have heard that concert the other night to realise how true that is. For all the music was as bad as it could be, listened to in cold blood, but probably excellent with the film. So I don't care where Major Barbara is or any other of my films. The music should never be heard without the film.

yrs ever
William

To Arthur Bliss   24 March 1942

Ashby St Ledgers, Rugby

Dear Arthur

As soon as I'm up from my bed of sickness ('flu is very vicious this year) I'll do your piece[3] as a thanksgiving offering. That is perhaps a rash statement as I've to start on the Leslie Howard film as soon as I'm up & immediately after that I['m] supposed to be do[ing] the music for a play for your august corporation [BBC]. About 80 mins music by the end of May & I don't see how it is going to be done. So I hope that there is no real hurry for your piece, or suite. Incidentally my commercial eye thinks there is too great a discrepancy in the fee of 10 gns

1 English composer. As the BBC's Director of Music in 1947, he was to commission Walton to compose *Troilus and Cressida*.
2 English musician, best known as a conductor of light music.
3 Bliss, at this time the BBC's Director of Music, had asked Walton to compose a suite for brass band, based on folk songs. It remained unwritten.

[guineas] for 4 mins & only 15 for 12. You won't get anyone doing a
suite except me who has no nose for money.

Anyhow I should be pleased to do a suite & if you would ask Dr
Thos. Wood[1] to send me the requisite amount of tunes necessary & the
instructions for what is exactly needed I will do my best to comply.

I should like, when I'm recovered, for us to have one of our periodical
illiterate "non sequitur" meetings.

Yours ever sincerely
William Walton

To Dallas Bower   1 April 1942

Ashby St Ledgers, Rugby

Dear Dallas,

I heard from Muir [Mathieson][2] last night and he said we shouldn't
be through with the film [*The First of the Few*] before the middle of
May, which is what I calculated myself and mentioned to you in my last
letter. It will possibly be even later than that and I shall need a day or
two's rest so it would look as if I could'nt be certain to be able to start
on C.C. before the beginning of June. I might get it done in less than
6 weeks but I shouldn't like to guarantee it.

This will upset all your plans, I'm sorry to say, so will you let me
know what you decide. Whether to put it all off to very much later
(Sept.) or whether you get someone else. John Ireland. Hely[-]Hutchinson
or even Loof Lirpa!

I think this last instalment the best part, but I'd like to discuss the
whole thing with you anyway.

I'm trying to get to the sea for a long week-end & hope to return by
London sometime in the middle of next week & will ring you.

Yours ever
William

1 Thomas Wood, English composer, mainly of choral music; also writer, critic and, from
1949, Chairman of the Music Panel of the Arts Council.
2 English conductor, much involved at this time in recording film music.

To Cecil Gray   [June/July 1942?]

Ashby St Ledgers, Rugby

Dear Cecil,

I've sent off your notes to be typed and they should be ready Tues or Weds.

Meanwhile I'm sending you a synopsis of the Prologue [of the Gesualdo opera]¹ which I've sketched out, but I don't intend that you necessarily follow it in any way if you disagree about it.

It's a bit on the spectacular & costly side and would require a fairly hefty chorus. Also it may be too much of a climax to start off with especially as there is no other scene of the same kind in the opera, but it may be alright for that reason as the other climaxes are of such a different type.

Will come round to the pub one morning next week.

Yrs
William

To Dallas Bower   12 July 1942

Ashby St Ledgers, Rugby

Dear Dallas,

Would you do me a favour, (a hard one I admit) and go & see "Macbeth" or part of it again fairly soon, & let me know how the music is sounding. And would you go & see John G. [Gielgud] & tell him if you have any suggestions to make. I've warned him that I am sending you as I haven't the time to spare to come & see about it myself just at the moment. I've told him you know something about the sound apparatus at the Piccadilly [Theatre, London].

I should be very grateful if you could manage to do this. C.C. progressing, slowly I admit, but progressing.

yours
W

1 See Appendix 2.

[142]

To Dallas Bower [August 1942]

Ashby St Ledgers, Rugby

Dear Dallas

[. . .]

Saw the War Office yesterday[.] 13 films on the tapis & three for the middle of Aug. What with Ealing these 3 & C.C. I don't know quite what will happen.

There is no room for me in the unit as an officer but I think I'm to be made civilian music adviser to the Army Film Unit. They had obviously been enquiring about it & apparently the unit is not allowed any more [officers] & I can't say I mind. Also I can say what I think, speak out of turn [*sic*] etc in my present status than if I had to remember I was speaking to a general & minding my ps & qus. My first experience of a government department, it stank of red tape but [I] found everyone very nice. But will talk to [you] more about it when I see you.

Yrs
William

To Sir Adrian Boult [October 1942]

The Hotel Portmeirion, Penrhyndeudraeth, North Wales

Dear Sir Adrian,

Thank you so much for your letter. As far as I could judge from the very inadequate set on which I was listening, the performance of "Christopher C" [on 12 October] could not have been better, and came off far better than I had dared to hope.

With many thanks for all the trouble you must have taken over it, and again I apologise for my absence, but it would not have gone **any** better if I had been there.

Yours very sincerely
William Walton

To Cecil Gray   14 December 1942

Ashby St Ledgers, Rugby

Dear Cecil,

Thank you for the last scene [of the Gesualdo opera]. It ought to be very effective if I can do my stuff. I'm all for the ghost scene from reading the extracts and I think it would be dramatically right.

I'm slightly worried about the many scene changes in Act I.

There will be a break of about 5 mins after the Prologue. Which is as it should be, but I feel there should be no more [breaks] in the music & that it should carry on between the scene changes which shouldn't take more than 1½ [minutes] at the most.

If the changes are going to take more than that perhaps it might be an idea to interpolate two extremely short scenes between 1&2, 2&3 before a drop curtain, and have some courtiers or somebody (Ping[,] Pong & Pang)[1] discussing the situation. In fact anything to stop the lights being put even half up & the continuity being broken, by the chattering of the audience. One has only to think of "Don Giovanni" to remember how even that masterpiece (to me at least) becomes a bore from that technical weakness.

Is there any expert you know whom we could consult on these technical stage points? I'm inclined not to trust young Michael [Ayrton][2] entirely on these questions, and I'm rather against it being assumed definitely that he is doing the scenery etc. If and when the time comes I think it would be better to get two or three artists to submit designs, (including M of course) to see for ourselves which we like best.

Yours ever
William

Is Act I going to be too long? Assuming that the Prologue & the 3 Scenes average 15 mins each that is an hour & with changes several minutes more – say an hour & a quarter before being able to get to the bar!

1 The trio of Chinese courtiers in Puccini's opera *Turandot*.
2 English artist and designer. He painted Walton's portrait during a holiday in Capri in 1948.

To Norman Peterkin   24 January 1943

Ashby St Ledgers, Rugby

Dear Peterkin,

I've already been in touch with Linnit & Dunfee (Mr Clifton) about the ballet [*The Quest*] & they have arranged terms with Albery. £4 a performance I believe.

It is a bit awkward as I hadn't realised that the O.U.P. were agents for my stage works. Perhaps you could <u>ring Clifton at Mayfair 0111</u> & see what can be arranged as regards splitting the boodle. It looks as if there won't be much by the time it gets to me.

Yrs
William Walton

To Roy Douglas   [May 1943]

Ashby St Ledgers, Rugby

Dear Roy,

I've been meaning to write to you for ages to thank you for your letter. A.A. [Anthony Asquith][1] did'nt want to see me about films at all. Muir [Mathieson] misinformed me, & when I did see him it had already been settled about Brodsky.[2] I made a few comments about it to him & to Larry Olivier[3] about B. I've been working on the battle of Agincourt [in *Henry V*], & luckily did'nt get very far as all the footages were rearranged two days ago & they forgot to tell me! So I must now start again. I am by way of recording it on the 21st but doubt if I'm ready. 10 mins of charging horses bows & arrows. How does one distinguish between a crossbow & a long bow musically speaking? Will you be available some-time round then to play for the guide track?

About the ballet [*The Quest*] – when I've time I shall rescore the "7 deadlies" [section portraying the Seven Deadly Sins] also make some

---

1 A leading British film director at this time. One of his best-known later films was *Orders to Kill* (1958), for which Paul Dehn, future librettist of Walton's *The Bear*, was to write the screenplay.
2 In his memoir in the Walton Archive, Roy Douglas writes: 'Brodsky was a so-called composer: I had actually composed entire film scores for him, which went under his name.'
3 Laurence Olivier. The already internationally famous English actor was currently star-ring in and directing his film version of Shakespeare's *Henry V*. Walton had been engaged to compose the music.

cuts in all the scenes. Having seen it three times I think I know just what is needed to tighten it up. I may see you next Fri. at the M.U.N.M.C.[1] committee. What about bringing up the question of composers who don't even write their own music?

yours
William

To Roy Douglas [July 1943]

Nethy Bridge Hotel, Inverness-shire, Scotland

Dear Roy,

You may well ask what has happened to Agincourt. The answer is the usual one. However I've done half of it – as much as I['m] going to do till I see how it works out – about 5½ mins & I propose if it is convenient to you, to record it on the morning of July 15ᵗʰ. I will send you the copy so you can have a look at it. Pretty grim!

I don't look forward to looking through those scores [for the CPNM] – I should have liked one to have been by Chris. Darnton, what a nasty piece of work!

[. . .]
More when we meet
yours ever
William

To Sir Henry Wood 7 November 1943

Ashby St Ledgers, Rugby

My dear Sir Henry,

I am much honoured that you should ask me to write a work for the 50ᵗʰ anniversary of the "Proms" and I shall be delighted to do so.

I'll let you know presently what it will be. Would you mind if it's first performance is in the last week, as I know from my film schedule that I may be a little pressed for time.

With kindest regards

1 The Musicians' Union New Music Committee, later renamed the Committee (subsequently the Society) for the Promotion of New Music.

Yours sincerely
William Walton.

To Roy Douglas   23 December 1943

Ashby St Ledgers, Rugby

My dear Roy,

Guilty is hardly the word for what I feel for having been so dilatory in answering your letter of Nov 20<u>th</u> – the only extenuating excuse I've got is that I've been taking the opportunity during a lull in Henry V to re-score the Vl. Con. I started out to do a little patching here & there but found it not a satisfactory way of doing it, so more or less I started from the beginning & I have even gone as far as to introduce a bass clarinet! on

instead of the timp. I sent it to be copied next week in the hope the parts will be ready for a performance at Birmingham on Jan 17<u>th</u>. If they are ready you must come down & hear it. I think now that I've got it as good as I can get it.

It is also time that I've re-vivified the Sin. Con. [*Sinfonia concertante*] chiefly by eliminating [sections of] the Pfte [part] & making it easy enough even for Harriet Cohen to play & doing it for a smaller orchestra, but alas I can't use it for Henry V, that idea was just a "Walterism".

Henry V is being more of a bloody nuisance than it is possible to believe – our masterpiece[1] went for nothing & no attempt whatsoever has been made to use it & I'm not surprised. I need hardly say they are not yet off the floor & won't be till mid-Jan, & everything is at 6s & 7s & I seem to get no chance of settling down to the music & of course there is going to be the usual hell of a rush.

Im delighted about your picture. I'll have a good deal to tell you about Brodsky when I see you. In my capacity as music adviser to Two Cities [a film company] it is going to be my duty to have to tick him off!

---

1   The earlier version of the music for the Battle of Agincourt, conceived for the film images to fit the music. The music eventually used was composed to fit the finished film.

When I'm more in the saddle there I hope to get you a picture of your own.

I'll let you know about the Birmingham perf. of the Con. [Violin Concerto] & you must come down.

With all good wishes for Xmas & the New Year
as ever
William

P.S. I'm embarking on a "Te Deum" for Sir H.J.W. 50th prom season!

To Sir Henry Wood   23 December 1943

Ashby St Ledgers, Rugby

Dear Sir Henry,

Though I can't say I've got very far as yet, I can tell you that I am safely launched on a "Te Deum" for chorus and orchestra[1] which I feel would be appropriate for the 50th anniversary of the "Proms". I trust that this will be agreable to you.

With best wishes for Xmas & 1944
Yours sincerely
William Walton.

To Walter Legge   5 Jan 1944

Ashby St Ledgers, Rugby

Dear Walter,

The parts of the Sin.Con. [*Sinfonia concertante* revised version] only turned up this morn. having been mislaid by the R.A.F. in their move. The score has not yet been found!

The rehearsal & performance of the Vl. Con. is on Jan 17th at 2–30 p.m. at the Civic Hall, Wolverhampton. There is another at Birmingham on the 18th & the other at Liverpool on the 19th. I hope you will be able to get to one of these, preferably the one at Wolverhampton when I'll be there. On the other hand if you can't manage any of those dates there is

---

1 This was never completed.

another perf. with Eda Kersey on a[n] as yet unspecified date sometime in March.

Will you be kind & forward the enclosed Pfte copy of the Sin. Con. to Cyril Smith[1] as I don't know his address. He has no need to memorise it – in fact – I['d] sooner he did'nt so as to try & emphasise the point that the Pfte is not really any more important than any other instrument in the orch. If he has any alterations to make as regards the way it is laid out, I hope he'll make them. The perf is on Feb 9th, at Liverpool & I hope you'll be able to come.

as ever
William

To Leslie Boosey[2]   1 August 1944
[handwritten by Alice Wimborne]

Ashby St Ledgers, Rugby

Dear Mr. Boosey.

I am writing this for Dr. Walton who has had an accident to his eye. The cornea is cut in two places & so he is utterly "hors de combat" for some time. The following sentences are dictated by Dr. Walton:

Alice Wimborne

The fact that the original announcement of the Committee was incomplete (which though mentioned was ignored or not understood by most people) and contained no name of an authority on opera itself makes me feel strongly that it would be wise to issue the full list of the completed Committee as soon as possible. Otherwise the mischief & rumours

---

1 English pianist, much admired both as a soloist and in piano duets with his wife, Phyllis Sellick.
2 English co-founder, with Ralph Hawkes, of the London music publishing firm Boosey & Hawkes. Covent Garden Opera House was in use as a dance hall during the Second World War. Boosey & Hawkes had made arrangements to lease the Opera House after the end of the war and to oversee its restored role as the nation's leading opera house. Leslie Boosey had approached Walton for his views on how the new house should be run and on a choice of possible members of the committee to plan this, particularly regarding the projected presence of Sadler's Wells Ballet there alongside the opera company, and the additional use of the auditorium as a cinema. Evidently Boosey had also asked Walton to join the committee.

already circulating might prevent people we have in mind & who are essential to the enterprise & its success, from joining the committee!

The names I suggested in consultation with Sir Kenneth Clarke [Clark][1] were –

Lord Keynes,[2] naturally, Chairman.
Captain Oliver Lyttelton,
Professor E. J. Dent.   J. Arthur Rank,[3] or Mr. Samuel Courtauld.

It also seems to me important, that it should be made quite clear that this committee is the governing committee & that the actual production of opera etc should be carried out by three technical-expert committees, one for opera, one for ballet & one for plays & films.

This I consider is as far as the contemplated announcement in the press should go; & it should be sufficient to allay for the time being any mischievous cavilling that may have occured.

However, for the consideration of the committee the following names are some that come to mind for the expert-committees. Opera, – E. J. Dent (I see no reason why he should not serve on both committees if willing) Miss Joan Cross,[4] Percy Hemming & Gerald Cooper. Ballet. Constant Lambert[,] Ninette de Valois[5] & Frederick Ashton.[6] Plays & Films. Lawrence [Laurence] Olivier, Ralph Richardson,[7] Tyrone Guthrie[8]

1 English writer on the arts, and an international authority on fine art.
2 John Maynard Keynes, English economist. His book *The General Theory of Employment, Interest and Money* (1935) advocated government-sponsored full employment as the best way of relieving the economic recession of the 1930s. In 1925 he had married the ballerina Lydia Lopokova. He served in the British wartime government, and died in 1946.
3 English industrialist and film distributor and producer. His J. Arthur Rank Organisation was incorporated in 1946.
4 English singer and opera producer. At this time she was also director of the Sadler's Wells Opera Company. She was to appear as Ellen Orford in the first production of Britten's *Peter Grimes* at Sadler's Wells Theatre in 1945, and in the title role of his *Gloriana* at Covent Garden in 1953.
5 Founder and General Director of the Sadler's Wells Ballet Company, which was eventually to become the Royal Ballet.
6 English dancer and choreographer, closely associated with the Sadler's Wells and Royal Ballet companies.
7 English actor, who had made his name in stagings of Ibsen and Shakespeare at the Old Vic in the 1930s. His films included *The Fugitive* and *Doctor Zhivago*.
8 English theatre and opera director, who had worked at the Old Vic and Sadler's Wells in the 1930s. He directed the first performances of Britten's *Peter Grimes* at Sadler's Wells in 1945.

& Dallas Bower. As Sir Thomas B. [Beecham] has not bitten,[1] it might be worth while the committee considering acquiring the services of Eugene Goossens as conductor-in-chief. I need not dwell on his capabilities for fulfilling the position & I think he would be a great acquisition from all points of view both in front & at the back of the "house".

You will note that I have added "plays & films", as a suggestion on my own account. Not only would they be a means of keeping the theatre open for as many weeks in the year as possible but it would add to the stature of the institution. As a permanent Orchestra is part of the scheme, such productions as "Midsummer night's dream" (Mendelssohn) "The Tempest" (Sibelius) could be given with their incidental music properly & adequately performed for once.

During my enforced inactivity I am thinking out a memorandum[2] (full of startling suggestions!) which I will forward to the Committee for their consideration – if & when completed!

With best regards

yrs. ever

P.P. William Walton

To Edward Dent   19 August 1944

Ashby St Ledgers, Rugby

Dear Edward,

I am so glad that you have consented to come on the Cov. Gar. opera committee & I enclose a memo[3] I've done on the subject, just to show we are'nt there as window dressing only.

I hope it will have your approval because important as the years 1945–50 may be, what is to happen after seems to me to be the crux of the whole matter.

I should welcome any advice and help from you about it, so don't hesitate to say forcibly what you think about the contents of the memo.

Looking forward to seeing you

yours ever

William Walton

1 Beecham had been invited to be the opera house's music director, and had turned down the approach.
2 See Appendix 3 for the complete text.
3 See Appendix 3.

To Edward Dent   9 September 1944

Ashby St Ledgers, Rugby

Dear Edward,

Owing to unforeseen circumstances I shan't be able to get up to London next week, but shall be there on Thurs. Sept 21st.

Will you lunch with me at the Savoy Guild room [Grill Room] at 1–oclock on that day? I will invite Guthrie at the same time & we can talk over everything.

I agree with you it would be a good thing for actors to develop some lungs and learn to fill a house like Covent Garden in preference to whispering down a microphone – that mechanical device is ruining all speech & singing.

Yours ever
William Walton

I shall only be in London for a day as I'm trying to get on with a quartet – rather vainly I'm afraid.

To Roy Douglas   30 January 1945

Ashby St Ledgers, Rugby

My dear Roy,

[. . .]

Yes, I've read Guys article & I heard arse over tippett[1] throughout.

I'll refrain from comment till I see you which I hope will be soon, or perhaps never as I'm in a suicidal struggle with four strings [String Quartet in A minor] & am making no headway whatever. Brick walls, slit trenches[,] Siegfried lines bristle as never before. I'm afraid I've done film music for too long!

But if I ever break through you must come down here & see it[,] also some pfte pieces, but it will have to be before its finished as that may be another five years.

Yrs ever
William

1 Michael Tippett. Possibly Walton had heard a radio broadcast of Tippett's First or Second String Quartet (see next paragraph).

To Roy Douglas   5 February 1945

Ashby St Ledgers, Rugby

My dear Roy,

Thank you for your letter. I'm delighted you will undertake [the piano reduction of the orchestral part of] the Sin. Con. – but there's no hurry about it, as I've reccommended you to Larry Olivier to do the music for a play by Thornton Wilder, so I trust you will be busy with that for the next few weeks.[1]

I've captured a trench & overcome some barbed wire entanglements – but every bar is a pill-box.

[. . .]

yrs

William

To Benjamin Britten   21 June 1945

Ashby St Ledgers, Rugby

My dear Benjamin,

I was so very sorry that I couldn't get to "Peter Grimes" last Friday.[2] But on arriving back from Cheltenham I found a message from my brother who had unexpectedly turned up on leave & so had to take him down here on an earlier train.

I got through to someone at Sadler's Wells and I hope you got my message. I could'nt get the box office and whoever it was I spoke to seemed to know nothing about any tickets being left for me[,] in fact seemed hardly to know who you were and certainly my name meant nothing!

So I thought you might have forgotten but I left a message saying I could'nt come.

I hope very much to see P.G. again before the end of the season.

It is always embarrassing to say things I find, but I should like to tell you how much I appreciate your quite extraordinary achievement, an achievement which makes me look forward to your next opera.

1 Douglas was not asked to compose the music.
2 The world première of Britten's opera had taken place on 7 June. Walton had evidently planned to see a later performance also.

It is just what English opera wants and it will I hope put the whole thing on its feet and give people at large quite another outlook about it. Not I am afraid, that you will find many other composers, if any, emulating your success. But it may be something if it encourages them to try.

Anyhow, you are quite capable of creating english opera all on your own.

I meant to have written you before but have these last days been overwhelmed by proofs of my Violin Concerto & I fondly but vainly hope to get the score out in time for the "Prom" performance which I hope you may be able to hear.

I say fondly and vainly as I have been four months getting the 2nd proofs. I shall have to move to B&H. [Boosey & Hawkes]!

Hoping to see you again soon
Yours ever
William

P.S. This is a "fan" letter!

To Roy Douglas   25 July 1945

Ashby St Ledgers, Rugby

Dear Roy,

I've taken the liberty of altering your account & even now I think I['m] underpaying you!

Peterkin informs me you wish to do the Childrens Pieces [*Duets for Children*] as solos. Please do so whenever you like.

No very encouraging news of the 4tet. Did you see or hear "Grimy Peter"?

yrs
William

To Harry Blech [1]

26 July [1945]

Ashby St Ledgers, Rugby

My dear Harry,

Here are the parts & score of the slow movement. [of the String Quartet in A minor] I'm sorry to have been so long but the O.U.P. did them so badly that I had to do them again. But they are now I think satisfactory.

The news of the rest of the work is very dismal & I've been at the point of chucking the whole thing. Progress is practically nil & I can only hope that my trip to Sweden next month will put some new life into me.

If the quartet [Blech String Quartet] is together before I go (about Oct 20th) perhaps you could play me through this movement, but don't bother about it if it entails too much trouble.

I shall be in my house 10 Holly Berry Lane NW3 [2] at the end of the month & I will ring you.

Yours ever
William

To Lady Wood [3]

12 January 1946

Ashby St Ledgers, Rugby

Dear Lady Wood,

I have not written to you before as I have been wavering about making a decision on Mr Masefield's poem. But having gone as far as setting two verses of it I am now sure that my first reaction was the right one & it is really not possible, for me at any rate, to make a worthy work out of it.

I am lo[a]th to make this decision as I have so much respect for Mr Masefield and the last thing I want to do is to offend or hurt his feelings.

1 English violinist and conductor. Leader of the Blech String Quartet, in which he played between 1933 and 1950. In 1949 he founded the London Mozart Players, a chamber orchestra specializing in music of the Viennese classical composers.
2 Walton's flat in South Eaton Place had been destroyed by German bombing. He had subsequently moved to this address in Hampstead, where he stayed when not at Lowndes Cottage or Ashby St Ledgers.
3 Jessie Wood, the widow of Sir Henry Wood, who had died in 1944.

Nor do I think it wise to ask him to write another – the same thing might happen.[1]

Accordingly I am pleased that you approve the idea of my writing a non-choral work instead, as a tribute to Sir Henry.

I have not yet communicated my decision to Mr Masefield and I won't do so until I hear from you what course I should take as regards the situation.

I am so sorry to be such a nuisance.
Yours sincerely
William Walton

To Lady Wood   20 January 1946

Ashby St Ledgers, Rugby

Dear Lady Wood,
I return you Mr Masefield's poem, and I am very pleased that you will let him know what has been decided. Before too long I hope to be able to report progress on the piece I have proposed to write.
With kind regards
yours sincerely
William Walton

To David Webster[2]   16 February 1946

Ashby St Ledgers, Rugby

Dear David,
Two suggestions. ① The Delius Trust is I gather fairly flush & it might be a good idea for them to finance performances of "A Village Romeo".[3] As it wouldn't be our responsibility Sir T.B. [Thomas Beecham] could be allowed "carte blanche" even paint the scenery if he wished! It would be a good thing to do putting us right with the public regarding T.B. as well as, in all probability having an excellent show. If

1 Masefield however agreed to do this, and provided the text of Walton's 'Where Does the Uttered Music Go?', first performed in April 1946.
2 The newly appointed General Administrator of the Royal Opera House, Covent Garden.
3 Delius's opera A Village Romeo and Juliet, based on Gottfried Keller's novella.

you think it worth pursuing you could get in touch with Ernest Irving[1] (Ealing 2110) as he is one of the trustees. I've already mentioned it to him & he[']s all for it.

② That we might "touch" the Co-Operative Society for a 7 year covenant. The "Lord" could manage this through A. V. Alexander at the Admiralty, also I think that K. Clark knows the gen. sec.

Incidentally Sixten Ehrling[2] is here. He might be of some use to us.
[. . .]
yours
William

I should like tickets for March 20ᵗʰ!

To Lady Wood   11 March 1946

Ashby St Ledgers, Rugby

Dear Lady Wood,
    The copy of the poem ['Where Does the Uttered Music Go?'] is with the copyist for checking up in case of doubt about the words. I will send it you as soon as that is through, though I am sorry to say it will be in a rather soiled condition what with my markings etc on it.
    Yours sincerely
    William Walton

To Lady Wood   2 May 1946

Ashby St Ledgers, Rugby

Dear Lady Wood,
    Thank you so very much for the cheque & your very kind & appreciative letter. I am forwarding the cheque to the Memorial Fund.
    I am so pleased you liked the Masefield setting, it turned out much better than I expected & was most beautifully sung.
    It would, I think, be a good idea if it was performed sometime during

1 English conductor. He had recorded Walton's scores for the soundtracks of the films *Next of Kin*, *The Foreman Went to France* and *Went the Day Well?*
2 Swedish conductor, already known for his work at the Royal Opera, Stockholm. He subsequently became Music Director there.

the "Proms". The more often the better as I have assigned all monies ac[c]ruing from it to the Memorial Fund.

I received a batch of press-cuttings this morning, & one must admit that it hardly received an overwhelming reception. But I have given up all hopes of critics a long time ago.

Yours very sincerely
William Walton

To Lady Wood 20 May 1946

Ashby St Ledgers, Rugby

Dear Lady [sic],

I am honoured that the committee of the H.W.C.S. [Henry Wood Concert Society] should wish me to become a member, but I must regretfully refuse. I am on far too many committees as it is & I am sorry but I cannot undertake to become a member of yet another. In fact I am resigning from most of the ones I am on as I find they get so much in the way of my work, so I am sure you will understand why I don't wish to join.

Yours very sincerely
William Walton

To Griselda Kentner [1]   [postmarked: Ascona, Lake Maggiore, [postcard] 17 June 1946]

I like your muse very much & hope for some more poetic efforts. I've finished a movement (scherzo) of the 4tet. [String Quartet] so you can pat yourself on the back. I hope you are not too depressed at your return to the "rothaus" [sanatorium] & that you are being good & quiet & getting better. The "Auxiliem" [?] arrived safely[,] thanks so much & I'm now a terror to all mosquitoes of either sex.

My love.
W.

Love from Alice too!

---

1 Née Gould; wife of the pianist Louis Kentner. Her sister, Diana Gould, was to become the second wife of the violinist Yehudi Menuhin.

To Lady Wood   [postmarked: Ascona, Lake Maggiore,
[postcard]   14 July 1946]

I am sorry to have been so long in answering your two letters but they
were delayed in being forwarded to me. I don't quite know where the
score ['Where Does the Uttered Music Go?'] is or to whom it belongs,
but if it should belong to me I would be delighted for you to have it, if
you should so wish. I shall, alas, be back in London shortly. It is very
lovely here.
    With kind regards
    yours sincerely
    William Walton

To George Barnes[1]   31 January 1947

Ashby St Ledgers, Rugby

Dear Barnes,
    Perhaps the following suggestions [for BBC radio music programmes]
may be of some use to you.

① That Eric [Erik] Tuxen (conductor of the Danish Radio Orch. at
Copenhagen) should be brought over to conduct a series of the Nielsen
symphonies.
    They are almost unknown here & I was much interested by a rather
poor recording of one, a week or two ago in a programme on Danish
music. He is regarded as much superior to Sibelius as far as I could
make out, throughout all Scandinavia & the symphonies might become
a good alternative now that the Sibelius are overworked.
    Tuxen is on the whole regarded as the best of the Scandinavian con-
ductors & is I understand an authority on Nielsen.

② Having thrown a crumb to [Bernard] Van Dieren, by performing a
few songs & piano pieces, might not half a loaf be added by the performance of one of his quartets, No 3 or 6 are I think the most accessible
& the Zorian [Quartet] might like to tackle one if properly subsidised! It
would I think be a 1ˢᵗ perf & not before its time. The Chinese Symphony
& The Diaphony[2] might be revived also.

1 Head of the BBC's newly founded Third Programme; later Controller, Third Programme.
2 Bernard van Dieren's *Diafonia* for baritone and chamber orchestra.

③ As the 3ʳᵈ P. [Third Programme] seems intent on an orgy of atonalism & whatnot (very enjoyable & I hope an early repeat of the Berg Concerto Vl. & Pfte [Chamber Concerto] will be forthcoming) why not indulge in a few works of Kaikhosru Sorabji¹ either played by himself (he's a magnificent pianist) or another.

Though he was supposed to be the last word in the days of my youth, it may sound as tame as Schönberg by now.

④ To do a little chiselling on my own behalf – if, as I doubt, there should be another performance of the original "Facade" could it be put on by itself & with no Concerto or speech beforehand? Either the Concerto or Facade, but not both, as C.L. [Constant Lambert] was obviously exhausted by his exercions on the former, as to be at times almost incoherent. And he can do it so well especially if he has been on a diet of bread & water, at any rate on the latter if not the former.²

⑤ Further chiselling on my behalf. Would it be possible to bring over David Oistrakh³ the Russian violinist? I heard him in a quite stupendous performance of my Vl. Con. from Moscow last week. He has been giving a series of concerts there, devoted to concertos from Bach to Prokofiev. I believe he would make a tremendous sensation, nothing like him having been heard over here since Kreisler at his best. I know it is difficult to make the Russians part with their artists, but [Nikolai] Malko⁴ seems to be able to get here periodically, so it might be possible to get Oistrakh.

Failing that, – a big drop, – perhaps Thomas Matthews might be given a broadcast of the work. he has been playing it a great deal lately in the provinces with Barbirolli,⁵ but I've not heard him.

Forgive this long letter with its probably useless suggestions.

Yours sincerely

William Walton

---

1 English composer of Spanish–Sicilian–Parsi ancestry. His intricate and often exotic works included *Opus clavicembalisticum* for piano, which lasts for approximately three hours without a break.
2 Lambert's alcoholism was increasingly undermining both his health and his capacity to perform and conduct. He died in 1951 at the age of forty-five.
3 Subsequently to become world-famous as one of the great violinists of his time. Prokofiev, Shostakovich and Khachaturian all wrote works for him.
4 Russian conductor who in 1940 had settled in America. (Walton had evidently not realized this.)
5 John Barbirolli, English conductor. Formerly music director of the New York Philharmonic, in 1943 he had been appointed conductor of the Hallé Orchestra in Manchester.

To Frederick Ashton   13 February 1947

Ashby St Ledgers, Rugby

Duckie,

Don't crack your little whip at me!

I'm not whoring about with L.M. [Leonid Massine] Being a director of Dallas Bower Prods. Inc. (£1 share) all I've done is to bring those two together as D.B. has a mad hatter idea of doing the Berlioz "Damnation of Faust" as a film-opera.

Think up a better one than that if you can!

J.C. [Joan Cross] has got it wrong I'm afraid. These are my commitments for the next 18 months or so. First finish this bloody quartet (the end is faintly in sight). Second, the music for Larry's [Laurence Olivier's] "Hamlet" film. Third, as I know you can keep a secret, I've accepted a commission from the B.B.C. to compose an opera for them. What it is to be & for when is all a bit hazy at the moment. But not a world! [sic] So "Agie" will have to be fitted in, so to speak.

But I could let you know definitely about that when I've talked with the B.B.C. that is – about the end of the month. I agree with all you say about "Agie"[,] as you know I am yours to command.

Love
William Oskar

To Cecil Gray   [February/March 1947]

Ashby St Ledgers, Rugby
or 10 Holly Berry Lane, N.W.3

Dear Cecil,

Thank you so much for your letter. I agree with you entirely about the quartet!

I will certainly go into the idea about Inez de Castro[1] or get a slave to do so. I've forgotten whether I told you that the B.B.C had commissioned me to write an opera (not specifically for "broadcasting") & reccomended Christopher Hassall[2] whom you may know of to go into the

1 Another idea for an opera suggested by Gray, after the plan for the one about Carlo Gesualdo had failed to work out. Nothing was to come of *Inez de Castro* either.
2 English poet and writer. Hassall had written the lyrics of several musicals by Ivor Novello, including the hugely successful *Glamorous Night* in 1935.

question of the libretto. And I believe that we have a[t] last hit on one in "Troilus and Cressida" – not founded on Shakespeare but on Chaucer, Henryson & Boccaccio.

When it has got to a little further detailed condition, I would like to send you the synopsis, as I should value your opinion before definitely embarking on such a hazard.

Love to you both
yours
William

To Christopher Hassall   31 March 1947

45 Clarges Street, w.1
As from: Ashby St Ledgers, Rugby

Dear Charles [sic] Hassall,
Many thanks for your letter. I will look forward to receiving the librettos when they are ready.

I have had another idea which I will let you have when we next meet, which I hope will be soon.

Yours sincerely,
William Walton

To Christopher Hassall   [postmarked: Kilsby, Rugby,
[postcard]   7 April 1947]

Thanks for the synopsis. Just finishing off my 4tet [String Quartet] & then will look into them seriously & let you know what I think.

Regards
W. Walton

To Griselda Kentner [September 1947]
[letter begun on two postcards, then completed on headed notepaper]

Hotel Royal Lucerne

Darling G.

Here is I am creditably informed your favourite piece of sculpture![1] It was sweet of you to ring up. I was going to write to you anyhow to tell of Diana and Yehudi [Menuhin]'s angelic behaviour to poor needy friends – it will be a very good Sonata[2] & 1st perf with Lou & Yehudi & dedicated to those world famous sisters Di & Gri.

Here is a phallic thimble[3] to keep you going when Lou's away.

It has been a pretty grim week what with one thing & another. Luckily Walter [Legge] was here. A [Alice] was with him & some of his swagger Swiss friends when she collapsed. They were very kind & told her the best doctor to go to etc. I'm now in a biergarten getting slightly tiddly on red wine, which will account for the inconsequence of this communication. I must say it is a pretty good hell-hole to be stranded in – full of people from Liverpool.

I bath[e] twice a day & walk up the mountain side to the Kurhaus twice also so I ought be to be pretty good by the time I'm out.

I think it may be at least a month with Alice. It is as far as I can gather chronic bronchitis & pneumonia which was so bad that she couldn't breathe, which was why the doctor at first suspected a tumour or cancer.

She has her arse jabbed every 2 hrs with penicillin & inhales same for hours on end. I think there is a slight improvement.

If I could find a piano I'd write a piano piece or even a Violin Son.

[Joseph] Szigeti[4] comes tomorrow which will be a slight change.

How awful Swiss girls are! I know there are lots of things I've forgotten to say but it can't be helped & I will write again when I remember them.

Love
Will

1 Picture postcard of the Lion Memorial, Lucerne.
2 Diana Gould, Yehudi Menuhin's fiancée, had commissioned Walton's Violin Sonata for performance by Menuhin and Louis Kentner.
3 Picture postcard of the Chapel Tower, Lucerne.
4 Hungarian-born violinist, resident in America from 1940.

To David Webster   22 September [1947]

Hotel Royal Lucerne

Dear David,

I shall be back on the 30th & not the 28th as I told Miss Kerr[1] so I shall only want tickets for performances on the 30th till Oct 4th. I hope that that will be all right.

Our whole trip has been rather unfortunate. Alice fell ill the second day here & has been in a clinic ever since. We were going on to Portofino & Capri & Rome but that had to be abandoned. However she will be well enough to travel to Milan on Weds & we fly back from there [on] the 29th.

However it has been mildly pleasant here (better than England I expect) & out of sheer self protection I've started on another work [the Violin Sonata].

I hope the Vienna Opera has done well & that everything prospers with you & Cov. Gar.

Yrs ever
William Walton

To Griselda Kentner   [late September 1947]

Hotel Royal Lucerne

Dearest Gri,

It doesn't look so good for the 30th after all. A. can't make up her mind whether she will be well enough to come or not & she's in the state of mind when it might upset her if she thought I wanted to take someone else. I'm sure you will understand.

In any case I doubt if we shall be back on the 30th. The weather has broken & the airfield at Milan apparently bogs up very quickly & the planes can't take off.

We leave this morn. for Milan. A. is better up to a point. The doctors still won't say whether it is cancer or not, but there is, it seems, undoubtedly something very abnormal at the base of the right lung.

I'll ring you as soon as I get back.

Best love to you both
Will

---

1 Muriel Keir, Webster's assistant at the Royal Opera House, Covent Garden.

To Mrs Elgar Blake [1]   30 November 1947

Savile Club, 69 Brook Street, w.1

Dear Mrs Elgar Blake,

May I thank you most cordially for your gift to the Savile Club of
Sir Edward's tie. The Secretary of the Art Committee has handed it to
me & I am honoured to have the privilege of wearing [it]. I happen to
be a member of both the Savile & the Garrick clubs as Sir Edward was.

   yours sincerely
   William Walton

To Cecil Gray   27 December 1947

Ashby St Ledgers, Rugby

Dear Cecil,

Thank you for your pics & more especially for "Contingencies"
which I have read & re-read with much profit & enjoyment.

Alice & I had every intention of coming to Capri in September, but
alas, on the way, at Lucerne, Alice fell ill and had to go to a clinic & she
has been ill ever since – in fact now the doctor's final verdict is due in
the next day or two & I fear it may well be the worst. All of which is
very depressing & gloomy, added to the other ordinary material difficulties of the filthy age we live in.

How I envy you & your lovely house & how right you were to make
a get-away. For everything here is much the same, but worse than when
you left. In fact I cudgel my brains to find some even slightly illuminating
piece of news.

Constant [Lambert] is as you may have heard, happily married &
back composing if even only for the film "Anna Karenina". But he's
altogether much better.

I've been doing much the same[,] doing the music for the "Hamlet"
film.[2] Not uninteresting – I've had to do nearly an hour of appropriate
but otherwise useless music. I'm also engaged on a Violin Sonata for
Menuhin who advanced me 1000 francs in Switzerland! The third &

1 Carice Elgar Blake, daughter of Sir Edward Elgar.
2 Directed by and starring Laurence Olivier.

last act of the libretto of "Troilus" has just arrived. I think it may eventually plan out well.

[. . .]

If ever you are so unwise as to return here for some months you might let me have first option on renting you[r] house!

Love to you both & best wishes for the New Year

yours ever

William.

If by any chance you come across two nice Swedish sisters called Bergson[1] remember me to them.

To Ernest Newman   1 March 1948

Ashby St Ledgers, Rugby

Dear Mr Newman,

Here is the first draft of the libretto of 'Troilus'. I shall much appreciate your advice about it, as I realise it still needs much improvement.

Yours sincerely

William Walton

To Griselda Kentner   3 March 1948

Ashby St Ledgers, Rugby

Dearest Griselda,

Belatedly and surprisingly I answer your letter (a french or red letter-day?).

I suppose & hope you are still where I am sending this. It is splendid that you are so well – mind you keep it up (whatever that may be). Which reminds me to ask – how are the lovers?

I've not much news. Hamlet took far too much time & even now (though Larry [Laurence Olivier] departed thank heaven, to Australia Feb 14th) there are odds & ends like gramophone records to see to.

The premiere is May 8th in presence of the King & Queen preceded by the Coronation March [*Crown Imperial*] – what-ho!

---

1 Walton was soon to find himself involved in a liaison with Ann Bergson, a talented painter then in her late teens.

I don't suppose you'ld be back from your dangerous drive round Italy with Lou & his "black" Triumph. Though I don't suppose he'll pass his driving test in time.

I meant to lunch with Lou the other day, but instead had to rehearse the quartet [String Quartet] which was being recorded.

Alice is, I think better for the deep X ray treatment. But the doctors say very little except that air is now definitely passing into the lung which would I presume, mean that the growth has subsided a little. But for how long is the question. Meanwhile we are here & she is better for it though terribly weak & suffers a good deal from a cough which noone seems to be doing much about. Doctors are awful & I suspect incompetent.

I'm working on the Vl. Son a bloody combination.

I may be at Edinborough (Belshazzar) for the lying-in! Yes Auntie.

This is now enough except I long to see you & mind you are looking pretty & plump when I do, or I shall pinch your bottom which doubtless I shall do in any case.

ever yours
W.

I hope to buy a ravishing new house but fear I shall be outbid so cross your heart for me on the 17th, auction day.

To Ernest Newman   6 March 1948

Ashby St Ledgers, Rugby

Dear Mr Newman,

Many thanks for your letter. I am so very sorry to hear of the trouble with your eyes from which I trust you will soon recover.

There is no hurry at all about your reading the libretto.

There are a few things I must clear out of the way before embarking on the opera & at the moment I am writing a Violin & Pfte Sonata for Menuhin – the consequence of his having advanced me 1000 francs whilst in Switzerland last summer!

But I look forward to hearing what you think about the libretto, as I am full of doubts (I always am) & shall almost certainly abide by what you think.

Yours very sincerely
William Walton

To Cecil Gray   28 March 1948

Ashby St Ledgers, Rugby

My dear Cecil,

I am most distressed to hear from Michael [Ayrton] the tragic news about poor Margery. One is completely at a loss in the face of such circumstances & it seems completely inadequate to extend one's sympathy, which indeed you have.

The only saving grace, if such a thing has to happen, is that it happened suddenly.

I wish to heaven almost, that the same could be true about Alice, instead of her lingering on in misery. She has a cancer on the bronchial tube & though she has undergone deep X-ray treatment the result seems to be that she is iller than she was before it.

The only hope now is in an operation – a drastic one neccessitating the removal of the right lung. It is a terrific gamble but she would apparently be alright if it is successful. We shall hear if it is possible or not in the next few days.

Anyhow I must'nt depress you further with my troubles.

Again all my sympathy in your great loss.

Yours ever
William

To Helga Cranston [1]   [postmarked: Capri, 22 May 1948]
[postcard]

I begin to recover rapidly with not being bullied & with the aid of good food, wine – sun-bathing etc. I wish I could avoid my life becoming so complicated.

    W.

---

1 Film editor. She and Walton had met during the filming of *Henry V*, which she edited. She was also to edit Olivier's film of *Richard III*.

To Christopher Hassall   15 July [1948]

Ashby St Ledgers, Rugby

Dear Christopher (enough of this "Dr" stuff!)

T&C is excellent. I've been reading it on & off all day & find very
little to suggest which might be an improvement, & I think now the time
has come when the actual text might be got under way. Doubtless doing
this, many new ideas will crop up which will make for the smooth
working of it.

[. . .]

It should I think work out at about 3 hours including 40 mins for
intervals, or as near as possible to that.

Remember that only about a ⅓ of the words is necessary for a libretto
to what there would be if it was a play.

Let us meet very soon, I may have some further suggestions by then.

Yrs
William

To Christopher Hassall   19 August [1948]

Les Novalles, Blonay, Vevey, Switzerland

Dear Christopher,

How are you & how is T&C? I am here until about Sept 5ᵗʰ & sail
from Genoa for Buenos Aires on Sept 13ᵗʰ & I am wondering if it would
be possible for you to let me have a copy of the revised version for me to
study on the voyage. It would be a good opportunity for me, perhaps to
get some ideas down on paper.

I tried vainly to get in touch with you by phone before I left, either
you were away or in the throes of house moving – a position I'm in
myself but I've left it to others & hope to be more or less in at Lowndes
Cottage¹ by the time I return in mid-Nov.

Let me have a word even if it is not possible to let me have a script of
T&C.

Yours ever
William

1 Alice Wimborne had left Lowndes Cottage, her London home, to Walton in her will.

To Griselda Kentner   19 August [1948]

Les Novalles, Blonay, Vevey, Switzerland

Dearest Gri,

Thank you for your rude epistle. I dare say I deserve it but I had no idea where you were you little b——.[1] When I got your letter I rang up Le Press & was told you'd left for the Savoy at Zurich – tried there & they said they'd never heard of you. So I gave it up.

The Furtwangler's [Furtwänglers] came to dine the other night & she told me of Yehudi's or is it Diana's happy event. But they['d] forgotten what sex the little brute is – hermaphrodite perhaps?

Anyhow congratulate all concerned [for] the strenuous & successful effort. I wish my delivery was [not] being so difficult.

The weather continues to be appalling so I've be[en] driven to work on Y's Sonata & it is not going at all well – in fact if I hadn't got too far into this movement I would start all over again – but I fear it is not going to work out too well. If only I could play the fucking piano!

I suppose Edinburgh is pretty bloody too.

I leave here about the 5th Sept & sail from Genoa the 13th. Shall see Ann [Bergson] whom I'm gently but firmly going to give the push. I think it wisest in the long run. Have given up sex chiefly from lack of opportunity. Furtwangler incidentally had an orgasm about your charm wit & beauty & it didn't at all go with a swing with Frau F.

Best love
W.

To Christopher Hassall   31 August [1948]

Les Novalles, Blonay, Vevey, Switzerland

Dear Christopher,

Thank you so much for the wads of libretto & letters etc.

I shall certainly have something to get my teeth into on the voyage.

There is some uncertainty now whether I shall actually go as there is trouble about the Treasury as the fare has to be paid in dollars. However the P.R.S [Performing Right Society] are trying to arrange it somehow so I hope to get away [on] the 13th leaving here the 6th.

---

1 As written by Walton, not an editorial amendment.

If I dont go to B.A [Buenos Aires] I shall stay in Italy till Lowndes Cot. is ready.

Best regards
as ever
William

To Griselda Kentner [September 1948]

M.V. *Italia* [at sea]

Darling,

What a surprise[,] a letter from me. You might think it was because I was hard up for something to do, but it is'nt – just <u>pure</u> affaction.

This up to now has been a wonderful voyage & comfortable sedate ship, calm seas & perfect weather.

I was glad to get away from dreary Schweiz [Switzerland]. I didn't really work well & I fear the Sonata is a dud, but don't as yet tell Yehudiana in case she wants the 1000 francs back!

I had an enjoyable week in Venice & Milan with Ann. I'm now completely flummoxed as to where I am with her. The only certain thing is that she more than ever wants to get married & I am less sure about it.

I'm the only English person on board which is heaven[,] the rest being "dagi assorti" brazils argentines Italians Swedes germans! The only conversation I have is with the nice barman & a rather sympathetic Brazil[ian] who on learning I was a composer said – "Ah the London Symphony, who's that by" – "V.W." says I – "Ah" says he "a pendant to the Warsaw Concerto[1] eh?" "Yes" – says I – "but not quite so popular."

We're allow[ed] off at Las Palmas & I hope to see a performing donkey! No senoritas[,] all either under or over age or heavily chaperoned or husbanded.

I hope you are well. Love to Yehudiana Lou & your infant nephew.
as ever
Will

1 By Richard Addinsell.

To Alan Frank[1]   31 October 1948

Claridge Hotel, Tucuman 535, Buenos Aires

Dear Alan

Kleiber[2] may want to do both Façade suites in Vienna on Dec 1ˢᵗ as a counter-attack to Furtwängler doing the Sym Dec 4ᵗʰ. So would you send the scores & parts (corrected ones) to Herr Kleiber c/o Herr Seefelden Konzerthaus Lothringer Strasse Vienna.

I think this is the right address but perhaps you'd better confirm it from the <u>Brit Con</u> or H.M.V.

I've <u>another concert here</u> (radio) on the 17ᵗʰ & a work as yet unnamed is being included in the last prog. of the season.

At the moment I should be returning to London – but it may be possible to get to Para(guay) & Chile in which case I shall be arriving sometime in Jan. It is exceedingly pleasant here with an excellent opera – in fact I'm enjoying life for once a good deal & doing some work as well.

as ever
William

---

1   Head of Oxford University Press Music Department, in succession to Hubert Foss.
2   Erich Kleiber, Austrian conductor. In 1925 he had given the world première of Alban Berg's opera *Wozzeck* at Berlin's Staatsoper Unter den Linden, where he had been music director. From 1937 he had been directing the German opera seasons at the Teatro Colón in Buenos Aires.

1949–1954

WILLIAM Walton and Susana Gil Passo were married on 13 December 1948, in a civil ceremony in Buenos Aires. A church ceremony followed on 20 January 1949. Nine days later Mr and Mrs Walton embarked on their return journey to England. There the composer's many friends and admirers, not least the female ones, were suitably astonished by this sudden turn of events. The story of the couple's first encounter, high-speed romance, engagement and marriage is told in live-wire style by Susana Walton in her book *William Walton: Behind the Façade*. This pulls no punches regarding the difficult and sometimes selfish element of her husband's nature. The young Mrs Walton was wide awake to this from the start.

One of her revelations regarding their first days together is Walton's point-blank insistence, shortly *after* their civil marriage, that he did not want children, and that if his wife did want them, he was prepared to divorce her there and then. 'It crossed my mind', wrote Susana Walton, 'that, if this was so important to him, he ought to have mentioned it before.' (This must be one of the outstanding literary understatements of the twentieth century.) But she had already had some early evidence of how self-centred Walton could be. During the Performing Right Society's Buenos Aires conference, he had found himself staying in the same hotel as a former girlfriend (Alicia di Robilant, an Anglo-Russian ex-ballerina) who had since married a now conveniently absent husband. Walton appears to have had no qualms about renewing this relationship on a temporary basis, while simultaneously pursuing his courtship of the impressed, but admirably stubborn Miss Gil. Allowing for Walton's instinctive talent for getting others to do as he wanted, his behaviour can have left his young bride with no illusions as to how calculating he could be when it suited him.

The couple's thirty-four-year marriage could hardly have begun more bizarrely. Walton had no illusions, and offered none, as to how difficult an individual he was going to be to live with. Nothing, after all, had ever been allowed to stand in the way of his work, and nothing was going to be allowed to do so now. Yet despite the twenty-four-year age difference between the couple, and with no children to provide the particular kind of emotional focus that only children can, the marriage was to survive periods of major difficulty with outstanding resilience. Walton's preceding relationship with Alice Wimborne always retained a special place in his heart. But surely the truest love of your life is the one who looks after you as you grow old.

When the Waltons arrived in England early in 1949, the enthusiastically welcoming atmosphere did not entirely disguise the various degrees of response, ranging from scepticism to hostility, of many of the composer's acquaintances. On their way to a party together, Christabel Aberconway remarked to Susana Walton, 'My dear, of all the women you will meet tonight, I will probably be the only one that William has not been to bed with. Such a pity.' The two women seem to have decided from this point onwards that they were firm friends. Another agreeable encounter was initiated by Osbert Sitwell, who invited the Waltons to visit him at the composer's old haunt in Carlyle Square. The two former comrades-in-arms had barely met since the start of Walton's relationship with Alice Wimborne in 1935. All was now evidently forgiven.

Elsewhere, there was sometimes a darker undertone to the mood of feverish goodwill. As Susana Walton remarked many years later, 'Most people couldn't believe that William had gone and married this Indian from South America.' Then, as now, elements of English society were not always as instinctively welcoming as they might have been to individuals from foreign lands. The new couple's early awareness of this was surely one of several factors that had led Walton already to say to his wife, 'Come on – we're going to live in Italy.'

Walton's return to England had plunged him back into the administrative work that now accompanied his status as one of England's senior composers. His position on the board of the Covent Garden Opera House Trust and other commitments were between them threatening to take up a dangerous amount of his time. There were other considerations too. Throughout most of the pre-war era – after the first performance of the Viola Concerto in 1929, and even more so after that of *Belshazzar's Feast* two years later – Walton was seen to be England's leading composer of his generation, with a broadly supportive critical consensus to match. Streetwise as ever to the way the wind was blowing, he had sensed that the spectacular rise of one Benjamin Britten was on the point of changing this. The composer of *Peter Grimes* was now being lionized as, for most

[176]

of the preceding twenty years, Walton himself had been. Walton's genuine admiration of Britten's talent did not prevent him from realizing that, on a personal level, he was going to find this shift in adulation difficult to live with. It was going to be particularly difficult to live literally within its midst. And besides, he had an opera of his own to write.

Troilus and Cressida had been constantly in Walton's thoughts since he, Alice Wimborne and Christopher Hassall had first begun to discuss its possibilities in 1947. Its slow germination must have been a necessary psychological sheet anchor during Alice Wimborne's illness and death, his own subsequent departure from Ashby St Ledgers, and the period of emotional confusion that had followed. He had taken an early draft of Christopher Hassall's libretto with him on his journey to Argentina, and his desire to start serious work on the music was now becoming impossible to suppress. Like many composers before and since whose musical power base was in London, Walton had generally found that he needed to remove himself from the city and its distractions when a major work was to be composed. Much of the Viola Concerto had been written in Amalfi with the Sitwells; much of *Belshazzar's Feast* and the First Symphony in Switzerland with Imma von Doernberg; and much of the Violin Concerto in Ravello with Alice Wimborne. *Troilus and Cressida* was going to be a far larger project than any of these.

The aim of spending at least six months of the year living and working in the country of his heart – the Italian south, in and around Naples – had been in Walton's mind for some time. Susana Walton relates that he mentioned the idea to her two days before their ship from Buenos Aires arrived at Tilbury Docks in February 1949. A visit to the travel agency of Thomas Cook turned up only the possibility of renting a house in Forio on the island of Ischia, on the northern fringe of the Bay of Naples. (Walton knew Capri and the Italian Riviera well from his pre-war visits with the Sitwells and Alice Wimborne, but it seems that he had not visited Ischia before. Did that perhaps make the prospect of living there seem all the more attractive to a composer now embarking on a new life?)

Off the couple set in October 1949, driving south across Europe via Monte Carlo, in the Bentley that Alice Wimborne had bequeathed to Walton. In their luggage was a hot-water bottle packed with pound notes – a deft circumvention of the draconian currency restrictions in place at the time. Conditions at the Convento San Francesco turned out to be run down and Spartan in the extreme. But at least during the winter the island was free of holiday-makers and therefore quiet, and Walton found the necessary equilibrium to compose. Serious work on *Troilus and Cressida* began.

The love affair between the rain-drenched Anglo-Saxon spirit and that different, sun-warmed world south of the Alps is time-honoured and enduring. Walton's wish to put down roots there (inasmuch as he ever put down roots anywhere) might appear to be yet another case of an Englishman falling in love with Chiantishire or the Bay of Naples and dedicating himself to the ensuing romanticized idyll. But dreams of this kind were not in Walton's nature. He went to Italy to work. And life at the Convento San Francesco in that first winter was the opposite of idyllic. Shortages and rationing were even more severe than in England. The roof leaked, and water had to be collected in pails from a cistern. The only way of heating the rooms was with charcoal braziers. Yet in these surroundings Walton found himself making early progress on his opera.

He began with sustained work on Act II, the emotional kernel of the story. Now, too, began the epic correspondence between the composer and his librettist. Walton must have realized almost at once that, as if there were not enough difficulties involved in trying to compose a full-length opera on an Italian island in a house without a telephone, he and Hassall were not truly on a mutual wavelength regarding the challenges ahead. Hassall's experience and accomplishment as a writer of lyrics for Ivor Novello's musicals seems to have blinded both him and, at least initially, Walton himself to the altogether more demanding set of problems involved in creating a full-length opera libretto. A situation soon developed where Walton's requests about virtually every line of the text meant that, in effect, he was himself writing the libretto by proxy. This was part of the reason why an opera that Walton thought would take about two years to compose in fact took nearly five.

Why then did he persist with Hassall as his librettist? As ever, his reasons were intelligent, realistic and practical. Hassall was a personable and likeable man and, apart from the occasional more than usually serious disagreement, he and Walton got on well. He consistently and conscientiously responded to Walton's demands as best he could, with a degree of patience that the composer always appreciated. Above all, Walton was in his preferred position regarding anything to do with his composing: he had the whip hand. Perhaps this had been the underlying problem with the projected Gesualdo opera that he had worked on with Cecil Gray during the war years. Walton probably felt that Gray was too keen to prescribe the kind of music that each scene would require, and that a genuine two-way collaboration of this kind would not suit him, however superior Gray's literary skills and musical knowledge might be. Hassall was a willing worker who would not attempt to influence the composition of the opera at arm's length. In this all-important respect at least, Walton had his ideal librettist.

The tale of Troilus and Cressida is set in the Trojan War of Greek legend. Hassall's and Walton's primary source was Chaucer's poem *Troylus and Criseide*, rather than Shakespeare's now more familiar play, although Hassall added some salient twists to his own version of the story as work on the opera proceeded. The theme is the timeless one of love set against the background of war, where the two main characters find themselves within the grip of a tragic fate they can do nothing to alter. Troilus, a son of King Priam of the city of Troy, is in love with Cressida. She is the widowed daughter of the Trojan high priest, Calkas, who is convinced that, after ten years of war against the Greeks besieging the city, further resistance is pointless. While Calkas prepares to desert to the Greeks, a Trojan captain, Antenor, is captured by them in a skirmish. Troilus promises to persuade Priam to negotiate for an exchange of prisoners. Pandarus, Calkas' brother, decides to indulge his liking for romantic intrigue by arranging a meeting of Troilus and Cressida at his own house.

In Act II, set in Pandarus' house, Troilus and Cressida meet. While a storm breaks outside, they become lovers. Diomede, a Greek commander, appears and announces that Calkas has demanded that his daughter join him with the Greeks, and that Cressida must therefore leave Troy in exchange for the return of Antenor. Impressed by Cressida's beauty, he leaves. Troilus and Cressida exchange vows of faithfulness, with Troilus promising to send messages to her across the Greek lines. Act III is set ten weeks later in the Greek camp, where Cressida is distraught at having heard nothing from Troilus. She does not know that on Calkas' orders her maidservant, Evadne, has been intercepting these messages and concealing them. Confused, lonely and desperate, she agrees to marry Diomede. Troilus and Pandarus arrive during a truce between the two armies, with the news – too late – that Cressida's ransom is being arranged. Diomede insists that she give up Troilus, but she cannot. Troilus attacks Diomede, but is killed from behind by Calkas. Cressida, denounced by Diomede and left alone in her despair, stabs herself.

As the opera began to take shape, the Waltons' lives together began to do so also. Winters were for working in Ischia, where Walton kept 'office hours': up early, working through from seven o'clock until lunchtime, and then for longer if things were going well. Summers were the time for visits to London and elsewhere, either to attend or conduct performances, or to 'live it up' in the way that was not (on the whole) considered desirable at home when there was work to be done. Even this adventurous couple, however, could not face the prospect of staying in the Convento San Francesco after that first winter. In March 1951 they moved into Casa Cirillo, a disused wine cellar which they had converted and extended into the home that they would live in for the next eight years. It was here that *Troilus and Cressida* was completed in 1954.

The opera's progress is charted with something close to self-sufficient completeness by the enormous correspondence between Walton and Hassall. Hardly a line of the text or a phrase of the music is not discussed at some point within the twenty-three volumes of papers now in the Walton Archive at La Mortella in Ischia. Eight of these alone are needed for the letters between the composer and his librettist, quite apart from the numerous outlines, drafts and revisions of the libretto that take up the rest. Future scholars and researchers may well have cause to thank the long-postponed arrival of the telephone in Walton's Ischian home, for perhaps no other opera's genesis has been charted in quite such meticulous, written-down detail. The editor of a book of this kind is therefore presented with an intriguing problem.

Troilus and Cressida was the love of Walton's creative life. Not only did it mean more to him personally than any other work of his: it also cost him more time and effort, by far, than anything else he composed. The overall perspective of Walton's life, as told here in his own words, would therefore be distorted if his letters from this period were not presented in a way that reflected his relentless dedication to the creation of his opera. But large parts of his correspondence with Hassall consist of the kind of fine detail that risks alienating the reader who does not have a score or recording of the work to hand. So I have not set out to chart the opera's growth continuously in the selection of letters published here. This has already been most expertly done, in a biographical context, by Michael Kennedy in his *Portrait of Walton* – and, besides, my own emphasis has been different. As mentioned earlier, this selection of Walton's letters has been guided always by a preference for those which show the reader something of his personality. Many of his letters to Hassall are so exclusively concerned with technical matters that they do not do this. Many others, however, do so in the composer's typically entertaining and characterful style. They also fill in a colourful portrait of the Waltons' life together on an Italian island in the early 1950s, before television, telephone, air travel and hydrofoil ferries transformed Ischia into the brimming cosmopolitan community of today. It has therefore seemed best to include here those letters which combine the small print of the process of creating an opera, bar by bar, with Walton's awareness of life going on both in the island world around him, and in the musical world back home in England.

During the later stages of *Troilus and Cressida*'s creation, from 1953 onwards, it seems remarkable that Walton was able to find enough hours in the day and night both to finish it (each scene having already been composed in more than one different version) and also to write so many letters of such tireless length. Besides Hassall, other *dramatis personae* – Walter Legge, David Webster, Laurence Olivier, Alan Frank, Henry Moore – now became involved in the opera's progress towards its première at the Royal Opera House, Covent Garden. Once again Walton's entertaining flair for long-distance manipulation came into play, as he skilfully played the leading characters off against each other. If challenged on this he would surely have responded, and with justice, that his purpose was simply to achieve the best he could for his opera by whatever means were at his disposal. He would have been equally justified in maintaining that for all the bonhomie and goodwill of David Webster, Covent Garden's general administrator, it had become clear that if Walton himself did not strain every sinew to see that *Troilus and Cressida* was cast and staged adequately, no one else could be relied on to do so either.

Walton's letters to Webster and to Walter Legge show his acute awareness of the problems of finding a suitable cast for a work he had conceived from the start as a true 'singers' opera' – one that drew directly on the musical and dramatic values of Bellini, Rossini and their successors. (Even today, Rossini is still widely thought of as a composer mainly of comic operas. Walton, with his knowledge of the then largely unfashionable field of Italian opera before Verdi, was familiar with the very different kind of stylized mastery that these composers had brought to their operas on tragic subjects.) The idea of an Italian tragic opera written in English by an English composer is unusual, to say the least, and it remains the source of much of the critical misunderstanding with which *Troilus and Cressida* will perhaps always have to contend. It is therefore little surprise that those involved at Covent Garden failed to perceive the likely difficulties ahead as clearly as Walton himself did.

Walton had always imagined the role of Cressida with the voice of

Elisabeth Schwarzkopf in mind. Her decision to turn it down (although she had been a member of the Covent Garden company between 1947 and 1952, singing many roles there in English) was a setback that sealed the opera's initial fate more finally than anyone could have foreseen at the time. The rehearsals were beset by difficulties, during which Walton realized that his attempts to secure an adequate cast had not worked out as he had hoped. Magda László's Cressida was overstretched by the vocal demands of the role. Sir Malcolm Sargent's contribution on the podium betrayed the fact that he had not conducted opera for many years. Meanwhile the orchestral parts were so littered with mistakes that the rehearsal schedule was in danger of being seriously disrupted. It was this situation that triggered Walton's angry and exasperated letter to Oxford University Press in November 1954.

The first night on 3 December was outwardly a success: the audience responded warmly, as it did during the remaining run of performances. Resistance to Walton's later music has generally come not from audiences, however, but from areas of the musical press, and from those who administer orchestras and opera companies. The critical response to *Troilus and Cressida* was, with exceptions, generally dismissive. The opera was seen to be old-fashioned, dramatically inert and out of step with the vivid new genre being developed by Britten, whose *Billy Budd* had been premièred at Covent Garden three years earlier. The essential point of *Troilus and Cressida* – that, far from being old-fashioned, it was a conscious re-creation of an earlier operatic tradition in a modern context – was missed. Instead, a critical mantra began to be chanted: Walton's post-war music was 'behind the times'. If anything he was ahead of them, as the late twentieth century's less didactic view of what constitutes 'modern' music has since shown. The musical world of the mid-1950s was simply not ready for the opera which contains some of the finest and most inspired music that Walton was ever to write.

To Alan Frank   26 January 1949

Claridge Hotel, Tucuman 535, Buenos Aires

Dear Alan

Can I trouble you to get in touch with the Leeds & Cheltenham Festivals & tell them that I don't want to write works for them but if I happen to have one about I'll let them know in good time.

[182]

We return Sat. due mid-Feb in London[.] Looking forward to seeing you[.]
Yours
William
Walton

To Yehudi Menuhin   30 July 1949

Lowndes Cottage, Lowndes Place, s.w.1

Dear Yehudi,

Thank you so much for your letter.

The end of your Sonata is nearly round the corner. Do you want me to send the copies to you now, or do you wish to pick it up here when you come to rehearse with Louis [Kentner]? I have got parts of the score all complete, and the second movement should be, in about ten days.

I am glad you enjoyed your trip to South America. The places you went to are much more exciting than the places I went to.

My love to Diana, yourself and Smithy,[1]
William

The 2nd mov. is a Theme & Vars. 8 in all & I'm on 7 so purgatory will be soon over till next time.

To Christopher Hassall   20 November 1949

Convento San Francesco, Via Cesotta, Forio d'Ischia

Dear Christopher

After being here for nearly a month I'd better report progress – & I hope I'm not going to prove too big a nuisance & a bore, as I'm about to ask you a lot.

For one reason & another I have got going on Act II & I've now got as far as I can without consulting you about some changes. The actual point I've reached is where Cres: [Cressida] is about to get to bed. I now want to make some radical changes in the script.

Act II Sec. [Section] 4 p. 17 (I hope your pages tally with mine) This is what I propose should take place if you agree.

---

1   The nickname of Yehudi and Diana Menuhin's son Gerard, born in August 1948.

Cres: seats herself at the foot of the bed (the curtains are not drawn by Evadne) & lets the audience into the secret of her growing love for Tro: [Troilus]. This should be in the form of a recitative & aria the latter maybe in rhyming verse (about 2½ mins).

Pan's [Pandarus'] entrance interrupts this & we then proceed as on p. 17 as far [as] "on jealousy's hot grid he roasts alive". This line might be developed as an aria for Pand: & should contain references to Tro's supposed jealous feelings (about 2 mins). (This could be in blank verse or if you prefer rhyming verse.)

During this song of Pand:'s Troilus should discover himself to the audience, but not the stage, & to be listening at the door & on the references to himself he can contain himself no longer (he can even have a few "asides" during P's song if you think it would be effective) & bursts out & interrupts P. He explains to C. that P appears to be trying to set them at odds etc & that he was present because he had been sent for by P & hearing that C was in the house he only wanted to thank her for the scarf etc. He gets to the kneeling stage & P exits on the "cushion" excuse, pleasurably discomfited to see how well it is going. Now should follow a love duet developed from "Oh strange new love?" in verse – rhyming probably. Then should come the avowals "as true as T" "as false as C" [. . .] A slight extension of "Now close your arms" & they should be on the threshold of the bed as the curtain falls for the Orchestral Interlude. This means cutting pages 18.19 & most of 20.

The reason for these new suggestions are chiefly these – as the script stands there is no chance for any of the principal parts to get going, or the music either.

I've discovered this by what I have already done & as it stands the script continues in much the same way till the end of the Sc. [Scene] & would result in a very tiring sort of tennis match with the ball (the music) being hit from one character to another without intermittance & never getting in to any kind of a flow.

In Sec. I it does not matter much this cross-talk as it does not last very long (longer than I thought having just timed it about 5 mins – too long I fear – but it can stand for the moment.) but the only people who have anything to sing are the most unimportant people: ie the women! with "Put off the serpent girdle".

So I think the whole Sc. should be planned thus:

Sec. I   (Scena Concertante) From "Pand. Does talking put you off?" to Evadne "Good night dear lady."

Sec II   Monologue & aria   Cressida [added in Hassall's hand: Less serene]

Sec III   Pand's "Jealousy" aria with interjections possibly from both Tro. & Cress.

Sec IV   Troilus' entrance developing into a Trio for Tro. Cress & Pand.

Sec.V   Love duet & "avowals" for T&C.

Orchestral Interlude.

I fear this may be a fearful bore & nuisance but I see no other way round. You need'nt let me have it all at once – but if I could have Cressida's recit & aria fairly soon so I can get on I should be very grateful.

It is very pleasant here & today one's almost complaining of the heat – but it has been fairly stormy the last 10 days.

With love from us both to yourself & your wife

Yours ever

William

P.S. I realise that I'm largely to blame for the short sentence technique & that I ought to have realised its shortcomings before – but being both novices at this opera game, one can only discover by trial & error!

Please don't think I am absolutely stuck on these new suggestions & if you can think of something else I'm sure it will be all for the good. I'm also coming round to more strict verse[.] I think it will stiffen up the form of the thing.

To Christopher Hassall   8 December 1949

Convento San Francesco, Forio d'Ischia

Dear Christopher

Thank you for your letter & emendations. First thing I suggest so that we know, more or less, where we are as regards lengths timing etc is that you should go to Boosey & Hawkes & buy the libretti (in english) of Aida & Otello & send me one of each. The 1st Act for instance of Aida is exactly the length this 2nd act of ours should be – & I think Cress: aria "At the haunted end" should correspond to the tenor recit & aria "Celeste Aida" in length – about 2'45" – so this will give you a model to work on. As it is – it is not quite long enough & I think it needs a middle section of say 4 lines. Also perhaps it is not quite direct enough.

I feel this aria should be balanced by "Good night dear night" in Sc 2: desire – unfulfilled – then fulfilled.

Cress: should be angry with herself for falling for T. & perhaps full of presentiments but she can't help herself. This should come out in the recit (about 45") & might run something like this. "How can I sleep! I couldn't keep my mind on that silly game for thinking of him, Troilus who now ever fills my thoughts blast him, why must I fall for him I thought never to love again" etc. (2–45.) Then the aria "Celestial Troilus"!¹ Then we have p. 17 to "On jealousy's hot grid" which I think a splendid line for an "Allegro" piece as a contrast to Cress's aria (about 1½' to 2'). What I think more difficult to manage will be T's entrance & denunciation of P's tricks & how P had sent for him – but on the other hand the audience knows that C is only now too ready to fall for him.

I think that [the] "Oh strange new love" duet should be the highlight of the scene & that everything has been working up towards it, & the avowals should be the coda of the scene & the climax to the Act should be in the pornographic interlude! – as to Sc II more anon.

This is what I conceive of the shape of the Sc. to be.

| sec.1 | sec 2. | sec 3. | Interlude |

Sec 1. is to Evads exit
Sec 2 " " P's "
Sec.3. to the Interlude
I'll try to explain what I've done in Sec 1.

There is 24" till the curtain rises to find P. walking up & down pre-occupied & restless, between the two tables. etc at 50" he starts a roulade "Does talkⵡⵡⵡing put you off?" repeated quasi parlando & staccato dóes tálkíng pút yóu óff? I've interpolated Cress: "No no kind uncle – chatter away as you please it does not disturb us at all" (1 min). (from here till "we're in for a storm" everyone remains oblivious of P'[s] chatter & are absorbed in their games though C. should try to act as if you [she] was thinking of something else). P's phrases are always fast, sung rather elaborately then repeated staccato & angrily gesticulating as

1 Cressida's 'At the haunted end of the day'; Walton is referring to his earlier comparison of this with 'Celeste Aida' from Verdi's *Aida*.

no-one pays any attention. After "the sky looks very nasty" I've interpolated this: P: (aside) But wait I have an idea! & during Hor [Horaste]:
& C. oh dear what can I do now, what can I do now? he goes to desk &
hastily writes on a tablet. P. Take this to Prince Troilus. hurry hurry
hurry (aside to slave).

I've put this in as I think it important that it should come out that P
has summoned T to his house – in fact to emphasise his pimpishness.

Then there comes the storm very short & sec 2 p.15 I've developed
into a quartet with Eva. & Hor joining, "come fill up the bowls" "we
must go home" so that it is quite an animated little ½ minute. P. makes
quite an elaborate to-do about the bed followed by extended farewells.

The timing works out thus.

Opening	0"	
Curtain	24"	The good nights are there
P.'s first sing	50"	C. Good night kind uncle goodnight
C "at all"	1'–0.	P. Good night, my niece
P. "outer wall"	2"	H. Good night dear lady (P. & H. exeunt)
P. "shillings"	2–37	E. Good-night
W. "so lightly"	3–0	C. Good night
P "soft"	4–0	Women. Good night good night
P. Satin	4–28	& P turns at the door & does an
P "dreams"	5–25	elaborate roulade on "And sweet dreams"
E "dear lady"	6–40	

Sec 2	to P's exit should take about 7. mins
Sec 3	to interlude " " " 8. "
Interlude	" " " 2½ "

Which makes this Sc. about 25 mins so Sc 2 must somehow be got down
to about 15 or 20 at the outside.

I don't see any point in your coming here yet – say perhaps in Feb
when the weather's improved. Thank you for being so sympathetic &
helpful. Meanwhile I can score what I've done.

yours ever
William

P.S. Perhaps W. Legge would lend you records of Aida & Otello which
would be a help with timing.

To Walter Legge   14 December 1949

Convento San Francesco, Forio d'Ischia

My dear Walter,

I was on the point of writing you for Xmas when your none too
cheering letter arrived. It indeed makes very depressing reading & bar
sending the whole correspondence to Sir J.A.[1] I don't see what I can do
further from this distance. I shall ask that [Peter] Brook[2] is not reap-
pointed – but I don't suppose for a second that any attention will be
paid to what I say – they never have in the past & I see no reason why
they should begin now.

We've had no papers at all since being here so are completely out of
contact with the horrors without. Each time I've see[n] a Con. Dai. Mail
it is just too much[,] first Neveu[3] – how ghastly[,] then heaven knows what.

I did see a snappy account of Salome in Time & it sounded the end.
Of course K. Clark is responsible for Dali [Salvador Dalí] in the first place.

As for my opera – the less said the better – I'm having a hell of a time
with the libretto & with the post being what it is it takes ages to get
anything altered.

As it stands noone has anything to sing at all except a sentence of
some 3 or 4 bars at a time. However C.H. is very amenable & I hope to
get straightened out soon. But I've got something down – not a vast
amount & am now waiting for C.H.s latest effort.

Otherwise it is pleasant here – the house fairly tolerable likewise the
food & wine – the weather variable, not cold & one can swim about
one day in four.

I'm sorry the Philharmonic Con was such a financial disaster – but I
imagine no concerts are doing too well – but they ought to pick up once
it is realised how good they are.

I hope this will reach you before you leave for India. Enjoy yourself.

---

1   Sir John Anderson, Chairman of the Directors of the Royal Opera House, Covent
Garden. In 1952 he was created the first Viscount Waverley of Westdean.
2   The English director Peter Brook had already built an international reputation with his
boldly radical theatre stagings, when he was appointed Director of the Royal Opera House
in 1947 at the age of twenty-two, effectively as head of productions there. His staging of
Richard Strauss's *Salome* at Covent Garden in November 1949, with designs by Salvador
Dalí, had been sharply disliked by much of the press and public. Brook left his Royal
Opera House post in 1950 and did not work there again.
3   The French violinist Ginette Neveu had died in an aeroplane crash on 28 October
1949, aged thirty.

This brings you all good wishes for Xmas & the New Year from us both.

Su. wants to know if you're married yet?[1] When & where? So do I.

as ever

William

P.S. Keep an eye on the Hungarians for recording the quartet[,] also on Yehudi for the sonata[,] that is if you are back.

To Christopher Hassall   25 December 1949

Convento San Francesco, Forio d'Ischia

Dear Christopher,

Thank you for your strenuous efforts[.] The new aria for C. is a great improvement & I am forthwith proceeding with it. Also I like the revised last sec of Sc 1 Act II & I think it is just what is needed.

What I still find unsatisfactory is "On jealousy's hot grid". First of all I think we could abolish the secret door – there seems to be little reason for it being there & it is not used again & only complicates the scenery – I feel unnecessarily.

P.'s aria should be on the subject of "Jealousy" per se. (about 1 min or 1½ mins). You know the kind of thing.

> Jealousy that all consuming fire
> That gnaws at the vitals etc. etc.

It should be as if P. realises suddenly that he dos'ent quite know how to explain away T's unexpected arrival & extemporises something to gain time to collect his thoughts. Cres. can make appropriate interjections. "What does this mean? Is he bereft of his senses?" etc.

About half way through the aria T. opens the door & concealed by it adds his interjections. "He's gone mad" – "I must stop him" – "he'll ruin everything" etc. You might finish P.'s aria by the four opening lines - - - - - - Is it dead or alive you would have him?

Then T. should burst in. "Cres. forgive me – your uncle is trying to stir up trouble between [us] instead of being as I thought our friend & helper." Then let P. explain "I made it all up – it was just a little

---

1 Legge married the German soprano Elisabeth Schwarzkopf in 1953.

strategem of mine to bring two lovers together." (Cutting the trio which I think will be too difficult to bring off effectively – nevertheless I think we could make a trio out of this bit but more on the lines of what I' ve done with "Fill up the bowls".)

Perhaps on P'[s] exit we still need a few lines before starting "O strange new love", as if T&C. were not quite reconciled by P'[s] explanation & taking the blame for the "scene" and C is in one key & T in another which gradually coalesce on to a unison note – if you see what I mean – I hope you do – or this may not be neccessary. One can clearly see when one gets nearer to this part.

I dare say you are right & this whole scene won't take as long as 25 mins – but love music is apt to move slowly – but at the moment exact timing is not so important – there'll be a pruning stage when the whole Act is through.

As for Sc.2 up to now I've only thought out one thing to be done, p. 24 (till then it is fairly O.K. though possibly p. 23 could be condensed). I think P. should belie his brave words & should be slightly terrified & grovelling when Diomede appears & be more or less silent. Sec 12 p. 24 should be condensed into a dramatic aria recit. for D. alone with only interjected asides from P.

A happy New Year to you both.

Yrs
William

P.S. Unfortunately I can['t] find any paralell(?) in Aida unless it be the trio you may remember, in the 1st Sc. between Rad Amn. [Radames, Amneris and] Aida. mid p. 7 & p8.

To Sir John Anderson   29 December 1949

Convento San Francesco, Forio d'Ischia

Dear Sir John,

I have been considering for some time whether to send you the enclosed letters or not. I have decided to do so as I think the Trustees should know about such a serious matter, so perhaps you would be so kind as to read them at the next committee meeting that is if the matter has not already been discussed.

I know nothing as to the rights or wrongs, but to me at least, it would appear that [Peter] Brook must be singularly obtuse not to have taken the opportunity of learning something about an opera he evidently knows so little.

I sincerely hope that Brook's contract is not going to be renewed. He seems to me one of our major blunders & we should be much better off without him, even if it does mean another hunt for suitable producers.

None of his productions that I have seen is satisfactory, & though he has improved some of the earlier productions such as Carmen, nobody could fail to do otherwise.

It is essential that an opera producer should not only have knowledge of the theatre but a good knowledge of music as well, & Brook has next to none.

If, as was under discussion when I left, Barbirolli, is to take over in 1951, I should like to suggest that Kleiber be invited to come to Covent Garden[1] say for three years for four or five months in the year. Erhart [Otto Erhardt] who has been producer with him in Buenos Aires for the last fifteen or so years might also be invited.

He may not be the ideal man but he is vastly experienced & one of the better producers existing at the moment & it might be possible to find some young men who would study with him & so ultimately solve our production problems.

I think if we had these three, Barbirolli, Kleiber & Erhart in charge, things might begin to look up a little at C.G.

If these suggestions have not already been put forward perhaps you would mention them.

It is time too that [Reginald] Goodall[2] & [Peter] Gellhorn[3] were prevented from appearing so often on the rostrum & some other conductors, I've already suggested Harry Blech, should be given a chance.

With best wishes for the New Year,

yours sincerely

William Walton.

---

1 Erich Kleiber was engaged for three months in 1950–51.
2 English conductor. He had joined the Sadler's Wells Opera Company in 1944 and had conducted the world première performances of Britten's *Peter Grimes* there. In 1946 he joined the Royal Opera House company.
3 German-born pianist, choirmaster and conductor, now resident in England.

To Walter Legge   18 January 1950

Convento San Francesco, Forio d'Ischia

My dear Walter,

Thank you so much for your letter. I am indeed, most sorry to hear about your accident, how dreadful for you & I trust that three weeks with Furtwängler won't bring it on again & that you will soon be alright again.

I duly sent off all the [Boris] Christoff[1] correspondence but I need hardly say, I've not heard a word – not even an acknowledgement from Sir J.A.

I've heard further from Parry Jones about the state of things at Cov. Gar. He actually does mention that Christoff was very rude, but it's the other things he mentions [about Peter Brook] – lack of discipline & coordination etc. Wants 19 rehearsals for Salome[,] 18, I ask you! for Lohengrin, & typically enough 3 for Boris [*Boris Godunov*] & you mention 2 for Butterfly [*Madama Butterfly*]. P.J. has been asked to be a more or less permanent member of the Co. So keep all this under your hat as I don't want to get him into trouble!

Thank you for the welcome news about "Scap" [*Scapino*] & Bs.F. [*Belshazzar's Feast*]. I'll certainly join the artistic directorate as soon as they are out of the way.

I'm sorry about Kubelik [Rafael Kubelík][2] – it would have been a help to have one decent conductor permanently in the country.

We went to Naples last week ostensibly to see [Berg's] "Wozzeck". But it turned out that it had been such a flop, though [Vittorio] Gui[3] told me the performance was good, with [Tito] Gobbi[4] & Bohm [Karl Böhm][5] conducting, that it was changed & we were let in for "Zaza" [Leoncavallo's *Zazà*] instead. The Zs are the only things in common I fear.

---

1 Celebrated Bulgarian bass, who was appearing in the title role of *Boris Godunov* at the Royal Opera House. He was a neighbour of the Waltons on Ischia.
2 Czech conductor resident in Switzerland. He had conducted the Glyndebourne Festival Opera company during its visit to the 1948 Edinburgh Festival. Legge had evidently informed Walton that Kubelík had since been appointed music director of the Chicago Symphony Orchestra, a post he held from 1950 to 1953. He was eventually to hold the position of music director at the Royal Opera House from 1955 to 1958.
3 Italian conductor, who had been appearing at La Scala, Milan since 1923.
4 Italian baritone and opera producer. He first sang at the Royal Opera House in 1951.
5 Austrian conductor. Twice music director of the Vienna Staatsoper during the 1940s and 1950s.

[Eugene] Goossens was there – incidentally he might do for the B.B.C as he has to decide in June whether to renew his contract in Australia.

There's to be a performance in Rome of the original Facade in March with K. Falkner[1] reciting. He might be good, but we shan't go because of the expense & the impossibility of getting a room being Anno Santo.

The opera is beginning to move & I hope to finish Sc I of Act II by the middle of next month. I shall then set to on Act I.

I started on Act II as I felt that if I could'nt do that it was no use bothering to try with the rest.

However having got at least, the libretto for this scene more or less right things have not gone too badly.

There is quite a good concerted Sc. to open with – the chess game & the song for attending maids (lifted from Hamlet film-theme) a recit & aria for Elizabeth [Elisabeth Schwarzkopf,[2] as Cressida], about 3½ mins with a nice top C at the end – a bit sailing near the wind, slightly Neo-Puccini, but what can one do with a very Neo-Novello poem. A "Jealousy" aria for Pandarus followed by a love duet which ends the Sc & leads to the pornographic Interlude.[3]

So I contemplate having two thirds of Acts 1 & 2 done before I return. When I say done, I mean a very sketchy sketch.

Our love to you & Elizabeth & let us know the happy day.

As ever

William

To Alan Frank   18 January 1950

Convento San Francesco, Forio d'Ischia

Dear Alan

I can't think why the proofs[4] haven't arrived. I sent them on the 9th by ordinary post as I couldn't afford the Air mail about 4500 lire. Air mail

1 Keith Falkner, British Council representative in Rome.
2 German soprano. One of the leading singers of her time, especially in Mozart and Richard Strauss operas and lieder, she married Walter Legge in 1953. She was a member of the Royal Opera House company between 1947 and 1952 and sang many roles there in English. Walton created the role of Cressida with her voice in mind.
3 The interlude between Scenes 1 and 2 of Act II, where the music describes the love-making of Troilus and Cressida, left alone together in Pandarus' house.
4 Of the *Scherzetto* for violin and piano, originally part of the Violin Sonata, and published separately in 1950 as the second of the *Two Pieces for Violin and Piano*.

is on the gold standard here! But they should have arrived in a week –
so I was told.

No I'm not going to America & refused K's [Koussevitsky's] offer.[1]
Teaching very knowledgeable students is beyond me! It was the fourth
offer of its kind I've had in the last months. In fact I don't see my getting
to U.S before 52 or 3 & then it must be a properly organised do. The
longer I put it off the more they'd like to see me – maybe!

About Sir Les B. [Leslie Boosey] I only asked as it was always understood around Cov. Gar. that he'd be dubbed [knighted] for having rescued
it from Mecca Cafés when B & Hs [Boosey and Hawkes's] lease was up
which it was at Xmas.

Yrs
William

Keep an eye on the recording of 4tet & Son.

To Harry Blech   22 January 1950

Convento San Francesco, Forio d'Ischia

My dear Harry,
   [. . .]
   As I'm sure he has been doing nothing in respect of his promise to
give you a chance at the "Flute" [*The Magic Flute*], I've been making
[David] Webster's life a burden to him – but have evoked as yet no
response.

I've no[t] much news from here as life is very quiet & pleasant if it
wasn't for this foul opera writing I've undertaken. A lot of libretto trouble
which has taken time to get right at this distance. However it is on the
move & at moments I think it no worse than any other British opera.

Our love to you both.
William

1 Koussevitsky had asked to Walton to teach composition at the Tanglewood Summer
School of Music in July and August 1950.

To Yehudi and Diana Menuhin   27 January 1950
[from Susana Walton
with postscript from William Walton]

Convento San Francesco, Forio d'Ischia

Dearest Diana & Yehudi,

We are greatly excited at the approaching 5th of Feb.[1] and ever so diss-appointed not to be there. But how are both of you and big old Smithie?

We are very well, William as adorable as usual and slowly getting along with his work. When our life gets unbearably monastic & monotonous we cross over to Naples. We've been to the opera & heard a most divine performance of Bellini's "Sonambula" [*La sonnambula*] by a young girl from Puerto Rico, of all places, with the most beautiful voice.

And mentioning the Americas when are you off to South America? I warn you that my dear sweet 'ma' and 'pa' will probably pounce on you, if Yehudi has a morning off they will try to smuggle him out to the country place, I hope you can manage something of the sort and have a peep at the wild PAMPAS that so horrified William at first! Dad's name is Enrique Gil so don't be too surprised.

Dear Diana I know you won't have time to write but please tell Griselda [Kentner] to do the effort & send us news of all of you & of the concert and a few jokes to keep William smiling.

Best luck & our love
William & Susana

Alles güt for Feb 5th. Of course if you don't play it [the Violin Sonata] in B.A. I'll see that none of my 113 new relations go or if they do they will boo! I hope you record [it] whether the great Walter [Legge] is back from Vienna or not. Best love to you both
Will.

1 The date of the first performance of the revised version of Walton's Violin Sonata, to be given by Yehudi Menuhin and Louis Kentner at the Theatre Royal in London's Drury Lane.

To Yehudi and Diana Menuhin
and Louis and Griselda Kentner   7 February 1950
[from William and Susana Walton]

Convento San Francesco, Forio d'Ischia

[begun by Walton]

Dear Yehulougridiana,

Thank you all a thousand times for the telegrams letters etc.

We are delighted and rapturous that the Sonata went so well & only too sorry we we'rent there to hear the marvellous performance, (we've had eye-witness accounts of that from others not only yourselves) of the wonderful work – it was those three extra bars in the coda that worked it!

The weather is playing up & being disagreable for having been so delicious last week. Otherwise our lives are somewhat placid & tranquil & I write about a bar a day[,] some days even two! I've been trying to explain to Susana the meaning or rather the double-meaning of some of Griseldas less decorous poems – not too easy without demonstration!

[continued by Susana Walton]

Demonstrations are easy enough though! but W's pornographic mind is unexcusable!!! you should have seen him giggle over Gri's letter.

We are in very high spirits after receiving your telegrams because we had been feeling rather sad at not being able to be in London and losing all the fun. so we are overjoyed & dance about the house (at least I do) with all the good news.

I hope Diana received my letter and please let us know when & if you are leaving Bs.As. [Buenos Aires]

I am glad to say that the tapestry is almost ready and therefore [I] will not take 8 painful years over it as poor Queen Mary, & neither will I give it to the nation!

So our four dears a big hug & best love.

William and Susana

To David Horner   19 February 1950

Convento San Francesco, Forio d'Ischia

Dear David,

Thank you so much for your letter. We are well & happy & T&C
progresses if somewhat slowly & fitfully. What I shall be in for from the
highbrow critics when it appears, I hardly like to contemplate, as it con-
tinually hits below the belt in the worst neo-novelloish taste!

I am glad you liked the [Violin] Sonata – it will take a year or two
for it to come into it's own. If I have too much back-chat from D.S.T.
[Desmond Shawe-Taylor]¹ & his girls – he's for it – so you better warn
him next time you see him!

We leave here on May 15ᵗʰ. Su's brother is joining us then (with some
dollars) & we are motoring him to Paris taking in everything on the way
& arriving back in London about June 10ᵗʰ. According to our schedule
we leave Perugia on May 22ⁿᵈ via Urbino-Arezz[o] to Siena where we
stay the night & I was going to write to Osbert proposing ourselves for
the 23ʳᵈ for a couple of days or so² – we could park little brother in
Firenze if inconvenient. We could motor you round places if you liked. If
this is alright will you let us know.

It is very agreable here & we've been enjoying marvellous weather the
last [few] days.

Naples is only 2 hours off so we've been able to get to the opera quite
a lot.

Auden³ comes here next month. We've met once his two friends one
Kalman [Chester Kallman]⁴ & another whose name eludes me (they're
poked by the local postman who does very well out of it as they pay on
a generous scale so local gossip says!).

"Facade" had quite a success in Firenze & is being repeated in Milan
& Rome.

Love from us both.

as ever

William

1 Music critic of *The Sunday Times*.
2 To stay at Castello di Montegufoni.
3 W. H. Auden. English poet and opera librettist, with a deep knowledge and love of music.
4 Chester Kallman, American poet, and Auden's partner and collaborator. Together they wrote the libretti of Stravinsky's *The Rake's Progress* and Henze's *The Bassarids*.

Have just been re-reading "Escape with me".[1] It is too depressing to think what has happened since you were there.

I saw Osbert's excellent letter on the H-bomb in a stray "Times". We don't as a rule see any newspapers so remain compar[a]tively calm & oblivious to what is going on outside.

To Christopher Hassall   22 February 1950

Convento San Francesco, Forio d'Ischia

Dear Christopher,

I am sorry to have been so long without writing to you. Yes! I have received safely all the bits & pieces.

I've had a lot of trouble, like you, with the "Jealousy" scene [Act II, Scene 1] but have at last reached the love-duet. I am just "funking" that for the moment, finding love music extremely difficult to get any originality into – Wagner, Verdi, Puccini, Strauss always "popping" their heads round the corner & I hope to pick up something from Act I.

The "jealousy" scene is still not quite right especially when T&C begin to join in. I've brought in C. [Cressida] at "By dawn he's dead" & T [Troilus] at "alive you would have him" & the trio proceeds till T. bursts in. But it is not very satisfactory but I think we can get it right if we work at it together. I've taken a few liberties with the text!

T. bursts in with the following. "Enough of this mischievous lying" C. Troilus! T. Cress. forgive me I must break in or stifle, I heard him every word. Nothing but bare-faced lying. (to P) [Pandarus] Chattering magpie how dare you plot to ruin us? Pand: Cooler, dear boy, calm down, I will explain. - - - - - I've always said there's nothing like a brisk misunderstanding for bringing young lovers together. This being so, to provoke the necessary quarrel I made it all up, every word. But I hardly dared hope I'd deceive you. Cress: Fools, both of you making the night a madhouse. Tro: You must believe him for once he is telling the truth. Pand. Oh this is going finely if not in all particulars according to plan. He seems to have reached the kneeling stage. I will fetch him a cushion! (exit P). Tro. Cressida! - - - - Cress: Troilus. - - - - .

Anyhow the scene is right for length (I use the 2nd verse of "jealousy" as well, 4 in all.) being about 4½ min – so one can afford to expand a bit on the love-duet, up to now the time being about 16 mins. It doesn't seem much after all this slaving – but I hope to progress quicker now I'm getting to learn the technique of the thing a bit.

I am now starting on Act I. We are in the same predicament over this act as we were over Act 2. Sc 1. that the hero & heroine especially the latter have next to nothing to sing. T's better off with the arrival of the new song but C.'s position is bad still, consisting as it does of some 15 or 16 short fragmentary sentences (in the whole act) with which little can be done musically speaking. This is bad from the point of view of the audience & the singers, both expecting a good deal of singing from the two chief parts. (I don't explain myself very well.)

Everything should be comparatively plain sailing till "Is that her name" p. 5. Somehow it must be contrived that both T & C have each something to get their teeth into in Sec 6. T's song "My name" is good but it can't stand alone – C must have something & I find it difficult to say quite what. And of course making something of this Sec. is going to add to the length so we shall have to condense elsewhere – also not easy. (I should say it will take me at least a month to get to this point so there's no great hurry.) In fact I fear the rest of this Act from p. 5 will need considerable re-modelling & for the moment I must leave it to you as I'm bereft of ideas as to how it is to be done. But the defects in the script as it stands are the same as the ones we have successfully (I hope) overcome in Act II Sc 1.

As for the other questions – the end of the opera & the rest of Act 2. [–] we can leave to talk over when I get back.

We saw "Tosca" in Naples & I timed it. Act I 42 mins Act II 46 mins Act III 27 mins. Admirable lengths which I keep in view – though I doubt getting the last Act to 27" – but Act 2 won't be more than 40.

I heard from Ernest [Newman] that you'd gone with [him] to hear the Vl. Son. How did it really go? The press seems to be a series of "damns" of faint praise.

Yours ever
William

To Christopher Hassall [March 1950]

[Forio d'Ischia]

Dear Christopher,
    Further work for you! I'm having a lot of trouble starting off Act I.
I despair!
    Yrs
    William

To Roy Douglas [early March 1950]

[postcard]

Convento San Francesco, Forio d'Ischia

Will you let me know how the changes in B.F. [*Belshazzar's Feast*] come
off (or not) in M.S. [Malcolm Sargent's] perf next week. He's using 6
Trpts a side instead of the bands![1]
    I don't much take to opera writing & I fear it may turn out to be a
colossal waste of time, especially as I['m] sure Cov. Gar. will have been
"axed" in the economy drive by the time I'm ready. How are you?
    as ever
    William

To Christopher Hassall 17 March 1950

Convento San Francesco, Forio d'Ischia

Dear Christopher,
    I am still having trouble with [the] opening.[2] As it stands it goes like
this: – Curtain up after 20 secs. intro. Wors. [Worshippers] kneeling
muttering "Vir. of T" [Virgin of Troas] as a reiterating background. Bells
from the Temple & Cal: [Calkas] begins Vir of T. answered by priests
& priestesses. (I've cut from "Taste" to "Abydos".) This is repeated 3
times each more intensified. Then the Ps & Ps [Priests and Priestesses]

---

1 Besides baritone soloist, chorus and orchestra, *Belshazzar's Feast* also requires two
brass bands, including trombones as well as trumpets, on the left and right of the concert
platform.
2 Of Act I.

take up "Mount Ida" followed in canon by the Wors. At "Pallas as she flows." the Wors. reiterate very quickly "Pallas awake" while the Bys. [Bystanders] start "P. is dead". There is a big cresc. made out of this, leading to "Pallas awake. Gird on" etc. Now I fear I must ask you to re-write this. It wants to be a chorus rhythmically precise. "Balance the spear" throws it out & it is too short for what I want. Look at the "Otello" libretto p. 6. & model it on "Dio, fulgor". "We are accursed etc" should be given to the Bys. who infect the Wors. with it leading to Cal. entrance.

I like the hexameters & I think after all it would be better sung. If it is spoken it will spoil the effect of "Beat flat" which should be spoken. I don't think the "hexes" will be too long. Also singers are notoriously bad speakers.

P.5. I still think that T. should have an aria at "Is that her name" like I mentioned in my last letter. But maybe you are right about C. [Cressida] confining her to a slightly longer version of "Morn[ing] & eve[ning]."

I agree that No 2. is the best place for her to have something further.

Since writing the foregoing page your letter has arrived, for which much thanks bearing the new material.

If you are feeling like having a "break" from the english winter do come & spend some days here – the weather is now pretty good. However I warn you the house is pretty uncomfortable no bath & only cold water – so you are warned!

If you decide to come you can fly to Naples (get you[r] return ticket in London) in about 8 hours. You would probably have to spend the night in Naples & catch the boat at the Porto at 2–pm for Porto d'Ischia where we would meet you.

Again if you come can you bring me as much "No Name" tobacco as you can conveniently carry & if you don't need all your lire I will be delighted to buy them from you!

The only thing of urgency now is the new version of "Pallas awake". Send us a wire if you come, any time will suit us.
Yours ever
William

To Alan Frank 21 March 1950

Convento San Francesco, Forio d'Ischia

Dear Alan,

There seems to be a distinct possibility of a perf. of B.F. [*Belshazzar's Feast*] at the San Carlo [Opera House] in Naples next season under Karl Böhm. He's very keen on it & if there is a spare score could you have it sent to him with the Pfte score as well. Walter L. who breezed in some ten days ago can give you his address. As he is also conductor at the Colon B.A. [Teatro Colón, Buenos Aires] he will probably get it done there too.

Now there's the question of translation. There was some talk once of the B.C. [British Council] having one done but I don't know if it was ever started but will find out from K. Falkner.

Will you have copies of the following works sent to Guido Pannain[1] "Il Tempo" Roma. He's Italy's chief music critic & is desirous of acquainting himself with my music as he is writing a book of some sort. You've probably got his address, but the above will find him, as he says he regularly receives V.W.s but has never had one [of] mine sent him from the O.U.P.!

Symph.	score
Vla. Con.	min score
Vl. " .	score.
Sin. Con.	2. Pftes
Façade 1.2.	scores
P.P.	min. score
B.F.	Pfte
Quart[et].	
Vl. Son. when ready	

There seems to be a tolerable amount of Walton about. Coming over on the boat the other day we were regaled with a broadcast of the Vl. Con & well it suited the landscape.

---

1 Italian composer, musicologist, critic, and Professor of Music at Naples Conservatory from 1915 to 1961. He was an authority on the music of Monteverdi, Domenico Scarlatti and Bellini. His own works included the operas *Beatrice Cenci* (1942) and *Madame Bovary* (1955).

The [String] Quartet is being broadcast from Rome & Naples tomorrow by the Rome Radio Qt. Then there is Facade on April 9th.

Yrs
William

To David Horner   21 March 1950

Convento San Francesco, Forio d'Ischia

Dear David,

Thank you for your letter & the invite to Montegufoni. We look forward to it & I'm sure my young b-in-law will be in his 7th heaven.

Not much news. As yet Auden hasn't arrived but I'll put the 'tecs on him. The tariff for the postman by the way, is 1000 lire for the girls & 600 lire for the chaps. He makes a fortune during the season.

We've been rather rash & taken a lease on a house here for 10 years. Its cheap enough[,] 50,000 lire a year, but we've to furnish it etc. but that should'nt be too difficult if done gradually.

It is the most divine spring. No rain for some weeks & the water shortage is becoming rather acute.

The op. is at a slight standstill. However C. Hassall is I think coming here for some days & I hope to bully him into writing something & getting the libretto more or less straight.

Best love from us both & to Osbert

yrs
William

To David Webster   [postmarked: 11 April 1950]
[postcard]

Forio d'Ischia

Of course I will become a subscriber to the new Cov. Gar. Co., & I hope you have taken it for granted as your letter of March 23rd has only now reached me. Opera progress is variable, but what there is of it I'm occasionally inclined to think rather good – sometimes very good.

yours
William Walton

To Alan Frank   19 April 1950

Convento San Francesco, Forio d'Ischia

Dear Alan,

I'd got it in my head that I'd answered your letter. By now, you will
have discovered that I returned the Scherzetto proofs at the same time as
those of the Sonata.

Don't send me the "Scapino" proofs as I want all the time I've left
here to continue with my "mag op". If Foote has discovered a lot of
mistakes perhaps it would be better to return them to the engravers now,
and I'll read the second set on my return.

I shan't be back till early June though we leave here on May 13th.
Susana's brother joins up then & we shall do a sight-seeing tour back.

If the Vl. Son. is ready will you send me 4 copies & I'll try & distribute
them to some deserving violinists here. Keith [Falkner] is going to try to
persuade Gioconda de Vito to take it up. M [Menuhin] has I hear been
playing it often in Switzerland.

About the Spanish translation of B.F. [*Belshazzar's Feast*] On the
whole I think it would be best to drop it & concentrate on an Italian
one. As I mentioned to you, I think, before, there's an idea that it may
be done in Naples sometime, & the Spanish & the Argentines can certainly read & pronounce Italian without serious difficulty, so we could
kill two "wops" with one brick so to speak.

Will you see that the score of "Facade" entertainment is ready for me
when I get back as I must swot it up for Aldeburgh!

The Blech's [Blech Quartet] did the Quintet [String Quartet?] in Rome
I gather.

That is about all for the moment I think.

Yrs

William

(It isn't!)
You might send a couple of copies of the Vl. Son. to
    John Hind
      The Brit. Cou.
        Centro de Música
          Juncal 1207
            Buenos Aires
& one to

Thomas Magyar
  Hanenburglaan 160
    Den Haag   Holland

& one to W. Schneiderhan[1]

Walter L. will give you his address & maybe the names of some other players who might be interested.

To Benjamin Britten   10 July 1950

Lowndes Cottage, Lowndes Place, s.w.1

My dear Benjamin,
  I arrived back from Cheltenham [Festival] to find your charming letter.
  We both enjoyed the [Aldeburgh] Festival[2] very much & have every intention of attending next year, whether or not there should be anything of mine in the programmes. I found the general atmosphere most pleasant & stimulating & I am happy that you should think my appearance there helped things a little.
  I should like to have a shot at a chamber opera or a piece of some kind for you.[3] It seems to me that there is a real future for that medium from all points of view – that is, if there is a future for anything, which at the moment seems doubtful!
  I am beginning to get things straightened as regards the libretto of T&C & hope to get down to it seriously again very soon.
  It will, I hope, be finished before World War III descends on us!
  We shall be delighted to come & see you & if you are in London do come & lunch or dine with us.
  Best regards from us both
  Yours ever
  William

1 Wolfgang Schneiderhan, Austrian violinist. Leader of the Vienna Philharmonic Orchestra from 1937 to 1951, from when he concentrated on a solo career.
2 Britten and his partner, the tenor Peter Pears, had settled in the Suffolk town of Aldeburgh, where they founded the Aldeburgh Festival in 1948.
3 Walton's chamber opera *The Bear* was composed between 1965 and 1967, when it was premièred at Aldeburgh. This reference indicates that he and Britten may well have discussed the idea much earlier than that. Britten had already composed his opera *The Rape of Lucretia* (1946) for chamber forces.

To Christopher Hassall   10 February 1951

Convento San Francesco, Forio d'Ischia

My dear Christopher,

I had been hoping that when I took up my pen to write to you, that I should be able to tell you that I had completed Act I.

This alas, is not the case, though it is now well on the way & I hope to complete it by the middle of next month or so.

There is only one major disaster in the libretto & that is that I'm quite unable to cope with "Child of the grey sea wave".[1] It evokes the worst type of music from me, real neo-Novelloismo,[2] which I fear cannot be tolerated on the operatic stage. Though the substance is right it is the regularity the <u>tum</u>-tum tum, <u>tum</u> tum, <u>tum</u>, which gets me down.

To proceed, I by-passed it, but I've kept returning to it, with alas, the same results.

It seems to me there are two solutions.

① for you to re-write it entirely or

② to extend the previous bit "Is Cressida a slave" to include the substance of "Child of the gray sea wave" [sic]. Of the two the former I think is better.

The other minor snags are ① Tro.'s [Troilus'] last par. p. 7. & ② Cressida's dramatic scene p. 11.

As regards ① it is the sentence, "Oh, let us bring our names where they belong, together, yours & mine", which trips me. Ive tried it all ways round. "Oh, let us bring our names together yours & mine". & Oh, let us bring together your name & mine. None of which seem to work & tend again to evoke this appaling streak of neo-Novelloismo. As for ② p. 11. it is just too long & needs a third of it cutting in each stanza which I find too difficult to do myself. I don't find Eva: [Evadne's] interjection too happy. In each case I've by-passed them so am proceeding, but they will have to be faced in the end.

It would seem that each page averages about 3 mins. so at a glance you can see that it is tending to be overlong as some pages for instance p. 7 works out at about 6½, which is what I suspect to be the length of p. 11 as it stands. It is all right for p. 7 as there are two of them at it.

When you have tinkered away at this (I'm most anxious for p. 11)

---

1 The opening text of Troilus' Act I aria eventually became 'Child of the wine-dark wave'.
2 Hassall had been the librettist of several musicals by Ivor Novello.

you might take a look at Act II Sc 2. Could you cut half or a third of Tro's bit [at the] bottom of p. 7. the same out of Cressida's p. 9. I'm very much perturbed about the length of Act II. as it stands I think it will play about 55 minutes, at least 8 too long.! So get out the blue pencil.

Ive done some rather drastic cutting of p. 8. 9. Act I.

"There was a time" & "Leave Cressida to me" have gone. I think it works better after "what do you know of love". Pan: ignores the implied insult with a (musical!) shrug. & proceeds "I have come here this morning, Troilus".

After Tro's "racked with misgivings" Pan: proceeds "Leave the wooing of Cressida to me dear boy. I'm an old hand at this game & can guarantee results".

The time factor again is the snag. This sc now works out at about 4 mins[,] about right.

I must rush for the post.

Our best love to you both

William

To Christopher Hassall   19 February 1951
[postcard]

Convento San Francesco, Forio d'Ischia

Thanks a million times for your speed & efficiency. The alterations will be a great help. Forgive the neo-Novelloismo but I meant it to refer to the music not the verse. If still on go & see the "Volpone" film – it may produce a few ideas for our next effort! – if & when I ever get through this one. Also you might give me an account of the "Consul."[1]

Love from us both

Yrs

W.W.

1 *The Consul* (1950), opera by Gian Carlo Menotti.

To Christopher Hassall   12 March 1951

Casa Cirillo, Forio d'Ischia

Dear Christopher,

I was deeply shocked to read of the death of Ivor N [Novello] & I [am] sure you are most frightfully upset about it. The only thing to [be] said, is that it was so sudden that he can have known nothing about it.

Your graphic account of the "Consul" arrived with the score which I sent for, so I look forward to studying it.

We are in the middle of moving to new quarters (see above) so life is a bit hectic & T&C slightly in abeyance owing to the noise of work-men etc. But we shall settle down in a day or two.

It is just as well that you postpone Sicily till next year as we are much on the rocks owing to our move. But it is an excellent idea that you come here for a spell of work. Alas we can't put you up but there is an excellent and cheap hotel (400 lire a day) & you could eat with us. So do come. It would be a great help with T&C having you about as well. We're here till the end of June so suit yourself as to the time, the later the better I should say as the weather is awful – snow rain wind, but it must change soon.

as ever
William

To Christopher Hassall   31 March 1951

Forio d'Ischia

My dear Christopher,

This is splendid! We could meet you in Naples & escort you to Ischia – the boat leaves at 2–30 arriving Porto d'Ischia 4–30.

Do bring with you your full £100 allowance or could you get a busi-ness one (£10 a day for 15 days)? I'd buy what you don't need (you won't need very much as we can put you up hear [sic]) as we are getting very short what with one thing & another as you will see when you arrive. Anyhow the whole trip goes against Income Tax as it is of the utmost importance that you come to work with me[.]

Best love to you both & looking forward to seeing you
Yrs
William

To Alan Frank   [early June 1951]
[postcard]

[Ischia]

I wonder if the two wooden stands designed for holding up the curtain of "Façade" still exist? They may be lurking in the cellars somewhere but as they've not been used for years, they may be mislaid. If you can lay hands on them would you let Basil Douglas[1] know as there are no facilities at all for hanging the curtain for the Liverpool performances.
  Yrs
  William

To Muriel Keir[2]   25 October 1951

Lowndes Cottage, Lowndes Place, s.w.1

Dear Miss Keir,
  Would you be so kind as to occasionally give tickets for the opera or ballet to Miss Sheila Perry,[3] my secretary, whose address is 52 The Manor Drive, Worcester Park, Surrey.
  You might confirm this with Mr. Webster.
  Yours sincerely,
  William Walton

To Alan Frank   [postmarked: Casamicciola, Ischia,
                                19 November 1951]
[postcard showing illustrated map of Ischia]

If you want to see the photos by Glass get hold of my sec. Mr Jefferson 42 Eaton Terrace sw1 Slo 4975 & use what you like.
  I dare say it would be as well if I had a quick look thro' the proofs of the Sin. Con.[4] It is always a mistake not to, boring tho' it may be.
  Yrs ever
  William

1 English promoter and artists' agent.
2 David Webster's assistant at the Royal Opera House.
3 The letter is typed by Sheila Perry herself.
4 The revised, 1943 version of *Sinfonia concertante*.

To Christopher Hassall   21 December 1951

Casa Cirillo, Forio d'Ischia

My dear Christopher,

Thank you for the detailed account of B.B's B.B. [Benjamin Britten's *Billy Budd*][1] I heard with a great deal of difficulty [on radio] Acts 3 & 4 & what I could hear I thought good (I had the score to help) especially the part you don't like [. . .] But I think the opening of Act 4 is a near thing, but being the genius he is, he managed by the orchestration & little phrase on the flute to avoid the maudlin bathos which it really ought to have been. [Ernest] Newman which is the only criticism besides [Eric] Blom[2] that I've seen must have come as a bit [of] a cold douche to the hysteria of the earlier press.

However to get down to business. I need hardly say I am doing worse even than usual and am at the moment at a complete standstill & see no signs of a move.

To get going I started revising Act 2 from the start & that took me about a month. It is much better than it was & may be said to have reached its final form. "At the haunted [end of the day]" much better with a new middle section, though I still fear it is the 'all time low'.

The "jealousy" scene I'm still a bit doubtful about as I fear it may be a little unconvincing from the dramatic point of view. And to make it more personal & clear the opening line of verse 3. might substitute "Unhappy Troilus" instead of "Unhappy boy".

But I come to a full stop at the last bit of p. 7. "If one last doubt". Nor have I found anything for p. 8. So in fact the most important scene in the whole opera is non-existent. However I can make headway from p 10 onwards.

I believe the crux is in the para. "If one last doubt". It is too flat & English!

We've now arrived at the point in the plot where the audience know more so than Troilus that C. [Cressida] has a yen for him. He has only been given a scarf by P.! [Pandarus] So I think that if I were in his position I should be inclined to be more impassioned & insistent & not so self excusing so as to tip her over into "O strange new love". The time factor is alright, up to this point it is 16 mins., so we can afford to spread

1 Premièred at the Royal Opera House on 1 December 1951.
2 English music critic (of the *Observer*), writer and editor.

[210]

ourselves a bit. Say pages 8 & 9 take from 12 to 15 mins the rest can be covered in about the same & Act 2 should be around 47 mins in all.

So I think instead of "If one last doubt" something on the lines I've suggested might be substituted. T. has comparatively little in this act so we can afford him something here, not too long say 1½–2 mins & I shan't mind if it involves your recasting "O strange new love" for as I've said it has not as yet evoked a spark of any kind.

I know it is a fearful bore & I hope not to have to trouble you further during this act.

I've got some views on Act 3. but they can [wait] for the moment.

We've been having a spell of the most heavenly weather & at the moment of writing this I've had to draw the curtain it's so hot!

With all seasonal greetings to you both

as ever

William

To Christopher Hassall   9 January 1952

Casa Cirillo, Forio d'Ischia

My dear Christopher,

Thank you for your letter & the new version of the Love Scene. Alas! I fear it will not quite do.

[. . .]

I see in my synopsis of Chaucer's T&C that it says this: – "This idyllic situation is brought abruptly to an end by Crs Father Calk. demanding his daughter in exchange for Ant. [Antenor] Cres. has to go & T's grief is heartrending. He & C. have a terrific farewell, in which C. is quite as heartbroken as T. & faints away. T. is sure she is dead & takes out his sword to kill himself, but C. sees him just in time; she turns to comforting him, tells him she will soon be back again & plights her troth that she will never love anyone but him & he must put his trust in her. There is a terrible parting & T. leaves the room."

Now may be there is something in this. C has already fainted into E's arms & after D's [Diomede's] exit. T could enter & find her as dead & he could rave & draw his sword to kill himself, as she comes to. P. & E could be got rid of to find some smelling salts!

Then T could proceed with an enlarged version of "I'll corrupt the sentries". But I'm not particular about this & only hand it out as an idea, being still in two minds about the quartet. I believe it may be too static & spoil the impetus for the curtain. Also the words as they stand won't do. The verses I suspect should be of varying length, otherwise it could become like the verse of a hymn with each voice saying different words if you see what I mean. Get the libretto of "Rigoletto" & look at the words for that – there couldn't be a better model. Also it might not be a bad idea to look at the libretto of "Un Ballo in maschera" though I doubt if its in english. (both Ricordi) There's a good love scene between Amelia & Riccardo in Act 2.

On the whole I incline to think that the best way to end the act is for there to be an extended scene of farewell between T.& C. & for E & P just to put their noses in to see her off.

[. . .]

One thing which we musn't lose sight of is the question of form particularly the musical form of Act 2 [which] should be borne in mind. We've more or less proceeded on the plan of recit & aria the latter being more or less self contained, such as "How can I sleep" followed by "At the Haunted end of the day" (incidentally still more improved – it will end up by stealing the act but we must make the love scene the best & highwater mark not only of the act but the whole op.) & "Is anyone there" culminating in "jealousy". I feel the same pattern should be more or less kept up throughout.

I saw the Bartók [*Bluebeard's Castle*] last year & found it rather dated – marvellously scored but on the whole rather unsatisfactory dramatically being both too short & too long (its about 55 mins in all). As it was sung in Hungarian I perhaps missed many points. In fact the words of an opera I'm inclined to think (more & more) are almost as important as the music, especially in T&C where the music almost invariably stems from the words. A weakness maybe on my part. However there it is.

Our love to you both.
as ever
William

There is I think no need for you to make a dash here, better wait for Santa Restituta[1] to whom I feel I ought offer a burnt-offering for help. We managed very well before by correspondence.

1 Patron saint of the island of Ischia. Her feast is celebrated over three days in May in the village of Lacco Ameno, next to Forio.

To Christopher Hassall   14 February 1952

Casa Cirillo, Forio d'Ischia

Dear Christopher,

First to business. I've received the love-scene & like it much better. The iron-curtain had descended on my inspiration after the words "Tro. & Cress" & I did not see how it was to be raised. But I've managed to raise it an inch or two & hope shortly it will have ascended for good – but I fear that's asking too much & it is bound to crash down again at some unexpected moment catching my big toe at the bottom! All this means is that I've sketched out the first twelve lines, but at any rate I've made the transition – perhaps not very convincingly. The only slight fear is that the scene is going to be too short!

I am always in a hurry for the alterations, but I wanted to give you time to get this all important scene right. Once I'm on the other side of the Interlude the rest of the Act should be plain-sailing as I've sketched pretty well to the end. But the wait wasn't time wasted as I did that chunk of scoring, the only thing about doing that though, is that it is something I can do anywhere. We will still leave the question of the Quartet in abeyance till I get to it, but I see your points & it maybe that I had an instinct too about the verses but I didn't connect up with "In Memoriam["]. So you might work out the prose version – there really is no hurry about this as I doubt reaching that part before six weeks time.

About the opening of Act III – not as you've noted a "Rolling down to Rio" but a good old sentimental nostalgic yearning one with a lot of alls-welling from the watchmen echoing back stage from post to post & an odd remark or two from the other soldiers. As I think I mentioned I want it to connect up with "No sign"[1] acting as the introduction to that. The words for that can wait till you come.

I'm glad you appreciated [Berg's] "Wozzeck" & "Mathis".[2] There's no doubt they are two masterpieces of their time – one really can't mention "Budd" I fear in the same sentence – not that mind you it has'nt its moments, but it has'nt the consistency or substance of greatness that the other two have.

Wozzeck I've not seen on the stage for twenty years but have heard 3. or 4 concert perfs. since & I've got the score with me just in case! Mathis

---

1 Cressida's 'No answering sign on the walls'.
2 Hindemith's opera *Mathis der Maler*.

we heard in Rome last year & you'll be able to hear it at Edinburgh this year. How splendid about your play. I'm delighted & you must feel very cock-a-hoop.

About Alan Frank & the O.U.P. This is a tricky business.[1] The first point being that I've been with the O.U.P right from the beginning of my career & they have always behaved well & I don't exactly have the face to leave them now for no reason at all.

I was approached about 6 months ago by big-boy Boosey himself & I wrote him what I've just said. Now this new fumbling by [Anthony] Gishford (who incidentally I don't much care for) means that I didn't fob of[f] Boose[y] as well as I imagined.

Now, without doubt, there is a lot, in fact everything, to be said for B & H [Boosey & Hawkes] for this particular work. The O.U.P possess no operas – thats not quite true they have the original & uncommercial version of "Boris" which is hardly ever done in that version nearly always the Rimsky[-Korsakov version][2] – & that great commercial proposition V.W.s Pils. Prog. [Vaughan Williams's *Pilgrim's Progress*]

Now B.H. possess a large number of successful operas. Strauss Bartók as well as more popular ones. I believe the basis for launching a new opera is this kind of bargaining – we'll perform "Budd" for instance 4 times at £25 a time if you'll let us have 6 perfs. of Rosenkavalier for £10 a time instead of £60 a time.

Not only has B.& H that card, but they are highly organised operationally speaking the world-over. & doubtless could guarantee T&C. (that is if it isnt a most awful flop) 200 in the 1st season. – like they have with the Stravinsky [*The Rake's Progress*] & doubtless with "Budd". The O.U.P have neither of these cards. & Frank is inclined to exaggerate how well known my name is amongst the operatic world – but the fact is – is that it isnt at all – in fact my reputation abroad is uncomfortably small as far as I can gather. Whether that is so or not my name is not enough to launch an opera on & we need an operatic "Helen", though god forbid we write 1000 operas.

I pointed this out to A.F when I told him about Bs approach & it just dawned on him that the operatic field is a quite different one to the

---

1 Boosey & Hawkes had made another approach to Walton regarding the possible publication of his music by them.
2 Over the past half-century, Musorgsky's original score of *Boris Godunov* has almost totally supplanted Rimsky-Korsakov's later version. But Walton's assessment at the time of writing was correct.

symphonic one. He nevertheless felt that some special effort would have to be made, & on the whole I'm inclined to stay with the O.U.P even if we don't get quite the same out of them as from B&H.

Also being suspicious minded would'nt B&.H do the dirt on one & sit on the bloody thing as being possibly the only rival to B.B.? Maybe I'm too suspicious!

What do you think now that you have more or less got the facts? I think we ought to keep an eye open on the Coronation! Another March! & this time a really singable tune in the middle, with words! I ought to have done it with [the] old one & then I was young compar[a]tively innocent & high minded in 1937 now I approach my 50th birthday March 29th things have changed!

So let me have the date when settled.

Even if you ca'nt get a business allowance the £25 should be enough for a fortnight or so. We are descending to a maccaroni & water diet more or less, so as to save to come out in the autumn to complete T&C. & I fear I shan't get farther than the 1st sc of Act III if as far by the time I leave. And I['m] sure I'll get no allowance next time from the Treasury & I doubt if you['ll] get one either. All the same I've suspected something of this kind might happen so have been saving (or rather Su. has) bits & pieces here & there enough to last at least 4 months. But not a word. Luckily Unesco have invited us to a 10 day conference in Venice at the end of Sept. all expenses paid & what I calculate my earning[s] would [be] for that period. [. . .]

[. . .]

Hope you get rid of your cough & that Ev[e']s operation will be successful. Not very pleasant I fear.

Love from us both

Yrs ever

William

To Walter Legge 3 March 1952

Casa Cirillo, Forio d'Ischia

My dear Walter,

I am sorry to have neglected writing you for so long, but my news of the op. [opera] was so depressing that I did not feel like writing anyone. Libretto trouble as usual, at last I think more or less satisfactorily ironed out & the end of Act II is at last in sight. I now understand why noone has attempted an opera with "love" interest since Puccini. Scyllas and Charybdises surround one at every bar. Give me Buddery every time – or even plain rape. Anyhow most of Act II is now scored as well.

I now aim to have it ready for the Coronation Season. Also I've got my eye on another Coronation March which as yet has only got as far as the title "Orb and Sceptre".

I'm sorry you could'nt get to see us & also, as Sue will have told you we missed Elizabeth.

It's good news that Karajan[1] is doing the "Symph" & I shall try to listen-in. Only hope it is not on the "Terza programma" [BBC Third Programme] which is on micro-waves & impossible to get [here] [. . .]

About the [Covent Garden] Co's agreement regarding T&C. I cannot grant them the score & parts as the O.U.P. are part owners, so I will send the copy to Alan Frank to see what he thinks.

[. . .]

I hope K. [Karajan] is conducting "Scap" [*Scapino*] on the tour some-time.

The only things of interest we've heard at the [Teatro] San Carlo [in Naples] were L'Assedio di Corinto, which is the only Rossini opera-seria I've heard [–] very interesting & full of lovely things divinely sung by [Renata] Tebaldi[2] [–] & Padmavati Rousell [Albert Roussel's *Padmâvatî*] which is quite interesting to hear if not an absolute masterpiece. Both well sung, but the productions – Cov. Gar. is heaven [compared] to the San Carlo!

I'm delighted you've got Harry Blech to do one of the Mysore con-certs. I'm sure he'll do well – I'm glad Karajan is taking on the other concerts. It is time he got going properly in London.

We don't return till the end of June. By which time pray heaven the end of this op. will be either accomplished or in sight.

as ever
William

1 Herbert von Karajan. The Austrian conductor's performances of *Belshazzar's Feast* in Vienna in June 1948 were in Walton's view among the best he had ever heard, but Karajan's subsequent interest in Walton's music did not extend beyond eventually conduct-ing the First Symphony in Rome in December 1953. Neither Karajan, nor Legge, nor OUP informed Walton that this was to take place, so the composer was not present.
2 Italian soprano. Maria Callas's only serious rival in the operas of Verdi, Puccini and other Italian composers.

P.S. When do the Symph records appear – For March 29ᵗʰ my 50ᵗʰ birthday?

To Christopher Hassall 6 March 1952

Casa Cirillo, Forio d'Ischia

Dear Christopher,

I trust you are not having too anxious a time over Eve's operation, & that all is going well & she is by now on the way to recuperation.

Thanks for Lewis's essay which I find extremely interesting, especially about Cs "fears". I'm glad we've made another reference to them as they were only just touched on in Act I.

Thanks also for the extra verses which after all I didn't need. I'm sorry to have put you to useless trouble.

[. . .]

Now a word on the Interlude.¹ Perhaps you'd reconsider it, in fact I wish you'd write the music as well! Because I'm fair flummoxed by it.

I think there should be some musical reference to what is going on or shall be, in the bed, some kind of orgasm or not? And to fit it in the outline as it stands is the difficulty. And the length, it can't be too short or it will be reffered to as a "premature ejaculation"!

And the timing for the "distant drum"?

[. . .]

So let me hear from you as soon as you can. The verses first & you[r] views on the other problems will do a bit later.

Dont you think it would be a good idea if you brought out Eve here to recuperate[?] There are two beds in the guest-room. so you won't have hotel expenses this time only the journey. So that £25 could be eked out a fair bit.

as ever
William

---

1 Between Scenes 1 and 2 of Act II (the 'pornographic interlude').

To Christopher Hassall   25 April [1952]

Casa Cirillo, Forio d'Ischia

Dear Christopher,
   [. . .]
   We are looking forward to your arrival on the 10th & trust that nothing like "mumps" will put you off.
   Unfortunately Pasquale[1] fell off a ladder about 10 days ago[,] luckily didn't break anything, but is in bed with bad bruising to his leg & he can't walk for some time. Misfortunes never coming singly, my father-in-law has come to stay & idiotically I allowed him to drive my Bentley to the baths for his cure & he of course charged the first rock he could find & has broken the oil shaft – a major operation.
   Don't let this put you off. We have Don P's sister to look after us so all's well on that score.
   Yours ever
   William

To David Webster   [postmarked: Forio d'Ischia,
[postcard]   18 May 1952]

[in reply to telegram dated 10 May 1952: HOW IS THE BABY? DAVID]

The "baby" is progressing & ought to be fully clothed by about Xmas, certainly out of it[s] swaddling clothes in fact should be possible for the baby show next June 53.
   Love from us both
   William

To Christopher Hassall   10 June [1952]

Casa Cirillo, Forio d'Ischia

Dear Christopher,
   Thank you for your letter & notes on Cs piece. I shall be approaching it, I hope in a day or two.

---

1 Pasquale Castaldi, the caretaker of the Convento San Francesco and owner of Casa Cirillo. On their first encounter in 1949, Walton had instantly christened him Don Pasquale, after Donizetti's opera.

[. . .]

I had a talk with D. [David] Webster from Milan. Owing to Harewood's[1] royal connections he has wangled that the Queen has commanded an opera for the Coronation season. It is I need hardly say not T&C. but a new one [*Gloriana*] on "Elizabeth & Essex" by Billy Britten. How he is going to get it done in 9 months (it must go into rehearsal at the end of March) I don't know. But genius will out. [William] Plomer,[2] Auden tells me is doing the libretto which is not ready yet. Auden's just returned from Paris where he'd seen both B.B'[s] & said he thought the opera absolutely the end & hadn't gone down too well.

So D.W. as far as I could gather, tactfully hoped that T&C would'nt be ready for the Coronation Season, but if it were could it open the season? That of course means having everything ready by the end of next Jan. instead of end of March, a vital two months difference & [I] doubt if it can be done even working 16 hours a day. So I think it is better not to hurry it & wait till the opening of the autumn season. It is all slightly irritating. B.B. has to give up all his engagements & Cov. Gar, which is already broke has to compensate him.

But there it is[,] we've no friends at Court so we must put on a smiling face & pretend we like it. But we shall not have such a glamourous opening as we might have had in next June. what with all the visitors distinguished & otherwise for the Coronation. Anyhow budder them!

We dined with Auden last night. Very aimable & wants to go thru' T&C with me. I think I will as it will be interesting to get an outside opinion, though I hate doing it, playing the thing as badly as I do.

It is very good of you to act as our temporary secretary [. . .] I hope the play is proceeding well. We are back on July 7th & are going to R.F.H [the Royal Festival Hall] on the 8th to hear "Facade"[,] [Schoenberg's] Pierrot Lunaire & a work by [Peter Racine] Fricker[3] – an amusing programme which you might like to come to.

---

1 The Earl of Harewood, a cousin of Queen Elizabeth II, was a director of the Royal Opera House, Covent Garden, from 1951 to 1953 and again from 1969 to 1972. He was also on the House's administrative staff from 1953 to 1960. He later became Managing Director of the Edinburgh International Festival, Sadler's Wells Opera and English National Opera, and edited and updated several editions of *Kobbé's Complete Opera Book* (compiled originally by the German-born critic Gustave Kobbé).
2 English poet, writer and opera librettist. He also wrote the libretti of Britten's three Church Parables between 1964 and 1968.
3 English composer, whose moderate modernist style, influenced by Schoenberg, brought him to prominence in the years after the Second World War.

I'm glad you both enjoyed your stay – it was reciprocal & got a lot under way[.]

With love to you both

William

P.S 2<u>nd</u> speech p6 Act III. Is'nt it now to[o] reminiscent of the love scene Act II. We have had perhaps enough of the gods!

To Lord Waverley[1]   7 November 1952

Casa Cirillo, Forio d'Ischia

My dear Lord Waverly,

Thank you for your letter. It has long been on my conscience that owing to my lengthy absences, I have been unable to carry out my duties as a Director of Covent Garden. I did mention last year, I think, that perhaps I should resign, but owing to one thing or another, the moment was not propitious.

So now it would be convenient to me to formally retire at the Annual Meeting, & trust that I shall be re-elected again next year. I am away till next October, but after that shall be in England for a considerable length of time.

With kind regards

Yours sincerely,

William Walton

To Walter Legge   12 November 1952

Casa Cirillo, Forio d'Ischia

My dear Walter,

I hear from the Brit. Cou. in Rome that the Symph is not included in the Herbert Von K programmes. Can this be so? You might ask him if he is going to do it (& I shall be very dissapointed if he's not) if he would be so kind as to let me know when & where.

Not much news, if any. Lord Waverly wrote me & asked if I wouldn't like to resign from Cov. Gar. so I said I would. I shall be asked to rejoin

1   Chairman of the Directors of the Royal Opera House, Covent Garden (formerly Sir John Anderson).

next Nov. when I'm back for a long time. I don't think it portends anything.

Is there any chance of seeing you & Liz [Elisabeth Schwarzkopf] in these parts?

Our love to you both & Herbert

yours ever

William

To Christopher Hassall   29 December 1952

Casa Cirillo, Forio d'Ischia

My dear Christopher,

After a spot of bother with the "Virgin's womb" (the kind of trouble I always seem to get into – don't tell the Archbishop!) the Te Deum[1] is complete & both full & piano scores dispatched. Quite a lot of work. It is not too bad for an occasional piece & should be right for the ceremony. The March is under way but not too bright as yet. Anyhow I hope to be rid of it in the next ten days. Everything I fear takes a bit longer than I think.

Now for T&C. I am sending you my old copy with the notes I've made on Act III. They will give you possibly a better idea than if I write.

[. . .]

I am all for shortening the end & think that your solution is probably right. However what happens to E. Should she stab herself during the chorus bit as T is being carried off? & then Cress begin from "Evadne dying".

What about the bit at the end of Act II about which I wrote you before? bottom p 18 new version.

This is about all for the moment. I long to hear what [Ernest] Newman says about it & what he suggests.

With all best wishes for you both for 1951.

as ever

William

---

1 Commissioned for the Coronation Service of Queen Elizabeth II in Westminster Abbey on 2 June 1953.

To David Webster 22 January 1953

Casa Cirillo, Forio d'Ischia

My dear David,

As noone has acknowledged my letter of resignation (purely temporary I hope) from the Board of Directors I don't know whether it was accepted or not. Presumably it was, which dose'nt prevent me from writing to ask if I may have four tickets for the Coronation Gala[1] on June 8th for ourselves & Heifetz & his wife. Paid for, of course, by me.

T&C after some good progress, had to be abandoned for some six weeks, while I indulged in an orgy of Coronation music – a superb Te Deum, a spanking March[2] & a piece for Aldeburgh.[3] Quite a feat for me to have got it over so quickly! So I am now back on T&C.

Walter [Legge] sent me a note asking for an approximate date as he wants to keep Elizabeth & Gedda[4] free. Perhaps the opening of the summer season in May 54 would be best as in Feb those two are at the Scala & in March when they would be free C.G. goes on tour, so it would seem the best solution. What do you think?

How has the season been going at C.G.? Well I hope.

There is a fairly enterprising one at the [Teatro] San Carlo [in Naples]. At the New Year we heard "Salome" preceded by Schonberg's [Schoenberg's] "Von Heute auf Morgen" which I found to be unexpectedly captivating.

If, as I expect you may have been bombarded with requests to put on Bartok's "Bluebeard" [Bartók's *Bluebeard's Castle*] the Schönberg would go admirably before it. It is short[,] about 45 to 50 mins & easy to stage, one simple set. It would be best to get the two singers who sang in Naples (the other two parts could be done by our locals as they were here) – Willy Krammer & Lidya Stix both of whom are first rate. [Hermann] Scherchen conducted & gave a marvellous performance of both the Schönberg & the Strauss. He would be equally good for the Bartok.

I should think they would be both quite cheap productions the

1 The world première of Britten's *Gloriana*.
2 *Orb and Sceptre*.
3 A variation on the theme 'Sellinger's Round'. Each of the six variations in the set commissioned by the Aldeburgh Festival was by a different English composer, among them Britten, Tippett and Lennox Berkeley.
4 Nicolai Gedda, internationally famous Swedish tenor.

orchestral rehearsals being the heaviest item (though the Schonberg is small not I imagine more than 30 players). There is as you know a fairly large & growing faction for Schonberg and I should say you could fill the house four times with the double bill.

But I forget I'm out of it & it is not for me to make suggestions!

After a very wet autumn we are now enjoying weeks of uninterrupted sunshine, though however there is a very cold wind.

We are giving a party on June 9ᵗʰ after the Heifetz concert I think thats the date so put it down provisionally in your little book.

Let me have a word from you.

Sue is well & sends her love

as ever

William

To Christopher Hassall — 4 February 1953

Casa Cirillo, Forio d'Ischia

Dear Christopher,

Forgive the delay in answering, but I've had to write a short piece 3 mins for Ben.[Britten] He's had the idea of asking some five composers to write variations on a theme by Byrd[1] & asked me to do the finale. I didn't see very well how I could refuse, so have got it over as soon as possible. It is for Aldeburgh Coronation festival celebrations. That is if after this appalling disaster,[2] there will be any. I'd just posted the piece & then bought a paper to see what was going on. I imagine Ben's house is completely inu[n]dated.

I am returning to London on March 17ᵗʰ to record "Orb & Sceptre" on the 18ᵗʰ either morning or afternoon, I don't as yet know which & shall return here the 19ᵗʰ or 20ᵗʰ. Kingsway Hall is the place & you might come along to hear it & we could have an hour or twos talk & possibly a play through of what I've done.

We return to Lowndes Cott. on May 24ᵗʰ till June 21ˢᵗ. I've not yet heard whether we're invited to the [Coronation] Service, but presumably McKie[3] is doing his best. Anyhow it will be as well to be at the rehearsal

1 'Sellinger's Round'.
2 Flooding in Suffolk.
3 Sir William McKie, Organist and Director of Music at Westminster Abbey.

of the "Te Deum" etc. & Heifetz plays the Vl. Con for the 1ˢᵗ time in England on June 9ᵗʰ. You'd better get tickets now if you want to hear it.

Why have you bought a house in the Vale of unhealth¹ – very damp in winter?

I'm glad about the play & that you've had no back-chat with the Dean & Chapter. You will be able to decide on March 18ᵗʰ whether you will have need of "O & S".

[. . .]

It was sad about Eddie [Edward Marsh], but he had a fairly good innings, though everyone these days seem[s] to have to be 90 & never stop writing chilly symphonies!² It may be just as well he didn't live to see Pandarus.³

Our love to you both

as ever

William

P.S. Read the life of Puccini by George Marek. Most interesting & instructive. I'm an angel in comparison to the time he gave his librettists!

To Christopher Hassall   22 February [1953]

Casa Cirillo, Forio d'Ischia

Dear Christopher.

Thank you for the bits & pieces & for the pleasant news [&] for the Zucherelli. It was nice of Eddie.

I fly back on March 16ᵗʰ[,] return on the 19ᵗʰ. The recording is at Kingsway Hall on the 18ᵗʰ at 2'oclock.

We might dine together at Lowndes Cottage on the evening of the 16ᵗʰ & we could try & straiten out any odds & ends about T&C. I can't think of any major snags but I'll try & cook up something for you!!

Meanwhile I finished orchestrating the whole love duet Act II but have not taken the plunge yet into the interlude. I've also orchestrated all to date of Act III & am now back on the grind so to speak.

Eve will enjoy this riddle rejected by the New Statesman for "This England", sent in by someone from the Children's Corner of a provincial newspaper[.]

1 Hassall's new address was The Old Cottage, The Vale of Health, Hampstead.
2 A reference to Vaughan Williams's *Sinfonia antartica*.
3 See p. 47, n. 3.

I am long & thin
I am covered in skin
My head
    is sometimes red
I am in three parts
I go into tarts   WHAT AM I?

"Rhubarb" believe it or not is the answer[.]
Yrs ever
William

To Christopher Hassall   5 May [1953]

Casa Cirillo, Forio d'Ischia

Dear Christopher.

I've not written as I've been scoring Act I so have had no reason to pester you. It's pretty tough going & rather slow going & needless to say I've not got as much done as I'd hoped. However I've got to "Is Cress. a slave" & managed to knock off nearly 3 mins. which is a great help to this opening sc. which I felt was overlong & made the Act lop sided. But its meant a lot of re-writing – however all an improvement.

I shall be back on the 20ᵗʰ & instead of returning here as originally planned in mid-June, we are going to the cottage at Notley which Larry [Laurence Olivier] has lent us. He was too tired & worried for me to bother him about T&C. but he read the script & we were about to get down to some hard thinking about the last 20 mins when he was re-called. However we should be able to do this at Notley when we can all have a series of sessions & try & polish it off.

I should like to finish the scoring of Act I & II before we come back here at the end of Sept. And if everything is fixed Xmas should see it more or less in the bag.

However I've been asked to do the music for the "Romeo [and Juliet]" film[1] & to fill my depleted purse I want to do it, & they will pay most of it here. But as yet I don't know the dates when I shall be needed, but I fear it may cut into T&C. But we'll see.

Our love
William

---

1 Planned by Olivier, but never made.

I hope this reaches you. I've not got your new address.

To Dora Foss

29 May 1953

Lowndes Cottage, Lowndes Place, s.w.1

My dear Dora,

I am dreadfully upset to read of the death of poor Hubert.

I'd only just heard that he had been so ill & I was looking forward to coming to see him as soon as the Coronation was past.

He was always such a staunch supporter & I can never forget what a help he was to me in the early days or for that matter, always.

The only small comfort would appear that his death was sudden & that he didn't suffer any lingering agony.

Susana & I send you all our deepest sympathy in your sad loss.

as ever
William

To David Webster

22 September 1953

Lowndes Cottage, Lowndes Place, s.w.1

Dear David,

I've been talking to Isabel Lambert[1] about the scenery for Troilus and Cressida. After consulting Kay [K, i.e. Kenneth Clark][2] we have all come to the conclusion that if Henry Moore[3] won't do it, she's the best person for it. Could you write to her and say that Covent Garden would be willing to pay for the sketches, regardless of whether we used them or not, as of course we may not like them when it comes down to it. I talked to Henry Moore last night on the telephone and he seemed very undecided about whether he wanted to do it or not, but much more favourably inclined than he was when I saw him last. Whether this is a good thing or not I can't make up my mind. We can hardly ask him to make sketches and then turn them down. But we could do that with Isabel.

I hope you had a strenuous and enjoyable time in America.

1 English artist and designer; widow of Constant Lambert.
2 Walton's secretary Sheila Perry, who typed this letter, evidently misunderstood the abbreviation in his handwritten draft.
3 English sculptor, artist and designer.

We are just off to Ischia, so please write to us there: Casa Cirillo, Via Cesotta, Forio d'Ischia, Italy.

Love from us both
Yours ever
William

To David Webster   [autumn 1953]

[postcard]

Forio d'Ischia

I've a telegram from Jane [Clark][1] saying that Henry Moore definitely won't do T&C, so you can proceed with Isobel [Isabel] Lambert, with a clear conscience. I don't think that I'm going to be late, in fact should be ready in May – all going well, which, of course, it wont[.]

love
William

To Christopher Hassall   [autumn 1953]

[Casa Cirillo, Forio d'Ischia]

Dear Chris,

[. . .]

After polishing off Act I I shall try & do the same with Act II & hope to get it out of the way by the New Year so I shall have till June for the rest of Act III. As the first part is already finished & scored the task of getting through in time ought not to be insuperable.

Wystan [Auden] is here till the end of Nov. He has a lot to say about Act III. But more of this anon when he's put down his ideas on paper. His main idea is that there should be a grand quintet so that everyone has a look in. I've an idea that the curtain should be much quicker after that & it should come thus.

Dio [Diomede] says at the moment[:] as for C. she has her uses. I propose he should say to the soldiers – "Take her. she's all yours" or something like that & the curtain comes down as they are about to pounce [on] her.

---

1 Wife of Kenneth Clark. In the past there had been an affair between her and Walton.

Perhaps a bit brutal, but makes it more dramatic & less Isolderish [Isolde-ish]. However we'll see.

As ever

William

I've written DW. about H.M's [Henry Moore's] refusal so all is clear for you to have fun with IL [Isabel Lambert] & get [her] to make some sketches quickly[.]

To David Webster   28 October 1953

Casa Cirillo, Forio d'Ischia

My dear David,

I am sorry to have been dilatory at answering your letter, but scoring at the moment has been taking precedence over all else.

On the whole the scoring has gone well & I shall be through with Act I by about Nov. 15th. About two thirds of Act II is already done, but I've still the interlude & the last three mins to write, so that, I hope will be complete in every respect by Xmas. This will mean that the Piano score (which Roy Douglas is doing) of Acts I & II will be available in photostat say by the end of January '54. So those concerned, if & when we have decided on them, can have their copies for study by then. The first 15 mins of Act III is scored & arranged for piano. So that leaves me with the remaining part of Act III to do, say between the New Year & June, which should not be impossible even for me.

Unfortunately I am still far from happy about the rest of the libretto of Act III. but luckily Auden & Kallman are here till the end of Nov. & theyve kindly offered to do something about it & I am sure we shall get it right in the end. I suppose it is slightly unethical on my part but I will square it somehow with Christopher H. but keep it quiet for the moment.[1]

I am glad you agree about Isobel Lambert. It struck me when I saw "Tiresias"[2] that she would be excellent for T&C. So I hope negotiations are under way. I've had a letter from H.M. [Henry Moore] crying off & on

---

1 Walton was not convinced that Hassall had the necessary technical and poetic skill to write the text for a culminating Quintet towards the end of Act III, and approached Auden to provide at least a provisional version for Hassall to emulate. Eventually the Quintet was to become the Sextet beginning with Diomede's words 'Troy, false of heart, yet fair!'
2 Ballet by Constant Lambert, first performed in 1951, with designs by Isabel Lambert.

the whole I'm not sorry. There are already too many beginners in this opera.

Regarding the casting. – Malcolm [Sargent,[1] as conductor] is, I think decided on, but you might have a word with him. This is what is needed.

Calkas (Bass)	Daghvell [Dahlberg]
*Antenor (Baritone)	?
Troilus (tenor)	Gedda
Pandarus (tenor buffo)	Parry Jones ?
Cressida (soprano)	Schwarzkopf
*Evadne (Mezzo-soprano)	?
*Horaste (Baritone)	?
Diomede (Baritone)	?

*These are all small parts. Evadne's is slightly larger & in fact has rather an important bit in Act III so she should be as good as we can find.

I'm not quite happy between ourselves about P.J. What is the voice like now or rather by next year? Also Pand: is an elegant middle-aged dandy & I'm not sure P.J. is quite the stuff for that. However I've written anything higher than F to be sung "falsetto". He might on the other hand be very good.

Gedda I'm not absolutely sold on – he seems a bit lightweight, though I'm told he's developing rapidly.

Diomede seems to be the real problem. He must not only sing but be good looking enough to make it seem possible for a girl to fall for him in five minutes. It struck [me] when seeing "Arabella" that Uhde[2] was the man & I'm told his english is good. But that makes three foreigners in the cast. I'm all ears for your suggestions.

Then there's the question of Larry. He is I think expecting & wanting to produce it. But of course he can't read music, nevertheless I think he would be all right if he had an underling who could & he would lend a cachet. Anyhow let me have a word sometime.

Love from us both.

William.

1 Sir Malcolm Sargent, who had conducted the first performance of *Belshazzar's Feast* in 1931, was at this time Chief Conductor of London's Promenade Concerts (the 'Proms'), a post he held from 1948 to his death in 1967. He was also Chief Conductor of the BBC Symphony Orchestra from 1950 to 1957.
2 Hermann Uhde, German baritone. He appeared with great success in the role of Mandryka in Richard Strauss's *Arabella* during the Bavarian State Opera's appearances at Covent Garden in 1953.

To Henry Moore   5 December 1953

Casa Cirillo, Forio d'Ischia

Dear Henry,

I am so sorry to have been so dilatory in answering your letter. I more than understand what you feel about T.& C – I almost feel the same myself! Though I can't pretend not to be slightly dissapointed I think you are quite right.

I'm glad you are recovered from your operation & are back at work. We've been & are blessed by an extraordinarily fine winter – continued sun for more than a month, though doubtless we shall pay for it later. We saw K. & J [Kenneth and Jane Clark] for a few hours last week – very enjoyable.

Our love to you both.
Yours ever
William

To Sir Laurence Olivier   [mid-December 1953]

Casa Cirillo, Forio d'Ischia

My dear Larry,

It would appear that owing to some mental abberation on my part I had not told you about Isobel Lambert. For some reason or other I'd got it quite fixed in my head that we had discussed her but I now realise we had'nt & I do apologise for having talked to her without your prior approval.

I didn't realise that you definitely always worked in conjunction with Roger [Furse][1] & I'm quite happy about him to do the scenery if you prefer him.

Lambert is very good – her work very normal but with a good deal of distinction & personality. She did Constant's last ballet "Tieresias" [*Tiresias*] & "Electra" [Richard Strauss's *Elektra*] for Cov. Gar. Both were excellent & it struck me when seeing them that she might be good for T&C. She is I'm told very practical & technically efficient. On the other [hand] she is a slightly awkward personality inclined to giggle for no particular reason, which is rather disconcerting I find.

---

1 English artist and designer.

Negotiations I may say are at an extremely tentative stage – 'if you will do some sketches & we like them' that kind of stage, so there will be no difficulty in putting her off if you should really dissaprove.

Personally I'm for her rather than Roger & so is, incidentally K. Clark who was in Naples the other week. But I am extremely sorry about not having let you know. I've been working madly but am already about a fortnight behind schedule.

The weather has been unbelievably fine & warm. No rain for six weeks – very serious.

How are you both? We hope the play has settled down to a long & prosperous run.

Our love to you both & respects from Don P. [Pasquale]

yrs ever.

William

To David Webster   26 December 1953

Casa Cirillo, Forio d'Ischia

My dear David,

I am sorry to have been dilatory in answering your letter of Nov 20th but I hope not so sorry as you ought to be for not having answered mine of about Oct 20th!!

About Larry – it was pure absentmindedness on my part – I definitely thought I had talked to him about Isobel Lambert. I've written to him explaining & that I've no objection to having Furse if he'd prefer him though I would prefer Lambert who I think is a fresher if not so experienced a talent. I've also written to Isobel L. explaining what has happened & that she may not be doing it, if Larry wants Furse. Because I think it would be a mistake to drop Larry in order to have Lambert. I had no idea Larry was so tied up with Furse. But however there it is [–] having put my foot in it I've tried to withdraw as gracefully as possible all round.

I'm a bit behind my schedule as I decided it would be wiser to revise the 2nd Act[.] It is tightened up considerably & I've made some beneficial "cuts" so it will now be a bit under 45 mins. The 1st Act is down to under 43 mins – the last I hope, about 38 mins. I expect to finish the full score of Act II by the end of Jan, so the Pfte scores of Acts I & II should be available fairly soon after that. I doubt if I shall have all of Act III in

Pfte score by the beginning of June, but I should think 2/3 would be available & the rest will follow at the latest by the end of July which should give those concerned time to learn the last 10 mins or so. The end is still a bit hazy but is gradually getting clearer.

I see you've had Udhe [Uhde] for "Lohengrin" so presumably we can get him for Diomede. Walter told me that Elizabeth is booked for America from Nov 10th to Dec 20th '54. so either we shall have to crowd the perfs together before she goes or find someone who can take her part. That is I think about all.

Our best wishes for the New Year.

yours ever

William

To Christopher Hassall   14 January 1954

Casa Cirillo, Forio d'Ischia

Dear Chris:

I have been hoping to hear from you as I have now reached as far as I can go regarding the orchestration. I am particularly anxious for the moment to have the bit of dialogue I mentioned covering "Put on" Act II p6, as that is delaying the dispatch of the rest of the score – also of the new version of "We were alone" Act II p.18. with the additional vows of "eternal love" etc. – that is if you approve the idea.

[. . .]

As to the suggestions I sent you about the rest of the Act [III], if you really are not convinced by them dramatically don't hesitate to take a firm line & have nothing to do with them. I'm not absolutely sold on Wystan [Auden]'s Quintet in fact it may possibly be quite out of keeping with the construction of the rest of the Opera, and I hope you've not embarked on it without arguing it out first with me.[1] What I do feel is that from III–9 on should be action without interruption[.] Even I think now that the duet III–13 "Time has not [yet passed]" should be regarded as an impediment to the action which of course it is & that if something more is wanted it should be a few lines after "What breathless joy". Having sent you the only copy of the suggestions I am now a bit hazy as

1 Understandably, Hassall had been upset by the news of Auden's involvement in the libretto.

to exactly what they were. But I do think the opera should be brought to a close on III–17. And if you don't like the idea of Cress: being seized by the soldiers for "garrison hack", would this idea be better? After Dio [Diomede] says "Soldiers take her" or something Cress should scream "Father" & Calk [Calkas] should break away from his guard & stab her followed by the curtain. Evadne is a bloody bore & I don't see the absolute necessity of her treachery being brought to Cress's notice, but knowing nothing of the rules of dramatic construction I'm doubtless wrong. However do let me here [*sic*] from you very soon, and now that I'm starting again on Act III a solution to all our problems may vouchsafe itself.

I've had a letter from Larry – without absolutely saying so – he says in so many words that especially under the circumstances he would prefer Furse for the obvious reasons. I think we had better agree, though I'd prefer Isobel[,] maddening though she may be & after all Furse is very good – knows his job & especially in conjunction with Larry.

Of course it will be too irritating if after all Larry finds himself unable to produce it for one reason or another & we find ourselves saddled with Furse without Larry.

But we shall just have to bear it. He's not heard from Webster nor indeed have I had a reply to my letter of the end of Oct regarding casting.

Best wishes for '54
as ever
William

P.S Regarding love-duet III p 7–8. Cres: "If there is blame" do you mean this "aside" to be sung at the same time as Dio's "No no my beloved" p. 7. I fancy not. Don't you think the lines – "A fathers anger - - - - - - hectic way" would be more appropriate in Cress's speech III – p. 5? I believe they would & the change from Tro[ilus] to Dio would not be quite so blatant if the audience felt it was more fear of father than entirely a bit of sex.

P.T.O
Before completely deciding about the scenery perhaps it would be better to wait & ask Larry & Vivien [Leigh][1] to come & see Isobel's exhibition which I understand is taking place next month, so L. can have an idea of what her work is like. Though I may add as far as I remember her paintings are quite unlike her stage sets. I have written her saying what has cropped up & that she may have to step down.

1 English actress, married at this time to Sir Laurence Olivier.

To Christopher Hassall   January 1?th [1954]1

[Forio d'Ischia]

My dear Christopher,

Thank you so much for the pantechnicon which arrived this morning. I wrote you yesterday so our letters have crossed again. At once before going into any detail, let me say how grateful I am [to you] for taking so much trouble over this new version [of part of Act III] & how much better it seems to be after having gone through it twice. It surely is an improvement?

The only thing is that you seem to have over-estimated Wystan [Auden]'s participation. That he did anything is entirely due to my asking him to look at Act III as I was'nt entirely happy about it. He took it & when next I saw him he said that both he & Chester [Kallman] had seperately reached the conclusion that a Quintet or Sextet or some concerted piece was needed. After some discussion I said, granted that a Sextet is the thing how & what is the proper way to lay it out because I don't know how it should be and am not at all sure that Chris H. (that's you) knows either (perhaps presumptiously assuming that you did'nt, though you remember we failed miserably when we tried to lay out a Quartet towards the end of Act II?) I continued – can't you do it now. just sketch out how the rhymes etc should balance etc & C.H. will cotton on in a trice. No, he said he could'nt do that & that in any case he would [not] dare to presume on to somebody else's territory & that he had a high regard for you & would'nt risk hurting his relations with you. Anyhow in the end I persuaded him that it would be of great assistance to us both if he would just do an outline of how he thought this sextet could come about & he reluctantly in the end said he'd try, but that it was to be considered nothing else but what is known in the film world as a guide-track & that is how & what I hoped you would take it for.

He never meant that I should set it & I never for an instant have ever thought of doing [so] & even less now. I thought you would do something on the lines laid down and only thought of it as being a way to help you do something which I imagined you'd never done before & that it would be a model for you to work on, for that is what it was intended to be & nothing more. And I may add he was terrified of being thought to be interfering & generally putting his foot in it, so to speak, with you.

In fact it is all my thought [fault], but I thought it would be a help &

---

1   The question-marked date is as written by Walton.

I hope this somewhat tardy & inexplicit explanation will clear things in your mind. I felt like Evadne: "It was I who stuck a pin in his letters".

But now to come down to it if there is to be a Sextet you will have to write it. On the other hand as I said in my last letter but one if you are not convinced about it (and being in uncertain mind about it myself you will now have to convince me) don't do it. It's sure not to be right if you are unconvinced.

You've certainly done a Dr Wolken cure on it & I'm sure that Act [III] has dropped more than 12 lbs! And I think it may have to be fattened up a bit here & there. Perhaps top of p. 2 E. "What breathless etc." Pan [Pandarus]'s new bit is excellent & justifies him & there should be possibly some more at the end as well [. . .]

We have both been smitten with the same idea that you should come here for some days & please don't refuse my invitation about the fare.

I said in whatever letter it was – the end of Feb – but perhaps the end of March beginning of April would be better, because by then I should be through with Dio's & Cress. love duet & any thorny problems which arise after that could be so much more quickly & satisfactorily resolved if you were here.

At the moment I'm feeling, probably rashly, fairly optimistic about finishing, by the time we are due to leave at the end of July. The orchestration of the remainder should not take at the most more than a month but I hope to have that done too before I leave.

One thing while we [are] at it[,] the fight between Tro & Dio. Is it right for Dio this great warrior to call for help when attacked by a youth? Dos'ent it belittle him somewhat. If we want the soldiers on he could call them on when he sentences Calk:. [Calkas]

We are indeed truly sorry to hear about the "bricks in the bladder"[,] nothing can I'm told be more painful & I hope they were small & smooth & not blocks of granite. Anyhow thank you again & we look forward to seeing you in about 10 weeks time & don't be a "mutt" about my offer.

Our love to you both.
Your[s] ever
William

P.S. I'm sorry you've been afflicted with Mr Marks[1] marital affairs. I

1 Possibly J. B. Marks, the Waltons' accountant (see p. 285).

knew she was liable to slight "dippiness" now & then & I suppose she's had a "bout". Anyhow I hope he's being efficient about your affairs. As for your saying Dallas [Bower] is flourishing, – believe me – I'm sorry to say – he's sunk himself beyond anyone's help as I fear you will see within the next months. I hope I'm wrong but fear not.

P.P.S. I think I'm going to be booted out of the P.R S. as they sent an ultimatum [. . .] that I'd got to be back by June. Why? Not because of the visit of the Queen Mother? Surely Sir Art. [Arthur Bliss][1] can cope with all that single handed?

PPPS.
The vows I asked for yesterday. False C & faithful T. [in Act II] will be I hope very handy in the <u>not</u> Interlude reffered to in D[.] Make much of them as they will also be useful in the <u>yes</u> Interlude Act II which is now at last assuming shape with the help of "We were alone".

PPPRS
Though while trusting dear Ernest N's [Newman's] judgement to a large extent, one must'nt forget that he can't help seeing things through rose-Wagnered spectacles,[2] & I can't help but remember that he passed the script as being perfect, god knows how many years ago when there were only sixteen insignificant lines for Cress. throughout the whole of Act I!!

To David Webster   January 1?<u>th</u>, 1954[3]

Casa Cirillo, Forio d'Ischia

My dear David,
    Thank you for your letter. If you are right in hearing that C.H. has been considerably exercised

[music quotation: the phrase 'Grimes is at his exercise!' from Act II of Britten's opera *Peter Grimes*, but with the text omitted]

(I will leave you to guess what that is) it has certainly been for the good, as I just heard from him, & with few emendations Act III should work

---

1 Sir Arthur Bliss was the current holder of the largely honorary position of Master of the Queen's Music.
2 Newman's four-volume biographical study of Wagner had made him an international authority on the composer.
3 The question-marked date is as written by Walton.

out pretty well – it won't be his fault if it dos'ent. The Auden intervention having acted in the way that it would act on me if someone had
said why don't you let B.B. finish your opera – but with this difference,
as I've a practical & unromantic mind, I should say "I wish to god he
would, but he can't have the royalties".

But to get down to tin-tacks. There is no choral work in any of the
Acts except in Act I[1] where there is a fair amount – say ten to fifteen
minutes, I've not worked it out. In Act II there is none, unless you can
call four women-attendants a chorus (there is not much of them). In the
third Act latest version, there is only this for a dozen Greek soldiers who
sing "An ambush! We are attacked! The Trojans are on us! Sound the
alarm!" all of which, will in all probability, be cut.

So you can have the chorus parts as soon as the O.U.P. are ready to
produce them which I hope should be before Easter. They are not being, I
think, very quick – I'm at the moment 150 pages ahead of them in scoring
meaning that they've not yet photographed my last 150 pages. But I'm on
to them about this. The position now as far as I'm personally concerned
is this – Act I complete Act II ⅔ complete Act III ⅓ complete with the
fact however regarding Act III, that I've as yet not written the music!

Now regarding Lambert & Furse – what I don't want & I'm sure you
don't either, is to be landed with Furse without Larry. I've heard from
Larry & he seems pretty definite, without actually saying so, about F. so
I've asked him to postpone a final decision till he has seen Lambert's
exhibition which I believe is to take place next month. Though I'm not
sure that this is wise advice, as, if I remember rightly, her pictures differ
very considerably from her stage designs & Larry is ever so slightly conservative – in fact he was horrified by the thought of H. Moore! But all
this we keep to ourselves.

I hope you can get a Pfte score (don't show it to my enemies – I leave
it to you to guess who they are!) of something fairly soon. Up to now I've
only got less than ⅔ of Act I whereas I've scored as far as ⅔ of Act II.

On Act I alone you can get a complete idea of what is wanted save
for Diomede who dosnt make his first appearance till the middle of Act II

---

1   In his letter to Christopher Hassall dated 14 February 1952 (p. 213), Walton had already
outlined the idea of 'a lot of alls-welling from the watchmen echoing back stage' at the
start of Act III. The libretto and first version of the score also have the watchmen specified
in the plural, which would imply at least some use of the chorus in Act III. But it is possible
that at the time of writing this letter to David Webster, Walton was thinking of using individual voices instead.

nor is Pandarus quite fully presented in Act I but flowers in Act II. But the king-pins as far as I'm concerned are Schwarzkopf & Uhde & to a less extent Gedda.

Think of me from time to time!
Yours ever
William.

To Alan Frank   16 January 1954

Casa Cirillo, Forio d'Ischia

Dear Alan,
[. . .]
No, I've not been playing for time about Schwarzkopf. I've definitely stated to David that I want her even if only for the first three perfs. Gedda for Troilus (though I'm not absolutely sold on him, – he seems to be just slightly lightweight – but Walter swears he can get through anything). Uhde for Diomede, Parry Jones for Pandarus, a big ? [i.e. a big question mark] though I'm slightly committed to him but that was some time ago. I don't know if he's still with Cov. Gar. or will be next season, otherwise [Hugues] Cuenod[1] would be good for it. Darghvell [Frederick Dahlberg] or however he spells his name for Calkas & then we should have a pretty good cast.

I don't think I shall be through completely before the end of July, but with the end of Act III I will send a Pfte [score] to Roy [Douglas] so he won't have to wait for the full score to do a transcription. Dos'ent it, by the way, take rather a long time getting the score photographed?

D.W. wants to see the Pfte score of Act I, but there is'nt a great deal of it ready, before he makes up his mind about casting. As there may be a bit of a delay over this, send him a copy of the full score & see how he gets along with that!!

Chris H. has sent me the new version of Act III. The Auden intervention seems to have put him on his mettle & he has produced something better than either A.'s solution or the previous version.

This I think covers most points up to now.
yrs ever
William

1 Swiss tenor, who appeared at Glyndebourne from 1954 onwards.

1 Louisa Walton, William Walton's mother.
2 Dr Thomas Strong, Dean of Christ Church, and one of Walton's first mentors.
3 WW and crew of the second boat, Christ Church College, Oxford, 1919.
WW is sitting cross-legged middle front.

4 *Top to bottom* Sacheverell, Osbert and Edith Sitwell, 1920s.
5 Margot Fonteyn and Frederick Ashton dancing the *Tango Pasodoble* in *Façade*.

6 Edith and Osbert Sitwell take some light refreshment in the 1920s.
WW is visible on the far left.

7 Imma von Doernberg.
8 Siegfried Sassoon (*left*) and Stephen Tennant, early 1930s.

9 *Left to right* Edwin Evans, Leslie Heward, WW, Dora and Hubert Foss.

10 Osbert Sitwell and Christabel Aberconway, 1930.
11 Alice, Viscountess Wimborne, at about the time that she and WW began their relationship, mid-1930s.

12 Benjamin Britten (*right*) and Peter Pears.

13 WW (*right*) and Laurence Olivier.

14 Susana Gil Passo, 1944.
15 Newly-weds Mr and Mrs Walton leave Buenos Aires for England,
January 1949.

16 Christopher Hassall, WW and Sir Malcolm Sargent at the Royal Opera House, 1954.

17 Magda László as Cressida, first Covent Garden staging of *Troilus and Cressida*, 1954.
18 Walter Legge (*left*), EMI's classical music supremo, and WW during the recording of *Belshazzar's Feast*, Kingsway Hall, London, 1959.

19 La Mortella, shortly after the house was completed, 1962. Walton's music room is at the top right, with the arched window.

20 Recording the Violin Concerto with Yehudi Menuhin and the London Symphony Orchestra, EMI's Abbey Road Studios.

21 WW with Edward Heath, the Prime Minister, early 1970s.

22 Walton aged eighty, 1982.

To Sir Laurence Olivier   16 January 1954

Casa Cirillo, Forio d'Ischia

My dear Larry,

Thank you for your letter. I had'nt realised that you had already talked to Roger, I remember discussing it when you were here, but I still thought we had left [it] rather in the air. But I may say I'm in complete agreement with you about him so let us take it as decided. Christopher has apparently talked to Isobel Lambert & she quite understands how muddled headed I am & is being docile about it.

I suppose David Webster has not as yet mentioned anything about anything to you, but I am working for a date between Oct 15th & 20th, and I trust you will be free enough round that date to take it on.

It has been going fairly well & I shall soon be through scoring Act II which mean that Acts I & II & a third of Act III will be complete as far as I am concerned – but I am doubtless in for some nasty moments.

The parcel has not yet arrived but I'm thanking you in anticipation.

Our best love to you both.

Yours ever
William.

To Alan Frank   21 January 1954

Casa Cirillo, Forio d'Ischia

Dear Alan,

Thanks for your letter. The last pages of Act I score arrived to-day. [...]

At the moment there is going to be a slight (? – I hope only) hiatus. This interlude [in Act II] (which has always been my nightmare) is proving difficult, but once it is past the rest of the Act all of which is musically (not scored) complete should not prove to be too arduous & I will send [it to] Roy [Douglas] in Pfte score as compensation for him having to do, I am sorry, almost all the first part again. It will be quicker that way than trying to stick bits together. The alterations are considerable & I think a vast improvement. When Act I is ready you might have a good look at it & let me know truthfully what you think. Not that I am going to alter anything now. But it might be a help if it has to be revised later on.

This thing about the date being possibly the end of Nov. is new to me. Do I suspect D.W. of not wanting Schwarzkopf? I think I do. I told him about her America dates [at that time]. And if the worst comes to the worst we shall just have to wait till she's back. Because it's an old, old promise & besides I've written it with her in view & in fact can think of noone else taking her part at the moment. Of course its (if I'm right) the old antagonism between D.W. & W.L. [Walter Legge] If E.S. turns it down, she might not like it, that naturally is another thing & one will have to look elsewhere. Malcolm [Sargent] as far as I know is definite as far as I & everyone else is concerned. You might let him have a score when convenient.

I can't think of anything else at the moment.

as ever
William

To David Webster   8 February 1954

Casa Cirillo, Forio d'Ischia

Confidential though I expect you know all

My dear David,

Thank you for your letter. I am not surprised or really pained about L.O., though as you say he would be of distinct value to the production, he will be more valuable to me personally if I do the music for his film which I hope to do. I've not heard definitely from him yet but I think they are both to appear in "Ant & Cleo"[1] in a production which is being set up in Rome & elsewhere in Italy. If I or rather Sue can be paid in lire here (she being an Argentine here), we can cock snooks at the Bank of E. for sometime to come; they have been particularly bloody-minded in the last year & show no signs of improvement. But this film is fraught with complications as it seems that it is a popular subject at the moment, there is L.O.'s production & one by Del Giudice with Michael Red. [Redgrave][2] & yet another with Warner Bros. with Brandon [Marlon Brando] & Ava Gardner! (& yet another remote one by Dallas Bower!) Both the former have asked me to do the music & I don't want to commit myself till I see who is really going to do it. So I [am] trying

---

1 Shakespeare's *Antony and Cleopatra*, with Olivier and his wife, Vivien Leigh.
2 English actor, particularly noted in stagings of Shakespeare, Ibsen and Chekhov at the Old Vic and the National Theatre. His films included *Mourning Becomes Electra* and *Goodbye Mr Chips*.

delicately to mark time on a tight-rope, as you know I am not at all clever at such accomplishments!

However this is nothing to do with T&C except as far as I can see it means that it is out of the question to avail ourselves of L.s services between July 15ᵗʰ this year & I should think about the same time next year. So we may count him as out, sad as it may be.

I have had noone else in mind, but think your suggestion of Michael Benthal to be first class. And of course we can have I. Lambert for the scenery as R.F. is sure to be in on the film.

I am very sad about Eliz. Schw. because as you know I have always had her in mind & have talked to her about it & played through bits of it to her.

I suppose it is hopeless to think of postponing the production till she is available? T&C couldn't swop places with "Midsummer madness" [Tippett's *The Midsummer Marriage*] for instance which I seem to vaguely recall is scheduled for Feb '55?[1]

However I don't insist, & welcome the suggestion of [Wilma] Lipp[2] which I think excellent. I've only heard her in Figaro but presume she is strong enough for a big dramatic part.

Alan Frank mentioned to me in one of his recent letters that you had mentioned as a date some day between the middle of Oct & the end of Nov. With Malcolm S. in view & for other reasons I will tell you, I'm inclined to a late Nov. date rather than the Oct. one. I'm definitely pro M.S. but I think if he could have his usual holiday after the "Proms" it would be better for him and for us, because it's going to be exacting work for him as he has not conducted opera for some time. I'm also rather against opening the season with T&C, the company would be still fresh but more settled towards the end of Nov. don't you think? It also gives a few weeks longer for the stage sets & incidentally for me but that is not why I'm suggesting this. Let me know what you think.

As ever
William.

The interlude in Act II which has preoccupied me for a long time is finished. Not so much of a "not-a-dry-seat-in-the-house" as I had hoped – but it will do.

1 *The Midsummer Marriage* was premièred at the Royal Opera House on 27 January 1955.
2 Austrian soprano. She had sung the role of Gilda in Verdi's *Rigoletto* at Covent Garden in 1951, but was better known in lighter *coloratura* roles.

To Christopher Hassall   20 February 1954

Casa Cirillo, Forio d'Ischia

My dear Chris,

Thank you for your letters etc. I don't know quite which I'm answering!

[. . .]

Your new suggestions [for Act III] I think tighten up Dio[mede]'s opening (I should express myself in a more decent fashion!) & I think it will now work till we get to the new arioso part profanely speaking.

I must say I think this is the most difficult scene of all & I shall be thankful to get it out of the way.

as ever
William

Motto for April: "Short lines mean pregnant music."

The Comets [jet aircraft] I see now go 4 times a week, so choose one as close as poss to May 1ˢᵗ[,] it won't matter if it's a day earlier or later.

I will send you a cheque for the tobacco as soon as my new cheque-book arrives.

To Christopher Hassall   9 March [1954]

Casa Cirillo, Forio d'Ischia

Dear Chris.

[. . .]

You don't mention in your letter if it is all right for [you] to come out at the end of April. I hope it is.

I saw David W. – not very satisfactory – except that I pointed [out] that Lipp was a coloratura & he tried rather unsuccessfully to think up some other names.

The only things that seem to be fixed are the date Dec 3ʳᵈ & Malcolm S. to conduct.

I've written to [Ernest] Roth[1] to see if he can help. Thank heavens

1   English music publisher of Czech birth. In 1938 he had left Vienna to join Boosey & Hawkes, and became the company's Chairman in 1963. An influential figure in the world of opera, he was responsible for securing for Boosey & Hawkes the rights to Richard Strauss's operas outside Austria and Germany.

we've got at least one who knows something about it. Alan F [Frank] is as I foresaw not much use for this kind of thing.

Meanwhile the [Teatro] San Carlo [in Naples] are very keen on getting it & I've had to be fobbing them off, not too hard in case La Scala falls through.

As ever
William

To Christopher Hassall   11 March [1954]

Casa Cirillo, Forio d'Ischia

Dear Chris,

[. . .]

I've heard to-day from Roth. He seems to favour an all english cast, on the grounds that the performances can be spread over a longer period & not have to follow in quick succession therefore in a limited time if we have a largely foreign cast. He is also inclining to the San Carlo rather than the Scala because of the hostile audience of the latter to any new work.

I['m] all for an english or Empire cast if one can be found – but can it? Let me hear from you soon

as ever
William

To Christopher Hassall   17 March [1954]

Casa Cirillo, Forio d'Ischia

Dear Chris.

Thank you for the two letters & enclosure – about the latter, if I have to, I will write when I've fully studied them.

First about the play-through on the 25th. I don't think we can make Cov. Gar. responsible for Franz [Reizenstein]'s[1] fee, but you, I & the O.U.P should be – in fact ask Alan F. to take charge of it all & we can settle it all up between us at some later date. We can charge it on income tax expenses!

---

1 German-born composer and pianist, now resident in England.

I think it a good idea to have tape made, wait however till Act II is complete. You could get in touch with Walter L [Legge] about this. Get two or three copies & bring one out here with you when you come as there is someone here who has a machine & we can play it through on that. If it is possible, which I doubt, without going to great expense, it might be worth while trying to collect four singers for the recording – you could for instance ask D.W. if he had some who would do it very cheaply – the understudies maybe. It would be useful to have, to adjust the tempi & for the producer etc.

At the playthrough I think it would be wiser & clearer if you arranged with Franz to stop every now & then, & you could explain what is happening on the stage, also it will give F. a rest; it is jolly tiring to play for 43 mins without a break. Incidentally tell him that I think I've marked "Slowly it all" too slow[:] ♩ should = 112 rather than 108 in fact it must have a feeling of a slow 2, not 6 in a bar, & that it mustn't flag. I've asked Alan F. to try & get Malcolm S. to come. He should be a help.

About Walter & Eliz. [Elisabeth Schwarzkopf] I don't attach any blame to them whatsoever,[1] because it would be asking too much not to accept [their decision] as there is still an element of doubt as to whether I shall be ready in time. This I think, is also at the back of D.W's mind and accounts up to a point for his dilatoriness.

I'm very pleased about F.'s [Reizenstein's] opinion about Acts I & II. I feel rather like John Ireland (you don't know him, but he invariably replies, if one says how much one liked[,] say, the last movement of one of his works "Oh I suppose that means you don't like the other movements"). F. dos'ent mention my most sensitive point almost, "Child of the wine-dark wave"[,] you might stealthily get his opinion on this! About the point he mentions on the orchestration I know what he means[,] it is due to "funk", in fact 'panic' scoring & he might keep an eye on it & point [out] these particular passages & we can discuss them when eventually we meet again.

I like [his comment] about "the acute responsiveness to the text"[,] he is quite right & that is where your appaling responsibility lies, when you're good I'm better when you're not so good Im much worse – so[,] rather late in the day to say so, bear that in mind! No-one has had such

1 Schwarzkopf had finally turned down Walton's request that she should sing Cressida. This seems to have been due more to her existing engagements elsewhere than to resistance to the role itself, which she sang in EMI's recording of highlights of the opera, conducted by Walton in April 1955.

a rotten time as you since Puccini's maltreatment of his librettists' lives! However look at the result! And don't think that you are going to have a moment's peace till the last bar is finished! What a life!

[. . .]

In one of your letters you said you had discovered a safe & painless way as to how to procure lire, but left it at that. Can you explain further – I'm all ears.

About you coming here, what about arriving on May 1ˢᵗ. You wouldn't contemplate flying instead of that cumbersome & expensive train? Try a Comet (no, I'm not urging you to do a Chester Wilmot!) I don't believe you'd feel any ill effects owing to the pressurization, much less so than in the ordinary plane which takes 7 hours & the Comet only 2 to Rome. If you took one that left at 8am you'd be in Rome at 11am take the express to Naples at 3pm arriving Naples 5pm take a taxi to Pozzuoli & embark on the steamer & you would be here at 7.45pm the same day. In fact you wouldn't know whether you were coming or going. Actually it is the least tiring [way] – I did it with Larry last year. But I dare say you have your sound objections to this particular form of 'whirlwind'! so I won't press the point on you.

And you can bring me some tobacco & no nonsense about showing it to the custom[s] official & having to pay thro' the nose, we cant afford it! What you do is this. Buy 2 lbs of "No Name" & 4 plastic pouches from Woolworths – empty the tins (a bit of a bore this but Eve will do it) pack 8oz into each pouch, by shoving hard this is quite possible as I know from experience[,] put a couple of elastic bands round the pouches. To travel you put one pouch in each of our overcoat pockets, the other two in your bag in the middle thus. ⬜ ⬜ surrounded by

shoes etc. When you are asked if you have anything to declare don't go white in the face & say "si" but smile in a superior manner & say "Niente" & you'll be left in peace[.] If you open your bag they only poke round the sides & if Eve is up to form with her deceptive genius nothing will be found. But in any case they wouldn't bother you as it is open & in pouches & for your personal use.

If you decide to take the Comet I will get Kennedy Cooke [of the] Brit[ish] Cou[ncil] to meet you & take you to lunch & put you on the train. If you decide alas for the train he would put you up for the night.

Cheer up.

as ever
William

Motto for May. "Comets for me"

P.S. Don't let F play the Interlude in Act II[,] let him say he has not yet transcribed it.

To David Webster   10 April [1954]

Casa Cirillo, Forio d'Ischia

My dear David

I am much delighted to receive your letter & to hear that you have not been dissapointed by what you have heard of T&C.

[George] Devine,[1] according to all reports, will be admirable as a producer. I am enchanted by the idea of della Casa [Lisa Della Casa][2] who will be first class if she will do it. Presumably her english is good enough. I also very much like the idea of Peter Pears[3] for Pandarus if he can be persuaded to take it – that may be a slightly delicate undertaking which I gladly leave to you.

If we can persuade P.P then I don't think [Richard] Lewis[4] would do for Troilus. Their voices are or were rather similar, Lewis, I always felt having been much influenced by P.P.

[David] Poleri[5] I know nothing about but am willing to take him on trust if you say he is good for the part.

Dalberg [Frederick Dahlberg] should be a more than adequate Calkas & [Otakar] Kraus[6] an excellent Diomede. So if all these will play we should begin to look fairly set.

The Pfte sc. of Act II should be ready any time now, so della Casa

1 Previously director of the Young Vic, and of the Old Vic Theatre School.
2 Swiss soprano. She had made her Royal Opera House début in the title role of Richard Strauss's *Arabella* in 1953.
3 English tenor. Partner and colleague of Benjamin Britten, and the first exponent of the title role of *Peter Grimes* and of many other leading tenor roles in Britten's operas.
4 English tenor, who had sung at Glyndebourne from 1947.
5 Tenor then singing regularly at the Royal Opera House.
6 Czech-born British baritone. A member of the opera company at Covent Garden from 1951 to 1968.

could get an idea of the part as far as the middle of Act III. which is her big bit in Act III bar the last couple of minutes.

I leave it to you to smooth the ruffled feelings of Parry J. if any – I hope not.

Greetings from us both
yours
William

To David Webster   6 May [1954]

Casa Cirillo, Forio d'Ischia

Dear David,

Will you look into the question of Magda Lazlo [László][1] for Cress:? Though I've only heard her on the radio in [Dallapiccola's] "Il Prigioniero" it struck me that she had an excellent voice though the part did not give her much chance.

But I hear from Hans [Werner] Henze[2] that she is a splendid singer, not only of the 12 tone boys but of parts like Isolde etc. She's good looking (I've seen photographs) young, intelligent, & a good actress & well disciplined at rehearsal & always knows her part. The only snag is the extent of her english. Hans thinks she speaks a little, but she could surely learn if we secure her early enough.

Anyhow look into it, and I'm sure you won't be dissapointed.

Act III progresses.

Our love to you
William.

Her address is
    66 Eaton Terrace
    s.w.1.

1 Hungarian soprano, at this time singing regularly in Italy.
2 German composer, who had settled in Italy in 1953, already very successful as a composer of operas (staged mostly in Germany).

To David Webster   18 May [1954]

Casa Cirillo, Forio d'Ischia

Dear David,

I have written to K. Clark to ask him to intervene with the King of
Sweden on Gedda's behalf so as to get G relieved of his 40 days military
service. Would you ring up K & give him details as to how long you
would need G. If K is successful there is no doubt we could get G as
Troilus which would be ideal.

Now what about Lazlo for Cress? Have you done anything about
her? The more I hear about her the more I like the idea of her as Cress:
Kennedy-Cooke knows her well & Keith Faulkner [Falkner] used to use
her a lot at the Brit Cou & it seems her english is quite good.

Chris H. has done an excellent closing sc. It however needs the chorus.
Nothing to be alarmed about it will be easy & short mainly accompanying the sextet.

Let me have some news
Our love
William

To Peter Pears   21 May 1954

Casa Cirillo, Forio d'Ischia

Dear Peter,

I gather that David Webster has written you regarding the possibility
of your considering to undertake the part of Pandarus in "Troilus &
Cressida". If he has done so (one can never be sure!) he has done so
with my highest approval, and I am hoping that you may find the part
worthy of you. If you do I shall be delighted, as I can think of noone
who could do it so well, also the relief that this tricky part would be in
your safe hands.

There is not much more of the part in Act III, just enough to round it
off.

Su sends her love as I do, also to Ben.
Yours ever
William (Walton.)

To David Webster   21 May 1954

Casa Cirillo, Forio d'Ischia

My dear David,

Thank you for the information about T&C. It would seem that for this comparatively early stage, that things look promising, except for the irritating snags which one can't expect to be absent.

I'm particularly happy about Peter P. – this tricky part should not only be safe in his hands, but positively brilliant. Gedda, I agree is a bit light, but I discussed this with Walter who said that in spite of its apparent lightness, he could be heard over fortissimo in the orchestra & on the whole, in fact entirely on the whole, his part is not overscored. There may be a bar or two where he may be overweighted if so these can be adjusted. I expect you will have communicated with K. about his 40 days.

Lazlo, would seem ideal except for her english. You'd better present her with a Linguaphone at once! I suspect she will blossom with a part which gives her an opportunity, which this certainly does. The 12 toners have kept her to themselves I suspect – lately she has only sung that kind of stuff. If the english is a fatal snag – what do we do? As you know I wrote it with Schwarzkopf in mind & anything that vaguely approximates to her, is what to aim for.

It is very awkward about Devine & Lambert. I think I'd better keep out of this & only hope that he has a good alternative.

As for the chorus, the women certainly I think can wear the same costumes as in Act I the men I suppose will have to be soldiers. But anyhow they will be right at the back covered in front by the six protagonists of the Sextet. So at the moment I won't charge that to myself!

Act III promises to be the best if I can only keep it up, so to speak. The Diomede–Cress love sc. has turned out much better than I thought it would – more thrust than the Act II sc.

Sue is recovering slowly[,] she's been very ill with of all things, a pollen allergy & she's been a fair sight, eyes, mouth, throat all swollen & a generally leperous appearance. Poor girl – however she is much better.

Our love
William

P.S. Pour soothing oil on P. Jone's [Parry Jones's] hurt feelings if any, also possibly the same for Barbirolli.

To Christopher Hassall   18 June [1954]

Casa Cirillo, Forio d'Ischia

Dear C.

Let me just get this right about "pomposo" [the Greeks' entrance in Act III]. I imagine it thus.

Trps [troops] chorus more or less together[:] Hail – Argos! backstage then

Tro[ilus]: What is this (sudden?) uproar? These voices? What are they calling? (you will notice slight cut which I think better rather) The orch[estra] in front then take up whatever tum tumtitum God gives me during which Cress says It's too late – Fate. followed by Pan. Tro. – – purpose. These latter will occur in the quieter bits of 'pomposo' which presumably is not for orch. alone but mixed up with a few Heil Hitlers etc. If this is the right idea just ok it & I'll proceed. I should be about there by the time there is a reply to this letter.

I wanted & have written an extra exquisite line after "Will he like me thus, hair loose & flowing". I doubt if you can better mine, in the ancient Minoan style[:] "Will he like me thus, tits boldly showing"[.]

I'm sure Lazlo has beauties & it would liven thing[s] up no end. And how this brightens up our correspondence when published! So send me your alternative or I'll leave it as it is.

Otherwise things are going smoothly, though I'm 3½ days behind schedule owing to having finished off Sc. I which I felt was a wise thing to do so everyone will realise that at least half of the last Act does exist & anyhow it had got to be done sometime.

We've now decided to stay here till the end of Aug. a wise decision I think because I'm almost sure I shall be able to finish completely orch & all by then & the 10 day break might be fatal for continuity. Of course we lose the rent, but what the hell!

You've no idea what bliss it is to have got rid of P. [Pasquale] The difference to the atmosphere of the house is quite extraordinary.

I had warned [him] last time that next time he was bloody-minded he was going. Of course he never believed me & said he wasn't going at any price. I then said I'd call the police & next morning he went like any angry lamb. It has cost a bit so I hope Peter M will be contacting you soon!

Let me hear from you soon

as ever

William

[250]

To Christopher Hassall   24 June [1954]

Casa Cirillo, Forio d'Ischia

Dear C.

I find your excellently vivid account of Lazlo slightly disturbing.

Her lack of English is [the] most disturbing feature. Do you really think that she can learn it parrot fashion & sing without a foreign accent in the 4 or 5 months remaining to us? Have you ever come across a similar case? If so well & good.

I think from looks she's a 100 per cent Cress. Of course you could'nt have heard [her] in anything less like T&C than [Gluck's] "Alceste"[1] & it can hardly be a fair criterion, & I can't help feeling that someone who looks like that can't pull it out or have it pulled out for her so to speak at the essential moments, but naturally a good deal of that will have to be the duties of Malcolm [Sargent] & George [Devine]. I can't believe a Hungarian (jewess?) lacks temperament – it can only be dormant & perhaps the music will help her to it. My music, on occasion, does have that effect on the coldest fishes – like Adrian Boult for instance!

But the point is, if we dont have her who in heavens name are we to have? You might speak to David W. about possible alternatives. You can say my only doubt is about her english, the rest I'm sure we can bring about to her satisfaction.

[Richard] Lewis I've not heard for sometime except in the "Rake" [Stravinsky's *The Rake's Progress*] on the air but I thought [him] excellent, but when I last saw him on the stage he seemed an awful clod, but he's probably improved since then. I['m] quite prepared to accept him if Gedda falls thro'.

How much of the music has she [László] seen? Enough to show what she's in for I hope. And she must know whether she can honestly sing it or not. If she is fixed can you see that she gets a copy of the german translation as then she can at least learn what she is singing about.

I once heard Joan Cross sing P. [Peter] Grimes in german & she had not the remotest knowledge of the language & she'd learnt it parrot fashion & one could'nt have been more convinced & the germans or Swiss rather were too. So I suppose it can be done.

To turn to the text.

1   At Glyndebourne, where László sang the role opposite Richard Lewis's Admetus.

[251]

Will he like me thus, hair loose & flowing?
– – – tits boldly showing? Will he like me thus?

I've then cut the next two lines & added instead "My wreath? My dress (gown)? Do the jewels become me?" O.K?
[not signed]

Isn't the transition from the wet dream to "Will he like me thus" a bit rapid?
No matter we'll leave it as I have already done it.
If she's engaged for T&C will you get her addres[s] in Rome as I could see her on my way back.

To Christopher Hassall   [June/July 1954]

Casa Cirillo, Forio d'Ischia

Dear C.
I hope you enjoyed your trip with Arturo pomposo.[1] It would seem I'm now doing a page of script a week & have finished Sc I [of Act III] & it is two thirds scored as well.
[. . .]
What are your views as to what should musically happen bottom p. 7 She falters, etc. I'm blank – & it's a v. important bit. pp or ff or cresc & dim or what?
I'm delighted to hear Lazlo is engaged. You must go & see her & arrange to teach her the script. Make her read, then sing it. You ought to do this every day & don't get into trouble!
It is essential she speaks beautiful Hassallese english – not like Lidia! Await your news about George & Isobel.
Livido fango nel tuo occhio!
That's "mud in your eye"!
as ever
William

1 Sir Arthur Bliss.

To Christopher Hassall   15 August [1954]

Casa Cirillo, Forio d'Ischia

Dear C.

About the dresses. I personally think it would be a mistake to have the same dress designer as Stratford.

I enclose some designs which have been done by a young but experienced French designer Jean-Pierre Ponnelle.

These are some of the costume designs for Nathan der Weise by [Gottfried Ephraim] Lessing.

He has also worked at the operas in Milan Rome & Naples Venice Berlin Paris Munich etc, so I'm not recommending someone who dos'ent know his job as anyhow you can see for yourself.

I suggest unless the dress designer is already settled by the time you get this, that you take the sc[ene] designs to [Sir Hugh] Casson[1] & George & see what they think. He is very adaptable & would of course fit in his designs with the stage sets. He would'nt I think be expensive[.] I don't know what Cov Gar pay but imagine £300–£500 & he certainly would'nt ask more.

I have seen other designs than these & consider him pretty good[.] There is also the advantage that he has already done dresses for Lazlo.

Anyhow find out how George & Casson feel.

More anon about other matters

as ever

William

The sultan would be a good dress for Calk. [Calkas] of course in a different style?

To Christopher Hassall   7 September [1954]

Casa Cirillo, Forio d'Ischia

Dear C.

Thank you for yours about nothing in particular. I expect to be sending off the last sheets at the end of the week. The last bit is proving a bit

---

1 English architect, artist and designer.

tiresome – it is not that it is really difficult, but that I'm just ever so slightly exhausted.

I've made the big cut in "Turn Tro:"[1] after trying it complete, with the 3 line cut, but have decided the 7 line cut is the best from all points of view, both for the verses & the music. As it is it lasts about 1'–50" so it's quite enough. After all I've gone back to your suggestion & put at [the end] "forgive me". So you can note these changes for your galleys. For all other changes verify from the full score which the O.U.P should have by now as far as the end of the fight. You will find they are very slight, a few things you've omitted in the typescript which are in the original which I'll return to you when I'm thro'.

George may or may not have had time to show you my solution to Act I. He's probably too engrossed in [Lennox Berkeley's] "Nelson".[2] I hope it will satisfy you both, as it is very simple from my point of view, entailing no orchestral chang[e] except for adding a few bars rest. It's not earth shattering literature consisting in the 1st instance p. 118 of adding (aside) I'll follow him too! for Pand: [Pandarus] (he goes after Calk but before Eva. [Evadne]) & secondly p 136. "Yes! He's fled to the Greeks" reappearing after Eva. The other bit "Either I rush" can go unaccompanied into the bar before 85 p 137. All clear? If so that would save a lot of messing about with Sc [score] & parts.

I suggest the preface should be simple & short chiefly stating where you've pinched it all from & how far you deviated therefrom. I also think it might be a good idea if you prefaced each act with a short synopsis such as at the beginning of each chapter in a Walter Scott novel! Useful for programmes!

As I have said before I'm feeling a slight holiday would not be out of place, so we have decided to stay on another week, not here but with some new friends of ours the Duca Cameroni who has that nice house you will doubtless remember at Porto [d'Ischia] which looks like a Moorish mosque. During which time the car will be being repaired in Rome where it goes with Mama [Lady Walton's mother] on the 11th.

The weather here is glorious after having been not so good thro' August in fact it's the first good [spell] this year so it seems stupid not to take advantage & have a slight break seeing what one is in for during

1 'Turn, Troilus, turn, on that cold river's brim': Cressida's aria before her suicide at the end of the opera.
2 Berkeley's opera was premièred at Sadler's Wells Theatre in 1954.

the next months. So I don't suppose we shall be in London before the 27ᵗʰ, which may well be too late for me to be of help on the "galleys" but I don't think I'm needed if you check carefully from the full score, where incidentally you will see (crescendo) that I have not buggered up (crescendo) your fucking verses in the way they (crescendo) bloody well deserve!!

   as ever
   William

To Christopher Hassall   [September 1954]

Casa Cirillo, Forio d'Ischia

Dear C.

   Thank you for everything. I'm finished. Next please!

   See you on the 27ᵗʰ. You will find all changes such as there are in the scripts enclosed herewith.

   as ever
   W.

To Geoffrey Cumberlege¹   6 November 1954

Lowndes Cottage, Lowndes Place, s.w.1

Dear Mr. Cumberlege,

   You may by now have heard of the unsatisfactory orchestral rehearsal which took place last Monday at Covent Garden. It was the first of the series of rehearsals for my Opera and the only one on the schedule allotted to Sir Malcolm for rehearsing the orchestra alone in Act One. He was, however, given no opportunity for interpr[et]ative rehearsal owing to the time wasted on correcting errors of the copyist. Had the chaotic state of Act One been discovered at a later stage, (and it was only by chance that this rehearsal was held at such an early date,) there would have been no choice for me but to cancel the Premiere, and in fairness to the Opera House I could not have withheld the reason from public notice.

   I would especially draw your attention to the fact that I carried out

---

1 Secretary to the Delegates of Oxford University Press; in effect, the firm's chief executive.

the delivery to your Press of Act One a year ago, and Act Two in February, thus giving more than enough time for the process of copying and checking. For the rest I had to rely on the co-operation of your firm, which I had a right to expect, and which I have not received. The result is that there now devolves upon me personally an enormous labour at a time when I'm in no state of health to undergo the drudgery of a copyist. You will understand that I have constantly to absent myself from rehearsals, and I may say I am only submitting to this strain because there is no alternative, if my work of five years (and incidentally the reputation of the O.U.P.) is to be saved from something like disaster.

Since Mr. [Roy] Douglas (an excellent and reliable copyist, who had been promised to me for the whole period involved,) and I began checking the parts of Act One we have detected no less than two hundred errors in the string parts alone. When I tell you that some twenty or so copies are concerned you will realise that this involves the making of several thousand corrections – and I repeat that this is of course but one section of the orchestra. The state of Act Two (where the parts are if anything more intricate and the same copyist has been employed) is bound to be such as to cause me the gravest concern. (We have not as yet had time to check this.) Even when not inaccurate this man's lay-out is well below the standard of clarity that a work of such complexity demands.

Only a fraction of Act One, the work of Mr. Douglas, is in a presentable condition. It is indeed a relief to find that he is responsible for most of Act Three, which has been delivered almost without a mistake. When I add that I was recently informed that the parts of Act One had been carefully checked, you will get some idea of the extent to which I can in future rely on statements made by the Music Department of your firm.

The persons concerned admitted at the outset to being inexperienced in Opera production, but I was given assurance that this deficiency would be overcome by an especial and conscientious effort. This assurance has not been honoured in the event. The adverse way in which this lamentable state of affairs reflects on the O.U.P. is only matched by the insult to myself, and to conclude I need hardly say that I am forced to consider resigning from any future association with your firm.

Yours sincerely,
William Walton

P.S. In the light of all this and the fact that the rehearsal of November 2nd was almost entirely wasted, I hope you will think it not unreasonable of me to suggest that the O.U.P., by way of some redress, might bear the cost of an additional orchestral rehearsal.

Finally, though I cannot sufficiently stress my aggravation, I must make it clear that I would be very sorry indeed if this protest led to your taking drastic steps with the director of your Music Department.[1] I would be grateful if you would bear this in mind.

To Geoffrey Cumberlege[2]   16 December 1954

Lowndes Cottage, Lowndes Place, s.w.1

Dear Mr Cumberlege,

I was very pleased to receive your letter of November 12 and was most interested in all you said. While thanking you for your offer to reimburse me for the considerable labour I had to undertake I will gladly take the thought for the deed.

As for the whole problem of copying, it looks to me as if the man who was chiefly to blame had checked the parts that he had himself copied. This is a most unsafe procedure, if I may say so, as we can judge from recent experience. I suggest that in future there should be a rule that all parts should be checked by someone other than the copyist himself.

I am grateful to you for your suggestion to meet me. I am sure you will understand that in recent weeks there has hardly been time. Now that the premiere is over we can proceed as we were, having, I hope, learnt a rather bitter lesson.

I much appreciated your letter and hope we will have occasion to meet in the near future.

1 Alan Frank.

2 Cumberlege had written back to Walton apologizing for the situation. He had meanwhile consulted Alan Frank, who had pointed out in a memorandum that of several copyists used by OUP, only one had been responsible for the vast majority of the errors in the orchestral parts of *Troilus and Cressida*, and that the normally acceptable standard of this man's work had been undermined by difficulties in his private life. Frank had also explained to Cumberlege that there was a subtext to Walton's letter. Roy Douglas was mostly working on the editing and copying of Vaughan Williams's scores at this time. In Frank's view, Walton had long resented both this situation and the perception within OUP that Vaughan Williams was the firm's 'senior' composer, whose requirements therefore tended to be given precedence over Walton's.

With kind regards,
Yours sincerely,
William Walton

To Dora Foss   17 December 1954

Lowndes Cottage, Lowndes Place, s.w.1

Dear Dora,
    It was kind of you to write such a nice letter about "Troilus and Cressida". I am touched to hear that you were there and that you saw the work on your own and on Hubert's behalf.
    With love to you all from us both,
    Yours ever
    William

1955–1963

THE opening run of performances of *Troilus and Cressida* at Covent Garden was followed by others – soon enough, Walton had reason to believe, to indicate that his opera might gain its hoped-for place in the international repertory, despite its dubious critical reception. Further performances with the original cast were given at Covent Garden in April 1955. The work was then taken on tour to other theatres in England and Scotland, this time with a substantially different cast and with a different conductor, Reginald Goodall. The same forces performed it yet again at Covent Garden in July. Walton's letters to Alan Frank and David Webster later that month show that he had begun to sense the worrying extent of the casting difficulties that had afflicted *Troilus and Cressida* from the start, and have continued to do so ever since.

The work's American première took place on 7 October 1955 at the San Francisco Opera, and New York City Center Opera staged it later that month and in March 1956. But the event for which Walton had the highest hopes was the Italian première at La Scala, Milan, on 12 January 1956. *Troilus and Cressida* was the first major work he had produced since he and Susana Walton had come to live in Italy, and it was natural that he should have expected a measure of visibility as a famous composer living and working in his newly adopted country. His initial optimism in the early stages of rehearsals at La Scala soon faded as a combination of administrative cynicism and, yet again, inadequate casting began to undermine the opera's chances of success with the notoriously critical Milanese press and public. The first night, while not entirely a disaster, gave more than enough free ammunition to those all too ready to dismiss *Troilus and Cressida* as a white elephant, much as their London counterparts had. The final indignity took place in the closing moments of Act III. Dorothy Dow, singing the title role, found that someone had removed or misplaced (on purpose?) the sword with which Cressida was supposed to kill herself, and ran around the stage in a panic looking for it, to the accompaniment of audience laughter. The applause after each act was mingled with boos and hisses. There is no reason to doubt Walton's reports that subsequent performances went better, and were much better received. But it is the cruel nature of the operatic world that if a new work is perceived to have been damned on its first night, a generation or longer may be needed to rebuild its reputation. At the time of writing, *Troilus and Cressida* has not been performed again at La Scala.

Despite the intelligently brave face that Walton put on the situation in his letters after this Milanese débâcle, he must have sensed that the prospects for his opera's long-term success were in serious trouble. He was right. *Troilus and Cressida* was not staged again anywhere until its revival at Covent Garden in April 1963. Walton had by then made a number of cuts and revisions to the score, in the hope that some judicious tightening would help to bring the dramatic structure into sharper focus. Yet again, however, an unconvincing staging and a cast of mixed quality combined to relegate the work to the perceived status of a 'flop', despite Marie Collier's widely admired performance as Cressida. The world of opera had apparently made up its mind that *Troilus and Cressida* was not to be taken seriously in the modern, post-war age.

The constant underlying theme of Walton's letters in the years after his opera's ill-starred London première was his increasingly exasperated disappointment at its lack of success, and his determination to do what he could to turn the situation around. Of course he needed to be seen to be believing in the work. But the evidence of his correspondence is that he really did believe in it, just as the evidence of the score and its various recordings show that he was right to do so. It is possible that the opera would have had a happier history if Walton had conducted the first performances or some of the later ones himself. He was by now earning a substantial part of his living as a successful conductor of his orchestral works. The extracts of the opera he recorded in 1955 with Richard Lewis (the original Troilus at Covent Garden) and Elisabeth Schwarzkopf (who had not been free to sing the role of Cressida on the stage) show his ability to generate the necessary intensity and atmosphere as few other conductors have. But he had not conducted an opera of any kind in the theatre, and he felt that the technical demands of co-ordinating the singers on the stage and an orchestra in the pit for hours on end amounted to a level of professional risk that was best avoided.

Oxford University Press's relative lack of influence and visibility in the world of opera, and for that matter on the European orchestral scene also, continued to concern him. At the time of *Troilus and Cressida*'s première, Boosey & Hawkes had made yet another approach to him, but a combination of genuine loyalty and hard-headed practicality made him decide to stay with the publishers who had, after all, given him his all-important first break in 1925. Walton knew that Boosey & Hawkes would continue to promote Britten as their leading composer, and he had no wish to find himself relegated to the position of just another composer within the same house as his perceived rival. Sure enough, after Vaughan Williams's death in 1958, Walton's standing as Oxford University Press's leading composer was unchallenged. He also appreciated the warmth of the relationship between himself and Alan Frank, the head of the company's music department. Their correspondence down the years combined the necessary shop talk of the composer and his publisher with an unmistakable mutual rapport which makes for richly entertaining reading.

Walton's relations with the critical press were a lot less happy. This was now the age of the official ascendancy of modernism in classical music. In critical circles Pierre Boulez, Karlheinz Stockhausen and the European avant-garde were widely regarded as the incontestable and uncompromising apostles of the future. In this brave new world, Walton's music was seen by many to be old hat. In fact his later works did not by any means receive the unremittingly hostile press that Walton's letters tend to make out. But his perception that many of the leading critics no longer rated his music as important or valuable was substantially accurate. The contrast with the near-adulation of the pre-war years was acute.

Walton responded to this with a less than convincing blend of bitterness, anger and irrationality. Naturally, no composer likes to be attacked in the press, even if those 'attacks' are often much more perceived than actual. But it is odd that his justified pride in his achievements as a composer did not bring with it a capacity to cope with what were, in truth, little more than the fairly normal slings and arrows of outrageous fortune. His irritation with 'the critics' also subverted his usually reliable and entertaining sense of humour more than he would probably have liked to admit. The situation crystallized in his bizarre, weathervane-like friendship with Peter Heyworth, the gifted, contentious, Boulez-supporting music critic of the *Observer*. On a personal level Heyworth and Walton found they got on well, to the extent that they stayed with each other regularly on their respective visits to Italy and London. Walton seems genuinely to have been able to distinguish between Heyworth's musical views, which he often disliked, and the intelligent skill with which they were articulated. But as his letters show, he could be contemptuous of Heyworth when writing about him to others.

The same uncertain mood swings can be charted in his relationship with Benjamin Britten. Again, on a personal level they remained friends, with a genuine level of mutual respect and admiration. Walton always felt welcome when visiting the Aldeburgh Festival which Britten and Peter Pears had so successfully started up, and this association was to bear rich creative fruit in years to come. But the competitive edge in Walton's nature often prevented him from responding to the stellar status of his younger colleague on a level that was more than grudging. At times the initials 'B.B.' seem to denote a kind of psychological incubus by which the older composer was both annoyed and fascinated. Britten's exceptional technical fluency and rate of production seemed in almost provocative contrast to the extreme difficulty that Walton himself found (or believed that he found) in producing his own music with any fluency at all. He always liked to make out that the actual process of composing was desperately difficult for him, and in many instances it undoubtedly was. But his insistence that he always struggled to get anything down at all on paper is part of a mythology that he himself did much to create. A glance at his catalogue of works shows that he was a more than respectably prolific composer. His large output included a high proportion of orchestral scores (which always involve more actual labour than, say, chamber music), besides two operas, one of them full-length, and a substantial number of film scores also. The trouble was that even he could not quite match the work rate and dazzlingly versatile all-round musicianship of 'B.B.'

It is arguable, however, that Walton's post-war music on one level achieved something that even Britten's did not (allowing for the fact that Britten's creative agenda and personality were of course quite different). The major works that Walton produced in the years after *Troilus and Cressida* – the Cello Concerto, the Second Symphony, and the *Variations on a Theme by Hindemith* – each show how strikingly and yet how subtly his music had developed since the pre-war years. The new works spoke with a musical voice that related quite clearly to the one that had spoken in the First Symphony and the Violin Concerto. But what had changed was the music's tone. This had become at once more economical and more elusive. Another development was an exceptional level of technical refinement which made the Second Symphony, in particular, demandingly difficult to play even by Walton's standards. This is part of the reason why Walton's post-war works are still performed much less often that their pre-war counterparts. Compared to the First Symphony's surging, applause-inducing rhetoric, the Second Symphony's precisely and beautifully judged range of light and shade is harder to bring out. And there is another, more intractable problem. It is strange that conductors and administrators, if only subconsciously, tend to want a composer to go on producing the same kind of music all the time. That the Second Symphony is a different work from the First, on every level, is its whole point. Like so much of Walton's later music, it was on the whole dismissed at the time as being 'more of the same'. Only a few perceptive listeners realized that what Walton's music had in fact done was to move ahead of, and beyond the current critical and political taste, rather than lag behind it. These obstacles to future performances soon began to be most successfully overcome by American orchestras, who were able to approach Walton's later works with a freshness of outlook their British counterparts seem to have lacked. Besides, the technical level of American orchestras at this time tended to be a class apart from that of most of their British counterparts.

Walton's stock in America began seriously to rise after the first performance, in 1957, of the Cello Concerto he had composed for Gregor Piatigorsky. The correspondence between the composer and the Russian-born cellist shows how much Walton seems to have savoured the opportunity of creating a work in such close contact with a solo artist of this order, even if (true to form) he was less generous about Piatigorsky in his letters to others than in those to Piatigorsky himself. Next came the *Partita*, by turns ebullient and exquisitely atmospheric, and the first of many happy experiences involving the Cleveland Orchestra and its formidable music director, George Szell. This was the outstanding team that did such exciting justice to the Second Symphony after its lacklustre première at the 1960 Edinburgh Festival, and to the similarly superb *Variations on a Theme by Hindemith*. It is in these four works that Walton's musical voice speaks most vividly and truly, at one of the happiest and most productive periods of his life.

Domestically, too, the Waltons' life together had begun to encompass new areas of interest. While renting Casa Cirillo they had bought and refurbished a number of small properties near by, in order to generate some reliable income by letting them out to friends and holidaymakers. When the lease on Casa Cirillo ran out in 1959 they moved into one of these houses, San Felice. Walton worked on his Second Symphony there, while Susana Walton looked around for somewhere to build a new, larger home and the garden she herself had long planned. Further up the hill above San Felice was a steep area of unused land which they decided to buy, undeterred by Laurence Olivier's description of it as a 'stone quarry'.

The Waltons were now officially permanent residents of Italy, and had been renting out Lowndes Cottage in London to friends, including Olivier and his wife, Vivien Leigh. They now decided to sell Lowndes Cottage and to put the proceeds towards the construction of their new home, La Mortella. In August 1962 the house was ready, and they moved in.

To Gertrude Hindemith   10 May 1955

Lowndes Cottage, Lowndes Place, s.w.1

Dear Gertrude,

Thank you for your letter. As it turns out we have not yet left for Spain, owing to the fact that Schwartzkopf [Elisabeth Schwarzkopf] got laryngitis during the recording of Troilus and we have had to postpone the recordings until next Monday. So we shall not be leaving until Tuesday.

This opera has absolutely ruined my life as regards work. I am going to America in October for the premiere. At the moment of writing I have not had the script for the ballet,[1] so I doubt if it will be ready in time for any of the dates you mention. However I am sending to Paul [Hindemith] a score of "Scapino", a short overture which he may, or may not, like to try. It would be fairly new in Germany, as I think it has only been broadcast once. If he doesn't like it he needn't hesitate to say so and throw it in the fire. I shall love him just as much as ever.

I shall eventually produce something new for him, before not too long I hope.

We shall be passing through Blonay in the middle of June on our way to Italy, but we shall be tactful about disturbing you.

With best regards to you both,
Yours
William Walton

1 *Macbeth*, planned for Covent Garden's 1955–56 season, with choreography by Frederick Ashton, who wrote a three-act scenario for it. The music was never composed.

To Lord Waverley

14 June 1955

Lowndes Cottage, Lowndes Place, s.w.1

Dear Lord Waverley,

Before leaving for another spell abroad I should like, on behalf of Christopher Hassall and myself, to put on record our appreciation of the way "Troilus and Cressida" was handled at Covent Garden.

We much appreciated the considerate and wonderfully competent way in which the organisation, which contributed so much to the success of the opera, worked.

Yours sincerely,
William Walton

To Alan Frank

18 July 1955

Casa Cirillo, Forio d'Ischia

Dear Alan,

Thank you for your various letters.

Re Hamlet[1] let us leave it till Nov. The chief difficulty as with all film music is to make coherent pieces out of it. There is, as you mention, the funeral march but it is scored for an enormous orch!

[. . .]

I am glad to hear that [the] T&C perfs[2] wer'ent too intolerable [. . .] I gather from C. [Christopher Hassall] that Goodall was pretty flabby. It is good that it is being [done] 4 times in Dec, but I agree with you [that Una] Hale is not sufficiently good & attractive from all points of view to be allowed to do it [again]. There must be a star of some sort for Cress & I believe that Joan Hammond[3] would be as good as anyone english. She was singing quite superbly when I heard [her] in Verdi's Requiem. Nielson [Raymond Nilsson, as Pandarus] must be abolished & D.W. [David Webster] will no doubt find someone. I've an idea he mentioned Arthur [Alexander] Young. [Jess] Walters I gather is better than [Otakar] Kraus.

1 The suite proposed by Walton from his original film score.
2 During a national tour of Britain by the Royal Opera House.
3 New Zealand soprano, famous for her performances of the title roles in Puccini's *Tosca* and *Madama Butterfly*. She had sung at Covent Garden between 1948 and 1951.

We went over to Capri the other say & saw Menotti[1] & Barber[2] with their appendages Theodore Shotter [Thomas Schippers] & Lance [Charles] Turner (a young composer). All nice & extremely aimnable & Shotter told me that Stockport [Joseph Rosenstock] was first class. He has worked with him for five years at City Center. So I expect the New York perfs won't be too bad. Curtin too I was told is very good.[3]

[. . .]

I hope all the business about the [Italian] translation has blown over. It was a very tiresome & sticky interview we had with Da Sabato [Victor De Sabata][4] & Ghiringelli.[5] Ravizza, [Ernest] Roth's go-between, in Milan seems to have been the one to blame, though I understand from Roth that [Eugenio] Montale[6] himself was the one. However he was very easy to deal with when I saw him, though his speaking english was not too good (he said he was out of practise) he must know it pretty well to have translated Eliot etc. And he is Italy's major poet so I'm told & he started his career as a singer, so he should be safe on the musical side.

Sonzogno [Nino Sanzogno][7] is to conduct & C tells me that [George] Devine is being asked to produce. Aldari who is 2nd in command at La Scala is staying in Ischia so I hope to be able to discuss casting more fully with him. De Sabata seems to be very enthusiastic about it & I was much impressed by his being able to sing innumerable quotations from it from memory. It is his first season as Sovrintendente so he is sure to be all out to make things go.

I've as yet not made much progress, if any with [the] cello concerto.[8]

1 Gian Carlo Menotti, American composer of Italian ancestry, already famous for his operas *The Medium, The Telephone, The Consul* and *Amahl and the Night Visitors*. In 1958 he was to found the Festival of Two Worlds in the Tuscan town of Spoleto.
2 Samuel Barber, American composer. His most well-known works at this date were his Violin Concerto, the *Adagio for Strings* arranged by him from his earlier String Quartet, and his song cycle *Knoxville: Summer of 1915*.
3 *Troilus and Cressida* was first performed at New York City Center Opera on 21 October 1955, conducted by Joseph Rosenstock. Cressida was sung by Phyllis Curtin. For Thomas Schippers, see p. 321, n. 3.
4 Italian conductor and composer, at this time the newly appointed artistic director of La Scala, Milan. One of the leading conductors of the time, he had taken the La Scala company on tour to Covent Garden in 1950.
5 General director of La Scala.
6 Italian novelist, essayist and poet.
7 Italian conductor, who had been working regularly at La Scala from 1939.
8 Walton had been asked to compose this by Gregor Piatigorsky. Born in Russia and by now resident in America, Piatigorsky was widely considered to be the leading cellist of his day.

I must admit I've not been trying very hard, but will pull myself together shortly I hope.

as ever,
William

To David Webster   23 July 1955

Casa Cirillo, Forio d'Ischia

Dear David,

A word or two if I may regarding the winter revival of T&C.

From the many accounts of the recent two performances it would seem that four things stand out. That Hale was not too bad vocally but that her acting & presence for Cressida was well below par. That Neilson was hell & Goodall worse than hell. That Walters was decidedly better than Kraus & would be very good when he had got more into the part.

I feel if the opera is going to continue to draw there must be a couple of stars, & I suggest that Joan Hammond would be good as Cress: In spite of drawbacks when I last heard [her] not long ago in the Verdi Requiem she was in really magnificent voice. If I remember rightly you suggested Arthur [Alexander] Young for Pandarus. [Hugues] Cuenod, alas, is out for Cov. Gar. & La Scala, as he's in America.

I hope you will persuade Raphael [Rafael Kubelík] to conduct if [Sir] Malcolm [Sargent] is full up. If not Raphael or Malcolm then who? Certainly not Goodall again & clutching at a straw I suggest [John] Hollingsworth as being the best of a bad lot.

Don't bother to answer this unless you feel inclined as you must be about to go for your "hol". But I will remind you about it in Sept, when I pass thro' London on the way to San F.[1] I need hardly say I've heard nothing from Fred [Frederick Ashton] or Ninette [de Valois] in spite of her public announcement of a ballet by me.[2] So the die is cast. Though not exactly in full spate, I've started on the Vlc. Con. Our best love

as ever
William

1 San Francisco, for the performances at the San Francisco Opera House of *Troilus and Cressida*.
2 The projected *Macbeth*.

P.S. Would you like to come & see me "doctored"[1] by the Queen-Mother at R.F.H. Nov. 24<u>th</u>?

To David Webster   24 August 1955

Forio

My dear David,

Thank you for your letter & your news about the casting of the next perfs. of "T&C".

About the ballet – I'm not adverse to the idea of "Macbeth" but it's length rather frightens me. Is'nt Lady M. a slightly odd character for Margot [Fonteyn][2] to play? – I feel about it in the same way as I feel about Vivien[3] playing it. But however I presume she & Fred know best.

However, if I do do it, it is obviously going to take quite a time – 6 to 9 months at least. And there is little chance of my being able to settle down to work on it seriously till after "T&C" at La Scala, which means the beginning of next Feb. So I can't possibly get it ready for the dates Ninette suggests – either April or June next year.

Also I think now I'm embarked on the Vlc. Con. that I ought to finish it. It is fairly well under way & if it wasn't for my visit to the U.S. & to Milan in Dec, it would be finished by Xmas.

It is an awkward medium to settle oneself into, & to break away on to an entirely different style of work for the so long period involved, would I feel be a mistake. Also I've made a verbal promise to try & get it ready for Edinburgh next year – and last but not least, a large amount of dollars are involved! And in these days of the weakness of "sterling" its something I can't afford to ignore.

So perhaps the wisest course is for me to finish the Con. as quickly as possible & then we can see how the situation lies as regards Margot's retirement,[4] or if that has happened, whether it is worth while doing it at all without her.

---

1   Walton's preferred description of being awarded an honorary doctorate, in this case by London University.
2   Principal ballerina with the Royal Ballet, and one of the greatest dancers of her generation.
3   Sir Laurence Olivier had evidently planned that Vivien Leigh should star opposite him in his proposed film of Shakespeare's *Macbeth*, with music by Walton. The film was not made, and the music remained unwritten.
4   A false alarm. In fact Fonteyn continued dancing for many years.

Love from us both
as ever
William

To Christopher Hassall   24 December [1955]

Via Soncino 2, Milano

Dear Christopher,

There has, I fear, been no offer forthcoming as yet from the Scala people, so you had better be prepared to pay your own way out here & we will try & find you some cheap hotel.

Otherwise than this (& the appalling cold kindly donated by Mrs Enid Blech[1]) things can be said to be going pretty well.

[Günther] Rennert is splendid as producer[,] full of imaginative ideas which makes everything & everybody become intensely alive & vivid in fact I've never realised what a producer can really do. The singers are to the most minor parts, first class especially [Dorothy] Dow [as Cressida] who acts almost as well as she sings. The translation is it seems very good & I've only had to make one or two suggestions for revision.

So far there have been only Pfte rehearsals & the orchestral of which I think there are at least 11 start in earnest at the end of next week. There are two general rehearsals on the 9th & 10th so you had better be here on the 8th.

We've seen "Il flauto magico" [*The Magic Flute*] & "Norma" with Callas who is fantastic, but all the same I prefer Dow for Cressida.

Let me know your plans.

Xmas greetings & what not
as ever
William

P.S Your genius for double meanings has even penetrated into Italian. "Impregnable Troy" when translated has an alternative meaning to whit "you unfuckable sow"!

1 Wife of Harry Blech.

To David Webster   20 January 1956
[postcard]

Casa Cirillo, Forio d'Ischia

Thanks for your good wishes. In spite of the disastrous opening & with few exceptions, a filthy press, the second performance was packed & enthusiastic, in fact if I'd not seen it with my own eyes I wouldn't have believed an audience could have been so different from the first one. However it is all good for the soul if not for the opera & the extraordinary part of it is, that the Scala people are delighted about it all!

    as ever
    William

To Helga Cranston   31 January 1956
[postcard]

Casa Cirillo, Forio d'Ischia

Thanks for your long letter & I hope this reaches you before you leave for "Old Jewry"! [Israel] Come & see us on the way back or forth. Tho' the 1st perf of T&C was all the english press made it out to be the 2nd 3rd & 4th perfs went better & better & were received with "molto applausi" from full houses. So I'm not so worried as you may have thought.

    Best love
    as ever
    William

To Alan Frank   31 January 1956

Casa Cirillo, Forio d'Ischia

Dear Alan,

    Thank you for your various bits & pieces of news. I have heard from various & reliable sources that the 3rd & 4th of T&C went increasingly well & was received with "molto applausi". So that is all right, so in the next Bulletin you can write something to efface the impression in England that it has been a complete "flop". I gather from Kenneth Cook[1] that there is a possibility of it being done in Rome next season.

---

1 Of the British Council in Rome.

The Roman press of course was much better especially Pannain.

We had tea with Callas before leaving & she seemed not averse to taking it up – but it was probably only politeness. I don't suppose it has been mentioned in the english press that they threw carrots & garlic at her on the 1ˢᵗ night of "La Traviata" & even Verdi was'nt left unscathed! At least nothing was thrown at us!

Unfortunately when we got to Rome we found Su had a fever of 102°. But it was in a way fortunate for a friend of ours lent us her villa here so Su could have a rest, for it turned out that Casa Cirillo had been left in a dreadful state by Henze & the Nonos[1] & we were only able to return here yesterday having got the house cleaned & made liveable again.

[. . .]

Love from us both

as ever

William

To Peter Pears   21 April 1956

Casa Cirillo, Forio d'Ischia

Dear Peter,

Thank you so much for your nice letter.

How we missed you in Milan. The Pandarus there was a disaster, so much so that the trio in the 2ⁿᵈ Act had to be cut. The rest of the cast & production was brilliant, bar Tro. (Poleri) & Cress (Dow) who didn't come up to expectations especially the latter, though she's got quite a good voice her looks & character were not too sympathetic.

The first night reception was a riot of hissing & booing & the Milanese press was foul – in fact I've never seen such a vicious press for anything, – the Roman press on the other hand was very good & serious. We went to the 2ⁿᵈ perf. in fear & trepidation, but to our surprise not only did the performance go much better, but it was received almost with enthusiasm. We didnt stay for the next two, but I was informed that they went even better.

---

1 Luigi Nono, Italian composer, prominent at this time in avant-garde musical circles, and noted for his Marxist political stance. He was married to Nuria, the daughter of Arnold Schoenberg by his second marriage. The Nonos were not asked again to stay at the Waltons' home.

I like the idea about the "one-man" opera & I'll see what Christopher [Hassall] thinks.

You are quite right in your surmise that I've my back to the wall with the 'cello Concerto, but at the moment I'm engaged on an overture for the Johannesburg Festival.[1] But I'm all for some little songs with guitar, when I'm finished with these works.

I hope you had a lovely time on your world trip. It must have been wonderful.

Our love to you & Ben if hes about
yours ever
William

To Gregor Piatigorsky   10 August 1956

Casa Cirillo, Forio d'Ischia

Dear Grisha,

Here is what I hope is the final version [of the Cello Concerto's second movement] – as far as it goes. I'm in a hurry to send it off so that you can have it on your journey.

This new version I think incorporates all your suggestions for which many thanks. It is as you will quickly see very different from what I've already sent you, so please destroy the former version.

The movement up to No $\boxed{19}$ lasts about $4\frac{1}{2}$ mins – now comes a coda of about a minute or so. I hope to send that to you in a day or two trusting that it will arrive before you depart – but anyhow here is the main bulk of the movement.

The cadenza can be played as freely as you like. I think I've covered most questions by alternative versions.

Have an enjoyable journey – it sounds most attractive.
Affectionately
William

P.S. Dr Ghiringelli the "boss" of La Scala Milano would like to know if you would be interested to give the concerto there in early June '57?

Marianna Leibl, who says she played your accompaniments many years ago wishes to be remembered to you. She has done my

---

1 *Johannesburg Festival Overture.*

"Horoscope", & says the concerto is going to get better & better & be a big success! I hope she's right!

To Gregor Piatigorsky   9 September 1956

Casa Cirillo, Forio d'Ischia

Dear Grisha,

By the time you receive this I hope the complete 2nd mov. will have reached you. I'm glad you like what you have got.

You will find it slightly different here & there. But your version of the cadenza seems splendid to me. The one in the complete version is more extended but you can easily work it out in the same way as the old one. [. . .]

I'm glad to hear that your tour is being so successful. No! I don't hate you for making me work! On the contrary I'm grateful for your patience & I'm sorry that I'm such a slow worker – but I'm always like that when I'm writing something I care about, and I shall try to make the finale worthy of you.

After many false starts & what is worse nothing happening at all, I'm at last launched on the finale. It opens with the solo Vlc. all on its own quite a while. Very "robusto".

I wo'nt send any more in case I change it! I think it will end quietly with a longish coda based on themes from the 1st mov. But we will see.

    as ever
    William

To Gregor Piatigorsky   6 October 1956

Casa Cirillo, Forio d'Ischia

Dear Grisha,

Here is part of the last movement for your approval or disapproval. There are three more "improvisations" to follow, (the next is for orch. alone) & a coda. I think you may safely learn these as I've scored them & sent them off to be copied in London.

Perhaps at 3 it would be better with the mute off & "sul pont" [*sul ponticello*] at 4 & similar passages. I'll leave it to you to decide.

I hope you will like what I've already done. I found it very awkward as to what should follow the 2ⁿᵈ [movement]. But I think this is the solution, something (but not too much) after the quick & hectic 2ⁿᵈ mov. I'll do my utmost to let you have the rest as soon as possible.

I hope you enjoyed & had a successful tour & that you are not too exhausted after it.

as ever
William

To Gregor Piatigorsky   [October 1956]
[postcard]

[Casa Cirillo, Forio d'Ischia]

I find I've omitted a ♮ to B in the 39ᵗʰ bar of the solo variation. It might in any case be better thus:

yrs.
William

To Gregor Piatigorsky   20 October 1956

Casa Cirillo, Forio d'Ischia

Dear Grisha,

I hope you have safely received long ago the entire 2nd mov & part of the 3rd. I now send you some more of the last mov & in the next few days will be sending the work complete.

I fear that it is difficult to convey the 3rd improv[isation] (that is from $\boxed{8}$) on the pfte but it will give you some idea of what is going on, & [I] hope that you'll find the 4th up to standard. After much misgiving I think it is turning out to be a good movement & the end though quiet will be just as effective if not more so, as a quick & loud one. Anyhow that you will be able to judge in a day or two after receiving this. It is by the way all scored & Munch[1] will be getting his score quite shortly.

Just one suggestion – in the 1st solo improv. 6 bars from the end perhaps it would be better thus

   or

   you decide!

as ever
William

---

1 Charles Münch, French (Alsatian) conductor, and Music Director of the Boston Symphony Orchestra from 1948 to 1962. The Cello Concerto's première was to be given by them with Piatigorsky as the soloist.

To Walter Legge   21 October 1956

Casa Cirillo, Forio d'Ischia

Dear Walter,

If you are now back, I hope you had an agreably busy time in the U.S.

About the Jo'burg Festival Ov. 1956 [. . .] A. Frank is asking about [a] recording.

It was by the way, a "wow" in Jo'burg, not [that] that means much (except for 400 smackers "tax free") & Malcolm S.[1] cabled "Overture complete triumph, repeating by request next concert, & in Pretoria".

Kurtz[2] who is doing the first English perf. on Nov 13th would like to record, so doubtless would Malcolm – so doubtless would I; as I havent a bean except "blocked" ones in England (of those I've quite an amount) a fee paid on the nail would probably [be] more than welcome when we return in Jan. for the 1st London perf. of the Ov. Jan 23rd & the Vlc. Con Feb 13th after which we return here for me to complete a work for Cleveland[3] (2000 dols taxfree!) & Su to carry on her building operations on our new acquisition which it is high time you visited.

But seriously my financial situation in England is very hazardous (I've even had a cheque for £10 R.D'd [returned to drawer], luckily only [made out] to Dallas Bower who was coming here & I wanted some tobacco) but I'm hoping to be allowed to sell some shares which can be put on what is known as a "transferable account" & if this goes thro' we shall be alright for the moment anyhow. But I think everything will settle down as soon as the routine is in working order.

I shall finish the Vlc Con in a couple of days or so as it is on the whole fairly satisfactory which from me is saying a lot. It is in fact the best of the three concerti.

The island is very quiet[,] all the great, Herbert [von Karajan], Callas [. . .] etc etc having departed & is divine with wonderful weather.

I suppose there is no hope of persuading Herbert to think about putting on T&C in Vienna. It is to be revived at C.G. in '58 for the

---

1 Sir Malcolm Sargent had just conducted the first performance of the *Johannesburg Festival Overture*, in Johannesburg's City Hall.

2 Efrem Kurtz, American conductor of Russian birth. He was Joint Music Director of the Liverpool Philharmonic Orchestra (later the Royal Liverpool Philharmonic Orchestra) from 1955 to 1957. In 1935 he had conducted Walton's score for the film *Escape Me Never*.

3 The *Partita*, commissioned by George Szell and the Cleveland Orchestra.

centenary. Could Elizabeth [Elisabeth Schwarzkopf] be persuaded to sing [Cressida] provided D.W. [David Webster] asks her in time?

Let us hear from you sometime

With our love

as ever

William

To Gregor Piatigorsky   21 October 1956

Casa Cirillo, Forio d'Ischia

Dear Grisha,

Second thoughts on what I sent you yesterday.

The 7th bar of the solo improv. is, I think, better thus:

& the last bar thus –

& at least one gets to the top slightly quicker & may be it is less boring than a long scale.

as ever

William

I'm about 10 bars from the end!

CASA CIRILLO
VIA CESOTTA
FORIO D'ISCHIA
ITALY   Oct 26th '56

Dear Grisha,

The inevitable emendations!

2 before [15] read on last two beats

last beat add # to G
L.H. P.fte.

Movendo at [19] more or less the same pace as the opening of 1st Mov.

4 after [19] ⟨— 1 —⟩

+ one extra bar of the low C at the end.

The score is now completely finished

as ever

William

To Gregor Piatigorsky   26 October 1956

Casa Cirillo, Forio d'Ischia

Dear Grisha,

The inevitable emendations!
2 before 15 read on last two beats

last beat add ♯ to G
L.H. Pfte.

Morendo at 19 more or less the same p[l]ace as the opening of 1st Mov.
4 after 19
& one extra bar of the low C at the end.
The score is now completely finished.
    as ever
    William

To Alan Frank   28 October 1956

Casa Cirillo, Forio d'Ischia

Dear Alan,
    I've been unduly & unnecessarily alarmed hearing from P. [Piatigorsky]
today.
    [. . .] There are alterations in the 2nd Cadenza of the 2nd mov. but they
don't really concern anyone except him [. . .] And there's something
about the last two bars of all but his explanation is undecipherable &
it will have to wait till he write[s] again, but it can't be anything much.
There are also other bits which have been changed but only concern
him. I presume it is not impossible to change the full sc. before printing.
    He writes that he's completely exhausted by his tour & has to embark
on another which includes 2 concerts in Pittsburgh 6 in Philadelphia 7 in
Canada & 1 in Connecticut before Dec 7th! How he can do it & learn
the Con as well I don't know, nor apparently does he! But they are all
like that, Heifetz was just the same.
    as ever
    William

[281]

To Gregor Piatigorsky   28 October 1956

Casa Cirillo, Forio d'Ischia

Dear Grisha,

What a relief to receive your letter, & to know that the music has safely arrived. I was about to imagine that it was chasing you round the Far East & never catching up with you! & you would think I was never going to finish.

I am sorry to hear that you are so tired & exhausted with your travels & that such a tough schedule is ahead of you. I only hope that you are doing works you can play in your sleep, so to speak.

There is only one thing that puzzles me (chiefly because I can't read it) in your list of queries & suggestions & that is the one about [the] last couple of bars. I enclose a piece of Ms paper to save you the bother of ruling lines so that you can put clearly what you do want.

The rest I answer on the enclosed sheet. I approve of all your suggestions, but maybe my counter suggestions are better, particularly about the five bars before 22 which now may be too easy!

I hope you will like the rest of the improvisations, but I am fearing that the Coda may be not what you want or expect. To me, musically speaking, it rounds off the work in a satisfying & logical way & should sound beautiful[,] noble, dignified etc though it ends on a whisper. Sometimes (& I hope this is one of them) an ending such as this one, is in every way just as impressive & evocative as a more spectacular & loud one, especially in this case, as I feel there is no other solution.

However I won't labour the point, in case you think I'm apologising for it! But I think & hope you will agree with me.

Let me know as soon as you can whatever you may need altering (in the 3rd mov). I hope it is not much, for your sake. Of course I'm not angry with you, but rather at myself for not getting things right the first time.

Trying to anticipate your wishes for the "uncomfortable" thirds & sixths – I've been trying to remember which they may be. Alas, I'm without a copy having sent it to London, but it will be back in a few days. But as far as I remember these may be the offending thirds – the sixths I hope are blameless!

Forgive my string indications[.] I've only put them in to help me figure [them] out for myself. You've no idea how difficult it is to write for some instrument one has no exact knowledge about. But here goes & it may be better.

[282]

or perhaps these are better.

Please keep in touch if you are not too tired.
as ever
William

To Helga Cranston   1 November 1956

Casa Cirillo, Forio d'Ischia

Dear Helga,

I wrote to you only last week & you will find the letter awaiting you on your return, that is if you do return.

It would seem that you have chosen a somewhat inopportune moment[1] to visit your father-or-mother-land [Israel] & I hope in a frenzy of misguided patriotism you won't hurl yourself into the fray by joining the Israelite Waafs, Wiifs or whatever they may be.

The whole affair which, pray Jahver, I trust will not spread & evelope [envelop] us all seems to a distant spectator like myself a reversion to mid '30s gangsterism, but this time with Eden[2] in the role of Mussolini.

I'm glad to hear about "St Joan" & hope you'll survive to return to do it. Gloomy, are'nt I?

---

1 The Suez Crisis had developed when Egypt's leader, Gamal Abdal Nasser, supported by the Soviet Union, had nationalized the internationally owned Suez Canal. Israeli, British and French troops attacked Egypt and had largely resecured the Canal when America and the Soviet Union, in response to the United Nations' condemnation of the invasion, sent in their own troops to enforce a ceasefire. After compensating the former Suez Canal Company, Egypt retained control of the Canal itself.
2 Sir Anthony Eden, British Prime Minister.

If you do manage to ever return to Rome look in here for a few days. Don't telephone[,] the nearest is miles off, but a telegram sometimes reaches us with[in] 24 hours. So do that if you can.

Look after yourself
As ever
William

To Gregor Piatigorsky   4 November 1956

Casa Cirillo, Forio d'Ischia

Dear Grisha,

I am so very happy to receive your cable, and [to] know that you approve the epilogue, and further that you should think the whole work "wonderful". It is to my mind, the best of my now, three concertos, but don't say so to Jascha [Heifetz]!

I must thank you in the first place for having commissioned the work, but more so for your patience with me in my darker moments (& some were very dark indeed) & I can assure you, that without the confidence & urge with which you inspired me, I very much doubt if I should have finished, at any rate in time for Dec 7th.

I only hope it will come up to your expectations when you come to playing it with the orchestra.

If anything in the orchestration (that vibraphone for instance) should irk you, just cut it out! It is not absolutely essential (though I might miss it!).

[. . .]

However I am still unable to fathom exactly what you intend in the last couple of bars of the 2nd mov. Please let me know if I can be of any further help.

Again with many thanks for everything
ever yours
William

To Alan Frank   9 November 1956

Casa Cirillo, Forio d'Ischia

Dear Alan,

Thanks for the clutch of letters.

① Your explanation about the £1400 cheque clears up everything & I've heard from Marks[1] that the B of E [Bank of England] has now agreed more or less to everything.

② I've written to P [Piatigorsky] for the [Cello Concerto] fee ($3000 by the way) to be paid to Su's a/c in N.Y. [New York]

③ Bach Partitas yes the keyboard ones.

④ Fl Con [Flute Concerto] for Mrs K[2] (yes we met her) very remote at the moment & not to be thought of till everything else I've on hand is out of the way.

⑤ Liverpool. Yes I was a bit uncertain whether it [the commissioning of the Second Symphony][3] was really clinched. What with Stiff's departure & having heard nothing further in writing – or had you got something? There was I remember in talking with Stiff no specified date for completion, but we talked of the 57/58 season. I shall aim for that & try & make it more or less coincide with the Manchester date in '58.

⑥ The Cleveland [Orchestra] work I doubt finishing by Feb, as we leave here mid-Jan[4] & shall be in London most of Feb which will mean getting little if anything done while there – but it should be through by early April.

I can then get started on the Symphony – but by experience I don't find summer the best time for working here – what with one's hide-out getting well known & people coming to stay etc. But one will just have to steel oneself & say no.

But though I'll try for late 57/58 season I make no definite promise.

1 J. B. Marks, the Waltons' accountant.
2 Probably Mrs Kurtz, i.e. Elaine Shaffer, the internationally famous flautist married to the conductor Efrem Kurtz (see p. 278, n. 2).
3 By the Royal Liverpool Philharmonic Orchestra.
4 To travel to London for the Cello Concerto's British première.

⑦ B's F. [*Belshazzar's Feast*] as there's no hope for a year it gives one time to think about conducting oneself. Is'nt [Wolfgang] Sawallisch[1] the one who did it in Aachen? Good about the American perfs.

⑧ Other works I plan to do in the next couple of years or so are a Sinfonietta for Birmingham (The Partita is the piece for Cleveland, that is why I want the Bach just to ascertain exactly what a P is!) Variations on a theme by Hindemith (for H. I've long promised him a piece – the trouble of course is [to] find the theme – in the end I shall probably have to think of one of my own).

A Sonata for Strings for noone in particular[.] Fl Con if sufficiently induced.

After that I could (having 7 or 8 comparatively new works to keep one going) take time off for another opera if Chris. [Hassall] has found a suitable subject by then.

Of course all one's plans will be blown sky high if – if! Anyhow that is the general overall-plan & I don't propose to take too long about carrying it out.

as ever
William

To Helga Cranston   13 November 1956

Casa Cirillo, Forio d'Ischia

Dear Helga,

Glad to know that you are still alive & that hysteria has not overcome your customary phlegm.

Yes, we'd be delighted to see you for Xmas & hope it will keep fine for you.

Of course, with my clear-eyed view on the situation the whole business is quite simply this. Are the Russians to be allowed to control Suez & the oil of the middle east or not? And however anyone may scream & yell, personally I feel for us & the whole of non-Communist Europe, they must be prevented by fair means or foul.

If they get Suez they've fairly got us by the balls (or testicles if you

---

1 German conductor and pianist. Music Director at Aachen Opera House from 1953 to 1958.

will) & they can cut (or bite) them off at any time they please. It's as simple as that!

We are by way of returning to London mid-Jan to hear my new works, but I doubt our being able to motor back as I see that France is already almost without petrol & we don't want to be stranded on the way. But by then maybe Messrs Onassis & Niarchos[1] may have got things going.

Look after yourself & keep away from uniforms of all kinds.

as ever
William

To Christopher Morris[2]   15 November 1956

Casa Cirillo, Forio d'Ischia

Dear Christopher,

Here is a list of mistakes, (not many) in Mov III. [of the Cello Concerto] I expect they've already been spotted, but in case not here they are.

If the parts are already gone to America perhaps it would be able [i.e. possible] to get Dowling or the Boston [Symphony Orchestra's] librarian to pop in the addition[al] 6 [bars] before the end of improv. III (see sheet).

P. [Piatigorsky] writes me that he lost all the music when he was changing 'planes in Chicago. It turned up however after three days. Perhaps we ought to have a spare copy on hand in case he does it again.

yrs
William

To Louis and Griselda Kentner   21 November 1956

Casa Cirillo, Forio d'Ischia

Dear Griselda & Lou,

You have been much in our thoughts of late especially poor Lou who must be much upset by these awful happenings in Hungary.[3] If, by the

---

1 Aristotle Onassis and Stavros Niarchos, Greek owners of their respective shipping lines (including oil-tanker fleets), and bitter rivals.
2 Alan Frank's assistant in Oxford University Press's music department.
3 The Soviet Union had responded to the advent of Hungary's independence-minded government by invading the country and ruthlessly suppressing the armed uprising that followed.

way, old Koch, should have been so fly as to make a get-away (I suspect he has) I will contribute to his support.

I fear a performance of Belsazár Lakomàja (Magyarországi bemutató) by the Budapestikoras és Magyar Allarmi Haugversenyzenekar Zene-akadémián which was frenziedly received, may have helped to touch things off. It was only a few weeks before the outbreak.

I finished the 'cello concerto to be precise on Oct 25th just in time for the perf next Dec 7th in Boston. It is, I think, the best of my concertos & Piatigorsky seems very pleased with it & cabled "entire work wonderful" etc – I only hope he's right.

We are returning to London mid-Jan to hear the overture I wrote for Johannesburg on the 23rd & the concerto on Feb 13th. If you've got nothing better to do, put the dates down & come & hear them.

How was the Tippett?[1] I read a few half-hearted notices about it.

We have become residents abroad & one has yet to see if it works out favourably or not. All my British income is now taxed at source at full rates, but everything I earn from America & other places I get here virtually tax-free as far as I can make out, but it's too soon to see if one really gains or not.

We have bought quite a piece of ground[,] 10,000 sq.m. so what with the intention of building three small houses for letting purposes (one can do very well on these) & one for ourselves, the muse will be kept pretty busy trying to cope with the outlay involved. And theres Su's mania for gardening to be taken into account as well. In fact I'm full of qualms about it – but we can always sell it (at a profit if only everyone would stop trying to make wars) if I find I can't cope. But Su's mad about it & I daresay she's right.

Let us have your news.

With best love from us both

as ever

William

---

1 Louis Kentner had played the solo part in the première of Tippett's Piano Concerto in Birmingham's Town Hall on 30 October 1956, with the City of Birmingham Symphony Orchestra conducted by Rudolf Schwarz.

To Helga Cranston   5 December 1956

Casa Cirillo, Forio d'Ischia

Dear Helga,

Gloom-doom-woe-woe etc ad inf.

Right – you stay in Naples Sunday night the 23rd. I doubt if the hotels are full, unless the whole of the American fleet turns up with its wives & families. [. . .]

Your boat leaves for Porto d'Ischia (2nd stop, don't get off at Procida) at 8–45am & arrives at P. Ischia at approx 10–45. I think you can easily get to Rome by 18–00 for the return journey in the day. But we can see about that later.

Just heard from Piatigorsky that he's had a break-down & the 1st perf of the Vlc Con which should have taken place on the 7th is postponed. Rather sad – but better this than that he should have collapsed during the work!

We look forward to seeing you
as ever
William

To Gregor Piatigorsky   6 December 1956

Casa Cirillo, Forio d'Ischia

Dear Grisha,

I was terribly sorry to hear of your breakdown. With your prolonged & exacting tour it is perhaps not surprising, but I only hope that you do not feel that my being behindhand with the Concerto, has been a contributory factor. Anyhow now, after an adequate rest you will be able to take the first performance in your stride.

Now that there is not such a rush about the first performance, do you think it feasible to have a photostat copy of the 'cello part made & sent to me. It would be a great help from the publishing point of view if I could have the part with all your emendations & phrasing[,] bowings, etc, & which of the several versions of some parts, you have finally decided on.

If however it is inconvenient to have this done it can wait till you come to London.

I hope you will allow it to be published with "edited by G.P".

Again I beg you to take it easy & above all not to worry.
Best love
as ever
William

To Gregor Piatigorsky   19 December 1956

Casa Cirillo, Forio d'Ischia

Dear Grisha,
    I am delighted to receive your letter & to hear that you are well on
the way to recovery.
    I am pleased that Jascha [Heifetz] is impressed with the Concerto, &
knowing that his critical acumen is not something to be sniffed at, I have
produced a shortened version (by about 20″) of improv. 2. also a new
ending.
    Both are I think an improvement though I'm in slight doubt as to
whether bars 4. – 6 – 14,15. are not better in the original version.
    The end is I think now more intense & if you should use it, it won't
involve much re-copying in the parts. As Jascha brought up these two
points perhaps you could show them him & he could give the final
verdict.
    [. . .]
    You will notice I've sneaked in the double-stopping as grace notes in
bar 20–21 & I feel them to be more of a climax in 23 – however if you
feel it is better without them – out with 'em.
    Take care of yourself
    love
    as ever
    William

To Sir Laurence Olivier   25 December 1956

Casa Cirillo, Forio d'Ischia

My dear Larry
    Thank you so much for your letter.
    This is the situation about Lowndes Cott. It has already been sold to
Dallas Bower Prods. (that is in reality that I've sold it to myself, as I'm a

director of D.B Prods, & with full approval of the Bank of England) so the tax obligations on the house are comparatively little. Marks, my accountant a co-director, is against my selling it, pointing out that by letting it it more than pays for itself & at the same time is more or less available to ourselves whenever we need it for our 93 days stay in London.[1]

He also said that when we are in London we can make our presence felt with more emphasis from our own house & entertain etc much more cheaply than if we were staying, say, at the Dorchester for three months.

That being our position as regards L.C, it would be pointless to let it for a period of years & store the furniture, in fact we might as well in that case, sell it, which at the moment at any rate is not what we want to do as we don't really need the money.

We shall be back in London between Jan 15th & 20th. & stay there till the end of Feb, so we have time to discuss it all.

We are motoring back so unfortunately shall need the garage (in fact I see we are making ourselves a bloody nuisance for you for which please forgive us). There's no rationing here & the allowance in France should be just enough to get us through.

[. . .]

We hope you enjoy your hol. & have found somewhere which is not so cold as it is here.

With our best love to you both

as ever

William

P.S. Marks says he needs about 6 weeks notice for letting L.C. There is a client nibbling about taking it from March 1st but I don't know for how long. After our stay in Jan–Feb, '57 I don't think we shall be returning to London till around March–April '58.

---

1 As foreign residents, the Waltons were allowed to stay only for this limited amount of time in Britain each year.

To Gregor Piatigorsky   25 December 1956

Casa Cirillo, Forio d'Ischia

Dear Grisha,

Just reading thro' your last letter I perceive that you quote the following bar thus

this F should be ♮ not ♯

I may not have made it plain in the M.s.s. A small point, but I thought I should mention it just in case.

After not having looked at the new endings for some days I looked today [and] I find I incline to A rather than to B. But who knows I might feel the exact opposite tomorrow.

As ever.
William

To Gregor Piatigorsky   [Rome, 16 January 1957]
[telegram]

AGREE TO ALL MODIFICATIONS LOOK AFTER YOURSELF LOVE
WILLIAM

To Gregor Piatigorsky   [Vatican City, 17 January 1957]
[telegram]

INVOLVED IN MOTORSMASH CANNOT MOVE FOR 40 DAYS SO DIS-
APPOINTED MISS PREMIERS BEST LOVE
WILLIAM

• | | LA217

L CDV055 21 PD INTL=CD VATICANCITY VIA MACKAY 17 1645=

=LT PIATIGORSKY=

=400 SOUTHBUNDY DR LOSA=

1957 JAN 17 PM 1 22

INVOLVED IN MOTORSMASH CANNOT MOVE FOR 40 DAYS SO
DISSAPPOINTED MISS PREMIERS BEST LOVE=

=WILLIAM=

26767

400 40=

To Gregor Piatigorsky [Rome, 22 January 1957]
[telegram]

IN BOCCA AL LUPO STOP SURVIVING AUTO ACCIDENT BUT BEDRIDDEN
FORTY DAYS LOVE
WILLIAM VIA TRIONFALE 228 ROMA

To Gregor Piatigorsky 4 February 1957

Clinica dello Spirito Santo, Villa Stuart, Via Trionfale 228, Rome

Dear Grisha,

Thanks so much for your cables, letters & cuttings. I'm so glad for us both that it[1] went so well in spite of the somewhat lunatic press – but one has to expect that – something would be seriously wrong if it were otherwise.

How hellish about this accident. I am, I fear in bed till the end of the month. As far as I can gather, all the bones down my left side & particularly the hip, are cracked without actually being broken. This makes it more complicated as I can't be put in plaster but have to lie prone on my back.[2]

R.A.I. (the italian radio) have very nicely offered to transmit the "broadcast" on the 13th[3] so I should be able to hear it well. But of course it is not the same thing as being there & we had both been looking forward to seeing & hearing you so much. Susana is on the mend quicker than I.

If there is anything you want to ask me about the work you can telephone me from London[,] in the evening would be best & it will be quite feasible for me to listen to any particular passage this way.

I hope you have nice stay in London & that everything works out well & look after those ulcers.

love
William

1 The Cello Concerto's world première, in Boston on 25 January 1957.
2 The collision of the Waltons' car with a cement lorry outside Civitavecchia had also left Susana Walton with a broken wrist. The ensuing litigation between the Waltons and Italcemento was to last for seven years, before they eventually received compensation from the cement company.
3 Of the Cello Concerto's British première on 13 February.

To Alan Frank   4 February 1957

Clinica dello Spirito Santo, Villa Stuart, Via Trionfale 228, Rome

Dear Alan,
      Thanks for your various letters. [. . .]
      [. . .]
      There is I fear not a hope of our getting back for the 13th. At one moment there seemed as if there might be a chance of my getting back in a chair but on 2nd thought the doctors have decided that I musn't put a foot to the ground before the end of the month in case of complications. Apart from the personal side of it with P [Piatigorsky] I don't think my presence or absence matters much either way.
      [. . .]
      Also would you drop a line to Szell[1] & Cleveland saying that in all probability with this accident taking 2 months out of my life I'm going to be later than June 1st with the piece.[2] I do'nt see now how I can get it done in time. At the moment I can hardly think without my head going round in a spin.
      [. . .]
      Love from us both. Sue's about in enormous boots & her sticks are out.
      Yrs
      William

I hope you can read this. Get Roy [Douglas] to see P. about the authentic version of Vl[c] Con.

To Gregor Piatigorsky   12 March 1957

c/o Alan Frank, Oxford University Press, 44 Conduit Street, w.1

Dear Grisha,
      I am sorry to have been so long in answering your letters, but what with getting back here for a few weeks everything has been an awful rush.
      You have made (& made for me) a terrific impression here with the Concerto & everyone is hoping that you'll be back here next season with it – indeed I hope so.

1 George Szell, American conductor of Hungarian birth. He was Music Director of the Cleveland Orchestra from 1946 to 1970.
2 The *Partita*.

I have heard the tapes of the "world premiere" & the "Philharmonic" & there are I think a few comments & suggestions I can make.

The timings –

	My timing	World Prem.	Phil.
I	7'–15"	9'–20"	8'–10"
II	6'–0	7'–7"	6'–30"
III	11–50"	15'–43"	15'–10"
Total	25'–5"	32'–10"	29'–50"

My timings are perhaps a little on the fast side, but the biggest difference is the last movement & to my mind the differences occur in the two solo "improvs".

To make it quite clear how I feel they should go, I'm making a tape which I will send to you very shortly. This I think is the best way. Mind you they are only suggestions & I hope you won't mind my making them.

I've got my publisher to find out from R.C.A. Victor if you could (that is if you wish to) re-record the unaccompanied parts for the record they're issuing. The answer is "yes you can" & there's plenty of time as the record is not to be issued anyhow till June.

I believe & I'm sure you will feel the same, that [it] is best to get the record as authentic as possible. All the re-recordings are easy & simple to fit in instead of the present ones.

I do so hate asking you to do this & I know you won't think it is because I don't appreciate your playing of the work as a whole but it is just these parts where the performance could be tightened up. Do forgive me.

We are getting on very well, now that we can get electrical treatment for our inert muscles & very soon I hope we shall be getting about without crutches.

You must be longing for the end of your season & I hope that the ulcers are not giving you trouble.

Ian Hunter[1] has suggested I write a double Concerto for you & Jascha! Not just yet I feel!

With best love from us both (my wife feels she knows you almost as well as I do)

as ever
William

---

1 English concert agent and impresario. Later chairman of Harold Holt Ltd., the agency that represented Walton as a conductor.

To Gregor Piatigorsky   4 April 1957

Casa Cirillo, Forio d'Ischia

[in reply to cable dated 2 April 1957: RE RECORD EVERYTHING WHERE
CELLO ALONE AS PLANNED BEFORE HUMILIATING REMARKS MADE ON
YOUR BEHALF BY OXFORD PRESS TO RCA LOVE GRISHA]

Dear Grisha,

I am so glad to receive your cable forwarded here by the O.U.P. & to
understand that you don't object to re-record the solo "improvs" in the
3rd mov.

I can't tell you how much I appreciate your going to all this trouble,
but I do feel that it may be worth it, & once done will ensure the record
being absolutely what we both want.

We have returned here & are getting well rapidly, in fact, I'm about
to begin on a new piece for the Cleveland Orchestra – unfortunately I'm
already some three months late & am sure that my usual panic will soon
set in.

Affectionate greetings from us both

as ever

William

P.S Regards to Jascha & Will[1] – what fun you must be having.

To Gregor Piatigorsky   12 April 1957

Casa Cirillo, Forio d'Ischia

Dear Grisha,

Thank you for your letter. True, I did not quite understand your telegram, as till now I had no idea of any "remarks addressed to a factory"
(I suppose the O.U.P. must have perpetrated them) & I can well understand your irritation about them, but I can assure you they did not
emanate from me. Anyhow as you say, let's forget it.

I will certainly change the indications, in fact I have already done so
when I realised quite how misleading they were. It is certainly all my

---

1   William Primrose, Scottish viola soloist by now resident in America, and a regular
colleague of Heifetz and Piatigorsky in chamber music and concertos. Bartók had composed his Viola Concerto for him.

fault, I see now, that you were misled, and I am sorry that I should have done so.

[. . .]

We are both getting well though still on crutches but hope to discard them soon. You've know [*sic*] idea how irritating they are.

With affectionate greetings from us both

as ever

William

P.S. Listening to various tapes I found various things not entirely satis-factory in the orchestra in both performances but [Roy] Douglas assured me (and he's quite a[n] expert) that it all sounded well in the actual hall.

To Alan Frank   15 May 1957

Casa Cirillo, Forio d'Ischia

Dear Alan,

Thank you for your letter. P. [Piatigorsky] sent me all the cuttings – all fairly good except one.

It is rather irritating about E.M.I. but I suppose they don't want to record it at the moment & till [ie. until] after the Decca one has been issued [for] some length of time. I hope that R. [Rostropovich][1] will take to it. P. says the record won't be out till the fall.

[. . .]

The Partita is being "bloody-minded" at the moment – in fact partic-ularly so – however we will see.

as ever

William

Karajan is here for a few days but will be coming for longer next month. I'll try & see how the land lies.

1 Mstislav Rostropovich, Russian cellist and conductor. He had made his London and New York débuts in 1956.

To Alan Frank   4 July 1957

Casa Cirillo, Forio d'Ischia

Dear Alan,

Thanks for the various communications. I've dispatched to-day the 1st mov of the Partita. The next will follow shortly but I fear it will be the end rather than the beginning of Aug before its complete.

Karajan has had a look at it & liked it & wants to do the 1st continental perf. with the Berlin Phil in Oct '58. He offered nothing about T&C so I didn't ask him feeling that he would say something if he had the intention to do it. I think it['s] still early days for it in Vienna, though he told me the Symph had gone very well.

The heat is terrific & if the score is somewhat blotchy you must attribute it to that as one's hand gets glued to the paper. Before photoing it had better be touched up. [. . .]

[. . .]

as ever
William

To Alan Frank   7 September 1957

Casa Cirillo, Forio d'Ischia

Dear Alan,

[. . .]

I shall I hope be sending you the finale of the P. [*Partita*] very shortly – a boisterously vulgar "ohne angst" jig. I had a nice letter from Szell in which he said "The 1st. mov. strikes me as very good indeed. If the others match it your P. will be by far the finest of our commissions and there are some very well known composers in the scheme." If that's so, heaven help him with the other compositions, if mine's the best – as indeed it probably is!

I'm going to Rome on the 18th to hear Ferrarese do the Vln. Con and help out at rehearsals.

Our case[1] which should have been heard on Aug 23rd is now postponed till Oct 29th. I suppose it will go on like this ad lib.

---

1 Regarding the Waltons' motor accident.

Michael Collins has turned up & is taking one of our houses for a couple of weeks. We are doing rather unexpectedly well with them which is cheering.

As ever,
William

Malcolm [Sir Malcolm Sargent] wrote to me saying that the Vlc. Con. went v. well & Bengtson[1] played marvellously, better than P. [Piatigorsky]. Timing 26½ mins! He's getting him over again for the studio perf.

To Alan Frank 7 November 1957

Casa Cirillo, Forio d'Ischia

Dear Alan,

Thanks for the conglomeration of letters & information. We returned yesterday having won our case at Civitavecchia. A minor triumph for Italian justice. The opposition lawyers did everything they could to blacken the character of whom they dubbed "La Valton" – false witness, followed false witness, including one with the appropriate name of Brigante! However they spoiled their case by overdoing it & the judge decided 100 p.c for us. Of course, this is'nt the end – there is an appeal & if we win that, another civil case, so one can't expect anything definite for about 18 months – but anyhow we have the satisfaction of having won the first round.

[. . .]

I feel a "classical" approach to the [Second] Symph. is the right one – so would you send me some Haydn & Mozart scores. I leave it to you what – the M. [Mozart] G minor etc, say ½ a doz of each!

[. . .]

As ever
William

After Civitavecchia we went to stay for a couple of nights with Osbert at Montegufoni. He was quite keen on doing a libretto for the oratorio for 'Uddersfield.[2] He however lacks a Bible (with Apocrypha) in large

1 Erling Bengtsson, Danish cellist. A pupil of Piatigorsky, he was also for a time his assistant at the Curtis Institute of Music in Philadelphia, US.
2 The Huddersfield Choral Society had commissioned Walton to compose a new work

enough type for him to read (so do I for that matter) so perhaps the O.U.P could go as far as presenting us both with one! His address is

> Sir O S.
> Castello di Montegufoni
> Val di Pesa
> Montespertoli (presso Firenze)
> Italy.

To David Webster   10 November 1957

Casa Cirillo, Forio d'Ischia

Dear David,

Thanks for the cable & the news that C.G is thinking of reviving the corpse.[1] The soprano is the crux & I personally don't think it worth attempting unless we can persuade a "star" or at any rate one with "star" quality to take it on.

Callas was here for a few days before leaving for Edinburgh. I didn't bother her as she said she was returning for a prolonged stay – however she didn't, so I missed the opportunity of talking to her about it. However I will write to her & see if she can be persuaded to do it, but I am, as doubtless you are, very dubious as to any hope of her doing it. But it will do no harm to try.

Failing her, could [Victoria de] Los Angeles[2] be persuaded or perhaps there is some American Swede or German? But it is essential that their English should be perfect – no more Lazlo [László] English! And certainly not Dow.

We return in mid-April. I'm conducting in Manchester at the end of that month, also maybe I shall hear the "première" of Symph. No 2. (at Liverpool) but I rather doubt that as I've not yet started it! So our visit would fit in nicely for the revival.

It has been quite a busy summer. I wrote my piece for Cleveland (you can hear it in London next May 3rd). We've built four houses (& let

---

for the Society's 125th anniversary season in 1961, and Walton had approached Osbert Sitwell to select the text (as Sitwell had for *Belshazzar's Feast*).
1 *Troilus and Cressida*. It was not in fact revived at Covent Garden until 1963.
2 Catalan soprano. She sang regularly at Covent Garden between 1950 and 1961 in French and Italian opera roles.

them quite profitably considering it is our first season) & won our case over the car accident, though of course there is an appeal & it will be at least another year before anything concrete results from it.

The accident has naturally put me back about 3 or 4 months with my work.

With love from us both.
William

To Alan Frank   12 November 1957

Casa Cirillo, Forio d'Ischia

Dear Alan,

I hear from Mr. Barksdale (Cleveland) that they can't afford to buy the Partita sc. I suggest it would be a nice gesture if we loaned them the original sc. for their Anniversary season. This should satisfy all concerned & who knows some lunatic or sputnikatic[1] might like to buy it.

As ever,
William

To Alan Frank   13 November 1957

Casa Cirillo, Forio d'Ischia

Dear Alan,

What a nuisance these programme note boys are! What can one say about a work like the Partita? The work is in three movements – 1. Toccata 2. Pastorale siciliana 3. Giga burlesca. These titles should provide the listener with sufficient clues as to what the music is about. They could I suppose be described as three essays in (I hate to use the term) "pure", or (as regards the last) "impure" music. Anyhow it has no programme or any ulterior motive behind it either deep or shallow (save perhaps making $2000!). The music, in both form and content is eminently straightforward & simple or even vulgar, too much so perhaps, nevertheless designedly so. It is meant to be enjoyed straight off & there is no attempt to ponder over the imponderables – in fact, I hope at any

---

1 The Soviet Union had recently launched Sputnik 1, the first man-made satellite to orbit the Earth successfully.

rate the last mov. will divert for a moment the hearers from thinking over too much the dire consequences of the launching of the "sputniks"!

That's all I can tell you and if you dish something together out of it, I'll admire you a lot.

But seriously, I think you had better do the notes for the Hallé & the Phil & I am dead against anyone from the "Listener" or any other journal being allowed a pre-view of the score. For once this is a work that does not need a pre-view. Anyone ought to be able to like it or dislike it after the first hearing.

as ever,
William

To Sir Laurence Olivier   15 November 1957

Casa Cirillo, Forio d'Ischia

Dear Larry,

A lot seems to have transpired since we saw you in Venice. How are you both? We are surviving after having built four houses, finishing my piece for Cleveland and having won our case about our car accident. Not that the latter has got us much further, as there is an appeal & heaven knows when that will come on. Anyhow it is something to have won the first & most important round.

You will see from the enclosed p.c. how we have changed the landscape (it is taken from the terrace of C.C.) The furthest one [house] to the right is not ours & the second from the left has yet to be re-done. But if either or both of you are feeling like a "break" any of them are at your command & we should be overjoyed to see you. Considering it's our first year we've done very well letting them – they were ready for August & we have quite a number of bookings for next season, including one from [Jean] Anouilh[1] for three months.

They are very pretty & comfortable & have everything so you would be much better off than when you were staying with us here.

I see in one of the papers that you have been in Scotland looking for "locations" for "Macbeth"[2] & failed to find anything suitable. This presumably means that production is fairly imminent. If you should have in

---

1 French playwright. Among his most famous plays are *Becket* and *Antigone*.
2 Olivier's planned film version of Shakespeare's play, which remained unmade.

mind, your old friend to write the music, could you possibly let me have the approximate dates. This [is] rather necessary, as with only our 93 days we have to look ahead. Unfortunately the year is counted as from April 5th to the following April 5th. We return to London round April 20th '58 as I am conducting in Manchester & the 1st London perf of my Cleveland piece takes place at a "Phil" on May 3rd. There is also talk of a revival of "Troilus" at the end of May. Now if the time for writing the music for "Macbeth" should occur between April 5th '58 & April 5th '59, it will mean curtailing our visit in April 58 so as to leave as much time as possible for doing the film. However if it should be after April 5th '59 there is no problem. Could you be angelic & let me know about this?

We saw the "Prince & the show-girl" in Rome (in English) & enjoyed it immensely (even without that ravishing "waltz"!). The music was good & appropriate in fact everything that was needed.

Our best love to you both
as ever
William.

To Alan Frank   21 November 1957

Casa Cirillo, Forio d'Ischia

Dear Alan,

Forgive my somewhat lengthy silence. This morning I dispatched the last pages of the P. [*Partita*] When you have a chance to see it as a whole, I think you will agree with me (I refer to [movement] III) that I have been sailing far too near to the wind in fact one could say, perhaps, that one has G.T.F. [gone too far]. However, if it does come off, it should make a rousing & diverting finish to the work. It is meant to divert, & also to annoy, & I shall be intensely dissapointed if I get a kind word from either P.H.[1] or D.M[2] or anybody else. "Vulgar without being funny" (in the words of the late Sir G. Sitwell in reply to some inane remark of Osbert's,) – is the best I can hope for. Incidentally the lyric that goes with the middle tune (A maj.) is not, as you might at first think, "The flow'rs that bloom etc" but, (& if you should have to dispute

---

1 Peter Heyworth, music critic of the *Observer*.
2 Donald Mitchell, at this time music critic for *Musical Times*, subsequently of the *Daily Telegraph*.

it with anyone) "There was a young woman of Gloster, who's parents thought they had lost her" etc.

And now I have to look a 2$^{\underline{nd}}$ Symphony in the face! I sha'nt do that, at any rate, for the next 10 days as our case [over the car accident] comes up on the 29$^{\underline{th}}$. If we win, it should be a pretty hilarious one, if not, full of the popular "angst" & gloom. Apropos of the symp. the other night we had dinner with some people which included an Italian painter called Pagliaccio (I need hardly add he's known as Rusticana) & his American wife (who I need hardly add is in fact a Russian). After dinner she, through the aid of a tea-cup, got in touch with the spirits & to her guide in particular & invited us to ask questions. My questions were these:– Q Shall I finish my new S. by April 1$^{\underline{st}}$ '58? A. No. Q When will it be finished? A. June. Which seems to me a fairly accurate estimate. Q. Why can't I finish by April? A. Because of difficulty with the last movement (typical!) – but you could finish by April if you cheat & so throw it away. Q. Will it be better than the 1$^{\underline{st}}$? A. Yes indeed. Q. Will my not finishing by April create a lot of trouble etc? A. Not at all don't worry. I then switched to T&C. Q When will T&C be revived? A. Never (which I have been suspecting for some time to be the truth) however it continued to say not to bother, as in a few years time I should produce another masterpiece! Then I asked Q. Shall we win our case? A. Yes. So, one can have a better idea by the 29$^{\underline{th}}$ as to how to judge the other answers. – One more question – Q Have I also got a guide? A Yes & her name's Salome! – Next time I get through I shall ask her what she thinks of Richard Strauss! Anyhow it was quite a diverting & amusing evening.

To answer your questions now. About the Pfte Qt [Piano Quartet], I don't know what to say. Best perhaps leave it as it is[1] except for correcting the vast amount of mistakes in the sc & parts. (I was only allowed one proof & it was my first experience!) Otherwise one might get involved in all sorts of cutting & re-writing & it might emerge (& is it worth it?) as an entirely different work!

[. . .] It would I think be worth while following up [Josef] Szigeti's[2] arrangement of the Façade waltz I did before the war & don't remember if it was ever completed.

This would seem to be all.

Have I got any money coming to me? – I fear not!

1 Walton eventually revised his Piano Quartet in 1973–74.
2 Hungarian-born violinist, resident in American from 1940.

as ever
William

P.S Cleveland have asked for notes on the P. & could they have the sketches for the work. I've replied that apart from never writing about my own work, this, I should have thought of all works, needs the least explanation. That my sketches, quite unintelligible to anyone save myself, I destroy as I go along but suggested that they could have the original score if the O.U.P. permitted. And I suggest the O.U.P. might submit it, for a consideration say of $500, to be split by us! Anyhow I leave it [. . .] to you to do as you think fit.

To Alan Frank   24 November 1957

Casa Cirillo, Forio d'Ischia

Dear Alan,
   Bravo – I couldn't have done it better myself! It says everything that is needed. Thanks.
   [. . .]
   I've had a letter from Szell saying he's delighted with the whole work & hopes that in the near future I will accept another commission from the C.O. [Cleveland Orchestra]
   As ever,
   William

To Alan Frank   28 November 1957

Casa Cirillo, Forio d'Ischia

Dear Alan,
   Thanks for the various letters. It's good about Szell even if he has a vulgar mind. I think you can safely go ahead with the engraving of the P. There won't be any cuts, it's short enough as it is, & I doubt if there will be many re-adjustments if any.
   [. . .]
   I heard from Callas very sweetly saying "no" [to singing the role of Cressida] – that she has'nt a date free next year etc. I must say it is only what I expected & I'll write to David [Webster] informing him & see

whether he has thought of anyone. Incidentally I heard over the air Jon Vickers[1] in Gerontius[2] with J.B. [John Barbirolli] from Rome – he's magnificent, better than [Richard] Lewis & would make, if he can act, a splendid T. [Troilus]

[. . .]

Glimmerings of the Symph are beginning to stir slightly, but I've been too preoccupied with planning our house to have really got down to it. Architects are worse than or as bad as conductors with their "take it or leave it" attitudes! Luckily both Su & I are not without our architectural talents & the result is, I think, going [to] be pretty good. You must arrange a tour of your Italian agencies in about a years time & stop off here to see what progress is being made on the new oratorio![3]

As ever
William

To David Webster   29 November 1957

Casa Cirillo, Forio d'Ischia

Dear David,

I have had a sweet letter from Callas saying "No" as expected to T&C. So that[']s one eliminated. Have you had any ideas?

I heard Jon Vickers in "Gerontius" from Rome & thought him magnificent & would make splendid Tro[ilus].

Just off to Naples for the opening of the [Teatro] San Carlo [season] – "Nerone"![4]

As ever
William

---

1 Canadian tenor. He was to sing the role of Troilus in a radio performance of the opera in Canada in 1963, but did not perform it on the stage.
2 Elgar's oratorio *The Dream of Gerontius*.
3 The commission from Huddersfield Choral Society.
4 The second and last, unfinished opera by Arrigo Boito (1842–1918), the composer of *Mefistofele*, and the librettist of Verdi's *Otello* and *Falstaff*.

To Alan Frank 2 December 1957

Casa Cirillo, Forio d'Ischia

Dear Alan,

We went to the opening of the San Carlo, Saturday – Nerone – dire – scenery like Alma Tadema[1] & Lord Leighton[2] & the music might as well have been by one or the other as well. [. . .]

I have the Double Con. [Concerto] on my list, but starting as from "Joburg" [*Johannesburg Festival Overture*] it is 10th! Fourth on the list is Symph. 2. 5th a piece for Hindemith which I promised him ages ago 6th the oratorio – true I could move up the D. Con to 7th place, but even so, it is still very much in the future, as I think I sha'nt get through the Oratorio before the end of '60.

And of course a double con, however spectacular the kick-off might be [. . .] has not much chance in the ordinary way. How often is the Brahms played? Not very often & one could hardly expect to equal that. However if the spirit was moved & the dollars jingled who knows?

[. . .]

as ever
William

To Paul and Gertrude Hindemith

[postcard] [postmarked: 21 December 1957]

Casa Cirillo, Forio d'Ischia

Don't think I have forgotten about the work I intend writing for you [*Variations on a Theme by Hindemith*]! But I have had four other works to do including a Symphony on which I'm working now – after that the one for you. We have also been building these houses & were in hospital

---

1 Sir Lawrence Alma-Tadema (1863–1912), Dutch-born painter of historical idylls and scenes, especially of Greek and Roman antiquity and Egyptian archaeology. After moving to England he became a naturalized British citizen, was knighted, and was elected a member of the Royal Academy.
2 Frederic Leighton (1830–1896), painter and sculptor, shared a taste in subject matter with Alma-Tadema, as titles such as *The Bath of Psyche* and *Athlete Struggling with a Python* witness. One of his paintings was bought by Queen Victoria and several became bestsellers in photogravure reproduction. He was a President of the Royal Academy, knighted in 1878 and created a baronet in 1886. He is buried in St Paul's Cathedral.

for 10 weeks after an appalling motor accident from which we are now more or less recovered.

With our best wishes to you both for Xmas & the New Year.
William & Susana Walton

To David Webster   31 December 1957

Casa Cirillo, Forio d'Ischia

Dear David,
    Alan Frank suggests that failing to find a "star", T&C should be done by the resident company with Elsie Morrison,[1] Vickers, Pears etc & with Kubelik conducting. I'm inclined to agree with him, but should like to know what you think. Or has the idea of the revival been dropped altogether?
    With our best wishes for 1958
    as ever
    William

To Alan Frank   4 January 1958

Casa Cirillo, Forio d'Ischia

Dear Alan,
    [. . .]
    As it is a very short visit in April, Su is not coming with me. Apart from doubling the expense she'll have to stand, whip in hand, to see the workmen get on with it! I don't suppose I shall be more than 10 days in England, just enough to cover my commitments, as, I think I mentioned, Larry wants me for "Macbeth" in Nov. so I must keep as many days as poss for that.
    Presumably the O.U.P can get my tickets & defray expenses as last year? I will let you know later about exact dates.
    As ever
    William

1 Elsie Morison, Australian soprano. She sang regularly between 1953 and 1962 at the Royal Opera House, where her roles included Mimì in Puccini's *La bohème* and Blanche in the British première of Poulenc's *Les dialogues des Carmélites*. She was married to Rafael Kubelík, the Royal Opera House's Music Director from 1955 to 1958.

Osbert's text for the choral work[1] has just arrived – called "Moses & Pharaoh". Not very satisfactory at first glance – very diffuse. It's about the plagues & the exodus through the Red Sea etc. In fact a bit of Cecil B. de Mille! But I think that something can eventually be made from it.[2] Could you send me a copy of "Israel in Egypt" (Handel), it might prove useful to look at the libretto! It covers, if I remember rightly, the same kind of ground & is out of copyright!

To Alan Frank   12 February 1958

Casa Cirillo, Forio d'Ischia

Dear Alan,

I think for the moment we won't do anything about Symph 2. In fact it is going so badly, that I fear I must start all over again & it might be wise to ask Liverpool[3] to put off the date till after April 5th '59. so that I can attend the performance (if any!).

Sorry to be so unhelpful & gloomy.

As ever
William

To David Webster   .   1 March 1958

Casa Cirillo, Forio d'Ischia

Dear David,

Thanks for the cable. Before I accept to conduct T&C[4] (that is if I feel capable of doing it, which needs some thought.) there are a few things I'd like to know.

① Where are the preparations to take place, London or Buenos Aires?
② What orchestra would play?
③ If I decide I can't do it, who would conduct instead?

---

1 For the Huddersfield Choral Society.
2 The oratorio was never composed.
3 The Second Symphony had been commissioned by the Royal Liverpool Philharmonic Orchestra.
4 The Royal Opera House company was planning to visit Buenos Aires with *Troilus and Cressida* and other productions. The project eventually fell through in April 1958. Walton never conducted his opera in the theatre.

Also the situation is complicated by my having accepted, (though I've not yet signed the contract so could squirm out of it), to do the music for Larry's film of "Macbeth". This will be ready for music in Nov.–Dec.

As I'm only allowed in England for 93 days of the year I have reserved 80 for that & the other 13 I use on my visit on April 21ˢᵗ –May 3ʳᵈ. If the preparations for T&C take place in London it will mean another 30 days, & so [I] should have to abandon the film, as it would be too much of a risk, knowing what films are like, to think it could be finished in 50 days. That is why I want to know whether the preparations are to be in London or B.A.

Added to this I've to get a move on with my symphony for Liverpool. So you can see it is a bit difficult to give you a precise answer offhand.

If you will let me know about these questions, I will let you have a definite answer.

With best love from us both
as ever
William

To Paul Hindemith   17 March 1958
[postcard addressed to 'Maestro Paul Hindemith']

Casa Cirillo, Forio d'Ischia

I've just seen about your concert in Rome in the "Radio Corriere", & we wonder if you would like to come here (you would have this house) for a few days. Perhaps the Labrocas would like to come too! If you should come by car go to Pozzuoli where there is a ferry direct to Porto d'Ischia. I wish we had known sooner as I fear we may have left this invitation too late. I hope not.

With best regards from us both
yours ever
William Walton

To Griselda Kentner   17 May 1958

Casa Cirillo, Forio d'Ischia

Dearest Griselda,

I find your nice letter on my return. I'm so glad you both enjoyed the Partita.

How irritating that we did'nt meet in the interval – but Mr Bean[1] wafted one away to a secret bar in which I hoped everyone who wanted to see me would be wafted too. However I was mistaken.

With our best love to you both
as ever
Will

To Alan Frank   10 June 1958

Casa Cirillo, Forio d'Ischia

Dear Alan,

Herewith the contract duly signed. I've no news except bad news. Many rows over our house, in fact we have had to suspend building operations, consequently not much progress with the [Second] Symph. which however does show some signs of gathering momentum.

I wrote to Malcolm S. [Sargent] withdrawing from writing "Moses" for the Huddersfield Centenary. He's written very kindly about it & suggests I might do a smaller scale work. Thinking it over, & while making no rash promise of delivery, I have suggested that a "Gloria in excelsis" might fit the bill. I think it would, at least one knows w[h]ere one is regarding the words – I propose doing it in Latin so there will be no bother about it if some other countries should happen to want to do it. So would you send me a Latin version of the Prayer book[,] also the English prayer book so I know what it is all about!

yrs
William

---

1 Ernest Bean, General Manager of the Royal Festival Hall.

To Gregor Piatigorsky   10 July 1958

Casa Cirillo, Forio d'Ischia

Dear Grisha,

   The record of the 'Cello Concerto has just arrived. I've already played
it several times & hasten to thank you for an absolutely superb interpretation & performance. Everything about it is as it should be & your
playing magnificent. Also Munch [Charles Münch] and the [Boston
Symphony] orchestra could hardly be better. In fact it seems to me to be
an exceptionally good record ([Ernest Bloch's] Schelomo as well, which
is new to me) & I hope that it goes well.

   I hope you are keeping well. For my sins, I'm embarked on a second
symphony & miss your sympathetic guidance [and] help to spur me on!
For you indeed spurred me on with the concerto, with the result that it
is I consider, one of my best works – certainly the best of the three concertos, though don't say so to Jascha!

   With many thanks again for everything & incidentally for recommending Bengtson [Erling Bengtsson]. We gave quite a good performance in Manchester at the end of April.

   As always
   William

To Griselda Kentner   2 August 1958

Casa Cirillo, Forio d'Ischia

Dearest Griselda,

   I've been meaning to write you for ages, but there's too much "dolce
far niente" to even write music, let alone letters.

   About Freccia, whom I've not met, but know about as a conductor, will
you tell him to write to our accountant, J. B. Marks 17 Fleet Str, E.C.4 as
he runs Lowndes Cott[age] & will know if it is vacant when he wants it.

   There is nothing much to write you about. Local gossip, though
funny, would hardly interest you. In fact life is slightly dreary though
our houses are all full & from that point of view all goes well.

   I was sorry to hear about the Sonata, but it can't be helped. In any
case it may be better for next year as I believe I'm opening the Ed. Fest
[Edinburgh Festival], with an all W. Concert. Yehudi did say something
about re-recording it for L.P. – he's probably forgotten.

The Piatigorsky record of the Vlc. Con has just been sent me from the U.S. Pretty good from all points of view.

I shall probably be coming to England mid-Oct for the Leeds Fest. Sorry for this dull letter.

With our best love to you both
As ever
Will

To Alan Frank   17 January 1959

San Felice, Forio d'Ischia

Dear Alan,

Owing to various complications we shall not arrive in London till Tues. 27th & shall go direct to Lowndes Cott. which should be vacant by then.

Meanwhile I've made a fairly fair copy of mov I [of the Second Symphony] which I send you, so that you can tell me the worst when we meet. Actually now that I've got some sort of birds-eye view on it, it may not eventually turn out to be quite so intolerable as I have been suspecting. To me it's great weakness is in the 2nd sub[ject] (which however can doubtless be improved when scored, which of course also goes for it all) & a certain harmonic monotony as the whole piece turns on the 1st bar almost throughout. There is also no recapitulation strictly speaking, of the main theme (bar 222). Whether this will appear skimped I find it hard to judge. I do know how to recapitulate if necessary in full but I incline to think it all right as it is. However we will see.

The thing is that I have only really settled down to work in the last couple of months having frittered away a lot of time chasing the shadow of the beautiful blonde Mrs Sidney Beer! She was on her back for weeks (but alas, only because she had fractured it!). In fact, a bad workman always blames his tool!

[. . .]
As ever
William

To Mrs Ernest Newman   14 July 1959

San Felice, Forio d'Ischia

Dear Vera,

We are so very sorry to read of the death of Ernest. Though it cannot have been unexpected, it nevertheless, must be a most brutal wrench for you & both Su & myself send you our condolences.

He was always a good friend to me & I always paid strict attention to his fair, penetrating, (& what is so rare amongst his colleagues) & helpful criticisms. He was helpful of course, because he really knew & understood the difficulties facing a composer.

Again with our deepest sympathy.

Yours ever

William Walton

To Alan Frank   7 January 1960

San Felice, Forio d'Ischia

Dear Alan,

Regarding "Facade" in Naples will you send the part for two 'cellos as well, so as to be on the safe side.

Despite that it will, I'm sure, be a bit of a nightmare, & doubtless the firemen will be called out, I think we had better go & see what goes on.

[. . .]

yrs

William

To Alan Frank   17 January 1960

San Felice, Forio d'Ischia

Dear Alan,

[. . .]

Please don't mention perfs of Symph 2 at the moment. It fair gives me the "willies" as it seems to get remoter & remoter. In fact I'm feeling extremely low about it. I think Szell would have replied by now if he felt any enthusiasm for mov. I. He did when I sent him only mov. I of Partita.

I suffer from nightmares of irate mayors & corporations!
Cheer up – I'll do my damndest – but –
yrs
William

To Alan Frank   4 February 1960

San Felice, Forio d'Ischia

Dear Alan,

Just back from Naples after hearing "Facade". It was a really excellent perf. one of the best, if not in fact, the best I've heard. Gracis[1] had a first rate lot of players & he knew the score & what it was all about. For once the balance couldn't have been better. Alvar Liddell[2] turned out to my mind to be the best reciter since he knows his microphone technique & spoke quietly though every word could be heard & at the same time it didn't butt into the music so there wasn't the confusion of sound that so often occurs. Apart from a whistle or two (as there should be) it was very well received. Gracis took some half-dozen calls & I arrived just in time for the last. Altogether rather satisfactory. [. . .]
   [. . .]
   As ever
   William

It would seem that I may have to contemplate doing another film. I had either forgotten or not realised that they were such money-makers after the initial payment. Fenn wrote to me not long ago saying that Wilcox would like me for "The reason why". Charge of the Light Brigade! I more or less turned it down but perhaps should see what it is all about. Maybe I could discover another "Colonel Bogey"[3] of the 1855s! And that would be out of copyright & with no widow to take the cream.
   It would'nt be till Nov. But I expect someone else has got it by now.

1 Ettore Gracis, Italian conductor. A noted specialist in eighteenth-century Italian opera and modern works.
2 Alvar Lidell. Famous for his reading of BBC radio news bulletins during the Second World War.
3 March tune used by Malcolm Arnold in his score for David Lean's film *The Bridge on the River Kwai* (1958).

To Alan Frank   7 March 1960

San Felice, Forio d'Ischia

Dear Alan,

[. . .]

I will send you a crumb very shortly – in fact I could send you the 2nd mov [of the Second Symphony] now, but I'm waiting to show it to Hans [Werner Henze] who's coming for the next weekend. All I can say about it, is that it is very slow & very long – getting on for 10 mins. It demands a Scherzo (very short about 3 mins) which is on the way out of its shell. The last mov I think will be a Passacaglia. It may have a "cereal" [serial note-row] in it, because up to now there's not a cereal in the sc. – not a "Post-Toasted" or even Quakers Oats (& the wild ones seem to have been sown long ago).

Seeing as how I'm not above or below taking a winkle from anyone at this juncture I'll even sink to having a squint at Rubbadubdubra's [Edmund Rubbra's][1] Passacaglia & Fugue mentioned in the American cutting (v. good) if you can send me a copy[,] that is if it is printed. Let me know my various conducting dates – I seem to have mislaid them. Also as J.B. [Julian Bream][2] is coming to Ischia we could get thro' the proofs of "A in L" [*Anon in Love*] while he is here.

As ever
William

To Alan Frank   27 March 1960

San Felice, Forio d'Ischia

Dear Alan,

To-morrow or the day after I dispatch I & II movs of S.2. I has been entirely redone & has turned out pretty well. In fact Hans H. who is here (recovering from a somewhat intimate operation) is quite enthusiastic about both – which cheers me considerably. [. . .]

Julian B. has plonct [*sic*] himself on us indefinitely – having developed a duodenal & felt like a rest! We thought he was "in passagio"! However

1 English composer, pianist and teacher; lecturer in music at Oxford University from 1947 to 1968.
2 English guitarist and lutenist, and a regular recital partner of the tenor Peter Pears.

we've got through the proofs & when I asked him if he wanted to see the 2nd proofs – they'd take a month maybe – he said 'Oh I shall probably still be here'! What can one do? But he's not much of a nuisance – except for another slight change (enclosed) to No 6, which is really as much my fault as his.

He is no good for an American perf – nor is P.P. [Peter Pears] However he is all for my orchestrating them sometime.

Have received also the Rub. [Rubbra] sc. I am now also more than slightly horrified at having asked for it. Surely no one, except intentionally, could be quite so boring. As such it is an undoubted masterpiece!

[. . .]

As ever

William

To Alan Frank   31 March 1960

San Felice, Forio d'Ischia

Dear Alan,

[. . .]

Hans who is still with us (he leaves to-day) is not at all sure that a Scherzo is needed & thinks I should proceed with the last mov. – a Chaconne (that is, if I can manage it!). Anyhow if I can get the last mov. out of the way it may be easier to judge if a scherzo is needed or not. I shall be interested to hear what you think when you have had a look at I & II.

[. . .]

He thinks a short "scherzo" might upset the balance & that 3 monumental(?) movs. would stand best alone. So another 8 to 10 minutes should be aimed at! When it has been photostated can I have a copy for reference?

As ever

William

To Alan Frank   12 April 1960

San Felice, Forio d'Ischia

Dear Alan,

The Liverpool people want me to conduct Symph 2 at Hanley Sept 23rd. I've accepted. Can the B.B.C rehearsal be in the afternoon or evening of the 24th as I don't know if I can get back in time for a morning one. Anyhow a night in the train would probably be mor[e] sufferable than a night in a Hanley hotel!

yrs
William

This is the Passacaglia theme.¹ All 12 notes – but we don't mention it!

I think it follows II well enough [–] though it is slow, it gets going fairly quickly.

To Alan Frank   16 April 1960

San Felice, Forio d'Ischia

Dear Alan,

Thank you so much for your letter about movs. I & II.

I, too, think II is all right. It has also struck me as being shorter than in fact it is. Having timed it several times over, even with hurrying I could'nt make it much under 9 mins.

As to I, I've gone back to what it was, more or less originally. The first scored version was a bit too truncated & gave me the feeling of being so. However I stuck to the foreshortened recapitulation which I feel, works, as well as making it more interesting formally speaking. That is more or less all I've done to it except for getting rid of the brush-wood in the scoring & generally gingering it up a bit. [. . .]

---

1   This sketch is different from the theme as it appears in the finished score: there the rhythms, time-signature and octaves have been altered, although the actual pitches and their order are the same.

[319]

III is getting on. It has it's points & I'm not being too pedantic with working it out serially! But I'm beginning to see that there is something after all to be said for that method, even if in the end it works back to old tonic & dominant!

[. . .]

As ever

William

To Alan Frank   19 May 1960

San Felice, Forio d'Ischia

Dear Alan,

It dos'ent exactly break my heart to hear that Hanley is off, though I daresay I shall regret 50 quid.

[. . .]

The 3rd mov. moves on it's plodding & more than slightly boring way. You know the kind of thing – Roast beef on Sunday – cold on Mon – hashed on Tues. stewed on Weds rissoles on Thurs & Fish on Fri – fish salad Sat. Boiled beef Sun with a carrot thrown in etc ad inf. In fact it's not at all exciting, as yet.

Everything seems pretty gloomy – like May '39! And I hope we shall all still be here for Sept 2nd.[1] I hate to think of doing all this slaving for nowt!

By the way, someone told me that he had seen in an Italian paper [news] of a Concorso of Military bands at Bari & that an English band (he didn't know if it had won a premio) had played "La Marzia Imperiale"[2] di Walton, received with much applause!

As ever,

William

It might be a small gold-mine if we could get "La Marzia Imp." into the

1 By May 1939 the much dreaded and anticipated prospect of a Second World War had moved closer than before, with Mussolini's aggressive invasion of Albania and the introduction in Britain of the Conscription Act. The hope of 'Peace in our Time', as proclaimed by Prime Minister Neville Chamberlain after signing his agreement with Hitler in Munich the year before, now seemed more remote than ever. Walton was evidently remembering the palpable sense of time running out. 'Sept 2nd' refers to the forthcoming first performance of the Second Symphony.
2 Probably *Crown Imperial*.

Italian Mil band rep – there are hundreds of them. Perhaps a suggestion to Ricordi[1] might help.

You might also have a word with Sansogno[2] if you get a chance & give him my regards & say why the hell etc etc.

To Alan Frank   28 July 1960

San Felice, Forio d'Ischia

Dear Alan,

I dispatched the Coda last Mon by B.E.A. [British European Airways] so presumably by now it has almost been photographed.

That's the lot & I hope that it will come up to your expectation when you see it as a whole movement.

The Fugato & Coda are effective enough, but I am conscious (perhaps too much so) that there is more than a slight likeness (rhythmically speaking) between them & the 2nd fugal episode of the last mov. of Symph I also a smattering of the Scherzo, not to mention the tutti in the 1st mov of the Vl. Con. & the Interlude in T&C. In fact that kind of 6/8 [tempo] is more than a mannerism – its a vice which must be checked in future! However there it is, its too late now to do 'owt about it.

When I cabled about Schippers[3] I had got it into my head that Szell was having cold feet about it, & I am delighted to know that I am wrong in my conjectures.

[. . .]

I append some dubious remarks <u>not</u> to be quoted on the three movs. I'm not at all keen on any publicity till I've heard it!

As ever
William

There is also a short list of corrections & additions.

1 Italy's leading and most powerful music publisher.
2 Nino Sanzogno had conducted the performances of *Troilus and Cressida* at La Scala in 1956.
3 Thomas Schippers, American conductor, at this time appearing regularly with the New York Philharmonic Orchestra, at New York's Metropolitan Opera House, and at La Scala, Milan.

To Helga Cranston   7 September 1960

Lowndes Cottage, Lowndes Place, s.w.1

Darling Helga,

How rash of you to become an Israelite. In fact the Arabs will be after you any minute so you'd better think twice about it. But I suppose something stronger than your fear of Arabs is calling you there.

We are here on and off until about October 4th. If you are in London at all ring us up on Sloane 9248 and we will try and arrange something.

Hoping to see you soon,

Your old, old friend,

William

To Alan Frank   12 February 1961

San Felice, Forio d'Ischia

Dear Alan,

We arrived safely back on Thurs. – just a week away. On the whole it was well worth going. Szell did the Symph really splendidly[1] & it was tremendously well received by the audience & strange to say, by the critics as you will have seen. J.W. [John Ward][2] gave us a jolly party afterwards. He was a real help & companion in some slightly trying situations.

[. . .] But the trip to Washington was entirely pointless. The great excuse was the snow & none of the so called programme existed at all. We did not see the "famed mansion providing gracious surroundings". But we lunched with the ambassador & attended a dinner & concert at Dumbarton Oaks.[3] It then started snowing again so we used that as an excuse for a dash to N.Y. & [I] suspect we only just got away before everything was again shut down.

N.Y. was gay enough & we saw Larry in [Jean Anouilh's play] Becket & Irene Worth[4] in her play. And Kostelanetz asked us to supper. He &

1 George Szell had conducted the Cleveland Orchestra in the Second Symphony's American première at Carnegie Hall in New York. The world première had been given by the Royal Liverpool Philharmonic Orchestra under John Pritchard at the Edinburgh Festival on 2 September 1960.
2 Oxford University Press's representative in New York.
3 Mansion in Washington, DC, owned by R. W. Bliss, a keen patron of the arts. Stravinsky's Concerto in E♭, known as 'Dumbarton Oaks', was first performed there.
4 American actress who worked often in England after the Second World War, in particular at the Old Vic and with the Royal Shakespeare Company.

his new wife are extremely nice & he presented me with a[n] acetate [recording] of Jo'burg [*Johannesburg Festival Overture*] which is excellent.
[. . .]

It is slightly boring that Poulenc has just come out with a "Gloria" at Boston[1] – a great success it seems. You might try & obtain a copy. Let me have the Mss back as soon as possible. I'm just getting going again.

As ever,
William

To David Webster   5 July 1961

San Felice, Forio d'Ischia

My dear David,

Thanks for your note. Life is like that and it can't be helped.[2] As a recompense I hope you open the 62/63 season with T&C & throw a party in honour of my 60th year!

Love from us both
as ever
William

To David Webster   19 September 1961

San Felice, Forio d'Ischia

My dear David,
[. . .]
We've just returned from a long week-end on Lord Camrose's yacht, where Garret D.[3] was, for a day, a fellow-traveller!
[. . .]
[. . .] I did ask Garret[t] to find out ① if Solti[4] could not be persuaded

---

1 Poulenc's *Gloria*, commissioned by the Koussevitsky Foundation, had been given its première by the Boston Symphony Orchestra under Charles Münch on 20 January 1961. Walton was currently at work on his own *Gloria* setting.
2 A plan to revive *Troilus and Cressida* at Covent Garden in the 1961/62 season had fallen through.
3 Garrett Moore, eleventh Earl of Drogheda, Chairman of the Royal Opera House from 1958 to 1974.
4 Georg Solti, Hungarian conductor, already appointed as Music Director of the Royal Opera House, a position he was to retain until 1971. He was later to become a British citizen.

to conduct at least the 1ˢᵗ perf of T&C. ② that it should open the 62'–63' season. He thought the 1ˢᵗ unlikely as S. has so much on his hands already, and has doubts about the 2ⁿᵈ. But bearing everything in mind, perhaps you could achieve the desired result. But don't think I shall take umbrage or bear malice etc.etc, if it can't be brought about, because I shan't. However all the same try & bring it about. At any rate try & have the perfs in '62 rather than '63 which, if things don't improve (they won't) will see the great holocaust start in earnest, if not before!

   Bless you
   William.

To Malcolm Arnold [1]   10 December 1961

San Felice, Forio d'Ischia

Dear Malcolm,

   Thank you for your note [. . .] The horrortorio [Walton's *Gloria*] didn't, I think, remove the gilt from the gingerbread, at least to me!

   I, presumptuously, would like to hope that you will soon devote your genius (it is not a word I often use) to writing a comic opera. If (always the question) you could find a good libretto Ive no doubt that you would produce a masterpiece of its kind. So do have a look around.

   Not more than 30 mins for each act! Less if feasible!
   With best seasonal greetings
   yours ever
   William

To Alan Frank   22 December 1961

San Felice, Forio d'Ischia

Dear Alan,

   [. . .]

   The Vars [*Variations on a Theme by Hindemith*] are beginning to move a bit. If you know the theme you will see that it is not entirely

---

1 English composer, conductor and trumpeter. The composer of a large output of works for the concert hall and also of many film scores, most notably that of *The Bridge on the River Kwai*, which won an American Academy Award in 1958.

my fault if it turns out to be a late Vic. or early Edwardian work!

[. . .]

All blessings for Xmas & the New Year

. As ever

William

A very funny letter from Hans H. [Henze] about Nono, who when Hans's name came up at a dinner party at K. A. Hartmann[1] in Munich upset his table full of rare Nymphenburg china worth over 2000 mks saying la putana Tedesca ['the German whore'] etc. etc. And all because he had written "Ondine".[2]

To Helga Cranston   30 December 1961

San Felice, Forio d'Ischia

My dear Helga,

How very Irish of you to have an address like that!

I am delighted to hear that yet again you are living in sin even if he's only a Jazz musician (they have that steady beat) & I am happy to think that I imparted the necessary training as to how to win the heart(?) of a composer. Anyhow I hope it is jolly nice & that you will enjoy him throughout 1962 if he can stand it. – as I hope you will enjoy everything else for the New Year.

My hopes of coming to Israel are rather remote. They should do "Belshazzar". Absolutely made for you all, even if I'm a "goy". It might spark off a new war with the neighbours. See what you can do about putting [it] into the heads of whoever is responsible. I might even conduct it myself if asked!

As always

William

What about Larry's new son![3]

1 Karl Amadeus Hartmann, German composer.
2 Henze's ballet *Ondine* had been premièred at Covent Garden in 1958, with Margot Fonteyn in the title role.
3 Richard Kerr Olivier, Olivier's son by his third wife, Joan Plowright.

To Sir Laurence Olivier   10 March 1962

San Felice, Forio d'Ischia

My dear Larry,

How dissapointing that I can't write the music for you. But it is impossible at this moment as I come to London on the 18th for my 60th birthday celebrations, which means conducting concerts at Manchester Bristol Bournemouth Cardiff etc until I return April 8th. In addition I've to finish a song-cycle for [Elisabeth] Schwarzkopf [*A Song for the Lord Mayor's Table*] by May 1st for the City of London Festival.

I suggest Malcolm Arnold because he's very quick & very good. Alan R. [Rawsthorne] I know is also writing a work for the London Fest so is probably busy also.

I hope you will both be coming to the cocktail party to which the Oxford Univ. Press have asked you on the 26th[.] Su joins me on the 25th & we shall be at 20 Chesham Place so I do hope we can contrive to meet.

With our best love to you both

As ever

William

To Peter Heyworth   13 April 1962

San Felice, Forio d'Ischia

My dear Peter, (or tormentor-in-chief)

I have only just got round to getting through my b&b letters, so forgive my tardy but nonetheless grateful thanks for the delicious pot of caviar which was highly appreciated by us both.

I did as a matter of fact telephone you but with no success. Once on Sun morn. April 1st pointing out you had split an infinitive & hoping you would have to bore yourself blue by reading through your contribution to find it. However you were'nt there.

It is about time you came to see us again. Surely a book on the deficiencies of Italian opera houses is within your scope.

Blessings, and don't pull your punches!

As ever

William

To Helga Cranston   14 April 1962

San Felice, Forio d'Ischia

My dear Helga,

Thank you again for your letter & birthday greetings. I'm all set for the 120th – in fact there's life in the old dog yet.

I'm glad you appreciate my Hebrew – blood will out you know.

We've just returned from a triumphal tour of England conducting W.W. concerts all over the place. Doubtless you have read the pages & pages in the press! In fact I'm inclined to believe they rather spoilt it from overstatement. However it was quite refreshing after the cloud I've been under with the new young critics.

I've just managed to avoid doing the music for Lawrence of Arabia.[1] 2½ hours for £5000 – not on my life. Anyhow the cutter-in-chief though female was not half attractive enough & you know how susceptible [I am] to the charm of "cutters". A lot of the film was shot in Jordan on the condition that no[o]ne with Jewish blood could enter. There was quite a sale for plastic fore-skins! I only saw a very rough cut but I could tell I was being taken for a camel ride. Wait till you see it.

Otherwise I'm writing a song-cycle for Schwarzkopf for the City of London Festival in July & some Variations on a Theme by Hindemith & I'm contemplating accepting to go to Los Angeles to conduct my new "Gloria" there. So the old boy is still quite active in more ways than one.

We spent a night in Brighton with Larry who is in his best form. She's delightful & they are dotty about the baby.

Incidentally no choir can call itself a choir these days unless it can sing "Belshazzar" almost by heart!

With lots of love
as ever
William

1 The music for David Lean's film was instead composed by Maurice Jarre.

SAN FELICE
FORIO D'ISCHIA

11. 5. 62

Dear Dr Szell,

This morning I received the record of
your recording of my 2ⁿᵈ Symphony, and have already
played it several times.

Words fail me! It is a quite fantastic a stupendous
performance from every point of view. Firstly it is
absolutely right musically speaking, & the virtuosity of
the performance is quite staggering, especially the Fugato;
but everything is phrased & balanced in an unbelievable way,
for which I must congratulate you & your magnificent orchestra.

I can only sink into banality & say that I thank you
really & truly from the bottom of my heart, & for once this is
not an empty phrase.

With our best regards to Mrs Szell & yourself, and with
many thanks again.

Yours very sincerely
William Walton.

To George Szell 11 May 1962

San Felice, Forio d'Ischia

Dear Dr. Szell,

This morning I received the record of your recording of my 2$^{\underline{nd}}$ Symphony, and have already played it several times.

Words fail me! It is a quite fantastic & stupendous performance from every point of view. Firstly it is absolutely right musically speaking, & the virtuosity of the performance is quite staggering, especially the Fugato; but everything is phrased & balanced in an unbelievable way, for which I must congratulate you & your magnificent orchestra.

I can only sink into banality & say that I thank you really & truly from the bottom of my heart, & for once this is not an empty phrase.

With our best regards to Mrs. Szell & yourself, and with many thanks again.

Yours very sincerely
William Walton

To Peter Heyworth [postmarked: Forio d'Ischia,
[postcard] 3 July 1962]

[American newspaper cutting, headed *Composer's Complaint*, pasted on to the postcard:

The following cable from Igor Stravinsky in Hamburg, Germany, was received by the editor of the *Herald Tribune* following Paul Henry Lang's review on June 15 of the television premiere of the composer's "Noah and the Flood" [*The Flood*].

'Of hundreds of reviews of my New York work most of them, like every opus since 1909, were gratifyingly unfavourable. I found only yours entirely stupid and suppurating with gratuitous malice.

'The only blight on my 80th birthday is the realization my age will probably keep me from celebrating the funeral of your senile music critic.']

Even "big fleas" suffer from their P.H.'s! See you soon.

as ever
William

To Alan Frank   23 August 1962

La Mortella, Forio d'Ischia

Dear Alan,

[. . .]

I am somewhat lazily settling down to the Variations. It is very hot &
there was an earthquake two days ago but we did'nt notice it[,] nor did
the house.

A dead secret for the moment is that Patrick Hughes[1] has written
suggesting the "Importance of being Earnest"[2] as a libretto. I think a
very possible idea but I don't see [myself] getting down to it till after the
round-the-world trip.

As ever, William

To Alan Frank   1 January 1963

La Mortella, Forio d'Ischia

Dear Alan,

Happy New Year!

Re: publication of film scores. You will recall that it was with considerable reluctance & against my better judgement that I consented for the
arrangement & publication of some of my film music. If I had realised
that it meant losing performance fees on the films in question, I should
certainly never have considered it. I note that I received £479 for "Hamlet"
this year. That in itself is a tidy sum but when divided amongst three it
becomes a bit measly. In fact I can see no justification whatsoever for
M.M. [Muir Mathieson] & the O.U.P muscling in on the perf rights
from the films as neither have had anything to do with them at the time
(except of course M.M. conducted the sessions, but that has nothing to
do with it). Of course M.M. & the O.U.P. are entitled to their P.R.S
[Performing Right Society royalties] on the perfs which emerge from the

---

1 Patrick ('Spike') Hughes, English composer, writer and critic. An expert on opera, he
also founded and played in a jazz dance band. He and Walton had been friends since
Walton's years with the Sitwells in the 1920s; and Hughes had arranged the meeting
between Walton and Heifetz, at London's Berkeley Hotel in 1936, during which Heifetz
had commissioned the Violin Concerto.
2 Oscar Wilde's play *The Importance of Being Earnest*. The opera was never written nor,
apparently, discussed further.

published scores, but to me those scores have no connection with the film rights, & I can't agree that the P.R.S should include the film royalties as part of the publication rights. Especially as all the films involved were made long before there was any question about publishers acquiring rights in film scores by publication of the music.

I'm sorry to write so strongly about this, but when discussing the business of publication the question of P.R.S regarding the films never cropped up, or I should, as I've already stated, have refused to consider it.

To turn to more pleasant topics. [. . .]

I've been asked & [have] accepted to conduct 4 perfs of B's F [*Belshazzar's Feast*] in Israel between July 16ᵗʰ & 25ᵗʰ – in Hebrew with a Cantor as soloist. It should be quite something if the chorus is up to standard. I then go to Ravinia (Chicago) to conduct all 3 W. cons. [Walton concertos] & on to Vancouver for another 2. The two at Hollywood Bowl have unfortunately fallen through. But it will I hope, all help.

I'll write to D.W. [David Webster] about T&C. I didn't hope for a new prod [production] but I did hope for a [new] producer. Is there any one who's any good amongst the residents?

The Vars are getting on. I start on the Finale tomorrow. I've, I fear, slightly evaded Var IX, but it is there, but is used as an Introduction to the Finale so it is perhaps not quite a Var. in its own right so to speak, but it completes the key scheme of (1 E) (2 A♭) (3 F♯) (4 B) (5 C♯) (6 D) (7 A) (8 C) (9 B♭) Finale F with Coda in E. I've also tried for a little internal balancing of the Vars [so] that 6 has an affinity with 2, 7 with 3, 8 with 4, (9 with 5?).

[. . .]

As ever, William

To Alan Frank   8 January 1963

La Mortella, Forio d'Ischia

Dear Alan,

How sad & what a desperate disaster for us about G.S. [George Szell] "Newsweek" have just been round to interview me about him & I trust I said the right thing.

It must have been very sudden as you were in communication with him just the other day.

I suppose the 1ˢᵗ perf. [of the *Hindemith Variations*] in the U.S. will now not take place on April 8ᵗʰ. I may add I'm having a good deal of difficulty with the Finale but hope to send you a page or 3 in a few days. The thing is for the copyists to keep up with me so in case I'm late they are finished & ready to tackle the last pages.

As ever,
William

To Alan Frank   9 January 1963

La Mortella, Forio d'Ischia

Dear Alan,

You must think my letter of yesterday to be a bit dotty – poor chap's crazy from overwork!

But as I told you "Newsweek" sent round a couple of journalists to inform me of Szell's demise & would I say a few words. Luckily they came rather late so we couldn't get to the post. However this morn. Su was on her way to Porto [d'Ischia] with a cable & condolent letter to Mrs S when she saw the journalists who came & said they'd been trying to telephone us, in vain as the telephone was struck by lightning a couple of days ago & was yet to be repaired. But they said S. was not "morto"[,] in fact it was about a celebration for his 50ᵗʰ anniversary as a conductor! Imagine everyone's surprise if the cable had gone off & it was just luck that Su met them, though they did say they had asked the police to come & inform us, which of course they did'nt do.

I don't think I'd better tell S. about it – funny as it may be – he might not be amused.

Yrs
William

Herewith a few wrong notes.

To Helga Keller[1]

4 February 1963

La Mortella, Forio d'Ischia

Dearest Helga!

I am a bit late in congratulating you on having made a dishonest man of your husband, but all the same I do. Its about time you settled down – that is of course, if you have'nt parted by now.

I'm a bit "gaga" from answering a whole drawerful of letters which have accumulated since I started my piece which I finished two days ago – just in time for perf. next March 8th. I left it a bit late for me – starting mid-October as I suspect you did too! Anyhow I've only taken 3½ months – a record for me.

I expect you will already know that we are coming to Israel mid-July for 4 perfs of "Belshazzar's F." – in Hebrew – with a Cantor singing the solo part. So I hope you will be there to welcome me with at least, – open arms.

I am looking forward to it tremendously & only hope it won't start a war (it touched off the Hungarian Revolution!) & long to see you & meet your husband.

Blessings
William

I hope I shan't have to conduct upside down & I hope my foreskin will be allowed to remain as it is!

To Alan Frank

9 February 1963

La Mortella, Forio d'Ischia

Dear Alan,

I hope that by the time you receive this the last double bar will have arrived safely. I'm feeling ever so slightly gloomy about the work – the Coda, I fear, may sound like the Salvation Army outside the "pub" on a cold and frosty Sun. morn. with a long Sullivanesque "Great Amen" at the end.

It will last, I think, well over 20 mins, but I've not timed the last 20 or pages so am not quite sure.

1 Formerly Helga Cranston. A longstanding friend of Walton, whom he had met when she was working as a film editor during the making of *Henry V* between 1943 and 1944.

When you have sent off a score to P.H. [Paul Hindemith] let me know by telegram so that I can bung in a letter to coincide with it's arrival. I can't imagine how he will take it. Being at the same time a kind-hearted but honest character, he won't want to hurt, but at the same time he won't be able not to say it's "bloody awful". Perhaps it won't be necessary & he will not object to it & will conduct it, I hope, at Lucerne [Festival].

[. . .]

When you've had a chance to have a look let me know what you really think about "l'œuvre" – the Vars – I mean! Sorry to see that Poulenc has, as the Americans say, paaassed on. He was only 64 – it seems only just round the corner!

As ever
William

To Alan Frank   15 February 1963

La Mortella, Forio d'Ischia

Dear Alan,

Thank you for your appraisal of the Vars. I hope you are not right about the end, but you easily may be. The only alternative I could see or can see would have been to recapitulate the theme in toto which I think would have been a bit much & in fact unfair to all concerned. [. . .] That it will have "popular" appeal I doubt, or for Mr Heyworth either. But I did not see it ending loudly or excitingly.

Having to learn my beats I've been going thro' it daily & I must confess I find it a trifle dull.

I don't think I've got far enough away from the Theme especially the form. On the other hand the Theme has such a well defined form that it would be very difficult – even wrong to have tried to have done so. The only bad Var. & that in its context is not really so, is VI – & context can & should count for a lot. I'm not worried about the strings, unless they are exceptionally bad, as it all lies under the fingers & is nothing like as difficult as S.2 or Partita. But of course the more rehearsal the better. Anyhow I'm much too near & involved in the piece as I'm conducting it to give you a sound or just opinion as to whether I think it good, bad or indifferent. It may be the latter, I fear. However we'll see[,] & see what the great master himself thinks.

[334]

As ever
William

To Paul Hindemith   21 February 1963

La Mortella, Forio d'Ischia

Dear Paul Hindemith,

My publisher informs [me] that he has sent you a score of the Variations I have written on the Theme from the slow movement of your 'Cello Concerto (1940).

This at long last, fulfils the promise I made to write a work for you, & I need hardly say how much I hope that you will approve of it, & that sometime you will give a performance of it yourself. I should feel very honoured if you would.

We go to London on March 1st for the first performance on the 8th at the Royal Philharmonic Concert conducted by myself. It is being broadcast by the B.B.C if you should wish to hear it.

My wife joins me in [sending] best regards to you both.
Yours sincerely
William Walton

To Sir David Webster   1 April 1963

La Mortella, Forio d'Ischia

My dear David,

Have just receive[d] the following cable from Walter L. [Legge] "Karajans accept first night Troilus please secure box" – which I hope will be forthcoming as it might be important for the work. Perhaps Garrett [Lord Drogheda] might invite them to his box!?

Also I suppose I must ask for a box for "little me" & co. I'll pay for the lot (if necessary).

Have a good time in the U.S.

With love from us both (& tell M.S [Malcolm Sargent] who will be present!)
As ever
William

To Walter Legge   1 April 1963

La Mortella, Forio d'Ischia

My dear Walter,

Thank you for the cable & for your success in inveigling the Karajans to attend the first night of "Troilus". I have written at once to Sir D.W. asking for a box which I am sure will be forthcoming.

Peccato! that Szell is unable to accept the invitation[1] for next year, but I am sure he would accept for the following season. He has written saying almost embarrassingly laudatory things about the H. Variations [which] he does on the 8th.

I hope we can induce you to return here with us about May 8th.

With our best love to you both

as ever

William

To Paul Hindemith   23 May 1963

La Mortella, Forio d'Ischia

Dear Paul Hindemith,

Thank you for your entertaining postcard.

I hope that by now the score & record of the 1st performance of the Variations (not too good, taken over the air) have reached you & they are not still belatedly following you around the U.S.

George Szell writes me that he has recently given it it's U.S. première in Cleveland & other places, & seems to be immensely pleased about the work & it's success, so much so that he is giving quite a number of performances of it next season in various places, including New York.

It would be good to have a word from you about it, & whether you may conduct it yourself sometime. I certainly tried my best to make it a worthy tribute to you both.

If ever you come to Naples, I trust you will not fail to come & see us.

With our best regards to you both,

Yours ever,

William Walton

1 Probably Legge's invitation to Szell to record the *Variations on a Theme by Hindemith* for EMI.

To Ian Kemp[1]   13 August 1963

Lisbon
as from La Mortella, Forio d'Ischia

Dear Mr Kemp,

I must admit that I find your request to be, as you put it, a bit of
a pest & suggest that a subscription, such as was done for Lennox
Berkeley's 60th to be more welcome to both the victim & the victimised
& much less embarrassing for all concerned.

The names were mentioned of the subscribers but not the amounts.
Give this idea consideration.

With best regards
yours sincerely
William Walton

To Helga and Melvin Keller   2 September 1963

La Mortella, Forio d'Ischia

Dear Hel & Mel,

We thank you for your letter & for the "cuttings" [of reviews of *Belshazzar's Feast*] which seem very good if you've translated them correctly.

The concerts in the U.S. went on the whole very well & I even got a
"tusch" (that is a fanfare on the brass – a rare & unexpected honour)
from the Chicago [Symphony] Orchestra at the end of the last concert.
New York not so good – too blasè [*sic*] to rehearse – in fact, I only had
two instead of 3 hours rehearsal. But it was wisest to give in & not
antagonise them or heaven knows what tricks they might not have
played at the concert. Anyhow I came back with quite a wad, enough
to make our stay in Portugal very enjoyable.

Glad to hear that Mel is hard at work. (We both took to him immensely
& think you are both very lucky.) Did you hear anything about Sir
Somebody Somethings (whose name I can't recall for the moment) film.

Our best love to you both
As ever
William

1 Teacher and writer on music, at this time working at the London office of Schott & Co.
Ltd, Michael Tippett's publisher. Kemp was currently editing *Michael Tippett – A Symposium on his Sixtieth Birthday* (Faber, 1965) and had asked Walton to contribute to it.

To Ian Kemp   9 September 1963

La Mortella, Forio d'Ischia

Dear Mr Kemp,
   If you must persist will this do: –

Dear Michael,
   Many happy returns and welcome to the 60s, and damnation &
everything else to those, such as P.H. [Peter Heyworth] who in their
crass ignorance & lack of instinct, presume to teach you your vocation.
   ever yours
   William (Walton)

I suspect it won't, but that is as far as I can go at the moment.[1]
   Yrs
   W. Walton

To Benjamin Britten   23 November 1963

La Mortella, Forio d'Ischia

Dear Ben,
   You must almost by now be suffering from a surfeit of adulation &
praise, so I won't add to it. All the same I should like to tell you, that I
celebrated your [50th] birthday in my own way by playing my favourite
works – Spring Symphony – Nocturne & War Requiem – each in it's different way a masterwork, particularly the latter – a non-stop masterpiece
without blemish – in fact, on a par with the two great Requiems of the
19th century, or for that matter, any other century.
   In the last years your music has come to mean more & more to me –
it shines out as a beacon (how banal I'm becoming!) in, to me at least, a
chaotic & barren musical world, & I am sure it does for thousands of
others as well.
   I know that I should understand what is going [on], but I suppose it
is a matter [of] age – old age maybe; but there it is – I don't. But I do
understand, appreciate & love, I hope, nearly everything about your
music, not only the ingenuity & technique but the emotional depth of
feeling, & above all the originality & beauty of sound which permeates

1   Walton's contribution did not appear.

these works. The War Requiem is worth 100's of Lord Russells & Aldermaston marches & it will surely have the effect which you, possibly sub-consciously have striven for, for you have made articulate the wishes of the numberless inarticulate masses.

Now I must stop before I descend to complete drivel, but I write only (purely selfishly, but from the heart) because I should like you to realise that I am (this being a "fan" letter) one of your most enthusiastic "fans" & I look forward to your next works, especially "Lear".

Please don't bother to answer this (unless you should happen to want to) as I know that you must be snowed under with letters to answer, & if by some mischance you should be again afflicted with "conductor's elbow" or whatever it may be & think of taking the "cure" here, we should be more than delighted to entertain you.

Su joins me in all good wishes to you & Peter,

As ever

William

1964–1976

WALTON began 1964 with a three-month tour of New Zealand and Australia, during which he conducted concerts of his works and visited his sister, Nora Donnelly, who had emigrated to New Zealand many years before. Meanwhile Susana Walton stayed at home to nurse the knee joint she had broken just before the start of the tour. By now the building and planting of the garden at La Mortella had become a major project, and Walton took advantage of his antipodean journey to collect some rare plants and send them home from halfway round the world. According to Susana Walton, however, no letters or postcards from her husband ever reached her from Australia or New Zealand, nor a single telephone call, until a telegram in May announcing that he was on his way home. Could it really have been true that he had written regularly, as he told her, and that the money for the stamps had been pocketed by the Australian hotel staff, so that none of his letters had reached her? One hopes so.

Early the following year two new projects surfaced. Walton had long been considering the idea of a double concerto for violin, cello and orchestra. This had been suggested to him by Gregor Piatigorsky, the dedicatee of the Cello Concerto. Considering the amount of music that Walton worked so hard to create, it would be churlish to make too much of regretting that, as far as is known, he never wrote down a single note of the proposed double concerto. Despite the tantalizing prospect of Heifetz and Piatigorsky playing it together, the problems of its genesis proved intractable. Fortunately this was not the case with the next area of Walton's interest. During one of his summer visits to the festival in the Suffolk town he always liked to describe as 'Aldebugger', the idea first proposed by Benjamin Britten many years beforehand – that Walton should compose a chamber opera – had evidently been discussed again.

Peter Pears then suggested that Anton Chekhov's short story *The Bear* would be an ideal subject for a one-act comic opera, with its abundant opportunities for the kind of roguish pastiche at which Walton had proved

[343]

himself so adept as far back as *Façade*. What followed was one of the happiest and most satisfying tasks of Walton's life. Within a short time a librettist had been found: the versatile writer Paul Dehn, whose literary skills and intelligence were complemented by his alert awareness of an opera composer's needs. Over the next two years the score of *The Bear* materialized with relative ease and speed, at least by Walton's painstaking standards. The contrast with the long and troubled creation of *Troilus and Cressida* could not be more marked. Indeed the reason why there appears to be so little surviving correspondence between Dehn and Walton is precisely because work on *The Bear* on the whole went so swimmingly. If they had both had to struggle with it more, then more letters about its creation would surely exist. Besides, Dehn stayed in Ischia for much of the time that he was working on the libretto, so that he and Walton were able to resolve problems as they came up.

Soon after serious work on the new opera was under way, Walton was on a visit to London when he began to have trouble breathing. Medical checks revealed a shadow on his left lung. This was diagnosed as cancer – probably, though not certainly, the consequence of Walton's many years of pipe-smoking. In January he underwent surgery to remove the tumour, and a month later he was back home in Ischia and working again on *The Bear*. In the summer, however, he began to have severe pain in his left shoulder, and a further check-up in London revealed a recurrence of the disease. Several weeks of cobalt ray treatment followed. Nevertheless Walton recovered from the debilitating after-effects of this in time to complete *The Bear* for the 1967 Aldeburgh Festival. For once even he had to declare a temporary ceasefire in his usual hostilities towards the critical fraternity. The première was a virtually unqualified success with press and public alike. And despite the composer's usual anxiety about Oxford University Press's limitations as a publisher capable of promoting an opera effectively, *The Bear* was to achieve a satisfying number of performances in the years to come. The award of the Order of Merit later that year was an honour of which Walton was deeply proud.

Ideally, a benign Indian summer of creativity should have followed. But Walton's next commission – a short orchestral work for the New York Philharmonic Orchestra, of the kind of which he had more than forty years' experience of composing – now proceeded to cause him extreme difficulty. Walton's ritual lamentations in his correspondence about the trials of the creative process were by now entirely familiar, and did not disguise the fact that he had almost always been able to complete his commissioned works to his satisfaction, if often a little late. But in Walton's letters to Alan Frank about his problems with *Capriccio burlesco*, the tone is different from before. Instead of mere worry, there is something close to panic at his inability to focus on what he was trying to achieve. *Capriccio burlesco* did eventually materialize, without any audible trace of failing powers: indeed its characteristic brand of understated virtuosity makes it one of the most deftly brilliant of Walton's later works. But the experience seems to have scarred his creative confidence more than similar difficulties had before. His diffidence about reworking his String Quartet in A minor as a Sonata for Strings, and his co-opting of Malcolm Arnold's skills as an arranger, hints at a new and deeper kind of uncertainty.

Much more is known today about the risks and side-effects of the various conventional types of cancer treatment. With hindsight it is only too easy to perceive that while cobalt radiation had been effective in treating Walton's cancer, it had permanently undermined his health in other ways. Outwardly he often seemed to be his usual self, and as his letters in this section show, his sense of humour had lost none of its usual roistering form. But those letters from now on also complain increasingly of the depredations of old age, and of his increasing exasperation at what he feared to be his waning creativity. After his motor accident in Civitavecchia in 1957 he had recovered his usual ebullience with remarkable speed. From now on, however, he was to write steadily less music, and seemed genuinely to have ever more trouble in composing any at all.

His seventieth birthday celebrations involved many concerts of his music in England and elsewhere, and the atmosphere of affection and goodwill surrounding these gave him and Lady Walton much pleasure. The occasion that probably meant the most to him was the private, late-night concert given in his honour at 10 Downing Street, and hosted by Britain's music-loving Prime Minister, Edward Heath (who had himself been an organ scholar at Oxford's Balliol College before embarking on his political career). The closing item on the programme was the work by another composer Walton had said he would have most liked to have written himself: Schubert's Piano Trio in B♭. But the most far-reaching event of the year was the concert performance, at an Albert Hall Promenade Concert, of Act II of *Troilus and Cressida*.

This was conducted by André Previn, who in recent years had emerged as one of Walton's most enthusiastic supporters among the world's leading musicians, with influence to match. Walton's faith in his opera was undimmed, and he had recently decided to speed its progress towards a hoped-for new lease of life by revising it yet further. In addition to the cuts and revisions that he had made for the 1963 staging, he now made some more. He had also begun to transpose the role of Cressida to a lower vocal register. This radical step had been taken with a view to persuading the great mezzo-soprano Janet Baker to sing Cressida in a planned revival of *Troilus and Cressida* at Covent Garden in 1974. In May 1972 Baker warmly agreed to this. The version of Act II heard at the Proms that year was therefore the one that used these revisions, although Cressida was sung on that occasion by the soprano Jill Gomez. The music's enthusiastic reception encouraged Walton to proceed with revising the rest of the score even when the Covent Garden revival was postponed to 1976.

Fortunately Janet Baker was still available for that date, as was Previn, but the casting of the role of Troilus proved as problematic as it had before. Then, once again, the opera's ill-starred past seemed to be resurrected. An unwell André Previn withdrew a week before rehearsals were due to begin. He was replaced by Lawrence Foster, who achieved good results considering that he had had so little time even to learn the score. Far from giving Walton's opera the adequate resources that it both needed and deserved in a so-called 'new production', the Royal Opera had been prepared to spend only the equivalent amount that a revival of the 1963 staging would have cost. This meant that the stage set had literally to be assembled piecemeal from those of other opera productions in the company's repertory at the time.

Even the presence of one of the century's outstanding singers in the role of Cressida did not help to convince a generally sceptical press of the work's merits. After the first night on 12 November there were indeed some warm and supportive notices along with other indifferent and even contemptuous ones. And the audience's response to the opera, throughout all six sold-out performances, was as warm as it had always been. But the underlying strain had taken its toll on the composer, who had been increasingly unwell during the rehearsal period. After the final performance he collapsed with a suspected stroke. Back in Ischia, plagued by nightmares and hallucinations, he was able to recognize only Susana Walton and a few others. He slept for most of the next few weeks, and did not realize that Benjamin Britten had died on 4 December. In *Behind the Façade*, Susana Walton wrote, 'Nature had protected him from recalling the treatment meted out to his beautiful work with what I believe was a serious nervous breakdown. But he did recover.'

To Benjamin Britten   2 January 1964

La Mortella, Forio d'Ischia

My dear Ben,

I was so very, very pleased to receive your letter & to learn that I
have been of some help to you both in your work & in other ways in
your early days.

It seems hard to imagine your ever being depressed about your works –
perhaps that is partly why it is what it is, for at it's best, it always to me
gives an impression of complete spontaneity & freshness of inspiration.

As for myself, I must admit to have been suffering from a prolonged
bout of depression & for months have hardly put down a bar worth
keeping. All my later works always receive such a drubbing from the
press, especially my last one, which incidentally I consider one of my
best "The Variations on a Theme by Hindemith". I am rather diffidently
sending you the score which is just out. His death is a great shock to me.

A few days ago Su fell of[f] a rock in the garden & unfortunately has
broken some bone in her knee. We were to start on our journey to New
Zealand & Australia on the 22$^{\underline{nd}}$, but I fear it will now have to be postponed or curtailed. Anyhow I have to conduct my first concert in
Auckland on Feb 22$^{\underline{nd}}$ & the tour ends in Perth on May 22$^{\underline{nd}}$ so we
shant be back till the middle of June.

We shall be delighted to have you both to stay during your sab[b]ati-
cal year, also any time you are feeling like a short break. Ischia is now so
near – you leave London at 9–30 & are here in time for lunch & vice
versa.

With our best wishes for 1964
yours
William

To Gertrude Hindemith   4 January 1964

La Mortella, Forio d'Ischia

Dear Frau Hindemith,

I cannot express to you how very sad and shocked I am by the death
of your illustrious husband, and my thoughts go out to you for what
this loss must mean to you, and in fact means also to the whole world
of music.

Though we met but infrequently I always had a great feeling of association and friendship with him and you know, also he knew, how tremendously I admired his work.

I was so pleased when he wrote so appreciatively about the Variations that I had the honour to dedicate to you both, and I was so looking forward to hearing him conduct the work as he said he would one day.

My wife joins me in sending you our deepest sympathy.

Yours very sincerely

William Walton

To Alan Frank   6 January 1964

La Mortella, Forio d'Ischia

Dear Alan,

[. . .]

Bad news about Su's leg. The doctor here says sh'ell be laid up for a couple of months. But we have sent the X rays to London & I think sh'ell still have to go there for an operation – far too risky here & in London there's B.U.P.A.[1] There will be no point in my coming with her as I've nothing to do in London except hang around & spend money. So we've decided I stay here till I go to N.Z. But of course all our arrangements are in the air, & I only hope that she will be fit enough to join me at the Adelaide Fest on March 10ᵗʰ.

It maybe that I can join Solly Zuckerman[2] in Delhi. He will be there for the Republic day (Jan 26) but I'm waiting to hear from him. If I can't I shall cut out India (too depressing sight-seeing on one's own) & Bangkok & join Terry Rattigan[3] in Hong Kong around Feb 5ᵗʰ & proceed to Auckland via Sydney about the 15ᵗʰ. Shall have to tackle N.Z. on my own – also rather a depressing thought – but they are keeping me very busy.

As ever

William

1 British United Provident Association, a private medical insurance company.
2 Distinguished South African-born scientist, anatomist and zoologist, resident in England from the 1930s onwards, and a longstanding friend of the Waltons. He wrote two volumes of autobiography, *From Apes to Warlords* (1978) and *Monkeys, Men and Missiles* (1981).
3 Terence Rattigan. English playwright, and a personal friend who had stayed in one of the Waltons' holiday houses in Ischia.

To Nora Donnelly [Walton]   24 January 1964

La Mortella, Forio d'Ischia

My dear Nora,

Thanks for your letter. I fear Su's recovery will be slow, 8 weeks in plaster then to London again for the specialist to see what progress has been made in the building up of the fracture – then another 6 to 8 weeks in plaster, so there is not a hope of her being able to join me in Australia.

I arrive in Auckland on Weds. 19ᵗʰ Feb from Sydney, Flight QF 352 arriving Auck. 18–45. I don't know as yet what hotel I've been booked in, but doubtless someone official will be there to welcome me & show me round. I look forward to seeing [you] & much appreciate your coming to Auckland. The rest of the plans we can settle when we meet.

love
William

To Alan Frank   23 April 1964

Belvedere, 81 Bayswater Road, King's Cross, Sydney, Australia

Dear Alan,

The 5 cons. [concerts] here have been a huge success – good notices & large & enthusiastic audiences in spite of a week of tropical rain.

I've made friends with the two best young critics here[,] Roger Cornell the "Herald" & Martin Long the "D.Tel".

Would you do me a big favour? Martin Long (the most learned) has discovered an Elizabethan composer, Frances [Francis] Cutting, a contemporary of Dowland & has transcribed the lute works (quite a number) for Pfte, written what's known of his life, in fact it struck me as a v. scholarly effort worthy of possible publication by the O.U.P. I think you'd get the money back from University musicologists the world over.

So would you be kind & write to him saying you've heard from me & would be interested to see the work. His address is

Martin Long
81 Bent Street
Lindfield
New South Wales
Australia

[349]

I think you will find it worthwhile.
   As ever
   William

To Alan Frank   27 May 1964

La Mortella, Forio d'Ischia

Dear Alan,

   I got back on Sunday – what a relief! Enjoyable as the tour was in many ways, I was just about getting to the end of my tether. The Perth concerts went well – S.1 very well played by the excellent if somewhat small orch, small in the number of strings which was the same trouble with all the orchs, bar Sydney & Melbourne. But they all played with enthusiasm & verve & I've become quite a conductor!

   I think that in spite of the many hours of desperate boredom that it was well worth doing, even if only for a change, being treated as a "great man" with enthusiastic audiences & good press, in fact all very good for the "morale". The A.B.C.[1] are very keen on my doing another tour – I would'nt mind if Su was with me. She is much better than she thought she would be & can get about slowly without a stick for short spells.

   I may say I got to know my own works pretty thoroughly & I must say that I thought that I should become absolutely sick of them, but both Symps, the Vars, & the Concertos wear very well & go down well also rather to my surprise, but I found myself getting irritated by the smaller works Joburg, Partita Facade etc.

   [. . .]

   Thanks for writing to Martin Long. He was very pleased. No you did'nt tell me about [David] Willcocks's[2] all W. concert. I'll do my best to be there – I might even consider conducting the Gloria. But if I do this I can't also manage M.S's [Malcolm Sargent's] birthday concert. One or t'other.

   [. . .]
   As ever
   William

1 Australian Broadcasting Commission.
2 English conductor and organist: for many years he was Organist at King's College, Cambridge, and also Conductor of the Bach Choir.

To Alan Frank [12 February 1965]
[telegram sent from Forio]

PLEASE SEND EXPRESS AIRMAIL TWO COPIES PENGUIN BEAR WILLIAM

To Malcolm Arnold 20 February 1965

La Mortella, Forio d'Ischia

Dear Malcolm,

Sorry to have been so dilatory in answering your letter, but believe it or not I've been having a bout of work, after a very long interval – an Anthem with words by Auden [*The Twelve*] for our Alma Mater Ch. Ch. [Christ Church College] Oxford. Also a "Missa Brevis" (very brevis) for Coventry [Cathedral Choir]. But don't think I've got religious mania!

I was pleased & proud to [hear] about your conducting the "Spitfire" music[1] & that it made such an impression. But I was furious to read what the damn fool of a critic said about your new piece. They are really insufferable – all of them.

I've heard from Dallas [Bower] & he is coming to stay in early April on his way back from Darkest Africa bringing with him I should like to think his black-black mistress!

With best wishes from us both
As ever
William

To Benjamin Britten 25 March 1965

La Mortella, Forio d'Ischia

Dear Ben,

Our best congratulations on receiving the O.M. Noone could deserve it more than you.

Incidentally I am seriously thinking of embarking on "The Bear"[2] which Peter [Pears] suggested I might do for the English Opera Group. But it falls into that rather awkward category of a "Curtain-raiser" & I

1 The *Spitfire Prelude and Fugue*, Walton's concert-hall adaptation of his score for the film *The First of the Few*.
2 The short story by the Russian writer Anton Chekhov.

25. 3. 65

Dear Ben,

Our best congratulations on receiving the
O.M. Noone could deserve it more than you.

Incidentally I am seriously thinking of embarking on 'The
Bear" which Peter suggested I might do for the English Opera
Group. But it falls into that rather awkward category of a
"Curtain-raiser" & I don't know if it would fit in with
something else. I don't think it could last more than 45
mins, if that. And what kind of an orchestra should I do
it for?

A few days ago I received the record of 'Amor in
Tore". I don't think Peter can have any qualms
about it. It is altogether an excellent record. especially

your part of it.

If you have a moment, let me know what you think about the "Bear" idea.

Still love from us both & to Peter & again many congratulations

Yours ever

William

don't know if it would fit in with something else. I don't think it could last more than 45 mins, if that. And what kind of an orchestra should I do it for?

A few days ago I received the record of "Anon in love". I don't think Peter can have any qualms about it. It is altogether an excellent record, especially your part of it.

If you have a moment, let me know what you think about the "Bear" idea.

With love from us both & to Peter & again many congratulations
Yours ever
William

To Walter Legge   21 April 1965

La Mortella, Forio d'Ischia

My dear Walter,

As you seem to be safely settled down in Ascona, I presume you have managed to get out of the clutches of the Inland Revenue & I should very much like to know how you managed it & to whom you went for advice.

I'm now in a desperate situation (having this morning had to pay £500 for Italian income tax & which I've to go on doing every two months) as the Inland Revenue won't let me go. I seem to be paying still about £5000 p.a in England plus £3000 to the Italians so you can see that pretty well my whole income is going on tax. And of course the In. Rev. owe me a vast sum for all the British tax I've been paying over the last three years.

Marks seems somehow to have made a balls of it as he seems to be unable to make the In. Rev. even answer his applications, so I would be vastly obliged if you would tell me to whom you went & perhaps he could help me out.

Meanwhile it is appallingly cold here & of course we've both had the flu. We go to London on May 9th. I've an all W. prog with Bach Choir[1] at the R.F.H. on the 18th. So if you could let me know to whom to go before then I'd be very grateful.

1 Probably the one to be conducted by David Willcocks, mentioned in Walton's letter to Alan Frank of 27 May 1964.

With our best love to you both
As ever
William

To Walter Legge   3 May 1965

La Mortella, Forio d'Ischia

Dear Walter,
   Thank you for answering so promptly & informatively my "cri-de-coeur", & I am sorry indeed to learn that you are almost in the same boat as I am.
   I must say that Ascona is about the most expensive bit of Switzerland you could have hit on & the "status" tax unbearable. Why not come here? There are a number of plots of land about half a mile from here where it is going for 4 or 5 thousand a sq metre. I won't say it is cheap but compared with Ascona it is as nothing. Nor should it be more out of the way than Ascona – 2¼ hours to London, 65 mins to Milan, 45 to Rome, so it's not so far from the centre of things as one might think. [. . .]
   I see Elizabeth [Elisabeth Schwarzkopf] is giving a recital on the 20th, so perhaps we can meet. We are by way of going to N. Wales to stay with Christabel Aberconway that day, but I'll try to put it off to the next day.
   I go to London on the 9th for rehearsals with the Bach Choir & to Oxford for the week end of the 16th to hear my bloody Anthem [*The Twelve*] I've written for Ch. Ch [Christ Church College] with Auden. Back on the 17th for the concert on the 18th.
   [. . .]
   I can see an inactive life for you more than anyone is intolerable. Writing your memoirs is a solution. You might even threaten E.M.I. with that. But seriously, I think you could write a marvellous document of your period.
   Hoping to see you and with our love to you both
   As ever
   William

To Walter Legge   13 June 1965

La Mortella, Forio d'Ischia

Dear Walter,

We go to London on the 19th to see & hear George Szell do the H. Vars (the record is just out) & return the 29th having heard "Mo.&Aa"[1] on the 28th – after that we shall be here to look after you. I hope that Elizabeth will join you later.

You might bring along the Mines of Sulphur.[2] I've not seen it or know a note of R. R. Bennett's music.

Looking forward to seeing you. Love from us both
As ever
William

To Nora Donnelly [Walton]   24 August 1965

Oxford University Press, Music Department, 44 Conduit Street, w.1

My dear Nora,

Thank you very much for your letter. Lovely to hear from you and we are delighted to think of Hannah [Nora's daughter] coming to see us some time next year. It would be great fun for her to go round the world with Alec.

The Pohoutakawas[3] are flourishing.

All love and best greetings from us both.
William

To Gregor Piatigorsky   4 October 1965

La Mortella, Forio d'Ischia

Dear Grisha,

Thank you for your letter. I like very much your idea for the lay-out of the proposed Double Concerto, but alas I can't get on with it until I

1 Schoenberg's opera *Moses und Aron*, at Covent Garden.
2 *The Mines of Sulphur*, the newly completed opera by the English composer Richard Rodney Bennett.
3 Bushes sent from New Zealand by Walton during his antipodean tour, and planted in the garden of La Mortella.

get at least some of these others out of the way, those with fixed dates, which are now too late for me to get out of. I do hope that you & Jascha [Heifetz] will understand.

With very best regards
yours ever
William Walton

To Paul Dehn[1]   11 October 1965

La Mortella, Forio d'Ischia

Dear Paul,

How splendid of you to have written such "smashing" verses [for *The Bear*] – & how quickly – if I could only set them so quickly. Maybe I shall now that I've to cease worrying about the printed text.

I'm just getting to Smirnov's entrance.[2] Up to that point the duration is nearly 10 mins. Too long? But it seems to work out and move fairly smoothly.

I think it may be a good thing that up to this point, it has been in prose, so to speak. And the whole thing will wake up with S.'[s] entrance & your verses, & there should'nt be any discrepancy between the 1st 10 mins & what follows. Anyhow there will still be a certain amount of recitative prose I imagine. But it may be that by the time we've reached the end, the beginning may have to be reconsidered.

[. . .]

I'm much taken with "Madame, je vous en prie". I must brush up on my Massenet. Incidentally I think of making the "Grozdiov" aria a Stravinsky pastiche.

1 English writer, poet and critic. Educated at Oxford's Brasenose College (one of whose boats a young cox called Willie Walton had been so delighted to defeat during his time at Christ Church College), Dehn wrote many acclaimed film scripts, including those of Anthony Asquith's *Orders to Kill* (winner of the British Academy Award for Best Screenplay in 1958), *The Spy Who Came in from the Cold*, Franco Zeffirelli's version of Shakespeare's *The Taming of the Shrew*, some of the *Planet of the Apes* series, and *Murder on the Orient Express*. He also wrote the libretti of Lennox Berkeley's one-act operas *A Dinner Engagement* and *Castaway*. He and Walton had met while Dehn was staying independently in Ischia.
2 The plot of *The Bear* is simple. The widow Yeliena Popova, still notionally in a state of soulful grief for her recently deceased husband, is confronted by the rough and boorish Smirnov, one of her late husband's creditors. They quarrel and threaten to shoot each other, but find that instead they have fallen in love. Luka is Popova's old, outwardly loyal, privately grumpy servant.

Don't cut the reference to "Tamara"[,] I can do a lovely "quote" for that[1] (bottom p. 410 & top. 411) or on p. 412 Louka's "They've gone to pick strawberries" as it refers back to his opening speech. But we could have a fine Trio with material of p's 412 & 413.

Again I can't thank you enough for having undertaken to do all this. Come out whenever its convenient for you. Of course I'll stand you your fare. Go to the ticket agents – Ashton Mitchell & Howlett's deal with our's & I'll write them to send the bill into the Oxford Univ. Press. They are in Dorland House[,] Lower Regent Street.

Love from us both & to Jimmy
as ever
William

Can we somehow introduce the "chair breaking" during the verse "Lord! What wasted time". Perhaps right at the end?

To Paul Dehn   15 October 1965

La Mortella, Forio d'Ischia

Dear Paul,

Thank you for your letter & the welcome news that you can come out on Thurs Oct 28th.

If by chance there's no fog & your 'plane should arrive on time you would be able to catch the helicopter & have lunch here. In any case the Aliscafo [hydrofoil] leaves around 3-oclock & takes only 25 mins instead of two hours. I'll let you know the exact times later. Three cheers for Zeffirelli![2]

I think that a week should be ample to elucidate the "Bear" problems.

I like your solution of the bottom of p. 403 & I hope that I shall get as far [as] the end of the "Grozdiov" Aria by the time you arrive.

It seems to me that it is necessary to include the gist of p's 406–7. From the end of S.s [Smirnov's] speech p 406 "You there. L. [Luka] What is it? S. Bring me some kvass or a glass of water" to p 408 S. "Well this is a surprise" is somewhat of a non sequitur. P. 407 "I cut a

---

1 Possibly from Balakirev's symphonic poem *Tamara*. A large part of *The Bear*'s appeal to Walton lay in the opportunities it offered for parodying earlier styles of music in the context of his own.
2 Franco Zeffirelli, Italian theatre and cinema director.

fine figure" could be quite funny & Pop. [Popova] must make her entrance somewhere.

I must say I sympathise with your life, being hen pecked by me, Lennox[1] & Franco [Zeffirelli] & I can't tell [you] how pleased I am about your cooperation which I hope you don't find too irritating & disturbing.

Will write again about your journey.

love
William

To Alan Frank   13 November 1965

La Mortella, Forio d'Ischia

Dear Alan,

Thanks for all your various letters which have been unanswered till now.

Paul Dehn has been here & the libretto has taken on very nicely. It could turn out to be a winner on a small scale. He's going to ring you on his return from Rome & report progress. I shall have a good shot at finishing at least in sketch before I come to London about Dec 27th. It is full of parody's anything from Tchaikovsky to Stravinsky via Massenet etc. & maybe will be quite funny if it's not a damp squib.

Meanwhile can you have sent me [Britten's] Albert Herring (I've the record – funny in parts but too-too long) & Stravinsky's Mavra & Lieutenant Kitje Prokoviev.[2]

I've heard from Mr Hochhauser[3] that Rostropovitch has expressed a desire to meet me. I'm moving up!

As ever
William

---

1 Lennox Berkeley's opera *Castaway*, also to a libretto by Dehn, was premièred in a double bill with *The Bear* at the Aldeburgh Festival on 3 June 1967.
2 *Lieutenant Kijé* by Prokofiev.
3 Victor Hochhauser, London-based agent and promoter with strong links with Russian artists.

To Walter and Elisabeth Legge [February 1966]

17 Harley St, w.1

Dear Walter & Elizabeth,

My prognostications I fear were only too correct & here I am[,] about to begin my 3<u>rd</u> week of "cobbalt" [cobalt] rays. The treatment itself involves nothing but the effects are variable to devastating making one feel ghastly & occasionally v. sick. However if they accomplish what they are supposed to it will be well worth it – I may be rid of this fell disease permanently – but I'm full of doubts. It's so hard to get anything from the doctors – they themselves can hardly say anything more definite than that it should do the trick. But so should have the 1<u>st</u> op.!

Meanwhile everything's in the air. I've still time I hope to finish the Bear as it need not be ready before the end of April.

Su's bearing up very well & for that matter so am I considering what a bloody bad temper I'm in about it all.

Our best love to you both

As ever

William

To Helga Keller 3 March 1966

La Mortella, Forio d'Ischia

My dear Helga,

Thank you so much for your letter. The operation itself was'nt too bad, not half as bad as the "piles"! Anyhow I've been v. lucky as it was caught in the early stage & the doctors say that it won't reccur. I'm not even having deep X ray as it is not considered necessary.

And the luck of having discovered it in the very few days I happened to be in London. I was feeling quite well & no symptoms as far as I could see & if I'd not met a girl-friend who happened to be a doctor, I should have come back here & I don't suppose it would have been discovered till it was to[o] late to stop it spreading. So as you see, the Devil looks after his own.

I'm glad life is working out well for you all.

After that dreadful London Clinic we pretended we were millionaires & spent 3 weeks in the Savoy! Very pleasant & rewarding & not more expensive than the clinic where I should have had to stay as I was'nt allowed to travel.

Our best love to you both
as ever
William

To Gregor Piatigorsky   4 March 1966

La Mortella, Forio d'Ischia

Dear Grisha,

Thank you so much for your cable & good wishes. We've been back here for a couple of weeks now & I am beginning to feel more like my normal self.

I've been extremely fortunate that the cancer on my lung was found in it's early stages & the doctors were able to get it completely away & with little chance of recurrence.

I am bearing in mind the Double Concerto & hope that it won't be too long before I can start work on it.

Yours ever
William

To Benjamin Britten   17 March 1966

La Mortella, Forio d'Ischia

My dear Ben,

Thank you so much for your letter & the good news of your conva-lescence.[1]

All had been going well with me, till I managed to catch a cold & cough about ten days ago – under the circumstances, slightly disastrous. But I've managed to evade any serious consequences, such as pleurisy etc. – but it just shows how careful one must be & not, because one was feeling pretty well, overdo it.

No more thoughts of work for the moment. I shall just lie about in the sun which is now at last consistently shining.

I hear from Alan Frank that the Aldwych season is off which is sad for all concerned, though for my part I'm slightly relieved at not having to press on at the moment.

---

1 Britten had had an abdominal operation the previous month, and convalesced in Marrakesh in Morocco.

[361]

Paul Dehn is coming here for some days at the end of April, so we will have a chance to re-polish the end of the "Bear" which at the moment I don't feel is very satisfactory.

With best love from us both & to Peter & may you continue to progress & not have any relapses – though I must say there is nothing to be done about the inevitable depression, but it seldom I hope, lasts for very long.

Blessings
as ever
William

To Sir Osbert Sitwell   1 April 1966

La Mortella, Forio d'Ischia

My dear Osbert,

We are so glad to get your letter. We must have missed the Sunday Times so did not read of your unfortunate experience on the "Antilles".

In all probability we may be coming to Florence over Easter arriving possibly next Wednesday – I'll let you know for certain & we can come over & see you. We'll be staying in a hotel.

The doctor who spotted my 'cancro' is coming to stay with us to-morrow. She is a pathologist & is going on to Florence. There are some very expert specialists at the Cobalt Institute – not that I've any need of them at the moment, as the doctors in London couldn't have been more pleased with me – & I'm feeling very well, if a bit inclined to go to sleep with or without the slightest pretext – all the same it is just as well to know of someone just in case.

Anyhow we look forward to seeing you sometime after Wed's next.

With our best love
as ever
William

To Walter Legge
29 April 1966

[postcard]

La Mortella, Forio d'Ischia

Just returned from Florence, where we had gone so that I could be X-rayed by an eminent Prof. They have luckily turned out to be very satisfactory so I can be calm for the next 3 months. Sorry I can't get to the Philharmonic meeting or to Elizabeth's [Elisabeth Schwarzkopf's] recital.

Is there any likelihood of your coming here during the summer?

Our best love to you both

William

To Peter Heyworth
29 April 1966

La Mortella, Forio d'Ischia

My dear Peter,

I was delighted to get your letter. The news is good. I've just had the report on the X-rays which is excellent. Also I am beginning to feel more like my old self & have even looked a piece of Mss paper in the face! – not with very promising results however. But it's wonderful to have an excuse not to work!

One way of your coming here would be to attend the Festival at Cava Tirreni. It's a classical "jazz" festival. That sounds awful & I'm sure it is awful. [. . .] But the Festival would I'm sure be frightfully flattered if you attended it – whether the Editor of the "Observer" would allow you is another question. But it might be a change from Salzburg. But the point of Cava is that it is very central – it is south of Naples on the way to Salerno & you can get to places like Paestum[,] Ravello – Amalfi from where there is in the summer a steamer direct to Ischia where you would find yourself very welcome. Anyhow give it a thought.

I hope by now that you are recovered from your mixture of cold and Addison's – it sounds most unpleasant.

Give our love to Wystan [W. H. Auden] and yourself.

William

To Walter Legge   23 May 1966

La Mortella, Forio d'Ischia

Dear Walter,

How nice to hear from you.

According to the latest x-rays I am keeping very well with no sign (as yet) of a recurrence. The doctors do'nt seem to expect one which is encouraging – but one never knows. Anyhow I shall continue with the X-rays every 3 months.

I'm hardly doing anything – even listening to music let alone composing. There's a sort of delayed shock & one will have to start all over again I feel, which I think may be a good thing. I was actually in the middle of an opera on Tchekov's "The Bear" for Aldeburgh. It's for next year & could be quite funny. Do you know the play? Very short – about 40 mins.

I think you are right about Ascona – Salzburg will be far more congenial I suspect.

With our best love to you both
As ever
William

Let me know when you move.

To Sir Osbert Sitwell   22 June 1966

La Mortella, Forio d'Ischia

My dear Osbert,

Thank you for your letter. I'm sorry [you] are not going to Amalfi.

I returned from London a couple of weeks ago where I had gone for a check-up. Everything satisfactory & I was given a clean bill of health.

Delighted to see that Francis[1] has got married. I hope with S & G's approval this time!

I'm trying to settle down to work. I've a commission for an overture[2] from the New York Phil[harmonic]. Any ideas for a title? If one should occur to you please let me know.

1 Sacheverell and Georgia Sitwell's second son.
2 Eventually named *Capriccio burlesco*.

With best love from us both
as ever
William

To Walter Legge   27 June 1966

La Mortella, Forio d'Ischia

Dear Walter,

I am delighted to hear that your check-ups have been satisfactory. I returned from London about 3 weeks ago after having had also a satisfactory check. It's all a bit nerve-racking, I find & I think I'm becoming a hypochondriac!

The press for the "Mines of Sulphur" [opera by Richard Rodney Bennett] was not at all good & I've not come across anyone who thought really well of it. It seems to have had the same kind of reception at La Scala as did T&C.

Are you going to Salzburg to hear Hans H's [Hans Werner Henze's opera] "The Bassarids"? I saw the libretto – quite incomprehensible, I thought – but I know I'm exceptionally stupid. If you hear it let me know what it is like.

Paul Dehn is doing the libretto for the "Bear" – on the whole very well if just a bit too witty here & there.

With best love from us both
William

To Benjamin Britten   21 July 1966

La Mortella, Forio d'Ischia

My dear Ben,

I was so sorry to have missed you when I came over to Aldeburgh or rather Orford, but it was too complicated to change the appointments with the doctors, who thank heaven gave me a satisfactory check-up.

I am very happy to read & hear of your complete recovery & that you are back to full activity. But what with Michael [Tippett]'s operation it would seem to be the composer's year of adversity.

I can't tell you how impressed I was & how much I enjoyed the Burning F.F. [*The Burning Fiery Furnace*] Besides it's beautiful & dramatic form it was so intensely moving & convincing & achieved with such small forces.

It didn't surprise me at all that you had found it so difficult to do, but it sounds so spontaneous that one would never guess the agony it must have cost you – you brought it off triumphantly. Though the performance & production was excellent I would like to have heard it with Peter [Pears] & hope to do so sometime[.]

We shall be in London at the end of Sept. for yet another check-up & it is just a possibility that I will bring the "Bear" with me.

With love from us both

yours ever

William

I was pleased to read some very good notices of the [Ronald] Stevenson Passacaglia.[1]

To Walter Legge   19 September 1966

La Mortella, Forio d'Ischia

Dear Walter,

I don't [know] where you saw that I was to conduct the N.P.O. [New Philharmonia Orchestra] but it's off. There was talk of my doing "Facade" but they could find no reciters, luckily as I feel unfit to conduct anything even with one finger. I'm having a good deal of pain from the operational area & my left arm. The doctor here says it is rheumatism! Well, I go to London next week for a check-up.

I don't think I'd better undertake the little piece for Gerald.[2] I've only just begun to resume work on the "Bear" & I assure you I'm not at all in form. Sir Michael T. [Tippett] I think is the answer & very appropriate too.

Our best love to you both

as ever

William

1 *Passacaglia on DSCH*, a large-scale piano work by the Scottish composer Ronald Stevenson, based on the initials of Shostakovich's name as represented musically by the notes D, S (German for E♭), C, H (German for B♮). Walton had been much impressed by a recording of the work and had tried to raise interest in further performances of it.
2 Gerald Moore, English accompanist. With Elisabeth Schwarzkopf he had given the première of *A Song for the Lord Mayor's Table* in 1962.

To Gregor Piatigorsky   17 November 1966

[London, as from:]
La Mortella, Forio d'Ischia

Dear Grisha,

How kind of you to write to me.

Alas it has been a very troubled year for me. Just as I thought I had recovered from the operation I underwent in January, there was a recurrence & I have been undergoing for the last eight weeks [a course] of cobalt rays. However I'm happy to be able to tell you that the doctors say (do I believe them?) that I'm completely cured & the chances of a further recurrence are very remote.

I return to Italy next week & hope to be able to get started on some work at last.

Fascinating to hear about your New York concerts with Jascha, & I'm keeping in mind about a Double Concerto.

The last address I had of Gertrude Hindemith is: Villa la Chance, Blonay, Vevey, Switzerland. I went to see her some 18 months ago & she seemed well – but lonely, living in that large villa on her own.

As ever
William

To Walter Legge   28 November 1966

La Mortella, Forio d'Ischia

Dear Walter,

Thank you for your kind enquiry.

Just a week ago (we returned here next day) I was examined by Sir Thos. Ashes Sellors & I had been previously examined by Sir Brian Wendeyer (very expert) & they both pronounced me to be rid of this fell disease. Personally speaking I'm not all that sure I believe them, but at any rate I am much better than I was a couple of months ago. It is said that the rays continue their activity for sometime after the treatment has stopped. Anyhow it was all rather disagreable, but I seem to have suffered less than most people do & I'm definitely better.

[. . .]

There's a mad situation. Without warning – suddenly E.M.I & Decca have decided to record Symph. I[,] E.M.I with Sir M.S. [Malcolm

Sargent] & the N.P.O. [New Philharmonia Orchestra,] Decca with [André] Previn[1] & the L.S.O. [London Symphony Orchestra] Both records come out in Feb & I've had to write "blurbs" for them both! Both recordings are very good, naturally in parts one is better than the other, but on the whole Decca is the best. But what a "pasticcio" after all those years to bring out both at the same time.

The "Bear" gets more difficult as it goes on. In fact the end is the end in all senses of the word & I do[n't] quite know how it will turn out.

With our best love to you both – bless you

As ever

William

Come & see us

To Alan Frank   19 December 1966

La Mortella, Forio d'Ischia

Dear Alan,

Thanks for your letter & for looking after the bits & pieces.

[. . .]

About Chris.Colomb. [*Christopher Columbus*][2] I can't believe that there is anything worth while resus[c]itating from that vast & boring score. I don't remember a thing so I had better have a look at those songs – not that I can do much about them as I think the BBC bought the whole thing outright for next to nothing. But let me have look! [. . .]

[. . .]

It would seem that E.M.I have missed the Xmas sales in spite of it's pretentious ad. They really do spoil the case by overstatement. That sentence is enough to get the backs up of everyone, not only the critics, but of the Elgarites, the Mahlerites, the V.Williamsites the Sibelius-ites – the Hittites, the Satellites & every "ite" including me. However I suppose they know their own business best.

Sir M. [Malcolm Sargent] seems to be having a bad time.[3] Poor man. I

---

1 German-born composer and conductor, who became an American citizen in 1943. He was Principal Conductor of the London Symphony Orchestra from 1969 to 1979.
2 Frank had asked Walton whether any of Walton's incidental music might be suitable for publication.
3 Sargent died of cancer on 3 October 1967.

had a word from Lilias[1] & she said the situation was very grave. I am sorry.

Meanwhile I seem to be keeping alright but with considerable discomfort at times, but I don't think it is anything to worry about, which of course one does.

All seasonal greetings,
as ever
William

To Alan Frank   12 January 1967

La Mortella, Forio d'Ischia

Dear Alan,

One must draw a line somewhere about the horrors of one's past being allowed to be dragged up & I am for a complete ban on those songs[2] even to destruction of the Mss! I'm not at all sure that MacNiece [Louis MacNeice] would'nt feel the same about his lyrics!

[. . .]
As ever
William

To Alan Frank   6 March 1967

La Mortella, Forio d'Ischia

Dear Alan,

Your letter to P.D. [Paul Dehn] evidently had the desired effect. Bravo! For he sent a revised ending which will make all the difference. Can you send me his address in Mexico so that I can write & thank him.

For the sake of speed I'm sending the rest in Ptfe [sic] sc. & will catch up with scoring later. Roy [Douglas] informs me that he is going away on May 1st so I'll have to be ready before that!

I expect P.D. will have sent you a copy of the new version.
As ever
William

1 Lilias Sheepshanks, a friend and supporter of Britten, Walton and many other composers and musicians.
2 Walton eventually allowed 'Beatriz's Song' from *Christopher Columbus* to be published in 1974.

There is a postal strike in progress, so letters may be a bit hectic.

To Walter Legge   9 March 1967

La Mortella, Forio d'Ischia

Dear Walter,

Sorry to hear about your relapse & I hope you are now fully recovered.

In about 10 days time I shall have finished the "Bear". Your theory that 12-toning is on the way out pleases me, especially as the "Bear" gets more tonal & frivolous & vulgar as it progresses.

Though I would like to think you are right I was slightly horrified by the enthusiastic reception given to the N.P.O. concert of atonal music, but it was I like to think more for Mr [Edward] Downes[1] who conducted extremely ably.

Incidentally Previn is a splendid conductor & did Symph I proud & it & I got a huge ovation. Sylvia[,] Malc's [Sir Malcolm Sargent's] sec. told me sometime ago that his [recorded] version had already topped 5000 & Mr Angle[2] told me that Decca were outselling H.M.V 5 to 1. I wonder.

I hope E.M.I will bring out a record of Geralds [Gerald Moore's] last concert with those 19 lollipops. I read I thought strangely enthusiastic notices about Walter Legge? So it must have been super.

Look after yourself

As ever

William

To Walter Legge   20 April 1967

La Mortella, Forio d'Ischia

Dear Walter,

Forgive my being so long in answering your letter – but it has been another case of the late Sir W. & I only finished the vocal sc. of the B. yesterday & I've still quite a few pages of scoring to get through.

I hope you are not going to live in France. I'm told that the tax situation is going to be much more difficult there. It is incidentally getting a bit more difficult here.

---

1 English conductor, at this time a company member of the Royal Opera House, Covent Garden.
2 Robert Angles of RCA Records, which had made Previn's recording of the First Symphony; at this time the RCA label was distributed in the UK by Decca.

I think possibly near Rome might be a better choice. After all you can get to anywhere from there. And near Rome there [are] lovely places to be found & often not so v. expensive & Fiumicino is v. accessible.

We should be delighted to have you here any time you like to come except for Aldebugger[1] from about May 20th to about June 12th. But let us know nearer the time.

I'll bear in mind about the nursing home. At the moment I seem to be all right. The only thing is I get dreadfully tired & sleepy[,] in fact I'm off as soon as I set eyes on a piece of Mss. paper!

Our best love to you both
As ever
William

To Paul Dehn   4 May 1967

La Mortella, Forio d'Ischia

Dear Paul,

I've finished the B.B. (stands for the bloody Bear – not what you think!). I don't know what to think of it so I've asked A. Frank to send you a Pfte sc. so Jimmy [James Lockhart][2] can play it to you, so you can vaguely know what to expect when it comes to rehearsal time.

There's no doubt I fear that I'm not what I was & have been & am feeling very exhausted over the work which has taken me far longer than necessary – but it is I think sufficiently in time. Noone would have thought of looking at it if it had been ready last year anyhow.

I've taken some unpardonable liberties with your text – but I've taken them all the same.

I see from the rehearsal list that you will be torn in two as the "Castaway's" rehearsals are in Aldeburgh & the "Bear's" in London.

We come to London [. . .] on the 22nd & look forward to seeing you. I shall have to do a round of doctors. I've just seen my local one – he's not too happy about me – nor for that matter am I.

[. . .]
As ever
William

1 Walton's preferred name for Aldeburgh.
2 English conductor. The world première of *The Bear* was conducted by Lockhart at the 1967 Aldeburgh Festival on 3 June.

To Helga Keller   11 May 1967

La Mortella, Forio d'Ischia

My dear Helga,

I'm sorry not to have thanked you before for your birthday greetings, but I've been busy with finishing the scoring of my operatic farce on the Bear of Tchekov.

[. . .]

The garden flourishes & we have been, I think stupidly extravagant & built ourselves a swimming pool. In fact it is almost a necessity as the beaches are so filthy & crowded these days.

You couldn't by any chance send us the name of a Sunray Heating firm for the pool. We got a quotation from England for 8 mirrors £450 – too much! Possibly they are to be had more cheaply from Israel.

With best love to you both
William

To Paul Dehn   13 May 1967

La Mortella, Forio d'Ischia

Dear Paul,

Delighted to get your letter & that there's hope that the libretto [of *The Bear*] will be on sale at the 1st perf – because as you may or may not know there is many a truth spoken in jest & I think apart from the unaccompanied recits [recitatives] that it is quite on the cards that not one – not one of your exquisite words will be heard – & then what will be the point of the opera? Certainly not the not very pretty or witty music. (William in his Facade vein! I'll bet.)

I suppose you mean well when you say you are going to Aldeburgh on April 29th or are you like "Alice where art thou?" In the middle of next week! as the old music-hall song had it!

We will certainly lunch & I hope after a successful interview with the docs.

Our love to you both
as ever
William

I hope we have circumvented the copyright of the various translations. I took infinite trouble avoiding the various words and sentences & even invented a mythical "groom" as you may have noticed & used only one pistol, not two.

To Roy Douglas   17 May 1967

La Mortella, Forio d'Ischia

My dear Roy,

Thank you so much for all your work on the "Bear". I thought for a moment I should never finish it, but however I got thro' somehow, & hope it is not quite so awful as I was inclined to think. A.F. [Alan Frank] seems to think he has a winner on his hands.

I hope that you a[re] quite recovered from your strenuous efforts with the Pfte. Sc. & parts & that you are having a well earned holiday. Enjoy yourself.

As ever
William

To Helga Keller   10 June 1967

La Mortella, Forio d'Ischia

My dear Helga,

Thank you for your letter of the 5th. Is'nt it incredible what has happened in the last five days![1] How thankful you must be, in fact we all must be, for Dayan[2] & the Israeli army.

I really imagined we were in for the 3rd G.W. [Great War]. When I wrote you on what must have seemed a very trivial matter, there was hardly any sign in the Italian press of what was afoot otherwise I would'nt have bothered you & thank you so much for the address. We will leave it awhile for things to settle down, which presumably they will do.

The "Bear" went v. well & had a good press. It's unfortunate that the

1 The 'Six-Day War' between Israel and the surrounding Arab states was about to end in a comprehensive victory for Israel, which had invaded and occupied the West Bank region of Jordan, the Golan Heights in Syria, and the Sinai peninsula in Egypt.
2 Moshe Dayan, Israeli general.

critic in the "Observer" [Peter Heyworth] is bound to be bad. He's never had a good word to say for me yet. However it dos'ent matter as up till now the rest has been v. good.

And I'm fortunate with my lung. I saw two specialists & they both gave me a clean bill of health. So I am I hope alright for some while to come.

Our best love to you both
As ever
William

I've just seen it – not at all so bad! And don't stand any rot from the Russians!

To Paul Dehn   13 June 1967

La Mortella, Forio d'Ischia

Dear Paul,

I've now seen the Sunday's [newspaper reviews] & on the whole I don't think any of us have much to complain about.

I tried often to 'phone you before I left, but you we'rent in, to tell you of a 90% possibility of the "B" being recorded by E.M.I after the S.Ws [Sadler's Wells] perfs. Perhaps A. Frank has told you about it.

The thing is, is there anything we want to emend before recording. Is 'dismal Desmond'[1] right about there being too many verses for "I was a"[2] & that I've smothered some of your jokes? The point is which? He may well be right. Do you know him well enough to ring him up & ask him before it's too late?

It is v. difficult for us knowing the words to be able to say what has been mucked up.

We'll be in London about July 10th.
William

1 Desmond Shawe-Taylor, music critic of the *Sunday Times*.
2 Popova's and Smirnov's duet in *The Bear*, 'I was a constant, faithful wife'.

To Paul Dehn   16 June 1967

La Mortella, Forio d'Ischia

Dear Paul,

I am indeed disturbed to hear that Aldeburgh gave you bronchial pneumonia though I'm not at all surprised. I escaped with a high powered cold.

[. . .]

About giving up smoking, there are some german pills obtainable at Boots which are of considerable help. Ive unfortunately forgotten the name.

I'm glad the "B" went well on the "air". Perhaps we should'nt bother about the plaints I mentioned in my last letter.

Lilias [Sheepshanks] arrives to-day with a recording of the broadcast perf. & I'll go through it with a musical tooth-comb to see if & where it can be improved. I expect that the critics had'nt realised that where they couldnt hear the words was because everybody was several bars out at times. Never mind. Get well quickly

 & our love to you both
William

To Sir Osbert Sitwell   27 June 1967

La Mortella, Forio d'Ischia

My dear Osbert,

Thank you so much for your letter about the "Bear". It does indeed seem to have gone down well, I'm even off to London to-morrow to record it. I should like to think that it may bring in lots of money, what with T.V. & those opera work-shops in American universities, it may.

How are you? I seem to be well, in fact touching wood, rather better than I was before the operation.

With best love from us both
William

To Walter Legge   12 August 1967

La Mortella, Forio d'Ischia

Dear Walter,

I was about to write you & tell you how much I missed you during the recording (E.M.I) of the "Bear". I hope it will turn out better than I fear. Hard luck on the singers etc, for there didn't seem to be any time for any play-backs during the recording – only during the interval or after the session. However it is too late to start bothering about it now.

I'm much interested by the "Frogs" idea.[1] I will re-read it & have a talk with Paul Dehn. He is, I think one of the better, if not the best of the librettists about at the moment – especially if there is a sound structured basis there already was in the "Bear" where he had only to cut & adorn the text with his (more often than not) witty & amusing & to-the-point lyrics, & I've got him in control! I don't think I want a commission as yet from Cov.Gar. It may sound a bit conceited, but I've got or could have so many commissions that I don't know where to begin – in fact I'm giving them all up & when I write another piece I'll put it up for auction!

We've been invited to a cruise to Greece & the islands & to Istanbul in early Sept. which will I hope be entertaining & instructive. We shall be back here about the 20ᵗʰ [. . .]

How boring that you have to go house-hunting again. Let me know when you find it & your new address.

With our best love & to Elizabeth when she gets back.

as ever

William

To Walter Legge   2 October 1967

La Mortella, Forio d'Ischia

Dear Walter,

I have only just returned from Montreal where the "Bear" was being performed at "Expo" [Expo 67]. [. . .]

I will certainly look at Baruffi Chiozzotti [*Le Baruffe Chiozzotte*] & the other Goldoni plays. It [*The Bear*] was done with [Handel's] "Acis

---

1 Legge had evidently suggested to Walton an opera based on the play by Aristophanes.

and Galatea" in Montreal – much too long for another opera in the same programme. However it was quite a successful evening in spite of competition from the Vienna State Op, the first rain (heavy) for about a month & an extensive bus strike, so the audience was rather meagre – but not noticeably more [so] than for Britten's "Midsummer night's dream" when things were normal!

I've heard the record. Not too bad, but lacking in brilliance in parts. However I'll send it you when its out in December.

Our love to you both
William

To Benjamin Britten   23 November 1967

La Mortella, Forio d'Ischia

Dear Ben,

Thank you all for your telegram of congratulations.[1] It is indeed very gratifying.

We were delighted to get your P.C. from the Argentine & to hear of your great success.

With love from us both & to Peter
yours ever
William

To Sir Osbert Sitwell   27 November 1967

La Mortella, Forio d'Ischia

My dear Osbert,

Thank you so very much for your kind letter of congratulations on my receiving the O.M. All very surprising. I vaguely knew that something was on the "tapis" but it had been going on for so long that I'd forgotten all about it – so we are both naturally excited and delighted that it should be the best of all.

I never forget what I owe to you Sachie & Edith for your help when I most needed it. In fact, I dread to think what would have been my lot. And your help with Alec too – who would have thought that he [would

---

1 Walton had been awarded the Order of Merit.

become] a Director of the Bank of Canada & a very rich man to boot.

I hope you are keeping tolerably well. My last check-up about a month ago was highly satisfactory & the doctors think that I may have got away with it. But one always has to keep an eye on it – which you can well imagine I do.

We have had a marvellously fine six weeks but to-day torrential rain – so to work! I must make some dollars to counteract the efforts of the appalling Labour [Government] boys.

With best love from us both
as ever
William

To Alan Frank   6 December 1967

La Mortella, Forio d'Ischia

Dear Alan,

Thanks for your letter. I forgot two important people for the Bear record – Lilias Sheepshanks & Roy Douglas.

What an unusual Xmas present![1] And what a grisly tale! I always disliked D [Delius] & his works, so it dos'ent really surprise me that he behaved like that on his death-bed! Nor incidentally (I can't tell for why) do I take to young V.D. Is the O.U.P going to publish the Symposium on his father? [Bernard van Dieren] I side-stepped[,] for though I knew him off & on for quite a long period, I can hardly pretend I knew him well enough to write about him even if I could write. In fact on thinking over about V.D. & the Warlock[2] lot I don't think they were a very savoury lot or really produced anything in particular. W. is either "Elizabethan hearty" or non descript wanderings in the V.W. [Vaughan Williams] & Delian styles. As for V.Ds music it is as far as I remember so invertebrate that it could hardly stand up. So that being what I now think, I think I had better keep it to myself!

[. . .]
William

1 Frank had sent Walton a copy of Eric Fenby's book *Delius As I Knew Him*. This tells of Fenby's work as the blind Delius's amanuensis, and of Delius's death in 1934.
2 Peter Warlock, *nom de plume* of the English composer Philip Heseltine.

To Alan Frank [7 December 1967]
[telegram]

Forio d'Ischia

PLEASE PERSUADE PRS EXPRESS WARRANT AT ONCE DEVALUATION
SCARE = WILLIAM

To Roy Douglas [postmarked: 12 December 1967]
[postcard]

Forio d'Ischia

Bless you & thank you for taking time off to write to me about the
O.M. What a life you lead owing to me, & I can't thank you enough,
nor I'm sure could that other O.M.[1] whose script was worse than mine!
    William

To Alan Frank 15 December 1967

La Mortella, Forio d'Ischia

Dear Alan,
    Well all I can say is that our bank manager put the fear of old G in
us about the £ – also the Italian press & for that matter worst of all, the
British press gave one to think that it might happen again before the
N.Y.[2] [. . .]
    Am fascinated with the cutting about K.L. [Kit Lambert][3] I've not
seen him since I held him in my arms as his god-father & a fat lot of
good I've been to him. That is only too obvious to see. I've not taught
him his catechism etc. – but he seems to have prospered all the better for
my neglect.
    However there is something which I think you could profitably suggest
to him, as coming from me (I[t's] too difficult to do it myself owing to
my neglect) [which] is that his record co. should do a new record of

1 Ralph Vaughan Williams.
2 The British government had devalued the pound sterling in relation to other currencies
earlier in the year.
3 Constant Lambert's son.

[Constant Lambert's] "The Rio Grande". He can't lose money on it & everyone concerned might make a bit, especially if he could include some of his "Who" players[1] in it – only those who can read music! And if he handles it with his obviously spectacular P.R. it might work. Anyhow I think it worthwhile suggesting it to him as from the O.U.P. – Pop's only publisher to Polydor records & filial duty! Also they must want to lose some money for tax purposes! See what you can do.

William

Get John Ogdon[2] or R. R. Bennett for the Pfte part.

To Walter Legge   6 March 1968

La Mortella, Forio d'Ischia

Dear Walter,

I hope that you are both back safely & well after your sojourn in the U.S.

I'm well, in fact we both are, but I get terribly tired, especially if I have to force myself to look at a piece of M'ss paper. I'm consequently well, very well behind with my overture [*Capriccio burlesco*] for the N.Y. Phil [New York Philharmonic] which is unfortunate as they are paying very handsomely & it will be quite a wrench if I have to forego it.

We are thinking [of] & are almost certainly going to the Scala on the 26th for the 1st night of Hans H.'s [Henze's opera] "Bassarids". Is there any chance that you might be going too? I hope so – it would be so nice to see you again at long last.

I found two easy & excellent "cuts" for the "Bear" & have done as you suggest in the printed score which should be out soon. A pity I could'nt do them before it was recorded – but one is so stupid about "cuts". I never see how to do them till too late. But now it will be some 8 mins shorter. Rather necessary.

Hoping to see you in Milano
Our best love to you both
William

1 Kit Lambert was manager of the British rock group The Who.
2 English pianist and composer, with a strong interest in contemporary works by both British and foreign composers.

To Walter Legge

22 March 1968

[postcard]

La Mortella, Forio d'Ischia

We sha'nt after all be coming to Milan for the Bassarids, we've already seen it at Salzburg. But Larry & Joan [Sir Laurence and Lady Olivier] are coming on Sunday for some days & we must look after them. Also my old complaint (not cancer, but musical impotence) is at me & I'm very late with my overture for N.Y. & I need the dollars as we have let ourselves in for a number of "cambiali" [financial drafts]. But I see little hope of my being ready with the piece. We are both desperately sorry to miss you, but perhaps [will see you] on our way back from London early May. Our best love to you both as always

William

To Alan Frank

4 April 1968

La Mortella, Forio d'Ischia

Dear Alan,

I've just written to Kostelanetz[1] telling him that I think it most unlikely that I shall have his overture ready in time for June 18th. It has just not occurred. I['m] trying for the fourth time, & though it is slightly more promising it dos'ent really get off the ground. There's no material. Anyhow unless I finish the sketch by the time I come to London (the 25th) I still have the scoring to complete & the parts etc have to be done. I need hardly say in what despair I am, & how humiliated I feel & not to mention those dollars I so sorely need. But I'll go on trying till I return.

[. . .]

On the 26th I've to attend my being doctored[2] & a rehearsal in the evening.

I presume I shall get this piece finished for the "Proms". I don't quite know now what about the 1st perf rights. Anyhow I've said to K, that I'll write him another piece – fool that I am.

1 The conductor André Kostelanetz, the dedicatee of the *Johannesburg Festival Overture*, had commissioned the *Capriccio burlesco* for his concerts with the New York Philharmonic Orchestra

2 The award of Honorary D. Litt. by Sussex University. (See also p. 270.)

yrs
William

In addition I'm suffering from an appalling attack of rheumatism – too much practising Bs F.

To Helga Keller   13 April[1] 1968

La Mortella, Forio d'Ischia

Dearest Helga,
   As for my birthday don't give it a thought – I never do!
   We've just returned from London, where I had a v. satisfactory check-up 100%. I had opened the Brighton Fest. with Belshazzar's Feast & was a bit scared that it might have been too much for [me]. But I was alright in spite of the new chorus (not much better if any than that of the Israeli – they ought to have a good one by now & ask me out again). I like to think that the last 2 mins of it might be played to celebrate the victory![2] The next one!
   We saw Larry & Joan. He seems to be also quite O.K. He came to stay with us about a month ago with his vast family of children & nurses!
   I am delighted to learn that Mel is getting on so well & is having a great success. He surely deserves it. When you come over bring some of his records with you, I'd love to hear some.
   I've had a very bad off-period with my work in spite of vast bribes from the U.S. I don't seem to be able to get going after the "Bear" which is more than a year ago.
   [. . .]
   Let us know when you can come
   as ever
   William

I had a 20 min interview with the Queen to receive my O.M. She was divine.

1 Evidently 13 May.
2 Of Israel over the Arab nations in the 1967 Six-Day War.

To Alan Frank   24 July 1968

La Mortella, Forio d'Ischia

Dear Alan,

I sent you 9 pages of the new ov. [*Capriccio burlesco*] Don't let me lead you up the garden path into thinking I am anywhere near the end – it's about half way. Maybe I shall have the rest with me when I come to London on Aug 13th but I doubt it. It is, I fear, not very good – it may get better – it can hardly get any worse!

By the way, I forgot to thank you for the Elgar book[1] which I found excellent & very interesting. I was so pleased to discover that he hated music almost as much, if not more, than I do. I must now read his V.W. book.[2] I know next to nothing about him & it is perhaps time I got to know his music a bit, though I can't say I really look forward to doing so. [. . .]

Incidentally Michael Tip. [Tippett] has taken one of our houses for the 1st fortnight of Sept (with his family). It will be fun having him here as I'm very fond of him, though I'm more often than not completely baffled by his music. But I persevere – but have little hope of catching up with any of them. All rather depressing.

As ever
William

To Malcolm Arnold   8 September 1968

La Mortella, Forio d'Ischia

Dear Malcolm,

I have accepted, perhaps rashly, to write the music for the film of the "Battle of Britain".[3] I say rashly since I've done nothing of the kind since Richard III, some many years ago. Would you by any good chance be willing to conduct the sessions?

There will be about twelve, with any orchestra we like to have, the recording would be in May–June of next year. May be a bit earlier. I do

1 Michael Kennedy's *Portrait of Elgar*.
2 Michael Kennedy's *The Works of Ralph Vaughan Williams*.
3 Produced by Harry Saltzman for United Artists, with Sir Laurence Olivier as Air Chief Marshal Dowding leading a large cast.

hope that you will be able to do this. I should feel much more confident with you about if things should go wrong.

I saw a very very "rough cut" last time I was over but having now completed the film the next roughcut should be much better.

I'm coming to London on the 23rd to conduct at the R.F.H. & at Croydon the 28th with L.S.O. & we shall be off & on in London till Oct 12th, so perhaps we could meet, perhaps on the 26th on 27th if agreeable for you & I'll see if we can see the "rough cut" that is if you will undertake to do it. I mentioned the idea to Salzman [Harry Saltzman] & he was delighted at the idea.

as ever
William

To Benjamin Britten   9 September 1968

La Mortella, Forio d'Ischia

Dear Ben,

I hope that you will not think that I am making a too strange request – namely that you will allow me to attempt to write Variations (orchestral) on the theme of the 3rd movement of your Piano Concerto. I realise that you have used it as a passacaglia but not strictly speaking as a theme & variations & hope very much you will let me have a try. It is not a new idea of mine but one which I've been thinking about for some time.

I am delighted to hear from Lilias [Sheepshanks] of your huge success at Edinburgh[1] & fear you may be too exhausted to write, but a postcard with "yes" or "no" will suffice & I wo'nt complain if it is the latter even if I shall be very dissapointed.

With our best love to you both
yours ever
William.

1 Britten's works had been extensively featured at the 1968 Edinburgh Festival.

To Benjamin Britten   14 October 1968

La Mortella, Forio d'Ischia

My dear Ben,

We have only returned yesterday from a three weeks stay in England, & consequently I have only just received your kind letter consenting to my attempting variations on the 3<u>rd</u> movement of your Pfte Concerto. I much appreciate your allowing me & for writing to B&H. [Boosey & Hawkes] I will get the O.U.P to communicate with them & hope that they will be in a more generous mood.

I am delighted to hear that Peter [Pears] has recovered from his operation successfully. Lilias told me of it & that you'd both gone away for his recuperation. She, poor thing, has to undergo a severe operation on her back. One of those beastly kill or cure ones. She's had a rotten time & one can only hope for the best.

Our best love to you both & many thanks again
William

To Malcolm Arnold   [January 1969]

La Mortella, Forio d'Ischia

Dear Malcolm,

I have taken you at your word & have sent you the top lines (perhaps a little more) of two pieces almost identical with 4M1.[1] So you must try & make them sound quite different!

I think they should be fairly loud (I've put in no expression marks) as I imagine there [are] a lot of background airplane noises to overcome. On the other hand it is probably better the other way round.

I'm getting in a bit of a panic, but I'm aiming to finish all the small bits by the end of the week so I've time to devote to the big stuff. No sign of a tune! Every time I think of one I find I've written it before.

[. . .] What a pest (but a very grateful one)
I am
Yours
William

---

1   A sequence in the film score of *The Battle of Britain*.

To Malcolm Arnold   28 August 1969

La Mortella, Forio d'Ischia

Dear Malcolm,

Thanks for your letter. We were delighted to read such excellent notices of your concert but didn't see the Financial Times! I've got a tape of your concerto [Concerto for two pianos (three hands) and orchestra] & am waiting impatiently to hear it. It sounds a riot.

Interesting about the "B of B" poster. I am now in touch with Ron G. [Goodwin] He is terribly upset (quite why it is a bit difficult to ascertain) about the whole business & has got <u>his</u> solicitors on to U.A. [United Artists] Anyhow we seem now to console one another! A bit late.[1]

[. . .]

We come to London on Sept 12th for about 10 days & shall be at 32 Chester Terrace. Perhaps you will be there also or are you too occupied with your film? I will telephone.

Our love to you both
William

To Malcolm Arnold   5 September 1969

La Mortella, Forio d'Ischia

Dear Malcolm,

We have a box at Cov. Gar. for the "Trojans" [by Berlioz] on Sat. Sept. 20th. Lilias Sheepshanks was coming in her invalid chair, but is now too ill to move. Would you and Isabel [Isobel Arnold] like to come? We should be delighted if you could. It means 5 ½ hours! But I think we are allowed out for dinner. Will you cable me so that I can get it all organised.

---

1 In the summer of 1969 United Artists had decided to replace Walton's score for *The Battle of Britain*, notionally on the grounds that he had not composed enough music to fill the two sides of the long-playing record that was to be released at the same time as the film. Walton was not informed of this decision, and first found out about it when an English newspaper reporter telephoned him in Ischia to ask for a comment. A new score was composed by Ron Goodwin. Sir Laurence Olivier threatened to have his name removed from the film's credits, posters and associated publicity unless Walton's score was reinstated. Eventually Walton's sequence 'The Battle in the Air' was retained. Some prints of the film also retain Walton's 'Battle of Britain March' during the closing credits.

Our love to you both
William

Ought I to address you as the bard of Cornwall?[1]

To Walter Legge   21 December 1969

La Mortella, Forio d'Ischia

Dear Walter
   Delighted to hear from you. I would have written sooner but I've
been up to the eyes with music for Larry's film of the "Three Sisters".
Not much music but very difficult to do.
   [. . .]
   It's getting rather grim here.[2] Luckily on the island we are unaffected
but in the towns it is getting boring & slightly dangerous. I remember it
being rather like this in '23 before Mussolini appeared. One of the great
irritations personally is the shutting of the Post at 2-o'clock every day
except Sat when it shuts at mid-day. They say everyone has too much
money but it will soon dissapear if the present situation goes on. I think
it will but only worse.
   All seasonal greetings & our love to you both
   as ever
   William

I'm well & I hope you are. My last blood test was for the first time completely normal & healthy.

To Benjamin Britten   19 January 1970

La Mortella, Forio d'Ischia

Dear Ben,
   I've just received the following cable, "Your work enthusiastically
received an excellent composition Josef Krips"[3] – which is all to the

1 Arnold had recently moved to Cornwall, and had been awarded the honorary local title
of Bard of the Cornish Gorsedd.
2 As in America and Europe, the late 1960s in Italy was a time of politically motivated
unrest, strikes, demonstrations and terrorism.
3 Krips had conducted the première of *Improvisations on an Impromptu of Benjamin
Britten* in San Francisco on 14 January.

good as I was rather frightened that it was'nt going to be up to standard.

I understand that it has also been released for Aldeburgh. I hope that you will conduct it.[1]

I hope the new hall is going to be ready in time for the Festival & that the money is rolling.[2]

It is wonderful news that Lilias Sheepshanks is apparently well on the way to recovery. It seems quite miraculous after what she has been through.

Our best love to you & to Peter,
As ever
William

To Malcolm Arnold   20 February 1970

La Mortella, Forio d'Ischia

Dear Malcolm,

We are sorry that you can't come to stay. I really thought it might be a good opportunity to produce a masterpiece (it will be one anyhow I'm convinced) for the E.C.O [English Chamber Orchestra] without the noise of plumbers!

[. . .]

I could'nt face that film [*Upon this Rock*] after seeing it twice in Rome. Doing background music for Ralph Richardson, not my favourite actor, about 70 mins of it did'nt seem a pleasant way to spend ones time however profitable.

Our best love to you all.
William

My check-up was 100% O.K.

---

1 The British première of the *Improvisations* at the 1970 Aldeburgh Festival was conducted by Sir Charles Groves.
2 Snape Maltings Concert Hall had burned down during the 1969 Aldeburgh Festival. It was immediately rebuilt, and reopened in time for the next Festival in June 1970.

To Yehudi Menuhin   4 April 1970

La Mortella, Forio d'Ischia

Dear Yehudi,

Thank you both for your cable. I didn't spend my birthday in such an agreable manner as E.M.I never send me any records till I chivvy them & then one arrives six months late. I've heard nothing at all of the Vl. Con. I'm sure it is splendid.

I shall be in London on the 12th for a week or so & will ring you up.

Our love to you both,

William

To Yehudi Menuhin   21 April 1970

La Mortella, Forio d'Ischia

Dear Yehudi,

After my few days recording in London I returned here with our recording of the Concertos.[1]

Your playing is absolutely astounding, in fact I am unable to conjure up adequate superlatives for your interpretation & performance – nor can I thank you enough for having brought to life a dream which I thought would never come true. Bless you & I hope to see you soon.

Our love to you both,

William

To Griselda Kentner   21 April 1970

La Mortella, Forio d'Ischia

Dearest Griselda,

You must get the recording your brother-in-law has made of my Viola & Violin Cons. Both performances are fantastically good – I can hardly believe it - & won't J.H. [Heifetz] be cross.

We come to London about May 17th & we must meet.

Our best love to you both,

William

1 The Violin and Viola Concertos: Menuhin played the solo parts of both.

To Malcolm Arnold   8 June 1970

La Mortella, Forio d'Ischia

Dear Malcolm,

Thank you for keeping me in touch about the Browning project.[1] Except that I am somewhat dilatory (am being v. much so about scoring those guitar songs [*Anon. in Love*] – I don't know what to do with the 'armonys which are so often implied on the "box" – whether to fill them in or not) there is really no great hurry.

Very sorry to hear about the gout. Osbert Sitwell had a theory that only geniuses suffered from it – a theory certainly borne out in your case. Larry O. is also a fellow-sufferer – but he has discovered some pills or other that have completely cured him. I will find out about them. (It must have been the lobster – it can't have been the booze – as George Robey used to sing.)

We are delighted that you are all coming for Xmas. Hope that by now the end of the "Prom" fantasia[2] is well within sight.

We come to England the 19ᵗʰ & head straight for Aldeburgh staying with Lilias & shall be in London at our old haunt on the 28ᵗʰ till about July 12ᵗʰ.

Would you like to come to the Mansion House to hear those "Songs for the L.Ms Table" on July 2ⁿᵈ, that is if recovered from the P.R.S. lunch.

Our love to you both & to Edward[3]
William

1 At Arnold's suggestion Walton was considering an opera called *The Villa*, loosely based on an episode drafted from Robert Browning's verse play *Pippa Passes*.
2 Arnold's *Fantasy for Audience and Orchestra*.
3 Arnold's son.

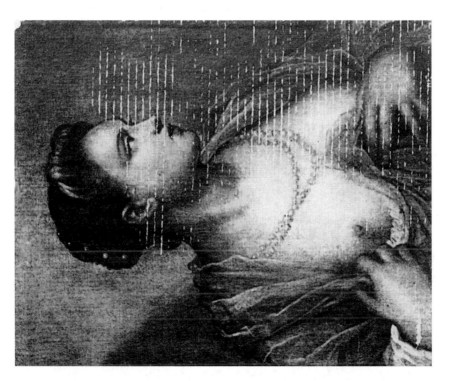

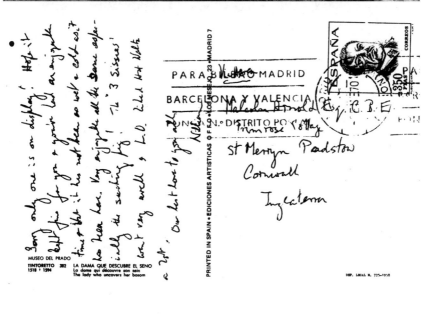

PARA BILBAO MADRID

BARCELONA Y VALENCIA

N.º DISTRITO PO

St Merryn Padstow
Cornwall
Inglaterra

ESPAÑA   CORREOS
3'50 PTAS

To Edward Heath   22 June 1970

Festival Office, Aldeburgh
as from La Mortella, Forio d'Ischia

Dear Prime Minister,
   Thank God you're in! It was a beautiful performance[1] worthy of a
Toscanini, & though it seems to have been a surprise to some people it
was not to either my wife or myself & we can't congratulate you enough.
Keep up the good work with Arts (one of the few commendable efforts
of the late government) & especially with music.
   Yours sincerely
   Sir William Walton, OM

To Malcolm Arnold   [postmarked: Madrid, ?September ?1970]
[postcard]

Sorry only one is on display! Hope it kept fine for you & you've had an
enjoyable time & that it has not been as wet & cold as it has been here.
Very enjoyable all the same especially the sucking pig! The '3 Sisters'
went very well & L.O. [Laurence Olivier] liked that Waltz a lot.
   Our best love to you all.
   William

To Malcolm Arnold   1 October 1970

La Mortella, Forio d'Ischia

Dear Malcolm,
   Yes, Tunisia was splendid – not least because of the vino – the best
I've come across outside of or for that matter, inside France. Well worth
a visit for that alone.
   I well understand your feeling that you have had enough conducting.
My own experience in New Zealand was comparatively pleasant chiefly
because the person[n]el of the orchestra was so nice, otherwise there is

---

1 Possibly referring to a performance conducted by Heath, a former organ scholar at
Balliol College, Oxford, who had recently begun to appear as conductor with the London
Symphony Orchestra. But it seems more likely that Walton is referring to Heath's victory
as leader of the Conservative Party in the General Election of 18 June 1970.

precious little to be said for it or its inhabitants as far as I could pick up.

We come to London on the 6th (the Ritz) & shall be there till the 10th, when we go to Shrublands for a thinning cure! I return the 18th to London for the rehearsals of "Improvisations on BBs theme". The performance is on the 20th Festival Hall. We come back here at the end of the month.

I will ring you on our arrival & fix meetings. I seem at the moment to be only booked for the dentist (Crack – bang).

Our love to you both
William

To Malcolm Arnold   5 November 1970

La Mortella, Forio d'Ischia

Dear Malcolm,

[. . .]

Glad you didn't come to 'Uddersfield.[1] Though Wyn Morris is by no means the bad conductor he has been made out to be (in fact he's v. good) how can anyone hope to obtain a performance of any worth if the chorus & orch meet for the 1st time at the actual perf [of *Gloria*] which is what happened. So it was not very impressive but v. depressive. Anyhow I'm not sure that it is at all a good work, in fact not perhaps worth the hard labour necessary to make it really come off.

Marvellous weather here. Only hope it will continue over Xmas.

Our love to you both
William

To Malcolm Arnold   21 May 1971

La Mortella, Forio d'Ischia

Dear Malcolm,

The answer to your thought may be where the cork was put in the first place. Not necessarily in a bottle! [. . .]

We've just returned from staying with Hans W.H. [Hans Werner

---

1 Concert by the Huddersfield Choral Society, for whose 125th anniversary season Walton had completed his *Gloria* in 1961.

Henze] to hear his new piece.[1] I don't quite know what to think, except that I wish he'd take to writing music again & not indulge in electronic (very good) noises.

What about joining us at Djerba where Hans has a house? And may I dedicate my guitar pieces [*Five Bagatelles*] to you? And when would [you] like to come here for a few days? Anytime you like. I don't think that we are coming to London during June after all.

love from us both
William

To Malcolm Arnold   1 June 1971

La Mortella, Forio d'Ischia

Dear Malcolm,

Thank you for your long & interesting letter.

I'm beginning to have cold feet about dedicating the "Bagatelles" to you – I don't think they are good enough or worthy enough for you – from which you may gather they are not going at all well. I shall dedicate something else if these are'nt up to the mark.

I am interested and slightly surprised at your enthusiasm for "Hamlet".[2] True I only saw the first Act & then it was stopped – & also in the worst company for that piece – Irene Worth. I don't suppose I shall have the chance of seeing it again.

I'm delighted to hear that the B.B.C are doing you proud for your 50th as well, indeed, as they should do. We'll be over for at least a part of the celebration.

Ischia is not much fun at the moment, very cold & wet & no "crumpets". I expect it will cheer up as soon as I leave for London. I shall be arriving at the Ritz (alone) on the 16th & leave the 23rd or so. There are perfs of the "Imps"[3] the 17th & "Anon in love" (string version) on the 21st.

[. . .]
as ever
William

1 Henze's theatre work *Der langwierige Weg in die Wohnung der Natascha Ungeheuer*.
2 Opera by the English composer Humphrey Searle, première at the Royal Opera House in 1968 and subsequently revived.
3 *Improvisations on an Impromptu of Benjamin Britten.*

To Malcolm Arnold   6 July 1971

La Mortella, Forio d'Ischia

Dear Malcolm,

Thanks for the Cook book! We'll try it out next time you are here, which I hope will be very soon.

I hope this reaches you before a letter from Neville Marriner or Alan Frank as I should like to be the first to ask you about the proposed project of doing my String Quartet for String Orch (ie. with Double bass).[1] During our discussion about it & about who was to do it, naturally enough your name cropped up. I said I couldn't think of anyone I'd prefer more, but I said that I thought it was too much of an imposition to ask you to do it especially as I knew you were busy with conducting dates & going to Vancouver & eventually to Ireland. They wanted me to "cut" it. I said I['d] do that (this was about 10 days ago) but I've been through it time & time again (it's the 1st mov. they were interested in cutting) & I've found it impossible to do without it sounding as if it had been castrated, had it's stomach out, with hysterectomy thrown in. I must say I rather agree with them that it is a bit long, that is if it is played by the Allegri Quartet whose performance is a bit sluggish and lifeless – it is I think the record I once played to you. However the record of the Holly-wood Quartet is altogether a different affair. I played it this morning & was pleased with it. N.M. asked that it should be "cut" to 23 mins & lo & behold without any cutting the Hollywood lot play it in exactly that length of time, so the cutting element is eliminated except for the repeat in the 2nd mov. which is easily removed & is better for it.

You have doubtless perceived what all this long preamble is about – that is to ask you to undertake the scoring of the work for St. Orch.

I know it is a lot to ask, but I'm too involved with it myself to do it really well otherwise I'd do it (or rather try to do it). You need'nt do it all – just those parts which you think would gain by more volume of Strings & it might have a solo String Quart[et] in it, as in the Intro & Allegro [*Introduction and Allegro*] of Elgar. The copying out of the score could be done by someone like Roy Douglas if you just indicate where & what changes would be necessary.

Don't hesitate for a moment to refuse what I think is an imposition to ask you, but you've no idea how pleased I'd be if you could see your

---

1   *Sonata for Strings.*

way to undertake it. Meanwhile I've asked Alan Frank to send you a copy of the work.

Come & see us soon & we could go over it together.

It is cold windy & wet – a most peculiar July for here. Also there's Sir Robert Mayer[1] in the offing.

With our best love to you both.

as ever
William

To Malcolm Arnold   20 July 1971

La Mortella, Forio d'Ischia

Dear Malcolm,

Thank you so much for your letter. I am so delighted that you will arrange the 4tet. I would'nt dream of asking anyone else to do it. There's no hurry about it at all. Neville Marriner would like to do it at the Bath Fest. I'm not quite sure when it is but I think it's held in early July '72.

We shall be delighted to come to hear the new work[2] & to the party after. We should like to give a party for you on Trafalgar Day the 21st [October] – your real 50th birthday. We could all come here to recover!

I am so glad that you have definitely decided to reside in Dublin.

[. . .]

Our love to you both
William

To Malcolm Arnold   30 August 1971

La Mortella, Forio d'Ischia

Dear Malcolm,

Thanks for the postcard [from Canada], presumably sent after [a] drunken bout with I. [Isobel] & Alec – at least I hope so.

[. . .]

It's all the fault of the O.U.P. that I can't come to London in Oct. The

---

1 English philanthropist, and founder of a concert series devised to interest young people in music.
2 Arnold's Concerto for Viola and Chamber Orchestra.

O.U.P. is doing a de lux[e] edition of Facade & signed by the composer. The copies are supposed to be ready for signing in Oct but now can only be ready Armistice Day (Nov 11th) & it is too much to come to London twice for such a short time.

I've finished the Guitar pieces (5)^1 with dedication to yourself. I'm inclined to think they are rather good, but Julian [Bream] will let you know about them. He's coming to inspect them on Sept 1st.

[. . .]

Our best love to you both

William

To Malcolm Arnold   15 September 1971

La Mortella, Forio d'Ischia

Dear Malcolm,

Thank you for your letter. I was delighted to hear that you enjoyed your sojourn in Vancouver so much. I heard from Alec [Walton] also who was highly delighted to see you.

In a few days I shall be sending you a copy of the Bagatelles. Julian [Bream] on the other hand when he saw the dedication was very pleased. After all what is important to him is his rake-off as Editor!

N[eville] Marriner^2 seems to want the Str. Orch version of that 4tet by the end of the year. In which case as you are very busy till then & I seem to have eff-all to do I might as well pull myself together & do my own dirty work! However I would dearly like to consult you & have your advice about it. It seems that it gets less & less likely that I shall be able to get [to] London in Oct. but I shall do my best about [it]. Any hope of your being able to get here for Oct 21st?

Our love to you both

William

1 *Five Bagatelles* for solo guitar.
2 English conductor and violinist, who had founded the Academy of St Martin-in-the-Fields, London, in 1959.

To Malcolm Arnold   26 September 1971

La Mortella, Forio d'Ischia

Dear Malcolm,

We are absolutely delighted & looking forward to your arrival on Oct 25th. By then I shall I hope have got this boring 4tet [arrangement] out of the way & all you will have to do is to point out where it can be improved to the accompaniment of popping corks. I know that critics & others will ask why can't he write something new instead of rehashing an old 4tet – in fact, I'd like to know too. But I'm not going to!

I'm delighted the 6th [Arnold's Sixth Symphony] went so well. I hope it will soon be recorded.

[. . .]

With love from us both
William

To Alan Frank   26 September 1971

La Mortella, Forio d'Ischia

Dear Alan,

I thought it would be a congenial birthday present for Malcolm A. to give him the Mss of the Bags. [*Five Bagatelles*] as they are dedicated to him, suitably bound. Can it be done by Oct 15th for his concert at the [Queen] Eliz. Hall 7.45. I['d] like him to get it by then tho his actual birthday seems to be on the 21st. Anyhow he's coming here on Oct 25th, & will cast a fatherly eye over this 4tet which is on the way. Arranging is a fearful bore, but better than doing nothing – doldrums. I know I ought to have written a new St. piece. But there it is[,] I havent.
William

To Edward Heath   12 October 1971

La Mortella, Forio d'Ischia

My dear Prime Minister,

John Peyton informs me that you would like to transfer the [70th] Birthday Dinner that he was intending to give for me to 10 Downing

Street. I much appreciate the kindness and the honour you show me by doing this, and I accept with the greatest of pleasure.

Yours sincerely,
William Walton

To Malcolm Arnold   2 November 1971

La Mortella, Forio d'Ischia

Dear Malcolm,

Your telegram arrived just as I was about to write & thank you for your invaluable assistance over the string piece & for the pleasure we have always in your society.

[. . .]

The funicular goes careering up & down, everyone wants to have a go.[1]

We shall be coming to London [. . .] & will ring you from there.

Love from us both
William

To Edward Heath   22 November 1971

Ritz Hotel, Piccadilly, London
as from La Mortella, Forio d'Ischia

My dear Prime Minister,

John [Peyton] telephoned me to ask if there was anyone else that I wished to invite to the Birthday party you are so very kindly giving for me. Would it be in order if the following people were asked?

Yehudi Menuhin
Andre Previn
Lord Goodman
Ian Hunter
Dr Jean Shanks

If all these make the party too large, please don't hesitate to say so.

---

1 A small funicular had been built between the house at La Mortella and the swimming pool and upper levels of the garden further up the hillside.

All my best wishes for the concert on Thursday. What a difficult piece[1] you have selected to conduct.

    yours sincerely

    William Walton

To John Tooley[2]   31 December 1971

La Mortella, Forio d'Ischia

Dear John,

    Thank you for your letter of the 23rd. I agree with you that H.H. [Heather Harper][3] is a very strong & acceptable candidate [for the role of Cressida]. Having been through the part carefully it strikes me that it could easily be done, & beautifully done by Janet Baker.[4] It would I realise, entail my re-writing bits & pieces of it here & there, a by no means insuperable task (chiefly drudgery) in fact there are a few places I might re-do anyhow, whoever sings it.

    The B.B.C. "prom" on Sept. 14th of Act II will be a great help in deciding on a definite casting. William Glock[5] may have helpful views on it. I am by no means definitely against [Alberto] Remedios.[6] It may be that I expected too much from the accounts I had had of him. Would [Ronald] Dowd[7] be a possible? He was in very good voice when I last heard him & thought what a good Troilus he might make, but that of course was some time ago[.]

    With all the best seasonal greetings,

    your[s] ever

    William

I spoke to Janet sometime ago about the possibility of her singing Cressida & she seemed pleased & interested with the idea when I said that it could be re-written for her.

---

1 Elgar's overture *Cockaigne*, with the London Symphony Orchestra.

2 General Administrator at the Royal Opera House, Covent Garden, from 1970, in succession to Sir David Webster.

3 Northern Irish soprano, noted for her radiant expertise in contemporary and other styles of music.

4 English mezzo-soprano.

5 BBC Controller of Music, and *de facto* director of the BBC's Henry Wood Promenade Concerts at the Royal Albert Hall.

6 English tenor, with many appearances with English National Opera. He had sung the role of Mark in the 1970 recording of Tippett's *The Midsummer Marriage*.

7 English tenor.

To Malcolm Arnold 24 January 1972

La Mortella, Forio d'Ischia

Dear Malcolm,

Thank you so much for your letter & the welcome news of the recording of the 5th S. [Symphony] Yes, indeed the way of critics & recording companies can knock "God" into a cocked hat about moving in mysterious ways their wonders to perform.

[. . .]

I'm glad you were impressed by [Edward] Heath's rendering of [Elgar's] "Cockaigne". No other P.M. could do it nor think of giving me a 70th birthday party, from which I propose to be carried out as I shall have been on the waggon from March 6th.

Our best love to you both
William

To Walter & Elisabeth Legge 1 April 1972

La Mortella, Forio d'Ischia

My dear Elizabeth and Walter,

Thank you so much for your greetings telegram.

The birthday celebration could not have gone better. "Sold out" everywhere (at the Fest. H. within two days much to everyone's surprise (& irritation?)). Previn did Bs.F [*Belshazzar's Feast*] really wonderfully & recorded it the next day.

The culmination was a marvellous party given by the P.M. [Edward Heath] at Downing St with the Queen Mum [HRH The Queen Mother]. Most enjoyable & non-pompous.

We shall probably be calling in on you at the end of the month as we are motoring out with all the loot! Will let you know later.

Our love to you both
William

We go to Oxford on the 15th.

To Yehudi Menuhin   4 April 1972

La Mortella, Forio d'Ischia

My dear Yehudi,

    It was such a kind tribute from you to play my Viola Concerto at my Birthday Concerts and I couldn't be more grateful to you.

    I hope you enjoyed the P.M.s party as much as we did.

    With our best love to you both

    As always

    William

To Leopold Stokowski [1]   [20 April 1972]
[telegram]

[Forio d'Ischia]

SORRY I AM LATE FOR YOUR 95TH STOP I AM WAITING FOR THE 100TH STOP BEST REGARDS WILLIAM WALTON

To Malcolm Arnold   2 May 1972

[London]

Dear Malcolm,

    Dining [. . .] the other night I asked about my letter which should have reached you with the vino – but no sign of it, – perhaps it's in the boot of your car! However this is more or less what it said as it was a spontaneous burst of thanks from the heart.

"Dear Malcolm,

    This is a small token of my affection esteem & regard & thanks for your help & support both practical & moral, for I was often at the point of cancelling before we started as I was feeling very low about everything etc etc."

I can't remember the rest of it but it was in a similar strain & I just want to you to know in writing how I feel about it all.

---

1 British-born American conductor of Polish ancestry. The date 18 April 1972 had in fact been his ninetieth birthday, not his ninety-fifth.

Su's written you about our arrangements & we are much looking forward to seeing you.

as ever
William

To Janet Baker   8 May 1972

La Mortella, Forio d'Ischia

Dear Janet,

I can't tell you how pleased I am that you are to do Cressida in '74 at Covent Garden, it really is a tremendous weight off my mind and you know you are one of the singers most admired by me.

Your suggestions for alterations are not half drastic enough and I have taken it upon myself that for Act 2, 26–31 [rehearsal nos.] should be transposed down to A flat or to G minor which I think will be effective for you and for others as well.

About the two bars before 68 I will have [these] done and send [them to] you and in Act 3 we can get it down a tone at 103, so the rest need not worry you.

I love you for ever.
Yours,
William

To Malcolm Arnold   8 May 1972

La Mortella, Forio d'Ischia

Dear Malcolm,

Can't thank you enough for your contributing to my wonderful record player,[1] which will be a great source of happiness to me for the rest of my life.

Meanwhile we are coming to Ireland on the 2nd June and shall be there on and off until about the 20th. How are we going to meet? I haven't got your address so I'm sending a copy letter to the Savile Club as well as the Gresham Hotel.

---

1 A seventieth birthday present from Walton's friends and colleagues.

Do you think you could get us a room at the Gresham Hotel for the
2<u>nd</u> June?

Best wishes from us both.

William

Think of those Rachmaninov debauches.

To Yehudi Menuhin   8 May 1972

La Mortella, Forio d'Ischia

Dear Yehudi,

Thank you for everything, but not in the least your kind contribution
to the plate of John Piper,[1] not that I need to be reminded by [of] you,
[but] it's very nice to have you in mind when I look at it.

Best love to you both

Yours,

William

To Lord Olivier   19 July 1972

[with postscript from Lady Walton]

La Mortella, Forio d'Ischia

Dearest Larry,

At last the famous gramaphone player has been fixed up and is in full
function, it gives a most wonderful sound and gives me and Su great
pleasure and I thank you for your contribution to this splendid machine,
I am sorry that the last time I wrote to you I thanked you for a plate!

I think that you must be finished [with] your film and I don't see why
you can't come to stay here for a few days. Anyway, tomorrow we shall
be in London and probably will be in touch with you before this letter
[reaches you].

Yours as ever,

William

Lots of love to both, please come out, the "funicolare" takes you out &
up to the pool with no effort, we shall be back here August 1<u>st</u>.

x x Su

1 English artist and designer.

To Benjamin Britten   3 August 1972

La Mortella, Forio d'Ischia

Dear Ben,

It was really noble of you to provide such a handsome 70th birthday present. The B. [*The Bear*] couldn't have gone better and as for Peter – he was superb. He must record it [*Façade*] for there is'nt, in spite of the number made, a really vaguely good one amongst the lot, in fact one has to go back to the one he did with Edith [Sitwell] years ago.

With best love from us both and many thanks again.

As ever
William

To Malcolm Arnold   8 August 1972

La Mortella, Forio d'Ischia

Dear Malcolm,

We were pleased to hear that you had enjoyed yourselves in [the] West of Ireland & that we had not been exag[g]erating.

We are just back (till Sept 7th when we go to London again) from King's Lynn. An enjoyable festival including, I need hardly say, Facade, – not very well done & the Sonata for St. orch. Good. Marriner now seems to have really got it going & it sounded extremely well. Then on to Aldeburgh for a W.W. evening consisting of the Bear[,] Siesta (a new ballet by Fred. A. [Sir Frederick Ashton]) Facade (in its original form[,] poems recited by P.P. & the original scoring – very good & effective). Ben incidentally extremely aimnable about you.

Lilias managed to persuade the Prince of Wales to attend the opening night which added to the glamour. What a charmer – but he must be a mixed-up-kid what with studying the workings of a submarine – flying a jet – playing the cello etc. He turned up with several girls & it would seem that he alone of the whole lot had seen an opera before. As it was very well sung & played & produced, it went down with a bang. You must come & see it when it comes to London in Oct. No, I forgot you can't till next year. Get it over to Dublin instead!

[. . .]

Best love from us both

As ever
William

To Benjamin Britten   17 August 1972

La Mortella, Forio d'Ischia

Dear Ben,

It was most kind of you to send me the quite superlative recording of
"Gerontius".[1] It has almost overcome my antipathy for it. At any rate
my protestant hackles didn't rise quite as much as they usually do when
I listen to this work. Any how, I am most grateful to you both for sending it to me.

As ever
William

To Malcolm Arnold   4 October 1972

La Mortella, Forio d'Ischia

Dear Malcolm,

Back again – what a relief – and its tolerably warm & fine.

I meant to telephone you before I left, but life was a bit too hectic
what with the performance & recording of the Violin Concerto with
Previn & Chung.[2] What a girl! She has to be heard to be believed. In
addition she's very easy on the eye. I will have the record sent you when
it is out. Did you receive the one of B.'s F.?

Our love to you all
William

1 Elgar's *The Dream of Gerontius*, conducted by Britten.
2 Kyung-Wha Chung, Korean violinist.

To Malcolm Arnold   9 October 1972

La Mortella, Forio d'Ischia

Dear Malcolm,

Your two letters, for which many thanks, arrived simultaneously.

I'm glad you like the S.A.T.B. piece [the carol 'All This Time']. I'm getting to like it a bit myself & so[,] he writes me, does the great B. himself.

I look forward to hearing the new overture [*The Fair Field*] & I couldn't be more delighted to think of it being dedicated to me. Thank you very much indeed.

Unfortunately I can't tell you that my Symph. III is progressing & I don't suppose it will if I continue like this! However I hope something will turn up fairly soon.

[. . .]

With best love to you all & thanks again for the dedication
William

To Malcolm Arnold   15 October 1972

La Mortella, Forio d'Ischia

Dear Malcolm,

Thanks for your letter. I've just been playing (for the first time) the record of B's F [conducted by André Previn]. How right you are! Conductors never seem to realise that in Bs F there is no need to add to the excitement – on the contrary, it should be kept on a very tight rein, otherwise it becomes a shambles, as unfortunately, this recording often does. It just shows how necessary it is for the composer to be present for a recording. Owing to the P.Ms party I couldnt be there, but I just had the time to instruct him about "the trumpeters & pipers" & the very end which had been completely wrong at the perf the previous night. These bits are O.K. but the speed in other places completely defeats its object. However it can't be helped – it's too late now. It's so irritating, because he is so quick (& sensitive) to act on a hint about pace or any-thing, & if only I had been there it would have been splendid, I feel.

Our love to you both
William

To Malcolm Arnold   24 February 1973

La Mortella, Forio d'Ischia

Dear Malcolm,

I have been vainly trying to telephone you in Dublin.

Thanks for your telegram & letter, neither of which explain your unseemly and hasty departure. Su with feminine prescience had wanted to go over & see you early (9–30) that morning, but I dissuaded her saying she would not be very popular so early – a mistake on my part. I went over at beer time to discover you had gone to Naples – I thought for what? When Su discovered your note about the car, we set about trying to discover your whereabouts & managed to contact you at the Airport.

True we had had a bit of mix-up the night before but what is a fall-out between friends? The only conclusion we came to, was that you had believed and been upset by something George (and possibly Gunda) had said,[1] as you kept on re-iterating that Su was ruining me by charging too much for the houses, that Su was so intolerably tough that it was, or is, impossible to find girls to remain with us etc. All of which if you had considered it for an instant you must have seen was quite untrue, and that George was out to butter up Gunda & denigrate Su, by insinuating that everything would fall to pieces without George's beloved Gunda. Believe me we did well enough before G&G were ever heard of. So I find it tragic that your mind has been poisoned against the unfortunate Su who has always gone out of her way to be kind to you & help you, & is most sad and distressed about it all.

So as you still have a long time on your [rented] house, till mid-March, I think you might think about coming back to finish off at least one movement of your Symphony [No. 7]. It distresses me to think that anything that has happened here should have stopped you composing

---

1 George and Gunda Tait were friends of the Waltons; Gunda Tait ran the rented houses at La Mortella. While arranging for Arnold to rent San Felice (in which the Waltons themselves had formerly lived), George Tait took him out to dinner and praised Gunda's administrative abilities, while presenting Susana Walton's in a less favourable light. At dinner a few days later, Arnold relayed this to the Waltons. Walton angrily told Arnold to desist. Arnold left the table and next morning left Ischia, leaving a note to Susana Walton (who had been silent throughout the altercation) saying that she could never manage to induce him to have a fight with her husband. The friendship between Arnold and Walton did subsequently recover, but without regaining all of its former warmth.

further. As for mine it is in an even more paralytic state! Our best love to you both.

William

To Malcolm Arnold   5 March 1973

La Mortella, Forio d'Ischia

Dear Malcolm,

Thanks for the Expresso which arrived to-day in very bright sunshine. I'm sorry you are missing it. Actually your departure started off a rather bad week weatherwise. Snow & terrible cold, disastrous for the garden. Snow halfway up Epomeo¹ but we survived!

What marvellous progress about your Symph. I wish I could say the same for mine. It was obviously the psychological moment for you to leave, I doubt if you would have picked up the threads of the music if you had remained here.

[. . .]

Gunda is not yet back but George is! Gunda's father is ill so she has had to go to Hamburg to see him. George is rightly in a flap about the dollar. It will affect us all I fear through our P.R.S & lots of other ways I suppose.

Dallas [Bower] I feel must have finally gone quite off his head. Well it is at least something to know where you are with him.

This brings our best love to you all & don't let it be too long before you are back.

William

To Malcolm Arnold   9 August 1973

La Mortella, Forio d'Ischia

Dear Malcolm,

I enjoyed the recording of S.5 [Symphony No. 5] – what about 3 & 4? not to mention 7. Presumably finished by now.

We are coming to Ireland at the end of April next year. Cork Univ. desires to doctor me (I'm not sure I've anything left!) & I have to write a

---

1 The volcanic mountain peak which is the highest point of Ischia.

little piece for it. Being, I presume a Catholic Univ. I thought of setting "Cantico del Sole" by St Francis of Assisi. Anything to put off the evil day of tackling a third S.!

Our love to you both
William

Perhaps we could meet in Cork?

To Malcolm Arnold   21 December 1973

La Mortella, Forio d'Ischia

Dear Malcolm,

Just back from London. What a relief to be in one piece! And the gloom there – just like the beginning of the late great wars. The only thing to be said for it is the comparative lack of bombs which deficiency the I.R.A are trying to rectify. Here owing to the lack of benzine it is strangely quiet – hardly any lorries & not many cars.

I'm in fearful disgrace with Dallas [Bower] over my resigning from the Savile [Club], & according to him, all the other members also which I can hardly believe as I hardly ever put my nose inside. He writes a lot about Sodality[,] a word of which I did'nt know the meaning – luckily I looked it up in the Dictionary & it does'nt mean what I thought it did!

Not much news otherwise. Cov. Gar. keep on procrastinating over T&C so I've persuaded the Coliseum [English National Opera] to take an interest, which they are doing, but there's the bother of getting the dates right. Janet B. [Baker] was marvellous in [Donizetti's] "Maria Stuarda" & I formed a very high opinion of the whole company. It is much more of a unit than Cov. Gar.

This brings our love & seasonal greetings to you all.
as ever
William

To Malcolm Arnold   2 February 1974

La Mortella, Forio d'Ischia

Dear Malcolm,

Delighted to get your letter for which many thanks. Indeed Rome was quite a success from all points of view. And about time too say I having lived here for more than 20 years. But how much I should have disliked being drawn into Italian musical life, so it is just as well to live in quiet obscurity!

Dallas is the end. I've just been doling out Danegeld so I'm not going to help buy the studios of Bray.

I'm mad that I am going to have to miss the 1st perf of the 7th [Symphony] on May 5th (but there'll be plenty of others) but have promised to go to hear the "Bear" which I must say I would willingly avoid doing, in of all places – Lisbon. But it is pointed out to me that it would be a wise thing to do as it is under the auspices of the Gulbenkian Trust. I want to persuade it to help out with the finance of recording T&C. We are terribly sorry that you can't get to Cork, but from a musical point of view you won't miss much for the "Cantico" has worked out a deplorably dull & unexciting piece & one for which I need "doctoring" in the other sense. Needless to say you have all our good wishes for May 5th.

I'm glad you wrote to Sachie Sitwell about his book. I should like to see his letter sometime. (a photocopy perhaps.)

Delighted about Edward.

With best love from us both
William

To Gregor Piatigorsky   20 March 1974

La Mortella, Forio d'Ischia

Dear Grisha,

This letter is to introduce you to Gillian Widdicombe. She is the music critic for the London Financial Times & also happens to be engaged in writing my biography, so anything you can tell her about our work on my 'Cello Concerto (luckily I've kept all your letters) would I'm sure be of great help to her. I am sorry to bother you about this & I shall be very grateful to you if you can see her for a few minutes.

How are you? There seems to be little chance of our meeting these

THE SELECTED LETTERS OF WILLIAM WALTON

days. I am delighted that R.C.A. has re-issued the Concerto as my record was getting worn out. It still I am glad to say gets played a fair amount by various people.

    With all good wishes

    yours ever

    William Walton

To Malcolm Arnold   12 July 1974

La Mortella, Forio d'Ischia

Dear Malcolm,

    Thank you so much for having S.6 [Symphony No. 6] sent me by F&F [Faber Music]. It seems to be a pretty good S. at least to me. My no.3 is a non-starter! I'm doing Mag. & Nunc. [*Magnificat and Nunc dimittis*] for Chichester [Cathedral] – about all I can manage – if I can even manage that.

    Su is recovered from her op. but gets easily tired & depressed which is not really her style.

    We shall be in London for the last night of the "Proms" so may see you then.

    As ever

    William

To Walter Legge   24 July 1974

La Mortella, Forio d'Ischia

Dear Walter,

    [. . .]

    I fear Ted[1] has also got it wrong about Herbert [von Karajan]. '76 is the 25th anniversary of the opening of the Fest. Hall. In order to celebrate the occasion the G.L.C. (the greater London Council) have invited several orchs. including the Berlin Phil. with Herbert, & the idea is that I should write a piece for the occasion with Herbert conducting the B.Phil. I'm not at all sure it is a good idea. It is all very hazy & even if I write a piece I[']d bet anything that H.K would squirm out of it, just as he has

---

1 Edward Greenfield, music critic of the *Guardian*.

avoided ever doing "Belshazzar" ever since that marvellous perf. in Vienna[1] – it was unforgetable, but alas, not to be repeated. Every time it has been scheduled he gets out of it at the last min – leaving someone called Abravandel(?)[2] (a Mormon?) to do it the last time it was announced in Berlin. So I'm not inclined to get excited about writing a new piece for him – someone else can do it – Malcolm Arnold, Sir Lennox B. [Berkeley] or even Sir Michael T. [Tippett] & I hope he enjoys it.

Poor Elizabeth slimming! She should come here. Sue sheds kilos, on lemon-water. Three days of it & two on fruit & one is hardly here at all, & one dos'ent feel at all hungry on it.

Our best love to you both

as ever

William

To Gregor Piatigorsky   24 July 1974

La Mortella, Forio d'Ischia

Dear Grisha,

How delighted I am to receive your letter. My wife & I were both very dissapointed that you could'nt come here on your way from Israel.

Our "charming lady"[3] has not, I hope, put false ideas into your head about a Double Concerto. What I thought of might be a piece in the nature of Chausson's Poème – a piece of some ten to fifteen minutes. But who knows what may turn up.

Having looked at the 'Cello Concerto I feel a bit doubtful about that also.[4] It may seem as if something had been stitched on, like adding a new hem to an old skirt! However, I will keep you informed. Perhaps for the moment not to tell Jascha would be wiser. I've been asked to write so many pieces, but I think I shall chuck the lot & concentrate on the piece, whatever it may be, for you both.

With our affectionate greetings

as ever

William

---

1 On 12 and 13 June 1948. Karajan had earlier written to a colleague that *Belshazzar's Feast* was 'the best choral music that's been written in the last fifty years'.
2 Maurice Abravanel, American conductor of Greek birth.
3 Gillian Widdicombe.
4 Piatigorsky had asked Walton to compose a new ending.

To Walter Legge   16 August 1974

La Mortella, Forio d'Ischia

Dear Walter,

Thank you for your letter. I think the idea about B's F. absolutely brilliant & I am writing off to J[ohn] Denison[1] & A Frank to pursue it. It would be marvellous if it could be brought off & K[arajan] could be persuaded. He could do the Ninth [Beethoven's] in the second half! Do please urge him to do it in London with his Berliners & for E.M.I to record it. It would be sensational.

I am sorry Elisabeth is upset about the house. Maybe air conditioning would be the answer. It's such a nuisance to change again. It will be all right in the winter.

I don't think Italy will go Communist. The party would rather stay in opposition so we hear, as the situation is so difficult. Too difficult for anyone to extricate themselves from. And I should stick to your Swiss residency as it is very difficult to get now.

With our best love & thanks to you both
As ever
William

To Malcolm Arnold   28 September 1974
[postcard]

La Mortella, Forio d'Ischia

[. . .]

Just returned from a marvellous week in Venice & happened to hear Mehta[2] with the L.A. orch. He's a splendid conductor & the orch. first class. Quite a revelation for the Italians. Music is rapidly disintegrating as is everything else for that matter. The [Teatro La] Fenice is occupied by the orch as protest at not having been paid for 3 months & the opera in Rome is shut.

With love from us both
William

1 General Manager of the Royal Festival Hall.
2 Zubin Mehta, Indian conductor, and Music Director of the Los Angeles Philharmonic Orchestra from 1962 to 1977.

1964–1976

To Malcolm Arnold   27 October 1974

La Mortella, Forio d'Ischia

Dear Malcolm,

I am so pleased that you like the Bagatelles.[1] They are indeed beautifully produced.

I went to London last week for [Hans Werner Henze's] the "Bassarids" which he conducted. It is a most wonderful piece as done by him. I had seen it twice before in Salzburg & at La Scala in Milan – both inadequate performances – so much so that I had had no high regard for the opera & I am so glad that I went to hear it in the Coloseum [Coliseum]. It[2] is a first rate company. Excellent soloists chorus & orch. (the least good part, but very adequate). It just shows one how devastating a bad performance can be. I heard also his new piece – Tristan – which I didn't enjoy so much – spoilt for me at any rate by an electronic tape which confused the whole sound.

It has been fairly nasty weather here – cold & beastly, most unlike it for Oct.

With our best love to you both
As ever
William

To Malcolm Arnold   19 November 1974

La Mortella, Forio d'Ischia

Dear Malcolm

The cutting has amused us vastly. As it happens I've just been reading a notice of a new piece by that ghastly man Stockhausen[3] which bears out everything you say about him. It's a Japanese religious piece called "Inori". Keep away from it.

Delighted that the domestic hiatus is past. Give her our love & to Edward.

William

1 Oxford University Press had at Walton's request made a specially bound copy of the *Five Bagatelles* for Arnold, their dedicatee.
2 English National Opera.
3 Karlheinz Stockhausen, German composer.

[415]

To Benjamin Britten   9 December 1974

La Mortella, Forio d'Ischia

Dear Ben,

Your card arrived more or less as I was about to write saying how very happy we both are at hearing that you are so very much better, in fact according to the interview in the "Times" with Rostropovitch that your recovery is almost complete.[1] How wonderful but don't take it too much for granted & continue to be very careful.

With our best wishes for Xmas & the New Year,
as ever,
William

To Gregor Piatigorsky   17 December 1974

La Mortella, Forio d'Ischia

Dear Grisha,

I was so happy to receive your letter & to discover what you want for the new ending of the [Cello] Concerto, but I'd got the wrong idea & thought you wished for a loud pyrotechnical ending, but your description of what you really want has been of the greatest help & I send a sketch of what I've done – but it's only a sketch & if it appeals to you I'll work it out properly. I hope you will approve.

I received a short while ago the R.C.A. re-issue of the record. I'd forgotten how good it was. Your playing & understanding of the piece is absolutely stupendous.

Please don't hesitate to let me know if you don't like the new ending, – there is still a lot of time for a new attempt to get it right.

I am delighted that you intend to do so many performances. Zubin Mehta who I got to know slightly in Venice when the L.O. orch [Los Angeles Philharmonic] was there in Sept, I am sure will do everything he can to help it. I only heard him in old "favourites" but I was very impressed with his freshness of outlook. Please give him my regards[,] also to other members of the orchestra I met. [. . .]

The atmosphere here is full of gloom, but nothing like it seems to be in London.

---

1 Britten had undergone major heart surgery the previous year.

[416]

Let me know what you really feel about the new ending. As I said – there is lots of time to try others – but you must suggest as far as you can what you want.

Our love to Jacqueline & yourself

Yours ever

William

To Malcolm Arnold   19 December 1974

La Mortella, Forio d'Ischia

Dear Malcolm,

Thank you for your letter about your monumental piss-up with Dallas. I hear he is trying to convert the Arabs to Wagner. It will serve them bloody well right if he succeeds.

With all seasonal greetings to all

William

To Gregor Piatigorsky   18 January 1975

La Mortella, Forio d'Ischia

Dear Grisha,

Thank you for calling & I hope this time I shall get it right about the [Cello Concerto's] new ending – I think I see what you want and I will send it you in a few days. Do you know the slow movement of my 2nd Symphony? Maybe it is something like that you need, & I'd be very happy if you could let me know as soon as you can. [. . .] You might get Zubin [Mehta] to take it up! If he would, I would modify the unnecessarily difficult passage between 166 & 227 which I suspect hampers the piece from being done more often.

Blessings

William

To Gregor Piatigorsky   24 January 1975

La Mortella, Forio d'Ischia

Dear Grisha,

I am sending this by a good friend of ours, George Tait. I meant to send with it a new version of the end [of the Cello Concerto], but alas! it has not turned out too well. Next attempt will I hope be all right, though whether it will be as good as the original I'm a bit doubtful, but anyhow that is always there to fall back on. You incidentally are the only person I've come across who has doubts about the end as it stands – about other parts I've had lots of criticism. But I'm sure you are right & I will go on seeking & hope I shall find it. After this try I give up!

Our love to you both
William

To Alan Frank   6 February 1975

La Mortella, Forio d'Ischia

Dear Alan,

Everything in the garden seems lovely so I've written to John D. [Denison] accepting to do the piece,[1] now what remains is to write the bloody thing. I for one shall be v. interested to see & hear what turns up as I seem to be absolutely impotent – I think that is the word, that is musically speaking. Anyhow having committed myself I'll do my best not to let the side down.

I've done a new end [of the Cello Concerto] which I hope will be alright. I don't suppose P. will approve as it is to all purposes the same as the original – but he can't say I have'nt tried. [. . .]

W.

I'm rather off Mahler & V.W. for that matter. Back to square 1, retro-grade perversion like M.T. [Michael Tippett] – at his age getting himself a new boy-friend – he ought to be ashamed of himself! Poor Karl,[2] being cut-off with a shilling!

My spy service is v. up to the mark, dont you think!

1 The orchestral commission for the twenty-fifth anniversary of the Royal Festival Hall in 1976.
2 Karl Hawker, Tippett's partner and companion for many years, and the dedicatee of his opera *King Priam*.

To Alan Frank   8 February 1975

La Mortella, Forio d'Ischia

Dear Alan,

Thanks for yours of the 3rd – it arrived the 7th. So we are catching up.
I'm sorry that James Lockhart won't be in charge of the B. [*The Bear*]
at Kassel.[1] His not being there makes it more unlikely that we shall be
there. Never mind, I'm sure it will go well enough without us. I'll write
to Schippers & urge him to take an interest in T&C. If you do publish
it do it in as cheap a form as possible. If this letter is a bit distracted it's
because I'm listening to Rach [Rakhmaninov] Pfte C. 3 – a v. underrated
composer at least by the notes! Is there by the way a good book on him.
I am catching up one way & another. In an album of his recordings
there is what may be the second half of the "Bear", or rather the companion piece to it, in the literature about it. – Writing about the "Crag"[2]
one Michael Williamson says that it emanates from a short story by
Chekov called "In Autumn" (1883) recast as a one-act play "On the
High Road" (1885). It would appear from the short description of it
that it is for a cast of 2, a man & a woman (strange as that may be). If
you could somehow discover a copy it is just possible that it might be
what one wants.

Paul Dehn is thank heaven well on the way to recovery. He had the
same operation as I had – about 10 weeks & it might give him something to do.[3]

The record album is Melodiya issued by E.M.I.

William

To Gregor Piatigorsky   25 February 1975

La Mortella, Forio d'Ischia

Dear Grisha,

I was delighted to get your cable & yesterday your letter, & I'm most
happy to learn that my new ending is more or less what you want.[4] Why

1 Lockhart was Music Director at Kassel Opera House.
2 Rakhmaninov's early symphonic poem: its title is more usually translated as *The Rock*.
3 Dehn died of cancer in 1976.
4 Piatigorsky died in 1976, without having performed the Cello Concerto with its newly
composed ending.

[419]

it bothered me so much I don't know. I'm losing confidence in my powers & find composing increasingly difficult. I never found it easy, but it's the very devil. But there it is – I must persist – that's all I can do. We are of course coming over for June 24ᵗʰ & I can't tell you how much we are looking forward to hearing you do the Concerto in the flesh, for you will remember that we were smashed up in our car just before the first London performance so could'nt come to London for it.

I am glad you took to George Tait. There are very few people about on the island, & he is one of the nicest. We shall be staying at the Ritz.

With our affectionate best wishes to you both,
William

To Lord Olivier [28 February 1975]
[telegram from Lacco Ameno]

WEATHER LOVELY PLUS WARM BED COME NOW LOVE WILLIAM SU

To Malcolm Arnold 26 March 1975

La Mortella, Forio d'Ischia

Dear Malcolm,

Your unanswered letter lies before me – but just to remind me, a not-too-distant motor-horn is tootling

etc in an ever more drunken & dislocated fashion. I hope you get royal-ties on it.¹ I thought it had died out, but no – it's got a new lease of life & will doubtless soon be on all motor horns! The [holiday] season in fact has started & one can't hear anything but German being spoken!

[. . .] I've let myself in for this fucking piece for the R.F.H. but I've still got a bit of time to get out of it if I make up my mind quickly. Ideas

1 The motor horn was sounding the first few notes of the march 'Colonel Bogey', used by Arnold in his film score *The Bridge on the River Kwai*.

are sparse, bare & ugly so "per forza" I think I shall have to give it up. In fact I must face it that it is highly probable that I shall never write a note again. It dos'ent depress me too much – nor I imagine anyone else.

Delighted to hear that the marital difficulties have been smoothed out. Forgive this boring letter, but you can judge from it what kind of state I'm in. Su's recovered completely.

ever
William

You are probably right about returning to England. One does get at moments very out of touch. I was 5 years paying double tax – in fact the buggers have just returned to the attack.

To Malcolm Arnold   24 May 1975

La Mortella, Forio d'Ischia

Dear Malcolm,

Thank you enormously for your encouraging letter & I believe it has [had] some effect for I believe I've started, but I'm not too sure & will have to wait to see how it goes on. But I think it's going to be alright.

[. . .] Unfortunately, as well as having trouble with my muse, I have been having a lot of bother with my blood-pressure – up & down like a see-saw – most unpleasant. Luckily there's now a very good young German doctor here & of course the 1st thing he's done is to knock me off all alcohol, which sounds a bit of a bore, but I'm sorry to say that I think I feel a bit better for it.

We are coming to England next month. We go to Shortlands[1] for a cure almost as soon as we arrive but are in London (the Ritz) the 22nd June till the end of June when we come back here so we can I hope meet any time between the 22nd & the 2nd of July.

Our best love to you both
William

---

1 Walton means Shrublands Hall, the health clinic that he and Lady Walton had visited before: see letter to Malcolm Arnold dated 1 October 1970, pp. 392–3.

To Malcolm Arnold
[postcard]

15 July 1975

La Mortella, Forio d'Ischia

It was marvellous seeing you, but I dread to think of the size [of] your bill at the Connaught. I hope you thought it was worth it.

I forgot to tell you about Elizabeth Frink. Would you write to her c/o The Waddington Galleries Cork Str. W1 (I've lost her private address) if you should still want the bust of W.W. which I think is terrific & I'm sure you'll think so too. Order it through her & not through the Gallery so that you can get it at the right prezzo!

It's frightfully hot here.

With lots of love & thanks from us both
William

To Walter Legge

3 August 1975

[La Mortella, Forio d'Ischia]

Dear Walter,
[. . .]
Yes T&C is being revived – in fact I've rewritten & cut it quite a bit & now believe it may be O.K. Janet Baker is Cress. (necessitating a lot of rewriting) [Alberto] Remedios Tro: Colin Graham[1] producing an entirely new production. So I have hopes. The "Bear" seems to have got off the ground in Germany. – First at Kassel, a month or two ago. Next season it is being repeated there, & at Wiesbaden[,] Münich & two or three other places. And B's F is being done twice in Munich next Nov.

I'm sorry that you are finding life so difficult at Cap Ferrat. It is not too bad here & I suspect that there's more nonsense about the Communist threat than actual fact.

I'm delighted to say that my mother-in-law is not here. She was getting too much of a good thing.

I'm well as is Su also, in spite of the doctors here thinking I was about to have a stroke. We made a bee-line for London & the doctors here had got it all wrong. Unfortunately our young German doctor was not here

---

1 English opera producer, whose work had included widely admired stagings of Britten's Church Parables at the Aldeburgh Festival.

at the time. You can now come here with safety. He's taken one of our houses which is only about a 100 metre[s] away.

I'm busy on a piece for the 25ᵗʰ anniversary of the R.F.H. [–] not a very inspiring idea.

Our best love to you both
William

To Walter Legge   15 September 1975

La Mortella, Forio d'Ischia

My dear Walter,

I have been meaning to reply every day to your letter & on the receipt of your justly reproachful card I'm now at last doing so. The barest excuse I have to offer is that I have been trying to get going (I fear vainly) on this work I've stupidly accepted to do for the "Consecration" of the 25ᵗʰ anniversary of the R.F.H. The only thing to be said about it is that the sum offered is quite acceptable for these days. But it's a difficult style of piece to get going on – for one thing the length 10–15 mins is a good deal to cope with even if inspired – & there's not much inspiration in the R.F.H or in one John Denison C.B.E. But somehow I must finish by Xmas – good, bad or indifferent.

I am glad you appreciate "la Widdicombe" [Gillian Widdicombe]. It is a great help having her as a biographer rather than, say, Michael Kennedy. Who is not at all bad, but I can talk to Gillian far easier than I could to him. And thank you for your excellent suggestions about T&C. Alas the cast is all set, I fear unchang[e]able. It is on the whole, about as good as Cov. Gar. can find or afford. But I think the recording is the really important thing. [Tippett's] Midsummer Marriage's success to me is one of the mysteries of life. But Philips & Schotts mounted a really devastating P.R act, especially in the U.S. & it paid off very nicely, with extraordinary sales. So I feel if the record of T&C is what it should be it should at least equal M.M. in sales. What with Janet & André. I've not heard Remedios except on the record of M.M. Not at all bad & I'm told he's improving considerably & if he can overcome the difficulties of M.M. he ought to find T&C more sympathetic. Of course T&C's sex-appeal is nowadays of the wrong sort! [. . .]

The new version of T&C should be & is at least twice as good. All the awkward bits of Hassalese & Walton having been eliminated. As soon as it is in print, I'll send you a copy. A great help has been Colin Graham who is producing [it] at C.G. He's excellent.

It will be splendid if you can come here next spring. We must arrange for la Widdy to be here – not easy as she seems occupied always in one position or another. We shall still I hope have the German doctor occupying one of the houses.

Our love to you both

William

Give H.K. [Herbert von Karajan] my regards and tell him to go and f—¹ himself. He's refused to record B.'s F. Blast him! He's probably getting too old for such a strenuous piece, tho' Adrian Boult is doing Sinf. 1 shortly & he's 86!

To Sir Adrian Boult   12 October 1975

La Mortella, Forio d'Ischia

My dear Adrian,

Though your letter is dated 28 Sept. it only reached here the day before yesterday, so my letter is somewhat belated.

I can't tell you how delighted I am that you are conducting my "first" for the B.B.C. I've been thro' the work with your "Nixa" record & tho' the record "qua record" is abysmal, you've got it all right.

The answers to [your] three questions are right & the metronome markings correct – perhaps the "Maestoso" in the last movement might be a shade less so. The parts, marked B.B.C parts should be correct. I warned Christopher Morris (the new head of O.U.P. Music Dept.)² that they should be checked so I think everything will be all right on that side & if the performance (which I am sure it will be) is even nearly as good as the record it should be a splendid performance & I am only too sorry that I am unable to be present.

I've been having an interesting & enjoyable time with [Elgar's] the "Apostles" & the "Kingdom" neither of which I had heard before. I like them both more than "Gerontius" – perhaps your recording will convert me! I hope so for I find Elgar's choral works rather inferior to the

---

1 Walton writes a clear 'f', followed by an indeterminate scrawl which is not quite an 'expletive deleted' dash.

2 In succession to Alan Frank.

orchestral ones. Apart from a chronic attack of Sciatica which I['m] suffering from at the moment I['m] keeping on the whole very well if not very musically productive. Very glad to hear of your recovery.

With best regards from us both

Yours ever

William

To Malcolm Arnold   14 October 1975

La Mortella, Forio d'Ischia

Dear Malcolm

I too am very dissapointed that the wrong Malcolm[1] should have been chosen as the new M. of Qs M [Master of the Queen's Music]. I did my best but nowadays cementing the cracks in the Commonwealth obviously take[s] precedent. I know nothing about it & for all I know it may be a good appointment. I've even considered trying to shove off onto him this dreadful R.F.H. piece which is ruining my life & dose'nt progress at all. And to add to my horrors I'm at the moment afflicted with a chronic bout of sciatica so all in all I'm feeling pretty low.

I look forward to hearing your 2nd Str. 4tet. Who knows, we may go to Aldeburgh next June.

[. . .]

Alas we shan't be in London in Nov. In fact I don't think we shall be there before May. It's so bloody expensive.

Our best love to you both.

William

To Sir Adrian Boult   5 December 1975

La Mortella, Forio d'Ischia

Dear Adrian,

I am furious with myself at having mistaken the date of the concert & failed to send off the telegram of good wishes for the Symphony which I had intended to do, but we were in München for the 1st performance there of "Belshazzar" & what with travelling & one thing [and] another, it

---

1 Malcolm Williamson, Australian composer resident mostly in London since 1950.

was only a chance look in the "Times" that displayed a photograph of your rehearsal that I realised that I missed sending you greetings. I hope, in fact, I am sure it was a superb performance & I look forward to hearing the tape. I do so appreciate you having undertaken to perform it. With many thanks & good wishes

Yours ever
William Walton

To Walter Legge   17 December 1975

La Mortella, Forio d'Ischia

Dear Walter,

Thank you enormously for your kind & helpful letter. It was awaiting us on our return from Munich where we attended two extremely enthusiastic & successful perfs. of B's. binge with the Münich state orch & chorus, conducted very well by James Loughran.[1] It may lead to a lot in one way & another, as with perfs of the "Bear" in Cassell [Kassel], Wiesbaden & Münich [. . .] next season, the name of W.W will begin to be known in Germany & I hope his music played.

Now about T&C. The only way to get it recorded is by recording every performance & making a choice from them. It is the only way open for it to be done, I know it may not be entirely satisfactory but as things are, we'd have to wait till 1978 at the earliest, & heaven knows what inflation will be by then. Also none of us is getting any younger & Janet [Baker] is agreeable to recording the work that way.

The great question at the moment is for a tenor who can speak English well enough to get by & of course be able to sing! [Sir Georg] Solti has collared our tenor [Alberto Remedios] for at least six months (in spite of his contract to Cov. Gar.) to learn the "Ring". I [can't] say I am devastated by the news, but it at the moment leaves a hole which has to be filled & filled very well. Colin Graham (the producer of T&C) has got two names of tenors whose English is perfect – but noone has heard them yet. They are Josef Kostlinger (Tamino in I[n]gmar Bergman's film[2] – an Austrian) & Jonny Blank – a Swede who is too grand to give an audition. Both are said to be excellent. Do you know of either or have

1   Scottish conductor.
2   Of *The Magic Flute*.

you any further suggestions? It would be a marvellous help if you knew someone, as I know you are to be trusted about singers!

I've been trying vainly to trace you in Berlin & hope you are back by now & will get this letter safely & will be the help you have always been.

With our best love & seasonal greetings to you both,

As ever,

William

To Sir Adrian Boult   4 January 1976

Taormina
as from La Mortella, Forio d'Ischia

Dear Adrian,

I got the recording of S.1 [the First Symphony] [. . .] The first & second movements are excellent. However I found the third movement too fast, but that is probably my fault – I must have given you the wrong metronome markings & as soon as I'm within distance of my metronome I will check these. Again at the end of the fourth movement I found it too fast, most likely for the same reason so I will go into it.

I hear from Robert Ponsonby[1] that you will probably be doing it later on in the "Proms" when I hope I may be present. With many many thanks for the performance

Yours sincerely
William Walton

To Harry Blech[2]   15 February 1976

La Mortella, Forio d'Ischia

Dear Harry,

Thank you for your letter.

It is, or so I like to believe, the prerogative of old age to change one's mind continuously, & I'm going to do it again. After all, I think I will

1 BBC Controller of Music, in succession to Sir William Glock.
2 Founder and conductor of the London Mozart Players, a chamber orchestra which now performed other works along with the Viennese classics.

conduct Façade. It was the first piece I conducted so it might as well be my last! The only thing is, what about the players? I'd like those who have played it before, if that is possible. Also I'd prefer not to dress up in full regalia, just a black sweater, & of course, trousers!

The reciter – always a problem, but I've a very bright idea about that, that is to see if Cathy Beberian[1] could be persuaded to do it. That would be feathers in our caps! I don't know how to get hold of her, but doubtless your agent would know how to lay hands on her. As Façade will occupy the 2nd half, I think Mozart [Symphony No] 34 in C & Haydn 102 in B$\flat$ would be an admirable 1st half. Anyhow I will leave that to you to decide. With Cathy B. there would certainly be a full house. We might even get it recorded!

We shall be in London the 29th for the Italian week at Cov. Gar. & will ring you up to see what you have decided. It is a great mistake to be 70. Only the great reaper to look forward to. However, it is one thing we all have in common. A somewhat trite thought (as I've already said, it is a great mistake to be 70!).

Affectionately,
William

To Malcolm Arnold   15 February 1976

La Mortella, Forio d'Ischia

Dear Malcolm,

We come to London (the Ritz) for the Italian week at Cov. Gar. and seem to pretty occupied except for Fri. the 5th of March[,] if you are in London then we could dine perhaps? A <u>Sober dinner</u> – more or less!

The Times, I thought, let itself go in an unseemly manner about Symph. 2. Just like the 1st time, under the same conductor etc. etc.

I hope Troilus will come off. We are having great tenor trouble. The fact is at the moment there aren't any, but I'm hoping one will turn up from Sweden who can speak English fairly decently & can sing also[.]
William

1 Cathy Berberian, American soprano. Exceptionally gifted as a singer of contemporary works, she was married to the Italian composer Luciano Berio.

To Walter Legge   18 February 1976

La Mortella, Forio d'Ischia

Dear Walter,

I can't tell you how grateful I am to you for all the trouble you have
taken to find a Troilus. Gedda,[1] alas, feels he's too old to start learning a
new role, and I suppose he knows best. A Swedish tenor by the name of
Gosta [Gösta] Winbergh – he's apparently very good – so good, in fact
that the Intendant of the Stockholm Opera is loath to let him go. Colin
Graham has seen but not heard him, but says he'd suit the part
admirably. Then there's an American Jack [Jacque] Trussel who C.G.
heard in Santa Fe. Quite good & would be possible if noone better is
found. Richard Lewis[2] told Alan Frank who kept it to himself, that he'd
like to do Pandarus. I'm sure he'd be a splendid P. & a tower of strength
as he knows the whole opera v. well. But there it is.

We go to London the 29th till March 7th for the Italian week at C.G.
The Ambassador in London is a great pal of ours so we are going to
help out so to speak. No chance of your being there I suppose.

With our best love to you both
William

To Walter Legge   25 February 1976

La Mortella, Forio d'Ischia

Dear Walter,

Do you know anything about a tenor called Richard Cassidy? or is it
Cassily?[3] He's not even a name to me, but he's been chosen to sing Tro:,
& everyone is happy about him, except Colin Graham. Who I gather
isn't worried about his voice, but says he's too tall for Janet [Baker], or
at least that is what I understand. But anyhow that's settled, & we've
now got to get down to the performance whether we like it or not.

We go to London (The Ritz) on the 29th & stay there till March 6th.
We shall be much occupied with the Scala set-up, as the Italian

1 Nicolai Gedda, Swedish tenor.
2 English tenor, who had sung Troilus at the first performances of *Troilus and Cressida*
in 1954.
3 Richard Cassilly, American tenor.

Ambassador is a good friend [of] ours & has asked us to dine with H.M. the Queen!

What with Sig. Crociani[1] no wonder, Breshnev[2] is cock-a-hoop. It is this time, I think, a real muck-up & I doubt if the D.C. [Christian Democratic Party] can survive till the election which is not till next year. What with the Italians & the Americans (who I think are the worst of the two) we can only slide, not too gently, into the lap of the Russians!

Let us know when you'd like to come & stay. I think life will go along, at any rate for the moment, & I hope not too unpleasantly.

Love to both
As ever
William

To Malcolm Arnold   16 April 1976

La Mortella, Forio d'Ischia

Dear Malcolm,

Thanks for yours of March 22nd & I'm so sorry to be so long in answering – but I've been much occupied & preoccupied by scoring those 5 Bagatelles for a large orchestra & they appear or rather re-appear under the name of "Varii Capricci". They are to be done at the F.H. on May 4th at its 25th anniversary concert. I fear I've not done them very well, in fact I should have asked you to do them, but having let myself in for something for F.H. I thought these would [be] easy. I couldnt have been more mistaken. I found them full of pitfalls especially the last one which is musically very much changed & hurriedly scored (& full of wrong notes!). I'd left it to the last minute as the O.U.P were panicking about part-copying. The only thing that is intact is the dedication![3]

We are pleased to hear that Edward is settling down in London. Perhaps you'll be in London early May. We shall be at the Old Ritz if it's still there. Luckily the Labour Gov put it on the scheduled list so it should be alright for the future tho' I'm sure the inside will be fairly buggered up.

As ever
William

1 Prime Minister of Italy.
2 Leonid Brezhnev, Chairman of the Communist Party of the Soviet Union.
3 To Arnold.

To Harry Blech   27 April 1976

La Mortella, Forio d'Ischia

Dear Harry,

   Life's full of dissapointments & for me C.B [Cathy Berberian's] decision [not to appear in *Façade*] is one. The other competitor would be Bob Tear.[1] He does it beautifully.

   But the other prog. would do as long as I have'nt to conduct anything!

   We saw Cov. Gar. in Milan in [Berlioz's] Benvenuto Cellini. Excellent & an enormous success. Let me know what you decide.

   As ever
   William

To Christopher Morris   28 September 1976

La Mortella, Forio d'Ischia

Dear Christopher,

   [. . .]

   Just back from the Como Fest. Facade was terrible – I've never heard such appalling playing, the Fl. Cl. & Tr were good but the others were dreadful especially the Vlc. Cathy B. [Berberian] & Jack B.[2] were excellent & I can't think what would have happened if either of them had lost their heads. Luckily they didn't, but to me the worst thing about it was that it could not have had a more resounding success if it had been played under Toscanini! It was conducted by a young man of 23 called Chailly.[3] He's being taken on by the Welsh [National] Opera. If he'd had really good players he would have done it excellently. On the other hand the Vl. Son. was marvellously played by a young Neapolitan. I should like him to record it. But the journey especially going completely exhausted me. Instead of arriving at 8–30[,] owing to a derailment (not of our train!) we arrived at 4am next day!

   Now to business.

   [. . .]

1 Robert Tear, English tenor.
2 Jack Buckley, of the British Council in Rome.
3 Riccardo Chailly, son of the Italian composer Luciano Chailly. Subsequently Principal Conductor of the Royal Concertgebouw Orchestra, Amsterdam.

It's useless to try to get the Brit. Cou. to help with anything to do with me. Buckley in Rome is the only one who will help. [. . .]

I never had much hope of a T.V. showing of even a bar or two of T&C, but we might keep the idea in mind for another year, that is, if it has a real success in Nov. [at Covent Garden] If that happens we might even try to get it on in Germany as well. What a hope!

If the B.B.C don't like my suggestion of Margarete Zimmermann, [as Cressida] I think it very possible that Soderstrom[1] would find [the version for mezzo-soprano] more possible than the old version. She's getting on & voices dont get higher & higher.

[. . .]

Enough for now[.]

William

To Peter Pears   23 December 1976

La Mortella, Forio d'Ischia

Dear Peter,

My thoughts have been with both of you frequently, and with the tragedy that such a genius as Britten died so young. I'm relieved to hear that at least for Ben it was peaceful, gradual, and not too painful. My heart goes out to you, and my best wishes for your own health and happiness.

With love

William

1   Elisabeth Söderström, Swedish soprano.

1977–1983

IT was not in Walton's nature to mellow into a serene old age, gracefully or otherwise. He bitterly resented the loss of so much of his former irrepressible energy, and his last letters are full of this sense of his life being lived under a shadow. Nor is there any mistaking his near-terminal despair at his inability either to compose at all or, when he could, to come up with fresh ideas, rather than what he considered to be tamer, recycled versions of what had come before. The irony that this was precisely the failing of which his critics had so long accused him was not lost on him. Yet even the notion of 'retiring' was not an option. Throughout his life, Walton had lived for his work. There were no compensating emotional resources to draw on, such as the pleasure of keeping in touch with the lives of the children he had chosen not to have. However successful or otherwise his continuing efforts to compose might be, it would have been psychologically impossible for him finally to stop.

But for all his capacity to immerse himself in a world of exasperated unhappiness at these problems, not all was gloom. Walton's last letters show that his sense of humour could crackle into life whenever the clouds parted. His waspish comments about the living and the dead (not forgetting B.B.) are rendered more entertaining by the fact that as he had got older, his language, in his correspondence at least, had got worse. Happy memories, too, were allowed to resurface and spread a mood of warmth and, sometimes, a measure of satisfaction with what he had achieved. Tony Palmer's television film *At the Haunted End of the Day* (the words are those of Cressida's aria in Act II of *Troilus and Cressida*) presented a figure whose sense of fun was undiminished. The same roguish quality had earlier shone throughout the BBC's 1977 television documentary about the creation of the First Symphony, during which Walton discussed the work with André Previn. The will to live and to thrive, however embattled, remained as strong as ever.

Walton's own fixation about his inability to compose anything substantial related, naturally, to works whose progress was fitful or non-existent. True to form, he wrote much less in his letters about those that had given less trouble, or had even emerged to his satisfaction. In March 1977 he travelled to London to hear a performance of some of the *Façade* settings which, some fifty years earlier, he had dropped from what became the final version of the score. Reading over the proofs of these rejected numbers before their publication, he felt sufficiently in touch with the idiom of the young composer who had created them to replace three of the settings with completely new ones. He also reworked those that he chose to retain. The result appeared as *Façade* 2 and showed that, given the right conception, Walton's creativity had lost nothing of its vividness and flair. The quintessentially English composer of the past half-century had, seemingly without difficulty, reconnected with the adventurous young radical whose early music had been more in touch with the European worlds of Stravinsky and Les Six in between-the-wars France, and the Schoenberg circle in Austria. It is probably no coincidence that while working on *Façade* 2, Walton asked Oxford University Press if the company still possessed a copy of his early String Quartet – the one played at the 1923 ISCM Festival in Salzburg, and which had so impressed Alban Berg.

Did Walton regret, on any level, the different direction in which he had chosen to take his music ever since then? Surely not. But there is perhaps something revealing in his deft re-creation of the world of *Façade* in its subtly brilliant successor, so near the end of his life. This can have happened only because, perhaps unknowingly, he had been carrying that world intact within him down the years. The contrast between this quietly achieved success and his unhappy struggle to complete other works could not be more marked. André Previn had asked him to compose a Third Symphony in 1972. Walton eventually sent Previn a sketch of the first page of the work, which shows the music's idiom – shimmering, mercurial, rapier sharp – to be connected (perhaps too closely, Walton may have felt?) to that of the Second Symphony. He always destroyed his sketches as he composed, and the fact that no more music from the Third Symphony appears to have survived does not mean that it did not exist. We shall never know whether Walton felt that his material was simply 'not up to scratch', as he would have put it, or whether he simply knew that he would never finish it and so destroyed it for that reason.

His awareness of the world around him remained alert, particularly when it came to denouncing the increasingly unstable political climate both in Italy and in England. And as his letters to Oliver Knussen show, he was still insatiably curious about the work of other, younger composers, even if he found their music as bewildering as he had probably suspected he would. It is difficult not to feel regret at his reluctance to allow this innate curiosity – always one of the most appealing parts of his nature – to lead his own work in the new direction that he evidently felt it needed. He had lived in Italy for years, and had a wide and affectionate knowledge of the country's music. It is therefore interesting that early in 1977 we find him suddenly asking his publisher to send him scores of some choral motets by Palestrina. Why, one wonders, had it taken him so long to sense a possible affinity here, while his attempts to compose yet more orchestral works were proving so difficult? But in the end it is not possible to second-guess the mind of an artist whose self-knowledge was as shrewd and complete as Walton's had always been.

In 1975 he had met the conductor Owain Arwel Hughes, who had pleased him with a fine performance of *Belshazzar's Feast*. They had kept in touch, and when Hughes was appointed Conductor of the Huddersfield Choral Society, he asked Walton for a new choral work, suggesting a *Stabat Mater* as a possibility. On 7 March 1983 Walton telephoned Hughes to say that he was keen to compose this, and could see the beginnings of how to proceed with it. He died the next morning.

It is poignant to think of the renewed creative resources that Walton might have been able to discover within himself if he had thought of composing a work of this kind about fifteen years earlier. But perhaps he had. And perhaps he had sensed that at that point, a *Stabat Mater* was not yet a viable project for him. No one, after all, had ever known better than Walton himself what he did best. It is not possible finally to establish whether his undated letter to Sir Frederick Ashton – about an extended ending that the choreographer had requested for his new ballet based on *Varii capricci* – is the last letter that Walton wrote. But it stands as a quietly appropriate finale. Seventy-three years after young Billy from Oldham had lost his ball during a day out in the winter gardens, Walton the working composer is standing at the ready, and, as always, looking to deliver.

To Christopher Morris[1]   9 February 1977

La Mortella, Forio d'Ischia

Dear Christopher,

[. . .]

I've just been reading a dismal journal called the "Composer". What a title! Anyhow I was much struck by the thought of being awarded a "prize" – not one of those measly native prizes but one like the Aspen [Award] for my 75th annniversary! (Ten percent to the O.U.P.) [. . .] The good name of O.U.P would not be besmirched at all, any way. B & H. [Boosey & Hawkes] must have pulled the strings like hell, for Ben B. has won all the prizes & that can't all be for his musical genius. So I think you might see what can be done for the brightest star in the galaxy of O.U.P. (at the moment). Let me know when the ball starts to roll. Who knows I might be able to give it a little prod?

Talking of prod the Sod. What shall I do about her "S—ship?"[2] A good kick in the cunt, I think! Or better leave well alone. But it is a bit much at my time of life.

William

But I'm quite serious about prodding someone into giving me a prize. There's not all that [much] time left & then they'd be sorry. Ha-ha. Ha-ha.

To Christopher Morris   14 April 1977

La Mortella, Forio d'Ischia

Dear Christopher,

In the end we got home safely & I'm trying to settle down to work.

Perhaps Psalm 130, De Profundis, would be a good choice for St Albans [Cathedral Choir]?[3] In Latin (a bigger field)? But perhaps Latin is not allowed there.

Can you send me a copy of Palestrina's 'Veni Sponsa Christi'. I don't know who publishes it but it's recorded by Argo with the St John's College Choir. Also V.W.s 5 Mystical Songs (Stainer & Bell that was).

1 Head of Oxford University Press Music Department, in succession to Alan Frank.
2 Editorial emendation. The reference is to a (male) editor, author and music critic.
3 This commission was later abandoned.

Lo Mortella

14. 4. 77

Dear Christopher,   In the end we got here safely
& I'm trying to settle down to work.
Perhaps Psalm 130 "De profundis" would be a good choice
for St Albans? In Latin (a tongue-fried)? but perhaps Latin is not
allowed there.

Can you send me a copy of Palestrina's "Veni Sponsa Christi"?
I don't know who publishes it but it is recorded by Argo with the
St John's College Choir. Also V.W.'s 5 Mystical Songs (Shirley-
Quirk featured) And the other Palestrinas on Act record. In
fact, Brush up your Palestrina!   £1 Slnumm + Read
                                         ordered
                    W.
Also 'The Short Stories of Chekov. — I'm trying to find a
companion for the "Bear"

And the other Palestrina's on that record. In fact, brush up [on] your Palestrina!

W.

Also the short stories of Chekov. I'm trying to find a companion for the "Bear".

To John Amis [1]   [postmarked: Lacco Ameno, 17 May 1977]
[postcard]

Thanks for the LSO book. I seem to have left the wheeled-chair for good except for taking journeys. V. useful at airports.

Love from us both

William

To Lady Diana Cooper [2]   19 May 1977

La Mortella, Forio d'Ischia

Dear Diana,

You must think me the most frightful boor, for not having thanked you before for the three volumes [3] you so kindly gave me. I am horrified to see that the inscription is 1976! I remember posting them to myself because of over-weight, but they only turned up in the post to-day. So much for both the English & Italian postal services – further excuse I cannot offer.

I can't tell you how I look forward to reading them and I can only offer my further humble apologies for not having written to thank you before.

If by any chance you should be visiting these parts, I need hardly say how very happy we should be if you came to stay with us.

1 English writer and broadcaster on music.
2 Born Lady Diana Manners, daughter of the eighth Duke of Rutland. In 1919 she married the Conservative politician and biographer Duff Cooper, who was created the first Viscount Norwich in 1952.
3 Lady Diana Cooper was a nurse at Guy's Hospital in London during the First World War. She then had a famous career as an actress, notably in Max Reinhardt's play *The Miracle*, in which she performed for many years in Europe and America. Between 1958 and 1960 her three volumes of autobiography were published: *The Rainbow Comes and Goes*, *The Light of Common Day* and *Trumpets from the Steep*.

Yours ever
William (Walton)

To Malcolm Arnold   4 June 1977

La Mortella, Forio d'Ischia

Dear Malcolm,

I am so delighted to get your letter and hear of the splendid success of your new Pfte. Concerto. If, as you say, it was the greatest success you have ever had, it must have been something quite terrific. I look forward to a recording which I hope will be done very soon.

I'm sorry you have to endure the boredom & horror of losing so much weight – it is losing that useful tool! But take care about the weight, it was while Su was trying to do the same that I started my collapse & I think if she hadn't discovered the acupuncturist I should have been completely paralised by now – as it is, I am fairly well, if I only hadn't let myself in for composing some piddling music! Fucking fool, – or rather non-effing fool that I am.

I'm glad Andrè P. [André Previn] has thought fit to include us in the same programme together.

With our best love
as always
William

Regards to Larry Foster[1] if you should see him. He's good, isn't he!

The weather is absolutely crazy. Mid-summer in mid-May, then cooler & autumn seems to have started with a 12 hour downpour. Lovely for the garden!

---

1 Lawrence Foster, American conductor, who had replaced the unwell André Previn just before the rehearsals of *Troilus and Cressida* at Covent Garden in 1976.

To Lady Diana Cooper   14 June 1977

La Mortella, Forio d'Ischia

Dear Diana,

I've just finished reading the three volumes of your autobiography &
I would like to tell you what enormous pleasure I have had in doing so.
You have, if I may say so, a positive genius for bringing your numerous
friends & acquaintances most vividly to life – those I knew of only by
hearsay, I feel I now know; but the best of all is [the portrait] of yourself, which you have quite uncon[s]ciously drawn.

I so well remember seeing an astonishing vision of a large straw hat
coming out of the sea on the beach of San Francesco – it was you,
another Venus! Those were the days when the island was still green. It is
now being rapidly over[r]un by concrete, & luckily we did buy quite a
large piece of ground when it was still fairly cheap. We have a really
lovely garden. You must come & see it sometime.

Thank you again for the books which I shall continue to dip into with
the greatest pleasure.

With admiration & (may I dare add) love.

yours ever

William

To Roy Douglas   8 December 1977

La Mortella, Forio d'Ischia

Dear Roy,

I hope that this will arrive in time for wishing you very many happy
returns for your 70th birthday. It is I may tell you much better to be 70
than 75 which dos'ent suit me at all in all sorts of ways, mostly unpleasant. I have asked Christopher Morris to send you a set of the recording
of T&C. and I would like to thank [you] for the help you have been
when I was harried by film producers etc.

As ever affectionately

William

P.S. I'm not sure that you are still at your Tonbridge [Tunbridge] Wells
address, so am sending this c/o O.U.P.

To Christopher Morris   12 January 1978

La Mortella, Forio d'Ischia

Dear Christopher,

I am extremely sorry that my letter about "The Bear" should have upset you. You can rest assured that it was not meant to. The full score of it in fact, was an unexpected pleasure if slightly blemished for me by the lack of the Italian translation. I'm told that Gillian Hunt, organiser of the Barga Festival was awarded an O.B.E in the New Year Honours, which gives me an excuse to write her & ask her about the translation, it's whereabouts etc. I heard from Hilary Griffiths who conducted the Barga perfs [in 1976] & who is now in Cologne saying that "the Bear" was "a great success here & has entered it's 2nd season – I conduct it again to-morrow". Already German & Italian, what other languages must I learn before I can conduct it in English! I've suggested Swedish & Russian. It would be a real laugh if it returned home to it's land of origin! Any further news about that?

Im still seeking a companion piece for it. Colin Graham has done a treatment of "The Tempest" called "Prospero" for which he would like me to do the music, but I don't feel that it would come off, though the Opera Theatre of Saint Louis[1] would like to have the 1st perf, with T.V. etc inducements. It would take me a long time, and as Ive still to do the Brass Band & Wind Band pieces, I see no prospect of taking anything else on. In fact Ive written to the Brass Band people[2] putting it off indefinitely. As I've hardly got it going at all I can see it won't be ready in time for the bands to have time to learn it – at any rate for the next Festival. Roy D. has taken to the B.Band he tells me. Perhaps he'd write a piece – I'm sure it would be excellent. Anyhow I'm mentioning this to E. Howarth.[3] [. . .]

I'll pass Mrs Waters' message over to Su. We've been taking her mother round Sicily otherwise I would have written before. We only returned yesterday.

> yours
> William

1 Colin Graham was working regularly with this company.
2 Grimethorpe Colliery Band.
3 Elgar Howarth, English trumpeter, conductor and composer, closely associated with Grimethorpe Colliery Band.

To Christopher Morris   22 January 1978

La Mortella, Forio d'Ischia

Dear Christopher,

Thank you for your various communications. There is not a hope of writing a Mass for San Francisco or a piece for Lennox [Berkeley]'s 75th – I don't expect to put a note to paper ever again. It has been a very depressing decision for me to make & I am having a serious bout of depression about it. Also I realise I must withdraw from the promised wind band piece. I should like to think it is a passing phase, but I fear not. However one can only wait & see.

The [photographed] pages of B's F [*Belshazzar's Feast*] you sent me are in the fist of Archie Jacobs [Jacob], if I'm not mistaken (brother of Gordon J.).[1] There were two scores of that dimension – a size difficult to lose, I should have thought. One of them, had the first two movements in my M.s.s. & written by me – the other the 1[st.] 2. movs were copied by someone else (possibly A.J. but I can't remember) & the last by me. I can't remember why there were two different scores, but there were big ones in Mss. until it was printed, & everyone used the printed one, except I believe (I may be maligning him) Malcolm Sargent, who could'nt read such small print! [. . .]

By the way, does O.U.P have any photostat copies of that horrible early Str. Quartet (the one played at Salzburg 1923). I'd like to have them if they exist.

I'm sorry to write you such a depressing letter.
William

To Roy Douglas   17 February 1978

La Mortella, Forio d'Ischia

Dear Roy,

Thank you so much for writing. I quite agree with all you say of the recording of T.&C. Personally I still would like to cut even more, but it was difficult enough to do, not having Chris. Hassall to help cutting the libretto.[2] He dissaproved madly about cutting any of it & I suppose we

---

1 Gordon Jacob, English composer and teacher.
2 Hassall had died in 1963.

should have had much fighting over it. In fact both the first and the last Acts need re-modelling & rewriting, but it was beyond me to do both on my own, so I did the best I could with it. It is to me at any rate, much better than it was originally, and I don't miss at all "Put off" & "who will pick up"[,] in fact they had both been in my mind for years as being the bits I'd first cut. Actually the best perf. of it was of the Second Act at the "Proms" a couple of seasons ago,[1] with Richard Lewis (a bit old, but alright nevertheless) & André Previn conducting. It was a great blow that A.P. was too ill to conduct at Cov. Gar. but [Lawrence] Foster did well under the circs. But the whole business was for me a great trial – in fact it made me ill. I was very lucky not to have had a stroke & was cured by an acapuncturist doctor (fully qualified medically). But that I hope is all past & over. I've rather foolishly said I was writing a 3rd Symph. Not a hope! though I have done a few sketches lately. Still more stupidly I said I'd do some piece for the American wind bands, before I realised what scoring for it would be like, let alone thinking about the music. I had to get out of that too! Not having tried to compose, except for an odd anthem or two I find it more difficult than ever & as you know only too well how difficult I found it always to get going, even I myself am now completely horrified at my impotence, there's no other word for it, and I am afraid it won't pass & that I shall never be able to put pen to paper again. I would much like to do a Brass Band piece, for they are such wonderful players, especially the Grimethorpe & Bess o' the Bann bands. There is a splendid record with Elgar Howarth conducting them in various pieces by such composers as Henze & Birtwhistle.[2] If you've not already got it, get it at once, since you have gone brass bandy too! You'll be very surprised & taken by it – it's fantastic.

On the whole I'm much better than I was, especially now that I've come to face that I've no real responsibility to write anything any more. After all better composers than myself stopped, Verdi for instance soon after 70 & didn't start again till he was about 78 or so.

I am so glad to hear that in spite of that nasty accident you are well & flourishing. Susana is well (I don't know what I'd do without her) & sends regards.

Write to me sometime, when you have nothing better to do.

1 In September 1972.
2 Harrison Birtwistle, English composer. His *Grimethorpe Aria* was commissioned by Grimethorpe Colliery Band and Elgar Howarth.

As ever
William

To Walter Legge   23 February 1978

La Mortella, Forio d'Ischia

Dear Walter,

How kind of you to write. Health is on the whole fairly good, but I get very depressed about my work. I don't seem to be able to get any-thing worth-while, down on paper – otherwise I'm still doing well enough to allow Sue to follow her ideas out, her latest being to have a trout stream in a new bit of land we bought a few weeks ago. Not quite so balmy as it seems to be at a first glance.

I can hardly believe that the Vl. Con. is having such a success. I must look more carefully at my P.R.S. returns.

I am sorry that you are having trouble getting rid of your house. With luck the elections in France may veer to the right, tho' that seems very doubtful. Here it is very much in the same state but more violent, tho' it has been very quiet here on the island. We came back yesterday from Rome where we stayed a few days with Enrico d'Assia & heard a performance of "Boris" [Musorgsky's *Boris Godunov*] in the original version. How marvellous it is without Rimsky[-Korsakov]'s touchings-up. But it is a lousy Opera House, orchestra v. 2nd rate, but the chorus which plays an enormous part in this version, was surprisingly good. A young Pole was "Boris", as was the conductor – terribly slow – it lasted over 5 hours, but was a great success with the public in spite of that.

The "Bear" has been having quite a success in Germany, in Kassel, Munich, Köln, Passau etc & on the Hungarian T.V. Quite a help. And now O.U.P tells me that Russia has bought the rights! I wish I could find a subject for a companion piece for it. It is being done here as well.

[. . .]

Enough about my goings-on. Now that there are distinct signs of spring why don't you both come here for a bit?

With our best love to you both
as ever
William

I've only just heard that Peter P. [Pears] has been dubbed a knight. Did you know?

[446]

To Walter Legge   18 April 1978

La Mortella, Forio d'Ischia

Dear Walter,

I'm in gross defect in not writing you before, but both your P.C. &
your letter arrived at virtually the same time, though the P.C. is dated
1.3.78 & the latter 8.3.78, but it is surprising that they've arrived at all
considering the state of everything here. [. . .]

Odd you mentioning Rostropovitch. I'm not on the best terms with
him! You may remember that he gave, a few years ago, a series of progs
of Vlc. Cons. including idiotic ones like Sauguet[1] – but not a mention of
W.W. On reproaching him a year or two ago about this, he said he knew
it very well, in fact taught it to his pupils. Then [he] said "You write me
new concerto & I play both" & I did'nt feel terribly enthusiastic about
the idea. However thinking about it again it has struck me that a
"Poëme" a la Chausson, might be an idea to do instead. You'll doubtless
remember Ginette Neveu playing [it]. What an artist! It's a pity there's
no recording of it. Or is there? Talking of recordings have you heard
Jung-Wha Jungs [Kyung-Wha Chung's] recording of mine. Superb! as
good as Heifetz or Francescatti.[2] Perlman[3] has said (but so far few signs)
that he wants to record both the Vla. & Violin [Concertos].

Unfortunately theres a bit of bother on with Gillian W. [Widdicombe]
about her biography of me. She's got a lot on tape, but not a word in
writing. Hamish Hamilton who wants to publish it (he's given her quite
a large advance[,] how much I don't know) has lost patience and given
her the push. I must say I think he's right. She's been at it (or rather not)
for about 4 years, without anything to show, not even the first sentence!
So he asked me to think again. I can only suggest Patrick Hughes. [. . .]
Can you think of a name? What about yourself? Anyhow I do hope that
you are writing your memoirs.

We are both horrified to hear about your accidents and hope that by
now you are well on the mend. The waters here are marvellous for those
kinds of breakages. So don't forget that we are here, save for a week
May 22–28 when we go to London for the [Chelsea] Flower Show.

1 Henri Sauguet, French composer. A pupil of Canteloube and an admirer of Satie, he
produced a large output including a ballet for Sergei Diaghilev's Ballets Russes company,
La chatte, and four symphonies.
2 Zino Franchescatti, French violinist.
3 Itzhak Perlman, Israeli violinist resident in America.

[. . .]
With our best love to you both
William

To Malcolm Arnold   16 June 1978

La Mortella, Forio d'Ischia

[. . .]
   Our sojourn in London was mostly occupied in seeing doctors. I for
my old aesophagus (?) for which has been found a cure. It seemed to be
going to be most unpleasant. It was'nt at all & has had a most beneficial
effect & I can now eat anything without choking, & what's more important, I can drink almost anything with moderation!
   Su also was most fortunate. She went for her usual check-up & it
was discovered that she had something on the breast. Cancer? of course
sprang to mind. After an operation & four days of agonised waiting it
turned out to be benign, but in a very early stage. So except for 6 monthly
check-ups, she should be O.K.
   [. . .]
   Distressing news about Hans H.s [Henze's] heart attacks. I'm about to
telephone him.
   As ever
   William

To Walter Legge   7 September 1978

La Mortella, Forio d'Ischia

Dear Walter,
   I grovel & apologise abjectly in being such an unforgivably long time
in answering your letter.
   The situation regarding the biog: remains the same. La Widdicombe,
who proposed that she should come here for the whole of Sept. to work,
is now ill with something wrong with her fallopian(?) tubes [. . .] so
there will be another delay. Not that I mind all that much, having seen a
transcript of the tapes she took long ago & they are fairly accurate.
What I should like you to do if you would consider it, is something like
the piece you sent me on Callas. After all you are about the only one left

[448]

who knew me at the time I was [*illegible*], so to speak, & knew Alice [Wimborne] well, whereas these others, there's another bobbed up who wants to [. . .] but it is all based on hearsay & not real knowledge that you have. But I do'nt like to ask you unless it would really interest you doing it. Give it a thought. It would be much less taxing than doing an official biog with date of birth etc.

We are going to London at the end of the month for our check-ups. Su seems to be, & according to our local doctor is, alright. So am I, I think. It is old age which is my affliction & noone can do anything about that. We've just returned from a few days in Siena where the 50ᵗʰ anniversary of the I.S.C.M performance of "Facade" was being celebrated. That gave me something to think about. It was on the whole quite well done with Cathy Beberian [Berberian] reciting. Of course, it was nothing like it was 50 years ago, with Constant [Lambert] on the megaphone instead of a loud-speaker. In fact, I've arrived at the reminis[c]ing stage – a sure sign of old-age!

On the way to England we may stop-off at Florence as I'm invited to judge a concorso of young conductors. I['m] only going in the hope that I might persuade the "Maggio"[1] to do "Troilus". Just a faint hope of succeeding.

Otherwise stagnations. The projected 3ʳᵈ symphony dos'ent seem to be forthcoming & any other bits & pieces, such as a piece for a Brass Band, don't seem to come to anything. In fact, it is all a bit depressing.

We hope you are both bearing up & are enjoying life,

With our best love to you both,

William

To Walter Legge   14 October 1978

La Mortella, Forio d'Ischia

Dear Walter,

We came back a few days ago & found your very welcome letter.

Your hard work on C.G. seems to have borne fruit up to a point, that being that the F. [*Façade*] ballet is being revived. But I'm all for the F. entertainment [original version] being linked with "Carmen Burano"

---

1 Florence's Maggio Musicale Fiorentino festival. One of Italy's major festivals, held every year between April and June.

[Carl Orff's *Carmina Burana*] which I liked very much when you played me a recording years & years ago – (more than I like to think of!). I must get another recording as I've not heard it since then.

We were invited to Siena for the 50ᵗʰ anniversary of the perf. there. It went very well, especially considering the implications of the Int. Soc. of Con. Mus. with which it was associated in 1928.[1] Now it was done by Cathy Beberian [Berberian] your telepathic suggestion. She has done it a number of times now, with Jack Buckley of the Brit. Cou. in Rome helping out – quite a good combination. She has quite taken the piece to heart & is doing it a lot, all over the place, so C.G. would have no difficulty in getting her if the dates were all right. In fact I've just finished re-hashing eight old pieces [*Façade* 2, revised version] from the original 30-odd, which I've had lying about, for her. They are quite up to standard now.

Apart from that, I've been my usual non-productive self. I think I shall do the Brass Band piece.[2] The B.Bs are tremendously popular & if one wrote the right kind of piece, it would produce the P.R.S. very vast & fast, so I'm told.

I doubt very much that I can get the tapes out of Gillian. She did a prècis [*sic*] of them for me, but of course kept the one & only copy. But there was, up to now nothing very new or interesting. Anyhow it is all obtainable in Michael Kennedy's preface to "W.W." a thematic catalogue – Stewart Craggs, O.U.P.[3] [. . .] if you can bring yourself to write a 4000[-word] piece about me. I should be very grateful to be included in the book with the one about Callas!

Our check-ups turned out to be benign for both of us, which is just as well.

I am back on Sibelius due to Herbert [von Karajan]'s recordings of [Symphonies] 4, 5, 6 & 7. Wonderful.

With our best love to you both
William

---

1 On 14 September 1928 Walton conducted *Façade*, with Constant Lambert reciting, at the International Society for Contemporary Music's annual festival, held that year in Siena. The performance went well until the 'Tarantella', which according to Walton's recollection in 1951 had its audience 'in an uproar. Things were being thrown onto the stage, people whistled and shouted and protested in the name of Mussolini and the entire Italian people [. . .] The trouble was that they considered they'd been mortally insulted. I had parodied Rossini and poked fun at a composer who, heaven knows, I love above all others.'
2 Walton had decided to make a brass band arrangement of his ballet score *The First Shoot*.
3 Stewart Craggs, *William Walton: A Thematic Catalogue of his Musical Works*, with a critical appreciation by Michael Kennedy (Oxford University Press, 1977).

Received a record of Ida Haendel[1] playing my Vl. Con. coupled with B. Britten's – a really splendid early piece – if he had only continued in that vein.

To Helga Keller   5 November 1978

La Mortella, Forio d'Ischia

Dearest Helga,

It is indeed a long time since I heard from you and I am very very sorry to hear about Mel. What else is to be said about such a situation except that I'm happy that you are getting over it – and you still have your daughter to cheer you up.

Certainly you may use my [name] as a reccommendation to whom it may concern about obtaining a "professorship". Noone could be a better "prof" than you in the techniques of "cutting" etc.

Larry comes to see us now & then. He has been terribly ill & Sue looked after him here for some weeks till he was well enough to face the world. They [Lord and Lady Olivier] were both here about six weeks ago. She'd lost her voice playing a Neapolitan woman in a di Felippo play [Eduardo de Filippo's *Filumena*] but recovered it, thank goodness after being completely silent for all the time she was here. Larry was v. upset. And those children. He has to keep on doing any film that will pay the price he needs. He has to keep the children at school & it costs the earth. He's now doing "Dracula" & loathing the thought of it.

I'm surviving – very old! & Sue is marvellous. We both send our best love.
As ever
William

To Walter Legge   5 January 1979

La Mortella, Forio d'Ischia

Dear Walter,

I am sorry that there was noone about to answer the telephone when you called, but Xmas and all that, what can you expect? We have now only one to look after us, & never on Sunday or Festas, which may account for the lack of response.

---

1 English violinist of Polish birth.

The B&H [Boosey & Hawkes] mag.[1] nearly had the desired effect as an emetic. That kind of thing puts me off from ever again putting a note on paper. I know what kind of a reception anything I wrote would receive & I don't think it worth while asking for it. Silence is preferable & more profitable!

I could'nt agree more about Carlos Kleiber.[2] I have the recording of "Traviata". Marvellous – with Placido Domingo. The "Carmen", with him, conducted by Abbado,[3] is excellent, perhaps not as good as it would be with Kleiber – but good enough. Also the production by Piero Faggioni[4] (Gillian's boyfriend!) provides a French slant, but I've not seen it, but it was a great success in Edinburgh.

We are sorry that you seem to have nowhere to go. Tho' the political situation is not exactly stable, there seems little likelihood of anything drastic like in Persia[5] happening. Here the Communists are I think, just as docile as the English Labour [Party] – in fact I should think even more so. If Elizabeth wants to live in Switzerland why not somewhere in the Ticino, where there's a little of both worlds. Not California, think of those earthquakes!

Our best love to you both and all good wishes for the New Year
As ever
William

Let us know when you change your address[.]

To Christopher Morris   3 March 1979

La Mortella, Forio d'Ischia

Dear Christopher,
I am delighted to receive confirmation from you about the "a cappella" for Llandaff.[6] I feel it may be just the thing to "turn me on", as they say somewhat crudely these days! You never know.

1 *Tempo.*
2 German-born Argentinian conductor, son of Erich Kleiber (see p. 172 n. 2).
3 Italian conductor, at this time Music Director of La Scala, Milan.
4 Italian director and opera producer.
5 In 1978 the Shah of Iran and his government had been overthrown by a popular revolution orchestrated by fundamentalist religious leaders.
6 Walton subsequently considered composing *Three Odes of Horace* for the Llandaff Festival. They remained unwritten.

I've just finished playing thro' again (I've only played it once) the Harty perf. of Sinf.1. Excellent re-processing. [. . .] After 30 years or so it seems to me to be still rather a good specimen of its kind – and not all, I find like Sibelius! In fact I wish it was. Will you send me the min. scores of S. [Sibelius's] Sinf 6 & "Tapiola" neither of which I seem to possess, tho' I've got the marvellous Karajan recordings of both works.

[. . .]

To revert to Llandaff – Latin is the thing (not Biblical preferably) & if any awkward bits of scansion can be marked – in fact the rhythm of the lines anyhow would be a help. What is the size of the choir?

yours
William

To Roy Douglas   21 April 1979

La Mortella, Forio d'Ischia

Dear Roy,

Sorry to have been a little dawdling about thanking you for your kind, (both encouraging & depressing) letter for my birthday. I would like to be able to say it is because I have been seized by a frenzy of inspired work, but I fear that that is not quite true. However I have done about 3 mins. of a piece for Br. Ba. competition, which in all probability will be sent to you by O.U.P to discover if I'm still in my right mind!

I know only too well about commissioned works; the only thing I can say about them, is if I'd not had a commission I should have produced nothing at all, which would be probably just as well. I shall proceed with the dotty Br. Ba. piece as I'm getting rather intrigued by it.[1] Anyway it won't frighten the Bands, for though the piece is slightly Henze-ish, it is not at all Birtwistle-ish! Which leads me to Elgar Howarth – a remarkable young man who I suspect will turn out to be a remarkable composer. You know of course [his] "Fireworks" for Bra. Ba. without which I should'nt be attempting to compose this piece. It is interesting for me to learn that he is the conductor for the Tun. Wells S.O. What excellent experience for both parties – for you too, filling in the missing instruments. The kind of experience I've missed & miss now more than ever.

1 It was not completed. Instead Walton made a brass band arrangement of his 1935 ballet score *The First Shoot*.

I looked through the piece you sent me[1] – a good chip off the old block – none the worse for that. [. . .] And to recall Henry V. I saw V.W. [Vaughan Williams] about the time I was writing it & happened to mention that I was in a bit of a dilemma about identifying the French musically speaking – (I could hardly use the "Marseillaise") & he suggested, if I remember rightly "Reveillez vous Piccars" & told me where to find it, not mentioning that he had used it himself.[2] It is in fact to me a rather typically English V.W. tune & I nearly used it instead of using the "Agincourt Song". What a long time ago it all seems.

Now I must stop boring you blue. Let me hear from you again & give my regards to Gary H. [Elgar Howarth] And I promise to get down to work on this rather silly piece.

As ever
William

To Nora Donnelly [Walton]   29 May 1979

La Mortella, Forio d'Ischia

Dearest Nora,

Thank you for your letter. It is really too sad for words the news about Alec. I've not yet heard any details from Jo, tho' I spoke to her on the telephone & she said she would write as soon as she could. I expect she's completely devastated by his death, tho' it would appear to be, not entirely unexpected, the doctors, not having as far as I know, said anything about heart trouble when there was that scare about his having cancer of the lung, but he hadn't, & I feel they must have said something about his heart condition. However there it is. At this time of life, if it is not one thing it's another. He was older than I remembered – 72, quite a good age. Being 77, I feel it's just one day to another. Here I have in front of me an invitation to the Festival Hall for a tribute to Sir Rob[ert] Mayer on the occasion of his 100th birthday on June 5th! He seemed hale & h[e]arty when I last saw him & I have written a short fanfare to go before the Nat. Anthem. Some people seem to have all the luck, but would it be good to live so long. I rather doubt it, but will try to do the best I can to circumvent the "old reaper.", & all things considered I'm

1 Douglas's *March for Brass Band.*
2 In his overture for brass band, also entitled *Henry V.*

not feeling so bad & Noel seems to be doing well. Thank heaven for Enid, she's really splendid. We were looking forward to having Alec with us. He was about to come & stay some 4 or 5 weeks ago. But things seem to be turning out well for my nephew & niece, which will cheer you up.

With our best love to you & Patrick etc.

as ever

William

To Helga Keller   20 November 1979

La Mortella, Forio d'Ischia

Dearest Helga,

I had a request from a Prof. Smilansky (tho' sent on Sept 20th it only arrived here a couple of days [ago] & I answered immediately) for details of your murky past, as it would seem you've applied for a lecture-ship at Tel Aviv Univ. I did my best to butter you up & hope that it will be duly awarded you.

Life is very nerve-wracking these days. One really should never open a paper – its always full of horrors – kid-nappings – the P.L.O – no petrol – Iran etc. etc. In fact, it would appear that Mrs Thatcher is the only fairly stable thing about & may she long be!

It is fairly quiet here, but I'm getting old much more rapidly than I anticipated, & I seem to have run out of ideas, musically speaking, which is annoying & frustrating.

Larry & Joan & the children were here for a few days at the end of August. In spite of everything, continuous bad films to make enough money to keep the children in their v. expensive schools, he seemed to be in good spirits tho' looking v. thin & run-down. I hope you asked him to help over the Tel-Aviv appointment.

Best love from us both

William

To Harry Blech [January/February 1980]

La Mortella, Forio d'Ischia

My dear Harry,

How very nice to hear from you. I should like to think that I should be able to get to London for your 70th[1] but I fear there's not a hope of my being able to achieve it. I don't really miss not being able to go to London so often. I'd very much like to hear you do a Brahms, but there seems so much (too much) going on in the musical world.

There's nothing to be said for being 70 & it gets worse with each succeeding year, but I suppose if one was Sir Robert M. [Mayer] one would be exceedingly happy to be 100 – but somehow I doubt if I should be. On the other hand, I don't much relish the idea of 'popping off' just at present, 'bloody' though the world seems to be.

I'm writing (nearly finished) a piece for solo vlc for Rostropovitch. Very difficult to do I find but better than have to face a lot of scoring!

Our love & best wishes for the 70th[.]

as ever
William

To Michael Vyner[2] 23 February 1980

La Mortella, Forio d'Ischia

Dear Michael,

How very nice to hear from you. Su is well & I am as well as can be expected at this rather gloomy time of life. Very cheering to hear of the success of "Facade" in Amsterdam. The [London] Sinfonietta is most highly regarded & eulogies always greet it in the press as you must know, when it's here or near here[.]

We shan't be coming to London at all this year, as after a bu[r]st of re-decorating our houses, bankruptcy is only just round the corner. However all five of them have been taken over by a firm called "Villa Venture". If this goes well for one year, it will take them over for five years at a very good rent following the cost-of-living index, so perhaps next year will see us in the "blue".

1 Blech was born on 2 March 1910.
2 General Administrator of the London Sinfonietta.

Ive done or rather re-done an old ballet "The First Shoot" for Gary Howarth for his brass boys. It will, I hope, be rather popular! What a hope. If spared, I shall be celebrating (if that's the right word) my 80th in two years time & I hope to produce something for it. But I doubt it.

With our love,

As ever

William

To Christopher Morris   27 February 1980

La Mortella, Forio d'Ischia

Dear Christopher,

I hope that by now the final pages of the "First Shoot" [brass band arrangement] will have arrived. – sorry to have taken so long over such a simple task, but old age is beginning to, or rather has taken over! I don't think that we should get very far wrangling over the music of the B.of B [*The Battle of Britain* film score]. They're a tough lot, & elephant minded! I don't think it can be very good as I can't even remember a bar of the "March" & it's not included in the music Mr Heath got back from them[1] & I don't think we should get it turned into a 'hit'. Even if we did, they'd get the brass! So lets leave it, but have a "go" if you are feeling pugnacious about it. Let Gary [Elgar Howarth] have a look at the "First Shoot" & if [he] gives an O.K. then go ahead with whatever plans you may concoct for it. Gary has some I believe.

Did I tell you that I heard from Sir Rudolf![2] & it would seem that it is very very likely that the Miami Opera will put on T&C in '82. They want Janet B. [Baker] . . . Its the tenor that is the worry. John Tooley has an idea to put it on at C.G. as a concert perf with Placido Domingo & Colin Davis[3] – that indeed might be something worth living for.

William

---

1 In 1972 Edward Heath had been instrumental in obtaining United Artists' release of Walton's score, most of which had not been used in the film.

2 Sir Rudolf Bing, Viennese-born impresario and administrator. General Manager of Glyndebourne Festival Opera from 1935 to 1949, and Artistic Director of the newly founded Edinburgh International Festival from 1947 to 1949. From 1950 to 1972 he was General Manager of the Metropolitan Opera House, New York. In 1973 he became a director of the artists' agency Columbia Artists Management.

3 English conductor, at this time Music Director of the Royal Opera (in succession to Sir Georg Solti).

To Christopher Morris   29 April 1980

La Mortella, Forio d'Ischia

Dear Christopher,

I fear I can't work up any enthusiasm for the B. of B. music & hope
that you have no success with the solicitors! I received yesterday from
them £3–52p. so it will take many years to make anything further out of
it. I'd drop it if I were you!

[. . .]

I'm plodding away at the Rostropovich solo piece [*Passacaglia* for
solo cello] – it's about 6 mins gone – it should be about 8 mins. The
plan for perf, I gather is that it will be included in a programme in a
concert for the Queen Mother's [80th] Birthday sometime in early Oct.
but I've not heard for sure.

I've heard from Gary H. about the "1ˢᵗ Shoot" – O.K. as a "pop"
piece but no good for a [competition] Test piece – so I'll leave it for the
time being, until I hear about the piece for Rostropovich & Washington.[1]
If there is little enthusiasm for the price asked we will drop that also! As
you see – I'm not too keen on trying to write music so-called. I shan't do
it if they don't like the price!

The cello suites by B.B.[2] have arrived – very depressing I find them, –
full of tricks & not much else, – or am I being blasphemous? I'll ask R
[Rostropovich] when I see him – he ought to know.

As ever
William

To Harry Blech   11 June 1980

La Mortella, Forio d'Ischia

Dear Harry,

If your plan to go to Capri matures, don't forget that there's a boat
going, between there & here, I think every day during the summer
months, so you have no excuse in not coming to see us. It would be very

---

1   *Prologo e Fantasia*, commissioned by Mstislav Rostropovich in his position as Music
Director of the National Symphony Orchestra of Washington, DC.
2   Benjamin Britten's Suites Nos. 1 and 2 for cello, recorded by Rostropovich.

agreable if you could manage it. Let us know. The telephone does work
occasionally!

As ever
William

To Griselda Kentner   9 October 1980

La Mortella, Forio d'Ischia

Dearest Griselda,

Help! Help! I've inadvertently let myself in for contributing to – as far
as I can see – a series of views on Alan Rawsthorne,[1] as an old pal it
seemed to me to be unavoidable. Here is the result of my effort. Pretty
feeble, but perhaps you could be prevailed on to fill it out a bit, or if you
think it to be alright, just correct the grammar, spelling etc. & I am your
slave, not that I'm not already.

It was lovely to see you both during our very short sojourn in
London. I must say that otherwise, I don't take to being there very
much.

I must now try to think up something for this piece I'm supposed to
be writing for Washington [*Prologo e Fantasia*], but ideas don't sprout
easily these days, not that they ever did.

Love to you both & I apologise for being such a bloody pest.

As ever
William

I've got a copy of this, so you can put whatever you like or not, in the
empty lines & return to me.

To Griselda Kentner   24 October [1980]

La Mortella, Forio d'Ischia

Darling Griselda,

You are an angel to have vetted that article with your very helpful
suggestions which I've used, I need hardly say.

1 English composer and pianist, and a former colleague of Walton during their wartime
work as film composers.

How very distressing about poor Georgia [Sitwell]. Though I knew she was ill, but not all that bad, however I was wrong. It will be awful for Sachie. I'm sure he will be quite lost without her.

I'm delighted to hear about Lou [Louis Kentner] & the Chopin competition.[1] How splendid of him to walk out on 'em. Perhaps it will learn them to behave better next time.

I adore Ely. Norwich I don't know so well. It was lovely seeing you both. I'm like you & dislike London a great deal now.

It's dreadful that you have not yet completely recovered from the bloody shingles, perhaps you will have by the time you get this.

I didn't know that the French admire Alan's music – the best thing about them that I've heard for some time & I quite see why.

With best love from us both & many thanks again for your help
as ever
William

To Helga Keller 6 January 1981
[postcard]

Forio

Dearest Helga,

Kind of you to enquire about our survival.[2] Luckily tho' everything shakable was shaken for about 90 seconds, but nothing on the Island collapsed. I wish I could say the same for the mainland. To add to everyone's miseries the weather is beastly – cold & wet.

I'm glad your love life has taken a turn for the better, may it long continue, not only for 1981.

love from us both
William

1 All the main prizes in the Warsaw International Chopin Piano Competition that year were awarded to competitors from the Soviet bloc.
2 There had been a major earthquake in central Italy.

To Oliver Knussen[1]   9 March 1981

La Mortella, Forio d'Ischia

Dear Oliver K.

Indeed I remember you well. In fact, it has often occurred to me to write you a word or two of encouragement when I've seen mention of you in the press.

I am very happy that you should still listen to & like my 2nd Symphony, to me very surprising, since it had the worst reception from the press that any work of mine ever had, in fact if it had'nt been for the Szell recording, the work would I believe, never have been heard of again. So don't ever pay any attention to what the critics say.

I should like to know what the young are up to, so please send me some cassettes (preferably) of what you think interesting. I've ploughed through some Ferneyhough,[2] & not much better, the 1st Symphony of Max Davies[3] but that is about all I know. Better Richard Rodney Bennett, I think.

With best wishes & thanks for writing
Yours sincerely
William Walton

To Oliver Knussen   15 March 1981
[postcard]

La Mortella, Forio d'Ischia

Dear Oliver K.

In case you may be feeling modest, I hope that you won't forget to send cassettes of your own music.

Not that I set much store on what either Stadlen[4] or Northcott[5] write,

---

1 English composer and conductor, born 1952, and a leading musician of his generation.
2 Brian Ferneyhough, English composer of music of an uncompromising modernist complexity.
3 Peter Maxwell Davies, English composer now resident in the Orkney Islands of Scotland.
4 Peter Stadlen, Austrian pianist and critic resident for many years in London, where he was a music critic on the *Daily Telegraph*. He had given the first performance of Webern's Piano Variations Op. 27 in Vienna in 1937.
5 Bayan Northcott, music critic of the *Sunday Telegraph*.

for the two of them to enthuse about your piece,[1] I shall look forward to seeing if I agree with them.

Yours,
William W.

This depressing card[2] was done at Capri over 30 years ago!

To Peter Heyworth   25 April 1981

La Mortella, Forio d'Ischia

Dear Peter,
    Thank you for your kind words about that T.V. biography.[3] [. . .] I may add that your articles in the "Observer" which is occasionally obtainable, are the only bits of music criticism that are worth paying attention to.
    Come & see us whenever you feel like it. It could be a good place for you to finish your book.
    love from us both,
    William

To Helga Keller   [1981]
[postcard]

La Mortella, Forio d'Ischia

Dearest Helga
    Thank you for writing. I'm glad to hear that things are going well with you & that you are surviving the very nasty times we are living in. With luck I shall see my 80th on 29.3.82 but I'm not too sanguine.
    With best love from us both.
    as ever
    William

1   Knussen's *Coursing* for chamber orchestra.
2   Michael Ayrton's sketch for a portrait of Walton, painted in 1948, shortly after Alice Wimborne had died.
3   Tony Palmer's *At the Haunted End of the Day*.

To Oliver Knussen

3 March 1982

[postcard]

La Mortella, Forio d'Ischia

Dear Olly!

Thanks for the record. I'm too muddled up to give you a sane opinion, that is if you want mine, but I'll do so later on.

yrs
William

To Sir Frederick Ashton

[early 1983]

La Mortella, Forio d'Ischia

Dear Fred,

I hear from John Tooley that your intentions regarding "Varii Capricci" are strictly honorable, but that you would like the last number to be longer.[1]

If that is so, I would be delighted to do it.

How much longer and where do you think the interpolation ought to be?

Hope that everything is prospering with you.

Love from us both,
William

1 Ashton was choreographing *Varii capricci* for a forthcoming Royal Ballet season at the Metropolitan Opera House in New York. The ballet was first performed there on 19 April 1983, six weeks after Walton's death.

APPENDIX I

It has long been known that the London-based music-publishing firm of Boosey & Hawkes made a determined attempt, in 1954, to lure Walton away from Oxford University Press. Walton was at that time sufficiently exasperated by what he viewed as the Press's incompetence in preparing the performing material of *Troilus and Cressida* to give the idea serious consideration. His unease was heightened by his awareness that his current publishers had neither the connections nor the expertise in the operatic world that would give his opera the best possible chance of international success. Boosey & Hawkes had much stronger credentials in this area. Besides the first operas of Benjamin Britten, including *Peter Grimes* and *Billy Budd*, the London company owned the worldwide rights, outside Germany and Austria, for virtually all of Richard Strauss's operas. Regarding non-operatic works, Boosey & Hawkes also had a more powerful presence in continental Europe than Oxford University Press, despite the best efforts of Hubert Foss and his successor, Alan Frank, to build up the Oxford company's standing and visibility outside Great Britain. Walton none the less decided to stay with the Press, on the grounds that to leave the company might not, after all, yield the results that Boosey & Hawkes was promising. His loyalty was rewarded by the status and influence with his longstanding publishers that came from being the biggest fish in a smaller pool.

What appears to have been unknown until recently is that much earlier, in 1937, Boosey & Hawkes had made a similarly serious attempt to attract Walton to their publishing operation. This was long before Benjamin Britten had achieved the international reputation, after the première of *Peter Grimes* in 1945, that made him the brightest star among English composers. Walton had every reason to be interested. In 1937 he himself was seen to be the leading English composer of his generation, and his music would have had a similarly unchallenged profile in Boosey & Hawkes's catalogue. He was already impatient with the apparent slowness with which his major scores up to that point – notably the Viola Concerto, *Belshazzar's Feast* and the First Symphony – were making progress in the concert halls of Europe, and he was well aware of Boosey & Hawkes's strengths in this field. His letter to Hubert Foss of February 1937 refers to the London company's approach, in a way that suggests that he and Foss had already discussed the situation, either in person or by telephone. Foss promptly drafted a memorandum to Sir Humphrey Milford, Publisher to the University of Oxford (the head of the Press's London-based operation, including the music department), asking for instructions. Milford sent it back with the words 'You must keep him' scribbled at the foot of the page.

Foss's business letters were almost always dictated in the Press's office and typed out there, with a copy of course being retained for the company's files. Foss's response to Boosey & Hawkes's approach to Walton was, however, dramatically different. The letter printed below has not been published before. Indeed it appears to have remained undiscovered, or at least unnoticed, until very recently in Oxford University Press's files of the company's correspondence with Walton.

The letter is handwritten throughout, and has been authenticated by Hubert Foss's daughter, Mrs Diana Sparkes, who has confirmed that the writing is that of her mother, Dora Foss. Hubert Foss had evidently decided that what he wanted to say to Walton was too personal to be dictated to anyone in the company office. Instead he appears to have written the letter during an evening or a weekend at home. Mrs Sparkes has confirmed that her mother often helped Foss by copying his letters written from home, so that he had a record of his personal correspondence.

The letter's contents show how personally Foss felt about Walton's possible defection (as he saw it), and how strongly he was prepared to express himself in order to try to retain his major 'find' as a music publisher. The letter, and doubtless the conversations between the two men that followed, had the desired effect: Walton decided to stay. If Foss had not made his case so passionately and indeed so angrily, all of Walton's music from then on might have been published instead by Boosey & Hawkes – including, of course, the Violin Concerto, whose firm place in the repertory of virtually every international soloist has ever since made it one of Oxford University Press's highest-earning Walton scores.

Hubert Foss to William Walton[1]   7 February 1937

My dear William.

Of course it was inevitable: no one in his senses could expect anything else. And, no doubt, this rather wretched form of commercial bargaining could go on indefinitely, for naturally your name, which I assert was made largely through the Press's work for you, is now worth losing money for. You are not the first one that has been in the same position: Wells is a good case. Why has he always changed his publishers? Because they couldn't afford his terms consistently and there was always a new publisher willing to pay for the publicity of his name – once!

But for you the position is entirely different. I am quite sure that if you were at B.& H. you would want to come to the Press. Has the Press nothing that makes it valuable for you? Surely it is today a step up to gain the Oxford imprint & not a step up to leave Oxford for B. & H?

You asked my advice in your letter. I took the chance when I was seeing a leading agent for authors on Friday (Ralph Pinder) to put the case to him, for his advice from your point of view. We eliminated money terms, for I'm sure you are not going to change your whole way of life to bargain over £50 a year. His attitude – and don't forget agents fight publishers! – was that you would be very

---

1   © Oxford University Press. Reproduced by permission.

foolish to change now. You've got a publisher who has spent money on you: a publisher with an international imprint, and a world wide reputation: a publisher who has backed you for ten years. Why run away? What good does it do you? Do you honestly think that B & H will do as much for you in the next 10 years as we have in the past? Do you find them philanthropic? Are they really interested in your music – or in the other things that your name will help them to sell? Do you really feel that you will have a sympathetic correspondent who will understand your music there? And if you go the way you have during this last ten years, do you think you'll find them very keen after the [next] five years?

Of course, it may be that you are not going that way, that you have it in mind to write shorter and less costly works. If that is so, I most definitely suggest that you owe us enough from the past to give them to us – I have never pursued you, nor has Milford. But you cannot like the idea that you should give us all your big works and another publisher your profitable small works!

God, who would be a pioneer? It's no job, it seems: bearing the burden and heat of the day, for what? – to be told that H. P. Allen[1] advises you to have another shop window. I regard that remark, from the Oxford professor about the Oxford Press as about the unkindest thing that that man has ever said, and I should be delighted for him to know it.

As for divided allegiance to publishers, that is commercially rubbish. When has such a scheme ever worked? I should have thought that your suddenly leaving the Press would be tantamount to saying to the great public that you were not wanted. Did Hardy,[2] having been found by MacMillan's [Macmillan], leave them? You're lucky, you were found by the right house first.

And there's another point. I wanted you to see Sir Humphrey Milford about it direct, but he's not been well and goes away on Wednesday so he cannot see you till you are back from Ashby St Le[d]gers. Surely there is some little obligation on you, isn't there? We've printed you entire[.] I nursed you and made you available. Now, at the height of your younger fame, is it right or even grateful to go whoring after strange gods? I feel it is the record of my own personal failure if you do: apart from the Press's capital expenditure, I feel I personally have not done enough for you. You must tell me on Thursday what more I am to do: you know I'll do it if it is in my power. I take it as a strong personal criticism that you should want to consort with a rather unmusical rival: to whom, dear William, postcards containing fugue subjects will not, I fear, be wholly intelligible!

Another point. We've got V-W [Vaughan Williams], Tovey,[3] Constant [Lambert] and Scholes[4] – four prominent names in different spheres, but all sellers. We've

1 Sir Hugh Allen, formerly Organist at New College, Oxford, and from 1918 Professor of Music at Oxford University.
2 Thomas Hardy, English poet, novelist and dramatist.
3 Donald Francis Tovey, Scottish composer, now better known for his writing and teaching as Professor of Music at Edinburgh University.
4 Percy Scholes, English composer and writer, best known for his compilation of *The Oxford Companion to Music*.

let go to B & H a number of lesser men.¹ You're in exclusive company, I suggest: you have no rival, in your own sphere, on our attention.

As for the lines of music that are outside our scope – brass, military band stuff, jazz etc – I am only too anxious to lease you out, when I get the music: I've made all the arrangements to do so, but you never send me the stuff – I could have sold for you the two older jazz tunes, I can sell the 'Dreaming Lips' stuff² & I will sell the Coronation March [*Crown Imperial*] – when I get the material. But you never send it! So I am powerless. Nor do you send me 'Under the Greenwood Tree'³ and 'Tell me where',⁴ which might make money for us all. You do realize, don't you, that if you leave us, you really must get down to the lesser works you owe us before you get going on works for other folk?

I'm unhappy about it all. Elgar left Novellos⁵ and was a failure: and I can't see, on this present contract, what you want to leave us for, except Allen's shop window. And there was a time when you did not think so highly of his advice!

Don't worry about the stage works – we'll do what you want about that, & follow the clause you quote.

No, I'm quite clear in my own mind that you would be foolish to desert us, & would make a wrong impression in many quarters: give lots of performing people the wrong idea.

If you feel you need a new start of some kind, let's have a new cover, a new format generally (you had that in [the] Façade semi-miniature [score]) and some new ideas. I'm not sure what you really want in your present mood of restlessness. Of one thing I'm quite sure: I can make you less restless than ever B & H can. And you must tell me what you really want. Don't forget and deny my work for you, William!

As for Thursday. I shall be at Cambridge in the morning but back at the office about 3 and I am of course going to the Phil. Will you stay the night with us here after the concert? Choose your time for a meeting, and your place, after 3. I'll be there. Do come and stay. Please ring me Monday or Tuesday.

I've put all this very mildly, in friendship.

Yours.

Hubert.

1 Some of Benjamin Britten's early works, including the cantata *A Boy was Born*, Op. 3, and *Holiday Diary*, Op. 5, for piano, had been published by Oxford University Press. Britten then joined Boosey & Hawkes.
2 Walton had been commissioned to compose the score for the film *Dreaming Lips*, and had evidently discussed with Foss the possibility of arranging a concert suite from this.
3 Song for voice and piano, composed by Walton in 1936, and arranged by him for unaccompanied voices in 1937.
4 'Tell me where is fancy bred?' (from Shakespeare's *The Merchant of Venice*) for soprano, tenor, three violins and piano, set by Walton in 1916.
5 Novello and Co. Ltd, London-based music publishers.

APPENDIX 2

While none of the music of Walton's planned opera about Carlo Gesualdo, Prince of Venosa, seems to have been written, there are quite extensive surviving drafts of its scenario and libretto in the Walton Archive in Ischia and in the British Library.

In 1941 and 1942 Walton and his librettist, Cecil Gray, were in regular correspondence as the opera's plot began to take shape. Set in Naples in the late sixteenth century, the story tells of the aristocratic prince and gifted amateur composer whose name survives today for two reasons. The daringly radical approach to chromatic harmony in Gesualdo's music was in some respects several centuries ahead of its time; and Gesualdo is known to have personally authorized the murder of his first wife, Donna Maria, and her lover, the Duke of Andria, for their adultery. Both aspects of the story had the makings of a powerful and colourful opera.

Along with his literary knowledge and expertise, Gray was himself a composer. His early exchanges with Walton included his ideas for the plot, outlined in some detail, and in entertainingly humorous style. As work on the project progressed, his own ideas about the kind of music called for in each scene of the opera became clearer. Perhaps too clear: Walton may well have begun increasingly to feel that he would not have a sufficiently free hand to compose his own music as he wanted. Instead, he may have thought, he would have to deal with what amounted to intelligent but excessive interference on Gray's part.

Whether for this reason or for others, he appears to have written down no music for the opera at all, or none whose whereabouts is currently known. But the vividness of his interest in the subject, in its early stages at least, is clear from the outline scenario that he himself drafted, in the summer of 1942 for the Prologue of the first of the opera's three acts. Handwritten in pencil on some lined leaves apparently taken from a school exercise book, this outline includes suggestions for the action on the right-hand pages and, on the left-hand ones, ideas for the music, as shown below. Walton also included a pencil sketch of a design for the Prologue's stage set. Several years later, his letters to Christopher Hassall during the creation of *Troilus and Cressida* show an equally sharp theatrical imagination. In the Walton Archive there is a draft of a kind similar to the one below, but more detailed, in which Walton sketched out ideas for both the music and the action of Act II of the later opera.

Prologo

Notes for the music	In the Piazza di San Severo. [Naples] morning
Prelude	[sketch design by Walton of a symmetrical stage set, with a *Palazzo* in the background and a house (marked *casa*) each side-stage right and left:]
Street music possibly a song sung back stage during back-chat of beggars against it	Stage empty save for crossing sweepers, beggars, old cronies & general neapolitan coming & going.
	Back-chat about how many soldi they will pick up during the wedding festivities – the new principessa a bit of a 'fast' one – nevertheless what a beauty – would'nt charge her much etc. in fact low "lazzarone" talk.
The music always gay & chattering will take on a more cynical & sniggering tone	Enter the aristocracy – their wives gossiping about Carlo – They never expected he'd marry – he was always so in love with music it's only the death of his brother that's forced him to do it – he must have an heir – he's so proud of his family – he's hardly the marrying sort, or what a poor girl really needs but she can surely find consolation elsewhere.
	The courtiers chip in – You know that this is her third husband although she's only 21 – They say her first died from a surfeit of love – that her second could'nt stand the pace & divorced her by his doctor's orders
Settling down to a more dignified measure for the Tasso[1] poem, perhaps unaccompanied. This may be a little	By this time the piazza will be completely filled by the crowd bar the space needed for the wedding cortège. The

1 Torquato Tasso (1544–1595) is considered the greatest Italian poet of the late Renaissance. Born in Sorrento in what was then the Kingdom of Naples, he was exiled in childhood with his family, but is known to have returned there intermittently to work in the 1590s. His most famous work was the heroic epic poem *Gerusalemme liberata* (1581). Tasso was one of the major roles in Gray's draft libretto for Walton's opera.

too static. – in which case one could have comments from the crowd about – "how beautifully they sing" – the great Tasso has written a poem. etc

Another Tasso poem here – a slow sarabande for the chorus, while the orchestra keeps up the excitement

cathedral bells, salutes, fireworks etc. can be heard in the distance & the chorus (of maidens?) from the balcony of the palazzo sing one of the Tasso poems.

With increasing excitement in the crowd, the wedding procession headed by monks, priests etc and finally with Carlo & Maria on a chariot followed by Don Giulio, the Duke of Andria members of the families etc.

Carlo throws gold to the lazzarone & the procession after proceeding round the stage enters the palace gate to cries of "Evviva", bells cannon etc – in fact, una vera festa napolitana!

Curtain.

The procession should look like one of those lovely 17th-cent marriage engravings.

This kind of rhythmical basis

[music notation: three lines of super-imposed rhythms]

APPENDIX 3

When Walton was approached in 1944 about his ideas for the future of Covent Garden's Royal Opera House in the post-war era to come, he responded with this meticulously worked-out memorandum. It is published here complete for the first time.

His original draft was typed out at Alice Wimborne's behest, with a near-immaculate accuracy that mirrors the clarity of his vision of the opera house's role. On the few occasions that Walton could ever be persuaded to write a formal article or document – a programme note, or a memorandum of this kind – he reverted to a conscientious, deliberate style which is quite different from the spontaneity of his letters. In this case it underscores how seriously he assessed the issues at stake.

A substantial degree of self-interest was involved. Walton had long been thinking of composing an opera of his own (witness his extensive work a few years earlier on the *Gesualdo* scenario that he and his librettist Cecil Gray had devised). His plea for a realistic level of support for potential composers of English operas was therefore not entirely altruistic, and was probably not intended to be so. But his awareness of what such a concept as 'the nation's post-war musical life' might mean in practical terms rings true. Whether his logistically intricate plan would in fact have worked is difficult to assess. But something very like it would have been at least feasible.

Some of the ideas are particularly striking. Late twentieth-century London heard endless discussion of the merits, or otherwise, of state funding of the arts. But the simplicity of Walton's solution to the problem of raising adequate and pre-dictable long-term funding – by adding a farthing a week to everyone's National Insurance payment – is a reminder of how absurdly little money is needed to fund a national opera house realistically, compared to other areas of governmental responsibility. It is also intriguing to see that Walton had alighted on the concept of parallel funding by the public and private sectors, several decades before this became a serious part of the nation's cultural agenda.

Walton's openness to the humane values of the wider world around him was not always one of his strong points. It is remarkable how far the spirit of his mem-orandum reaches out beyond the self-sufficient containment that was typical of his dealings with the classical music business in other respects. The contents of the document were no doubt worked out in conversations between Walton and Alice Wimborne, whose generous spirit seems to have been such an entirely good influ-ence on his own nature. Their joint vision of what Covent Garden could and

should offer modern audiences was a world apart from the genre of expensive
society entertainment that opera, in particular, has struggled for so long to develop
beyond (and to some extent still does). If Walton's plan had been implemented in
anything like its entirety, the story of opera, ballet and drama in post-war London
might well have been very different.

Memorandum

Projected Scheme, Royal Opera House, Covent Garden

PREAMBLE

The following suggestions (and it must be borne in mind that they are only
suggestions, unsolicited, but humbly and diffidently put forward) cover a far
wider field than that probably envisaged by Messrs. Boosey & Hawkes when
they, with enterprise and public spirit acquired a five-year lease on Covent
Garden and invited the co-operation of C.E.M.A.[1] and this committee with a
view to the production of opera and ballet.

It must, however, be emphasised, that this project, excellent and stimulating
as it undoubtedly will be, is nevertheless but a temporary solution, since it leaves
the entire question as to the future of opera in this country virtually unanswered.

The writer proposes nothing less than that Covent Garden should become the
permanent State Theatre for Opera, Ballet, concerts, *Drama and Films, with the
theatres of Sadlers Wells and the "Old Vic" as its satellites.

The ensuing sections deal with not only the potentialities of the proposal, but
also offer some suggestions as to how it might be financed, organised and brought
to fruition.

To this end, the Sadlers Wells opera and ballet Companies, as also that of the
"Old Vic" would be essential, and for the purposes of this memorandum, their
willing collaboration is assumed. None of them would lose their identity, and
each, when not at Covent Garden, would function either at its own theatre or on
tour (vide Sect. 2).

1. FINANCE

A. Interim Plan 1945–50

The funds already at the disposal of the Vic–Wells Companies would not be called
upon, on the other hand they would be supplemented from a Central Fund.

To acquire the means for this Central Fund, on the scale needed for financing

* These two arts are included with a view to the theatre remaining open for as
many weeks in the year as possible; and to give it wider appeal, as it could not
be run on opera and ballet the whole year round.

1 Council for the Encouragement of Music and the Arts. Later reconstituted as the Arts
Council of Great Britain.

such a project, involving as it would the provision for three theatres (vide Sect. 2), a double five-year plan might be initiated.

It is suggested that the committee invites some fifty leading industrial concerns to contribute or guarantee £500 per annum for five years, the Treasury on their part, contributing through C.E.M.A. £1 for £1 thus subscribed.

In this manner, £50,000 per annum as well as the contribution from Messrs. Boosey & Hawkes, which includes the lease of Covent Garden, would become available.

In addition, if required for a particular and outstanding production, a firm might be induced to sponsor it, in the manner of the American broadcasting systems, with an announcement (in the press) that "This opera is presented through the generosity of ——— & Co."

As some material recompense for the concerns thus subscribing, free advertisements in the programmes might be given, and some scheme of priority and reduced prices be introduced for the employees of these various concerns, such as existed for the Co[u]rtauld–Sargent concerts.

B. Permanent Plan 1950–

To make the proposed institution a permanent asset for the country, the following suggestion might be gone into, which, if feasible, though of wider scope, would be simple to work and painless to all!

After some scrutiny of the Social Insurance and Allied Services Report, it is noticeable that while providing for almost every contingency, there is no mention of any provision for the contentment and happiness of people through recreation and entertainment. Opera, ballet and the drama, under the auspices of the State could provide at least a part – perhaps an ever growing part – of this need.

On the grounds of not only health for the body but also for the mind, it is proposed that an emendation be made to the National Health Services bill, to the effect that one farthing per week be added to the weekly insurance contribution. Estimating 20 million as the number of insured people – a conservative estimate – over 1 million pounds per annum would be forthcoming by this means. This would be handed by the Ministry of Health to C.E.M.A. for distribution.

With such a sum and the funds already at the disposal of C.E.M.A., there would be adequate financial resources, not only for the National Theatre in London, but for others of a similar kind in the provincial centres. Also there would be the means to support music societies of all kinds in addition to the kindred arts of painting, sculpture and architecture throughout the country.

It is, of course, realised that this emendation would require the sanction of Parliament, but the individual contribution is so infinitesimal that it should not be an insuperable task for it to be passed by the House.

That it should be attached to the National Health Services bill may at first sight appear slightly eccentric, and the argument, perhaps, rather plausible. Nevertheless, it is not really so – a doctor or psychologist would confirm the good effect on a depressed patient, of the relaxation afforded by a visit to the opera or drama (though it must be conceded that the contrary might result if the performance was of a low standard).

That the Government recognise the need for such relaxation and entertainment is manifest by their support of the orchestral concerts (of the highest standard, both as regards programmes and performances) to the munition workers through E.N.S.A.[1] and the numerous other concerts organised by C.E.M.A.

This emendation, if passed, should come into operation on January 1st 1950 on the expiration of the scheme outlined in Section A.

Other indirect sources of income would be forthcoming from gramophone recordings and broadcasts (both sound and television) – nor would the box-office receipts be negligible though "Popular prices" should be the rule.

On the whole, the method indicated in the foregoing paragraphs seems preferable (to the writer at least) to awaiting the possible formation of a Ministry of Fine Arts, or the promotion of some special Opera and Entertainments Act.

The writer, realising on what dangerous ground he has been treading, apologises for his amateur intrusion into the province of the expert, although he is not without hope that there may be something practical in his suggestions.[*]

2. RESOURCES

For both opera and ballet Sadlers Wells would be the source of supply – for drama the "Old Vic".

The Sadlers Wells Opera Co. should be so built up as to possess (by 1950) enough personnel to form two companies, A. and B., so that the Companies A. and B. combined would be large enough for performances at Covent Garden. When the Company (A. & B.) is not at Covent Garden, A. company would be at Sadlers Wells, B. company on tour. For tours to the larger provincial centres with adequate stage facilities the combined companies could be sent.

The same plan would apply to the Sadlers Wells Ballet Company, though it would be necessary to retain a portion semi-permanently at Covent Garden for the operas in which ballet is an integral part.

Two permanent orchestras would be essential, the larger at Covent Garden, the smaller at Sadlers Wells, also a permanent chorus which could be divided between A. and B. companies when not at Covent Garden. The nucleus of a third orchestra might be required for the touring company (it could be augmented by instrumentalists from the towns visited).

For the drama at Covent Garden, any additional personnel needed by the "Old Vic" company could be obtained from outside sources. Films create no problems.

* The figures quoted in the above section are of necessity purely arbitrary; the sums involved may be larger or smaller, but that does not affect the proposals put forward.

1 Entertainments National Service Association.

The whole plan could be organised on some such schedule as is roughly sketched below:-

	Covent Garden.	Sadlers Wells.	The "Old Vic".
Jan.	S.W. Opera (A & B Cos.)	S.W. Ballet. A Co. (B on tour)	Plays.
Feb.	S.W. Ballet (")	S.W. Opera " (")	Plays.
March	O.V. Plays	All Cos. on tour.	Empty.
April	Empty for rehearsals. Films in the evening?	Empty.	Plays or Co. on tour.
May)	International Opera and	"	"
June)	Ballet Season.	"	"
July)	Mid-May – Mid July	"	"
Aug.)		Vacation.	Vacation.
)	Promenade Concerts.		
Sept.)		Rehearsals.	Rehearsals.
Oct.	O.V. Plays	S.W. Opera. B Co. (A on tour)	Empty.
Nov.	S.W. Opera (A & B Cos.)	S.W. Ballet " (")	Plays.
Dec.	S.W. Ballet (")	S.W. Opera " (")	"

This distribution is not quite evenly balanced, but this could be easily rectified by the expert co-ordinator.

It is, of course, realised that it will be impossible in the early post-war years, to adhere to the plan outlined in the preceding paragraphs, until the all-round standard of the Sadlers Wells Companies (and this applies particularly to the opera company) is raised to a level comparable with any. The question of how this is to be achieved, though of immediate concern, should be gone into by the opera and ballet executive committees (vide Sect. 3) and not here.

Provisionally, use will have to be made of whatever material comes to hand, whether from this country or overseas, and foreign opera and ballet companies should be invited "en bloc".

However, the substance of the plan remains, and it is the goal to be aimed at, and should be attainable within three to four years.

3. ADMINISTRATION

The above heading is not strictly relevant to this memorandum, beyond noting that three executive committees would be formed to deal with the departments of opera, ballet, drama and films respectively. Their functions need not be gone into.

However, the appointment of Music Director is of paramount importance. One has only to reflect that the quality and reputation of the State run opera houses of Milan and Vienna was largely due to their having in command

[476]

conductors of the calibre of Toscanini and Mahler; and it would seem that Sir Thomas Beecham, almost alone amongst English conductors, could co-ordinate and provide the necessary stimulus and inspiration that an organisation of this conception would demand. Therefore it is suggested that on his return to England he should be asked to reconsider his former refusal to accept the post[1] (that is, of course, if anything should take shape as a result of this memorandum).

4. GENERAL POLICY

All opera to be sung in English, with the exception of the International Season, which, on the whole, it would be expedient to retain at any rate for some years. Not only would it be useful as a yard-stick by which to measure our own achievements, it would also supply the necessary variation and afford the opportunity of hearing opera in its original idiom, besides satisfying that element which can only enjoy opera in some language it barely understands. The precedent of inviting foreign companies (vide Sect. 2) should, in fact, be continued from time to time.

The repertoire should be as catholic as is consistent with the resources available. Contemporary opera should not be allowed to suffer the neglect it has in the past, while comic opera should have a large part and it might be that Sadlers Wells Theatre became eventually a counterpart of the Paris Opéra-Comique.

With the view to creating an English school of opera in all aspects, particular regard should be reserved for operas by our own composers. The worthy few already existing would obtain, it is to be hoped, a permanent place in the repertoire as soon as is feasible.

To momentarily divagate, the rarity of English operas is partly due to the conditions existing in the past – to find their works fobbed off with, at most, a half-dozen performances was not exactly encouraging to the composers. Of their ability to compose operas the writer has no doubt, for from early times to the present day English composers have excelled in the setting of words. Though this is not sufficient in itself the dramatic instinct might surely emerge if given adequate opportunity.

Composers, therefore, should be encouraged to write new operas, and as some aid to the impecunious composer whose problem is how to obtain both a livelihood and the necessary leisure in which to compose, an "advance on royalties" scheme could be instituted to enable him to achieve this.

What has been said of opera applies in greater or lesser degree also to Ballet.

For the drama the plays requiring the facilities Covent Garden could supply, particularly those with incidental music ("A Midsummer Night's Dream" for example) should be the general rule.

No effort or expense should be spared to make the various productions of the highest standard. The best casts and scenic artists should be employed and while no undue extravagance would be justified, no tinge of meanness or parsimony should be allowed to creep in.

1 During the Second World War Beecham had been conducting in America. After returning to England, he founded the Royal Philharmonic Orchestra in 1946.

Films would occupy the smallest place in the scheme, and showings confined to the type of those of the pre-War Film Society and the Museum of Modern Art in New York. There exists an interested and growing audience for this kind of showing.

Concerts, given chiefly by outside orchestras, could make use of the permanent chorus. A Covent Garden Choral Society might eventually be formed to supplement this for such occasions.

Until the "Henry Wood Hall" is built the "Proms" would find a "temporary home" at Covent Garden in preference to the Albert Hall.[1]

A restaurant and café should be provided, as the majority of the "new audience" would attend the performances on their way from work.

It might be that eventually Covent Garden could be acquired for the nation, perhaps by public subscription with help from the Government.[2]

5. POLITICAL AND SOCIAL REPERCUSSIONS

If this plan were to come to fruition, its announcement might have considerable propaganda value, both at home – and perhaps more so – abroad. The stigma of "a land without music", in spite of many manifestations to the contrary, still persists, and would be effectively dispelled.

The interchange of companies from foreign lands with those of our own (when raised to exportable standards) would make for goodwill and mutual understanding.

It would mean the virtual creation of a new industry at a time it is most needed, and when ultimately expanded to the provincial centres, would create employment, directly and indirectly, for some thousands of people. It would also alleviate the demobilisation problems for musicians now in the forces, especially amongst orchestral instrumentalists.

The standards of tuition in the colleges of music would automatically be raised, with, it might be hoped, a consequent influx of students from overseas – it would also play its part in the attraction of foreign visitors.

It is possible that the post-War years may prove as irksome as those of the War, and the State Theatre could provide distraction to a not inconsiderable proportion of a maybe slightly disgruntled populace.

To take a long-term view, with the eventual advent of a forty, or even a thirty hour week, people having more leisure and better education will be inclined for higher standards in entertainment than the commercial theatre might normally supply. The phenomenon of the new and vast audience for music is common

1 The destruction of the much loved, acoustically fine Queen's Hall by German bombing in 1941 had left a void in London's musical life which to this day has not been satisfactorily filled. The 'Henry Wood Hall' was not built, and the Royal Albert Hall had to suffice as the city's main concert hall until the Royal Festival Hall was constructed for the Festival of Britain in 1951.

2 This was achieved in 1946 with the formation of the Covent Garden Opera Company, subsidised by the newly created Arts Council of Great Britain.

knowledge, and it cannot be doubted that it would show equal, if not more enthusiasm for opera and State Theatre, opera being virtually unknown to the younger generation.

In conclusion, the fact that opera has had a distinctly chequered career in this country should not invalidate the preceding paragraph. On the contrary, as a consequence of the conditions under which opera was formerly produced, it could of necessity only appeal to and reach a fraction of the population. If the opera was at "Popular Prices" the performances were as a rule inadequate, and the former International Season at Covent Garden, though of a high standard, was beyond the pocket of all except a well-to-do minority. Moreover, it was limited to a London audience.

Although the plan outlined above may have other limitations, it will at least avoid a repetition of those mentioned, in that the prices would be low, the standard high, and the touring companies sent to the provincial centres (until such time as they possessed their own opera and drama theatres) would bring performances of the three categories within the reach of all.

While there is everything to be said for the scheme at present in being (and it fits in admirably with the plan as conceived in these pages) all the same, taken by itself, to a certain extent it harks back unavoidably to the regimes of the inter-war years at Covent Garden. It should be regarded as a starting point whence it would lead to, and link up with, some more enduring plan of wider scope.

The constant changes of direction and management at Covent Garden during those years led nowhere; and only the stabilisation and continuity of management which the Government alone is capable of sustaining financially can provide the country with a State Theatre for opera, ballet and drama (though by no means necessarily on the lines suggested).

Owing to a concatenation of propitious circumstances, there has never been such an opportunity as the present to start afresh on a solid foundation, with collective, rather than individual effort, and so provide "opera for the people, by the people".

Aug 8th 1944

CHRONOLOGY

1902   29 March: William Turner Walton is born at 93 Werneth Hall Road, Oldham, Lancashire, to Charles Alexander Walton and Louisa Maria (née Turner).

1908   Sings in the local church choir directed by his father. Starts to learn piano, organ and violin.

1912   Charles Walton notices a newspaper advertisement for choral scholarships at Christ Church College, Oxford. Walton is accepted, and moves from school in Oldham, to become a boarder at Christ Church Cathedral Choir House.

1916   First known compositions, performed in Christ Church Cathedral, include a Fantasia and a Chorale Prelude for organ and the motet *Drop, Drop, Slow Tears*. Dr H. G. Ley, Organist at Christ Church, and Dr Thomas Strong, Dean of the College, arrange for these to be seen by the influential English composer Hubert Parry, Professor at London's Royal College of Music. Walton's voice breaks; Strong arranges for him to stay on at the choir school.

1917   June: meets Parry. Continues musical studies at Christ Church.

1918   With Strong's support and influence, enters Christ Church College as an undergraduate, funded by an exhibition scholarship for two years. Passes first part of B.Mus. examination. Composes early version of Piano Quartet.

1919   At Oxford meets Sacheverell Sitwell, Siegfried Sassoon, and Sacheverell's siblings, Edith and Osbert. The Sitwell family invites Walton to London during vacations. There he begins to meet major figures in the musical world: Ernest Ansermet, Sergei Diaghilev, Eugene Goossens, Igor Stravinsky. Fails general Responsions examination for third time. Composes String Quartet.

1920   Now living with the Sitwell family at 2 Carlyle Square, Kensington, London. Visits Italy for the first time with the Sitwells; his trip is paid for by Dr Strong. Passes second part of B.Mus. examination. Renewal of exhibition scholarship 'postponed' (permanently, as it turns out) by the College governors. Begins work on overture *Dr Syntax*.

1921   Begins work on *Façade* with Edith Sitwell. String Quartet performed privately. Piano Quartet completed.

1922   24 January: first version of *Façade* performed privately at 2 Carlyle Square. Begins work on *Fantasia concertante*.

1923   12 June: *Façade* is performed publicly, and controversially, at London's Aeolian Hall.
August: Walton visits inaugural festival of International Society for Contemporary Music (ISCM) in Salzburg for performance of revised version of his String Quartet. Meets Alban Berg and Arnold Schoenberg.

1924   Begins overture *Portsmouth Point*.

1925   Completes *Portsmouth Point*, dedicating it to Siegfried Sassoon.

1926   22 June: *Portsmouth Point* performed at ISCM festival in Zurich. Thanks to initial contact arranged by Siegfried Sassoon, *Portsmouth Point* is accepted for publication by Oxford University Press, the beginning of a lifelong association. Starts work on *Sinfonia concertante*.
3 December: conducts *Façade* Suite No. 1 at Lyceum Theatre, London.

1927   Completes *Sinfonia concertante*.

1928   5 January: *Sinfonia concertante* performed at London's Queen's Hall, conducted by Ernest Ansermet.
Meets Sir Thomas Beecham, who suggests a Viola Concerto for Lionel Tertis.

1929   Works on Viola Concerto during winter in Amalfi with the Sitwells. Meets and falls in love with Baroness Imma von Doernberg. Tertis turns down the Concerto.
3 October: Paul Hindemith gives the première of the Concerto at the Queen's Hall, conducted by Walton.

1930   Begins *Belshazzar's Feast* in Amalfi during the winter. Further work on this during the summer and autumn in England.

1931   Moves to Ascona, Switzerland to live with Imma von Doernberg. Completes *Belshazzar's Feast*.
8 October: triumphant première of *Belshazzar's Feast* at Leeds Festival. Starts work on a Symphony.

1932   Receives lifetime annuity in the will of Elizabeth Courtauld. Continues to work on Symphony No. 1 in Ascona.

1933   Further work on Symphony No. 1.
10 June: *Belshazzar's Feast* performed at ISCM Festival in Amsterdam.

1934   Runs into major creative difficulties over completion of Symphony No. 1. Composes first film score, *Escape Me Never*.
3 December: first three movements only of Symphony No. 1 performed at the Queen's Hall, conducted by Sir Hamilton Harty.

1935   Ends relationship with Imma von Doernberg. Begins relationship with Alice, Viscountess Wimborne, causing hiatus in friendship with the Sitwells and their circle. Completes Symphony No. 1, and dedicates it to Imma von Doernberg. Buys house in South Eaton Place, Belgravia, with mortgage financed by fee and royalties for *Escape Me Never*.
6 November: Symphony No. 1 performed complete at Queen's Hall, again conducted by Harty.

1936   Meets Laurence Olivier during work on score for film *As You Like It*. Meets Jascha Heifetz (in London), who commissions a Violin Concerto.

1937   Composes *Crown Imperial* for Coronation of King George VI at Westminster Abbey, 12 May.
28 July: meets Benjamin Britten.
Arranges *Façade* Suite No. 2 for orchestra.
December: enters London clinic for hernia operation.

1938   January: convalesces with Alice Wimborne in Ravello on the Amalfi coast. Stays there until June, working on Violin Concerto. Further work on this at Ashby St Ledgers, Alice's country home near Rugby.

1939   Death of Viscount Wimborne. Walton and Alice Wimborne now live together at Ashby St Ledgers or at Lowndes Cottage in Kensington.
May: visits US with Alice to work with Heifetz on solo part of Violin Concerto.
2 June: completes work on Violin Concerto, and returns to England.
3 September: Second World War begins.
7 December: Heifetz premières Violin Concerto in Cleveland, Ohio.

1940   Composes film score *Major Barbara*, and comedy overture *Scapino* for the Chicago Symphony Orchestra.

1941   3 April: *Scapino* performed in Chicago.
Walton's London house in South Eaton Place is destroyed by bombing in the Blitz. Works on various film scores and theatre projects. Also plans opera on the life of Carlo Gesualdo, Prince of Venosa, with Cecil Gray as librettist.

1942   Gesualdo opera project abandoned. Composes film scores *The First of the Few* and *Went the Day Well?*

1943   Begins work on score for *Henry V*, starring and directed by Laurence Olivier.

1944   12 July: completes *Henry V*.
August: drafts memorandum on the post-war future of the Royal Opera House, Covent Garden.

1945   Begins String Quartet in A minor, originally projected in 1939.
June: attends one of the first performances of Britten's opera *Peter Grimes* at Sadler's Wells Theatre.

1946   Joins the board of the newly established Covent Garden Opera Trust.
        June: holiday in Ascona with Alice Wimborne.

1947   The BBC commissions Walton to compose an opera.
        March: meets Christopher Hassall (through Alice Wimborne), and dis-
        cusses ideas for an opera with Hassall as librettist.
        4 May: première of String Quartet in A minor, in BBC broadcast.
        July: decides on *Troilus and Cressida* as opera subject.
        September: Walton and Alice are in Lucerne, on the way to a holiday
        in Capri, when Alice becomes ill with cancer and enters a clinic. Diana
        Gould commissions Violin Sonata for her future husband, Yehudi
        Menuhin, to provide funds for Alice's treatment.
        October: Walton and Alice return to England. Walton composes film
        score of *Hamlet*.

1948   19 April: death of Alice Wimborne.
        Walton resumes work on and completes Violin Sonata.
        July: Hassall submits first version of *Troilus and Cressida* libretto.
        September: Walton travels to Buenos Aires to attend international confer-
        ence of the Performing Right Society as British representative. Meets
        Susana Gil Passo.
        13 December: marries Susana Gil Passo in Buenos Aires.

1949   February: the Waltons return to England.
        Rapprochement with the Sitwells, to whom Walton introduces his wife.
        30 September: Yehudi Menuhin and Louis Kentner première Violin
        Sonata in Zurich.
        October: the Waltons drive across Europe to Italy and move into the
        Convento San Francesco on the island of Ischia in the Bay of Naples.
        Walton begins serious work on *Troilus and Cressida*.

1950   Works on *Troilus and Cressida*, mainly in Ischia.
        June: conducts recording of Violin Concerto with Heifetz in London.

1951   1 January: awarded knighthood.
        March: moves from Convento San Francesco to nearby Casa Cirillo in
        Ischia.
        Continues work on *Troilus and Cressida*.

1952   Further work on *Troilus and Cressida*. Commissioned to compose
        Coronation Te Deum and march *Orb and Sceptre* for the Coronation of
        Queen Elizabeth II.

1953   May and June: visits London for Coronation, and to hear performance
        of Britten's opera *Gloriana* at the Royal Opera House.
        Resumes work on *Troilus and Cressida*.

1954   13 September: completes *Troilus and Cressida*, dedicating it to Susana
        Walton.

Travels to London for rehearsals at the Royal Opera House.
3 December: première of *Troilus and Cressida*.

1955 Composes film score of *Richard III*, starring and directed by Laurence Olivier.
7 October: travels to San Francisco for the US première of *Troilus and Cressida*.
Begins work on a Cello Concerto commissioned by Gregor Piatigorsky.

1956 12 January: Italian première of *Troilus and Cressida* at La Scala, Milan.
Completes *Johannesburg Festival Overture* and Cello Concerto.

1957 17 January: the Waltons are both injured in a motor accident outside Rome, on the way to London for the Cello Concerto's British première (13 February); Walton is hospitalized in Rome with broken hip.
25 January: Piatigorsky gives the Concerto's world première in Boston.
April: back in Ischia, Walton starts work on *Partita* for the Cleveland Orchestra.
October: completes *Partita*.
Begins a Second Symphony.

1958 30 January: George Szell conducts *Partita* in Cleveland.
Walton continues work on Second Symphony.

1959 Composes *Anon. in Love* for tenor and guitar, for Peter Pears and Julian Bream. Moves from Casa Cirillo to nearby San Felice in Ischia.

1960 Completes Second Symphony.
2 September: attends première of Second Symphony at the Edinburgh Festival.

1961 February: visits New York to hear George Szell and Cleveland Orchestra perform Second Symphony in Carnegie Hall.
22 April: travels to Oldham, where he is made an Honorary Freeman.
The Waltons decide to sell Lowndes Cottage in order to finance the purchase of some land near San Felice, where they plan to build a larger house, La Mortella ('The Myrtle') and create a substantial garden; work starts on this in November.
24 November: Walton visits Huddersfield Festival for première of *Gloria*.

1962 Composes *A Song for the Lord Mayor's Table* for Elisabeth Schwarzkopf and Gerald Moore.
August: moves from San Felice into La Mortella.
Begins *Variations on a Theme by Hindemith*.

1963 8 March: conducts première of *Variations on a Theme by Hindemith* at London's Royal Festival Hall.
Revises *Troilus and Cressida* for revival performances at the Royal Opera, beginning 23 April.
July: visits Israel to conduct performances of *Belshazzar's Feast*.

1964 February to May: undertakes major tour of New Zealand and Australia, conducting his own works.
February: visits his sister, Nora Donnelly, and her family in New Zealand.
September: abandons work on new orchestral piece commissioned by George Szell.

1965 Begins *The Bear*, to a libretto by Paul Dehn.
December: visiting London, is diagnosed with lung cancer.

1966 10 January: operation to remove tumour.
February: returns to Ischia to work on *The Bear*.
June: visits Aldeburgh Festival.
August: visits Salzburg Festival for the world première of Hans Werner Henze's opera *The Bassarids*.
September: medical check-up in London reveals return of cancer in shoulder area. Has cobalt ray treatment.
November: returns to Ischia.

1967 Cancer does not recur.
30 April: completes *The Bear*.
3 June: attends first performance of *The Bear* at Aldeburgh Festival.
September: visits Expo '67 in Montreal for first overseas performance of *The Bear*.
Early, abortive attempts to compose *Capriccio burlesco*.
November: awarded Order of Merit by Queen Elizabeth II.

1968 May: major row with BBC over a planned television documentary's dismissal of Walton's post-war works. Protests to BBC TV's Head of Music, John Culshaw, who agrees to change the film's content and emphasis. Walton accepts commission to compose score for film *The Battle of Britain*, featuring Laurence Olivier.
5 September: completes *Capriccio burlesco*.
7 December: attends première of *Capriccio burlesco* by New York Philharmonic under André Kostelanetz in Lincoln Center.

1969 February to April: attends recording sessions for *The Battle of Britain*, conducting the March for the title credits; Malcolm Arnold conducts the other sections.
June: is informed by a newspaper reporter in a telephone call from England that United Artists has rejected his score.
15 September: *The Battle of Britain* is premièred with new score by Ron Goodwin, retaining only Walton's 'Battle in the Air' sequence; some later prints also retain the March during the final credits.
Completes *Improvisations on an Impromptu of Benjamin Britten* for San Francisco Symphony Orchestra, and his last film score, *The Three Sisters*, directed by Laurence Olivier.

1970   Considers, but turns down offer of film score for *Upon This Rock*.
June: travels to London for television recording of *The Bear*, and to
Aldeburgh Festival for UK première of *Improvisations*.

1971   April: joins the London Symphony Orchestra and André Previn on a tour
of the Soviet Union, where they perform his First Symphony.
Autumn: rescores much of his String Quartet in A minor (incorporating
substantial revision of first movement) as *Sonata for Strings*.
November: Malcolm Arnold visits Ischia and contributes to rescoring of
the finale of *Sonata for Strings*.
Walton begins to consider revising *Troilus and Cressida* for a planned
Royal Opera revival, with the soprano role of Cressida transposed and
amended for mezzo-soprano Janet Baker.

1972   Extensive seventieth birthday celebrations in UK include dinner at 10
Downing Street on 29 March, hosted by Prime Minister Edward Heath,
with Queen Elizabeth the Queen Mother among the guests. Among the
music performed are *Façade* extracts and Schubert's Piano Trio in B♭.
Autumn: begins work on a Third Symphony.

1973   12 June: conducts fiftieth anniversary public performance of *Façade* in
Aeolian Hall, London (his last conducting appearance).
Starts revision of early Piano Quartet.
November: correspondence indicates that he has destroyed existing
material of Third Symphony.

1974   Starts again on Third Symphony, sending copy of opening bars to André
Previn.
Completes *Cantico del Sole*, revision of Piano Quartet and, at
Piatigorsky's request, a new ending (never performed) for Cello
Concerto. Continues revision of *Troilus and Cressida*. Turns down
commission to mark 250th anniversary of Three Choirs Festival.
October: visits London and hears Henze's *The Bassarids* at English
National Opera.

1975   Attempts to work on *Adagio ed Allegro Festivo* for the Royal Festival
Hall's twenty-fifth anniversary, and on Third Symphony.
May onwards: increasing signs of declining health.
Continues revision of *Troilus and Cressida*.
September: abandons *Adagio ed Allegro Festivo*, and instead starts to
arrange *Five Bagatelles* for guitar as orchestral *Varii capricci*.

1976   Final work on revision of *Troilus and Cressida*.
November: travels to London for rehearsals at the Royal Opera.
Further signs of illness and exhaustion.
12 November: first of six performances of *Troilus and Cressida*.
30 November: collapses after final performance.
December: returns to Ischia and begins slow and only partial recovery.

1977   Attends seventy-fifth birthday celebrations in London, including the first performance for over fifty years of formerly rejected numbers from *Façade*. Starts to revise these as *Façade 2*.
November: attends seventy-fifth anniversary lunch for members of the Order of Merit at Buckingham Palace, hosted by Queen Elizabeth II.

1978   Attempts to resume work on Third Symphony, in three-movement form with *Allegretto* first movement, *Scherzo diabolico* second movement and slow finale. These sketches also appear subsequently to have been destroyed.

1979   June: attends Aldeburgh Festival for first performance of *Façade 2*.
Starts work on solo cello *Passacaglia* for Rostropovich. Abandons projected *Three Odes of Horace* for chorus, commissioned by Llandaff Festival.

1980   Completes *Passacaglia* and brass band arrangement of *The First Shoot*.

1981   Despite cataracts in both eyes, works on orchestral *Prologo e Fantasia*, also for Rostropovich.

1982   Completion of Tony Palmer's television film documentary on Walton, *At the Haunted End of the Day*. Visits London for eightieth birthday celebrations.
20 February and 16 March: attends premières in Royal Festival Hall of *Prologo e Fantasia* and *Passacaglia*.
29 March: attends eightieth birthday concert at Royal Festival Hall to hear Violin Concerto and *Belshazzar's Feast*.
1 April: attends lunch for members of the Order of Merit, hosted by the Queen at Windsor Castle.
Becomes ill at Savoy Hotel, is taken into intensive care. Later in April is able to return to Ischia for local birthday celebrations.
July: the Waltons appear in Tony Palmer's film *Wagner*.
August: Walton travels to London for operation to remove cataracts; afterwards is in intensive care again, but recovers, and returns to Ischia.
October: composes four bars of a projected *Duettino* for oboe and violin, for the two children of Stewart Craggs.
Starts work on a choral motet.
Spends Christmas at Ravello.

1983   Composes new extended ending to *Varii capricci*, for a ballet by Sir Frederick Ashton. Considers working on a *Stabat Mater* setting.
8 March: dies at La Mortella. His body is cremated in Florence, and his ashes are buried at La Mortella.
20 July: a memorial stone is unveiled in Westminster Abbey.

LIST OF WORKS

All writers on Walton today owe a considerable debt to Stewart Craggs's many years of meticulous compilation of material relating to Walton's life, works, and correspondence. The following list draws mainly on that in Craggs's *William Walton: A Source Book* (Scolar Press, 1993), which catalogues Walton's works in extensive detail.

The list below is a simple one, intended as no more than an essential guide to the references to Walton's music that occur in his own correspondence. Every independent work that Walton is known to have composed, completely or partially, is included, apart from a few, mostly very early ones that appear long since to have vanished, and whose past existence is known only from a single reference in Walton's letters of the time. Arrangements not worked on by Walton himself in his lifetime are omitted, such as the several suites later assembled from Walton's film scores and theatre and incidental music by Christopher Palmer and others. Their exclusion here is in no way intended to reflect adversely on their quality or artistic validity. Muir Mathieson's arrangements of Walton's music for *Henry V* and *Richard III* are mentioned, however; Walton would have had a say, at least, in the evolution of these.

Dates refer to the period during which, according to evidence in Walton's letters and elsewhere, he was working on the composition in question. Where a single year is given, this denotes either a work written during that year only or, sometimes, the date of completion of a larger work where the point at which it was begun is unclear.

Chorale Prelude on 'Wheatley'   1916
for organ
(unpublished)

The Forsaken Merman   1916
Cantata for soprano, tenor, double women's chorus and orchestra
Text: Matthew Arnold
(unpublished)

Tell Me Where Is Fancy Bred   1916
for soprano and tenor, 3 violins and piano
Text: Shakespeare, from *The Merchant of Venice*
(unpublished)

A Litany ('Drop, Drop, Slow Tears') 1916
for unaccompanied mixed chorus
revised 1930
Text: Phineas Fletcher

Valse in C minor 1917
for solo piano
(unpublished)

'The Winds' 1918
for voice and piano
First performances: probably 1920, 34 Queen Anne's Gate, London (private);
30 October 1929, Aeolian Hall, London, Odette de Foras (soprano), Gordon
Bryan (piano) (public)

Three Swinburne Songs 1918
for voice and piano
(unpublished)

Piano Quartet 1918–21
revised 1973–74
First performance: 19 September 1924, Liverpool, McCullagh String Quartet,
J. E. Wallace (piano)

String Quartet (No. 1) 1919
revised 1921–22 (with *Scherzo* movement added)
First performances: 4 March 1921, 19 Berners Street, London, Pennington String
Quartet (private); 5 July 1923, Royal College of Music, London, McCullagh
String Quartet (revised version)

'Tritons' 1920
for voice and piano
Text: William Drummond
First performance: 30 October 1929, Aeolian Hall, London, Odette de Foras
(soprano), Gordon Bryan (piano)

The Passionate Shepherd 1920
for tenor and ten solo instruments
Text: Christopher Marlowe
(unpublished)

Dr Syntax 1920–21
Pedagogic overture
(Unperformed and now apparently lost, apart from the title page; also planned
to be expanded into a one-act ballet, to a scenario by Sacheverell Sitwell and
Wyndham Lewis)

Façade   1921–22
An Entertainment for reciter and instrumentalists
variously revised and reworked 1922–28; definitive version 1942, published 1951
Texts: Edith Sitwell
First performances: 24 January 1922, 2 Carlyle Square, London, Edith Sitwell
(reciter), ensemble conducted by William Walton (private); 12 June 1923,
Aeolian Hall, London, Edith Sitwell (reciter), ensemble conducted by William
Walton (public); 27 April 1926, New Chenil Galleries, London, Neil Porter
(reciter), ensemble conducted by William Walton (first 1926 revision); 29 June
1926, New Chenil Galleries, London, Neil Porter (reciter), ensemble conducted
by William Walton (second 1926 revision); 14 September 1928, Siena (ISCM
Festival), Constant Lambert (reciter), ensemble conducted by William Walton
(1928 revision); 29 May 1942, Aeolian Hall, London, Constant Lambert
(reciter), ensemble conducted by William Walton (1942 definitive version)

Toccata in A minor   1922–23
for violin and piano
First performances: 12 May 1925, 6 Queen Square, London, K. Goldsmith
(violin), Angus Morrison (piano) (private); 23 March 1997, Werneth Park Music
Rooms, Oldham, Paul Barritt (violin), Catherine Edwards (piano) (public)

Fantasia concertante   1922–23
for two pianos, jazz band and orchestra
(unpublished and unperformed; score now lost)

Bucolic Comedies   1923–24
Arranged from *Façade* for voice and six instruments
revised 1931–32 as the *Three Songs* for voice and piano
Texts: Edith Sitwell
(unpublished)

A Son of Heaven   1924–25
Incidental music for the play by Lytton Strachey
First performance: 12 July 1925, Scala Theatre, London, conducted by William
Walton

Portsmouth Point   1924–25
Overture for orchestra, after an etching by Thomas Rowlandson
First performances: 22 June 1926, Tonhalle, Zurich, Switzerland (ISCM
Festival), Tonhalle Orchestra, conducted by Volkmar Andreae; 28 June 1926,
His Majesty's Theatre, London, Orchestra of Ballets Russes, conducted by
Eugene Goossens (UK)

Siesta   1926
for small orchestra
First performance: 24 November 1926, Aeolian Hall, London, Aeolian Hall
Chamber Orchestra, conducted by William Walton

Façade Suite No. 1   1926
Arranged for orchestra
First performance: 3 December 1926, Lyceum Theatre, London, Lyceum Theatre
Orchestra, conducted by William Walton
('Valse' arranged for solo piano, 1928)

Sinfonia concertante   1926–27
for orchestra with piano obbligato
revised 1943
First performance: 5 January 1928, Queen's Hall, London, York Bowen (piano),
Royal Philharmonic Society Orchestra, conducted by Ernest Ansermet

Viola Concerto   1928–29
revised 1936, 1961
First performance: 3 October 1929, Queen's Hall, London, Paul Hindemith
(viola), Queen's Hall Orchestra, conducted by William Walton

Belshazzar's Feast   1930–31
Oratorio (cantata) for baritone, double mixed chorus, orchestra and two brass
ensembles
Text: from the Old Testament, selected by Osbert Sitwell
First performance: 8 October 1931, Leeds Town Hall, Dennis Noble (baritone),
Leeds Festival Chorus, London Symphony Orchestra, conducted by Malcolm
Sargent

'Make We Joy Now in This Fest'   1931
Carol for unaccompanied mixed chorus

Chorale Prelude on *Herzlich thut mich verlangen* (J. S. Bach)   1931
Arranged for piano
First performance: 17 October 1932, London, Queen's Hall, Harriet Cohen
(piano)

Three Songs   1931–32
Arranged from *Façade* for voice and piano
Texts: Edith Sitwell
First performance: 10 October 1932, Wigmore Hall, London, Dora Stevens
(soprano), Hubert Foss (piano)

Escape Me Never   1934
Music for the film
Release: 14 October 1935, London
(Ballet music arranged for solo piano, 1935)

The Boy David   1935
Incidental music for the play by J. M. Barrie
First Performance: 21 November 1936, King's Theatre, Edinburgh

LIST OF WORKS

Symphony No. 1   1931–35
First performances: 3 December 1934, Queen's Hall, London, London
Symphony Orchestra, conducted by Sir Hamilton Harty (first three movements
only); 6 November 1935, Queen's Hall, London, BBC Symphony Orchestra,
conducted by Sir Hamilton Harty (complete, including Finale)

The First Shoot   1935
Ballet scene in *Follow the Sun* (revue by C. B. Cochran)
Scenario: Osbert Sitwell
Choreography: Frederick Ashton
First performance: 23 December 1935, Opera House, Manchester, conducted by
Frank Collinson
(See also *The First Shoot*, 1979–80)

As You Like It   1936
Music for the film of Shakespeare's play
Release: 3 September 1936, London
('Under the Greenwood Tree', for voice or unison voices and piano, not included
in the film and published separately in 1937)

Crown Imperial   1937
Coronation march for orchestra
First performances: 16 April 1937, Kingsway Hall, London, BBC Symphony
Orchestra, conducted by Adrian Boult (recording); 12 May 1937, Westminster
Abbey, London, Coronation Orchestra, conducted by Adrian Boult (Coronation
of King George VI and Queen Elizabeth)

In Honour of the City of London   1937
Cantata for mixed chorus and orchestra
Text: William Dunbar
First performance: 6 October 1937, Leeds Town Hall, Leeds Festival Chorus,
London Philharmonic Orchestra, conducted by Malcolm Sargent

Dreaming Lips   1937
Music for the film
Release: 11 October 1937, London

Façade Suite No. 2   1937
Arranged for orchestra
First performance: 20 March 1938, Carnegie Hall, New York, US, Philharmonic-
Symphony Orchestra of New York, conducted by John Barbirolli

A Stolen Life   1938
Music for the film
Release: 18 January 1939, London

Set Me as a Seal upon Thine Heart   1938
Anthem for unaccompanied mixed chorus
Text: from The Song of Solomon
First performance: 22 November 1938, St Mary Abbots Church, London,
St Mary Abbots Church Choir, conducted by F. G. Shuttleworth

Violin Concerto   1938–39
revised 1943
First performances: 7 December 1939, Cleveland, Ohio, US, Jascha Heifetz
(violin), Cleveland Orchestra, conducted by Artur Rodzinski; 1 November 1941,
Royal Albert Hall, London, Henry Holst (violin), London Philharmonic
Orchestra, conducted by William Walton (UK)

The Wise Virgins   1939–40
Ballet in one act to music from cantatas by J. S. Bach, selected and arranged by
Constant Lambert and orchestrated by Walton
Choreography: Frederick Ashton
First performance: 24 April 1940, Sadler's Wells Theatre, London, conducted by
Constant Lambert
Suite arranged from the ballet, 1939–40
First performance: 24 July 1940, Sadler's Wells Orchestra, conducted by William
Walton (probably recording)

Duets for Children   1940
for piano duet
First performance (probable): 7 May 1940, Columbia Gramophone Company
studio, London, Ilona Kabos, Louis Kentner (piano duet)
Arranged as *Music for Children* for orchestra, 1940
First performance: 16 February 1941, Queen's Hall, London, London
Philharmonic Orchestra, conducted by Basil Cameron

Major Barbara   1940
Music for the film
Releases: 21 March 1941, Nassau, Bahamas; 4 August 1941, London (UK)

Scapino   1940
Comedy overture for orchestra, after an etching from Callot's *Balli di Sfessania*
revised 1950
First performances: 3 April 1941, Orchestra Hall, Chicago, US, Chicago
Symphony Orchestra, conducted by Frederick Stock; 12 November 1941, Corn
Exchange, Bedford, BBC Symphony Orchestra, conducted by William Walton
(UK)

Next of Kin   1941
Music for the film
Release: January 1942, London (private screening); 15 May 1942, London

Macbeth   1941–42
Incidental music for Shakespeare's play
First performance: 16 January 1942, Opera House, Manchester, London
Philharmonic Orchestra, conducted by Ernest Irving (pre-recording for subsequent relay in the theatre)

The Foreman Went to France   1941–42
Music for the film
Release: 13 April 1942, London

The First of the Few   1942
Music for the film
Release: 20 August 1942, London
Selected and arranged for orchestra as *Prelude and Fugue ('The Spitfire')*, 1942
First performance: 2 January 1943, Philharmonic Hall, Liverpool, Liverpool
Philharmonic Orchestra, conducted by William Walton

Christopher Columbus   1942
Incidental music for the radio play by Louis MacNeice
First performance: 12 October 1942, Bedford, Joan Lennard (soprano),
Bradbridge White (tenor), George Elliott (guitar), BBC Chorus and Symphony
Orchestra, conducted by Adrian Boult (BBC broadcast)
('Beatriz's Song' for voice and strings, piano or guitar published separately, 1974)

Went the Day Well?   1942
Music for the film
Release: 1 November 1942, London

Fanfares for the Red Army   1943
First performance: 21 February 1943, Royal Albert Hall, London, Trumpets and
Drums of the Life Guards, Royal Horse Guards and Royal Air Force, conducted
by Malcolm Sargent

The Quest   1943
Ballet in five scenes
Scenario: Doris Langley Moore after Spenser's *The Faerie Queene*
Choreography: Frederick Ashton
First performance: 6 April 1943, New Theatre, London, Sadler's Wells Ballet
Company, conducted by Constant Lambert

Henry V   1943–44
Music for the film of Shakespeare's play
Release: 22 November 1944, London
Two Pieces for Strings (Passacaglia; 'Death of Falstaff' and 'Touch her soft lips
and part'), arranged 1943–44
Suites arranged by Malcolm Sargent (chorus and orchestra, 1945) and Muir
Mathieson (1963)

Memorial Fanfare for Henry Wood 1945
Expanded reworking for three orchestras of *Fanfares for the Red Army*
First performance: 4 March 1945, Royal Albert Hall, London, BBC Symphony
Orchestra, London Symphony Orchestra, London Philharmonic Orchestra, con-
ducted by Adrian Boult

'Where Does the Uttered Music Go?' 1946
Motet for unaccompanied mixed chorus
Text: 'Sir Henry Wood' by John Masefield
First performance: 26 April 1946, St Sepulchre's Church, Holborn, London,
BBC Chorus and Theatre Revue Chorus, conducted by Leslie Woodgate

String Quartet in A minor (No. 2) 1945–47
First performances: 4 May 1947, Broadcasting House, London, Blech String
Quartet (BBC Third Programme, broadcast); 5 May 1947, Concert Hall,
Broadcasting House, London, Blech String Quartet (public)
(See also *Sonata for Strings*, 1971)

Hamlet 1947
Music for the film of Shakespeare's play
Release: 6 May 1948, London
'Funeral March' and 'Hamlet and Ophelia' arranged by Muir Mathieson (1963)

Violin Sonata 1947–48
revised 1949–50
First performance: 30 September 1949, Tonhalle, Zurich, Yehudi Menuhin
(violin), Louis Kentner (piano)

Two Pieces for Violin and Piano 1948–50
(including material originally from the Violin Sonata)
First performance: 27 September 1950, Broadcasting House, London, Frederick
Grinke (violin), Ernest Lush (piano) (BBC Third Programme, broadcast)

Orb and Sceptre 1952–53
Coronation march for orchestra
First performances: 18 March 1953, Kingsway Hall, London, Philharmonia
Orchestra, conducted by Sir William Walton (recording); 2 June 1953,
Westminster Abbey, London, Coronation Orchestra, conducted by Adrian Boult
(Coronation of Queen Elizabeth II)

Coronation Te Deum 1952–53
for two mixed choruses, two semi-choruses, boys' voices, organ, orchestra and
military brass ensemble
First performance: 2 June 1953, Westminster Abbey, London, Coronation Choir
and Orchestra, Royal Military School of Music (Kneller Hall) Trumpeters,
Osborne Peasgood (organ), conducted by William McKie (Coronation of Queen
Elizabeth II)

The National Anthem   1953
Arranged for orchestra
First performance: 8 June 1953, Royal Opera House, Covent Garden, London,
Royal Opera House Orchestra, conducted by John Pritchard

Variation on an Elizabethan Theme ('Sellinger's Round')   1953
for string orchestra
First performance: 20 June 1953, Parish Church, Aldeburgh, Aldeburgh Festival
Orchestra, conducted by Benjamin Britten (Aldeburgh Festival)

Troilus and Cressida   1947–54
Opera in three acts
revised 1963, 1972–76
Libretto: Christopher Hassall
First performances: 3 December 1954, Royal Opera House, Covent Garden,
London, Magda László (Cressida, soprano), Richard Lewis (Troilus, tenor), Peter
Pears (Pandarus, tenor), Otakar Kraus (Diomede, baritone), Frederick Dahlberg
(Calkas, bass), conducted by Sir Malcolm Sargent, produced by George Devine;
23 April 1963, Royal Opera House, Covent Garden, London, Marie Collier
(Cressida), André Turp (Troilus), John Lanigan (Pandarus), Otakar Kraus
(Diomede), Forbes Robinson (Calkas), conducted by Sir Malcolm Sargent (1963
revised version); 12 November 1976, Royal Opera House, Covent Garden,
London, Janet Baker (Cressida, mezzo-soprano), Richard Cassilly (Troilus),
Gerald English (Pandarus), Benjamin Luxon (Diomede), Richard Van Allan
(Calkas), conducted by Lawrence Foster, produced by Colin Graham (1972–76
revised version); 14 January 1995, Grand Theatre, Leeds, Judith Howarth
(Cressida, soprano), Arthur Davies (Troilus), Nigel Robson (Pandarus), Alan
Opie (Diomede), Clive Bayley (Calkas), conducted by Richard Hickox, produced
by Matthew Warchus (1994 revised version by Stuart Hutchinson, restoring
Cressida as a soprano role within Walton's 1972–76 revision)
Three Solo Songs, arranged for concert performance, 1961
First performance: 8 August 1961, Hollywood Bowl, California, US, Elinor Ross
(soprano), Los Angeles Philharmonic Orchestra, conducted by Alfred Wallenstein
'Put Off The Serpent Girdle' for three-part female chorus, with extra verse by
Paul Dehn, 1972
First performance: 27 December 1972, London, BBC Chorus, conducted by
Peter Gellhorn (BBC Radio 3, broadcast)

Richard III   1955
Music for the film of Shakespeare's play
Release: 13 December 1955, London
'Prelude' and 'A Shakespeare Suite' arranged by Muir Mathieson (1963)

The National Anthem   1955
Arranged for orchestra
First performance: 18 October 1955, Royal Festival Hall, London, Philharmonia
Orchestra, conducted by Herbert von Karajan

'The Star-Spangled Banner'   1955
Arranged for orchestra
(unpublished)

Cello Concerto   1955–56
First performances: 25 January 1957, Symphony Hall, Boston, US, Gregor
Piatigorsky (cello), Boston Symphony Orchestra, conducted by Charles Münch;
13 February 1957, Royal Festival Hall, London, Gregor Piatigorsky (cello), BBC
Symphony Orchestra, conducted by Sir Malcolm Sargent (UK)
(revised ending, 1974; unperformed and unpublished)

Johannesburg Festival Overture   1956
First performance: 25 September 1956, City Hall, Johannesburg, South Africa,
South African Broadcasting Corporation Symphony Orchestra, conducted by
Sir Malcolm Sargent

Partita   1957
for orchestra
First performance: 30 January 1958, Cleveland, Ohio, US, Cleveland Orchestra,
conducted by George Szell

A History of the English-Speaking Peoples   1959
March composed for television series (which remained unmade) based on
Sir Winston Churchill's book
First performance: 25 May 1959, Elstree Film Studios, London Symphony
Orchestra, conducted by Sir William Walton (recording)

A Queen's Fanfare   1959
Composed for Her Majesty The Queen's entrance at the NATO Parliamentary
Conference
First performance: 5 June 1959, Westminster Hall, London, The State
Trumpeters

Anon. in Love   1959
Song-cycle for tenor and guitar
Texts: Anon. (sixteenth and seventeenth century)
First performance: 21 June 1960, Claydon, Ipswich, Peter Pears (tenor), Julian
Bream (guitar)
Arranged for tenor and orchestra, 1970–71
First performance: 21 June 1971, Mansion House, London, Robert Tear (tenor),
London Mozart Players, conducted by Harry Blech

Symphony No. 2   1957–60
First performance: 2 September 1960, Usher Hall, Edinburgh, Royal Liverpool
Philharmonic Orchestra, conducted by John Pritchard (Edinburgh International
Festival)

'What Cheer?'   1960
Carol for unaccompanied mixed chorus
Text: from *Richard Hill's Commonplace Book*

Gloria   1960–61
for contralto, tenor, bass, mixed chorus and orchestra
Text: from the modern Roman Missal
First performance: 24 November 1961, Huddersfield Town Hall, Marjorie
Thomas (contralto), Richard Lewis (tenor), John Cameron (bass), Huddersfield
Choral Society, Royal Liverpool Philharmonic Orchestra, conducted by Sir
Malcolm Sargent

A Song for the Lord Mayor's Table   1962
for soprano and piano
Texts: William Blake, Thomas Jordan, Charles Morris, William Wordsworth,
Anon. (eighteenth century)
First performance: 18 July 1962, Goldsmith's Hall, London, Elisabeth
Schwarzkopf (soprano), Gerald Moore (piano)
Arranged for orchestra, 1970
First performance: 7 July 1970, The Mansion House, London, Janet Baker
(mezzo-soprano), English Chamber Orchestra, conducted by George Malcolm

Granada TV Prelude, Call Signs and End Music   1962
for orchestra
First public performance of Prelude: 25 June 1977, St John's, Smith Square,
London, Young Musicians' Symphony Orchestra, conducted by James Blair

Variations on a Theme by Hindemith   1962–63
for orchestra
First performance: 8 March 1963, Royal Festival Hall, London, Royal
Philharmonic Orchestra, conducted by Sir William Walton

The Twelve   1964–65
Anthem for mixed chorus and organ
Text: W. H. Auden
First performance: 16 May 1965, Christ Church Cathedral, Oxford, Christ
Church Cathedral Choir, Robert Bottone (organ), conducted by Sydney Watson
Organ part arranged for orchestra, 1965
First performance: 2 January 1966, Westminster Abbey, London, Ann Dowdall
(soprano), Shirley Minty (mezzo-soprano), Robert Tear (tenor), M. Wakeham
(baritone), London Philharmonic Choir and Orchestra, conducted by Sir William
Walton

Missa Brevis   1965–66
for double mixed chorus and organ
First performance: 29 March 1967, London, BBC Chorus, Simon Preston
(organ), conducted by Alan G. Melville (BBC Radio 3, broadcast)

The Bear   1965–67
Extravaganza in one act
Libretto: Paul Dehn and William Walton, after the short story by Anton
Chekhov
First performance: 3 June 1967, Jubilee Hall, Aldeburgh, Monica Sinclair
(Yeliena Popova, mezzo-soprano), John Shaw (Grigory Smirnov, baritone),
Norman Lumsden (Luka, bass), English Chamber Orchestra, conducted by
James Lockhart, produced by Colin Graham (Aldeburgh Festival)

Capriccio burlesco   1968
for orchestra
First performance: 7 December 1968, Philharmonic Hall, Lincoln Center, New
York, New York Philharmonic Orchestra, conducted by André Kostelanetz

The Battle of Britain   1969
Music for the film
Release: 15 September 1969, London

Three Sisters   1969
Music for the film of Chekhov's play
Release: 26 August 1970, Venice

Improvisations on an Impromptu of Benjamin Britten   1968–69
for orchestra
First performances: 14 January 1970, War Memorial Opera House, San
Francisco, US, San Francisco Symphony Orchestra, conducted by Josef Krips;
27 June 1970, Snape Maltings Concert Hall, Royal Liverpool Philharmonic
Orchestra, conducted by Charles Groves (Aldeburgh Festival) (UK)

Theme (for Variations)   1970
for solo cello
Composed for HRH The Prince of Wales (contribution to 'Music for a Prince')
First performance: 29 April 1985, Villa Wolkonsky, Rome, Antonio Lysy (cello)

'All This Time'   1970
Carol for unaccompanied mixed chorus
Text: Anon. (sixteenth century)

Five Bagatelles   1970–71
for guitar
(edited by Julian Bream)
First performances: 13 February 1972, Queen Elizabeth Hall, London, Julian
Bream (guitar) (No. 2); 29 March 1972, BBC Television Centre, London, Julian
Bream (guitar) (Nos. 1 and 3); 27 May 1972, Assembly Rooms, Bath, Julian
Bream (guitar) (complete)

Sonata for Strings   1971
Arrangement (with Malcolm Arnold) of the String Quartet in A minor (1945–47)
First performances: 2 March 1972, Perth, Western Australia, Academy of St
Martin-in-the-Fields, conducted by Neville Marriner; 27 May 1972, Assembly
Rooms, Bath, Academy of St Martin-in-the-Fields, conducted by Neville
Marriner (UK)

Jubilate Deo   1971–72
for double mixed chorus and organ
First performance: 22 April 1972, Christ Church Cathedral, Oxford, Christ
Church Cathedral Choir, Stephen Darlington (organ), conducted by Simon Preston

Birthday Greetings to Herbert Howells   1972
(unpublished)

Anniversary Fanfare   1973
composed for EMI's seventy-fifth anniversary concert
First performance: 29 November 1973, Royal Festival Hall, London Royal
Military School of Music (Kneller Hall) Trumpeters, conducted by Rodney
Blashford

Cantico del Sole   1973–74
Motet for unaccompanied mixed chorus
Text: St Francis of Assisi
First performances: 25 April 1974, University College, Cork, Ireland, BBC
Northern Singers, conducted by Stephen Wilkinson; 14 September 1974, Milton
Hall, Manchester (same artists) (UK)

Magnificat and Nunc Dimittis   1974
for mixed chorus and organ
revised 1975
First performance: 14 June 1975, Chichester Cathedral, Chichester Cathedral
Choir, Ian Fox (organ), conducted by John Birch

Fanfare for the National   1974
Composed for the opening of the National (later Royal National) Theatre
revised 1976
First performance: 1 April 1976, de Lane Lea Studios, Wembley, London, Band
of the Life Guards, conducted by Harry Rabinowitz (recording)

Varii capricci   1975–76
Free transcriptions for orchestra of *Five Bagatelles* for guitar
First performance: 4 May 1976, Royal Festival Hall, London, London
Symphony Orchestra, conducted by André Previn
Finale re-written, 1977
First performance: 28 January 1981, Broadcasting House, Cardiff, BBC Welsh
Symphony Orchestra, conducted by Owain Arwel Hughes

Roaring Fanfare   1976
Composed for the inauguration of the Lion Terraces at London Zoo
First performance: 3 June 1976, Zoological Gardens, London, Royal Military
School of Music (Kneller Hall) Trumpeters, conducted by Trevor Platts

Antiphon   1977
Anthem for mixed chorus and organ
Text: George Herbert
First performance: 20 November 1977, Rochester, New York State, US, St Paul's
Church Choir, David Craighead (organ), conducted by David Fetler

'King Herod and the Cock'   1977
Carol for unaccompanied mixed chorus
Text: Traditional
First performance: 24 December 1977, King's College, Cambridge, King's
College Choir, conducted by Philip Ledger (Festival of Nine Lessons and Carols)

Title Music for BBC Television Shakespeare Series   1977
First performance: 26 January 1978, Lime Grove Studios, London, English
National Opera Orchestra, conducted by David Lloyd-Jones (recording)

Façade 2   1977
A Further Entertainment
Revision of discarded numbers from early versions of *Façade*, with new items
(originally named 'Façade Revived')
revised 1977–78
First performances: 27 March 1977, Plaisterers' Hall, London, Richard Baker
(reciter), English Bach Festival Ensemble, conducted by Charles Mackerras;
19 June 1979, Snape Maltings Concert Hall, Peter Pears (reciter), ensemble
conducted by Steuart Bedford (Aldeburgh Festival) (revised version)

Medley for Brass Band   1977–78
(unpublished)

Salute to Sir Robert Mayer on his 100th Birthday   1979
for twelve trumpets
First performance: 5 June 1979, Royal Festival Hall, London, twelve trumpeters
from schools of the Inner London Education Authority
(Later revised and amended as *Introduction to the National Anthem* for three
trumpets and three trombones)

Passacaglia   1979–80
for solo cello
First performance: 16 March 1982, Royal Festival Hall, London, Mstislav
Rostropovich (cello)

The First Shoot 1979–80
Arrangement of 1935 ballet for brass band
First performances: 19 December 1980, Goldsmith's College, London,
Grimethorpe Colliery Band, conducted by Elgar Howarth (television recording);
7 September 1981, Royal Albert Hall, London, Grimethorpe Colliery Band,
conducted by Elgar Howarth (public)

A Birthday Fanfare 1981
Composed for the seventieth birthday of Dr Karl-Friedrich Still
First performance: 10 October 1981, Recklinghausen, West Germany,
Trumpeters of the Westphalia Symphony Orchestra, conducted by Karl Anton
Rickenbacher

Prologo e Fantasia 1981–82
for orchestra
First performance: 20 February 1982, Royal Festival Hall, London, National
Symphony Orchestra of Washington DC, conducted by Mstislav Rostropovich

Duettino 1982
for oboe and violin
(unpublished)

Varii capricci [1983]
New ending to 1975–76 score, for ballet by Sir Frederick Ashton
First performances: 19 April 1983, Metropolitan Opera House, New York, US;
20 July 1983, Royal Opera House, Covent Garden, London (UK)

SELECT BIBLIOGRAPHY

Besides books about Walton himself and his music, this selection includes others exploring the background to the musical and literary world around him. For information on further material and details of articles in periodicals and newspapers, see Michael Kennedy's *Portrait of Walton*, Stewart Craggs's *William Walton: A Source Book*, and *The New Grove Dictionary of Music and Musicians* (1st and 2nd editions).

Aberconway, Christabel, *A Wiser Woman?*, London, 1966

Adams, Byron, 'Walton' in *The New Grove Dictionary of Music and Musicians*, 2nd edn, London, 2001

Bradford, Sarah, *Sacheverell Sitwell*, London, 1993

Burton, Humphrey, and Maureen Murray, *William Walton: The Romantic Loner*, Oxford, 2002

Campbell, Roy, *Light on a Dark Horse*, London, 1951

Craggs, Stewart R., *William Walton: A Thematic Catalogue of his Musical Works* (with a critical appreciation by Michael Kennedy), London, 1987

– *William Walton: A Source Book*, Aldershot, 1993

– (ed.) *William Walton: Music and Literature* (symposium), Aldershot, 1999

Elborn, Geoffrey, *Edith Sitwell*, London, 1981

Glendinning, Victoria, *Edith Sitwell*, London, 1981

Heath, Edward, *Music: A Joy for Life*, London, 1976

Hinnells, Duncan, *An Extraordinary Performance: Hubert Foss, Music Publishing, and the Oxford University Press*, Oxford, 1998

Howes, Frank, *The Music of William Walton*, London, 1965; 2nd edn, London, 1974

– *The English Musical Renaissance*, London, 1966

Hughes, Patrick ('Spike'), *Opening Bars*, London, 1946

Kavanagh, Julie, *Secret Muses: The Life of Frederick Ashton*, London, 1996

Kennedy, Michael, *Portrait of Walton*, Oxford, 1989; 2nd edn, Oxford, 1998

Lambert, Constant, *Music, Ho! A Study of Music in Decline*, London, 1934; 3rd edn, London, 1966

Lehmann, John, *A Nest of Tigers: Edith, Osbert and Sacheverell Sitwell in their Times*, London, 1969

Lloyd, Stephen, *William Walton: Muse of Fire*, Woodbridge, 2001

Lutyens, Elisabeth, *A Goldfish Bowl*, London, 1972

Motion, Andrew, *The Lamberts*, London, 1995

Ottaway, Hugh, *Walton* (Novello Short Biographies), Sevenoaks, 1972
– 'Walton', in *The New Grove Dictionary of Music and Musicians*, London, 1980
Pearson, John, *Façades: Edith, Osbert and Sacheverell Sitwell*, London, 1978
Reid, Charles, *Malcolm Sargent: A Biography*, London, 1968
Roberts, John Stuart, *Siegfried Sassoon*, London, 1999
Schafer, R. Murray, 'Walton', in *British Composers in Interview*, London, 1963
Shead, Richard, *Constant Lambert: His Life, His Music and His Friends*, London, 1986
Sitwell, Edith, *Taken Care Of*, London, 1965
– Selected Letters, edited by John Lehmann and Derek Parker, London, 1970
– Selected Letters, edited by Richard Greene, London, 1997
Sitwell, Osbert, *Laughter in the Next Room*, London, 1949
Sitwell, Sacheverell, *All Summer in a Day*, London, 1926
– 'Façade', in the limited edition of the full score of *Façade*, Oxford, 1972
Skelton, Geoffrey, *Paul Hindemith: The Man behind the Music*, London, 1975
Tertis, Lionel, *My Viola and I*, London, 1974
Tierney, Neil, *William Walton: His Life and Music*, London, 1984
Vaughan, David, *Frederick Ashton and his Ballets*, London, 1977
Walton, Susana, *William Walton: Behind the Façade*, Oxford, 1987
Ziegler, Philip, *Osbert Sitwell*, London, 1998

ACKNOWLEDGEMENTS

The copyright of letters written by Sir William Walton is held by Lady Walton and by the William Walton Trust. I am most grateful to them for granting me permission to reproduce the letters in this book, which is published with a subsidy from the William Walton Trust.

Every effort has been made to contact the addressees of letters. The publishers will be pleased to make good in future editions or reprints any omissions or corrections brought to their attention.

The texts of Walton's letters to the following individuals have been taken from copies and original manuscripts in the possession of the Walton Archive at La Mortella, Ischia, Italy: Lady Aberconway (pp. 38, 42, 43, 71, 86, 89, 97 [dated 31 January 1935]), Sir Malcolm Arnold, Dame Janet Baker, Harry Blech, Sir Arthur Bliss, Dallas Bower, Lord Britten, Alan Bush, Christian Darnton, Paul Dehn, Edward Dent, Nora Donnelly, Roy Douglas, Patrick Hadley, Sir Hamilton Harty, Christopher Hassall, Peter Heyworth, Leslie Heward, John Ireland, Oliver Knussen, Sergei Koussevitsky, Walter Legge and Professor Dr Elisabeth Legge-Schwarzkopf, Sir Henry Moore, Zena Naylor, Edward Newman, Sir Peter Pears, Gregor Piatigorsky, Siegfried Sassoon, Sir Osbert Sitwell (except p. 98), Sir Sacheverell Sitwell, Leopold Stokowski, Stephen Tennant, Michael Vyner, Mrs Louisa Walton.

Material from the Archives of Oxford University Press is reproduced by kind permission of the Secretary to the Delegates of the Oxford University Press. This material encompasses Walton's letters to Geoffrey Cumberlege, Hubert Foss, Alan Frank, Christopher Morris and Norman Peterkin, and also the music examples handwritten by Walton in the course of those letters. The copyright of Hubert Foss's letter to Walton reproduced in Appendix 1 (pp. 466–8) is held by Oxford University Press; this letter is reproduced in this book with their permission, and also with the permission of Hubert Foss's daughter, Mrs Diana Sparkes. Walton's letters to Diana Foss – individually, or jointly to Mrs Foss and her husband, Hubert Foss – are reproduced with Mrs Sparkes's very kind permission and support.

Walton's letters to the following are held in the Additional Manuscripts collection of the British Library: John Amis, George Barnes, Sir Adrian Boult, Edward Clark, Cecil Gray, and Sir Henry and Lady Wood. The letters to Lord Olivier are held in the British Library's Olivier Archive.

The Archive of the Royal Opera House, Covent Garden kindly granted me access to letters by Walton in their possession, written to the following individuals working in their official capacities at the Royal Opera House: Sir Frederick Ashton,

Leslie Boosey, Muriel Keir, Sir John Tooley, Viscount Waverley (Sir John Anderson), Sir David Webster.

Walton's letters to Lady Diana Cooper and David Horner, and the letter to Sir Osbert Sitwell on p. 98 are in the manuscripts collection of Eton College Library, and are reproduced by permission of the Provost and Fellows of Eton College. The letters to Dr Thomas Strong (later Bishop of Oxford) are in the collection of Christ Church College, Oxford, and are reproduced by kind permission of the Governing Body of Christ Church. The Beinecke Rare Book and Manuscript Library at Yale University, New Haven, US, generously allowed me to see and reproduce copies of Walton's letters to Ernest Newman as soon as was possible after the Library's purchase of these at auction in London, and their subsequent arrival in the US. Quotations from the letters of William Walton to Benjamin Britten and Peter Pears are reproduced courtesy of The Britten–Pears Library. Walton's letter to Sir Henry Moore is published courtesy of the Henry Moore Foundation.

Walton's letters to Paul and Gertrude Hindemith are held by the Hindemith Institut in Frankfurt, Germany; I am most grateful to the Institut's director, Dr Luitgard Schader, for allowing me to reproduce them here. The letters to Lord Menuhin are held by the Menuhin Archives and are printed here by permission. Copies of Walton's letters to Carice Elgar Blake, the daughter of Sir Edward Elgar, and to Bernard van Dieren were very kindly sent to me through the Elgar Society. The letter to George Szell is reproduced courtesy of The Cleveland Orchestra Archives.

I am especially grateful to the following for generously providing me with copies of Walton's letters in their private possession: Zamira Benthall, for Walton's letters to Griselda Kentner; Sir Edward Heath; Helga Cranston Keller; Ian Kemp; and the Hon. Christopher McLaren, for Walton's letters to Lady Aberconway on pp. 92 and 97 (dated November 1934).

In the course of compiling and editing this book, I have been fortunate in being able to draw on the work of those who have previously written about Walton. Michael Kennedy's *Portrait of Walton* (Oxford University Press) has been an indispensable source of information, as has Lady Walton's *Behind the Façade* (Oxford University Press). And all present and future writers on Walton are indebted beyond measure to Professor Stewart Craggs's years of meticulous work in gathering and cataloguing information on the composer, as published in Craggs's *William Walton: A Thematic Catalogue of his Musical Works* (Oxford University Press, 1987) and *William Walton: A Source Book* (Scolar Press, Aldershot, 1993).

Throughout this project I have been much taken with the goodwill extended in general towards a writer fortunate enough to be working on a book on Walton. Simon Wright, Melanie Pidd and Sophie Currie of Oxford University Press contributed to making each of my numerous research-related visits to the composer's former university town and *alma mater* a pleasure in their own right. Similar helpfulness was shown by Francesca Franchi at the Archive of the Royal Opera House. Kathryn Johnson, curator of the Olivier Archive at the British Library, very kindly succeeded in locating some letters by Walton among the Archive's vast and newly arrived collection of Olivier's papers, at that time still unsorted and uncatalogued.

For conversation and correspondence happily concerning matters Waltonian I am indebted to many more people than I have been able to mention individually here. I sincerely hope they will recognize themselves, and will accept my unnamed thanks to all of them. In particular I would like to thank: Susanne Baumgartner at the Menuhin Archives; Professor Craggs, who identified for me some exquisitely obscure references in Walton's earlier letters; Anthony Day; Roy Douglas; Suzanne Graham-Dixon; Michael and Joyce Kennedy; Hugh and Liz Macdonald; Martin Maw, Archivist of Oxford University Press; Michael Meredith, College Librarian at Eton College Library; Andrew Porter; Francis Sitwell; and Mrs Diana Sparkes. In the course of note-setting the music examples in Walton's letters which are not reproduced here in facsimile, Colin Matthews exchanged thoughts on the intriguing differences between these sketches and their counterparts in Walton's published scores. My colleague and fellow author, Humphrey Burton, helpfully applied his eagle eye and his formidable expertise on British musical life in general, and on Walton in particular, to the book in its final stages.

An edition of this kind amounts very much to a collaboration between editor and publisher, and the experience of working with the team at Faber and Faber could not have been happier. My warmest thanks are extended to Belinda Matthews, most supportive of editors; to Jill Burrows, whose virtuoso copy-editing skills coaxed my draft towards what appears in the pages of this book; and to Kate Ward, whose production expertise steered the entire project safely towards the finishing post.

As already mentioned in my introduction, this edition would not have evolved as it has without the assistance of my research consultant, Maureen Murray, who is also archivist of the Walton Archive at La Mortella. Besides her encylopaedic knowledge of the composer's life and work and her tireless instinct for locating possible sources, she has been the most genial and hard-working of companions on our various joint visits to La Mortella, the Royal Opera House Archive, the British Library, and the Archives of Oxford University Press. As editor, the responsibility for any errors lurking either in my own text or in the documentation accompanying the letters is of course entirely mine. Warm enthusiasm for the project has also been shown from the very start by Stephannie Williams and Martin Denny, respectively Artistic Director and Administrator of the William Walton Trust. I am most grateful to them both for their patient insistence in negotiating whatever obstacles might have stood in the way of the book's eventual creation.

This edition really has two presiding spirits. One, of course, is the composer himself. The other is Lady Walton, whose passionate support for this book has been a beacon of goodwill from the moment when, several years ago now, it was first suggested to her. Among the happiest of many memories of the past two years are her generous hospitality at her home at La Mortella, and her reminiscences of the life that she and her husband created there together – reminiscences shared as ' we talked on the house's plant-enshrouded balcony, with its view across Ischia towards Monte Epomeo in the distance. Her pride in La Mortella's wonderful garden also ensured that, whenever I surfaced between research sessions in the Walton Archive, my knowledge of rare species of tropical water-lily became at least a little broader than it was before.

M.H.
Ischia – Oxford – London
1999 – 2001

INDEX

Figures in italics indicate manuscript letters.

Aachen Opera House: *Belshazzar's Feast* performed 286
Abbado, Claudio 452
Aberconway, Christabel, Lady 355
  correspondence with W 32, 38–9, 42, 43–4, 71, 86–7, 89–90, 92, 97–8
  Viola Concerto dedicated to 38n, 87n
  and *Belshazzar's Feast* 43n
  friendship with Susana 176
Aberconway, Henry, Lord 32
Abinger, Surrey 72
Abravanel, Maurice 413
Adelaide Festival 348
Admiralty 157
Aeolian Hall, London
  first public performance of *Façade* 30
  first performance of *Siesta* 36
Aldeburgh Festival 204, 205, 264, 343, 371, 372, 375, 390, 425
  and *The Bear* 205n, 344, 359n, 364, 371n
  'Sellinger's Round' variations 222n, 223
  and *Improvisations* 388
  Snape Maltings burnt down and rebuilt 388n
Aldwych season 361
Alexander, A.V. 157
Alexander Nevsky (film) 136
Allchin, Basil 14, 19
Allegri Quartet 395
Allen, Dr (later Sir) Hugh 12–15, 17, 18, 22, 109, 124, 134, 467, 468
Alma-Tadema, Sir Lawrence 308
Amalfi 37, 48, 58, 363
  W works on *Belshazzar's Feast* 54–5
  Viola Concerto written 177
Amis, John: correspondence with W 440
Amsterdam: *Façade* a success 456
Amsterdam Festival 116
  Belshazzar's Feast performed 84n, 87, 88, 90, 99
Anderson, Sir John *see* Waverley, Lord
Angles, Robert 370
Anna Karenina (film) 165
Anouilh, Jean 303
  Becket 322
Ansermet, Ernest 28, 33, 112
  conducts *Sinfonia concertante* 44
Argentina 122, 177, 377
Aristophanes: *The Frogs* 376
Army Film Unit 143

Arnold, Caryl 133
Arnold, Edward 390, 411, 430
Arnold, Sir Malcolm 326, 413
  correspondence with W xiv, 324, 383–8, 390, 391, 392–9, 401, 402–12, 414, 415, 417, 420–22, 425, 428, 430, 441, 448
  and *Sonata for Strings* 345, 395–8
  and *The Battle of Britain* 383–4
  and *The Villa* 390n
  copy of *Five Bagatelles* 397, 398, 415
  cooling of relationship with W 408–9
  argument with Bower 417
  Concerto for two pianos (three hands) and orchestra 386
  Concerto for Viola and Chamber Orchestra 396n
  The Fair Field 407
  Fantasy for Audience and Orchestra 390
  Fifth Symphony 401, 409
  Fourth Symphony 409
  Piano Concerto 441
  Sixth Symphony 397, 412
  Seventh Symphony 408–9, 411
  String Quartet No. 2 425
  Third Symphony 409
Arnold, Samuel 8
Arts Council of Great Britain 473n, 478n
As You Like It (film) 101, 107n
Ascona, Switzerland 364
  W lives in 53, 54, 61–2, 67, 70, 158, 159
  Legge lives in 354, 355
Ashby St Ledgers, near Rugby 108, 109, 112, 117, 118, 120, 123, 124, 126, 127, 129, 131, 132, 134, 137–49, 151–9, 161, 162, 165–9, 177, 467
  the country house and estate of Alice Wimborne 105
  estate ploughed up for war food 119, 123
Ashes Sellors, Sir Thomas 367
Ashton, Sir Frederick 150, 269, 437
  correspondence with W 161, 463
  Macbeth scenario 266n, 270
  and *Siesta* 405
  and *Varii capricci* 463
Ashton, Mitchell & Howlett 358
Aspen Award 438
Asquith, Anthony 145
At the Haunted End of the Day (film) 435, 462n

Atkins, Ivor: 'Abide with me' 11
Auckland, New Zealand 347, 348, 349
Auden, W. H. 197, 203, 219
  and *Troilus and Cressida* 219, 227, 228, 232,
    234, 237, 238
  writes text for *The Twelve* 351, 355
Australia: W tours (1964) 343, 348, 349
Australian Broadcasting Commission (A.B.C.) 350
Ayrton, Michael 144, 168, 462n

B. Feldman & Co. 131n
Bach, Johann Sebastian 22, 75, 160
  6 *Partitas* (BWV 825–30) 285, 286
  'Jesu, joy of man's desiring' 13
  'When Jesus Our Lord' 8
Bach Choir 13, 354, 355
Bach Choir Orchestra 14
Baden Baden Festival 47
Bairstow, Edward: 'Save us O Lord' 11
Baker, Dame Janet 410
  correspondence with W 403
  and *Troilus and Cressida* 346, 400, 403, 422,
    423, 426, 429, 457
Balakirev, Mily: *Tamara* 358n
Ballets Russes 6, 25
Balliol College, Oxford 22, 23–4, 345
Bank of Canada 378
Bank of England 285, 291
Barber, Samuel 268
Barbirolli, Sir John 160, 191, 249, 307
Barga Festival 443
Barnes, George: correspondence with W 159–60
Barrie, Sir J. M.: *The Boy David* 98, 101, 107,
  108
Bartók, Béla 214
  Duke Bluebeard's Castle 212, 222
Bath Festival: and *Sonata for Strings* 396
Battle of Britain (film) 383, 385n, 386, 457
Bax, Sir Arnold 70, 114, 136
  Fourth Symphony 85
Bay of Naples 177, 178
BBC Symphony Orchestra 135
Bean, Ernest 312
Beaton, Sir Cecil 42, 47
Beddoes, Thomas Lovell: *The Duke of Melveric*
  (or *Death's Jest-Book*) 121
Bedford studio (BBC) 135
Beecham, Sir Thomas 61, 129, 151, 477
  W meets 39
  conducts *Façade* 41
  and the *Sinfonia concertante* 43, 56
  and the Viola Concerto 44
  and *A Village Romeo and Juliet* 156
  founds the Royal Philharmonic Orchestra 477n
Beethoven, Ludwig van 21, 85
  Ninth Symphony 414
Bellini, Vincenzo 181
  Norma 271
  La Sonnambula 195
Bengtsson, Erling 300, 313
Benjamin, Arthur 95
Bennett, Sir Richard Rodney 380, 461
  The Mines of Sulphur 356, 365

Benthal, Michael 241
Berberian, Cathy 428, 431, 449, 450
Berg, Alban 31, 76, 436
  Chamber Concerto for piano, violin and
    14 wind instruments 160
  Wozzeck 192, 213
Bergman, Ingmar 426
Bergner, Elisabeth 108
  and *The Boy David* 101
  and *As You Like It* 107
Bergson, Ann 166n, 170, 171
Berkeley, Sir Lennox 112, 222n, 337, 413, 444
  Castaway 359n, 371
  Nelson 254
Berkeley Hotel, London 330n
Berlin 56, 59, 60, 83, 90
Berlin Philharmonic Orchestra 43, 412
  and the Viola Concerto 77
  and the *Partita* 299
Berlioz, Hector
  Benvenuto Cellini 431
  The Damnation of Faust 161
  The Trojans 386
Berne Convention 122
Berners, Lord
  W stays at Faringdon House 54, 68
  The Triumph of Neptune 36
Bess o' the Bann 445
Bing, Sir Rudolf 457
Birmingham
  Violin Concerto performed 147, 148, 148
  Boult conducts *Portsmouth Point* 56
Birmingham University 125
Birtwistle, Sir Harrison 445, 453
Bizet, Georges: *Carmen* 191, 452
Blank, Jonny 426
Blech, Mrs Enid 271, 455
Blech, Harry 191, 216
  correspondence with W 155, 194, 427–8, 431,
    456, 458–9
Blech String Quartet 155, 204
Bliss, Sir Arthur 236, 252
  correspondence with W 90–91, 113, 140–41
  Britten as his protégé 91
  W's criticism of 93–4
  and W's Violin Concerto 113, 114
  Morning Heroes for chorus and orchestra 62
  Piano Concerto 90n, 113n, 114
Bloch, Ernest: *Schelomo* 313
Blom, Eric 210
Blonay 266
Boccaccio, Giovanni 162
Bodleian Library, Oxford 15
Böhm, Karl 192
Boito, Arrigo: *Nerone* 307, 308
Boosey & Hawkes 154, 185, 194, 438
  tries to poach W from OUP 108–9, 214,
    262–3, 465–8
  and Covent Garden Opera House 149n, 473,
    474
  compared with OUP 214, 465
  and W's *Improvisations* 385
  magazine (*Tempo*) 452

Boosey, Sir Leslie 194, 214
  correspondence with W 149–50
Borodin, Alexander: *Prince Igor* 25
Boston, Massachusetts 40, 43, 49, 107
Boston Symphony Orchestra: and the Cello
  Concerto 277n, 288, 313
Boulez, Pierre 263
Boult, Sir Adrian 76, 251
  correspondence with W 67, 91, 143, 424–5,
    425–6
  conducts *Portsmouth Point* 56
  and the First Symphony 91, 424–7
Bournemouth 326
Bournemouth Festival 43
Bower, Dallas 119, 151, 161, 236, 240, 278, 351,
    411
  correspondence with W xiv, 135–6, 138, 139,
    141, 142, 143
  and W's resigning from the Savile Club 410
  and Arnold 417
Bradfield College, Berkshire 12
Brahms, Johannes 21, 456
  Double Concerto for Violin and Cello in
    A minor 308
  Trio in B 17
Brando, Marlon 240
Braque, Georges 61
Brasenose College, Oxford 18, 20, 23, 357n
Bray Studios, Windsor 411
Break the News (film) 107n
Bream, Julian 317–18
  and *Anon. in Love* 317–18
  and *Five Bagatelles* 397–8
Brezhnev, Leonid 430
Brighton 327
Brighton Festival: *Belshazzar's Feast* performed 382
Bristol 326
Bristol University 125
British Broadcasting Corporation (BBC) 117,
    125, 129, 135, 136, 139
  Siesta played at Savoy Hill 41
  and *Belshazzar's Feast* 43n, 49, 55, 62n, 82
  BBC Dance Orchestra 69
  and *Three Songs* 83
  and the First Symphony 100, 424, 435
  W's projects in the Second World War 119
  and *Troilus and Cressida* 121, 161, 400, 432
  and *Christopher Columbus* 140, 368
  W's suggestions for radio music programmes
    159–60
  Third Programme 160, 216
  and the Second Symphony 319
  and *Variations on a Theme by Hindemith* 335
  and Arnold's fiftieth birthday 394
British Council 113, 114, 115, 118, 123, 204,
    248, 432, 450
  and *Belshazzar's Feast* 139, 202
  and the First Symphony 220
British and Dominions (film production company)
    99
British Library 469
Britten, Benjamin (Baron Britten of Aldeburgh)
  xvii, 130, 136, 215, 237, 435, 468n
  correspondence with W 110, 111–12, 153–4,
    205, 338–9, 347, 351, 352–3, 354, 362–3,
    365–6, 377, 384, 385, 387–8, 405, 406, 416
  lionized 176–7
  and *The Bear* 205n, 343, 405
  and 'Sellinger's Round' 223
  as Boosey & Hawkes' leading composer 263
  relationship with W 264
  W's opinion of his music 338–9
  abandoned *Lear* project 339
  Order of Merit 351
  health 361
  and W's *Improvisations* 384, 385
  death 346, 432
  Albert Herring 359
  Billy Budd xvii, 182, 210, 213, 214, 219, 465
  A Boy Was Born 91, 112
  The Burning Fiery Furnace 365–6
  Gloriana 219, 222n
  A Midsummer Night's Dream 377
  Nocturne 338
  Peter Grimes 120, 153, 154, 176, 236, 251,
    465
  Piano Concerto 384, 385
  Spring Symphony 338
  Suites Nos. 1 and 2 for cello 458
  Variations on a Theme of Frank Bridge 110,
    112
  Violin Concerto 451
  War Requiem 338, 339
Brook, Peter 188, 191, 192
Browning, Robert: *Pippa Passes* 390n
Buckley, Jack 431, 432, 450
Buenos Aires 169, 171, 310, 311
  Performing Right Society international con-
    ference (1948) 122–3, 175
  W marries Susana Gil Passo 175
  Menuhin plays the Violin Sonata 195, 196
B.U.P.A. (British United Provident Association)
    348
Bush, Alan: *Dialectic* 130
Bussaco 98

Callas, Maria 271, 273, 278, 301, 306, 307, 448,
    450
Cambridge 43, 134, 135
Cambridge University 125
Cameroni, Duca 254
Campbell, Roy 5, 19
Campion Hall College, Oxford 22
Camrose, Lord 323
Canti Carnaschialeschi 124n
Cap Ferrat 422
Capri 164, 165, 458
  W on holiday in 122, 144n, 168, 177, 462
  W meets Menotti 268
Cardiff 326
Cardiff University 125
Carl Rosa Company 21
Carlyle Square, London (No. 2) 27–9, 33, 35, 36,
    38–43, 46, 48, 67, 71, 72, 97
  W lives in the Sitwells' house xiii–xiv, xv, 29,
    32, 36n, 53, 54, 70

first private performance of *Façade* 30
Osbert lets the property 86, 88
and W's relationship with Alice 101, 105
W and Susana visit Osbert 176
Carnegie Hall, New York 322n
Carnegie Trust 75
Casa Angolo, Ascona, Ticino, Switzerland 60, 63,
    75, 76, 78, 79, 80, 83, 85–9, 99
Casa Cirillo, Via Cesotta, Ischia 180, 208, 210,
    211, 213, 215, 217, 218, 220, 221, 223,
    224, 227, 228, 230, 231, 232, 236, 238,
    239, 242, 243, 246, 247, 249–53, 255, 265,
    267, 269, 272, 273, 275–87, 289, 290, 291,
    297–304, 306–13
Casa Giachetti, Ascona, Ticino, Switzerland 84–7
Casamicciola, Ischia 209
Cassilly, Richard 429
Casson, Sir Hugh 253
Castaldi, Pasquale 218, 231, 250
Castello di Montegufoni, Montespertoli, Tuscany
    64, 85, 197n, 203, 300, 301
Castro, Inez de 161
Catterall Quartet 19
Cava Tirreni jazz festival 363
Cavalcanti, Alberto 130, 135, 137
C.E.M.A. *see* Council for the Encouragement of
    Music and the Arts
Chailly, Riccardo 431
Chapel Tower, Lucerne 163n
Charles, HRH The Prince of Wales 405
Charles I, King 7
Charpentier, Gustave: *Louise* 129
Chartres Cathedral 128
Chaucer, Geoffrey: *Troylus and Criseide* 122,
    162, 179, 211
Chausson, Ernest: *Poème* 413, 447
Chekhov, Anton 440
    The Bear 343–4, 351n, 364, 372
    'In Autumn' 419
    On the High Road 419
Chelsea Arts Ball, London 42
Chelsea Flower Show, London 447
Cheltenham Festival 153, 182, 205
Chenhalls, Cornwall 128
Chesham Place, London (No. 20) 326
Chester Terrace, London (No. 32) 386
Chicago Symphony Orchestra 337
    Portsmouth Point toured by 56
    commissions *Scapino* 119
Chichester Cathedral: *Magnificat and Nunc
    Dimittis* 412
Chile 172
Chopin, Fryderyk: Preludes 27
Christ Church College, Oxford
    W as a choirboy xvii, xviii, 3–19, 75
    W an exhibition scholar 5, 6, 19–28, 75,
        357n
    W does not finish his studies 6, 75, 76
    and *The Twelve* 351, 355
Christ Church College Cathedral, Oxford 3, 9
Christian Democratic Party 430
Christie, John 134
Christoff, Boris 192

Chung, Kyung-Wha: records the Violin Concerto
    406, 447
Cincinnati Symphony Orchestra 126n
City of London Festival 326
Civitavecchia, Rome 294n, 300
Clair, René 107
Clarges Street, London (No. 45) 162
Claridge Hotel, Tucuman, Buenos Aires 172, 182
Clark, Edward 62, 83
    correspondence with W 79–80, 129–30
    and the Viola Concerto 62n
    and *Belshazzar's Feast* 62n
Clark, Jane, Lady 227, 230
Clark, Sir Kenneth, Baron 150, 157, 188, 226,
    230, 231, 248
Cleveland Orchestra 306
    and the *Partita* 265, 278n, 285, 286, 295, 297,
        301, 302, 303, 306
    and the Second Symphony 265, 322n
    and *Variations on a Theme by Hindemith* 265,
        336
Clinica dello Spirito Santo, Villa Stuart, Rome
    294, 295
Co-operative Society 157
Cobalt Institute 362
Cochran, Sir Charles B. 56, 101
    Follow the Sun 56n, 59
Cocteau, Jean: *La machine infernale* (adapted as
    Queen Jocasta (or *The Scourge*)) 121
Cohen, Harriet 82, 83, 90
    and the *Sinfonia concertante* 69, 79, 147
Collier, Marie 262
Collins, Michael 300
Cologne 443
    The Bear performed 446
'Colonel Bogey' 316, 420n
Como Festival 431
Composer journal 438
Connaught Hotel, London 422
Connecticut: W visits Heifetz 107, 119n
Convento San Francesco, Forio d'Ischia 177, 178,
    180, 183, 185, 188, 190, 192–9, 202, 203,
    204, 206, 207
Cook, Kenneth 272
Cooper, Lady Diana: correspondence with W
    440–41, 442
Cooper, Gerald 150
Copyright Act (1911) 132n
Corfu 86, 88
Cork 410, 411
Cork University 409–10
Cornell, Roger 349
Coronation Service (1953) 223
Cortot, Alfred 27
Cothill House School, Abingdon 8
Council for the Encouragement of Music and the
    Arts (C.E.M.A.) (later Arts Council of Great
    Britain) 473, 474, 475
Courtauld, Elizabeth 70, 71, 78n, 87n
Courtauld, Samuel 70n, 71, 72, 97, 98, 109
Courtauld Concerts 82, 90, 115, 474
Covent Garden Choral Society [proposed] 478
Covent Garden Opera Company 478n

Covent Garden Opera House *see* Royal Opera House, Covent Garden
Covent Garden Opera House Trust: W on the board 121, 176
Coventry Cathedral Choir 351
Craggs, Stewart: *William Walton: A Thematic Catalogue of his Musical Works, with a critical appreciation by Michael Kennedy* 450
Cranston, Helga *see* Keller, Helga
Cross, Joan 150, 161, 251
Croydon, Surrey 384
Cuenod, Hugues 238, 269
Cumberland Hotel, London 92
Cumberlege, Geoffrey: correspondence with W 255–8
Curtin, Phyllis 268
Cutting, Francis 349

Dahlberg, Frederick 229, 238, 246
Daily Dispatch newspaper 68, 70
Daily Mail newspaper 188
Daily Telegraph newspaper 95
Dalí, Salvador 188
Dallapiccola, Luigi: *Il Prigioniero* 247
Dallas Bower Productions Inc. 161, 290–91
Danat bank 66
Danish Radio Orchestra 159
Darnton, Christian 146
  correspondence with W 116–17
  Piano Suite No. 2 116
d'Assia, Enrico 446
Davis, Sir Colin 457
Dayan, Moshe 373
The Daye House, Quidhampton, Salisbury 72, 73, 74
de Mille, Cecil B. 310
De Profundis (Psalm 130) 438
de Valois, Dame Ninette 150, 269
de Wills, Norman 90
Debussy, Claude 27
Decca Gramophone Co. (later Decca Record Co.)
  W records *Façade* 47, 48
  W's shares 70
  and the Cello Concerto 298
  and the First Symphony 367, 368, 370
Dehn, Paul 419
  correspondence with W 357–9
  and *The Bear* 145n, 344, 357–9, 362, 365, 369, 371, 372–5
  meets W in Ischia 357n
Delhi 348
Delius, Frederick 24, 378
  A Village Romeo and Juliet 156–7
Delius Trust 156
Della Casa, Lisa 246, 247
Denham Film Studios 133, 139
Denison, John 414, 418, 423
Denmark 93
Dent, Edward J. 28, 150
  correspondence with W 99, 134, 135, 151, 152
Devine, George: and *Troilus and Cressida* 246, 249, 251–4, 268
Diaghilev, Sergei 6, 47

Dieren, Bernard van 23, 24, 378
  correspondence with W 101
  Chinese Symphony 159
  Diafonia for baritone and chamber orchestra 159
  Down Among the Dead Men 101n
  String Quartet No. 3 159
  String Quartet No. 6 159
Djerba 394
Doernberg, Baron Hans-Karl von 53
Doernberg, Baroness Imma (Irma) von 47, 64, 68, 71, 72
  correspondence with Sassoon 53, 55, 62, 66–9, 79, 81
  relationship with W xiv, 53, 55
  personality 53, 55
  lives with W in Ascona 53, 54, 177
  financial position 54, 63, 66, 77, 86, 87
  health 55, 76–7, 80, 81, 82, 88
  W dedicates his First Symphony to 55
  leaves W 55
  a graphologist 61n, 64, 66
  stenography 64, 65
  stays with McEacharn 79
  marries McEacharn 79n
  job in Zurich 90, 98
Domingo, Placido 452, 457
Donizetti, Gaetano: *Maria Stuarda* 410
Donne, John 97
Donnelly, Hannah (W's niece) 356
Donnelly, Nora (née Walton; W's sister) 3, 7, 20, 343
  correspondence with W 349, 356, 454–5
Dorking, Surrey 69
Douglas, Basil 209
Douglas, Roy 132–3, 369, 443
  correspondence with W 133–4, 137, 145–6, 147, 152, 153, 154, 199, 373, 379, 442, 444–6, 453
  and *Troilus and Cressida* 228, 238, 256
  works on Vaughan Williams scores 257n
  and the Cello Concerto 295, 298
  and *The Bear* 373, 378
  and *Sonata for Strings* 395
  March for Brass Band 454
Dow, Dorothy 261, 271, 273, 301
Dowland, John 349
Downes, Sir Edward 370
Dowd, Ronald 400
D'Oyly Carte Company 22
Drogheda, Garrett Moore, eleventh Earl of 323–4, 335
Dublin 405, 408
Dumbarton Oaks, Washington DC 322
Dvořák, Antonín, Trio in F minor 17

Ealing film studios 133, 135, 136, 137, 143
Eden, Sir Anthony 283
Edinburgh 44, 167, 170, 214
Edinburgh Festival 384, 452
  Second Symphony premièred 265, 322n
  and the Cello Concerto 270
  and the Violin Sonata 313

Ehrling, Sixten 157
Elgar, Sir Edward 165, 424–5, 468
    The Apostles 424
    Cockaigne 400n, 401
    The Dream of Gerontius 307, 406, 424
    Introduction and Allegro for Strings 395
    The Kingdom 424
    Third Symphony [fragment] 86
    Violin Sonata in E minor 23
Elgar Blake, Carice: correspondence with W 165
Eliot, T. S. 268
Elizabeth, Queen (later the Queen Mother) 166,
    236, 270, 401, 430, 458
Elizabeth II, Queen 219, 382
Ely, Cambridgeshire 460
E.M.I. Records 298, 355, 367–8, 370, 389, 419
    and the First Symphony 367–8
    and The Bear 374, 376
    and Belshazzar's Feast 414
    and Troilus and Cressida 244n
English Chamber Orchestra (E.C.O.) 388
English National Opera: and Troilus and Cressida
    410
E.N.S.A. (Entertainments National Service
    Association) 475
Epomeo, Ischia 409
Erbach-Schoenberg, Prince Alexander von 53
Erhardt, Otto 191
Escape Me Never (film) 54, 98, 99, 101n, 135n,
    278n
Expo 67, Montreal 367

Faber Music 412
Faggioni, Piero 452
Falkner, Keith 193, 202, 204, 248
Faringdon House, Berkshire 54, 68, 69, 70
Fascism 88–9
Feldman, Bertram 131–2
Fenby, Eric: Delius As I Knew Him 378n
Ferneyhough, Brian 461
Festival of Britain (1951) 478
Filippo, Eduardo de: Filumena 451
Film Society 478
Financial Times 411
Firenze (Florence) 197
The First of the Few (film) 120, 133, 136, 139,
    141, 351n
First World War 5, 16, 25
Flecker, James Elroy: Hassan 121
Fleming, Joan 57
Florence 362, 363, 449
    Maggio Musicale Fiorentino festival 449
Fonteyn, Dame Margot 270
The Foreman Went to France (film) 135, 137, 157
Forio, Ischia 177, 351
Foss, Christopher 68, 83
Foss, Dora (née Stevens)
    correspondence with W 60, 68, 73, 74–5,
        81–5, 93–4, 111, 117, 119, 226, 258
    W stays with 54, 60, 68
    and 'Through Gilded Tresses' 68, 73
    on Bliss's studio 94n
    health 116

and W's mother 117
Foss, Hubert 61, 82, 91n, 258, 465
    correspondence with W xvii, 75–6, 83–5,
        99–100, 106, 107–8, 112, 114–16, 117,
        123–8, 131–3, 465–8
    decision to publish W's music xiv, 31, 35
    writes W's programme notes xv
    aims to build up a strong catalogue of com-
        posers 54
    W stays with 54
    broadcasts on Belshazzar's Feast 82, 84
    and Three Songs 74
    asks W for promotional information 75n
    Three Choirs Festival 80
    and the First Symphony 93, 94
    strong views on W's proposed 'defection'
        466–8
    death 226
Foss family 60n
Foster, Lawrence 441
    conducts Troilus and Cressida 346, 441n, 445
Françaix, Jean 130
    String Trio 130
Francescatti, Zino 447
Francis of Assisi, St: 'Cantico del Sole' 410
Frank, Alan 214–15, 361, 395, 465
    correspondence with W xiv, 122–3, 172,
        182–3, 193–4, 202–3, 204, 209, 238,
        239–40, 261, 263, 267–8, 272–3, 281,
        285–6, 295, 298–310, 312, 314–25, 330–35,
        349, 350, 351, 359, 368–70, 378–9, 383,
        398, 418, 419
    writes W's programme notes xv, 303
    and Troilus and Cressida 181, 216, 238–9,
        241, 243, 244, 257, 261, 429
    W appreciates his relationship with 263
    and the Johannesburg Festival Overture 278
    and the Cello Concerto 281
    and the Partita 304–5
    and the Variations on a Theme by Hindemith
        324–5, 331–4
    and Capriccio burlesco 345, 383
    and The Bear 371, 373, 374, 378
    and Sonata for Strings 396
    and Belshazzar's Feast 414
    Morris succeeds 424
Freccia, Massimo 313
French Embassy, London 130
Fricker, Peter Racine 219
Fried, Oskar 43
Frink, Elisabeth 422
Furse, Roger 230, 231, 233, 237, 239, 241
Furtwängler, Wilhelm 70, 170, 192
    and the First Symphony 112, 172

Gardner, Ava 240
Garrick Club, London 165
Garsington Manor, Oxfordshire 27n
Gatty, Hester 72n
Gedda, Nicolai 222, 229, 238, 248, 249, 251,
    429
Gellhorn, Peter 191
Geneva: Sinfonia concertante performed 56

Genoa 122, 169, 170
George V, King 9
George VI, King 166
Germany
  Imma's situation 63
  and the London Conference(1931) 64
  currency restrictions 66n
  and Troilus and Cressida 432
Gershwin, George 106
Gesualdo, Carlo, Prince of Venosa 120, 134,
  137n, 142, 144, 161n, 469
Gielgud, Sir John 142
Gilbert, Sir W. S. and Sullivan, Sir Arthur
  The Mikado 22
  The Yeoman of the Guard 22
Giorgione 125
Gishford, Anthony 214
Glasgow 44
Glenconner, Lady 25, 44
Glenconner, Lord 46n, 64, 78
Glock, Sir William 400, 427n
Gloucester 25
  Three Choirs Festival 80n
  Sinfonia concertante performed 43
Glover-Kind, John: 'I do like to be beside the
  seaside' 131n, 132n
Gluck, Christoph von: Alceste 251
Glyndebourne Festival Opera 251n
Gobbi, Tito 192
Goldoni, Carlo: Le Baruffe Chiozzotte 376
Gomez, Jill: and Troilus and Cressida 346
Goodall, Reginald 191, 261, 267, 269
Goodman, Lord: and W's seventieth birthday 399
Goodwin, Ron 386
Goossens, Eugene 6, 26, 28, 126n, 151, 193
Goossens, Janet 126
Goss, John: 'The Wilderness' 12
Gould, Diana, see Menuhin, Diana
Gounod, Charles
  Faust 21
  Petite Symphonie in B♭ for 9 wind instruments
  130
GPO Film Unit, Bennett Park, Blackheath 130
Gracis, Ettore 316
Graham, Colin 422, 424, 429
  Prospero 443
Grand Hotel Santa Lucia, Naples 37
Gray, Cecil
  correspondence with W 137, 142, 144, 161–2,
  165–6, 168
  longstanding friendship with W 119
  Gesualdo opera project 120, 134, 137, 142,
  178–9, 469
Gray, Margery 168
Greece 376
Greater London Council (G.L.C.) 412
Greenbaum, Hyam ('Bumps') 98
Greene, Maurice: 'God of my righteousness' 8
Greenfield, Edward 412
Gresham Hotel, Dublin 403, 404
Grey, Lady (formerly Lady Glenconner) 44
Griffiths, Hilary 443
Grimethorpe Colliery Band 443n, 445

Grosvenor House, London 89
Groves, Sir Charles: premières Improvisations 388n
Guernsey 127
Gui, Vittorio 192
Gulbenkian Trust 411
Guthrie, Tyrone 150, 152

Hadley, Patrick 69, 134
  correspondence with W 95–6
Haendel, Ida: records Violin Concerto 451
Haig, General Douglas, Earl 25
Hale, Una 267, 269
Hallé Orchestra 59, 70, 303
  and the Partita 303
Hamilton, Hamish 447
Hamlet (film) 161, 165, 166, 193
Hammond, Joan 267, 269
Handel, George Frideric
  Acis and Galatea 376–7
  'Comfort ye' 14
  Israel in Egypt 310
Hardy, Thomas 467
Harewood, Earl of 219
Harold Holt Ltd. 296n
Harper, Heather: and Troilus and Cressida 400
Hartmann, Karl Amadeus 325
Harty, Sir Hamilton 32, 55, 59
  correspondence with W 102
  and Façade 59
  and the Sinfonia concertante 59
  and the First Symphony 59, 70, 84, 85–6, 91,
  94, 95, 102, 453
  and Belshazzar's Feast 84, 85
  and the Viola Concerto 87, 94
  and the Courtauld Concerts 90
Hassall, Christopher 178, 274, 286, 444–5
  correspondence with W xii, xiv, 169, 170–71,
  180, 183–7, 189–90, 198–201, 206–8,
  210–15, 217–21, 223–8, 232–6, 242–6,
  250–55, 271, 469
  and Troilus and Cressida 121, 122, 161–2, 170,
  177–80, 183–90, 198–201, 203, 206–8, 210–13,
  217, 220, 221, 224, 225, 227–8, 232–6, 238,
  239, 242–6, 250–55, 267, 271, 469
  Byron 121
Hassall, Eve 215, 217, 224, 245
Haus Hirth, near Munich
  W composes Siesta 25n
  W looks forward to visiting 46
Hawker, Karl 418
Hawkes, Ralph 149n
Haydn, Franz Joseph 300
  Symphony No. 102 in B♭ 428
Heath, Sir Edward 345
  correspondence with W 392, 398–9
  Birthday Dinner for W 398–9, 401, 402, 407
  and the Battle of Britain score 457
Heifetz, Jascha 222, 281, 284, 296, 297, 343,
  357, 367, 389, 413, 447
  and the Violin Concerto 106, 107, 113, 114,
  115, 118, 123, 124n, 126, 127, 224, 330n
  and the Cello Concerto 290, 284, 313
Hely-Hutchinson, Victor 140, 141

commissions *Troilus and Cressida* 140n
Hemming, Percy 150
Henry V (film) 120–21, 145, 146, 147, 168n, 333n
Henry Wood Concert Society 158
Henry Wood Hall (proposed) 478
Henry Wood Promenade Concerts 158, 241, 427
  Viola Concerto performances 32, 65
  W asked for a work for 50th anniversary 146, 148
  Violin Concerto performed 154
  Troilus and Cressida performed (Act II) 345–6, 400, 445
  Last Night of the Proms 412
Henryson, Robert 162
Henze, Hans Werner 247, 273, 393–4, 445, 453
  correspondence with W 325
  and the Second Symphony 317, 318
  health 448
  The Bassarids 197n, 365, 380, 381, 415
  Der langwierige Weg in die Wohnung der Natascha Ungeheuer 394n
  Ondine 325
  Tristan 415
Hereford: Three Choirs Festival 80n
Heward, Leslie: correspondence with W 118
Heyworth, Peter 263, 304, 334, 338, 374
  correspondence with W 326, 329, 363, 462
Hind, John 204
Hindemith, Gertrude 367
  correspondence with W xvii, 266, 308–9, 347–8
Hindemith, Paul
  correspondence with W 308–9, 311, 335
  plays first performance of the Viola Concerto 32, 44n, 47, 62n
  and *Scapino* 266
  and *Variations on a Theme by Hindemith* 286, 308, 334, 335, 336, 348
  death 347–8
  Mathis der Maler 213, 214
  Das Unaufhörliche 79
H.M.V. 370
Hochhauser, Victor 359
Hollingsworth, John 269
Holly Berry Lane, Hampstead, London (No. 10) 155
Hollywood Bowl 331
Hollywood composers 106
Hollywood Quartet 395
Hong Kong 348
Horner, David 56, 66
  correspondence with W 87–8, 99, 120, 197
Hotel Cappuccini Convento, Amalfi 44, 45, 46, 49, 57, 58, 59
Hotel Continental, Paris 34, 98
Hotel Europa, Salzburg 34
Hotel Garni, Zurich 76n
Hotel Portmeirion, Penrhyndeudraeth 143
Hotel Royal Lucerne 163, 164
Howard, Leslie 133, 136–40
Howarth, Elgar 443, 445, 453, 454, 457, 458
  Fireworks 453
Howells, Herbert 5, 22, 96

Huddersfield Choral Society 300–301n, 307n, 310n, 437
  and the *Gloria* 312, 393
Hughes, Owain Arwel 437
  and *Belshazzar's Feast* 437
Hughes, Patrick ('Spike') 330, 447
Hungarian T.V.: *The Bear* performed 446
Hungary, Soviet invasion of (1956) 287–8, 333
Hunt, Gillian 443
Hunter, Ian 296, 399

'I do like to be beside the seaside' (Glover-Kind) 131n, 132n
India 348
Inland Revenue 354
International Society for Contemporary Music (ISCM) festivals 112, 116
  Liège (1930): Viola Concerto 76
  Salzburg (1923): String Quartet 31, 76, 436
  Siena (1928): *Façade* 76, 450
  Zurich (1926): *Portsmouth Point* 31, 76
I.R.A. (Irish Republican Army) 410
Iran (Persia) 452, 455
Ireland, John 136, 141, 244
  correspondence with W 127
Irving, Ernest 157
Ischia
  W moves to (1949) xii, xviii, 53, 177–8
  Henze lives in 54
  W works on *Troilus and Cressida* 178, 179–80
  W describes life on 180–81, 278, 394, 460
  Dehn works on *The Bear* libretto 344, 362
  W invites Britten 347
  Dehn meets W 357n
  Heyworth invited 363
Israel 283, 322, 325, 372, 382n
  and *Belshazzar's Feast* 325, 331, 333
Istanbul 376
Italcemento 294n
Italian Riviera 177

Jacob, Archie 444
Jarre, Maurice 327n
Joffre, General Joseph 25
Johannesburg 278
Johannesburg Festival 274
John, Augustus 101
Jones, Parry (Gwynn Jones) 125, 192, 229, 238, 247, 249
Jonson, Ben: *Volpone* 121
Juliana, Princess (later Queen of the Netherlands) 84

Kallman, Chester 197, 228, 234
Karajan, Herbert von 278, 450, 453
  and the First Symphony 216n, 220
  and *Belshazzar's Feast* 216n, 412–13, 424
  and the *Partita* 298, 299
  and *Troilus and Cressida* 299, 335, 336
Kassel Opera House: *The Bear* performed 419, 422, 426, 446
Keats, John
  Endymion 129n
  'La Belle Dame Sans Merci' 96n

Keir, Muriel 164
  correspondence with W 209
Keller, Helga (née Cranston), correspondence
    with W 168, 272, 283–4, 286–7, 289, 322,
    325, 327, 333, 360–61, 372, 373–4, 382,
    451, 455, 462
Keller, Melvin 337, 382, 451
Kemp, Ian
  correspondence with W 337, 338
  *Michael Tippett - A Symposium on his Sixtieth
    Birthday* 337n, 338n
Kennedy, Michael 423
  Portrait of Elgar 383
  Portrait of Vaughan Williams 383
  Portrait of Walton xvi, 180
Kentner, Griselda (née Gould) 122
  correspondence with W xiv, 122, 158, 163,
    164, 166–7, 170, 171, 195, 196, 287–8, 312,
    313–14, 389, 459–60
Kentner, Louis 158n, 167
  correspondence with W 196, 287–8
  and the Violin Sonata 122, 163, 183, 195n
  and *Façade* 109
  and the Chopin Piano Competition 460
Kersey, Eda 149
Keynes, John Maynard, Lord 150
Kilsby, Rugby, Warwickshire 162
King's Lynn, Norfolk 405
Kingsway Hall, London: *Orb and Sceptre*
    recorded 223, 224
Kleiber, Carlos 452
Kleiber, Erich 172, 191
Klemperer, Otto 70
Knussen, Oliver
  correspondence with W 436, 461–2, 463
  Coursing for chamber orchestra 462
Köln *see* Cologne
Korngold, Erich Wolfgang 106
Kostelanetz, André 322–3, 381
Kostlinger, Josef 426
Koussevitsky, Sergei 40, 43, 48
  gives the first American performance of the
    Viola Concerto 49
  conducts *Portsmouth Point* 56
  Tanglewood offer to W 194
Krammer, Willy 222
Kraus, Otakar 246, 267, 269
Kreisler, Fritz 92, 160
Krips, Joseph: conducts *Improvisations* 387
Kubelík, Rafael 192
  and *Troilus and Cressida* 269, 309
Kurtz, Efrem 285n
  and the *Johannesburg Festival Overture* 278
  and *Escape Me Never* 278n
Kurtz, Elaine *see* Shaffer, Elaine

La Mortella, Forio d'Ischia 330–38, 347–51, 352,
    354–90, 356n, 392–432, 438–44, 446–9,
    451–63
  Walton Archive xii, 145n, 180
  W and Susana move in (1962) 266
  swimming pool 372, 399n, 404
  funicular railway 398, 404

La Scala, Milan 222, 243, 268, 380, 415
  and the Cello Concerto 274
  and *Troilus and Cressida* 261–2, 268–73, 365
Labroca family 311
Lacco Ameno, Ischia 420
Lambert, Constant 150, 467
  and *Façade* 57, 160, 449, 450n
  a close friend and colleague of W 57n
  spreads rumours about W's parentage 75n
  conducts *Belshazzar's Feast* 90, 99
  alcoholism 160n
  Anna Karenina 165
  Eight Songs of Li-Po 124
  Piano Concerto 124
  The Rio Grande 23n, 59, 380
  Tiresias 228, 230
Lambert, Isabel 226, 227, 228, 230, 231, 233,
    237, 239, 241, 249, 252
Lambert, Kit 379–80
Lang, Paul Henry 329
Lassade 64
László, Magda: and *Troilus and Cressida* 182,
    247–52, 301
Lawrence of Arabia (film) 327
Leeds 65
Leeds Festival 61, 66, 182
  Committee 39
  Beecham conducts *Sinfonia concertante* 43
  first performance of *Belshazzar's Feast* 55, 90n
Legge, Elisabeth *see* Schwarzkopf, Elisabeth
Legge, Walter 112, 134, 163, 195, 360
  correspondence with W xiv, 148–9, 188–9,
    192–3, 215–16, 220–21, 278–9, 354–6, 360,
    363–8, 370–71, 376–7, 380, 381, 387, 401,
    412–13, 414, 423–4, 426–7, 429–30,
    446–52
  one of W's lifelong friends 112n
  and *Belshazzar's Feast* 138
  and *Troilus and Cressida* 181, 187, 238, 244,
    249, 335, 336, 423, 429
  and Webster 240
  and *The Bear* 364, 365, 366, 370, 376, 380
Leibl, Marianna 274–5
Leigh, Vivien 233, 266, 270
Leighton, Frederick, Lord 308
Leoncavallo, Ruggiero: *Zazà* 192
Lessing, Gottfried Ephraim 253
Lewis, Richard 246, 251, 262, 307, 429, 445
Ley, Dr Henry 13
  W's accompanist at his Christ Church voice
    trial 3
  an early supporter of W 3
  and W's music 4, 9, 11, 12
  and Noel's visit 17
  gives W organ and piano lessons 19, 20
Lidell, Alvar 316
Lion Memorial, Lucerne 163n
Lipp, Wilma 241, 242
Lisbon: *The Bear* performed 411
The Listener magazine 303
Liszt, Franz: Rhapsody No. 2 27
Liverpool 301
  Violin Concerto performed 148

Sinfonia concertante performance 149
Façade performances 209
Liverpool University 125
Llandaff Festival 452, 453
Lockhart, James: and *The Bear* 371, 419
London
  Sinfonia concertante performed 56
  expense of living in 61
  Conference (1931) 64
  musical activity suspended in the war 119
  Cello Concerto premièred 285n, 288
  Johannesburg Festival Overture performed 288
  W on 410, 460
London Coliseum, St Martin's Lane, London 415
  and *Troilus and Cressida* 410
London Philharmonic Orchestra 112
London Sinfonietta 456
London Symphony Orchestra (LSO) 384, 440
  committee 95
  First Symphony recorded 368
London University 270
Long, Martin 349, 350
Los Angeles 327
Los Angeles, Victoria de 301
Los Angeles Philharmonic Orchestra 414, 416
Loughran, James 426
Lowndes Cottage, Lowndes Place, London xvii,
  120, 169, 171, 183, 205, 209, 223, 224,
  226, 258, 266, 267, 313, 314, 322
  Alice buys 105
  left to W in Alice's will 122, 169n
  rented to friends 266
  sold to help buy La Mortella 266, 290–91
Lucerne 122, 165
Lucerne Festival 334
Lugano 63
Lytham St Annes 18
Lyttelton, Captain Oliver 150

McEacharn, Captain Neil 79, 79n, 90
McKie, Sir William 223
McLaren, Christabel *see* Aberconway, Lady
McLaren, Henry *see* Aberconway, Lord
Macmillan (publishers) 467
Macmillan, Sir E. 133
Macmillan, Sir Harold (1st Earl of Stockton) 64
MacNeice, Louis
  W admires 136
  Christopher Columbus 120, 135n, 136n, 369
Magdalen College, Oxford 11, 12, 16, 24
Magyar, Thomas 205
Mahler, Gustav 418, 477
Major Barbara (film) 133, 140
Malko, Nikolai 160
Manchester 25, 26, 285, 301, 326
  Viola Concerto performed 70
  Belshazzar's Feast performed 85
  W conducts *Façade* suite No. 2 124
  W records and rehearses (1942) 136
  Cello Concerto performed 313
Manchester University 125
Mansion House, London 390
Marek, George 224

Margaret, HRH The Princess 98
Markevitch, Igor 47
Marks, J. B. 235–6, 285, 291, 313, 354
Marlborough Club, Pall Mall, London 41
Marlborough House School, Cranbrook, Kent 4, 7
Marlowe, Christopher 468n
Marriner, Sir Neville: and *Sonata for Strings* 395,
  396, 398
Marsh, Edward 47, 224
Mary, Queen of Scots 196
Masefield, John 155–6
  W meets 22
  'Where Does the Uttered Music Go?' 156n,
  157–8
Massenet, Jules 357, 359
Massine, Leonid 98, 117, 161
Mathieson, Muir 121, 141, 145, 330
Matisse, Henri 61
Matthews, Thomas 160
Maxwell Davies, Peter: First Symphony 461
May, Nurse 61, 62
Mayer, Sir Robert 396, 454, 456
Mecca Cafés 194
Mehta, Zubin 414, 416
Melbourne, Australia 350
Melodiya 419
Mendelssohn-Bartholdy, Felix
  A Midsummer Night's Dream incidental music
  151
  'When Jesus was born' 8
Mengelberg, Willem
  and the First Symphony 112
  and the Viola Concerto 112
Menotti, Gian Carlo 268
  The Consul 207, 208
Menuhin, Diana (née Gould) 158n, 163, 170
  correspondence with Susana 195, 196
  correspondence with W 195, 196
  meets W 122
  and the Violin Sonata 122, 163n, 167, 170, 171
Menuhin, Gerard 183n
Menuhin, Yehudi (Lord Menuhin of Stoke
  d'Abernon) 170
  correspondence with W 183, 195, 196, 389, 404
  and the Violin Sonata 122, 163, 165, 167, 183,
  189, 195, 204, 313
  and W's seventieth birthday 399, 402
Metropolitan Opera House, New York 463n
Miami Opera 457
Milan 164, 270, 431
  W with Ann Bergson in 171
  Façade performed 197
  state-run opera houses 476–7
Milford, Sir Humphrey 131n, 465, 467
Milhaud, Darius 30, 130
Ministry of Health 474
Ministry of Information film unit 119, 128, 129,
  130
Ministry of Labour 138
Mitchell, Donald 304
Montale, Eugenio 268
Monte Carlo 177
Monteverità 64

Montreal 110, 376
Sinfonia concertante performed 69
Moore, Gerald 366, 370
premières *A Song for the Lord's Table* 366n
Moore, Sir Henry
correspondence with W 230
and *Troilus and Cressida* 181, 226–30
and Olivier 237
Morison, Elsie 309
Morrell, Lady Ottoline 27
Morris, Christopher 424, 442
correspondence with W 287–8, 431–2, 438,
439, 440, 443, 444, 452–3, 457, 458
and *The Bear* 443
Morris, Wyn 393
Mortimer, Raymond 42, 43
Moscow 160
Mosley, Cynthia (Cimmie) 88, 89
Mosley, Sir Oswald 88, 89
Mozart, Wolfgang Amadeus 300
'Dies irae' 17
Don Giovanni 144
The Magic Flute 194, 271
The Marriage of Figaro 241
Symphony No. 34 in C 428
Symphony No. 40 in G minor 300
Münch, Charles: and Cello Concerto 277, 313
Munich
Belshazzar's Feast performed 422, 425, 426
The Bear performed 422, 426, 446
Museum of Modern Art, New York 478
Musicians' Union New Music Committee (later
Committee (then Society) for the Promotion
of New Music) 146
Mussolini, Benito 387, 450n
Mussorgsky, Modest: *Boris Godunov* 192, 214,
446

Naples 177, 192, 195, 197, 199, 201, 204, 222,
231, 245, 289, 307
String Quartet No. 2 broadcast 203
Façade performed 315, 316
National Gallery, London 130
National Health Services bill 474
National Symphony Orchestra of Washington,
DC 458, 459
National Theatre, London 474
Naylor, Zena
correspondence with W xviii, 32, 34–5, 37,
39–40
relationship with W 32
Nethy Bridge Hotel, Inverness-shire 146
Neveu, Ginette 188, 447
New College, Oxford 13
New Party 89n
New Philharmonia Orchestra 366, 370
First Symphony recorded 367–8
New Statesman 224
New York 43, 107, 113, 337, 367
Koussevitsky conducts *Portsmouth Point* 56
W visits (1961) 322–3
New York City Center Opera: *Troilus and
Cressida* performed 261, 268

New York Herald Tribune 329, 381
New York Philharmonic Orchestra: and *Capriccio
burlesco* 344, 364, 380, 381n
New York World's Fair 90n, 113n, 114, 118
New Zealand: W tours (1964) 343, 348, 392–3
Newman, Ernest 40, 210
correspondence with W 48, 57–8, 93, 94, 166,
167
and *Troilus and Cressida* 166, 221, 236
and the Violin Sonata 199
death 315
Newman, Mrs Vera: correspondence with W 315
Newsweek 331, 332
Next of Kin (film) 133, 157
Niarchos, Stavros 287
Nichols, Robert ('Crikey') 62, 69
Nielsen, Carl 159
Nightingale Corner, Rickmansworth 60n
Nilsson, Raymond 267, 269
Nono, Luigi 273, 325
Nono, Nuria 273
Normandie, SS 119
Northcott, Bayan 461–2
Norwich, Norfolk 460
Nottingham: *Belshazzar's Feast* performed 85
Les Novalles, Blonay, Vevey, Switzerland 169, 170
Novello, Ivor 178, 193, 206, 207, 208
Novello and Co. Ltd. 468

O'Bryen, Linnit & Dunfee 107, 127, 145
Observer newspaper 263, 363, 374, 462
Ogdon, John 380
Oistrakh, David 160
Old Vic Company 473, 475
Oldham, Lancashire xv, 3, 29–30
Olivier, Edith 61, 62, 72, 80
W stays with 53, 54, 69, 70, 71, 72
Olivier, Lady (Joan Plowright) 327, 381, 451, 455
Olivier, Laurence (later Lord Olivier) 150, 153,
245, 265, 309, 325, 390, 392
correspondence with W 230–31, 290–91,
303–4, 326, 404, 420
becomes firm friends with W 120–21
Henry V 120–21
Hamlet 161, 166
and *Troilus and Cressida* 181, 229, 230–31,
233, 237, 239, 240, 241
lends W a cottage at Notley 225
and Moore 237
rents Lowndes Cottage 266
Macbeth project 303–4, 309, 311
in *Becket* 322
W visits in Brighton 327
stays with W 381, 382, 455
and *The Battle of Britain* 383, 386n
Three Sisters 387
illness 451
in *Dracula* 451
Olivier, Richard Kerr 325n, 327
Onassis, Aristotle 287
Opera Theatre of St Louis 443
Orchestre Symphonique de Paris: performs
Sinfonia concertante 44

Orff, Carl: *Carmina Burana* 449–50
Orford, Suffolk 365
Oxford 43, 134, 355
Oxford Book of Verse 129
Oxford University 125
Oxford University Press 93, 123, 202, 287n, 301,
 309, 326, 356, 358, 380, 438, 442, 453
 Foss's decision to publish W's music xiv, 31
 Frank as W's publisher xiv
 and royalties 45, 330–31
 contract with W 53
 Foss's aim 54
 and W's film business 107
 Boosey & Hawkes tries to poach W from
  108–9, 214, 262–3, 465
 W's subsidy 115
 and the Feldman royalties issue 131, 131n, 132n
 and *Belshazzar's Feast* 139
 agent for W's stage works 145
 and the String Quartet in A minor 155
 and *Troilus and Cressida* 182, 237, 243, 254,
  255–7, 465
 compared with Boosey & Hawkes 214, 465
 W decides to stay with 215, 465
 and the Cello Concerto 297
 and the *Partita* 306
 and *The Bear* 344, 446
 and Cutting 349
 and W's *Improvisations* 385
 deluxe edition of *Façade* 396–7
 special copy of *Five Bagatelles* for Arnold 397,
  415n
 and *Varii Capricci* 430
 and the First String Quartet 436, 444
 and the Violin Concerto 466

Palestrina, Giovanni Pierluigi da 437, 440
 'Veni Sponsa Christi' 438
Pallanza 79, 82, 90
Palmer, Tony 435, 462n
Pannain, Guido 202, 273
Paraguay 172
Paris 43, 45, 46, 197
 Portsmouth Point broadcast 56
 Sinfonia concertante performed 56
Paris Opéra-Comique 477
Parry, Sir Hubert 5, 9, 11–14
Pascal, Gabriel 114
Pascal Film Productions Ltd. 127n
Passau: *The Bear* performed 446
Peake, Revd Edward 16, 17, 19
Peake, Mrs 16, 17
Pears, Sir Peter xvii, 246, 264, 366
 correspondence with W 273–4, 432
 and *Troilus and Cressida* 248, 249, 309
 and *Anon. in Love* 318, 354
 and *The Bear* 343–4, 351, 405
 illness 385
 and *Façade* 405
 and Britten's death 432
 knighthood 446
Performing Right Society (PRS) 115, 128, 170,
 236, 379, 390, 409, 423, 446, 450

international conference (Buenos Aires, 1948)
 122–3, 175
 and *Façade* 132n
 and royalties 330–31
Perlman, Itzhak 447
Perry, Sheila xvii, 209
Persia *see* Iran
Perth, Australia 347, 350
Perugia 197
Peterkin, Norman 154
 correspondence with W 138–9, 145
Peyton, John 398, 399
Philips (Record Co.) 423
Piatigorsky, Gregor 343, 419
 correspondence with W xvi, 265, 274–7,
  281–4, 289–90, 292, 293, 294–8, 313,
  356–7, 361, 367, 411–12, 413, 416–17,
  419–20
 and the Cello Concerto 265, 268n, 274–7, 279,
  280, 281–5, 287, 288, 292, 293, 294–8, 300,
  313, 314, 413, 416–17, 419–20
Picasso, Pablo 61
Piccadilly Theatre, London 142
Pilgrim Trust 130
Pinder, Ralph 466–7
Piper, John 404
Plesch, Prof. J. 112
P.L.O. (Palestine Liberation Organization) 455
Plomer, William 219
Poleri, David 246, 273
Polydor 380
Ponnelle, Jean-Pierre 253
Ponsonby, Elizabeth 42, 44
Ponsonby, Robert 427
Porto d'Ischia 201, 208, 254, 289, 311
Portofino 164
Portugal 66, 337
Poulenc, Francis 30, 334
 Gloria 323
Powell, Mrs (Sitwells' housekeeper) 57–60
Pozzuoli 245, 311
Pretoria 278
Previn, André 441
 and *Troilus and Cressida* 345, 346, 423, 441n,
  445
 one of W's most enthusiastic supporters 345
 and the First Symphony 368, 370, 435
 and W's seventieth birthday 399
 conducts *Belshazzar's Feast* 401, 407
 records the Violin Concerto 406
Primrose, William 297
The Prince and the Showgirl (film) 304
Pritchard, John: and Second Symphony 322n
Pro Musica society 44
Prokofiev, Sergei 160
 Lieutenant Kijé 359
 The Prodigal Son 46–7
'Proms' *see* Henry Wood Promenade Concerts
Psalm 130 (*De Profundis*) 438
Puccini, Giacomo 193, 198, 224, 244
 Madama Butterfly 21, 192
 Tosca 199
 Turandot 144n

Pulver, Frau 66
Pulver family 64
Pygmalion (film) 106, 114

Queen Elizabeth Hall, London 398
Queen's College, Oxford 23
Queen's Hall, London 33, 95, 112, 115, 478n
  Belshazzar's Feast broadcast 77
Queen's Hall Orchestra 98n
Quidhampton, near Salisbury 53, 54, 72, 73, 74, 81
Quilter, Roger: *A Children's Overture* 128

R.A.I. 294
Rakhmaninov, Sergei 404
  Piano Concerto No. 3 in D minor 419
  The Rock 419
Rattigan, Sir Terence 348
Ravel, Maurice
  Daphnis et Chloë 6
  L'heure espagnole 25
Ravello 106, 113, 114, 116, 177, 363
Ravinia, Chicago 331
Rawsthorne, Alan 112, 326, 459, 460
R.C.A. Victor 296, 297, 412, 416
The Reason Why 316
Redgrave, Sir Michael 240
Reinhardt, Hans 83, 85
Reizenstein, Franz 243, 244
Remedios, Alberto 400, 422, 423, 426
Renishaw Hall, Derbyshire 89n, 90, 100
Rennert, Günther 271
Restituta, Santa 212
Richard III (film) 168n
Richardson, Sir Ralph 150, 388
Ricordi 321
Rimsky-Korsakov, Nikolay 446
  Boris Godunov 214
  Sheherazade 14
Ritz Hotel, Piccadilly, London 393, 394, 399,
  420, 421, 429, 430
Robey, George 390
Robilant, Alicia di 175
Robinson, Stanford 140
Rome 36, 164, 245, 292, 311, 371, 388, 411,
  414, 446
  W's 1932 visit 85, 86
  Façade performed 193, 197
  String Quartet No. 2 broadcast 203
  and *Troilus and Cressida* 272
  Susana's illness in 273
  Violin Concerto performed 299
Rome Radio Quartet 203
Rootham, Helen 25
Rosenstock, Joseph 268
Rossini, Gioachino 181, 450n
  L'Assedio di Corinto 216
Rostropovich, Mstislav 298, 359, 416
  and *Passacaglia* 456, 458
  and *Prologo e Fantasia* 458n
Roth, Ernest 242–3, 268
Rouault, Georges 46
Roussel, Albert: *Padmâvatî* 216
Royal Air Force (RAF) music department 136, 148

Royal Albert Hall, London
  Beecham conducts *Façade* 41
  acoustics 135
  British première of the Violin Concerto 135n
  Troilus and Cressida performed 345, 346
  proposed move of the 'Proms' 478
Royal Ballet 463n
Royal College of Music 11, 96
  and *Portsmouth Point* 56
Royal Festival Hall, London 384, 401, 454
  Façade performed 219
  W's honorary doctorate 270
  Bach Choir concert 354
  Improvisations performed 393
  Varii capricci commission 412, 418, 420, 423,
    425, 430
  constructed for the Festival of Britain 478n
Royal Liverpool Philharmonic Orchestra: and the
  Second Symphony 285, 319, 322n
Royal Opera House, Covent Garden 24, 152,
  164, 200, 209n, 219, 222, 230, 376, 386,
  431, 450, 463
  W's memorandum xv, 121, 151, 472–9
  Boosey & Hawkes' involvement 149n
  Committee 149–51
  and *Troilus and Cressida* 181, 182, 216, 243,
    253, 255, 261, 262, 267, 278–9, 301n,
    310n, 346, 403, 410, 423, 424, 426, 432,
    445
  Brook's directorship 188, 191
  W subscribes 203
  W resigns as a Director 220–21, 222
  Italian week (1976) 428
Royal Philharmonic Orchestra
  first performance of *Sinfonia concertante* 38, 40
  and *Variations on a Theme by Hindemith* 335
  founded 477n
Rubbra, Edmund: *Passacaglia and Fugue* 317,
  318
Rubinstein, Artur 79
'Rule, Britannia!' (Arne) 128
Russell, Lord [Bertrand] 339

Sabata, Victor De 268
Sadler's Wells Ballet 149n
Sadler's Wells Ballet Company [proposed] 475,
  476
Sadler's Wells opera and ballet Companies 473
Sadler's Wells Opera Company [proposed] 475,
  476
Sadler's Wells Theatre, London 120, 134, 135,
  153, 374, 477
St Albans Cathedral Choir 438
St Joan (film) 98, 283
St John's College, Oxford 22
St John's College Choir 438
Saltzman, Harry 383n, 384
Salzburg 364, 365, 381, 415
  ISCM festival (1923) 31, 436
  first String Quartet played 31, 76, 436, 444
Salzburg Festival 363
San Felice, Ischia 265, 314–29, 408n
San Francesco, Arezzo 442

San Francisco: *Improvisations* premièred 387n
San Francisco Opera: American première of
    Troilus and Cressida 261, 269n
Sanzogno, Nino 268, 321
Sargent, Sir Malcolm 90, 350, 444
    and *Troilus and Cressida* 182, 229, 240, 241,
        242, 244, 251, 255, 269, 335
    and *Belshazzar's Feast* 200, 229n
    and the *Johannesburg Festival Overture* 278
    and the Cello Concerto 300
    and the *Gloria* 312
    and the First Symphony 367–8, 370
    W on his illness 368–9
    death 368n
Sassoon, Siegfried xiv, xvi, 6, 40, 42
    correspondence with W 33, 35, 41, 44–7,
        55–8, 60–62, 63–6, 69–72, 76–9, 80, 85–6,
        100–101
    correspondence with Imma von Doenberg 62,
        66–9, 79, 81
    W meets 22
    one of W's closest friends and supporters 22n
    Portsmouth Point dedicated to 31, 33
    helps W on financial matters 36n, 45, 46, 53,
        54, 56, 70, 77–8
    and Imma von Doernberg 53, 55
    told of the Courtauld bequest 71, 72
    engaged to Hester Gatty 72
Satie, Erik 130
    Parade 27
Sauguet, Henri 447
Savile Club, 69 Brook Street, London 165, 403,
    410
Savoy Hotel, London 31, 152, 360
Savoy Hotel, Zurich 170
Savoy Orpheans 31, 33
Sawallisch, Wolfgang 286
Scherchen, Hermann 99, 116, 222
Schippers, Thomas 268, 321, 419
Schloss Monrepos, Ludwigsburg 128
Schnabel, Artur 43
Schneiderhan, Wolfgang 205
Schoenberg, Arnold 31, 76, 160, 436
    Moses und Aron 356
    Pierrot Lunaire 31, 219
    Von Heute auf Morgen 222–3
Scholes, Percy 467
Schott 423
Schubert, Franz
    Piano Trio in B♭ 345
    'Where thou reignest' 15
Schumann, Robert: 'Te decet hymnus' 15
Schwarzkopf, Elisabeth (Professor Dr Elisabeth
    Legge-Schwarzkopf DBE Kammersängerin)
    355, 356, 363, 413, 414, 452
    and *Troilus and Cressida* 181–2, 189n, 193,
        221, 229, 232, 238–9, 241, 244, 249, 262,
        266, 279
    and *A Song for the Lord Mayor's Table* 326,
        327, 366n
    correspondence with W 360, 401
Searle, Humphrey: *Hamlet* 394
Second Viennese School 31

Second World War 320n
    and the Violin Concerto 107, 119
    broadcasting and film-making 119, 120–21
    W proposes joining the A.R.P. 123
    W's view of its duration 127
Sengerphone 30
Severance Hall, Cleveland, Ohio 119
Shaffer, Elaine 285n
Shakespeare, William
    Antony and Cleopatra 121, 230
    The Merchant of Venice 468n
    A Midsummer Night's Dream 477
    The Tempest 443
    Troilus and Cressida 122, 162, 179
Shanks, Dr Jean 399
Shawe-Taylor, Desmond 197, 374
Sheepshanks, Lilias 369, 375, 378, 384, 385,
    386, 388, 390, 405
Sheldonian Theatre, Oxford 22
Sheridan, Richard Brinsley: *The Rivals* 20
Shrublands Hall Health Clinic, Suffolk 393,
    421n
Sibelius, Jean 159, 453
    Symphony No. 4 450
    Symphony No. 5 450
    Symphony No. 6 450, 453
    Symphony No. 7 450
    Tapiola 453
    The Tempest 151
Sicily 58, 443
Siena 197, 449, 450n
    ISCM festival (1928) 76, 450
Sitwell, Dame Edith 6, 35, 47, 377
    Façade 30, 35n, 57, 74n
    and *Three Songs* 73, 74
Sitwell, Francis 364
Sitwell, Sir George 57, 58, 59, 75n, 304
Sitwell, Georgia 42, 54, 66, 71, 88, 460
Sitwell, Sir Osbert 6, 34, 37, 38, 42, 46, 58, 81,
    120, 197, 304, 377–8, 390
    correspondence with W 98–9, 113–14, 362,
        364–5
    selects the text of *Belshazzar's Feast* 37n, 43n,
        301n
    and Horner 56, 66, 88
    lets the Carlyle Square house 86
    goes to Corfu 86
    and Fascism 88–9
    behaviour over W's relationship with Alice 105
    invitation to W and Susana 176
    letter on the H-bomb 198
    selects the text for an oratorio (*Moses and
        Pharaoh*, never composed) 300–301, 310
    and *The Bear* 375
    assistance to W and Alec 377–8
    Brighton 99n
    Escape With Me! An Oriental Sketch Book 198
    The First Shoot (libretto) 56n, 98, 101
    *Winters of Content. More Discursions on
        Travel, Art and Life* 89
Sitwell, Sacheverell ('Sachie') 6, 23, 34, 36, 42,
    46, 66, 88, 377, 411, 460
    at Oxford 24

visits Spain with W (1925) 31
W stays with 54
importance of his friendship to W 75–6
Sitwell family 76, 330n
W lives in their house in Carlyle Square
xiii–xiv, xv, 6, 23, 24, 29, 32, 36n, 53, 54,
70
W taken on trips abroad xv, 6, 29, 177
financial support of W 36n
rift with W 101n, 105
and the Viola Concerto 177
Les Six 30, 436
Slevin, Felix 131n
Smith, Cyril 149
Smyth, Dame Ethel 75n
Snape Maltings Concert Hall, Suffolk 388n
Social Insurance and Allied Services Report 474
Söderström, Elisabeth 432
Solti, Sir Georg: and *Troilus and Cressida* 323–4,
426
Somers, Debroy 33n
Somme, Battle of the 5, 9, 11
Sophocles: *Oedipus Rex* 135n
Sorabji, Kaikhosru 160
South Eaton Place, London (No. 56A) 101, 102,
105, 108, 110
W buys 105
destroyed in the Blitz 120, 155n
Spain: W visits (1925) 31, 33
Sparkes, Mrs Diana 466
Stadlen, Peter 461–2
Stainer, Sir John 8
Stainer & Bell 438
Stanford, Charles Villiers 12
'The Lord is my shepherd' 16
Steggall, Reginald: 'Remember now thy Creator'
12–13
Stevenson, Ronald: *Passacaglia on DSCH* 366
Stix, Lidya 222
Stockhausen, Karlheinz 263
Inori 415
Stockholm Opera 429
Stokowski, Leopold: correspondence with W 402
Strauss, Richard 198, 214, 305
Elektra 230
Der Rosenkavalier 214
Salome 188, 192, 222–3
Stravinsky, Igor 6, 27, 30, 129, 357, 359, 436
The Flood 329
Mavra 359
Petrushka 6
The Rake's Progress 197n, 214, 251
The Rite of Spring 6
Strong, Dr Thomas 3, 7, 8, 11, 14
correspondence with W 25–6, 27–8
an early supporter of W 3, 6
helps W financially 5, 19, 27, 36n
and W's exhibition scholarship 5
importance of his friendship to W 75–6
Suez Crisis 283n, 286–7
Sunray Heating 372
Swan Walk, London (No. 5) 25
Sweden 66, 155

Switzerland 122, 452
W lives in xiv, xvi, 73, 171
Menuhin's advance 165, 167
W works on *Belshazzar's Feast* and the First
Symphony 177
Menuhin plays the Violin Sonata 204
see also Ascona; Casa Angolo, Ascona
Sydney, Australia 348, 349, 350
Szell, George
correspondence with W xvii
and the *Partita* 265, 278n, 295, 299, 306, 315
and the Second Symphony 265, 315, 321, 322,
328, 329, 461
and *Variations on a Theme by Hindemith* 265,
336, 356
and *Newsweek* 331, 332
Szigeti, Joseph 163
and *Valse* 305

Tait, George 408, 409, 418, 420
Tait, Gunda 408, 409
Tanglewood Summer School of Music 194n
Tasso, Torquato 470, 471
Taylor, Valerie 42, 43–4
Tchaikovsky, Pyotr Ilyich 359
Tchelicheff, Pavel 47
Tear, Robert 431
Teatro Colón, Buenos Aires 202
Teatro La Fenice, Venice 414
Teatro San Carlo, Naples 202, 216, 222, 243,
307, 308
Tebaldi, Renata 216
Tel Aviv University 455
Tempo magazine 452n
Tennant, Stephen 25n, 42, 44, 46, 57, 58, 64, 65,
78
correspondence with W 40
at Haus Hirth 46
health 61, 80, 86
W wants him moved to Switzerland 64
his behaviour 66
Tertis, Lionel: and the Viola Concerto 44, 61, 62n
Thatcher, Margaret, later Baroness 455
Theatre Royal, Drury Lane, London 117
Thomas, Ambroise: *Mignon* 21
Thos Cook & sons 177
Via Tornabuoni, Florence 34, 60
Zurich 60
Three Choirs Festival 81
Portsmouth Point performed 80
Sinfonia concertante performed 43
Viola Concerto performed 80
Ticino, Switzerland 452
Time 188
The Times newspaper 39, 43, 124, 198, 416, 426
Tippett, Sir Michael 152, 222n, 365, 366, 413,
418
stays in one of W's houses 383
The Midsummer Marriage 241, 423
Piano Concerto 288n
Tooley, Sir John 463
correspondence with W 400
and *Troilus and Cressida* 457

Toscanini, Arturo 392, 431, 477
Tovey, Sir Donald 467
Toye, Geoffrey 90
Traunkirchen, Austria 31
Trussel, Jacque 429
Tunbridge Wells Symphony Orchestra 453
Tunisia 392
Turner, Charles 268
Tuxen, Erik 159
Two Cities film company 147

Uhde, Hermann 229, 232, 238
United Artists 383n, 386, 457n
Upon this Rock (film) 388

Vale of Health, Hampstead 224
Van Dieren, Bernard *see* Dieren, Bernard van
Vancouver 331, 397
Vatican City 292
Vaughan Williams, Ralph 96, 114, 128, 136, 138,
    202, 257n, 378, 379n, 418, 467
  and *Henry V* 454
  5 Mystical Songs 438
  49th Parallel 118
  Henry V (overture for brass band) 454n
  A London Symphony 171
  Pilgrim's Progress 214
  The Running Set 128n
  Sinfonia antartica 224n
Venice 171, 303, 414
Verdi, Giuseppe 198, 445
  Aida 185, 186n, 187, 190
  Un ballo in maschera 212
  Otello 15, 185, 187, 201
  Requiem 267, 269
  Rigoletto 212
  La traviata 273, 452
Vic–Wells Companies 473
Vickers, Jon 307, 309
Vienna 299
Vienna Konzerthaus 172
Vienna State Opera 164, 377, 476–7
Villa Cimbrone, above Ravello 106, 113, 114,
    116
Villa la Chance, Blonay, Vevey, Switzerland 367
Villa Taranto, Pallanza 79
Villa Venture 456
Vito, Gioconda de 204
Vivaldi, Antonio 27
Volpone (film) 207
Vyner, Michael: correspondence with W 456–7

Waddington Galleries, Cork Street, London 422
Wagner, Richard 198, 236, 417
  Lohengrin 192
  Der Ring des Nibelungen 426
Walters, Jess 267, 269
Walton, Alexander (Alec; W's younger brother) 3,
    356
  childhood 7
  W sends suits 36, 41
  W tries to get him a job 97, 98
  health 108

Alice's efforts to help him 110
and his son Michael 133
Osbert's assistance 377–8
Arnold visits in Canada 396, 397
death 454–5
Walton, Charles (W's father) 3, 30
Walton, Jo (W's sister-in-law) 454
Walton, Louisa (W's mother) 39
  correspondence with W 3–25, 10, 27, 28–30,
    33, 36, 41, 48–9, 59, 60, 108–11
  birth of W 3
  and Dora Foss 117
Walton, Michael (W's nephew) 133
Walton, Noel (W's elder brother) 3, 18, 28, 39
  childhood 7, 13
  visits W at Christ Church 17
  health 22, 23, 60, 455
Walton, Nora *see* Donnelly, Nora
Walton, Lady Susana (née Gil Passo)
  on W's persuasiveness xii–xiii
  works for the British Council in Buenos Aires
    123
  marries W 123, 175
  relationship with W 175–6
  friendship with Christabel Aberconway 176
  pollen allergy 249
  plans a home and garden 265, 288, 446
  car accident and convalescence 294, 295, 298
  and Szell 332
  broken knee joint 343, 347–50
  and the Arnold incident 408n
  health 412, 448, 450
  and acupuncture 441
  William Walton: Behind the Façade 175, 346
Walton, Sir William Turner
  birth (29 March 1902) 3, 75
  moves to Ischia (1949) xii, xviii, 53, 176–7
  lives in the Sitwells' house xiii–xiv, xv, 23, 24,
    53, 54, 70
  affairs with women xiv, 122
  relationship with Baroness Imma von
    Doernberg xiv, 53, 55
  interest in the arts xv, 29
  memorandum on the future of the Royal Opera
    House xv, 121, 151, 472–9
  letter-writing style xvi–xviii
  choirboy at Christ Church College, Oxford
    xvii, xviii, 3–19, 75
  early compositions 4–5
  exhibition scholar at Christ Church 5, 6,
    19–28, 75, 357n
  first visits Italy (1920) 29, 76
  meets Schoenberg 31, 76
  relationship with Zena Naylor 32
  health 38, 40, 41, 45, 91, 105, 111, 113, 139,
    344, 345, 346, 360–67, 371, 374, 378, 382,
    387, 421, 425, 441, 445, 446, 448, 450,
    454–5
  lives with Imma in Ascona 53, 54
  financial problems 53–4
  Imma leaves 55
  relationship with Alice Wimborne 55, 101n,
    105, 106, 122, 176

the Courtauld bequest 71, 78n, 87n
convalesces with Alice in Italy 105–6
visits Heifetz in Connecticut 107, 119n
film scores during the Second World War
    120–21
Covent Garden Opera House involvement 121,
    149n, 176
Alice's death 122
Performing Right Society conference in Buenos
    Aires 122–3
marries Susana Gil Passo (1948) 123, 175
the Feldman royalties issue 131–2
eye injury 149
a director of Dallas Bower Productions Inc.
    161, 290–91
liaison with Ann Bergson 166n
relationship with Susana 175–6
and the rise of Benjamin Britten 176–7
importance of *Troilus and Cressida* to him 180
resistance to his later music 182, 263
decision to stay with OUP 215, 465
resigns from Covent Garden 220–21, 222
response to *Troilus*'s performance at La Scala
    262
as a conductor 262
relationship with Britten 264
prolific output 264
change in his music's tone 264
technical refinement 264–5
moves in to La Mortella (1962) 266
honorary doctorates 270, 381, 409–10
house-letting on Ischia 288, 301–2, 303
car accident, convalescence, and litigation
    (1957) 292, 293, 294–300, 302, 303, 305,
    308–9, 345
enjoys a seance 305
admiring letter to Britten 338–9
tour of New Zealand and Australia (1964)
    343, 347, 349–50, 356n
Order of Merit 344, 377, 379, 382
loss of creative confidence 345, 383–4, 420, 459
seventieth birthday celebrations 345, 398–9,
    401–5
suspected stroke 346, 422–3
taxation problems 354, 355
rift with Arnold 408–9
biography 411, 423, 447, 448–9
the first page of a Third Symphony 436
houses taken over by Villa Venture 456
death 437
personality xii, xiv, 175
    competitiveness xii, 119–20, 264
    curiosity 436–7
    economy of expression 3
    generosity 54
    hard-working 54–5
    manipulativeness xii, 175, 181
    self-sufficiency xii, 5
    selfishness 175
    sense of humour xi, 263, 345, 435
works
'All This Time' 407
Anon. in Love 317–18, 354, 390, 394

As You Like It 101, 107–8
The Battle of Britain 383–4, 385, 386, 457,
    458
The Bear xii, xvii, 145n, 205n, 343–4, 351,
    354, 357–60, 364, 365, 366, 368–78, 380,
    382, 411, 419, 422, 440, 443
Belshazzar's Feast xvii, 37n, 43n, 49, 54–5, 57,
    60–61, 62n, 65, 67, 77, 79, 82–5, 87, 88,
    90n, 138–9, 167, 176, 177, 192, 200, 202,
    204, 229n, 286, 288, 325, 327, 331, 333,
    382, 406, 407, 414, 425, 444, 465
The Boy David 98, 101, 107, 108
Cantico del Sole 410, 411
Capriccio burlesco 344–5, 364, 380, 381, 383
Cello Concerto xiii, 264, 265, 268–9, 270,
    274–9, 280, 281–5, 285n, 287, 288, 289,
    292, 293, 300, 313, 314, 331, 350, 411,
    412, 413, 416–17, 418
Chorale Fantasia for organ 5, 9, 11
Chorale Prelude on 'Wheatley' 9
Christopher Columbus incidental music 120,
    135n, 136, 138–43, 368, 369n
Coronation Te Deum 221, 222, 224
Crown Imperial Coronation march for orches-
    tra 109–10, 166, 320n, 468
Duets for Children 154
Escape Me Never 54, 98, 99, 101n, 135n, 278n
Façade xiv, xvi, 30–31, 32, 44–7, 57, 59, 124,
    125, 126, 131n, 132n, 160, 193, 197, 204,
    209, 315, 344, 350, 366, 372, 396–7, 405,
    428, 431, 436, 449, 468
Façade Suite No. 1 36, 40, 109, 117, 131n,
    132n, 172, 202
Façade Suite No. 2 124, 172, 202
Façade 2 436, 450
Fantasia concertante for two pianos, jazz band
    and orchestra 31, 33
The First of the Few 120, 133, 136, 139, 141,
    351n
The First Shoot arrangement of 1935 ballet for
    brass band 450n, 457, 458
The First Shoot ballet 56n, 98, 100, 101, 113,
    450n
First Symphony xiv, 32, 55, 59, 70, 73, 77, 80,
    85–6, 88, 90–101, 102, 105, 112, 117, 118,
    124, 172, 177, 202, 217, 220, 264, 265,
    299, 350, 367–8, 370, 425–6, 435, 453, 465
Five Bagatelles for guitar 123n, 394, 397–8,
    415, 430
'For all the Saints' 12
The Foreman Went to France 135, 137, 157
Gesualdo project [abandoned] 120, 134, 137,
    142, 144, 161n, 178–9, 469–71
Gloria 312, 327, 350, 393
Hamlet 161, 165, 166, 193, 330
Hamlet (suite) 267
Henry V 120–21, 145, 146, 147, 333n, 454
*Improvisations on an Impromptu of Benjamin
    Britten* 384, 385, 387–8, 393, 394
Johannesburg Festival Overture 274, 278, 288,
    308, 323, 350, 381n
Macbeth incidental music 136, 137, 142
Magnificat and Nunc Dimittis 412

Major Barbara 133, 140

'Make We Joy Now in This Fest' 68, 70

Missa Brevis 350

Next of Kin 133, 157

Orb and Sceptre Coronation march for orchestra 215, 216, 221, 222, 223

Partita 265, 278n, 285, 286, 295n, 297, 298, 299, 301–4, 306, 312, 315, 350

Passacaglia for solo cello 456, 458

The Passionate Shepherd for tenor and chamber ensemble 468n

Piano Quartet 75, 305

Portsmouth Point xvii, 31–2, 33, 35, 38–9, 40, 44, 56, 58, 80, 202

Prologo e Fantasia 458n, 459

The Quest 145, 145–6

Scapino 119, 123, 129n, 135n, 137, 192, 204, 216, 266

Scherzetto for violin and piano 193n, 204

Second Symphony xii, xiii, 264–5, 285, 300, 301, 305, 307, 308, 310, 312, 313, 314, 317–22, 328, 329, 350, 417, 436, 461

Siesta 25n, 36, 41, 405

Sinfonia concertante xiv, 38, 39, 40, 42–5, 47, 56–7, 59, 69, 79, 147, 148, 149, 153, 202, 209

Sonata for Strings 345, 395–9, 405

A Song for the Lord Mayor's Table 326, 327, 366n, 390

Spitfire Prelude and Fugue 351

String Quartet (No. 1) xiv, 31, 436, 444

String Quartet in A minor (No. 2) 121, 125n, 126, 155, 158, 161, 162, 167, 189, 194, 202, 203, 204, 345, 398n

'Tell me where is fancy bred?' for soprano, tenor, three violins and piano 75, 468

Three Sisters 387, 392

Three Songs 68, 70, 73, 81n, 82, 83
  'Daphne' 73, 74
  'Old Sir Faulk' 69, 74
  'Through Gilded Tresses' 68, 73, 74

Toccata in A minor for violin and piano 33

'Tritons' 6, 28

The Triumph of Neptune (Berners, orch. by W) 36

Troilus and Cressida xii, xiii, xvi, 47n, 120, 121–2, 125n, 140n, 161–2, 165–6, 167, 169, 170, 177, 178–90, 193, 194, 197–201, 203, 205–8, 210–13, 215–17, 219, 221, 222, 224–58, 261–2, 264, 266–73, 278–9, 299, 304–7, 309, 310–11, 321, 323–4, 331, 335, 336, 344, 345–6, 365, 400, 403, 410, 411, 419, 422, 423–4, 426–9, 432, 435, 442, 444–5, 449, 457, 469

The Twelve 351, 355

Two Pieces for Violin and Piano 193n

'Under the Greenwood Tree' 468

Valse (from *Façade* Suite No. 1) 109, 305

Variation on an Elizabethan Theme ('Sellinger's Round') 222n, 223

Variations on a Theme by Hindemith xiii, 264, 286, 308, 324–5, 327, 331–4, 336, 347, 348, 350, 356

Variations for Violin and Pianoforte on a Chorale by J. S. Bach [abandoned] 75

Varii capricci 123n, 430, 437, 463

Viola Concerto xiv, 32, 38n, 44, 45, 47, 48, 49, 56–7, 62n, 65, 80, 85, 87, 110, 112, 176, 202, 331, 350, 389, 402, 447

Violin Concerto 91n, 106–7, 113–16, 118, 119, 123, 124n, 134, 135n, 139, 147, 148–9, 154, 160, 177, 202, 224, 264, 299, 330n, 331, 350, 389, 406, 446, 447, 451, 466

Violin Sonata 122, 163, 164, 165, 167, 170, 171, 183, 189, 193n, 194, 195, 196, 197, 199, 202, 204, 313, 431

'Where Does the Uttered Music Go?' 156n, 157–8, 159

'Where the bee sucks' 75

'The Winds' 6, 25n, 28

Walton Archive, La Mortella, Ischia xii, 145n, 180, 469

War Office 136, 143

Ward, John 322

Warlock, Peter (Philip Heseltine) 378

Warner Bros. 240

Warsaw Concerto (Addinsell) 171

Warsaw International Chopin Piano Competition 460n

Washington 322

Waverley, Lord (previously Sir John Anderson) 188
  correspondence with W 190–91, 220, 267

Webster, Sir David 194, 209, 219
  correspondence with W xiv, 156–7, 164, 203, 218, 226–9, 231–2, 233, 236–8, 240–41, 246–9, 261, 269–72, 301–2, 307, 309, 323–4, 331
  and *Troilus and Cressida* 181, 238–9, 241, 242, 244, 251, 261, 267, 269, 279, 306–7, 310–11, 331, 335, 336
  and Legge 240

Welsh National Opera 431

Wendeyer, Sir Brian 367

Werneth Hall Road, Oldham (No. 93) 26

Wesley, Samuel: 'Praise thou the Lord' 8

Westminster Abbey, London: *Crown Imperial* performed at the Coronation (1937) 109–10

Weston Hall, nr Towcester, Northants 38, 72, 91–5, 97, 99

Wheatley, Oxford 9

The Who 380

Widdicombe, Gillian 411, 413n, 423, 447, 450, 452

Wiesbaden: *The Bear* performed 422, 426

Wigmore Hall, London 82

Wilde, Oscar: *The Importance of Being Earnest* 330

Wilder, Thornton 153
  The Woman of Andros 121

Wilhelmina, Queen of the Netherlands 84

Willcocks, Sir David 350, 354n

Williamson, Sir Malcolm 425

Williamson, Michael 419

Wimborne, Alice, Viscountess 149, 449
  correspondence with W 106
  and W's memorandum xv, 472–3
  relationship with W 55, 101n, 105, 106, 122, 176
  and the Violin Concerto 106
  her estate ploughed up for war food 119
  and W's eye injury 149
  illness 122, 163, 164, 168, 177
  death 122, 177, 462n
  leaves Lowndes Cottage to W in her will 122, 169n
Wimborne, Viscount 105
Wimborne House, Arlington Street, London 105, 110, 111
Winbergh, Gösta 429
Wolverhampton Civic Hall: Violin Concerto performed 148

Wood, Charles 130
Wood, Sir Henry 39, 79, 148
  correspondence with W 146–7, 148
Wood, Jessie, Lady: correspondence with W 155–6, 157–8, 159
Wood, Dr Thomas 141
Worcester: Three Choirs Festival 80
Worth, Irene 322, 394

Yeats, W. B.: Oedipus Rex (trans.) 135n
Young, Alexander 267

Zeffirelli, Franco 358, 359
Zimmermann, Margarete 432
Zorian Quartet 159
Zuckerman, Solly (later Lord Zuckerman) 348
Zurich 63–4, 66, 88, 116
  Portsmouth Point performed 31, 76